The Actual Star

The Actual Star

A Novel

Monica Byrne

HARPER LARGE PRINT

An Imprint of HarperCollinsPublishers

Maps created by Monica Byrne

FIRST HARPER LARGE PRINT EDITION

ISBN: 978-0-06-311788-4

Library of Congress Cataloging-in-Publication Data is available upon request.

21 22 23 24 25 LSC 10 9 8 7 6 5 4 3 2 1

ti ch'ujul na'tak an bä ti ch'en,
bajche' jwa'täl jkuxtäl

para las diosas en la cueva,
como lo prometí

fi di gaads eena di kayv,
laik ah mi pramis

for the gods in the cave,
like I promised

CONTENTS

AUTHOR'S NOTE

This novel is set in real places in Cayo, the western district of Belize: the sacred cave of Actun Tunichil Muknal; the nearby site of Cahal Uitz Na; and the ancient city of Cahal Pech in modern-day San Ignacio. However, with the exception of Katwitz, we don't know what the ancient Maya called any of these places. The characters are also invented. There is no record of young monarchs named Ixul, Ajul, or Ket. However, I've made every effort to write their lives to be consistent with the most current research on the lowland Early Postclassical Maya, specifically in the Western Belize Regional Cave System.

The identities of the sacrificial victims in the cave are unknown, as is much about these specific people, and this specific time. There are many reasons why: the Spanish invaders' burning of vast libraries of Maya text; the jungle environment, which erodes stone and rots paper; the passage of a thousand years' time; and the prohibitive cost of archaeological research. So, even given the millions of modern Maya people, describing the specific Maya people who lived in 1012 lowland Belize is as much an act of imagination as research.

In all cases of lacunae, I borrowed from the closest available proxy in time and space. Sometimes that was Late Classical Tikal and Caracol (original names: Mutul and Oxwitza, respectively); sometimes that was the modern Maya of Monstantenego in Guatemala (as described by Barbara Tedlock in her ethnography *Time and the Highland Maya*); sometimes that was the Aztec, a civilization that arose several hundred years after and far to the northwest of, but was on a continuum with, Maya philosophies and practices (as described by Inga Clendinnen in *Aztecs: An Interpretation*). From the Olmecs to the Zapotecs to the Nahua, many ancient Mesoamerican cultures had commonalities—for example, the sacred calendar, concepts of the soul, and the belief in spirit animals—spread and reinforced by trade routes, migration, and conquest.

In terms of language, the term "ancient Mayan" covers a huge family of distinct languages over a large area over thousands of years, including Yucatec, Mopan, and Kekchi branches, as well as Nahuatl influences. Though it is not known what dialect was spoken among the lowland Postclassical Maya (that is, the characters in my book), the best proxy I could find in my research was Ch'ol, and so all ancient Mayan words are sourced from the 2010 Ch'ol Dictionary by Nicholas A. Hopkins, J. Kathryn Josserand, and Ausencio Cruz Guzmán. Spoken and transliterated Ch'ol uses glottal stops—like the *t*'s in the English pronunciation of "settle"—signified by a single apostrophe. Also, in Mayan pronunciation, *x* is pronounced like the English "sh." For example, "Ixul" is pronounced "ish-ool" and "Xibalba" is pronounced "shi-bahl-ba."

In terms of the calendar, there is considerable scholarly debate about which day names were used at which times, and no one knows for sure which convention was used by the ancient Maya population portrayed in this book. I've chosen to use a Ch'ol convention reconstructed from colonial manuscripts, and collected by scholars Lyle Campbell, J. Kathryn Josserand, and Nicholas Hopkins.

With regard to tourism in Actun Tunichil Muknal, there was a real-life accident with a camera in the high burial chamber, but the circumstances described in this book are entirely fictional. As for the Kriol in the book (one of the most common languages in contemporary Belize), I'm grateful for the translation work of Belizean artist Katie Numi Usher. In places where I chose to deviate from "pure" Kriol, it's usually because a Belizean character wishes to be understood by a native English–speaking character. As for High Spanish (the religious language of Laviaja), the terms are mostly preserved from contemporary Mexican Spanish, with exceptions for neologisms and the evolution of gender expression.

In all the above areas, I take full responsibility for all choices, mistakes, and inaccuracies.

Please be advised that this novel contains multiple depictions of self-cutting.

PROLOGUE

Submission to the Tzoyna
from Niloux DeCayo
Yazd, Persia
7 Ajwal 3 Ch'en, Long Count 15.10.13.11.0
14 January, 3012

As of 4:24 a.m. Persian Time, the last of the world's ice is gone. This means the Diluvian Age is over. We have to decide what the new age will be.

Over the last thousand years, Laviaja has remade the world according to the belief that we don't belong to this reality, and that our true and lasting reality is the Other World, Xibalba, which we can only reach through constant viaja.

But now I want to propose that Xibalba is not a real physical place at all. That rather, what we call Xibalba is just a shift in understanding of our lived reality. Also, I propose that Leah Oliveri never really disappeared. My guess is that, if we were to search the Great Cave, we'd just find her bones alongside all the others.

I understand what it means to say this. I understand it'll upset a lot of people. But now that the ice has melted, the climate will begin to stabilize, and I think it's the duty of any sofist to question whether the beliefs that have served us till now are still useful for a post-Diluvian era.

I'm requesting the standard discussion period of 36 hours. Thanks.

BOOK I

THE LIGHT ZONE

If we find ourselves with a desire that nothing in this world can satisfy, the most probable explanation is that we were made for another world.

C. S. LEWIS
1952

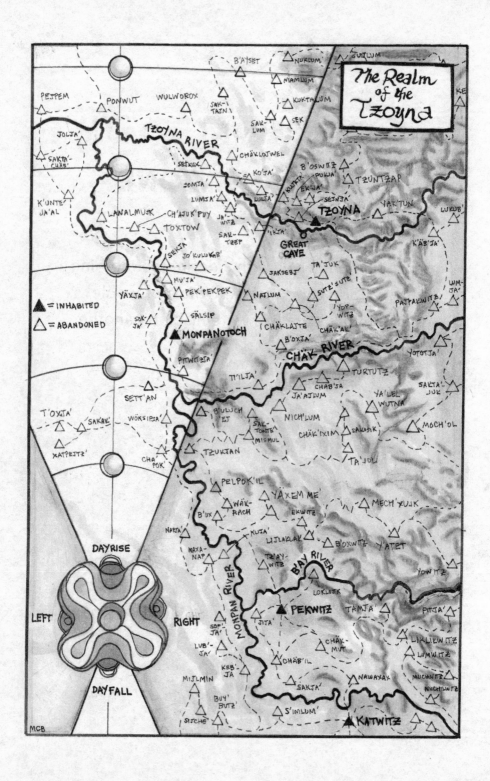

TZOYNA
3 Batz' 14 Pop,
Long Count 10.9.5.7.11

---

9 December, 1012

Ket set the obsidian blade to her skin, then heard a whistle. She looked up. Her brother, Ajul, was staring down at her.

"What are you doing?" he yelled.

Ket felt she'd been caught at something vulgar. She dropped the blade into its nest of moss.

Ajul slung his spear across his back and leapt down to the court. For a long moment he hung in space, dappled with sunlight, then landed and stood with the grace of a stag.

Ket kept her eyes down. Her brother was rarely angry, but he was still a giant, a hand taller than even their captain of the guard. He drew his spear and circled, the point leveled at her, as if approaching prey. Ket cowered. To make eye contact was an act of challenge.

"Ket!"

Ket looked up.

Ajul was smiling, exasperated.

She let her breath out. He'd been teasing her. He was still just her big brother.

He sat down and set his spear beside him. He said nothing about the blade for now. It was another windless, bright, blazing day. The grackles shrieked overhead.

Ajul asked, "Why this place, little sister?"

Ket sensed he was testing her.

"This is the old ball court," she said. "It's one of the four moorings of the Tzoyna."

"And what are the other three moorings?"

"The dayfall boulder, the dayrise ceiba, and the well to the right of the sun."

"In which direction are you facing?"

She frowned at the simplicity of the question. "Left of the sun."

"And which city lies beyond?"

"Chichen Itza."

"Yes, that is far away, but it is the biggest city. Good." He reached over, took hold of her legs, and pushed her a quarter round. She giggled. Her siblings were allowed to touch her body; no one else was. It felt good to be touched. "And now which direction are you facing," he asked, "and what city?"

She couldn't see past the next hill, but she knew. "Dayrise, and Katwitz."

"Good."

"Will I get to meet the stupid merchants tonight?"

"Do not call them stupid."

"Ixul does all the time."

"But only among us, little sister. Only among the royal family."

"All right."

He turned her another quarter, so that she was facing away from him. "Now?"

"Right of day, and Oxwitza."

He turned her another quarter.

"Dayfall, and . . ."

Ajul raised his eyebrows. "And?"

She wasn't sure. "The encircling water?"

Ajul smiled. "Good enough, little sister." He swung her one final time to face him.

Then Ajul picked up the blade and examined it. She wanted him to notice how careful she'd been, cushioning it in the moss. It was a family heirloom of rare green obsidian, shaped like the Great Star, Chak Ek'—four equal points, knapped as sharp as thorns. It had come to their lineage as a gift from some ancient royal house of the dayfall. When Ket had been a baby she hadn't even been allowed to touch it. But ever since their parents had disappeared, Ajul and Ixul overlooked their sister's transgressions, including stealing the blade from the family shrine and carrying it wherever she went, as other children would carry a doll.

Ajul held it up. "To me," he said, "with a piece as fine as this, the edge of the obsidian looks like the edge of water. See?"

It was something their father had once said. Ajul was repeating him, whether he realized it or not. But Ket said nothing of that, and only leaned forward and squinted at the blade and saw what he meant: that at the edges, the color faded from green to grey to clear, like a petal of water that surged up the sand and disappeared.

She nodded, bashful.

Ajul took note of all her other instruments: mushrooms, bark paper, cloth, herbs, water, censer, clay bowl, kindling stick, crumbs of copal.

"Were you going to let blood, sister?"

Now came the direct question. Ket crossed her arms. She knew she wasn't supposed to do it alone.

"Letting blood is a powerful act," he said, "and even more powerful under the influence of the god. You may be starting something you are not prepared to finish."

She pouted. "Then how can I ever prepare?"

"You are only seven years old."

"I want to do it anyway."

"Why?"

Ket focused on a snail oozing across the court, leaving a trail of sparkling slime. She wanted to tell her brother so much. But he and Ixul were very busy, the famous tall twins, meeting with farmers and merchants and slavers, or their daykeeper Mutna or their captain of the guard Upakal, or with emissaries from Pekwitz or Katwitz. They didn't have time to look after her. So she had a lot of time alone during the hot, bright, quiet afternoons. She talked to herself so often that she'd stopped realizing when she was talking aloud and when she was not. She had favorite secret places around the palace. She'd sit on empty thrones and command invisible servants, or drape herself with jade for an invisible suitor. She burned blue cakes of copal just to watch the smoke. She climbed up the terraces from the river to the hilltops, like climbing giant stairways; then up the path to the old slate altar, down the lime roads, along secret forest trails that led to crumbling red temples, the stones split by young ceiba trees. She wandered along the haunted road to Tuntzap, a long-abandoned city in the next valley over, though turned back when she started feeling scared. She walked up to calabash trees and held out her hand, hoping one of the fruits would spit in her hand and make her pregnant, like the Bloodmaiden, the mother of the Hero Twins in all the old stories. She walked in abandoned fields, careful not to step on the spikes of dead maize. She waded in sluggish streams and watched how the sun shone through the trees and made jaguar skin on the ground. She played at the mouths of dry caves, the Cave of Hands and the Cave of Bats, but never dared to go in. And when she was very, very sure no one was watching, she even crept within view of the Great Cave itself, the black flame out of which she and her lineage were born; and sat on a stone at the entrance, and let the bright road of rain part around her.

"Ket," said Ajul. "Answer me. Why do you want to let blood?"

"Because I want to help," she answered, and it was the truth.

Ajul ran a finger down her cheek. He looked sad.

"You are already helping. You're going to bowl the ball at our ascension tonight."

"I know. But—"

"You have stayed awake. You have fasted. You have done everything you need to help us. If you want to let blood also, you have to know where the gods are stationed in the sky, and who the day is, and—"

"I know all that!" said Ket, impatient to prove herself. She pointed to a spot low on the horizon. "Chak Ek' will appear there to bless your ascension." She shifted her finger a bit. "The moon will rise there, late at night, and bless it also." She dropped her hand to her lap. "Today is Three Batz', who fastens our lineage in the past and the future."

Ajul smiled and spread his hands. "I am impressed."

"Good," Ket spat before she could stop herself.

But Ajul just laughed. When he did, he was at his most lovely: he had the ancestors' classic beauty, with big blossoming eyes. Ket adored him—his warmth, his piety, his ease of being, his slowness to anger, the way his body sprang from rest to readiness. She wanted to be around him more often, though she knew that was impossible. She could never possess him the way their sister Ixul did. The twins' fame was beginning to spread. In the last year, embassies had arrived from as far as Chichen Itza, eager to see the young giants play the ball game. Ket had heard the servants whisper that they were the Hero Twins reborn, reincarnated in the lineage they founded.

"Is it true," said Ket, "that you're going to lead us into a new age?"

"Who told you that?" said Ajul. He sat up straighter and seemed pleased.

"That's what the servants say. They say you're going to end the drought and heal the land and bring everyone back to the way it used to be."

He nodded. "This is what we intend. We want to build a realm where all people will prosper."

"But you can't do it without my help!"

Ajul sighed. He brushed back her bangs and ran his thumb across the jade tattoo on her forehead. It was also a four-pointed star, the symbol of their kingdom.

When he spoke again, his voice was quiet and serious. "Then I will not stand in your way any longer," he said. "Have you expressed your intention to the gods?"

"I was waiting till I cut."

"Do you understand you may see things that frighten you?"

"Like what?"

Ajul looked pensive. Then he said, "Father once told me that you see the city beneath the city, and the star behind the star. Try to remember everything you see. It will guide you later."

Ket nodded. "I'll be all right," she said, "because you're here."

He smiled at her, cupped her cheek.

Then he got to his feet. "Eat one mushroom only," he said. "Chew it well so that the god comes quickly. Then light the copal. I'll prepare the rest."

Ket put one withered mushroom in her mouth and began to chew. It was sour and rubbery, but she made herself chew it to a pulp before she washed it down with water. Then she sat quietly. She couldn't back out now. That would be dishonorable. She had to be as brave as a captive facing the altar.

Ajul walked along the wall, his eyes on the ground. He picked up seven crumbs of limestone and then, murmuring the words of invocation, dropped four of them in a square around her. He took another crumb and threw it up to the Sun, who ate it. Another, he crushed in his hand, and scattered on the court as if sowing maize.

Finally, he sat back down and dropped the seventh crumb in her bowl. "Now the way is open," he said.

Ket looked down at her instruments. It was hard to think straight. She tried to remember what to do next. She picked up the paper, her hands shaking; broke the roll in two, and pushed the pieces down into her cup. Then she folded her cloth next to the bowl and lined up the herbs and the censer, all in a neat row. Then she murmured her own prayer of invocation, calling on the gods to attend, though she would not abide any that meant her harm.

Then there was nothing else left to do.

She felt Ajul watching her.

She took a deep breath. Then she shivered. It was real this time, not play, never again play. The vines were beginning to spiral across the court; the god was arriving. She picked up the star blade with one hand and extended the first finger of her other hand.

"I ask the god of this place," she said, "to heal the Tzoyna."

She put the blade to her finger.

Nothing.

"You have to press, little sister," her brother whispered, and she saw his hand reaching out to guide her, but before he could, she pressed hard and drew lengthwise.

Her finger split open, too deeply, already, she could see. Ajul hissed and got to his knees and was leaning over, now, telling her to let up and put it down and breathe and let it drip.

Ket's hand hung over the bowl like a palm tree in a downpour. She blinked back sudden and involuntary tears. The pain astonished her into silence. She'd cloven her own flesh. Now there was a blazing hot little slice in her finger. She couldn't hear anything. The blood made an unbroken stream for several heartbeats, then broke into shining kernels, each of which floated in space before hitting the paper and spreading from edge to edge.

Ajul was saying her name. But she couldn't focus on his voice. She was mesmerized by the slit in her finger. She pulled it apart and saw the star-white of her bone.

"Stop," said Ajul. He put the herbs in his mouth to wet them, pressed them to the cut, and folded the stanching cloth around her finger. She let him do it, watched him tie it off. She felt serene and detached. It was all right. He knew what to do. He picked up the copal, asking Xibalba's forgiveness for the improvisation, and blew on it till the smoke bloomed.

"Ket. Focus. You have to continue."

She looked up at him and squinted, as if peering from a great distance.

"Look into the smoke."

She looked into the smoke.

Then her mouth fell open, and she was looking at herself from below.

Ixul sat under a cohune palm with the daykeeper, Mutna. Between them was a red cotton mat and a pile of maize kernels.

"Ask your first question," said Mutna.

Ixul took one kernel and pressed it to her lips: a sign of respect. "Of Ajul and me, which is more like which Hero Twin?"

Mutna frowned. "That is not a proper question for divination. Besides, you can answer it yourself."

Ixul nodded, her intuition confirmed. "I'm more like Xbalanque."

"See? You already knew. Your nagual is a jaguar."

"And Xbalanque is covered in jaguar skin."

"Yes . . ." Mutna prompted.

"So Ajul is more like Hunajpu. I see. How long will we rule?"

"That is also not a proper question for divination."

Ixul glowered, though she knew it wouldn't do her any good. Mutna never let Ixul intimidate her. The tutor was proud and severe, of an ancient lineage of daykeepers. Her black braids made a glossy crown around her head.

"Recall," said Mutna, "that a soul lives many lives. All of those lives have the same essential character. You and Ajul are twins. You were born only a few minutes apart, but on different days, and different gods rule those days. This means you have different destinies. More than that, I can't say."

Ixul hated not knowing. She felt contempt for the gods, hiding knowledge from her. Also, she was fasting—as was the whole royal household—and hunger made her quick to anger. She stared down at the sacred river. The water sparkled, unaware of any drought.

Mutna pointed at the kernels. "Try another question."

Ixul pursed her lips. She thought of her little sister, probably lost in some fantasy above the city. "What is Ket's nagual?"

"That, we can try to answer."

Mutna grabbed a handful of kernels, swept the rest aside, and began placing them on her mat in groups of four. Ixul watched her work. The twins had learned their naguals long before. Ajul was a stag, Ixul was a jaguar—the daytime and nighttime faces of the Sun. Ixul hoped that Ket's nagual would also be a majestic animal, bespeaking a greater destiny than her plainness suggested.

"May this petition be received by Xibalba," said Mutna in a low and resonant voice. "May it be received in the day . . ."

A grackle passed low overhead. Ixul frowned, distracted.

". . . in the light, in the morning . . ."

Ixul thought: *Birds are not birds; they are messengers.*

". . . in the night, in the stars and the heavens . . ."

Ixul remembered the words of the philosopher: *This world is a world of deceptions.*

". . . in the wind and the cold . . ."

This world is merely a representation of representations.

". . . in the earth and the water . . ."

The sun we see is not the real sun.

". . . in every slice of the day upon the world . . ."

The star we see is not the actual star.

". . . I say, thank you to the day."

Ixul looked back at the mat, where Mutna had set twelve piles, each with four seeds. A perfect cast. That guaranteed a strong answer.

Mutna sat back. "Now," she said, "we must ask the day. Princess Ket Ahau was born on Twelve Ajwal, a very powerful day. Ask him directly."

Ixul didn't hesitate. The gods were her intimates; that was her birthright. She closed her eyes and said, "Dear Twelve Ajwal, tell me what you saw when my sister was born. What form crept into our mother's mouth?"

"Now," Mutna said, "soften your mind. Let the answer alight upon you, as a bee upon the hibiscus. You know more than you can tell."

Ixul closed her eyes and began the catalogue of royal animals.

Quetzal? No.

Howler monkey? No.

Ocelot? No.

Crocodile? No.

She floated, summoning each animal in her mind, down to the smell of feathers.

Scarlet macaw? No.

Vulture? No.

White eagle? No.

Rattlesnake? No.

Still she felt nothing. She began the catalogue of lesser animals, feeling frustrated.

Peccary? No.

Wasp? No.

Crab? No.

Spider?

Yes.

A whip spider. A harmless, awkward bug that spent all of its time alone, staring with big eyes. Just like Ket.

Ixul opened her eyes. "Spider," she said. "It's a simple whip spider."

Mutna raised her eyebrows. "Spiders can be noble," she said.

"But not *royal*," Ixul snapped. "Let's go on. I still have many questions to ask."

"I'll allow two."

"But—"

The look on Mutna's face stopped her. The day-keeper had been her tutor ever since she was a child, and her parents had given her free rein to administer discipline whenever Ixul became too insolent. Ixul would become queen, which meant she must keep her passions in check and not display them constantly, like a howler monkey baring its anus.

Mutna folded her hands in her lap, waited.

Ixul composed herself. She went through her questions in her mind:

Why did our parents disappear?

Is Ajul's and my carnal union offensive to Xibalba?

Why have all the great houses fallen in the lowlands?

Is there any royal blood left for Ket to marry?

What is Chichen Itza like?

What is Oxwitza like?

What is Tula like?

Ixul had philosophical questions, yes, but also questions to satisfy her curiosity—to know everything that Mutna had seen in her education abroad, to the dayfall and dayrise and left and right of the sun. She was jealous. She was impatient to start her own travels as queen. Until then, she'd gladly spend days interrogating Mutna, or anyone who had the fortitude to withstand her.

But her tutor was right: time was short. The delegations from Katwitz and Pekwitz were due to arrive by sundown. Pilgrims, farmers, and their families had been gathering all day in the city. She had to choose wisely. She had to ask the most important questions.

"What is Xibalba?" she asked.

Mutna's eye twitched. "You test me, child," she said.

Ixul shrugged to say: *This is your charge.*

Mutna turned and looked up the river. Ixul followed her gaze. Through the palm trees, they could see the entrance to Xibalba, the black flame in mid-ripple. Ixul feared looking directly at the Great Cave. Only noble blood was allowed even to come within sight of it.

"The Lakamhan school of thought," said Mutna, "stated that if you step over that threshold, into the underworld, you're in Xibalba. Whereas we who sit here are *not* in Xibalba. That there is a clear line separating this world from that world. But," she said, holding up her finger, "I believe the Mutulian school of thought, which said that Xibalba exists in the very same space as we do. It is with us, all around us, like two circles overlapping. Xibalba is the place behind the place. We cannot reach it; we can only sense it, but there are some places where the borders are thinner than in others. Ritual is such a time and"—Mutna nodded to the black flame—"the underworld is such a place."

"Where the Hero Twins entered to confront the gods of death."

"Yes." After a pause, Mutna said, "However, I do think the worlds have become farther apart in time."

Ixul frowned. "Farther apart? How?"

Mutna shrugged. "That is the way of creation. There have been many creations before. Each one failed, and then humanity tried again."

Ixul gazed at the slit in the mountain.

"You've been in there," she said. She spoke in a whisper, though they sat in bright daylight. "Were you scared?"

"Yes," said Mutna, and the swiftness of her answer was startling to Ixul. She had never known Mutna to be scared of anything. "That is its name, after all: the place of fear. But it is also a place of great wonder. When I assisted your father, the king, we followed the main avenue of rain up into the city. There were many turns of the avenue, and it took me many trips to learn them all, to learn the locations of the ladders and the markings on the walls, so I could lead the priestly retinue myself. You fear to disturb that which watches you, just beyond the torchlight. There are branches and false turnings everywhere. I have not explored them. In some places, the rain is so deep that you have to swim. You have to keep the torches aloft to protect them from the water."

"But if Xibalba is the place of fear and Xibalba is all around us . . . do we live in fear? I don't understand."

Mutna pointed across the river. "Go fetch me a calabash," she said.

The river was one of the only places where calabash trees still grew in the drought. Ixul got up and walked down the bank. She prostrated to the mountain and the sacred water, murmuring the words of permission; then gathered her skirt in one hand, waded across, plucked a young green fruit, and brought it back.

"Give me your knife," said Mutna.

Ixul handed over her flint knife.

Mutna stabbed the calabash, and it fell apart in two halves. She put down the knife and placed one half on top of the other, so that it looked whole.

"Think of it like this," she said. "The universe has three levels. What are they?"

"The underworld, the middleworld, and the heavens. The World Tree connects them all."

"Yes. Think of this top half as the heavens and the bottom half as the underworld, and both of them together are Xibalba, the Other World."

Ixul frowned. "But where is the middleworld?"

Mutna removed the top and held one half in each hand. "We live in the cut," she said.

Ixul took one of the halves. She drew her finger over the oozing white flesh. "Tzoyna, the name of our kingdom," she said, "means Mother's Cut."

"Yes, it does."

"And we can't escape it," she said. "We're reborn in the middleworld, over and over."

"So some say."

"Some?"

"There are different schools of thought on this subject, as well."

Ixul's mood darkened again. She wanted to know for sure. "If we've already lived many lifetimes, hundreds in the deep past, to the time of the Hero Twins and even before—why don't we remember them? Why aren't we born knowing the answer?"

"Every time we're reborn, we have to remember what we know through other ways, child."

"I'm not a child," said Ixul.

"No," said Mutna with sudden harshness, "you're right, you're not a child. You're about to become queen. After tonight, you'll be the one sending ambassadors. You'll be the one rebuilding the canals. You'll be the one leading the priests into the underworld. You'll be the one who the people turn to for answers, and you must be strong and confident, not sniveling and petulant."

Ixul pursed her lips at the grass, which was the closest she came to concession.

When Mutna spoke again, her voice was softer. "The Mutulian and Oxwitzan scholars both claimed that their empires would last forever. Their people are scattered now and their cities are empty, just like Lakamha and Saal and Kaanu'l. You must understand why they fell."

"I want to," said Ixul. "I want to succeed where they failed."

Mutna nodded. "You are bright and strong. Upakal and I will be here to advise you as you set about your work. There is much to be restored."

"But it *can* be done?"

Mutna hesitated. The water babbled behind them. They each held half a calabash, like bowls of balché.

Finally she said, "I think so, though it will be difficult."

Ixul knew she was telling the truth and not flattering her as a lesser tutor would.

They were both gazing at the mountain again. Now the sun shone into the entrance, lighting up the bright turquoise pool inside.

"I will permit one more question," said Mutna. "What do you wish to ask?"

Ixul was ready. She turned back and said, "What is Ket's role in the new age to come?"

ANOONG, MINNESOTA
12 Men 18 Mak,
Long Count 12.19.19.17.15

---

16 December, 2012

On the drive to the doctor's office, Leah fondly remembered a night from her past.

She'd been in seventh grade, watching a nature program. The narrator told her that the universe had originated in an event that caused the space between all matter to expand, and it was still expanding, and the expansion was in fact accelerating, and would continue until all the stars died out and disintegrated, and every speck of matter was separate from every other, and would stay that way forever, in eternal freezing darkness.

The narrator said: this is the law of entropy, the ultimate nature of the universe.

Immediately Leah knew he was wrong. This law was not compatible with her faith in a loving God. How could she reconcile the two?

She locked herself in the bathroom and turned up the heat. She tied her hair back in her usual black braid, then took off her clothes and looked in the mirror. She felt mad with a purpose she didn't fully understand, except that she needed to resolve the terrible thing she'd just learned, and return to a state of wholeness. She plucked at herself. The inner lips of her vulva were longer than the outer ones, and so, she thought, resembled a lamb that bites its tongue in death. Acting on instinct, she took her mother's orange Bic razor and drew it along her finger, quick, lengthwise. She didn't feel anything at first. But then the cut filled, bloomed, spilled over. In a long strange moment that seemed to draw away from her in all directions, she became aware of the separation of her thoughts like dewdrops on a spider's thread: the impulse, the act, the memory, the meaning, and the imposition of the meaning upon the memory. There'd been a moment when they were all one and the same, she felt sure; but it was already past.

She realized that entropy was the truth of this universe, yes; but not the ultimate truth.

She felt calmer. She could hear everything more clearly: the sound of water running, the yippy dog in the apartment above, and the sound of Fox News in the living room, where her mother heated up dinner. Her blood dripped onto the tiles like a metronome.

It wasn't true wholeness, but it was a step closer.

Upon commencing eighth grade, she decided to become the school slut. Sex seemed another good way to regain that lost state of wholeness. No one at Trinity High understood this, of course; as soon as she began having sex, the word spread and the bullying began. Leah tried to get along as best she could. Her cheerful embrace of the word "slut" was deeply confusing to her classmates. So while the bullying persisted, it also leveled off at a manageable rate. Leah could plan to be pushed into a locker a few times a week; there was no avoiding that. She usually ate lunch across from the only other brown-skinned kid at school, a Somali boy named Andrew, who always brought a book like she did. Sometimes they traded. She wrote lots of poetry and thought it good. She swam breaststroke for the swim team and usually won third place. When the school split up into teams for Field Day, each named for a member of the Trinity, she always chose Team Holy Spirit.

She spent a lot of time on the Internet.

She found sex partners there, mostly from the arts magnet high school in St. Cloud. She'd tried Craigslist once. Her ad read:

Teenager looking to experiment with other teenagers, any gender. No one over eighteen, please!!! I am not stupid.

This did not work. Her inbox was flooded with pictures of pale dicks peering up like turtle heads from under hockey jerseys. She took down the ad.

She also researched cutting on Internet message boards. She always included the word "safe" in her searches, and so found a community—mostly of other teenagers—who practiced cutting, not for the purpose of hurting themselves, but as a mild opiate.

Anything in excess is bad, said 1EqualTemper, and anything in moderation is ok. But yeah ok tell that to my parents. They'd freak if they knew.

So would my mother, wrote Leah. Nobody trusts me.

Nobody trusts teenage girls period.

rite?? and yet cutting is the only rational response of a teenage girl to this world.

I could be doing so much worse than this. I still get good grades. Cutting is nothing. Everything heals up. Meanwhile my cousin does heroin and no one says anything.

Why not??

cuz he's a dude

They traded tips on safe practices. Leah snuck the box cutter from her mother's toolbox and used that, though always first sterilizing the edge with a candle and then using rubbing alcohol, cotton balls, antibiotic ointment, and binding afterward. She never appeared around her mother without underwear on, because she had a series of cuts along each wing of her pelvic crest, where her potbelly met her thighs.

They talked about aftereffects. Almost everyone reported feelings of calm, attributed to the sudden opiates in the bloodstream. Leah was particularly interested in the history of cutting, and shrieked when she saw an article about the ancient Maya.

I'm Maya!!!!!!!!! she posted in response to hopeless-gamete77.

wait how r u maya

My biological father was Maya.

how is that possible were you born in 1000 BC

No, there are millions of descendants of the ancient Maya living in Central America.

ohhhh cool I didn't know sorry lol

That's all right.

well now u know why u cut

Leah sat back from her computer. She'd never thought of that.

She read everything she could about the ancient bloodletting ritual. She learned that it was never done lightly. The Maya let blood to bless a new venture like the beginning of a war or the healing of an illness or the ascension of a king. Blood was their divine offering to Xibalba. The first time Leah read that word—*Xibalba*—she went deep into the sparkling darkness behind her eyelids. What if her lost sense of wholeness could only be satisfied by entering another universe, a realm of divine forms, of which all things here were merely reflections and shadows?

She began to fantasize about what Xibalba would be like. She was sure it wasn't like the Roman Catholic heaven, with cherubs and cotton candy clouds. Her idea was more true, more real, a realm of stone and stars. She found it harder to be surrounded by only the shadow versions of things. Once, while with Sister Jean in the counseling office, she stared very hard at a picture of Mary Magdalene.

"My middle name is Magdalene," she said suddenly to the nun.

Sister Jean, who'd been in the middle of a careful explanation of how the female body was sacred and should not be defiled through premarital sexual contact, turned red in the cheeks. "Have you been listening to me?"

"Sort of," said Leah. "I thought I'd change the subject. Why did you choose Mary Magdalene to put here in your office?"

The nun's face became solemn. Leah knew she was thinking that this was a big opportunity for a teaching moment. "Because she was the greatest sinner," she said, "but Jesus made her among the greatest saints."

"How did Jesus *make* her great? Didn't she choose it herself?"

"Well, yes, but only because she happened to meet him."

Leah nodded, swung her legs, moved on. "My mother had premarital sex when she was a young missionary. That's how she had me. She was in Cayo, in Belize. She gave me the middle name Magdalene to remind her of her past sins."

Sister Jean blanched. "I'm sure it wasn't because of that," she said. "The name is a great honor. Mary Magdalene was one of Jesus's closest friends. She shows how you can go from the greatest depths to the highest heights. Which brings me to . . . your behavior. The way you . . . behave . . ."

Leah felt bad for the nun. How to deal with a girl who so clearly didn't want to be saved? Who'd never needed to be saved in the first place, from anything? She smiled and patted the woman's hand. "Sister," she said, "be at peace. There's nothing wrong with me."

There was only one teacher she trusted, her Spanish teacher, Ms. Fitzpatrick, who'd gone to the University of Minnesota and wore red cat's-eye glasses. Despite Leah's mediocre grades, she'd encouraged her to apply to college. But the very idea slid off Leah's mind. Ambition was foreign to her. Only her pursuit of Xibalba mattered, and only she knew how to pursue it. During her senior year, when she'd get home from work, she'd run experiments with layering sensory experiences. She went into her bedroom, turned up the heat, upended an hourglass, put on headphones playing Janelle Monáe at maximum volume, put on green-tinted sunglasses, lit cinnamon incense, put a bite-sized Hershey bar on her tongue, and then waited for the peak of the best chord change of the chorus of "Mushrooms & Roses" and then, only then, did she make a small cut on her finger. All of this was an attempt to shift herself to Xibalba.

She tried very hard. Sometimes she thought she almost got there.

But reality would always return. She'd find herself back in her mother's apartment, where the heat leached out the windows.

When Leah left the doctor's office, having learned what she'd learned, she exited through the sliding glass doors. The cold hit her face like a wall of freezing water.

She jogged sideways. She made it to a potted plant before throwing up her oatmeal. It hit the wood chips and stayed there. She heaved twice more before the nausea ebbed. A woman and her child, coming up to the clinic, stopped in their tracks.

"Don't worry!" said Leah, thumbing the last of it off her lip and stubbing it into the soil. "It happens all the time!"

The child began to cry.

"Jeez, are you all right?" said the woman in a faint voice. She was shielding her child as if from a threat. They were both wearing puffy Vikings coats, yellow and purple.

"Oh, I'm fine," said Leah, covering over the little pile, as if she were planting a seed. "I just ate something that disagreed with me, but now it's out of my system. Could be worse."

"Maybe you should go back in there, huh?" The woman nodded at the clinic doors.

"No!" she said more loudly than she meant to. "I'm not going back in there again. Ever, actually. I have plans."

The woman nodded, even more uneasy. She said, "Do you need help getting to your car?"

"Actually, my boyfriend's picking me up, but thank you so much! That's very thoughtful of you."

"Okay, well. I hope you feel better soon." She led her child up to the doors, which swooshed open and enclosed them in warmth.

Leah crouched by the plant, making sure she felt well enough to stand, feeling the sweat freeze on her forehead. Her boyfriend wasn't actually picking her up because she didn't have a boyfriend. She only had Nate, who didn't count. She felt bad. She hated any form of deception, including the practical jokes her mother's fiancé, Rick, was so fond of. Though her mother had urged her to lighten up, the tricks seemed unkind.

Except omission, she told herself. Omission was the only acceptable form of lie. Omission had a purpose.

With that in mind, she'd go ahead with the dinner tonight as planned.

She got in her car. The engine took four tries to turn over. She let the inside get warm before taking Interstate 94 back to Anoong. She spotted one of her own black hairs caught in the vent, waving like a sea anemone, and it made her think of Nate picking her hairs off his body. Nate was one year younger, a high school senior. He worked on a farm. They'd had sex eighteen times now. Leah had marked each occasion on her calendar with an asterisk. He was going to pick her up tonight, after dinner with Rick's family at the steakhouse.

She turned on Minnesota Public Radio and started to drive.

Along the highway, rising out of the snow fields, she saw great works of masonry jumbled together, as if a giant baby had been playing with blocks. She wondered whether this was what Belize was like, with ancient Maya cities everywhere: crumbling arches, fallen keystones, ramparts and causeways, flagstones on their side, pitted stone, weathered for centuries. Field after field, there they were, stone honeycombs, sometimes rising a whole wall high, but then crumbling back down to ground level before trailing away in the grass. They must have been great cities once. She hadn't spotted them before, though she'd lived in western Minnesota all her life. But it was like that sometimes, she thought. You only notice a place when you're about to leave.

It was still cold in the car. She turned up the heat full-blast, now that the engine was warm.

"Did you know that our blood comes from stars?" said the radio.

She looked at the radio.

"It sounds like science fiction, but it's true. What gives blood its red color is its iron content. You might say, *Well, I eat iron in my morning cornflakes*, and that's true. But where did *that* iron come from? How do you manufacture an element? It turns out that iron comes from stellar fusion. The enormous pressure inside stars is the only thing in the universe that can make it. Once that iron is made, the star itself reaches its dying phase—the supernova—and all of it is released into space. So when I say our blood comes from stars, it's not a fantasy, and it's not even an exaggeration. We are made of stars."

Leah's eyes filled with grateful tears. She decided that, despite everything, she was going to be all right.

ZEIN-O-DIN, PERSIA
8 Himux 4 Ch'en, Long Count 15.10.13.11.1

---

15 January, 3012

Niloux's tribunal was scheduled for the next morning.

She blamed Venus. The moment the last of the world's ice had melted—announced by viajeras in the Chersky Range, toasting their vodkas over the last smear of snow—Venus had cracked the horizon where Niloux sat. No one born to Laviaja could mistake the gravity of that timing. Not even Niloux. To the ancient Maya, the appearance of the morning star signaled change, and as she watched it rise over the pool in the oasis, she felt such a surge of purpose that she felt nauseated, as if the planet's beams were sending a message. Her body understood it at once. Her mind was still catching up.

In that state of euphoria, she'd submitted her proposal to the Tzoyna. She thought she'd get intelligent debate. But no. Everyone lost their minds. She got condemnation, calls for blotting, and a summons to a tribunal.

The wayhouse appeared in the distance, a circle of stone under a jagged ridge, lit only by the milk wash of stars.

Niloux walked into the wind.

She arrived at an arch in the wall. At its top was the Laviaja flag, a gold whip spider on a green field, over a curtain embroidered with Versa Uno from the Rule of Saint Leah, in Farsi script:

Ayuda a la personix que te acompañe

Help the one you're with.

A little hand pulled the curtain aside. A ninx in a white shift gazed out at her.

Niloux bowed, obeying the usual forms.

The ninx bowed back, nervous, but said her lines. "Buenas noches, en nombre de la Trinidad de Cayo," she said with careful formality. "¿Que necesita?"

"Una segura casa," Niloux replied in the traditional way, "y comida y descansa."

"Por favor, ven en paz." The formalities were finished,

but the ninx was still tense. "I'm on welcome duty. I'm supposed to bring you supper."

Niloux paused. "*Bring* it?"

"In your room."

"I'm imprisoned, then?"

The ninx flinched. "No! They just thought you would want to be alone before the tribunal, like you always are, in the wild."

Niloux snorted. "It's convenient for them to think so. They're scared of me. I'll take supper in the common room with everyone else." She moved to enter, but the ninx blocked her way.

"Why did you say Xibalba isn't real?" she asked.

Niloux shifted on her feet. She was exhausted from the long day of walking and impatient to get out of the wind, but restrained herself from snapping at the child. Versa Uno: *Help the one you're with.* Versa Dos: *This child is your child.* No matter her mood, she must care for her as if newly born from her own body.

"I didn't say that exactly," Niloux said. "I said that Xibalba isn't a real physical place, it's just a shift in thought. The meaning of Xibalba has changed many times. It's not going to stop anytime soon."

"Okay. What's the new meaning?"

Niloux almost laughed. "Kid, I don't know yet. Do you have any ideas?"

The ninx sensed a change in tone, looked coy. "My name is Daveed," she said. "It's my first time on welcome duty."

Niloux shrugged. "I think you're doing great. Welcome away."

Daveed said, "Come on then."

Niloux followed her into an eight-sided entry chamber. The walls sparkled with solar paint. On the far side of the chamber, there was another curtain, which she guessed led to the common room. Through a gap, she saw ninx playing and zadres lounging. Her jaw clenched. These were the people she'd have to face for her tribunal.

Daveed smoothed a moonball awake, then disappeared into another arch. Niloux dropped her gear and sat on a bench. There was a bowl of bubbling copal in the corner, giving off crisp honey smoke.

The ninx came back with a bronze ewer. "I haven't picked my first manéra yet," she announced.

Niloux raised her eyebrows. Strange way to start a conversation. "You're still a child. You don't have to."

"No, but I want to start thinking about it. What manéra are you?"

"Mopan maya," said Niloux. "Since I was ten."

"There are a lot of maya."

"Three hundred thousand, I think. Most common manéra on Earth."

"What do you have to do?"

"Lots of tutorials. Initiation, language, sims, religion. There are different kinds of maya too. I'm mopan maya, and that's the language I learned. And then there's the history to cover." She counted on her fingers. "Origins, metropolitan phases, dispersed phases, Spanish invasion, colonial occupation, Guatemalan genocide, neocolonial occupation, the Age of Emergency, Indigenous resurgence, the Hundred-Year Carnival, and then . . . well. Early Laviaja."

Daveed's eyes were wide. "All those tutorials would take months."

Niloux shook her head. "Two years. Plus recovery."

Daveed put a bowl on the floor, knelt with a cloth over her shoulder, and poured water from the ewer into the bowl. The two vessels matched, bronze chased with gold. They were probably thousands of years old. The ninx talked as she worked, already on to a new subject. "I'm always scared of new duties, but one of my zadres in China told me that everyone is scared of new duties, even adults, so I just have to do it, and then I'll find it's not so scary. Yesterday I learned how to fix agribots. Or at least, the ones that watch over the qanats. Can you fix agribots?"

Now Niloux was starting to smell supper. She could pick out warm curry, tangy tomato, and rich olive oil. Her capacity for small talk was diminishing. She forced herself to answer anyway. "Yes," she said.

"But mostly you're a sofist."

"Mostly. Yes."

"So you work alone all the time?"

"Not all the time. I do maintenance and cooking and cleaning like everyone else. And I communicate with other sofists."

Daveed took Niloux's foot and eased it into the rose-scented water. Niloux closed her eyes at the pleasure of it, feeling two weeks' dust float away. The child's chatter became a kind of background music. "The last wayhouse I was at," she said, "there was an este dane, and her hair was so pretty, all twisted up in braids. And then there's a dryad here—she's my zadre at this wayhouse, Chemy, you'll meet her—and she reconned her supper wear in Epirus. Everyone looks so beautiful. Lift your foot."

Niloux did. Daveed patted her foot dry with the towel, then took her other foot and lowered it into the bath.

"What's that around your neck?" asked Daveed, glancing up.

Niloux fingered the oval on her throat, an orchid carved on silver. "I'm a Child of Saint Leah."

Daveed cocked her head. "What does that mean?"

"It means I don't know my birth zadres."

The child's eyes went wide. "Why?"

"Because they didn't want to be known."

"Are you sad?"

Niloux shrugged. "No. I was given to other zadres like everybody else. About half choose not to be known."

"But I thought anyone could know anything about anybody."

"Birth zadres are one of the only exceptions. To discourage attachment to blood kin."

"Oh!" Daveed nodded, folding the new information into her growing brain. She started washing again. Niloux began to feel restless. She wanted to get on with things: on with supper, on with whatever shit she would face in the common room, on with sleep, on with the tribunal, on with her viaja, on with life. There was too much to do. But this child was still talking. "This is my three hundred and ninth wayhouse. See?" Daveed touched her thumb to her forefinger, and her halo sprouted from her head like dandelion fluff. Each sphere was the token of a wayhouse. Niloux recognized Yuxi, red-and-gold lacquer; and Lahore, gleaming brass.

Daveed blinked twice and her halo collapsed back against her head. "How many tokens do you have?" she asked.

Niloux tapped her temple to ask her ai, *How many wayhouses have I been to?*

The answer sprouted, text in the aug: *Nine hundred and eight.*

Daveed gazed at the number before it dissolved in midair. "Wow," she said softly, drying Niloux's other foot. She was comfortable now, seeming to have forgotten she was speaking to a heretic. "I want to get to Xibalba," she said. "All the other ninx say they want to find their cortada in Cayo, like Saint Leah did, but I think mine is in a desert . . ."

Niloux tuned out at the word "cortada." This was the same old prattle. It was as if she'd never made any proposal to the Tzoyna at all. She'd been naïve to think she could overturn a thousand years of tradition in one night. In Laviaja, cortadas were the theorized cuts in spacetime that allowed a viajera to enter Xibalba. Versa Nueve: *You know not the inch where you will cross.* Cortadas were believed to be exclusive to each individual. Those who disappeared were called saints. Disappearances began during the early Diluvian years, and most attributed this to the development of ojos-de-

Leah, the otracortex that was supposed to help a viajera sense the "thin places" where Xibalba was especially close.

Daveed was still talking. ". . . I think my cortada is in a desert because I had an adivinix in Lahore, and she said I need to pay attention to which gods are calling me, and I've always loved the desert, so I think my cortada is somewhere around here—"

"Do you know how unlikely that is?" Niloux snapped.

Daveed recoiled.

Niloux felt too stubborn to take it back. This kid needed to learn.

Daveed looked down at the ewer and recited, "'In the sum total of all our reincarnations, we would find our cortadas twenty times over.'"

"Sure," said Niloux. That was the standard line in the standard tutorial, world over. "But how many lives is that?"

Daveed wrung her cloth in her hand. "I don't know."

"A good ten million. Ten million lifetimes until the surface of the Earth becomes uninhabitable, even with fugitech that hasn't been invented yet. So yes, if Xibalba exists, you'd get there in your next ten million lifetimes, but how likely is it going to be this one?"

Daveed didn't look up. She finished wringing out the cloth, then slung it over her shoulder. "Well, it's got to be one of them," she said in a small voice, and carried the bowl away.

The honeymoon was over. So be it.

Niloux was ready to face the common room. She'd go in taking the summons at face value: that the purpose of tomorrow's tribunal was just to discuss her ideas. She couldn't imagine being blotted just for that. Surely the scrupes, the orthodox viajeras, hadn't drifted that far. But if she did end up being punished in any way, she wanted to make it perfectly clear that she'd obeyed all the forms. Who was here? She could harvest the basics from the wayhouse ai. It was just after Día de Pasaja, so lots of viajeras had recently changed their manéra. That made it a volatile season, socially. She touched her finger to her temple, and the chamber floor electrified with pistas, the paths each viajera had taken through the chamber. She selected for those colored indigo—the most recent, in her personalized aug—and the viajeras' faces, genéras, and manéras floated up. Pute DeLyon, norte odette. Chemy DeLampang, oeste dryad. Ahmed DeGrozny, sur persian. Niloux's ai informed her that this wayhouse was once the Zein-o-Din caravanserai, a stop on the Silk Road, built by the Safavids in the sixteenth century. It had become a tourist destination during the Age of Emergency, a refuge during the Hundred-Year Carnival, and then one of the first wayhouses in Persia. Also, her ai added: Ruth Okeke, one of the founders of Laviaja, had died here in 2041. Xander Cañul himself had traveled here to attend her deathbed. That made this place a shrine for scrupes. No wonder they wanted to hold the tribunal here.

Niloux put her palms over her eyes. The truth was, she didn't know what she'd started.

"Ven a cenar, Niloux DeCayo," said a voice.

She looked up. It was Daveed. The child looked a little older, now.

Niloux took up her gear and followed her across the chamber, where she pulled back the curtain to the common room.

Twelve stone arches circled a round supper table, open to the night sky. The adult viajeras reclined on pillows, floated on hoverdishes, or sat on cushions, talking in twos and threes; at the far end, ninx played near a fire pit, where two viajeras were cooking. Everyone was in their supper wear, their carefully curated social costumes. In old times, everyone was welcome at a wayhouse table regardless of how they looked; in modern times, it had become gauche to appear at supper in travel wear. But Niloux was already persona non grata. She might as well twist the knife.

Daveed abandoned her, running down the ramp and calling, "She's here! I brought her!"

Everyone looked up. Silence fell. Some stood up.

"Buenas noches," said Niloux.

There was a clang from the fire pit. Someone had dropped a spoon.

She took another step down.

One viajera rushed forward as if to stop her. Niloux stood still. Without touching her temple, she asked her ai to identify her, and the tag unfurled over her head: *Pute DeLyon*, the odette. She was tall and regal, and wore a white feather diadem around a black bun. Her interpretation of the manéra was uninspired. Apparently she was a historian who studied the transitional Magdalene Catholic architectures of the Hundred-Year Carnival. It sounded pretentious.

"Niloux DeCayo," said Pute.

"Yes."

"The author of the proposal to the Tzoyna."

Niloux raised her eyebrows. There was no mistaking which proposal she meant. "That's me."

Several of the viajeras murmured to one another. The ninx were alert.

Pute said, "We thought you might prefer to eat in your room."

"You thought wrong."

"We thought it might be more *prudent*—"

"I have nothing to hide."

Pute sneered. "That much is clear."

"And therefore, I refuse to be hidden."

Pute spread her arms like a swan displaying rank, though Niloux could sense her insecurity. Yes, she thought, Pute had just changed to an odette and was still growing into the performance.

"No one is stopping you from doing anything," Pute said. "Laviaja permits perfect individual freedom."

Niloux smiled, wry. "So it does."

Pute frowned again. "But it's irresponsible to say what you said."

"Irresponsible?" said Niloux. "The Tzoyna's entire purpose is to discuss questions that relate to the global good."

"You know better," Pute snapped. "It's not so simple when it comes from a sofist of your reputation. Your words threaten civilization itself."

Niloux scowled. She'd been in the wilderness for weeks and she'd reported to the summons like a good viajera. What else did she have to do? Right now she was hungry and didn't want to debate a scrupe on an empty stomach. So she switched to High Spanish and made her voice clear and strong. "Vengo en paz, sin violencia en mi mente, solo preguntas. Ojalá que pueda comer. ¿Tengo permiso o no?"

Pute blanched.

Everyone was staring at the odette now. By asking permission to eat in the ritual language of Laviaja, Niloux had shamed her. No matter the personal conflict, it was unthinkable to deny a viajera food upon arriving at a wayhouse. Versa Seis: *La extranjerix más extraña es tu hermanix.* Inhospitality was the strongest taboo.

Pute picked up a clay bowl and held it out to her.

Niloux let out a breath she didn't realize she was holding. She came forward to take the bowl. "Gracias," she mumbled, and sat on a cushion.

The cooks had been watching. After a few whispers, and a few more clangs and shuffles, they carried the pots to the table. The other viajeras cleared the room. The ninx climbed onto cushions or laps. The wind rose to a scream outside the walls, died down again. One viajera remarked on it, and then several were talking, and the conversation rose like a tide.

Niloux just listened. Right now she had that terrible hunger that came upon viajeras whenever they came in from the wild, having lived on foraging, bia, and photosugar for weeks. Here was hot food cooked by human hands: tomato curry, barley soup, and cracked tahdig with pomegranate sauce. Soon she was on her third helping. She ate and listened. The conversation didn't concern the Tzoyna, Xibalba, or the proposal; by unspoken agreement, the company seemed content with a moratorium. They talked about updates to the hoverdish—fugitechs had finally figured out how to maintain the magnetic cushion over rough water. They talked about the new australian manéra. Niloux sneered into her soup. Manéras that were descended from ancient ethnic groups were fine by her—she belonged to one—but those based on ancient nation states made her uneasy. They gossiped about the glucosis of the Pacific—purists who claimed to subsist on photosugar alone—though many supplemented with kelp. They talked about relations with the sedentix, the few thousand humans who opted to settle in one place instead of wander, "as is natural," said Pute. It occurred to Niloux to say that a thousand years ago, settling was the natural state of life and nomadism was the exception; but she didn't want to press her luck. She continued to listen. It was an exciting season for the luchas—the "battles" among manéras, conveyed by pitz or poetry—as so many viajeras had recently switched. So last year's manéras were out of favor and this season's, trending. Visigoths were out and miqunks were in. The miqunks were now courting the mermaids and clamor was building for a lucha between exemplars of each. Niloux had missed it all in the wilderness, ignoring the aug—augmented reality, the virtual world that was integrated with the physical world. She'd been deep inside her own head. But now she was among other humans again. She had to remember how to be with them.

All twenty-three viajeras at the wayhouse were present around the table. As Niloux ate, she observed them all. Murete was a minnesotan, wearing a puffy yellow-and-purple coat, sitting in a hoverdish. Rrimeq was a himba, bare-chested, her braids bound in red clay. Chemy was a dryad, wearing an olive garland, regrowing one of her fingers. Niloux noticed two jovenix who spoke together in low voices, glancing at her but seeming unsure what to say. Everyone observed each other at supper. That's what supper was for. Under normal circumstances, this would be her familia for the next few days, and she'd assume a relationship with each according to the seven relational classifications in Laviaja:

Six ninx and two jovenix, age three to seventeen. Niloux would be their tíax, as a rule, since all the ninx were already paired with zadres.

Thirteen adult viajeras, age twenty to one hundred and seven. Those could be Niloux's hermanix, encamadix, or ancianix, depending on whether their chemistry was more like that of brethren, lovers, or elders. Her ai asked whether she wished to know the preféras, the sexual inclinations, of those at the wayhouse. She blinked her right eye to say no. She wasn't here for sex.

When the tea arrived, the ninx returned to playing. The adults became more bold in their topics of conversation. Ahmed mentioned that yet again, there had been no new disappearances in the preceding year.

"Have you heard of that adivinix, Sembaruthi?" said Murete. "She's credited with the last disappearance in 3009."

"Credited how?" said Ahmed.

Pute jumped in, as if to stake territory. "Sembaruthi DeSiruvani was the last one to perform divination for Gemet DeGonder before she disappeared. That means her divination sent her in the right direction. And now she is in Xibalba."

There was an uncomfortable silence. The word had been spoken. Niloux just stared into her tea, not speaking unless spoken to. If anyone wanted to talk to her, she was right there.

"Niloux?" said Ahmed.

It hadn't taken long.

"I know the tribunal is tomorrow, but maybe . . . just informally . . . can you give us any more context for your proposal to the Tzoyna?"

Now even the ninx hushed by the fire pit.

Niloux looked up from her tea glass.

Ahmed drew back. "Only if you want to," she said. "I've read your submissions on cortada theory. The new proposal just seems like a total reversal of your previous work."

Niloux reminded herself that Ahmed was young. She was curious, not malicious. So she had to be gentle, but also understate her case. The euphoria she'd felt in the wild would not serve her here.

"My experience suggests," she said, "that the ideal existence we seek, what we call Xibalba, is merely a new understanding of this reality." She remembered Venus rising over the pool, sending a message. More words came to her. "That maybe it's a reconciliation of our past lives."

"But how can we know our past lives?"

Niloux shrugged. "Don't know yet."

Ahmed seemed surprised by the admission. "All right. But what would we do once we knew our past lives?"

"I'm guessing we would braid them."

"Like what we do with information in the Tzoyna," said Daveed, sitting on Chemy's lap.

Chemy put her arm around the child's waist and said, "This is your idea?"

"It's not new," said Niloux. "Plato proposed it in *Meno* three thousand years ago. He said that we know more than we can tell, because of our past lives. That we carry memories of them. But instead of surfacing in any predictable way, they surface in our instincts. I'm saying if we knew our past lives, we would reconcile them, and then . . ."

"Then what?" said Pute.

Niloux pursed her lips. "Transcendence," she said.

Pute narrowed her eyes at the mocking tone.

"But do you have any proof?" said the other jove-nix. Niloux asked her ai for her name: Rhett. She had a spiky red mohawk. Niloux saw Ahmed wincing, and guessed that the two were encamadix, and Ahmed was embarrassed by her lover's indelicacy.

Niloux went easy on Rhett, for the sake of Ahmed, whom she liked. "Proof is a westernist construct," she said. "I use westernist techniques when applicable, but often they're not."

"Oh," said Rhett, looking confused.

Ahmed rushed in. "Niloux works in older traditions than westernism," she said.

Rhett lit up and snapped her fingers. "Oh, I remember this now from tutorial! Westernism ended because of disappearances."

"It didn't end," said Ahmed, "it just stopped being the world's dominant epistemology. No one could deny that disappearances were real, but no one could study them, either, because they didn't fit westernist criteria for study."

"Meaning . . ."

"Meaning they couldn't be repeated or predicted."

"Yes," said Niloux, relieved to not have to explain everything herself. "In fact, most phenomena can't be. So we use techniques from the contemplative and fictive traditions."

"Fictive, meaning . . ."

"The science of learning the universe by creating it."

Pute leaned forward and crossed her arms. "So you decided to create chaos."

Niloux pressed her lips together and stared at the table, taking her time. No one spoke.

"I just asked a damn question," said Niloux, "which is what sofists do."

"A question implying that"—Pute gestured to the crusty pots—"this is all there is to reality."

"Yes." Niloux clenched her teeth. Now she remembered why she liked being alone in the wild.

People were hell. "We live in utopia. Right now. I hate to tell you, but this is as close as humankind is ever going to get. The world has been at peace for four hundred years. We can control our metabolisms. We have endurance and heat tolerance. We've reengineered the planet for freedom of human movement. We can learn any subject or skill in hours. No one goes hungry. No one is imprisoned. No one fears violence. No one lacks shelter or companionship or medicine. Everyone has an equal voice in local tzoynas or the global Tzoyna."

Pute blinked. "But people still—"

"Die? Experience pain? Feel dissatisfaction? Of course they do. A mortal is mortal. But everyone is free to live however they want, even scrupes."

The table became deathly quiet.

Niloux realized she was dealing with scrupes.

At last Pute said, "What a utopia, where such words are used."

Niloux tried to regain ground. "It's just short for scrupulous."

"And in the holy burial place of Ruth Okeke. How dare you."

"It's just a word, and it's not inaccurate."

"A coward's excuse," said Pute, quiet and furious. "We follow the Rule of Saint Leah, which was written to ensure peace for all humanity. You call it scrupulous. We call it basic."

Niloux sneered. "Maybe we're not so equal in La-viaja after all."

"I guess not," said Pute.

"But don't you see that's the point?" said Niloux. "Any system will fragment. That's entropy. Stratifications always form in any social system, no matter how hard we try to prevent them."

"So you're saying we should give up trying," said Pute.

"No. I'm saying that all systems change, but we can choose to direct that change for the good. Utopia is dynamic."

"That's the opposite of what utopia means. Utopia is an ideal. Our world is a communist—"

"Communist? Who told you that?" Niloux laughed. She couldn't help herself, even though she knew the argument was getting ugly, and was aware of children watching. She put her finger down on the table to emphasize each word. "Our world is a pacifist, no-madic, subsidiarist, anarchist gift economy that evolved in response to rapid, catastrophic climate change."

"You interrupted me."

Niloux pressed her lips together and gestured, magnanimous. No one else spoke. Their heads just went back and forth as if they were watching a pitz game.

"Utopia is not possible at all in this world," said Pute slowly, staring into space, "because even now, there's a gap between what we have and what we want. To obtain what we want, we have to make sacrifices." She seemed to gather herself, sit up straighter. "Sacrifice is a technology common to every human belief system. In the case of the ancient Maya, the sacrifice was blood. In the case of capitalism, time."

"I'm curious," said Rrimeq. "What would you say the sacrifice is in Laviaja?"

Pute turned to her. "Each other. We give each other up, according to the Principle of Dispersion. My nine days are over. Tomorrow after the tribunal, I'm going to leave this wayhouse and never see any of you again."

"So what you're saying," said Rrimeq, "is that because Laviaja still requires sacrifice, it is by definition not a utopia."

Pute looked ready to disagree, but then frowned, and nodded. "Yes. And that utopia isn't possible in this world, but we still long for it, so we must seek the Other World. Laviaja came from—"

"Climate refugees!" Niloux interrupted. "But as a *practical necessity,* not as a religion. The refugees had to let go of people and places, forever. They had to invent fugitech to survive the floods. They had to stay in small bands to survive the pandemics. Only *later* did viajeras start saying that Xander Cañul and Javier Magaña must be the reincarnations of Ixul and Ajul. Only *later* did Laviaja get mashed up with Maya mythology and the story of Saint Leah. Like the Catholics who invented the Immaculate Conception after the fact, to explain how Mary was born without sin. We made it up. We made it all up."

"Including disappearances?"

Silence at the table.

Disappearances. That was going to be the weak point of Niloux's argument, she knew. She still couldn't explain disappearances. She saw now that she'd underestimated Pute, and her overconfidence had trapped her in an unwinnable argument. Why not broadcast this, she thought. We don't have to wait until tomorrow for the tribunal. This is it.

Pute leaned in. "Meanwhile—to be practical, as you say—peace needs enforcement. Shared fear is the only thing that guards norms of behavior. Among the ancient Maya, fear of the gods. In capitalism, fear of the state. In Laviaja, what is the only thing we fear?"

Niloux snorted. "Bad sex."

"Entropy," said Pute, as if she hadn't heard. "Entropy is the most fundamental law of this universe.

Everything will be lost. All knowledge, all memory, all meaning. I refuse to accept that there is not a greater reality."

"So we just wander around." Niloux couldn't keep the bite from her voice. "We wander and wander until we 'cross over' to this mystical realm of Xibalba, which no one has ever seen, no one has ever come back from, and no one can confirm."

"The alternative is to settle like a sedentix. And then it's a quick slide back into hoarding."

"Not necessarily!" Niloux was yelling now. She felt like a cornered cat, all its tricks used up. "We don't have to go back! We can go . . . up." She gestured to the stars overhead. She looked for Venus but couldn't find it, then remembered that Venus was in its morning star phase. The planet had seemed to call to her at the oasis. Now she felt abandoned. "Humanity gave up on space travel entirely. Why? Because Laviaja says we need to stay bound to the Earth. What if we change? What if we listen to—what's their name—the sofist who . . ."

Niloux trailed off, having forgotten the name. She didn't want to rely on her ai. It was an obscure sofist from the twenty-eighth century who'd proposed space travel and been ridiculed, never taken seriously again.

The wind screamed in the silence.

Niloux felt hot blood rush to her face. She'd lost this argument and everyone knew it.

"Humanity left space travel behind," said Pute in a smug voice, "because it would require enormous accumulations of capital, which is also prohibited by the Principle of Dispersion—on grounds of practicality, which I know you value. But by all means, propose space travel to the Tzoyna, next time."

"Maybe I will. At the Jubilee itself."

Niloux said it on impulse. It was the first time she'd even thought it, much less said it aloud. But she realized she meant it.

Pute was speechless.

In the silence that followed, Daveed asked, "What's the Jubilee?"

Her sweet piping voice made everyone blink, as if coming out of a trance; they remembered a child was there.

Chemy answered. "It's a big party," she said, "that's going to be held in Cayo at the end of this year. You know how we gather every December, no matter where we are?"

"To celebrate Día de Pasaja."

"Yes. Día de Pasaja is on December twenty-first every year, but this year it's the thousand-year anniversary of Laviaja."

"What happened a thousand years ago?"

"It's the day Saint Leah disappeared in the Great Cave."

"How many people are going? A hundred?"

"No, many more."

"Thousands?"

"Possibly tens of thousands."

"Of people? Together in the same place? Is that allowed?" Her eyes were big as moons.

Pute had been quiet during this interlude, and now got up, her teacup empty. She'd decided to leave the field victorious. "Well, good luck, Niloux DeCayo, great and particular sofist," she said. "Thank you for sharing your thoughts. We'll see you at the tribunal in the morning."

She swished off to her room and closed the curtain.

No one moved.

Then Daveed said, "I think I was Bill Gates in a past life."

Everyone laughed, which made her cry, because she had been serious.

Niloux went straight to her assigned room.

She pulled the curtain shut so violently that it almost fell down. She didn't care who saw. Let them watch—small-minded reactionaries, all of them. But Niloux was frustrated with herself, too. Tomorrow was the tribunal. She had to have better answers by then. The whole world would be watching.

She tapped the moonball in the corner. The room filled with a milky glow. She unpacked her gear: printer, plate, kiln, canteen, pillow, bia to print organics, and pluripote to print inorganics. Like every viajera, she owned no more than she could carry. Versa Ocho: *Posee solo lo que cargas.* Fifteen pounds of fugitech for a human to survive anywhere on Earth. She took off her tunic and skirt, which stank of sweat. She'd compost them and print new travel wear. She set aside her supper wear for the tribunal: an embroidered cotton huipil, a layered skirt, a necklace of coral, and a pot of red ochre for her face, with enough clay mixed in to contrast with her dark brown skin. After twenty years of being the same manéra, her look was pretty simple.

Niloux sat on her bedroll, thinking.

A lion roared, far away in the desert.

She got up and stood at the wall. She touched her temple to activate the aug, so that the wall became a tablet, and started writing with her finger.

What are disappearances?

She stared at the words.

She didn't know what else to write. She was blocked.

She summoned the Tzoyna feed. An I-shaped courtyard appeared, a projection of the ball court at the ancient city of Tzoyna. She dragged her question into the center lane. Immediately, the court filled with a cloud of text, images, stories, streams, simulations, audio, and video, all linked to her original proposal. Niloux had asked for only thirty-six hours of discussion by the Tzoyna. Now they were on hour 355. She might have felt proud of raising such a ruckus if she didn't feel sick at the thought of having to deal with the fallout from scrupes like Pute for who knew how long.

She had to think. Head-on engagement was too stressful. She had to seek a reframing, an oblique strategy.

She turned the data cloud like a piñata. Other lobes represented other topics.

Can blotting still be considered a humane punishment for any crime when restorative, rehabilitative, and reconciliatory justice are available?

Niloux snorted. No, she thought, but good luck trying to get rid of the human urge to punish. When someone was blotted, anyone could remove her from view in the aug, thereby potentially removing her from mutual aid networks. But whether a person was blotted depended on the viewer and the offense. Niloux didn't blot anyone, even the violent. She knew what it was like to feel violent.

More topics:

Is it a violation of the Treaty of 2780 to print animal flesh in our kilns, because we're not actually killing a sentient being?

A lot of viajeras were printing meat these days. Niloux did, but deep in the wilderness so she didn't get nasty looks in person. No one could hunt real animals unless they consented to being hunted in turn, which meant permanently deactivating their shields.

Why do rummages still exist when they're clearly concentrations of goods in violation of the Principle of Dispersion?

Niloux rolled her eyes. It was telling that the questioner had used capital letters. Scrupes loved to use capital letters.

She continued turning the cloud with flicks of her finger.

Should birth zadres be required to be known to their birth children and vice versa, rather than it being a choice?

Can paragua algorithms ever be truly neutral, even given decentralization measures?

Should we restrain viajeras who put themselves in danger to find their cortadas?

Is voluntary manéra a triumph over whiteness or a triumph of whiteness?

Should birthplace determine manéra?

"Great idea!" Niloux said aloud. "Let's bring back ethnostates too."

She slapped the wall to close the feed.

She was angry at the last question. People were getting careless. The concórdia system of identity was so hard-won: the self-determined trinity of genéra, manéra, y preféra. She knew she was norte by the age of five, she'd declared her manéra when she was ten, and she was mostly an endotánte in bed, liking to give and penetrate. Other viajeras were other things, but all bodies were good. That was the important thing. Like other viajeras, she'd been epigenetically treated in the womb to grow a uterus, vagina, penis, and testicles—a legacy of the population bottleneck of the twenty-fifth century, when humans had had to take drastic measures to ensure survival of the species. Now that biological imperative had calcified into religious tradition. Versa Cuatro: *Las pluripotentix sobreviven.* Some chafed at it and addressed the incongruence by shrinking one set of genitalia in favor of the other. But the right to choose and change manéra was central to a peaceful society. The entire course of history demonstrated how rigid attachments—to nation, to land, to wealth, to kin—ultimately led to violence. Yet fools still asked questions like *Should birthplace determine manéra* as if no one had ever thought of them before, as if the entire fifteenth through twenty-sixth centuries weren't a repudiation of such determinism, as if—Pute was right—humanity couldn't so easily slide back into violence. People got comfortable. People forgot.

Niloux felt restless. She'd seen a stairway next to her door, so she left her room and took it up to the roof. The wind was so strong it nearly knocked her over, but it felt good, extreme, matching her inner state. She leaned on the rampart and looked toward the mountains. Jupiter was rising, due east.

A turtledove landed in one of the cubbies and startled Niloux out of thought. It was a real bird, not an aug messenger. The dove turned to the mountains and began to sing. Her ai translated:

> The poet is too near
> The poet is too near
> Eggs in the sky

It flew off.

What did it mean? Niloux didn't know. She wasn't a therolinguist, much less one who specialized in dove.

Alone at the oasis, she'd been sure of herself. But tonight had been a rude awakening. She realized she was only beginning. She knew that Xibalba was not real, and that society must stop being structured around an untruth. But she had to offer an alternative.

Her theology floated back to her: *The god of the place is time integrated over space.*

In Laviaja, "god" was the sum total of the natural history of a place, known and unknown, integrated over time. In this spot, where the caravanserai stood, the god was her experience of standing here, and of the refugees and scholars and merchants who had stood here before her, and the Safavid artisans who'd built the walls; and before that, the mouse plucked by the hawk, the snake en route to water, the cedars long dead, the bedrock unbroken, and the very earth that had slid into place a billion years ago. God was as small as a micron and as large as the cosmos. God as place. Pistas, meanwhile, were singular to each person; individuals' paths that formed an inscription upon the land, like a text that could be read. Niloux felt that she should start addressing disappearances by studying pistas: a contemplative approach, this time, instead of a quantitative one.

She softened her mind and said to herself, *Si pudiera ver con los ojos de Santa Leah.*

She realized she was invoking the name of the very saint she'd denounced. Her habits had calcified too.

Why ask help from a girl who died a thousand years ago? She needed new heroes. What was the name of the sofist she'd forgotten at supper, who'd proposed space travel in the twenty-eighth century? She flushed at the memory of forgetting it. She still wanted to remember without using her ai. When she was young, to remember a name, she'd go through all thirty-two letters of the Común alphabet, hovering over each letter like a bee over hibiscus, and ask—*Are you the one I seek? Yes? No?* And each time, she knew exactly which was the right letter, though she couldn't tell how she knew.

She tried it now.

Do you start with A? No.

Do you start with B? No.

Do you start with Bh? No.

She was the bee, going from letter to letter.

Ñ? No.

O? No.

P? No.

She would run out of letters.

R? No.

S? No.

T? Yes, yes, yes:

Ting Lee DeBrazza.

The name flowered across her mind with no effort. All she'd had to do was find the right starting letter.

Niloux frowned. She had a hunch. Ideas were connecting in her mind.

She focused on the horizon, and like a bee dropping to the flower, she let her eyes alight on a mountain peak. Instead of trying to remember a name, she was trying to remember a place.

God of the place: do you know me?

No especial feeling.

She shifted her eyes to the next peak.

God of the place: do you know me?

No especial feeling.

She shifted her eyes closer, to a patch of land beneath her.

God of the place. Do you know me?

Yes.

The answer was immediate and absolute. Just as with Venus at the oasis, her body flushed with a certainty that her mind reeled to understand.

Niloux had been here before. For the first time in the history of Laviaja, she'd concretely sensed a past life. All she'd had to do was graft a childhood game onto the landscape.

"Mark it," she told her ai. The patch of land below her blushed in the aug.

She smacked the stone. Now she had something to tell the tribunal.

TZOYNA
3 Batz' 14 Pop, Long Count 10.9.5.7.11

---

9 December, 1012

Ket fell backward in her trance, away from her own slumped body, and hit a clump of soil at an awkward angle, against her neck; the clump crumbled and gave way, her heels vaulted over her head, and she somersaulted through the earth. She scraped for a hold but couldn't find any, only more soil that burst in her hand. She couldn't scream because she couldn't get her breath. The light was fading, covered up by collapsing earth, and a big whip spider was leaping from clump to clump in her wake, following her progress with a bright yellow eye. Every time her body rolled to a stop, the soil strained and burst, and she was tumbling backward again. She stopped trying to find handholds. She drew in her limbs and let herself fall.

She hit open space.

She opened her eyes.

She was falling into a red city in a green valley.

She alighted in the main plaza, marked by a perfect grid of ceiba trees. It was twilight here.

She recognized the city as her own. There were her brother Ajul and sister Ixul, her mother and father, and their ancestors before them, all the way back to the Hero Twins, dim tall figures whose faces were obscured. They were all standing in the grid, aligned with the trees, and drawing their hands across their chests and pointing to the sky, but the motion was halting and inexact, as if they were trying to remember it. They wore masks, as if playing roles in an entertainment: the farmer, the priest, the dwarf, the scribe, the merchant, the warrior, the daykeeper, the lackey, the refugee, the king.

The plaza cracked open and she fell through.

The whip spider leapt after her, the hunt afoot again.

She hadn't wanted to leave that place. She'd wanted to watch the dance and maybe try it herself. But she had no control over anything. This earth wasn't soft soil, it was hard and broken rocks, stabbing her in the back as she tumbled. She drew in her arms and legs again, miserable. She shouldn't have let blood so young. She wasn't ready for this.

She hit open space.

She opened her eyes.

She was falling into a red city on a green hilltop.

Again, she alighted on the plaza in twilight.

It was still her city, but now it sat on an acropolis so high above the earth that she could see the mountains moving in the mists below, like herds of deer. In this plaza, the stars were nearer and brighter, and the trees were lower and fatter, shedding blood-red leaves in a circle around each trunk. A grey road began at the edge of the plaza and departed into an eternity that lapped the edges of the acropolis. Ixul and Ajul were standing at either side of the road like sentinels, rigid, holding matching spears.

She started toward them, wanting to be with them.

A black jaguar appeared on the road.

Ket froze.

But the twins didn't seem to notice the jaguar. Instead, they leveled their spears at each other, as if to attack.

Ket took a step forward.

They began to circle each other.

Stop, she tried to yell, but her voice got stuck in her throat. She started to run toward them, but then the jaguar charged her and scooped her up like a little doll so that she flipped head over heels to land on its back, and as the plaza collapsed and the jaguar leapt down, she saw the twins shoot up into the sky like a pair of hawks.

She held tight to the jaguar's neck. She couldn't see anything in the dark. But judging by the lurches and jolts, the jaguar was leaping from ledge to ledge, deeper into the earth. Then she heard the sound of rushing water. The jaguar slid into a channel that twisted and dropped and gathered speed. Spray splashed her face. Was she in the underworld now? Or still in her own city, in the Tzoynas beneath her Tzoyna; or in the city that had existed before any Tzoyna, far older, before the humans, with no name, when there was only stone and stars?

There was a moment of sickening free fall, and then a powerful splash.

Ket held on tight to the jaguar's neck, gripping her own wrist.

They began to swim downward. The water was warm, and Ket found she could breathe.

A glow appeared below them. The light was the same color as the light on the plaza—pink-orange, shimmering like the lip of a seashell. She began to be able to see. She made out the jaguar's huge paws sweeping, one and then the other, as if it were crawling down the column of water. The water tasted like cacao.

She relaxed. She felt that even though she was not in control, she was safe. She wanted to remember all these things: the ancestors, the red leaves, the green mountain, the grey road, the cacao water. She wanted to hold on to them and understand their meanings.

She was amazed to realize that, in one hand, she still held her obsidian blade. How had she not dropped it, so many years ago, with her brother on the ball court? How had it survived all this tumbling and sliding and swimming? She held it up to the seed of light that was growing beneath her, and as if delighted to see itself in a mirror, the blade began to turn so fast that its four spokes blurred into a circle that began to glow, and now she could see that this blade was not just shaped like a star, but was a real star, an actual star, which both signified all things and was itself all things.

Ket's eyes fluttered, but Ajul knew she wasn't there.

He laid the cloth over her eyes so she could better see what she was meant to see. She'd cut too deep, but there'd be no infection. He'd seen to that. Now he made sure her body was comfortable in the shade. He took off his outer esh and folded it, lifted her head, and slid it under. Her chest rose and fell rapidly.

He reclined next to her and looked up at the ceiba trees. The howler monkeys roared in the distance,

fighting their own wars, defending their own kingdoms. He felt lucky to have a little sister so sweet, she
would ingest the god and let blood—at seven!—for
the good of the Tzoyna. He wasn't worried about the
night's ascension ceremony, or ball game, or even the
sacrifices. It wasn't in his nature to worry. It was certainly Ixul's nature, though. When they were children,
they'd practiced the ball game on this very court, marking every hit with yells that echoed against the hills.
Any child born in these times was precious, but Ajul
and Ixul were both considered exceptional, so clever,
so tall, so pleasing to the eye, Ajul the hunter and Ixul
the scribe, both undefeated on the court.

Meanwhile, baby Ket sat on the sidelines in her
blankets, wobbling under the weight of her headboard.

They had all watched Ket from birth, waiting for
her gifts to manifest. But Ket was slow, clumsy, and
quiet. Her face was plain. She'd taken a long time to
crawl, stand, walk, and speak. She was born too cold,
always grasping for heat, so they kept her near the fire
to keep her spirit inside of her; Mutna kept the twins
away, as twins had a tendency to draw heat. Ket ate
mud for a long time and still ate termites when no one
was looking, which Ixul hated, because eating termites
was low and vulgar, a refugee's trick.

Ajul and Ixul noticed their father's disappointment in her. They copied it. They'd always been closer to their father, as the future heirs, while Ket had been closer to their mother. Now Ajul regretted that. Both their parents were gone, and Ket was trying to be brave and helpful. If he and Ixul couldn't produce an heir, maybe Ket herself could be their heir. He liked the idea. All he really wanted was a wife and child to love and serve, and weren't both already right in front of him?

But now that he'd thought of heir-making, he was restless for Ixul. Now were the few hours of midday when they always met. Today they had to abstain from coupling because of the ceremony, but surely, he thought, at least they could talk.

Ajul left Ket on the court, confident that no harm could come to her.

Whistling, he took the old path down the terraces, leaping from step to step until it led to the family garden. He broke into a bawdy Kaanu'li song he'd learned from eavesdropping on some guests of his father's, years ago, about "the butter and the cob." He hadn't known what it was about then, but now he did. He'd sung it to Ixul once, and expected her to reprimand him, but she just laughed loudly. He loved her for it. She always surprised him.

He remembered how, a year and a half earlier, they'd been waiting in this garden for their parents to return. They were away in Monpanotoch, holding a canoe race to mark the return of Chak Ek' as the evening star. Their father had raised them on stories of the great canoe races: teams traveling from as far as Tula to compete, ninety-nine canoes launching at once like so many leaves blown from the god's hand, the leaders spreading a skirt behind them and making the others capsize, and hecklers standing on the banks to taunt them and throw lima beans. Both twins had been unhappy about being left behind. But, their father argued, they needed to begin learning statecraft. They would act as regents in his absence and give a full report upon his return.

So here they were in the garden, cross-legged on a stone bench, fighting about which ball player was the greatest in history. Ajul was arguing for Jasaw Chan K'awiil, the great king of Mutul who'd captured his nemesis the Snake King, treated him as an honored guest, then defeated him in single combat. But Ixul was arguing for Saktelab, the mischievous rogue who'd abandoned her metate and wandered from city to city challenging their best players.

Then Upakal appeared on the rampart above. He looked somber. Ajul stood up immediately. Upakal was the captain of the guard, but even so, he was required to ask permission before entering their presence. The fact that he had not was a sign that something was wrong.

"Your parents set out from Monpanotoch three days ago," said Upakal. "They should have arrived by yesterday morning."

Ixul stood up too, angry at his breach of protocol. She only tolerated familiar speech from her family and her tutor. "Remember yourself," she said sharply.

Upakal's eyes widened. Immediately he leapt down into the garden and prostrated below them. When he spoke again, it was into the dirt. "May Your Royal Highness forgive your servant, Ahau. I will not forget again."

Ixul relaxed. She sat down on the bench with her back straight. At a look, Ajul sat down next to her.

"I forgive you, child of maize," she said, "and invite you to deliver your message."

Upakal continued talking into the dirt. "Ahau, I, your servant, do not know the whereabouts of your parents, Our Royal Majesties. We have only heard one report about the canoe race, from a farmer who left after the launch. We have sent scouts on the road, but no one has seen the king and queen on the road, nor any of their retinue."

"Then send the scouts to Monpanotoch."

"We did, Ahau. The merchant Letutz said they were not in his city."

"Then they're lying," said Ixul. "They're holding them captive. How dare common merchants lay hand on royal blood. We have to send our warriors."

Upakal paused. "I, your servant, would not advise that, Ahau, as it is not the season for war."

"I don't care!" shouted Ixul. "Prepare them!"

Ajul laid a hand on her shoulder, but Upakal was saying in a soft voice, "I, your servant, do not have enough warriors, Ahau."

Ajul asked him to sit up and repeat himself, and he did, his eyes downcast.

Then Ajul said, "What did you hear from the farmer who was at the race?"

Upakal hesitated.

"It's all right," said Ajul. "We will not harm you for reporting the truth."

"Ahau, I do not know if the farmer was lying."

"Just say what he said."

Upakal licked his lips. "The farmer said that only four teams arrived, two from Katwitz, one from Pekwitz, and one more from the scrublands, but the canoers were drunk."

The twins were silent. They knew their father had expected far more—twenty teams had been invited, and seventeen promised. He'd spent a year planning the race, wanting to unite the realm after another hard drought. This had been their chance to assert themselves as benefactors.

The grackles shrieked overhead. The sun beat down.

Ixul said, "We thank our servant, Upakal, for your message," in a composed and formal voice. "You may go now."

Upakal made an elaborate prostration and left the garden.

They were fourteen years old. Ajul started crying, saying, "We're the only ones left. What do we do?" But Ixul remained silent, thinking and chewing her lip.

Finally, Ixul steered him to the shade of a young cotton tree. Her movements were calm and ordered, even as Ajul's were heaving and shuddering. She pushed him gently down to the ground, then took the end of her esh in her hand and tucked it into her waistband, to reveal the seashell that covered her sex. Ajul averted his eyes. But then she unhooked the seashell from her waistband and put it in his mouth, to quiet him. She pressed her hand on his chest and he lay back, surprised, but doing what she wanted without question. She was the firstborn, even if only by an hour. He followed her in all things. Her heart-shaped face was dark against the canopy. Grackles snickered overhead.

What happened next was first surprising, then natural: an answer to his question. A hot grip, an unbearable tugging, the seashell splintering in his mouth. Then a wave of calm. He stopped crying.

Always they'd played games as children. They played in the garden, the palace, the ball courts. Of course they played the ball game itself, but whenever they got tired of it, they played war games, ritual games, and divination games. Ajul was the one who played by the rules; Ixul was the one who broke them and made up new ones. They held "concerts" with sticks and whistles, and "feasts" with guavas and maize cobs, with piles of rocks meant to be roast meat, and bowls of mud for cacao. They would smell each dish and describe the smells to each other as never-ending "poems." They would hunt each other in the jungle, with Ajul playing a refugee from Oxwitza and Ixul playing a Nahua warrior, and then take each other captive, and torture and sacrifice each other, performing cruelty and mercy in turn. They would switch back and forth between all the languages they knew: their native tongue High Ch'ol, elegant Lakamhan, haughty Yucatec, tongue-tripping Nahuatl, and handtalk, a sign language that only the royal family knew. They memorized the family tree that was carved in the public plaza, going back four thousand years, all the way to the Hero Twins; then they would reenact the highlights of their lineage over the course of days, forgetting to eat or wash or even sleep. They would invite Ket to join them, but only to make her worship them, which she did, without question, bringing wildflowers as tribute and offering them in prostration. And then they would dismiss her, and she would wander off to play games by herself.

Now their games were real. There was no time to mourn. They had no parents to teach them, only Mutna. She made them memorize the star almanacs, the seventy varieties of maize, the Kojkinia's *Ball Game*, the nine chronicles of *The Unity of the Senses* by Chenchup of Kaanu'l, and the philosophies of Tulum, the Place of Reeds, far to the dayfall. They memorized records of the ball-game leagues, in peace and wartime. They learned how to divine omens, especially from birds, the messengers of the gods—owl, macaw, quetzal. They read the chronicles of the great wars between Mutul and Oxwitza, and of the Saalian rebellion; and the Black Treatise, the manual on the treatment of captives; and the Epic of the Bloodmaiden, the mother of the Hero Twins. They read to each other from volumes of Lakamhan love poems, which were sad and elegant and watery, just like the city itself.

Ajul longed for Ixul, even when he was lying right beside her. Some days were worse than others. Today was very bad. He'd told her once, while inside her, in a moment of sincerest poetry, that his prick always felt like a torch that needed dousing. She started laughing so hard that her muscles squeezed him out. So he never said it again. But it was exactly how he felt when they met in the family palace at noon, when the day's heat was darkest. She took a long time, which made Ajul happy; he was content to linger with his head between her legs for hours. He, on the other hand, climaxed quickly and repeatedly. She joked, *I'm mostly made of you by now.* That made him laugh.

They no longer took pains to keep it a secret. Upakal and Mutna must know. They'd said nothing against it. So—Ajul thought—their closeness doesn't offend the gods, the underworld, or the heavens, as he'd first feared. Their closeness was understood: royal blood could not dilute itself with lesser lines.

Even though they wouldn't lie together today, Ajul washed himself in the garden spring, taking extra care with his armpits and crack. He peeled back his hood and put his penis directly into the stream of water and rubbed it over with his fingers so that there was no possibility of any smell left. He had a tendency to smell strongly. At his best, he smelled like woodsmoke, but Ixul had once remarked that he smelled like dog piss.

It hurt him. He never wanted that to happen again. He scrubbed himself raw and hoped she noticed.

Ajul wicked himself dry and then leapt up the stairs to the family quarters. All the bedchambers were arranged around a green courtyard. They usually met in Ixul's chamber, and sometimes she was already there, reading, naked, globed buttocks splayed casually on the blankets. He rushed to the door and pulled it open.

He looked both ways. No Ixul.

He felt hurt. He needed her. Maybe she was elsewhere in the palace.

Ajul heard a growl and turned around.

There was a face staring at him from the courtyard below, but not the one he was expecting: an enormous black face with white teeth, bared in a blinding rictus, like a painted stucco mask.

He made himself take a deep breath.

He felt the stone beneath his feet. He felt the earth beneath the stone. He felt the power in his muscles coursing, available as needed. He was glad for the rampart between them, which gave him some cover. The spear across his back was loose and ready.

The thing looked exactly like a black jaguar. But jaguars never hunted in daylight, and never grew this big. And Ajul hadn't seen it when he'd come into the courtyard. It seemed to have just appeared when his back was turned. That meant the jaguar could be Balam Ahau, a messenger of Xibalba, visiting him on the day of his ascension to impart some sign.

The white teeth were swallowed up by the face and gave way to eyes of pale jade, set in black fur made red by sunlight.

Ajul looked down at her paws, avoiding her eyes. "I, Royal Prince Ajul B'uluch Chab of the Tzoyna, greet you, Ahau. From where do you come?"

The jaguar opened her mouth and her tongue dropped like a pink scroll.

"Do you come from our world, Ahau, or from Xibalba?"

The jaguar turned broadside to him, walking, the shoulder bones alternating. A ridge of loose skin waggled along her underbelly. The end of her tail flicked back and forth, rasping on the plaster. As a hunter, Ajul could feel her body move as if he were inside it, even as he remained inside his own.

"You are welcome to drink from the well in the garden."

The jaguar seemed to notice the steps on the far side of the courtyard. She started up them with ease and grace, as if she lived here, as if she were no more than a family member come home. Ajul watched her ascend.

He felt strong and light. As in the ball game, so in the hunt: his body was his ally, his genius, the royal litter of his soul. He drew his spear and stood, waiting.

The jaguar rounded the corner and paced toward him, head low. Her black shoulders rotated: hill, valley, hill, valley. Her glossy black head was enormous. Her jaws bulged. They could bite his skull like an egg. Ajul stood his ground, spear leveled, waiting.

The jaguar stopped, turned, and sniffed. She was smelling the musky blankets in Ixul's bedchamber.

She walked right in.

Ajul watched it happen. The tip of her tail disappeared last.

Before he could think it through, he ran forward and pushed the door closed and barred it.

He pressed his ear to the door. There was no sound from within.

ANOONG, MINNESOTA
12 Men 18 Mak, Long Count 12.19.19.17.15

---

16 December, 2012

Leah was the first to arrive at the steakhouse, so she sat in the vestibule and stroked her braid. Tonight she was having dinner with her mother, her mother's fiancé, Rick, and his children. This restaurant was Rick's suggestion. It smelled like fresh paint.

Leah was willing to give it a try, as long as her mother promised they'd still have nights at Xquic's, their favorite Mexican place in St. Cloud. Her mother had picked it out because it was a Mayan name, pronounced *Shkik*, and Leah grew up obsessed with saying it. She'd ask to go there for every special occasion. The restaurant glowed pink-orange from puffy lamps, and Leah insisted on a booth where they could see the statue in the center of the room: a woman robed in orange and gold. When she was little, she thought it was the Virgin Mary, drawing one hand over her chest and pointing upward with the other in a gesture of praise. Later, she got up the courage to ask the waitress about it, and was told it was Xquic herself—the Maya goddess Blood-maiden, the mother of the Hero Twins. Leah asked for the same statue for her birthday. Her mother surprised her with a papier-mâché version she'd made with the ladies at church. At first Leah was disappointed that it wasn't an exact copy, but she learned to cherish it.

Those were good days, Leah thought. But her mother didn't feel the same way.

Now she came, blond bangs freshly cut, appearing in front of the glass doors of the steakhouse. She waved to Leah and paused to take off her mittens. Leah waved back. But then a big man came up behind her, bent double, hands twitching, wearing a black balaclava.

Leah yelled, "Mom, look out!"

The man grabbed her tiny mother off the ground and wrestled her back and forth so that her legs were swinging like a pendulum. Leah could hear him growling, but it was a strange growl, as if it were made by a sock-puppet dog, and Leah was halfway out the door when the man took off his balaclava to reveal his grinning face.

Rick set her mother down again.

Her mother was bent double, trying to laugh. "Oh, Rick!" she cried. "You scared me!"

"I got her good, didn't I?" Rick said to Leah.

"That was a horrible thing to do," said Leah. "Don't ever do that again."

Wrong answer, of course, as she was expected to go along with the presumed hilarity of the joke, but Leah never followed that script. Her mother rallied on Rick's behalf. "Oh Leah, come on," she said. "He was only teasing."

"It was deceptive."

Her mother's face washed serious. "Young lady. Rick has been through enough without your—"

"Hey, I apologize, Leah," Rick boomed, generous. "I'm sorry you feel that way."

"Rick," said her mother, "you don't have to—"

"It's all right, Toni. If we're going to be a family, I have to take input from everyone."

Up trudged Rick's children, Katie, Mackie, and Benji. The younger two wore matching puff jackets in navy and white, the colors of Our Lady of the Prairie. They didn't say hello, but rushed through the double doors and up to the hostess's podium in the warm interior.

The eldest remained.

"Hi," said Katie from under her scarf.

"Hi, Katie," said Leah, hugging her. "It's lovely to see you." She liked her soon-to-be-stepsister, or rather, was fascinated by her, especially since she'd been named the county Dairy Princess. Leah thought of Katie as an exotic doll she'd been lucky to acquire. But Katie's body went stiff. Leah knew Katie disliked her because of her reputation at school and her strangely formal speech. Leah didn't care.

"Yeah, you too." Katie extricated herself and brushed spider threads of blond hair out of her lip gloss and followed her siblings.

Rick pointed at Leah's jacket and said, "Aren't you cold?"

"A little bit, Rick, thank you."

"Leah, why do you insist on underdressing?" said her mother. "You underdress and then you complain about the cold." She turned to Rick. "She always does this."

"But isn't the style great?" said Leah. "I got it at a shop in St. Cloud for ten dollars. I love the colors. It's retro."

"It's December, is what it is," said Rick.

Mackie came back to the double doors and banged on the glass. She mouthed, *I'm hungry.*

They entered the steakhouse, carpeted with red-and-blue diamonds. The hostess was a friend of Katie's from Student Council, and Katie animated, briefly, while they were led to a corner booth. The young-est two dove for the back. Katie enthroned herself on the edge. That left for Rick, Leah's mother, and Leah to shuffle, half-bent, around the other side. As they settled in, Leah smelled a sour whiff of wine on her mother's breath. She stiffened. This wasn't uncommon. But it was going to make the night's business more difficult.

Rick said to the table, "Big changes coming soon around here."

Katie, Mackie, and Benji were already studying their menus.

"There are, there are!" said Leah's mother. "One chapter ending and—"

A server appeared. She wore a maroon polo shirt and black apron. "Hi, welcome to Anoong Steakhouse, can I get you all something to drink?"

"Toni," said Rick, squeezing her shoulder.

"I'll have a glass of red wine, please."

"Toni," said Rick in a different tone of voice. Leah glanced up. "Do you think that's wise?"

"Oh for heaven's sake, Rick, it's just a glass, I'm not an alcoholic." She turned back to the server. "One glass of red wine."

"Okay, would you like Merlot or Shiraz?"

THE ACTUAL STAR • 95

"A choice! I like this place," said Leah's mother, turning to Rick, but he was engrossed in the menu. "I'll have the Shiraz, please."

The server turned to Leah.

"I'll have your very best ginger ale, please, with a twist of lemon."

The server gave a nervous laugh. "I hope Schweppes is all right, it's all we have."

"That would be wonderful, thank you."

Katie closed the menu. "Just water for me," and looked elsewhere.

"Orange juice," said Mackie.

"Chocolate milk," said Benji.

Rick pinned the menu with a meaty finger. "Your beers . . ."

Everyone waited.

The server shifted her weight and twirled her pen.

Rick folded up the menu and tossed it across the table. "You know what, I believe I'll have a hot chocolate."

The server left. Leah watched her go. She was probably home from St. Olaf for Christmas break. She wondered what she was doing with her life. Who her parents were. Where she was going. Whether she spoke any other languages. Whether she had plans like Leah did.

"Dad, you're getting hot chocolate?" Katie said to Rick.

"It's a family night. I'm not going to drink on a family night."

"Why would you say that?" said Katie. "When Toni just ordered—"

"I enjoy a warm, frothy drink from time to time," Rick announced to the table.

Katie rested her head on her fists.

"Should we pray now, or—?" said Leah's mother.

"Good idea, Toni. Let's do it now before the drinks come."

Hands slithered out of polyethylene sleeves to grasp one another.

"Dear Lord," said Rick, "we thank you for the food we are about to receive—"

"But we haven't even ordered it yet," said Mackie.

Her brother thumped her.

"That we haven't yet ordered, but will receive after we do. We thank you for the money to pay for it, for secure jobs, for the wedding in just two short weeks—"

Leah saw her mother squeeze Rick's hand.

"And I thank you for this woman, this little Antonia, my Toni, who's brought so much—so much meaning back in—back into my—"

Leah saw Katie's eyes go wide in a silent scream.

"We ask your blessing on this new family," said Leah's mother, saving him. "And on other—family members who can't be here today."

"Yes, other family members." Rick nodded at his children, eyes wet. Leah knew he was only thinking of their dead mother. In her heart, she added her own dead father to the prayer.

"Mackie," said Rick, "would you like to say what you're grateful for?"

"My orange juice, if it ever comes."

"That's nice. Benji?"

"Spider-Man."

"Katie?"

"I'm too old for this."

"Excuse me, young lady?"

"I said, I'm grateful it's my senior year."

Leah was next. It occurred to her that now was as good a moment as any to make her announcement.

"I'm grateful that I'm going to Belize tomorrow."

It didn't have the effect she wanted. Leah's mother laughed and grimaced, as if she'd made a bad joke, but the others seemed to take it as just another eccentricity.

"I'm grateful for—" began Leah's mother, eyes closed.

"Mom," she said. "I said I'm going to Belize tomorrow."

Her mother opened her eyes and stared at the table-top. "Leah, that is not funny."

"I don't mean it to be funny. It's a fact."

"What on earth has gotten into you?"

"Let's finish the prayer," said Rick.

Leah's mother kept her eyes on the table. "I'm grateful for God's forgiveness," she said quietly.

"Amen," said Rick, and made the Sign of the Cross, and the rest followed.

"What's Belize?" said Benji.

"It's a country," said Rick. "In South America."

"Central America," said Leah.

"It's where Toni grew up," said Katie, who looked lively now, at the prospect of conflict.

"She didn't grow up there," said Rick. "Just a year, right, Toni?"

"Two years," said Leah's mother, who was now regarding Leah as if from a great distance. "I was nineteen."

"Toni was a missionary," Rick said to Benji. "Which means she gave food to poor people in Third World countries."

"Why can't they grow their own food?"

"Don't be difficult."

"What do you mean," Leah's mother said, "you're going to Belize?"

"Tomorrow I have a flight from Minneapolis to Houston, and then from Houston to Belize City, where I'll catch a bus to Cayo."

Her mother shook her head, unrolled her utensils from her napkin, and stared at them.

"Why?" she asked.

"Because I want to."

"How did you get the money?"

"I saved it from my job. Two thousand dollars."

"And you were living under my roof all that time and you didn't bother to tell me or ask me how I would feel about any of it."

"I know how you feel about it, Mom, but it doesn't have to be how I feel about it."

"What's wrong with Minnesota?" her mother snapped.

Their drinks arrived. The server could tell she'd intruded on a sensitive moment, so set down their drinks quickly, which made her spill one of them. She left, promising extra napkins.

"She's an adult now, Toni. She's nineteen just like you were," said Rick. "Leah, how long are you going to be in Belize?"

"Nine days. I'll be back in time for the wedding. I'm flying back on Christmas."

"*On* Christmas?"

Leah did feel bad about that. "I'm sorry. It was the cheapest flight."

There was a long pause.

"Nine days!" Rick exclaimed. "Well, it's pretty short notice, and a little weird, but in the end, it's no harm, is it, Toni?"

Her mother shook her head and said, "After everything."

Rick picked up the slack. "Heck, I'd kill for a tropical beach vacation at this time of year. You got your snorkeling gear?"

"No, actually, my father—"

Her mother took a gulp of wine and opened her menu.

"My biological father was from Cayo, inland near the Guatemalan border, so I'm going there. There are lots of famous Maya sites there, including a sacred cave! I've already booked my tour with a guide named Javier Magaña. He's the most popular guide on TripAdvisor."

"Magaña!" Rick said grandly. "What kind of name is that?"

"It's Maya," said her mother, as if telling a sick joke.

Mackie piped up. "I know about the Maya!" she said. "The Maya said the world would end next Friday. I saw it on the news."

"Then your stepsister will have a front-row seat," Rick said. "And she can tell you all about it when she gets back. Or should I say, *if* she gets back?" He laughed.

The server returned with extra napkins and asked for their orders. Rick indicated that they still needed time. The server left.

"Actually, Mackie," said Leah, "the Maya calendar is—"

"You know, I like to watch the Discovery Channel, and I see these documentaries," said Rick, now leaning forward, elbows on the table, gesturing. "Greeks, Romans . . . they gave so much to the world. Heck, they basically built the modern world. But the Maya, the Inca, and the Aztecs . . . I see documentaries about them, and you know, they had these amazing cultures, and then they just vanished. They weren't suited for long-term survival. Even their art is primitive. Greek statues look like living, breathing people, really advanced stuff, but with those cultures down south, it was all just . . . symbolic."

"How are the college applications coming, Katie?" said Leah's mother in a strained voice. Leah noticed she'd already drunk half her wine. She hadn't even seen it go down.

Everyone labored to redirect their attention. "Oh!

They're fine," Katie said. "I actually got them all out in November."

"And where would you most like to go?"

"St. Olaf. But U of M would be fine. They have more options in their study abroad program, especially for France."

"You wouldn't need a study abroad program if you were like this one here," Rick said, wagging his finger at Leah. "Just get born there! Lucky."

"She wasn't born there," said Leah's mother in a quiet voice. "She was born. In. Minnesota."

"Mom, what is the big deal? Why are you so ashamed of it? Are you ashamed of me?"

She could see her mother's hands shaking. She put down her menu and dabbed her mouth with her napkin, as if she were following a memorized sequence of gestures, normal, placating, and said, "Excuse me, I need to use the restroom," and Leah got up and her mother edged out and moved quickly down the aisle out of sight.

There was silence at the table. Rick sighed. Katie looked smug. The younger two were confused.

"Was Toni married before?" said Mackie.

"Not married, sweetie," said Rick. "She had a baby out of wedlock when she was young."

"She had sex?"

"Ewwww," Benji wailed.

"Sex, sex, sex, sex, sex, sex, sex," Mackie chanted.

"Enough, Mackie," said Rick, eyeing Leah. "God is forgiving. God loves us. God takes our mistakes and makes love out of them. Without it, Leah wouldn't be here, and Leah makes all of our lives a lot more colorful, now, doesn't she?"

"Are you Black?" said Benji to Leah.

Leah laughed before she could stop herself.

"Benji!" Rick said, seizing his shoulder. "That's not nice."

"But why—"

"Apologize to your sister."

"She's not my—"

"Benji." That was Katie this time.

Benji swung his head in her direction. "Sorry, Leah."

"It's okay, Benji. I don't think I am. My father was Maya."

"Didn't Dad just say they disappeared and didn't contribute anything?"

"Benji," snapped Katie. "Enough."

"Katie," said Rick.

"Dad," said Katie.

The server returned once again, hopeful.

Everyone placed their orders, wanting to get the evening over with. Rick ordered a chicken Caesar salad for his bride-to-be. After the server took their menus and departed, Leah said to Rick, "I do know it's weird that I'm leaving right before the wedding. But it's only nine days, and I wanted to be there for the big Maya celebration of the year 2012, and I knew Mom wouldn't want me to go no matter what, so I just . . . saved up and made the reservations." Leah looked at everyone around the table. "I'm sorry if it's going to cause inconvenience for you."

"It's fine," Katie said, not meeting her eyes. "You're already measured for your dress anyway. If we have any rehearsals I can just catch you up."

"That's very generous of you, Katie," said Rick.

Leah's mother returned without a word. Leah got up to let her in and then said, "Mom."

"What?" said her mother, in amused exasperation, as if the last ten minutes hadn't happened. "I suppose it was going to happen someday. It just came sooner than I expected, that's all, and not at a very convenient time, actually the worst time possible. But Rick's right! You're an adult, just like I was." She took another gulp of wine. "Since we're all going to be family soon, I might as well tell the story."

"I told them," said Rick.

"You told them what?"

"About the baby—about Leah."

"I want to hear about the father," said Mackie, with a mischievous edge to her voice.

"Mackie," said Rick, warning.

"Yes, the father," said Toni.

Leah stared at her mother. Not even when drunk had she ever divulged details about her biological father. It was just something they never talked about. Leah had learned that very young. Now her mother was casually telling their entire stepfamily what she hadn't told her, and it felt like a kind of revenge.

"I lived in Cayo," she said. "I worked at a church just across the street. I taught Sunday school, helped run Mass, and so on. Now, in Belize it's very normal to hire local Maya for certain things, like making repairs or doing yard work. They come by and ask you what you need, because they need the money."

She took another gulp of wine and gestured grandly. Leah didn't know how much she'd drunk before she arrived, but it was enough that she was not her normal self. "Now, one morning a chiclero comes to my gate. A chiclero is a man who goes into the jungle for chicle season to tap gum trees for the chicle that goes in your gum. Did you know that, Mackie? Now you do! Chicle makes gum, and it comes from Belize! Well, it wasn't the chicle season, so this man was in town and looking for work. His name was Pancho. My landlady invited him in for a cup of Nescafé and spoke Spanish with him. He asked us if we needed someone to come do yard work every week. He would pick the fruits, mow the grass, chase away snakes, and all the rest. My land-lady hired him on the spot. Pancho was so courteous, a perfect gentleman. And I thought he was very hand-some. He was twenty-three. I had a big crush on him."

Leah glanced at Rick, who appeared pale and sweaty. He seemed to have given up on interrupting her. Leah felt paralyzed.

Toni took another gulp. "Pancho came every Satur-day, just as promised. He left baskets of oranges on my doorstep. I started watching him from my room. One day he caught me watching him. And then it became a sort of game, me watching him watching me watching him."

The server arrived with a big brown tray and little folding table. She kicked it open with her knee and set down the tray, laden with seven white plates. She handed out each one, saying the name of the dish under her breath, but sensing the mood of the table. "Okay, you enjoy," she said, and was already running away, the brown tray tucked under one armpit and the fold-ing table tucked under the other.

The plates of food steamed around the table. No one moved.

"So!" said Toni, finishing off her wine. "You can guess what happened next! It all seemed very romantic. I got pregnant right away. I came back home and told my parents and they disowned me and I gave birth alone as a result of my sin. And you know what? I've always thought that that is why Leah turned out the way she did."

Toni turned to Leah with a fond look on her face.

Leah could not move.

She was outside herself, hearing Rick say, from a great distance, "That's quite enough, Toni," and then "Leah? Where are you going?" but she was already gone, floating over the diamond carpet, out the double doors, into the parking lot, past her car, and down the road. She couldn't get into her car right now. She couldn't trust herself to drive it. She just walked down the road in the dark, feeling dizzy, but strangely, no longer cold.

Beside her, a teal Honda slowed to a stop. The window rolled down. Nate was looking out at her.

"Hey," he said.

"Hi," she said, and balled her fists.

He opened the door, seeming to understand without having to ask. She got in and slammed it shut. They started driving.

"How'd it go?"

"Not well."

"Sorry."

"Mom is upset."

"Because you're going to Cairo?"

"Cayo," Leah corrected. "Yes, that's part of it. But it's also just in general because she hates herself. Her parents brainwashed her to think sex is bad."

"A lot of people think sex is bad."

"I don't," said Leah. "You don't."

Nate nodded and gestured expansively. "Yeah, I don't see how it can be."

There was a long silence, during which Leah calmed down. It was dark now. They were driving past all the brick storefronts of Anoong. She could be with Nate, and then she could go back to the apartment to pick up her backpack while her mother was on the night shift at the hospital. She'd been packed for days. Her flight to Houston was at six in the morning, and from Houston she'd fly to Belize. It was still all possible. She just had to take one step at a time.

She felt at peace again.

"Thank goodness you were driving down the road," she said.

Nate looked out the window, uncomfortable. "I was in the parking lot."

"Of the steakhouse?"

"Yeah."

"Why?"

"Because we were going to hang out, remember? And then I saw you walk out and it didn't look good."

Leah looked out the window and smiled to herself. He'd come early, because he liked her.

"I've been thinking," she said, settling in to her seat. "You know what sex is like for me? Because I keep trying to imagine what sex is like for you, and I can't, and I wish I could. But at least I can describe my side of it to you. You know when you have an itch deep under the skin, like in your thigh or your forearm, and you scratch at the surface but you can't reach it or satisfy it, and it's driving you crazy, and you think to yourself, 'If only I could actually slice open my skin and shred the muscle itself with my fingernail'?"

Nate stared ahead.

"Nate?"

"Yeah."

"You know what I mean?"

"I think so."

"Well, it's like that, except in sex, you actually get to do that."

Nate looked troubled. "So is that a good thing or . . ."

"Oh, it's a marvelous thing!" said Leah. "I wish you could tell me what it feels like for you."

She waited.

"I don't know," said Nate, collapsing against the far window as if trying to escape. "I guess I don't really think about it. I think some things are just for doing. Like, you just need to be in the moment, you know?"

"I agree! But at the same time, I want to understand it! I think sex is one of the nearest experiences of perfect wholeness, of Xibalba."

"You're weird."

Leah had to agree. She was certainly weird. She let it be, for now. She'd pushed him, so now she could be patient with him. He was only eighteen. He was still in high school. He'd played trombone when she'd marched down the aisle at graduation six months ago. From her seat on the stage she kept trying to catch his eye, to have a moment of mutual regard that the whole audience would see, but it never quite happened. He did pose for pictures with her, afterward. The photo was overexposed, and showed the white of his skin, the blue of his uniform, and the red of his acne.

"Where are we going?" said Leah.

"The river, I thought."

"Can you turn up the heat?"

Nate turned the dial from 1 to 2.

They drove a winding road through black woods, then turned onto a gravel road, descending. The car creaked and bounced. Leah put a hand on the door to steady herself.

They cleared the woods. The Mississippi spread before them, looking like a far blue meadow. Nate put on the brakes, got out, and shuffled onto the ice. He shone his penlight on it and hit it with his heel a few times.

"It was a foot this morning," called Leah from the car. She'd checked the ice report, because she knew he'd take her to the river.

"Has to be that, still," said Nate, getting back into the car. "At least six inches. We'll be fine."

He lifted the brake and eased the car onto the ice. It was smooth as glass, and he drove slowly. He stopped the car in the exact middle of the river and turned it off.

"Can you leave the heat on?" said Leah.

"It's bad for the car," he said. "You should just dress warmer."

She met him in the backseat. They pulled their respective doors shut, unzipped their coats, angled toward each other, and opened their mouths. His tongue was cold. Her mind was already outpacing her body, going sixty seconds ahead of her, like when she could see all the lane changes in her mind on the way to her job at the outlet mall. She worked at the bedding store,

Soft-A-Lot. Nate worked across from her at Waffa Cream. When they were both working at the same time, and business was slow, she'd watch him through the glass across the way, shoving metal paddles into the vats, wrestling out chunks of ice cream like clay, taming them on the marble slabs; and blond women in puffy coats leaned over the glass guard, fogging it up, insisting on various add-ins, like dusty Skor bar fragments, making sure he put in enough, and he always did, faithfully, wordlessly, torturing the ice cream with his metal paddles, and then stuffing the final product into a famous Waffa Waffle Sugar Cone so that there were imprints of the paddles' edges, like cuts, in the cream.

And now, her daydreams were manifest. Here he was, beneath her, smelling of malted milk balls. But she couldn't connect her heart to her mind to her body. She was distracted. The heat had leached out of the car now. The tip of her nose had gone cold. When he was here, now, actually below her, she couldn't connect. She felt nothing. Everything was too fragmented. In Xibalba, she imagined, all would be whole.

Nate pulled the neck of her underwear to the side and pulled her to fit her over him. It should have been sexy, but going in, he felt spiky. The angle was all wrong, and she had to shift, get over him, guide him in, and whatever happened to checking with the finger first? He used to do that. She wasn't ready. They both licked their hands. He repositioned himself. He still felt spiky coming up, and Leah winced but said *Just keep doing it*, and he did, silently. She willed the wetness to come. Slowly, it did. Her body came around. It's not that she didn't like sex. She loved sex. She just remembered liking it more with him the first time. She'd once said, *"Cunnilingus" is such a weird word*, to gauge his response. Nate pretended he hadn't heard. She was disappointed. She hadn't yet had oral sex or anal sex and she was getting impatient with this same routine, which she'd started referring to in her mind as the Ol' Stab. Leah squeezed her eyes shut and told him to keep going, that her body would catch up. His penis felt like a stinger. She grabbed the headrest to stay anchored. Meanwhile, he was already going into his plateau phase, arms rigid, using her body to climax, pressing her away and pulling her down at the same time.

She gave up on being present. She had a view out the back window, dusty with salt, through which she could see the frozen shore, the black woods, and the stars above. She was too cold. She was being blown apart, like the atoms of the universe. But in Belize I'll reconstitute, she thought. Belize will be warmer. Belize will be better.

PALAWAN
9 Ik' 5 Ch'en, Long Count 15.10.13.11.2

---

16 January, 3012

"Si pudiera ver," Tanaaj prayed, "con los ojos de Leah."

She pulled down her mask and walked into the torchlight.

The drums stopped.

At the other end of the court was another jugadorix, Li-Wei, wearing a white mask with yellow feathers for hair.

The two of them closed their eyes and pressed their palms to their chests. Tanaaj could feel the gaze of the audience. She invited the god of the place to enter her body. The god would direct the play. The god knew that tonight must be a powerful performance, because the audience was distracted: a thousand miles away, in

Persia, a tribunal was questioning the heretic Niloux DeCayo.

A mopan maya like her.

Tanaaj opened her eyes.

She spread her feet, squatted, and raised her palms to complete the personage of Leah la Putita.

Li-Wei, opposite, prostrated herself in the personage of Nate el Novio.

How pleasing, Tanaaj thought, that we ourselves are lovers, playing lovers who lived a thousand years ago on the other side of the world.

She called her opening line: "Who will go with me into Belize?"

Ninx in the front row recited: "No one goes with you."

Tanaaj turned to the other side, deepened into the same pose. "I seek a wholeness I cannot name. How do I find it?"

The children, again: "Seek out the flame in the mountain."

Tanaaj put her palms on the court in thanksgiving. Then she rose and turned and deepened into a lunge, her green silks fluttering around her legs. She waited. Roosters crowed in the dark.

Li-Wei rose as Nate, stamped and shuddered, then beckoned with a show of lust.

The drums began again, slow at first, encouraging their final coupling. This dance required close coordination and attention, because of the leaps at the end. It was only the first movement of the second act of *La Estrella Actual*, which recounted all the cities Leah had passed through: St. Cloud, St. Paul, Houston, Belize City, and finally San Ignacio.

For now, though, she was still in Anoong. Tanaaj broke away from her partner and turned to her audience in a show of distress, hunched and shuffling. The drums waffled, became disordered. Leah was hesitating in Anoong: should she really leave everything she's ever known, to fly to an unknown country?

"Go," said a ninx, and then they all took up the call: "Go!"

Tanaaj exploded up from her crouch and commenced the leaping twists around the perimeter of the court, and the crowd exploded, too, cheering her on to Belize. With each turn she could see Nate leaping after her, reaching for her, but she was careful to remain just outside his grasp, and then there was a shout that came down from the wayhouse, so sharp it cut through the drums:

"Mardom e Zein-o-Din!"

A handful of faces swiveled upward at the noise, which distracted Li-Wei, and though Tanaaj came to a graceful stop, her partner did not. Li-Wei stumbled and lurched, breaking her fall with her hands. Her wrist bent. Her mask fell off and cracked.

The drums faltered. There were gasps from the audience.

Time slowed in Tanaaj's mind. If this were a full traditional performance with experienced jugadorix, both of them would continue with their roles, adapting to the injury, taking it as direction from the god within the larger play that never truly ended. *The land has acted upon us, blessed be the land. The god saw fit to alter our path.*

But tonight was a mere showcase, and Li-Wei not as skilled a performer. She didn't want to assume that her lover would want to play through pain.

Tanaaj pulled up her mask. "Do you want to stop or continue, carnalix?"

Li-Wei's expression of agony told her all she needed to know.

"My medkit is in the common room," called Tanaaj, and a child's voice said, "I'll get it!"

She knelt by Li-Wei and helped her get on her back, clearing the mask from under her. One viajera put a bundle under her head, another under her wrist, another under her knees.

"I did badly," said Li-Wei through clenched teeth.

"Not at all," Tanaaj said. "Your interpretation of Nate was very original."

That made her laugh.

Tanaaj peered at the damage and said, "Broken wrist, carnalix, and deep abrasions on your knees. Skin quite gone. A very dedicated jugadorix indeed."

Her medkit was passed to her, hand to hand. Tanaaj opened it, rummaged through it, and pulled out a splint, bandage roll, and several small jars. She unscrewed one of them and pulled up a fingerful of honey-colored taffy. "Will you sleep while we set your wrist?"

Li-Wei stuck out her tongue to receive it.

Tanaaj stayed with Li-Wei in her room off the common room. It was just as well that the play had ended early; a hailstorm had moved in, each hailstone as big as an apple and bursting on the court. Li-Wei was sleeping through it all, still sedated. Tanaaj had told everyone she wanted to be here when she woke up, which was true; she liked taking care of people, especially those she'd had sex with. But she also wanted to gather her thoughts now that the news from Persia had come in.

Niloux DeCayo had refused to recant. She'd repeated her heresy and added to it. Some nonsense about a past life visualization technique. Tanaaj had always had a mild and loving nature, but this news had awakened something in her, a shadow of anger, and an urge to act on it. She wasn't the only one. Everyone in the wayhouse seemed restless, like bees in a beehive.

She listened to two viajeras talking nearby.

"If Niloux didn't recant this time, she won't in the future," said one. "It seems like the tribunal only made her more mad."

"What do you think of her technique?" said the other.

"For seeing past lives? Apparently it works for her. No one else has tried it."

"It's inevitable that people will."

"Will you?"

A pause. "I'm curious. Aren't you?"

Another pause. "Of course I am."

"There's already a movement rallying for her in the Tzoyna. They call themselves Mardom e Zein-o-Din."

Tanaaj leaned forward. That was the shout that had disrupted the play.

"What does that mean?"

"The people of Zein-o-Din. That's the wayhouse where the tribunal took place."

"Isn't that where Ruth Okeke is buried?"

"You're right. Whew."

"I also heard Niloux called for a special tzoyna at the Jubilee."

"Special how?"

"To debate the questions en vivo. Whether it's still useful to live oriented toward Xibalba."

Tanaaj remained calm, observed her thoughts rising like bubbles in a pond. Would a flower ask if it was useful to keep oriented toward the sun? Would a fish ask if it was useful to stay in water? Xibalba was not a myth; it was a real place to which thousands of people had disappeared, and Saint Leah had been the first. These disappearances had been witnessed, recorded, and documented. How could Niloux explain them?

But Tanaaj said nothing. She was not the kind to enjoin intellectual debate; it was not the way of a juga-dorix, the heir of the ancient ball game. She spoke with her body, her deeds, and her performances.

An eye blinked at Tanaaj through the lattice. She'd been noticed.

The first voice rose, brusque. "Well, it could just be that Niloux is having delusions of grandeur. She forgot Versa Doce."

Be not particular, said Tanaaj automatically in her mind. *No seas particular.*

"What happens now?"

"It'll go to the Tzoyna and they'll vote on whether she can be blotted."

"That's extreme. Would you vote to blot her?"

A pause, a muted gesture, a nodding of heads.

"I'd like some tea," said the first voice loudly.

"Yes, let's get some tea."

The two viajeras got up and departed in the direction of the refectory.

Tanaaj leaned back. They'd left because they didn't want her to overhear. She was known to be orthodox, just as she was known as a jugadorix; she could discourage fame according to Versa Doce, but not entirely. She could access their conversation later if she wanted to, but then the act of her accessing it would also be recorded, and doing so was frowned upon unless you had a good reason. She let it go. But she was bothered that these two viajeras had wished to hide their conversation from her, as if it belonged only to them. Since when was speech private? She stared up at the ceiling: an elegant lattice of chitin. She felt the ground beneath her: a grass bed on a packed dirt floor, built so that she never lost contact with the earth. The paragua knew her preferences and matched her with compatible people, compatible wayhouses. But it was difficult to shut out viajeras who were becoming so lax, like these. At the last wayhouse, Tanaaj had been stunned to discover

viajeras watching streams of *La Estrella* performances
halfway across the world instead of performing their
own where they stood. It negated the entire devotional
practice. That was only one of the ways in which Laviaja was slipping. She kept hearing rumors that viajeras
were printing meat, or staying at wayhouses for longer
than nine days, or reversing Versa Cuatro, the pluripo-
tency of their bodies. And then there were the worst,
the sedentix, the settlers who colonized one place and
used ih/ahn pronouns, rejecting the universal she/her
in honor of Saint Leah. The rot was creeping in.

Li-Wei stirred and smacked her lips.

Immediately Tanaaj attended her. "Hello, queridix,"
she said.

Her charge opened one eye. "Am I going to live?"

"I'm afraid not. Gangrene, you know."

She laughed, pillowed her head on her good wrist,
flexed the other a little. "I barely feel anything."

"I'm relieved. The fermites I gave you are from five
wayhouses ago, so they weren't fresh."

"Thank you for healing me."

"Por supuesto. You are a good patient." Tanaaj
rested her hand on Li-Wei's forehead, and closed her
eyes at the pleasure of it, just this reassuring touch of
skin. "Do you want to sleep alone tonight?"

Li-Wei smirked. "I could not cause you such pain."

"I have others."

"Putita. You love being loved."

"I suppose that is true."

"But you also love loving." Li-Wei tugged at Tanaaj's green silks, drawing her down, and kissed her on the mouth.

"Yes," said Tanaaj between kisses, "that is also true."

Tanaaj was startled awake when a bird landed on her breast.

It was a motmot, blue and green and gold. That meant the message was coming from Messe.

She leaned back and closed her eyes. It was no use sleeping anymore. She'd always been a poor sleeper, and then there'd been the commotion of last night, and now a holo from Messe on top of it all, yet another test of faith. She checked the time: 5:24 a.m. local.

She got up gently, so as not to disturb Li-Wei. The motmot fluttered behind her. She tapped the sunball once, then pulled on her usual tunic and drawstring pants. She made her way across the common room. The wayhouse was quiet. Most were sleeping where they'd lain down last night, zadres and children and elders all together, breath passing through them like wind over water.

On the far side, she walked up the ramp to a patio that faced the ocean. The eastern rim of the sky was deep violet. Venus blazed on the horizon, lighting a path across the waves.

For a moment she took in the beauty of the sight.

She bowed to the planet, Chak Ek', the Great Star of the Maya, the twin sister of Earth. She fingered the medal of Saint Leah on her throat. "Que la Mundotra esté conmigo," she whispered.

That said, she sat on a stone bench and let down the motmot. She mentally prepared for the trial of temptation. Then she nodded for it to deliver its message.

The motmot hopped away, turned back, and flowered into the shape of a ninx with dark brown skin and box braids.

Tanaaj steadied herself. It was always a shock to see her birth child.

Following the Rule of Saint Leah meant that Tanaaj avoided any direct contact with another person who was not en vivo, where they could sense each other with the faculties of their own bodies. This also meant that she avoided developing any particular attachment to blood kin, one of the oldest taboos of Laviaja. In truth, when Tanaaj had given birth to Messe on a boat off the coast of Spain, she should have decided then and there to make her a Child of Saint Leah, to cut her free.

But she had not. She could only explain it to herself in terms of moral failure, an original sin for which she needed to perform penance: to receive these messages from Messe and yet resist reaching back to her, grasping as if she owned her, like a hoarder of old. If they ever happened to meet in person, what a joyful meeting it would be! Sometimes Tanaaj allowed herself to fantasize about it—the embrace, the kisses, the tears. But for now, they were parted. And for now, Messe was still learning why.

The child waved to the space in front of her. She was so big now, este genéra, strong and broad-shouldered, wearing a purple jumpsuit with orange stripes. Her eyes were looking up and to the left. A reminder that this was a pre-recorded message.

"Hi, Tanaaj! It's Messe again! Um . . ." She faltered, looked down, but then rallied. "I know you might not watch this, but maybe you will. I just wanted to tell you some big news. I'm about to go on my first solo viaja. I looked you up and your profile says you did yours at thirteen, and I'm only twelve, so that means I'm going before you." The child grinned, then picked at a spot on the ground. "I also wanted to tell you that everything's fine. I haven't figured out my manéra yet, but maybe I will on this trip. I have good zadres, and they're going to monitor me in the aug in case anything happens. All my fugitech is up to date and I know how to forage. Oh! I want to show you." She sat up, animated. "Here's my route . . ." she said, and drew her thumb across the air. A translucent map flowered in its wake. "I'm starting here at Onigamiising," she said, pointing to a red dot, "and then walking around Mille Lacs, and then finally to . . ." She pinched the dot and drew it back toward her, then opened a new circle, which showed brick ruins and orange blossom trees.

Tanaaj recognized it at once. "Anoong."

Of course, Messe didn't hear her. "I've always wanted to see the place where Saint Leah was born. So I can understand more about Laviaja and grow in my faith, like you. Maybe I'll be able to feel some of what she felt. I'm going to watch the history filters and visit the archives. Did you know Leah's mother even preserved some of her lip glosses? Anyway . . ." The child looked uncertain; glanced behind her, as if self-conscious. "I've been taught well. I'm not afraid. Thank you for giving me to the Munda. I'm ready." She swallowed hard, as if gathering up courage to say something, but at the last second, she seemed to change her mind. "Anyway, I guess that's all the news I have, so goodbye. Hasta luego."

The child waved and disappeared.

Tanaaj put her face in her hands, allowed herself to cry, then dried her face and went to breakfast.

A few hours later, Tanaaj's work assignment arrived from the wayhouse bird, an orange tit:

Magandang umaga, Tanaaj DeCayo!
Your work today is:
0900–1200, Inducción guide to Pei-shan DeYushan.
All modules met.

She was not surprised. Her ai knew she was hurting over Messe, so it'd paired with the paragua to give her soothing work. Though Laviaja was built to disperse all things—including blood kin—it was also merciful to the ache of biology. If Tanaaj could not take care of Messe, she could be with another child Messe's age, who would be, for all purposes, her child. In this way, Laviaja fulfilled Versa Cinco: *The beloved always comes back to you.*

Tanaaj found Pei-shan in a semicircular courtyard, high on a cliff above the wayhouse. She stopped to take her in: small for her age, likely oeste like her, with a bowl cut and a bar of lapis in her septum. She'd been one of the children in the front row the previous night.

The palm trees swished in the wind, already warm and thunder-laden. This would be pleasant work.

"Buenos días," said Tanaaj, stepping in front of her.

Pei-shan waved. "Buenos días," she said, her words unraveling as a ribbon of text next to her face.

Tanaaj sensed she was shy and would need extra care to come out of her shell. This was the sort of challenge she loved. "You picked a very beautiful place to do your tutorial," she said, gesturing to the sea. "I have been here three days, hermanix, and not found this spot."

Pei-shan flushed at the use of the term *hermanix*, which named her as an equal. "I like the ocean," she said. "I always like to be near it."

Tanaaj sat down on the bench. "You seem as though you are apologizing," she said, "but it is very useful to know what kind of land you love. It means you already know which kind of god is calling you."

Pei-shan sat up straighter. Already she was a little more confident. "I walked the whole length of Palawan before this. Well, I mean, my familias did. And I said, always, I want to keep seeing the sea, so I kept going with zadres that were moving down the coast."

"And what is it that you love about the sea?"

The child considered. "I like watching the typhoons. You can see them coming from a long way off. There's nothing blocking your view."

Tanaaj nodded. "I had not thought of that. You are right, it's a grand sight to see the typhoons coming."

"I saw you last night," said Pei-shan.

Tanaaj realized she was talking about the performance. "Ah, yes. It ended too quickly."

"Is the other dancer okay now?"

"Li-Wei? Never better. The fermites knitted her back together."

"You were doing really good up until she fell."

Tanaaj laughed. "Thank you. She was doing well, too, she just got distracted."

"Distracted by what?"

The answer unfurled across her mind like a banner: *By Niloux DeCayo spreading a lie that threatens the peace of humankind.*

"By all the adorable children like you!" she teased.

Pei-shan giggled. "I played Javier Magaña once in a children's production. He's hard."

"Ah, yes. Javier was the very founder of *La Estrella Actual.* Did you perform the cave sequence?"

"No, just the ball court scene."

Tanaaj nodded. "Someday you'll tackle the more difficult material. Just pay attention to how the god directs you. Whenever I play Ajul or Javier, I pay especial attention to earth and water. Whenever I play Ixul or Xander, I pay attention to fire and air. You see?"

Pei-shan nodded, but Tanaaj had the sense it was a bit too abstract for her. "Are you going to do tricks for us tonight?" she asked.

"Perhaps," said Tanaaj, smiling. Her reputation had spread among children—how she could perform physical feats on command, like tumbling runs and trick shots. Once she'd bounced a pelota off parts of her body for ten minutes straight. Children told other children on the road: *If you meet Tanaaj DeCayo, ask her to do her tricks.* But she had to be careful. She must not indulge the pleasure she took in her own skill. Desiring fame was antithetical to Laviaja.

"But now!" said Tanaaj. "Let's get on to the real business of the day. What is the tutorial you're taking?"

"Inducción."

Tanaaj sat back in mock astonishment. "The fourth sacrament? You are to become a member of the Tzoyna today? You can *vote*?"

"I just turned seven! I don't want to wait anymore!"

Tanaaj laughed. The child's shyness belied her ambition. "That's good," she said. "We need ninx in the Tzoyna. You have points of view that we old folks don't have."

"How old are you?"

"Thirty years old, niñacita. I am ancient."

To Tanaaj's chagrin, Pei-shan merely nodded at this. "All right," she said. "I have some questions first."

"Of course you do." Tanaaj leaned against the trunk of a banana palm, wrenched off a bunch, started peeling. "Ask away."

"First: what is braiding?"

Tanaaj was ready. "Do you feel like sometimes you get too much information at once?"

Pei-shan nodded.

"Well, braiding is a way to take in all that information at once so that we don't feel too overwhelmed, but are also not too reliant on tech."

"Why would that be bad?"

That would take a whole day to answer. But Tanaaj said, "Humans have learned that it is better to rely on the human mind, and not external machines, which tend to accumulate. So we train the natural abilities of the human mind, and then induce otracortices to amplify those abilities."

"Like ojos-de-Leah."

"Yes! Ojos-de-Leah is one type of otracortex. It helps you sense Xibalba."

"Like Saint Leah could." Pei-shan thought hard. "So we can feel Xibalba more than people could in the old days."

"Exactly."

"Can we braid information if we don't induce otra-cortices?"

"Maybe," she said. "Most of us are not born with brains that can reconcile information in the same way. Everything changed because of the Age of Emergency."

Pei-shan became solemn. "Saint Leah's time," she said.

"Yes. The Age of Emergency began in the twentieth century. Within a generation, a human was receiving many more stimuli than she had evolved to receive. So in the twenty-first century, sofists invented a new way to reconcile multiple streams of information, called braiding. But only external computers could do it. And capitalism depended on the manufacture of external computers. Then, with the rise of fugitech over profi-tech, sofists developed otracortices, which helped us braid in our heads."

"Is there anyone in the world that doesn't have otra-cortices?"

Tanaaj nodded, thinking of the sedentix with distaste. "There are some. But mostly, zadres plant them within nine days of birth."

"Plantanda. That's the second sacrament."

"Sí, hermanix. But then some viajeras remove them when they are grown up."

"Why?"

Tanaaj shrugged. "It is their choice."

Pei-shan sat up straight, emboldened. "I don't know why anyone would live without them. Or without the aug. You wouldn't even be able to see me talk," she said, and pointed to the ribbon that curled from her lips.

"That's true. You and I would have to find another way to talk, like Cantosign."

Pei-shan brightened. Her hands flashed, "I know Cantosign! How many languages do you know?"

"Nine," Tanaaj signed back.

Pei-shan looked wistful. "I only know four," she signed, then switched back to text. "I know Cantosign, Común for conversation, High Spanish for ritual, and Mandarin for tutorial."

"That is plenty of languages, hermanix. You'll learn more as you need them."

"I hate having to sleep afterward," she said with a look of long sufferance.

"You will have to sleep a lot after this tutorial."

"But why?"

"Your brain needs to incorporate all the information it received. But oh, what dreams you will have! When I learned Urdu, I dreamt entire epic poems. I only wish I could have written them down, but whenever my zadres woke me up, it was all they could do to get a little soup in my mouth before I fell back asleep." Tanaaj mimed her head falling hard against her arms.

Pei-shan giggled. "What other languages do you know?"

"I know the ones you know. Plus two I learned along my pista—Urdu and Tamil—and then Ch'ol and Mopan, which I needed to learn for my manéra."

"I want to learn Kriol. Like what Saint Leah spoke."

"It is understandable to think Saint Leah spoke Kriol, but she did not. She only spoke Común and some Spanish."

"Oh. So only Saint Javier and Saint Xander spoke Kriol?"

"They did, but ah," said Tanaaj, wagging her finger, "do not call them saints. Javier and Xander are not saints, because they did not cross over to Xibalba. Their causes of death are well known. They merely entered new bodies and continued on their viajas."

Pei-shan stared at the sea, her eyes bright and serious. Tanaaj felt chastised, as if she'd referred too casually to something so sad.

In a more gentle voice, Tanaaj said, "The morning is getting on. Shall we start?"

The child nodded. "I'm ready."

"Sit as you were taught. Make sure your back is straight. Take three calming breaths . . ."

Pei-shan did it all. She was well trained, had had good zadres; Tanaaj wouldn't have to do any remedial work here.

"And now soften your mind."

The ninx nodded, and her eyelids went heavy. She was now prompting her ai for a microdose of psilocybin, to blur the ego, and practicing mindful breathing at the same time. This was the technique of receptivity, the induction of that fertile strip of consciousness between waking and sleeping, where forms flowered with no effort. Artists called it the realm of perfectly realized art, glimpsed but not grasped, like her dreamed Urdu epics. The surf sloshed below. The wind was warm and buttery. When Tanaaj saw that Pei-shan was ready, she tapped her heart and murmured to her ai, "Necesitamos Inducción, Lección Uno."

On the court, there blossomed a short, round viajera in a sapphire-blue sari.

Tanaaj grinned. She had so many memories of this beloved avatar. Meha pressed her hands together in greeting and, even though she was not the one being greeted, Tanaaj returned the gesture.

"Welcome," said Meha to Pei-shan. "I am an avatar

of Meha DeVellore, founding mother of the modern Tzoyna. I consented to the preservation of my likeness for the purposes of this training. Today, I will be guiding you through a tutorial on how to participate in the Tzoyna."

Tanaaj settled back to watch the lesson. It'd been a while since she'd seen it. But she had to be careful not to get dizzy; she wasn't in the same receptive state as Pei-shan.

Meha drew a timeline of human history. First she covered the original seventeen human species. Then the millennia of experimentalists, including communities that gathered and dispersed on a seasonal basis, as in Laviaja. Then the Agricultural Catastrophe, when egalitarianism was distorted by overaccumulation. Then monarchies, where basic needs were guaranteed only to a hoarding caste. Then came the experiments in democracy:

The Greeks at the agora in Athens, 510 B.C.

The English in the meadow on the Thames, 1215.

The Quakers on the peak of Pendle Hill, 1652.

The Americans in the hall in Philadelphia, 1776.

The Belizeans in the wayhouse in Cayo, 2050.

The delegates at the summit in Mexico City, 2099.

The jugadorix at the Carnival in Belmopan, 2129.

. . . and finally the Great Assembly in Delhi, called by Meha herself, the last prime minister of India—or of any nation, anywhere—in 2381.

Meha opened her palms with a little smile. "That is how," she said, "the practical nomadism of climate change refugees evolved into the philosophy of Laviaja."

Tanaaj regarded the ninx. Pei-shan was still in the trance state, her eyes heavy-lidded. Inducción was a multiday affair. Most children needed at least two sessions of this tutorial, plus three or four days of sleep after each, during which she needed to be watched and fed so that her body could finish the work of incorporation. As for Tanaaj, absorbing information at this pace was starting to make her feel sick.

She got up, walked to the edge of the cliff, and looked down. The foam swirled around limestone boulders. She looked out to sea, where a hundred islands were flung like pebbles, each circled in turquoise. The god of this place seemed proud and decadent, like a peacock. But, Tanaaj wondered, had it always been so? She tapped her heart to ask her ai: *What was the view during the Age of Emergency?*

The time filter spun backward. The sea level dropped and the islands grew upward, became hills. Cliffsides rebuilt themselves. Beaches emerged. Shirtless sailors pulled a boat into the shallows. The boat looked strange, like a white scorpion; her ai told her it was a paraw, an ancient fishing boat.

She was looking at Linapacan in the year 2012.

She laughed at herself. She'd been braced for some horror—skyscrapers on every island, crawling with people, dense as ants. But it was not so. The land had much the same character as it did now. She had to remind herself that the Age of Emergency was not awful for everyone, hard as it was to believe.

Tanaaj returned to the bench. As she watched Pei-shan, she remembered her own Inducción. She'd been in the dry upper neck of the Americas at the time. She didn't like deserts. She liked jungles and forests and river lands. She'd been a clingy child, too, and while communion was encouraged in Laviaja, particular attachment was not. It was something she needed to outgrow.

Her zadre was very devout. Her name was Yereft. She sat in a corner as Tanaaj took the tutorial—watching the same Meha press her hands together, wearing the same blue sari. After the history lesson came the practicum of braiding. It was so difficult the first time. How was it possible to find commonalities among streams of information that were so different? How was it possible to reconcile them, to apply them to a problem? How could anyone use this technique in the Tzoyna, the hallowed virtual space where a thousand viajeras were debating at the same time?

"At first it may seem impossible," said the avatar of Meha, seeing her skepticism. "But like with any skill—reading, cooking, or climbing—all it takes is practice. First, ask a simple question with a yes or no answer."

Little Tanaaj furrowed her brow, then asked, "Do you love me?"

Meha looked surprised. "Do I?"

"Yes."

"But I'm an avatar."

"But the real Meha. The original one. Would she have loved me?"

"That's . . . not quite right for this exercise," said Yereft from the corner gently.

But the avatar held up her hand. In that moment, Tanaaj realized two things: one, that the real Meha had been a colder sort than she had judged; and two, that Tanaaj would never receive as much love as she needed.

The avatar said, "She may have. She didn't have any children of her own, but by all accounts, she loved her nieces very much."

Tanaaj looked into her lap, abashed.

The avatar reset.

Meha gestured in invitation. "First, ask a simple question with a yes or no answer."

Tanaaj looked out the window, wishing the view were lush and green.

"Can I have just one familia that stays the same?" she asked.

This time, Yereft stood up and paused the avatar. "Child," she said, "maybe we should talk."

Tanaaj was chastened.

Yereft crouched in front of her. She was a mopan maya with gentle eyes, and the memory of her would inspire Tanaaj to become one, too, when it came time to choose.

"Why would you only want one familia?" said Yereft.

"Because then I'd always have someone to love me."

"But the whole world loves you," she said. "The whole world is your family. And if you chose just a few people to love and love you back, and you lose them, what then?"

Tanaaj hadn't thought of this, and it horrified her.

"What if they fell off of a cliff?" Yereft continued. "What if they drowned? Then you would have to start all over again, loving new people. But then you would lose them too."

Tanaaj was crying now. She'd always been especially scared of drowning, though Yereft couldn't have known that. The zadre put her hand on her shoulder.

"It's better this way, child. You don't understand it now, but you will." Yereft cocked her head, looked to the side. "Now that I think about it, it might not be such a bad question to ask after all. Do you still want to?"

Tanaaj sniffled. "Will Meha be angry with me?"

Yereft laughed. "She's an avatar! But if she gives you any trouble, I'll keep her in line."

That made Tanaaj laugh too. "Will you sit next to me?"

"Of course," she said.

Yereft sat next to her, and Tanaaj leaned against her, to make sure their bodies were touching. She wanted Yereft to like her. Besides, she was a kind zadre. She trusted that she must be right.

Meha came to life again, gestured in invitation. "First, ask a simple question with a yes or no answer."

"Can I have just one familia that stays the same?" Tanaaj asked.

Tanaaj saw a golden bubble drifting away from her mouth. Now, it seemed, her question had been accepted. Meha waved her arm to summon the virtual ball court. The bubble floated down to the stone and popped in a spray of sparks, which rose slowly, then multiplied until the whole court was filled with them, thick as fireflies.

"Now comes the yax che, the ancient Maya World Tree," whispered Yereft. "We use it as a visual aid."

A shoot cracked the stone and grew upward, thickening into a trunk, which divided into branches that spread outward. At the same time, roots trickled down and spread under the court. Then she noticed the golden sparks were clustering along the trunk. Tanaaj reached out in space and pulled the view closer, to get a better look.

"They're answering me!" she said in astonishment.

"Yes," said Yereft. "Those who say 'yes' cluster along the trunk aboveground. Those who say 'no' cluster along the trunk belowground."

Tanaaj noticed that there were far, far more data points belowground. "Who is 'they'?"

"Only sample data. The tutorial generates them."

Tanaaj was disappointed. She'd wanted real viajeras to answer her question. The tree disappeared, leaving only the answers, and then the answers thickened and stretched into lines, representing their change over time. And so the braid flowed like magma, spurting and glowing and cooling again, and she had to make sense of it.

After adult Tanaaj put Pei-shan to sleep, she looked for a place to pray.

She followed a gully down to the water. She climbed onto a palm tree whose trunk curved over the waves, lay back, and opened her legs in prayer position. The arc of the Milky Way rose in the east.

"Saint Leah," she said, "I am troubled."

A bird cooed in the brush behind her. She let down her leg and dragged her toes through the water.

"Niloux DeCayo wishes to break Laviaja," she said. "She wants to drag us back into the Age of Emergency. I don't understand why anyone would want to do that."

She shut her eyes and saw blood, guns, atomic plumes.

She opened her eyes again, to the sea and stars.

"All we have in this world is the family of the road," she said, "la familia de la carretera. There is nothing permanent. To grasp at this world will only bring suffering."

A rooster crowed on one of the distant islands, and the sound bounced back and forth across the water, as if they were in a small chamber and not on the open sea.

"And Niloux is going to the Jubilee. What if people start joining her?"

The starlight glimmered on the insides of her thighs.

"I have to find a way to stop her."

She craned her neck to look up at the sky. The universe glittered, a warm blanket. Venus was not visible now, so she picked out Aldebaran and addressed it.

"I can see you, lovely star. I know that you're real even though I can never touch you. This is how it is with Xibalba. Why can Niloux DeCayo not understand such a simple thing?"

A breeze sprang up and curdled the face of the water.

Tanaaj sat up, encouraged. She spoke to that which was invisible, behind the sea and the stars.

"What am I, if not your servant? How do I give courage to the faithful?"

The breeze grew stronger, blowing warmth in her face, and a faint scent of woodsmoke.

Tanaaj closed her eyes, having received her answer. She would go to the Jubilee to challenge Niloux. Laviaja had to know it had a champion.

She got down from the tree, walked back to the wayhouse, and found the children in the common room. She'd decided to perform her tricks.

TZOYNA
3 Batz' 14 Pop, Long Count 10.9.5.7.11

---

9 December, 1012

Ixul couldn't focus. She was still buzzing from the session with Mutna.

She took the path up to the city. She hid in a storeroom at the back of the temple. No one would bother her here. On a table there was a bowl of red clay. She watered it to make paint and stood staring at the wall.

Mutna had told her that there'd been many creations in the past, and there were many yet to come. But Ixul needed to know how to control the transitions. It was not an idle question. In the last ten generations, every royal house had fallen—Mutul, Oxwitza, Kaanu'l, Lakamha, Saal, Pachan. Their people were refugees, scattered in the countryside, forgetting how to read and write, speak to the gods, and mark the cycles of time.

Ixul wouldn't forget though. She had to plan for the future. She wasn't content to wait for the next creation; she had to be its creator.

She painted the cycles on the wall with her finger.

Lordly—9 days

Winal—20 days

Lunar—29 days

Natal—260 days

Solar—360 days

Milpa—365 days

Stellar—584 days

Compass—819 days

Katun—7,200 days

Sacred—18,980 days

Creational—93,600 days

Baktun—144,000 days

Long Count—1,870,625 days

These were the known cycles of time, handed down from the ancient dayfall peoples, who'd received them from the god. Each of her glyphs looked like seeds, curled up, their meanings waiting to unfurl. Ixul stared at the last number. How long that was! And yet the end of the Long Count was only a thousand years from now, at which point another cycle would begin. A daykeeper must be able to count a thousand years into the past and the future, rolling the sacred rounds like bracelets on her wrist.

Ixul had relaxed. Her shoulders had dropped and her breathing was even; when she was at work, she was at rest. She wrote the day's full date: 10.9.5.7.11. The day god was Three Batz', who governed along with the fourteenth farmer of Pop. Each day was a unique mix of influences. She must discern them as a hunter pulls apart entrails.

"Ixul," said a voice behind her.

She turned.

Ajul was in the doorway. He was breathing hard, his shoulders glossed with sweat, wearing only his under-esh.

Ixul frowned. "Has anyone seen you in that rag?"

"I was looking for you in the palace, wajmul." He used the term of endearment for a lover, which he was careful to use only when they were alone.

She said, "I was by the river with Mutna. Now I'm working something out." She turned back to her work. "I'll deal with you later."

"No. I have to talk to you."

"Not now."

"I just saw a jaguar, wajmul."

Ixul stopped, midstroke. "Where?"

"In the family courtyard of the palace. I turned around and she was there looking at me."

She turned to stare at him. "Spotted or black?"

"Black."

Then it was not Ixul's nagual. "Did you ask where she was from?"

"Yes. No answer. She went into your bedchamber and I locked her in."

Ixul stared. "You locked the god *in my bed-chamber*?"

Ajul spread his hands. "I did it quickly, wajmul! It seemed like the right thing to do."

"Is she still there?"

"I don't know. I listened at the door and heard no sound."

Ixul was speechless. Ajul could be both foolish and maddeningly lucky. The appearance of a black jaguar was a serious omen, but for good or ill, she didn't know. She would have to consult with Mutna. But she also wanted to finish this calendar work. There was too much happening.

Ixul pointed to the corner. "Sit there and wait until I'm done."

He did as he was told.

He rested his spear on the floor and watched her with that worried expression he had whenever he didn't want to provoke her. He had an erection. They both ignored it. He couldn't control his erections, especially around her. He could sit there, for hours, just watching her. His body was as strong at rest as it was in motion.

She'd lost concentration. She slammed her hand against the wall. Clay water splattered across her face.

Ajul remained quiet.

She wiped off the drops with the inside of her wrist.

He chose that moment to say, "I have to tell you something else."

She turned to him. "By all means."

"This morning, Ket let blood."

Ixul raised her eyebrows. "On purpose?"

"Yes."

"That was foolish of her."

"No, wajmul! I would think that too, if you'd told me, but she was very brave. She gathered all the instruments by herself. She even used the star blade. Ixul, I think we should take her more seriously."

Ixul looked up at the ceiling. She understood what he meant. All things would yet be made new in this future she was creating, and perhaps that included her relationship with her little sister.

"How did it go?" she asked.

"I arrived just in time. I guided her through it. She took a whole mushroom and cut to the bone. I bound it up right away. When she went into the trance, I made sure she was comfortable."

Ixul closed her eyes. There was so much to remember that was new today, on top of everything needed for the ceremony tonight. The calendars. The black jaguar. Ket letting blood. She moved the glyphs behind her eyelids, adding this, subtracting that.

"Did you see the jaguar in the courtyard before or after she let blood?" she asked.

"Just after."

"Then Ket must have called it. The jaguar was probably Balam Ahau."

"What does it mean?"

"I don't know. Balam Ahau does not serve us, he serves Xibalba. His reasons are not ours. Have you told anyone what you saw?"

"No. Just you."

"Then don't. Not even Mutna or Upakal. This is our knowledge to use."

"Ixul?" he said. "Do you think the omen is good or bad?"

"Ket was the one who summoned it," she said, "and you say we should take her more seriously. We'll ask her."

Ket opened her eyes on the court.

Immediately she wanted to remember everything. Everything she'd seen was important and prophetic. The star that both signified all things and was all things! How could that be? And yet she felt certain. She wanted to find the right words to convey the weight of her vision, but none were sufficient.

She shut her eyes again, and the darkness helped her remember: the pink-orange light, the cacao water, the red leaves. What else? She knew she was forgetting things. Is this what happened every time a royal ate the god and let blood? No wonder it was so powerful. She'd fallen through time itself, seen the deep past. Or was it the far future? She had to ask her brother and sister. Where was Ajul? How long had she been away?

The howler monkeys roared in the trees overhead. She tuned them out; she couldn't get distracted. She had to remember all the things she'd seen.

The pink-orange light.

The cacao water.

The red leaves.

She turned the star blade in her hand.

She sat up slowly. She felt nauseated.

From the light, it was past midday now. She got to all fours and knelt upright, slowly, and examined her finger. Ajul had applied herbs to prevent putrefaction. She resisted the urge to pull off the binding and examine it. Now it had to heal.

She gathered up her instruments in a bundle. She took the path that led down the terraces, up the lime road, past the old farmsteads, beneath the fortifications of the palace, through the market arches, and out into the main plaza. On the far side, the great temple reared overhead like a standing wave of blood. She loved the red against the green and remembered it from her vision: a red city in a green valley. And now she was here, in waking life.

She had to remember:

The pink-orange light.

The cacao water.

The red leaves.

Women and men were sweeping the plaza, getting ready for the night's feast. All of the dirt and leaves had to be removed so no one would get sick. There were cooking stations set up all along one side, and each station had its own array of pots and metates and cook fires. Women held handfuls of maize kernels up to their lips to kiss them before dropping them into the pots. Ket took stock: there was venison and river snails, chicken and papaya stew, red-and-green stew, tapir stew with cassava, pozole with chili peppers, atole with wild greens at the bottom, honey and cinnamon pops, cacao with vanilla and agave, candied pineapples and soursop tarts, turtles with blood gravy, pickled baby iguanas, spitted stingrays, and—she lingered by this pot—seed draught. It was her favorite. It was a special Nahua drink of little black seeds soaked in water, which swelled into slimy little balls that Ket had called "tadpoles" as a baby, though now she knew they weren't real tadpoles.

The cooks bowed to Ket as she strolled past. She nodded back at them, enjoying the attention, though she knew Ixul didn't like her to wander alone through public spaces like an urchin. She disagreed with Ixul on many things. Ket had her own way of handling people. She enjoyed the glances at her bandaged finger. No one asked her about it, but when she looked back, she saw them murmuring to each other, adding it up: Look, she's let blood. The baby princess is grown.

She came to the public ball court. This was where the twins would play against the captives tonight, who were staked on the platform at the far end, naked in the sun. In the old days, they'd have been nobles; now, Ajul captured what he could get. That usually meant refugees.

Upakal stood at attention on the platform. He bowed to Ket, and she smiled at him, letting him know he didn't have to do anything more than that. She squatted in the shade and studied the captives. One woman and two men. Ket's family shaped their heads like elegant cacao pods, and the merchants from Katwitz shaped their heads like pumpkins, but these captives had no shape at all. They were people of no lineage, no consequence. Their heads looked sad and bald, like eggs.

In her mind, she called the woman Fob, and the two men Gob and Dob. Their tongues had been removed. Bloodied strips of paper were looped through their earholes. They were all sedated to help them sleep through the heat; but when the sun went down, they'd be fed and watered, their faces washed by beautiful women.

Ket focused on Gob. He was tall, with lanky limbs and a soft belly that sloped to the side, like a pregnancy gone to seed. He was older than the others, probably a father. His penis rested soft on his thigh and breathed on its own. Ket wondered what had happened to his children. Maybe they were wondering what had happened to him.

She had seen her first captive when she was four years old, at Ajul and Ixul's presentation ceremony. The captive was a young Nahua prince captured on a raid. In her head, Ket had named him Nob. He was young, lean, and pretty, with long dark eyelashes. She fell in love with him right away.

Her mother tried to prepare her. She said, "We play the ball game for Xibalba. Blood is our gift to the other world, and the other world gives us gifts in return. A good captive is kind and beautiful, strong and healthy, trustworthy and honorable, with good eyes and no deception, who plays to the best of his ability and, at the end, offers no resistance."

"How can you tell when a captive is going to be good?"

"We can't know for certain. We can visit them, to test their disposition. Sometimes a captive is cowardly or sullen, or kicks away the food you bring them. Then you know they must be further conditioned. But the best captives know that only chance has made them a captive. If they have been brought up well, they know it is honorable to submit to their fate. We can only prepare them, and hope."

"What if they run away?"

"To run away is a terrible thing," she said in the slow voice she used when she wanted to impart something especially important. "A captive must never run away. Once they are captured, they are marked for Xibalba, and to accept that fate is what truly sets them free. If they run away, they lose all honor before Xibalba, the gods, and humans. No one would take them in. They would be no better than a monkey without a face, shitting in the jungle."

Her mother saw the distress in Ket's face, and spoke to comfort her. "Don't worry," she said. "This captive won't run away. And neither will your father. He's been practicing the ball game since he was a little boy."

And so Ket was comforted.

She was too young to understand, of course, that Nob would die.

They watched together from the royal dais, all four of them—Ajul, Ixul, Ket, and their lady mother—as their lord father faced the young captive on the court. Ket had seen lots of the twins' games by now, so she thought she knew what was coming. But there were already big differences. Ajul and Ixul played by day; this game was at night. The twins played on the old court in the jungle; this was happening on the big public court. The twins wore plain cotton to practice; her father and the captive were arrayed in gold, shells, feathers, and bright body paint.

She saw Ajul lean over to Ixul. "This is a good captive, sister," he whispered. "He is fully present to his fate. Look how he stands with his shoulders thrown back."

Ixul nodded, serene. "But what about his skill? See how he leans. He favors his left side, like you do."

"I do not."

"You do. Remember the game against the youth at Pekwitz?"

"That was a practice game. He was just a farmer's son."

"His name was Tatichwut. You'd do well to remember his name. He scored three points on your right side."

"Tatichwut was five years older than me, sister."

"It doesn't matter. You were far better than him, even then."

"I did humiliate him in the end. He ran off the court crying."

Ixul lapsed into silence, granting the point. Ket smiled to herself. She loved listening to the twins' banter. She looked out over the crowd. She felt bad for the people far away, angling for a look, and half of them with weak eyes anyway, so relying on the murmurs of their neighbors.

But she and her family were right up close. They could see and hear everything. They could even smell the sweat: her father's, musky like the dark honey of copal; Nob's sour, like milk gone bad.

That's when Ket knew that Nob might be afraid.

Afraid of what? she wondered.

Then the game began.

At first, it seemed an even match. Nob scored a point against her father, which made the crowd cheer. Ket was upset. She looked up and said, "Is Father going to lose?"

Her mother looked down with her big round moon face and smiled. "Don't worry," she said. "Your father is just tiring him out. It does no good to defeat the captive right away; everyone would be bored. He has to provide an entertainment as well as a victory."

"But the captive is so strong. How do we know he won't win?"

"We've conditioned him. Look, he's already dragging."

The ball game unfolded just as she'd said. Nob was allowed to score points, and so was encouraged to become bolder, thinking he had a chance to win. But this was when her father showed real skill. Suddenly he was twice as fast, twice as strong, twice as cunning. The court began to shimmer, as if seen underwater, and the crowd fell silent. Her mother whispered, "This is the sign. Xibalba is near." Then Nob was racing to keep up, desperate. He made mistakes. He dashed his knee on the stone, and his blood mixed with the blue paint, leaving purple smears on the stone.

It was over.

Ajul leaned over to Ixul again. "Father never even touched him," he said.

"Of course not," said Ixul. "It's beneath him to actually touch him. The captor must win by skill and strategy alone."

"But at every turn, Father let him get as close as he could."

"Yes," Ixul agreed. "That's the art."

Their father glided off the court, headdress still intact. Upakal and the other guards pulled Nob to his feet and half-walked, half-dragged him to the altar, as his knee was shredded. They cleaned his wounds. They repainted him in blue. They fitted him with a peaked headdress. All the while, the crowd was silent, and the air on the court shimmered.

Her mother pulled her close and said, "Don't look at them directly."

Ket's breath stuck in her throat.

Out of the corner of her eye, she saw four figures arriving from the direction of the Great Cave. They were the four blue chaakob, the rain gods. The guards fell back and the chaakob stepped in, and lifted Nob and pinned him down to the altar, which curved so that his chest bloomed upward. The crowd had gone still, as if turned to trees.

Now Nob looked panicked, like he wanted to run. But Ket didn't want that for him. She wanted him to continue just as he had played the game—with dignity. She stared at him, only him and not the gods holding him down; willing him to look back, wanting him to see her, so she could convey her admiration.

He turned and locked eyes with her.

She clutched her doll to her mouth. She couldn't look away.

Seeing her, he became calm. He bowed his head to her. She bowed her head back, ever so slightly, feeling that somehow, even though they were in such different positions, they were equals just now. She sensed that he needed her to anchor him through the next few moments. So she was with him, and he was with her, no matter what happened next, their faces licked warm by the same firelight.

Her father reappeared at the altar, now fresh, washed, and changed into clean garments. The air still shimmered. But Ket didn't search for the gods; it was bad luck. Instead, she had to anchor Nob.

First, her father took the captive's fingers. He put them in bowls held out by Mutna, who caught the blood, then went around the court anointing the ancestral guardians of the Tzoyna. She bowed before the royal dais and the twins rose to be anointed too. Ket could smell the heat of the blood, but kept her eyes on Nob. She would stay with him. She'd promised. Her father cut away more: his ears, his nose, his feet. Now he looked like a broken statue. Blood streamed down the sides of the altar. The gods kept coming, each taking their due, and Ket saw them as colored hazes at the corner of her eye: storm-blue Chaac, silver Ixchel, golden Itzamna. Nob seemed to relax into a more natural state he'd never known was available to him. When her father took his penis and testicles next, and put them in a bowl, he only winced a little. He never broke gaze with Ket, who finally understood, now, what it meant to be given to Xibalba.

Her father made two clean cuts in his chest cavity, one horizontal and one vertical, reached in, and pulled the heart free of its moorings. The red god Balam took it, steaming in the night air, and dissolved back into the darkness.

All the while, Nob made no sound at all. His eyelids just began to droop, as if he were falling asleep. By the time the warriors cut off his head and threw it into the court, his eyes were closed.

A light rain began to fall.

Xibalba's gift, in return.

At their father's beckoning, Ajul and Ixul rose and descended, because they had to learn what happened next. But Ket remained behind in a daze.

"Ket," said her mother. "Are you all right?"

"Yes," she said, and she felt as if she were answering from far away. "He died well."

Now, three years later, Ket wondered how these captives would compare. They weren't nearly as beautiful as Nob. But there were three of them, so maybe they'd add up to an equal gift.

The slope-bellied Gob seemed to sense Ket watching him. He opened his eyes and tugged feebly at his yoke, like he was trying to wake himself up from a dream. But, Ket imagined, he stayed within the dream. In this dream, the ball court was lined with people, young and old, royal and commoner, holding torches that bloomed like jungle flowers, while Ajul and Ixul circled him with spears leveled, and the weight of holy purpose inscribed itself on the court as if by a great obsidian blade at the end of a pendulum whose fulcrum was rooted in the sky, where the Sun pulled it back from the center of his petal throne and let it swing; and it wrote, and it wrote, and it wrote.

CAYO
1 Tznanab 0 K'ank'in,
Long Count 12.19.19.17.17

---

18 December, 2012

Xander didn't like his tourists today. In truth, he didn't like his tourists most days. If he were a good guide, he would indulge every question and laugh at every joke. But he'd never cared about being a good guide. So even though this couple had paid extra for a private tour of the cave, he didn't even pretend to like them.

The man was Chris, a six-foot-five gringo who took too many pictures. He'd already stopped Xander twice to make him unpack his knapsack and hand him his smartphone. Now they were deep in the upper chambers and Chris was taking pictures with the flash on.

"That rock formation," he said to his girlfriend, a shrinking blonde named Kassy. "That one looks like a—"

He paused to make eye contact with Xander, as if to ask permission to say the word, but then he said it anyway. "Dick!" he finished.

Good, good for you, Xander thought. *You said the word "dick" inside the sacred cave. You can go home and tell all your friends at the water cooler.*

But what Xander said was, "Yes, that's a stalagmite that took millions of years to form. And behind it is a pillar that some think was deliberately carved to re-semble the goddess Ixchel. See how the shadow looks if I cast my headlamp on it?"

Kassy cooed. "I see what you mean," she said.

"That looks like a dick to me too," said Chris.

Yes, Chris, everything looks like a dick to you. Thank you. Your insights are a gift to us all.

But what Xander said was, "Come on. The grand finale awaits."

"You mean where the skeletons are?" said Kassy.

"We're already surrounded by skeletons," said Xander. "And only eighteen individuals have been identified. There could be hundreds more in these dry pools. Keep to the rims, please—don't step inside them."

"I mean the Crystal Maiden on all the tourism posters."

"She's up in the final chamber, yes," said Xander. "But we can't tell much about her."

"Why not?"

"It's very delicate work, extracting—Chris! Don't go over there. Follow me, follow in my footsteps— it's delicate work extracting sample material from the bones, because they're crystallized in calcite. You make one wrong move, and the whole skeleton could collapse."

They stepped from rim to rim, their headlamps shining like stars in the darkness.

"Why shouldn't I have gone over there?" asked Chris.

"Because there are babies over there."

"What?"

"Little infant babies. They were brought here as sacrifices, too, along with older victims. Their remains are even more delicate."

"Dude. I can't believe we can just walk up to them like this."

"It's a great privilege," said Xander. "Many think the cave shouldn't be open to the public at all."

"What do you think?"

Ah, he had to ask. "I don't think it should be open."

"So what are you doing as a guide, then?" asked Kassy.

This is what it was like, day in, and day out. His culture, his motives, his personhood, all reduced to slides in a slideshow for the next white tourist. How could he boil it down for them? Should he tell them he wants to study abroad, but can't get a visa? Should he tell them he feels a compulsion to return to this cave, as if plowing a wound he can't leave alone? Were they paying him enough to know? Did they deserve to know?

"Because of money," he said. "Everyone needs to work. So I might as well work in a place I like."

"Do you believe in the ancient Maya gods?"

"Nope!" said Xander cheerfully. "TripAdvisor is our god now."

That shut them up.

Xander heard a cluster of voices behind them. He turned and saw a new group coming in. He knew it was his twin Javier's group, because he could hear his loud, happy voice. Everyone in that group was probably his best friend already. He had a following, including a Facebook group devoted to him, full of girls promising to bring him to the States to show him their natural wonders.

They were not alike.

"Come on," he said to Chris and Kassy. "There's another group behind us and we want plenty of time. We have to get through that tumbledown ahead."

After they made it through, only the final chamber was left, reachable by a ladder. Xander designated Kassy to hold it, went up first, then helped her and Chris onto the uneven rock. There were two sacrificial victims up here, including, yes, the Crystal Maiden, her glittery arms flung back, her glittery jaw yawning open. He'd seen her so many times, and answered so many questions about her, and invented so many scenarios at the tourists' prompting, illustrating them at length or even making them up in direct contradiction to known evidence, according to what mood he was in on any given day, and how much he wanted to satisfy the insatiable tourist gaze.

Yes, *it was a girl, we can tell by the hip bones.*

Yes, *it was a boy, we can tell by the jaw.*

Yes, *his throat was cut, that's how all of them were sacrificed.*

Yes, *she was pushed backward, you can see her crushed vertebra.*

Yes, *she was an elite, we can tell by the carvings in the teeth.*

Yes, *he was a peasant, we can tell by the degradation of the bone.*

Most guides spun a story that the skeletons were Ixul and Ajul, the legendary last two monarchs of the Tzoyna, the overgrown site downriver. Sometimes he indulged in the fantasy as well. But whoever the skeletons were, every time Xander came up here to see them, he was reminded that he was living in the world they'd created, whether they'd intended to or not. The Crystal Maiden was on every Belize tourism poster from here to the Cayes. She was the crown jewel of the industry, which was the crown jewel of the Belizean economy, which meant that his very ability to eat— much less to study, or leave the country—depended on this daily portage of gringos to gawk at the remains of a Maya teenager who died alone in agony.

Today, Xander was in no mood to linger. Javier's group was catching up with them—why was he going so fast?—and he felt rushed. "Watch your head, Chris— the ceiling's very low in here. Now we're at the end of the tour. This is the grand finale on the posters you saw in the airport. There are actually two individuals in this chamber. One is right behind you—" He pointed behind Chris, who swung his huge body around and drew up his smartphone and aimed. "Be careful," he said. "Don't get too close. Those remains are a thousand years old."

Chris was hovering, holding the smartphone right over the skull, his flash going off over and over like lightning bolts. "Cool," he said. "How'd they die?"

Xander was losing his patience. "Those bones are

consistent with the hands being tied, but—okay, now step away—"

Chris shifted and fumbled his smartphone, which slipped out of his hand and dropped through the skull with a delicate *clitch*.

Xander didn't move.

"Hello!" called a voice at the top of the ladder. Xander turned to look. It was Javier, his golden cross glinting on a chain against his chest.

"Sorry we are moving so fast, hermano—I have two trips to make today. We will just wait down here until you are finished, sí?" he said to Xander.

Xander didn't reply.

"Dude, I am so sorry," said Chris. "Dude. Whoa."

"What happened, amigo?" said Javier. Then he saw the hole in the skull and went silent.

"It was my fault," babbled Chris. "Mine. He was just telling me to step away. Though, dude! Shouldn't there be some kind of barrier here? Look, I'll tell anyone it was my fault."

Xander had gone cold. He knew what Javier knew: that tourists were not liable for any damage to historical sites. Their guides were.

Xander found his voice. "Someone has to tell Dr. Castillo."

"I will go," said Javier, selfless as always.

"No, I will," said Xander. He felt like he was speaking from a great distance outside himself. A cold sweat had broken out on his neck. "I can take—"

"I only have six with me, hermano," said Javier, "so I will take your two. Get out of the cave and call Dr. Castillo."

Xander nodded. He passed his brother, climbed down the ladder. "No, amigo," he heard Javier say to Chris, "He has to go report this to the Institute of Archaeology. You will go out with me instead. Don't worry! You will like me even better."

Javier was already making friends. Even with a dipshit like that.

Xander walked past Javier's gaggle of tourists, who were whispering to one another, aware that something was wrong. Xander didn't look at them. He felt sick. He was seeing his future recede from him. He started back through the tumbledown to get to the main burial chamber. He couldn't think straight. A tourist had dropped a camera into a thousand-year-old skull. There was a hole in the skull now. And he would be blamed, for letting the tourist get too close, for knowing he was a clumsy fuck and letting him hover and take pictures anyway. Xander should have seen it coming. He could tell from all the asinine questions Chris had been asking en route from the resort, like *What hap-*

pened to the Mayans? Was it aliens? We signed up for the overnight End-of-the-World package at Caracol, do you know if it'll be any good? Are the ceremonies they do authentic?

Authenticity, thought Xander, Oh authenticity. There's a topic too sophisticated for you. There's a whole subfield of sociology called tourist gaze, did you know that? And I want to study that, plus history and coding and political theory, but people born in Belize can't just get up and leave their country like you can.

Xander was rehearsing his angers again. He'd need a drink after this, or eight.

He came to the far end of the upper chambers and squeezed himself through the last opening. He heard the river below. He ran into another group of tourists.

Nine headlamps flashed his way. He squinted and shielded his eyes.

One dimmed, was turned up by a beefy hand. Ronald.

"Have you lost your guests?" he asked. "Or did you sacrifice them?"

That was a joke for his tourists, who tittered. But Xander didn't have time or good humor to spare. He spoke in Kriol.

"No taim bwai. Ah di ron bak."

Ronald frowned. "Wehpaat, breda?"

"Weh di dakta deh?"

"Dakta Castillo deh dah Belmopan, noh? Wai?"

Xander didn't know how to answer why. It was his fault, he knew, but he'd let it happen because he was stressed about Javier rushing him, so he wasn't watching his guests properly, and really it was this whole fucking 2012 tourist season putting the last remaining relics of a destroyed culture in danger and the horror of capitalism generally, so it was as much on anyone else as it was on him, really, and he'd better shut up for now.

"Aks Javier," he said, and shouldered past Ronald to climb down to the river.

Chris the tourist was in distress. "You can keep the phone if you need to look at it or keep it or anything. I'm so sorry."

Javier looked down the ladder at him. "I know you are, amigo," he called. "Just stay there and don't go off wandering while I retrieve your phone. That goes for everyone else, yes? Can I trust you to be safe and respectful?"

A chorus of yeses from the upturned faces.

Javier entered the small chamber. He crouched by the first individual, the one with its hands tied, the one most likely to be male. He'd been guiding since he was sixteen and porting since he was twelve, so he'd been in this chamber three or four thousand times. But he'd never touched the bones. Never even thought of it. Yesterday, this skull had been a smooth shell, undisturbed for centuries; now there was a big hole in it. Javier rested his forehead against the wall. He felt a headache coming on. This was very bad. He wouldn't want to be the one to tell Dr. Castillo about it. Dr. Castillo liked Xander more, anyway—the troubled young genius he was trying to send abroad.

Javier unclipped his flashlight. Steadying himself against the rock face with one hand, he pointed the flashlight down into the hole. He saw the phone—he'd be able to extract it from the skull if he was careful. Then a glint caught his eye: something green and glassy. Javier balanced over the skull, hearing his breath loud in his ears. He angled the flashlight to get a better look. He saw a sharp point, like a green shark's tooth. But that's all he could see.

He carried several tools in his bag. One of them was for retrieving smartphones from tight spaces. Tourists tended to drop them a lot; it was just part of the job. He had a pack of seven dogs at home, and he thought of his tourists like his dogs. It wasn't a derogatory thought, just a practical one: some dogs were smarter than others, but he had a responsibility to keep them all safe, secure, and fed. So it was with tourists.

This was a direct contrast to how Xander thought of

them: he was either hot or cold, depending on his mood, and depending on how he felt about them. If they were smart and easygoing, he nearly enjoyed himself. If they were pompous and demanding, Xander could dish as well as he got. If they were just dense, Xander considered them sport. It wasn't ethical. He knew that. They'd gotten reports that Xander had told credulous tourists all kinds of things: that he'd seen jaguars in the cave, that the ancient Maya built the first primitive radio, and so on. Javier wished he could tell him to knock it off. But Xander just wanted to leave the country and was angry that he couldn't. So he acted out.

Javier found what he was looking for: a long, skinny pair of pliers.

He looked toward the ladder. "Amigas y amigos! Is everybody still there?"

"Yes!" a few called back.

"I did not hear as many people as I would like to hear, so I will ask again, amigas and amigos, is everybody still there?"

"Yes!" A stronger, unified chorus this time.

"Nobody is peeing in any puddles?"

There were giggles, but he was serious. All tourists were supposed to empty their bladders before they went into the cave, but there was always some jerk who thought he was special. This point in the tour—the farthest point in—was a popular spot to sneak off. It didn't matter how much the guides warned them or waved the plastic baggies they carried for poop and pee. The tourists never asked. They just lingered overlong in some bend of the river with a distant look in their eyes. Once, Javier had let himself down into a pool, only to find a single hard turd swirling in it, as if in a toilet bowl.

"Turd!" he had said to the first tourist, who passed it back down the line: "Watch out for the turd." Someone took a picture of it and put it on Instagram.

Now Javier turned his headlamp to the strongest setting, angled it down, crouched over the skull, and slipped the pliers down into the hole. He'd always been good with his hands—balance, sports, dance—anything that required physical intelligence. He went into a fugue state while he clamped the phone and drew it out. He dropped it into a plastic bag and sealed it.

Now Javier could see what had been beneath the phone. It was a beautiful green obsidian blade—shaped strangely, like a ninja throwing star, with edges nearly as smooth.

His breath came fast and shallow. No one had seen this blade for a thousand years. He felt a passing urge to claim it, but he knew he mustn't. It was a good thing he was seeing it and not Xander. Xander's academic training and professed reverence for the cave meant that, paradoxically, he took liberties in it.

Javier made a mental note to tell Dr. Castillo about the blade. But he wouldn't move it. And neither would anyone else—he'd tell all guides to turn back for today. Those were the rules.

Javier came down the ladder and his tourists clustered around him. "Thank you all for waiting, amigas and amigos," said Javier, "and now we will have to turn back. I apologize that this matter is not up to me. It is the protocol of the Belize Tourism Board and the National Institute for Culture and History that if there is damage to one of the archaeological sites, we need to close it temporarily and assess how we are to be going forward. Thank you for your cooperation in this matter."

They reassured him it was all right. Chris was smart enough to stay quiet.

Javier led them back through the tumbledown, and saw another group standing over the remains of Individual 14. Their guide was Ronald. Javier could recognize him just by the shape of his body: thickset, beer belly. The cave guides were an intimate brotherhood.

"Hermano," Javier called.

Ronald looked up. His tourists turned, their headlamps swinging.

"Weh di goh aan?" he called. He sounded worried. He must have run into Xander down at the river.

"Weh Xander seh?"

"Ih noh tel mi noh ting. Ih seh, aks Javier."

Javier sighed. His brother could be so difficult. "Wahn kamara jrap eena Individual 12."

"Fu chroo? Weh?"

"Di hed."

Chris couldn't take it anymore. "It was me!" he said. "I did it."

Javier and Ronald ignored him.

"Soh wi noh gwehn eni ferda tudeh," said Ronald.

"No. Xander gaan bak fu fain di Dakta."

Ronald turned to his group, switched to English. "Friends, I have some bad news. There's been an unfortunate accident up at the Crystal Maiden."

One of his guests cried out: "Is she all right?"

A moment passed as everyone processed the question. "Well, she's still dead," said Ronald, "but there's been damage to the site, so in that sense, no, she's not. We're following protocol, which is to close down the site until our boss decides how to proceed. I'm very sorry you won't get to see the grand finale."

His tourists seemed despondent, but no one protested. Tourists were generally easygoing—just ordinary people, thought Javier, who responded to ordinary kindness like anyone else. But Xander had more complicated ideas. One of his projects was an ethnography of tourists: how they behaved, what they believed, and especially, their preoccupation with "authenticity." Whenever a tourist even breathed the word "authentic," Xander got a glint in his eye, like a butcher sharpening his knives. "What," he'd say with delicious slowness, "do you mean by 'authentic'?"

"I mean, what were Maya *really* like?"

"I'm Maya. I'm right here in front of you."

"Well, I mean the real Maya. What they really believed. Like, did they really believe that all the stars in the sky were gods?"

"You don't?"

"Ha!"

"I'm not joking. How do you know what a star is?"

"Because of science. Stars are made of gas."

"Have you set foot on one?"

"No. But scientists don't need to set foot on it to tell what it is. It's made of hydrogen."

"I'm made of hydrogen. And carbon and nitrogen and iron, but that doesn't tell you what I am. There's no way to prove that stars are not gods. So I ask: how do you know the ancient Maya weren't right?"

This was usually the point at which the tourist would start to look uncomfortable. He (it was always a he) would take another swig of Belikin, and then decide whether to ease off or press on. If the latter, every tourist on Burns Avenue would get their money's worth that night.

Javier led his group back down the river. He'd been through the cave so many times that he couldn't see it with new eyes; sometimes he wished he could. He had to be content to see the looks of wonder on the tourists' faces. The vast majority were impressed, one way or another, and felt they'd spent their day well. But there was a smaller population—usually one a week—who would be deeply moved, to tears or silence. He always looked for that one: the tourist who not only appreciated the cave, but shook their heads, too full to speak. It was a beautiful thing to witness.

Javier was feeling better already. Everything happened for a reason, after all. They passed through the shallows, the sinkhole, the canal, the first tumbledown, and then there was light ahead. He turned to narrate everything to his tourists. "Look, friends!" he said. "We have come back to the daylight!"

"Have you ever come here at night?" asked one.

"Yes, I have come here at night, amiga," he said. "Sometimes we do overnight trips. I sleep in a hammock with a big machete in my lap."

"Why?"

He winked at her. "Jaguars."

CAMPANIA
13 Wotan 6 Muwan,
Long Count 15.10.13.17.3

---

16 May, 3012

A black jaguar had been padding ahead of Niloux for an hour.

She didn't know where it had come from. Jaguars had been extinct since the twenty-third century. But here it was, solid and articulate. Maybe someone was cloning jaguars. Or maybe she was hallucinating after months of blotted exile. Or maybe it was an aug demon programmed by someone who wanted to punish her even more than she was already being punished. Pacifism still had its loopholes. Pacifism did not prohibit cruelty. Because of documented anarchy, any viajera could be watching her now—they probably were—because all information was available to anyone. Watching another person remotely was usually distasteful at best. But she was a notorious heretic now. Hundreds tuned in to watch her every day. Their very act of watching was also recorded, but they didn't care who knew they were doing it; it was fashionable. For five months now, because the Tzoyna had voted to allow it, Niloux appeared as only a blur on the landscape to all viajeras who'd chosen to blot her. She'd hoped that would be around five percent of the population. It was closer to forty. Enough to send her to very dark inner landscapes on her long walks alone.

The jaguar stopped.

Niloux also stopped, wiped the sweat from her face. It was 116 degrees, a warm spring day in the Mediterranean. The jaguar had to be feeling it too. Maybe it was searching for fresh water?

The jaguar flicked its tail, resumed walking.

She followed it. She had no choice. She was stuck on a narrow cliffside path on the Amalfi Coast and below her was a forty-foot drop to the Sea of Naples. Niloux pulled her gear around to her front, just in case she had to deploy her swair, the extensions of her pelt that would slow her descent if she had to jump.

The jaguar stopped.

Niloux also stopped.

It sat and looked out to sea, panting. She could see its muscles under the glossy black fur. It looked completely real. The Treaty of 2780 had set down clear rules for animal-human relations, the first being, *Let alone.* Viajeras couldn't harm them unless their lives were threatened or unless they were mutual hunters.

She was getting impatient. There was only another half mile to pick up the searoad to Capri—she could see it bobbing in the distance—but she was trapped here.

Niloux decided to backtrack, turned around.

A second jaguar was sitting on the path behind her.

It regarded her with bright jade eyes. Then it lifted its head and made its call, a yelping cough. Her therolinguist ai was silent, as if it hadn't picked up any sound at all. But she was sure she hadn't imagined it.

Niloux pressed herself against the cliff wall and looked at the first jaguar.

The first one had heard the call, turned to approach.

Now she was stuck between two jaguars.

Niloux swore. What the fuck was happening? Were they real? Or was she hallucinating? If they were real, what could they want except to eat her? She looked over the cliff edge. The drop was thirty feet now—not an impossible height—but the sea roiled and smacked against the rocks.

They were closing in, heads low.

She couldn't trust her shields. Even at full charge, she could hold off an attack for ten minutes at most; and she only had half a charge, because the last five days had been cloudy.

There was movement in her peripheral vision. They were trotting, gathering speed.

She touched her temple. Her swair unfolded from their resting positions against her upper back. The moment she could feel them catch the air, she jumped. She knew she was out of control as soon as she hit open space. She'd rushed and the swair weren't at the right angle to be much more useful than a sheet. She dropped like a stone, curled up to protect her vitals. The water rushed up and slapped her. Then she was under, sinking. She commanded her body to unfurl and started to climb to the surface. Then she felt her right leg twist like a stalk. Her foot was caught. Panicking, she tried to force it free. She felt a stabbing pain and screamed underwater. She shut her mouth. She could easily drown. Clenching her jaw, she bent double to see where her ankle was lodged. All she had to do was move it a little to the left. She did. Now she was free.

She pulled herself up with her arms.

When she surfaced, coughing, she saw she was too near the cliff—the waves would push her against the rocks. She saw a flat rock and swam toward it. Her right leg hung useless, ankle burning.

She got to the rock and dragged herself on top of it, facing Capri.

She asked her ai for a damage report.

Right ankle broken, it said pleasantly.

Niloux swore. She could reset it on her own, but her medkit didn't have taffies or fermites. She hadn't stocked up because she'd been blotted by so many people, she'd avoided wayhouses altogether. Without taffies or fermites, she wouldn't be able to move without pain for days, and even with her pelt compensating for heat and conserving her water, she didn't want to stay in the sun.

But her ai already knew all of this. It had detected the emergency and sent word to the paragua.

Niloux tried to guess how long it would take to hear back. Campania was a well-populated region—ten thousand viajeras passing through, last she'd checked. Lop off four thousand scrupes who'd blotted her, that left six thousand. Then the paragua had to skillmatch: Who was trained as a medic? Who had dealt with an injury like this before? Who was closest? Probably there were thirty or so within a mile. But what if all of them had blotted her? What if no one could hear her?

A lilac finch arrived.

Niloux felt a hot tear at the corner of her eye. She wiped it away. Isolation had left her raw.

"Stay where you are," said the finch. "Your ai is sending me your information. I'm twenty minutes away by water. Calling for backup." The finch took off.

Help was coming. Niloux would be interacting with another human en vivo for the first time in months. She was both relieved and apprehensive: she hated depending on anyone else, though that was a very un-Laviaji thought. Under other circumstances, it'd have been useful to find out how far she could get on her own with an injury like this. She was lucky she was in Campania, a well-traveled corridor, and not the Australian desert or the Kolkata Murk. Many who traveled those regions still died because there weren't other viajeras close enough to render aid.

She looked back at the cliff face. Both jaguars were still there on the path, heads cocked.

"Eat shit!" she yelled at them.

One looked at the other.

Niloux lay down and shielded her eyes from the sun.

She'd shut out the world for the last four months. She'd walked down out of Persia, then west across Cappadocia and Anatolia. Realizing how many had blotted her, she retreated inward. She kept close to deserts and away from people. She avoided looking at

Venus. She worried over the limits of panoptic justice, the corollary to documented anarchy. The rest of the world was watching her shit and eat and sleep and drop her menstrual blood, waiting for her to do something more interesting. So—paranoid—she did nothing. She took the searoads between the Aegean islands and rode out two cyclones underwater, suspended from gossamoor threads. She retreated deeper into bitterness. She avoided the news and ignored aug birds. She thought as she walked. The contents of her mind, at least, were still private. She started drinking too much. Her ai nudged her to induce cannaba or lysergia to get through the days. She searched for reports of new disappearances, but still there were none. She read the research feeds on geosophy, cortada theory, terraphenomenology, contemplative technique, fictive technique, quantum geometry, and linear relativity, all of which were relevant to the study of pistas. Niloux still felt that pistas were the key to her nascent technique. She'd made a breakthrough that night at Zein-o-Din, inventing the technique of seeing pistas from a past life, and the more she practiced, the more confident she felt. When she focused on a spot of earth and softened her mind and asked with clear intention, *God of the place: do you know me?* the answers were almost always no but the occasional yes was unmistakable, the answer surfacing as if always known. It was sheer luck that, in a past life, she had visited Zein-o-Din. What confused her was that these spots must have changed over the millennia—by erosion or sedimentation or plant growth. Were her past pistas visible only on landscapes that had remained unchanged? If a person had occupied a room above the earth, would her pista still register on the ground below her? What was the geometry of such a relationship? She had too many questions. Every night she lay down and slept six hours like a corpse. Every morning she woke up energized to find the answers. This was the work and it was all she had. She practiced the technique several times a day, and every now and then, got a positive result: once in the desert near the ancient ruins of Mosul, and once in the highlands of Greece. In fact, her pista had pooled there like a ball of yarn, circling over and over in an olive grove, which probably meant she'd lived there during the Sedentary Era. She called up a history filter and saw that she was standing in the ruins of ancient Sparta. What had she been here? A seasoned warrior? A slave for soldiers? A priestess of Artemis? She slept in the open, staring up at the sky, eating olives and printed pork.

But even as she developed this technique, she'd begun to doubt her resolve to go to the Jubilee at all, much less to hold a tzoyna there. On the other side of the world, a scrupe named Tanaaj DeCayo had begun to speak out against her. She was amassing a following that called themselves La Familia de la Carretera, the Family of the Road. How Tanaaj reconciled her fame with Versa Doce, the injunction against particularity, Niloux didn't know. But she was a jugadorix and claimed that she spoke for Xibalba. And people were listening.

While in Greece, Niloux was on the verge of turning back to Persia when she noticed a strange item in one of the more obscure feeds.

The Mardom e Zein-o-Din are gathering on Capri in mid-May, it said. It was signed: Ahmed DeGrozny. Niloux recognized that name. That had been the curious jovenix at the wayhouse in Persia.

Niloux ventured a bird to Ahmed and asked, with no preamble, *What the hell are the Mardom e Zein-o-Din?*

Ahmed sent back immediately: *You got the clue. I'm so glad. Word is you haven't been answering any birds, so the only way I knew to get your attention was to put an item in a feed I know you read. Look: you have friends. More than you realize. Mardom e Zein-o-Din just means "People of Zein-o-Din," after the wayhouse where you faced down the tribunal. We call ourselves Zeinians. There's a group of them planning to meet on*

*the island of Capri and I know you're headed west. So
if you want to join them, tell me.*

Niloux had said yes.

"¡Buenos tardes!" Niloux heard a voice call behind
her.

She turned and saw a tiny figure treading water. She
had silver hair and lilac skin—probably a mermaid.
This was good. She liked mermaids.

"Buenos tardes," Niloux called back.

"Soy Emelle. Quisiera acercarme."

"Soy Niloux. Sí, ven en paz."

Niloux appreciated that Emelle had used a custom-
ary greeting of two viajeras in the wilderness. Emelle's
ai must have told her to err on the side of formality.
The exchange was meant to establish goodwill, but
also consent, to enter another's space. She also noticed
that Emelle's accent was different from what was in her
head, and her ai had to correct for it. Dialect drift was
a consequence of traveling solo.

Emelle pulled herself up on the rock. She was slight
but well muscled. She first put her hand on Niloux's
forehead, and as she did, Niloux realized it was the
first time she was being touched in four months, and
an involuntary whimper escaped from her throat.

Emelle frowned. "Head pain?"

"No," said Niloux. She didn't want to say why.

Emelle tied back her silver hair and got to business. "The paragua knows you're here," she said, "and two others are on their way from Nerano Wayhouse. They're bringing a steadifoil. Did you jump from that path?"

"Yes," said Niloux, pointing. "Those two—"

She stopped. The jaguars were gone.

"Those two what?" said Emelle.

"Nothing," Niloux mumbled.

Emelle dropped it and rummaged in her pack. Niloux had an impression of profound competence. This was a trained and seasoned medic. "Your right ankle is broken," said Emelle, "but it's a clean break. You don't seem to be in shock but I'll elevate your leg anyway. The nearest wayhouse is on Capri, so we'll take you by steadifoil and treat your ankle there, but in the meantime I have anesthetic." She tore off a lump of blue taffy and Niloux opened her mouth to accept it. The taffy dissolved on her tongue, tasting of menthol. Soon the pain in her ankle began to ebb.

Emelle used her packs to prop up Niloux's leg, slow and gentle, then looked out to sea and sighed. "So now we just wait," she said.

"We wait," Niloux agreed. She was surprised that Emelle hadn't brought up her notoriety, and dreaded it. Didn't she know who Niloux was?

To forestall the topic, she broached another. She wouldn't be so forward as to ask about her preféra—not until they were in a place to do something about it—but in the meantime she could ask her manéra. "Are you a mermaid?" she asked.

Emelle beamed and stroked her hair. "Yep," she said. "Since a few years ago. But I don't have my tail on right now. Have you met any before?"

"A few."

Emelle nodded. She folded her legs, which brought her body closer. She smelled of brine and lilies. "And you're mopan maya," she said.

"You could tell?"

"No, my ai told me. Where were you going?"

"Jovis Wayhouse."

"Ah, well that's convenient! I was headed to Nerano. But I'll be happy to go to Capri."

Niloux took a risk. "Do you know about . . . the meeting of the Zeinians?"

Emelle looked confused. "What's that?"

Niloux didn't know what to do. She wanted to talk plainly, but she was so hurt from these past few months. She'd become afraid. She hated being afraid.

"It's a group," said Niloux, "who want to talk about the Zein-o-Din tribunal."

"Oh *that*," said Emelle, in a reverent way that gave

Niloux hope. "The Tzoyna has been discussing that since January. Around and around. I feel so sorry for what's-her-name who started it."

"You mean me," said Niloux.

Emelle focused on her, then sat straight up and clapped her hand over her mouth.

"Surprise," said Niloux.

Emelle drew her hand down to clasp it on top of the other, slow, penitent. "I feel like an ass."

"Don't. Thanks for feeling sorry for me, though. There aren't many wayhouses I can go to, because there are too many blotters everywhere."

Emelle shook her head in disgust. "Barbaric practice," she said, "and for something as simple as posing a question. You didn't murder anybody."

"Tell that to the scrupes."

She didn't flinch at the word, which confirmed to Niloux that she was in safe company. "I do," said Emelle, "whenever I can. I did Tzoyna duty just last week and said it there too. Blotting is barbaric."

"Thanks."

"How long is the sentence?"

"Four months. It comes up for a revote in a few days."

"I think there'll be a different outcome this time."

Niloux was surprised. "Oh?"

Emelle gazed at the surf, beating against the coast. "You tapped into something," she said. "There haven't been any new disappearances for years. There used to be one every week, in the 2200s. Even in the 2900s there was at least one or two a year. So viajeras are beginning to doubt, and well . . . you're the first one who's given credible voice to the doubt."

Niloux shrugged. "There's resistance too. Apparently this Tanaaj DeCayo and her Familia de la Carretera are going to challenge me at the Jubilee."

"Tanaaj DeCayo," said Emelle, drawing out the name, then laughed a little. "I've met her."

Niloux was about to ask her about it, but then they heard the distinctive pulse-tone of an approaching steadifoil, and turned to see it gliding over the water like a magic carpet. That was her ride to Capri.

Villa Jovis was a nicer wayhouse than most, because it was always occupied, which meant it was always maintained. Niloux could see the appeal. The ancient emperor Tiberius had run the Roman Empire from here, after all, and then the palace fell into ruin, and then came the millions of tourists during the Age of Emergency. The evening was pleasant, the air suffused with salt spray. When Emelle arrived to get her for supper, Niloux was standing in a courtyard overlooking a thousand-foot drop. She was so high up that the sea looked like a mirror.

"Come on," said Emelle. "Everyone wants to meet you. Do you need help walking?"

Niloux turned around. Emelle had put on her supper wear. Her silver hair was braided around a rayed head-piece, and she wore a white silk dress that offset her lilac skin and framed her bare breasts. Niloux was glad she'd put some effort into her own appearance. She'd combed her short black hair and added a virtual face tattoo that would be visible to anyone in the aug: a green star, symbol of the ancient Tzoyna.

Emelle helped her walk into a grove of lemon trees. In a clearing, there was a long pine table; it seemed too wide, almost as if it were a raft. Niloux counted four-teen viajeras sitting around it. Two were breastfeeding. All of them looked eager. So these were the Zeinians—Emelle included now.

Niloux was both glad to be around other people and feeling shy. She looked at her feet.

"Niloux DeCayo, everyone," said Emelle with a wave of her hand.

"Hi," she said. She wanted to sink into the ground.

"We have a seat for you," said a fat viajera, waving to get her attention. Niloux shuffled toward her, shrug-ging off Emelle's hand on her elbow. Emelle rolled her eyes, smirked, and took a seat on the other side of the table.

This was the first wayhouse Niloux was eating in since Zein-o-Din. It was the longest she'd ever gone. The wild hunger came on her again. She thought it must be some ancient feasting instinct—the Ice Age imperative to fatten up during hunting season, to make it through the winter. The fat viajera next to her—Demos, a yool, with a sleeping infant strapped to her back—made sure her plate was always full in a discreet and unobtrusive way. The other viajeras didn't bother her. They knew she needed to eat. Things felt different here. She let herself hope that she was really among friends.

After supper, they moved up a stone ramp into an intimate cella. The floor was grass, there were candles set in the walls, and above them, stars. They passed around cuvettes of lemon liqueur. Niloux felt she should say something.

She cleared her throat. "So. The Zeinians. Why did you all come?"

There were raised eyebrows, bemused looks.

"I know, I'm disappointing in person," she said.

To her surprise, there was laughter.

Demos said, "Not disappointing! Illuminating."

"You're too kind."

Demos sat forward, dispelling the tension. "Well, I'll start. I heard about the gathering in one of the Tzoyna forums. I think it was you, Miguel."

Miguel nodded. Niloux had noticed her at the table—a wide, commanding viajera with a neck as thick as her head, who used a handkerchief to dab the corners of her mouth. She was a taurus and, judging from her muscles, had been for most of her life. "It was me," said Miguel in a deep bass voice. "I thought the tribunal was unjust. I thought the ruling was unjust. I thought Niloux had said something worthwhile, but most viajeras around me reacted with cowardice."

These words were a balm to Niloux. Other people were saying the same things she'd been saying to herself all these months, angry and alone. She relished that those watching in the panoptica were hearing every word of this.

"So," said Miguel, "I started reaching out through the feeds, to find a place where people like me might gather en vivo. Especially if we were also heading to the Jubilee. Which . . ."

The question in her voice made Niloux look up.

"This special tzoyna you speak of. What are you planning once you get to Cayo? How can we help?"

Niloux let out her breath. She'd been on the verge of giving up on the idea. To have people on her side, willing to help, was more than she'd allowed herself to dream.

She also had to be honest. "I don't know," she said. "I've spent the last four months alone, just . . . thinking and refining the technique."

Demos was excited. "So it's real?"

"Yes, it's real."

"You can see your past lives?"

"Just positives over the spots where my feet once crossed, but you can join enough of them to make out a pista, or fragments of it. I found fragments near Zein-o-Din, Mosul, and Sparta. Whether they're from the same life or different lives, I don't know." She shrugged. "This whole technique is brand new. And I can't promise it'd work for other people. Contemplative techniques aren't necessarily transferrable. I can only tell you what I did."

Emelle said, "I want to hear more about why you think Laviaja won't work for the post-Diluvian Age." She leaned forward, refilled Niloux's cuvette. "Specifically how the story of Saint Leah was created after the fact. Maybe people knew at the time that she was special, but it's not like she was Muhammad, converting the Arabian peninsula during her lifetime."

Niloux nodded. "Right. The Rule of Saint Leah is a construction. It was invented after the fact, by viajeras who lived well after the founders died—all of them, Xander, Ruth, Ida, and Micah. It only sort of relates to her actual life and deeds. Like lots of religions with a human founder. Granted, the Rule has seen us through the last millennium—not always smoothly, there were still hoarders in the twenty-seventh century—but here we are today, eight million people in the world, living in peace. Now, though, I think the Rule is holding us back. I want . . ." Again, Niloux remembered the name of Ting Lee DeBrazza, felt the awareness of her own intention surfacing; her deepest desire was there, ready to be named, but she still didn't feel safe enough to say it out loud. She would suppress it and wait. She would choose something safer. "I want to find out more about what really happened the day Leah disappeared."

"Besides the accounts we already have?" said Demos.

"All historical accounts are incomplete."

"Do you think everyone in San Ignacio at the time was lying?"

"Not at all," said Niloux. She corrected herself. "Well, not necessarily. Just—everyone has motivations that aren't immediately apparent, right? *Cui bono*—who benefits from certain stories getting told? I don't think there's enough scholarship on why this story, the story of Saint Leah, became so important in the hell of the Age of Emergency."

"Because people needed to believe there was a way out of this world," said Emelle softly.

"Yes," said Niloux with sudden vehemence, locking eyes with her.

They all fell silent.

The cicadas rose to a swell. Niloux's ai translated:

The moon is a lemon too!

They ebbed all the way down before anyone said anything.

"Well, then you need to go to the Jubilee," said a new voice. Niloux turned to see an elderly viajera, with dark skin and golden bands across her hair. Her name and concórdia floated beside her face: Calliope, norte, roman, envolvánte. "But you have to plan for resistance. Tanaaj DeCayo is going too, with her LFC."

"LFC?"

"La Familia de la Carretera."

"Oh great, it's an acronym now?" Niloux shook her head. "DeCayo," she muttered. "What are the chances we were both born there?"

Emelle gave her a strange look, which unsettled her.

Niloux said, as if in riposte, "You said you'd met Tanaaj."

"Yes," she said. She addressed the group. "I crossed paths with her a few years ago, in West Bengal. She was"—her eyes drifted into the middle distance—"very passionate."

The way she said it made everyone laugh. Demos poked her in the shoulder, which made her spill her liqueur, and her lilac skin flushed to a deeper purple as she slapped back, and then everyone was poking her and laughing.

"Oh hush!" she said finally. "Everyone wanted to sleep with her, I was no different. There was a damn waiting list."

Niloux raised her eyebrows. She'd never had a problem landing an encamadix for a night, but she'd never had a waiting list.

"What was it about her?" asked Demos.

"Just charisma. She's warm and funny. I remember all the children loved her and fought to sit on her lap. She's childlike herself—kind of scrappy, and her hair is always messed up."

"And passionate how, exactly?" said Calliope, reclining for the gossip.

Emelle was giddy, half-smiling. She pulled a strand of silver hair behind her ear. "Well," she said, "she had stamina, for one thing. We were up all night. Sex was like a ministry for her."

"We need more details. Envolvánte, endotánte, what?"

"Omnipreféra. But she especially liked to give head. For hours."

"*Hours?*" said Demos. "That sounds so tiring."

"I would have said the same thing. But she was so present, you couldn't help but stay present with her. She had an instinct for touch . . . as if she knew how your body was feeling as much as she felt her own."

There was a pause, and Calliope said, "Is there a . . . fan up here or . . . ?"

Everyone laughed.

"Anyway," Emelle said, "I slept all the next day, but she just went on to the next."

Miguel whistled. "I'm sure it was nice to see her perform too."

"Oh yes," Emelle said. Her eyes went unfocused on the grass; she was trying to see it as she'd seen it then. "I saw her perform a ball game as Ajul." She opened her mouth, then bit her lip. She seemed hesitant to say the next thing. "She made the air shimmer."

Most in the circle knew the implication of that, but a jovenix was confused. "What, like she made a program in the aug?"

"No," said Niloux, "without it. There are stories of jugadorix being able to do that. The air starts to change, like . . ."

"Like how heat distorts things," said Emelle, "or like when you induce psilocybin or lysergia. It makes everything shimmer. Like you're watching it from the bottom of a river. When she danced, you just had the sense that . . . she was channeling the truth of who Ajul really was." She looked up, blinked. "She's famous for it."

"And she doesn't call herself particular?" said Niloux, with a bitter edge.

"No. She's incredibly strict about following the Rule of Saint Leah. She doesn't answer birds. She doesn't allow any pictures or streams of herself or stay anywhere for more than nine days. She doesn't even stay with the same people for nine days."

"When I was young," said Calliope, "that was much more common."

"According to scrupes," said Miguel, "it's simply the correct interpretation of Laviaja."

"Yes," said Calliope. "The ultimate dispersion of attachment. The only way to peace."

"So why don't you do it?" Emelle asked. But it wasn't a challenge; her voice was gentle.

Calliope sipped her liqueur. "It takes heretics to make a religion worth its salt."

After the drinks, Niloux wanted some time alone, so she went up to the roof. There was a single bathtub fed by a hot spring. There was even lemon-scented oil for the water.

While the bath filled, Niloux smoothed a moonball for light, and craned her head to read the spines of the books on the marble slab next to it. There was a volume of poetry by Esther DeBenque, a Divan of Hafez, and a *Popol Vuh*, the ancient creation story of the Maya.

She took it into the bath with her. She stepped in with one foot, then the other, clenching her teeth at the heat. She lowered herself and winced as the water touched her scrotum, then submerged up past her breasts. She let the water slosh over the sides. Her pelt adapted. Now her skin felt as if it glowed like an ember. Her ankle felt better. The only sounds were the laughter of those who'd stayed in the cella, and the waves a thousand feet below them.

She opened the *Popol Vuh* right to the page where the Bloodmaiden gave birth to the Hero Twins.

This, therefore, is the account of their birth that we shall tell. When the day arrived, the maiden Lady Blood gave birth. The Grandmother did not see it when they were born, for these two arose suddenly. Hunajpu and Xbalanque were their names. They arose in the mountains, but when they were taken into the house they did not sleep: "Take them away and abandon them, for truly shrill are their mouths," said the Grandmother. Thus they were placed on an anthill, and there they slept blissfully.

Niloux laughed, closed the book, and looked up at the stars. She wondered whether there had ever been a real set of mischievous twins upon whom the Maya myth was based. The Hero Twins were hardly unique to the Maya; twins were one of the most fundamental motifs in ancient Mesoamerican mythology. They still were, Niloux realized, if you counted Javier Magaña and Xander Cañul, the twin founders of Laviaja. But who had been the original? Had it been a set of twins among the first human settlers, twenty-five thousand years ago? Were they monarchs or athletes? Were they charismatics or recluses? Were they normal farmers, only venerated after some spectacular death?

Niloux sank deeper into the bath.

She thought about how humans occupied such a narrow, arbitrary slice of time in the universe, when stars were still visible from Earth. But as the ages went on—far beyond this age, into a distant future—the stars would disappear, one by one. The universe would expand until it froze to death. Xander Cañul had argued that, in the beginning of human history, dream, thought, word, and deed were all one and the same, in a point of singularity; now they were all separate and irreconcilable, like driftwood coming apart on the open sea. Even Laviaja itself was coming apart. Was it a religion? A philosophy? A system of government? An economy? A mathematical construct? An iterative science? A fictive technique? A deliberative process? Niloux was convinced it had become all of those things. Entropy could not be reversed. Neither could the dissolution of human experience. That is why—said Laviaja—we must ceaselessly travel, to search for Xibalba the unknowable, the greater reality, the reconciliation of all experience, the driftwood resurrected into the ship that plowed the eternal—

"Good evening," said Emelle.

Niloux sat up and water splashed everywhere. She'd been so deep in her thoughts that she hadn't even heard her arrive. She was conscious of her body; her nipples wrinkled in the air even as her cock was soft from the heat.

"Uh, and to you," said Niloux.

"Would you rather be alone?"

The truth was, Niloux would. Then again, she'd been alone for so long. And Emelle was still wearing her white silk dress.

"May I join you?" said Emelle.

Niloux waved, tried to sound nonchalant. "Sure."

Emelle sat on the edge of the bath, trailed her finger in the water. Sweat beads formed on her bare breasts, merged and ran together. "You looked deep in thought. What were you thinking about?"

"Reformers," she said, but her voice broke, so she coughed and tried again. "Reformers like Martin Luther, Ana Safavi, even Saint Leah. They don't think of themselves as reformers. They think of themselves as purists. Like they're getting back to some essential truth that everyone else is missing."

"You think that's what Tanaaj DeCayo is doing?"

Niloux laughed at the irony. "That's what *I* think I'm doing."

Emelle cocked her head. "Oh? What is the essential truth we're all missing?"

Niloux tried to avoid eye contact, to focus on the question. "That transcendence is real, but it's not what we think it is."

"What do you think it is?" Emelle said.

"I don't know."

"Look at me."

Niloux did. And now there was no way she could focus, with Emelle sitting like that, with her arms pushing her breasts together and the sweat running down them in rivulets. There was not enough written about the geosophy of human bodies, she thought, as she knelt upright and buried her face in Emelle's soft belly, letting herself touch and be touched this way after so long. We are also landscapes, she thought. We are also settled, abandoned, and resettled. Niloux peeled the silk gown down to her waist, then past her hips so that it pooled on the ground. Emelle's body was taut and sinuous. Her areolas were large and violet, and her cock was erect, but tiny. Interesting, Niloux thought: Emelle might be one of the viajeras who experienced incongruéncia, the mismatch between body and self, who felt so strongly norte that she shrank her penis and amplified the rest. The LFC had not condemned these modifications outright, but they certainly disdained them. No wonder Emelle was sympathetic to the Zeinians. Niloux observed how the topography of her body was shaping her thoughts, just as the topography of land did, to all viajeras.

Emelle was pulling her up out of the bath and kissing the side of her neck. "Stop thinking. Be present with me," she whispered in her ear. Niloux tried to be. But she was always elsewhere. Wasn't it strange that she was about to sleep with someone who'd also slept with her political enemy? Then again, that was probably a grand tradition. She tried to think of historical examples. She moved mechanically. She got out of the bath, picked up the silk dress, and put it down on the marble slab next to the bath for traction. She looked at Emelle expectantly.

Emelle looked amused. "I can't read your mind, you ridiculous person," she said. "What do you want me to do?"

Niloux closed her eyes, shook her head. "It's been a while."

"I can tell."

"I'm an endotánte. If you like, could you please lie on your stomach."

Emelle raised her eyebrows as if to say, *Knew it.* She lay on the slab, supporting herself on her forearms like a sphinx, and flexed her legs so that the shadows of her muscles appeared and disappeared.

Niloux knelt between her legs and drew her finger along Emelle's body, trying not to go too fast and failing. I am a norte maya endotánte, she thought, and Emelle is a norte mermaid envolvánte. Our bodies alchemize in this moment. We live in a world where identity is self-determined and sacred, after thousands of years of people dying for that right. This kind of change was good. So by challenging Laviaja, was Niloux putting this freedom at risk? She was so hard that she was in pain. She took the jar of bath oil, coated her hands, coated her cock, coated Emelle's bottom and spread it apart with her hands. She let her tip drag along the crack. She closed her eyes and opened her mouth. She'd forgotten the agony of it. Everything was oiled now, but she still went slowly, fitting flesh to flesh, and Emelle arched her back to help her, until she was sunken all the way in. She buried her face in the back of Emelle's neck, smelled the lemon oil and lily perfume and mermaid brine all mixed together. She thought and thought. This alchemy will never happen again, she thought. Is this utopia? Is this transcendence? Are we happy? She heard Emelle groan and felt her tighten, so she crouched low, finding her rhythm and rocking with her, pressing her whole weight into her back, practical, skilled, working the problem.

TZOYNA
3 Batz' 14 Pop, Long Count 10.9.5.7.11

---

9 December, 1012

Ket untied Gob, the fatherly captive with the soft belly, and led him around the city on a rope to see the sights.

"Here is the main plaza," she said, waving her arm. The cooks cast sidelong glances, but Ket didn't pay them mind. She was feeling confident. "You might remember that you came through this plaza when you first arrived. My family has lived here for thousands of years. My brother told me there used to be millions of pilgrims to our city. When he ascends tonight, they'll start coming back. See my ancestors on the wall? See those ribbons of words that are coming from their mouths? Those are the things they're saying. But don't look them in the eyes. I would take you to the palace, but the palace is only for the royal family. You can be here in the plaza, though. Last month we had a pilgrim all the way from Lakamha, city of the waterfalls."

She stopped and pointed to the stelae along the plaza. "Those are monuments to our family. They go back four thousand years. They say . . ." Ket paused. She didn't know how to read yet, but she didn't want to lie, so she aimed for what she was pretty sure was true. "They say we're going to be all right because we were born of the Hero Twins. Did you know my brother and sister are twins? They'll be king and queen tonight. They're going to build a whole empire from here."

Gob wavered in place.

"Are you tired?" she asked.

His eyes couldn't focus.

"Let's go sit in the shade."

She felt responsible for him. He wasn't young or beautiful like the Nahua prince Nob, but still, she wanted him to make a good showing tonight. She was worried that Upakal and the others had pushed him too far.

Still holding his rope, she led him to the great ceiba tree in the center of the plaza, which rose as high as the red temple. The sight reminded her of her vision, still fresh in her mind: the grid of ceibas in perfect lines, and the ancestors standing beneath them. She went to sit on a wooden bench under the tree. As soon as she sat down, it gave way. Ket cursed, using grown-up words. The wood was rotted. She kicked it over with her foot. Gob looked on, stoic. She stomped to the next bench, still leading him, and sat carefully. This bench was solid. She'd have to tell Mutna about the other. This whole plaza needed repaving—the plaster had begun to warp and rupture, and weeds poked through the cracks, then died for lack of rain.

Ket extended her hand into a shaft of sunlight. "The ceiba is the World Tree," she said to Gob, who slouched at her feet like a cat. "This is the center of the universe. The branches are in the stars and the roots go down into Xibalba. I was just there, I think, but now I'm back. You and me are here in the middleworld."

Gob peered up at her as if from a deep well.

"My brother and sister are going to marry each other," she said. "They don't think I know, but I do. They started to share a bed after our mother and father disappeared. They go to the palace at this time of day. It's disgusting. Do you want to go see?"

Gob looked confused. He hadn't expected to be presented with a choice about anything.

Ket tugged on his yoke. "Come on. I know I said you couldn't go into the palace, but it's all right if you're with me." The truth was, she didn't know if it was all right or not, but she was lonely, and she liked the companionship of the naked old man on a rope. If he was going to die tonight, she might as well make his last day interesting.

She led him to the path that ran around the city wall, which led to a tunnel of steps, at the top of which was a single doorway that led to the royal quarters. She paused, allowing Gob to admire it. The threshold was carved with vines and falcons and flames.

Ket tugged. "Come on," she said. "We can look at it more later."

But he didn't come. He looked worried.

"I told you," said Ket. "It's all right if you come with me."

So Gob suffered himself to be led through the doorway. Once they were in the courtyard, Ket turned and waved dramatically, signaling to hush.

Gob hunched, spooked.

Ket tilted her head and listened for sounds of her brother and sister panting. But she heard nothing except grackles cheeping. Something rustled in the branches overhead. A blossom dropped from a tree and splashed on the stone. She didn't hear anything human, just the soft hush of sunlight.

She led him farther in.

The floor was sunk. Around its raised perimeter were eight bedchambers. All the doors were open, except Ixul's, which was shut.

She turned back to Gob and held her finger over her lips. He nodded. She was pleased with his engagement. She felt like she was doing her part to prepare him, nursing him back to life.

She arrived at the door and pressed her ear to it. But she couldn't hear anything—no moans, no rustles, no heavy breathing.

Then she noticed that the door was barred from the outside.

Suddenly she was very worried. What if something had happened to her brother and sister? What if they were trapped in there? What if that was the meaning of her vision?

Ket dropped Gob's yoke, lifted the bar, and swung open the bedchamber door.

On the bed was an enormous black jaguar.

"Oh, hello!" she said.

Behind her was a scampering sound. Gob was trying to get away. She turned in time to see him go right over the edge into the courtyard below, but because his hands were tied, he couldn't break his fall, and smashed face-first onto the plaster. He got to his feet, his nose spurting blood. He scrambled away, across the courtyard, up the stairway, tripped, fell, hit his head again, pushed himself to his feet, looking behind him to see if he was being followed, ran under an archway, and—by the looks of it—jumped off the wall into the jungle.

There was nothing Ket could do about it.

She looked back at the jaguar.

It cocked its head at her.

She stared back. It was too late to avoid eye contact. She'd never seen a jaguar in real life before, only in the vision she'd just had. She'd been told they were very dangerous. But this one wasn't growling or snarling. It seemed tame, even gentle. If it meant to eat her, she reasoned, it would have done so already; and her blood-letting had emboldened her. Maybe this was the same jaguar from her vision. Maybe this was a sign.

She stepped into the chamber and climbed onto the bench next to the jaguar. It regarded her amiably, like a pet deer. She couldn't believe she was this close. Its nearness was thrilling. She lifted her right hand slowly—making no sudden movements—and patted its head. It was solid. This was a real jaguar. She smoothed the soft black fur. The jaguar still didn't recoil, and in fact seemed to like it. It sniffed Ket's other hand and licked at the bandage.

"Yes," said Ket with pride. "I let blood today."

The jaguar pulled itself closer to her, and laid its huge skull in her lap.

The skull was so heavy! Ket had to remind herself to start breathing again. It was like a boulder had been dumped on her legs. She could bear it for a little while, couldn't she? What choice did she have? This was the course of her life, now that she'd done the grown-up thing of letting blood. This is what it meant to be an adult. Now black jaguars appeared and put their heads in her lap.

The jaguar took a deep intake of breath, which she could see by its ribs rising; and then exhaled in a mighty push. She could feel the moisture of it on her hand and stifled the urge to wipe it dry. She didn't want to give insult.

"I wonder," said Ket, "if you're the same jaguar from my vision. The one that flipped me up to ride it. That was an actual jaguar, a real jaguar, more real than others, but right now I can't tell if you're the same kind of real. I saw so many things in my vision that I have to remember . . . like the red leaves and the whip spider. They all mean something."

The tip of the jaguar's tail curled up, curled down. It seemed relaxed and sleepy.

Ket had an idea. "Would you like to hear the story of the Hero Twins? They're our ancestors who went to Xibalba." She shifted a little so her bottom wouldn't go sandy under the weight of the jaguar's head. She cleared her throat and began. "Once there was a daughter of Xibalba named the Bloodmaiden. Sometimes storytellers skip her and start with the Hero Twins. I hate that. I always start with her because nothing would have happened without her. Anyway. She lived in the great city of Xibalba and had many adventures in its rivers and mountains and starlit forests. Then one day she came up into the middleworld and got pregnant when a calabash spit into her hand. The calabash was really the head of the dead hero, but that's another story. Then she gave birth to the Hero Twins, named Hunajpu and Xbalanque, and stayed with them in the middleworld. They lived in the forest and played the ball game all day, and their mother the Bloodmaiden liked to just sit on the sidelines and watch them. They were the best players in the world. But some lords of Xibalba lived underneath their ball court. They heard the twins playing and got mad at their noise and their pride. So they sent a falcon with a message that demanded the twins come to play a match. The twins said goodbye to our world, went down to the cave, and entered Xibalba."

Ket paused, for drama. The jaguar shifted its tongue in its mouth like a lapdog.

"The twins traveled on and on in the endless city of the underworld. Finally they met the king of the dead, who wanted the twins to show off their powers. He said, 'Kill me and bring me back to life.' But you know what they did? They killed him, but they didn't bring him back to life. He just stayed dead. So they won."

She fell silent.

She hoped she'd told the story well enough for a jaguar. She'd only ever told stories to dolls and ants before.

She wondered how long ago the Hero Twins had lived. She'd asked her sister once, and she'd answered, *Before time began.*

Ket asked, *When did time begin?*

Ixul said, *When the god revealed the cycles to the dayfall peoples.* But Ket wasn't satisfied with this answer. She liked to think about the time before that. Was there such a thing as before-time? If so, was there such a thing as after-time or no-time? And how would you know if you were in it? Ket remembered how she and Ixul used to nap together in this room. There had been moments of tenderness between them in the past. Ket would make Ixul put her head in her lap, then comb out her long black waterfall of hair and trace her tattoos, the star on the forehead, the rays along the jaw-line. Ket knew that she herself did not have the twins' beauty. But she didn't mind. It was enough for her to cherish theirs.

"Did you like the story?"

The jaguar lifted its head and stretched its paws. Ket shifted, relieved to get the blood flowing in her legs again.

"I suppose you can't tell me outright," she said, pulling at one tufted ear, staring into the middle dis-tance. She wanted Ixul to find her like this; she'd be so impressed. "I wish you could speak. I wish Gob could speak. That's the captive who ran away just now—I think he was scared of you. I'm going to get in so much trouble for that. But I couldn't very well go after him by myself, could I? I'm seven years old. Maybe it's meant to be. He disappeared. Like all the others. But my royal family still lives and guards the Great Cave. We're going to build an empire as big as the whole world. I can't wait to begin."

As if in answer, the jaguar nuzzled her neck. Ket giggled. The jaguar's tongue licked up her cheek, then up to her eye, which tickled Ket and made her plant her hands in its black fur. She turned to face it, and saw the jaguar's jaws open, and its long pink tongue and the deep black cave of its throat, and then she felt a stab-bing pain, and her left eye went dark.

She went still. Her hands floated away from the fur, somewhere out to the sides. With her right eye she saw the jaguar slip down off the bench, like a house cat banished outside for the night, holding something deli-cately in its teeth. It padded into the light and turned. The tip of its tail disappeared last.

She felt warm tears streaming down her left cheek, but wasn't crying. She couldn't see from her left eye and her right eye was turning red. She blinked but her vision kept turning red. She started to feel pain, like the sun was inside her head. She tried to remember the last few moments: pink tongue, black throat, sudden knife bite. She started to breathe rapidly. She had to find her brother and sister. She gathered up the blan-ket, balled it in her fist, stepped outside, and saw blood was coursing down the front of her body. The sun-light made it bright orange. The jaguar was nowhere in sight. There was no one nearby in the palace, just the grackles shrieking in the trees, and geckos scuttling along the steps, and leafcutter ants marching along all the silver threads of the world.

She felt woozy, as if the world were dilating. She walked down the rampart, off-balance. She stopped to take a breath. She looked up at the sun, looked down again, and a purple disc slid across the red field of her vision. She resumed walking. She had to find help. She was dragging the blanket behind her. She set a goal: to get down to the main plaza, where people would see her. All in all, she thought, the black jaguar's visit was a good sign. The gods were conspiring with them, not against them. No one should worry anymore.

She descended the stairs, the blanket trailing her like a royal train, leaving a cloud of dust in its wake.

"Wackan!"

The servant on the path below stopped and prostrated.

Ajul relaxed his voice. "Find the Princess Ket, please. We wish to speak to her before the ceremony."

"Yes, Your Highness. Where shall the Royal Princess Ket attend them, Ahau?"

"Here in the staging suite."

"As you say, Ahau. How else may I serve Our Royal Highness?"

"Tell Upakal to move the captives to the shade if he hasn't already. They should be washed, fed, and watered by sundown."

"It shall be done as you say, Ahau." Wackan got to her feet and rushed away.

Ajul went back inside the staging suite. It was a large room, paneled with mirrors on all sides, with a floor that sloped down to a corner drain. A handmaid set down a pot of hot water scented with orange blossoms. Another brought a stack of embroidered cotton towels. Women and men were not supposed to bathe together, but Ajul and Ixul had always been indulged. While the attendants washed them, the twins towered over them, checking their reflections from every angle and talking ceaselessly.

"We're royal, but we can't afford to be foolish," Ixul was saying. "We have to learn from the mistakes of the fallen. First we have to know how to present ourselves. You're too afraid of being disliked, but any king has to get used to being disliked sometimes. Another thing: you're too passionate. You can't be seen to be passionate."

"Even with you?" Ajul was having trouble concentrating, with her naked body right in front of him.

Ixul glanced at the handmaids, who kept their eyes downcast. She didn't feel as comfortable being so open. "Yes. And it's not just the commoners paying attention to how you act, it's the gods. After tonight, they'll watch us very closely. We are the intermediaries between our world and theirs. We always need to stay worthy of that. Remember how Father was, during ceremonies?"

"He said no word except what was needed."

"Yes. He controlled himself."

"Can there be different kinds of kings, though, waj—?" He glanced at the handmaids. "Sister? I might just be a different kind of king. Maybe all the great lines fell because their kings did not love their people enough."

"It has nothing to do with that. Those kings insulted the wrong gods and failed to do penance, so Xibalba punished them."

"But people want to follow you if you show them love."

"Or they'll think you're weak. Statecraft matters more."

Ajul felt offended. Sometimes Ixul spoke to him as if he were a child. But Mutna had always said they were equally bright, just with different sorts of intelligence. He was about to retort when Ixul turned to a handmaid and said, "We'll be ready for our ceremonial attire soon. Why is it not yet here?"

"It should be here already, Ahau."

"Who's in charge?"

The handmaid looked to a servant in the corner and said, "When is the gear coming?" and the servant muttered back, "I thought Chujuki was getting it," and the handmaid said, "Chujuki can't be trusted to shit in a hole."

Ixul backhanded her.

"Out," she snapped, "all of you. And don't come back until you bring our gear, oiled and polished."

Her words made Ajul wince, but he didn't stop her. According to Ixul, he was always softer on servants than he should be; though in turn he wished she could learn a more gentle tongue, as servants were people, who responded to ordinary kindness like anyone else. But the full truth was this: he and Ixul could learn from each other. They completed each other. This is why Ajul believed in the future of their realm. As servants retreated from the room, bowing, Ajul heard distant sounds—the clack of poles, the swish of brooms, the shrieks of children, the rhythm of metates, the squawks of turkeys, the barking of dogs, the whining of grackles, the belching of howler monkeys—and felt as if all were at peace, and he never wanted another moment than this one, ensconced in his home alone with her, his closest friend in the world.

Ixul turned to him as if to challenge him to say something.

Ajul held up his hands, indicating he didn't mean to.

Ixul looked awkward then, even self-conscious. Her whole body was swollen and reddened from the scrubbing. As if to compensate, she put her hands on her hips, the same way she would if they were fully geared and facing each other on the court. Ajul tried to keep his eyes on her face.

"Statecraft matters more," she repeated, as if nothing had happened.

"I know that, wajmul," he said. A gentle riposte, a return of the ball. "But I am telling you to consider other factors in how to lead. Showing our love, yes, but also our ability as ball players. That is an advantage that other lineages did not have."

"Recall the history of Yokib. A young queen who held lavish tournaments while her tribute states plotted. She died as a captive, butchered and planted in the four corners of the earth."

"But," said Ajul, "recall the history of Pachan. The last king secured the portage roads, but never set foot on his ball court. He was assassinated before a year had passed."

"True. Building a stela should have been the first thing he did," said Ixul, staring into the middle distance. Ajul felt as though he'd scored a point, though Ixul, true to her nature, didn't congratulate him; she merely continued the conversation. "We have to use tonight's ceremony to connect the past, present, and future. And tomorrow, we should announce our plans."

"First, we focus on our home. We should fortify the walls and rebuild the canals."

"No. First we need to make state visits, to build our alliances."

Ajul sighed. He suspected that Ixul really just wanted an excuse to see faraway exotic places. Whenever travelers came to their city, she would corner them, asking questions, until they begged off to rest.

Ixul saw his expression. "We need alliances," she insisted. "The Nahua remember how we took their prince captive. They've been gaining strength again, sacking the villages around Saal, leaving their white-feathered arrows. Why haven't they attacked us yet? Why haven't they even tried?"

Ajul frowned. "They know better. The Tzoyna is a holy place."

Ixul stared out the window. "You may be right. But we can't count on it. How is your speech?"

Ajul had practiced it until he knew it by heart, but the question still made him nervous. He had never spoken in front of a large crowd before. "I think it is good."

"Say it for me."

"Now?"

They were alone. He couldn't think straight. His pine torch was lit. He was helpless.

"Say it for me," she said again.

"Please, wajmul . . ."

"Now."

"All right. But I have to close my eyes, I cannot look at you."

"As you will."

Ajul shut his eyes and found his first word. Then it flowed.

"Tonight on Three Batz', the Great Star rises, and we gather to mark the triple alliance of Tzoyna, Katwitz, and Pekwitz. In the past, we have been rivals; but in the age to come, we are kin. We are bound by the rivers that course through our realm, even as veins course through flesh. We welcome you, our guests from Pekwitz. We welcome you, our guests from Katwitz. We welcome you from every corner of the kingdom. Now rise! Much will be seen and heard tonight, but first: rise, and eat until you are full. It is our promise to you, of the age to come."

Ajul opened his eyes. Ixul looked so pretty.

He shut them again and gestured to his right, where the captives would be staked when he'd be standing on the royal dais.

"We have three captives here, whom I have captured; I, Royal Prince Ajul B'uluch Chab of the Tzoyna, Servant of Xibalba, descended from the Hero Twins. These captives were fleeing the fallen houses that insulted the gods. We offer them to the gods of Xibalba in the sacred trust that, because we do them honor, their fate will not be our own."

"Good. Say the second piece now—after the game, before the sacrifice."

Ajul squeezed his eyes shut harder. She was merciless. He knew she was testing his strength of will.

"May their blood water the beginning of the new age. This is for the rebirth of the fields. This is for the reopening of the roads. This is for the return of the pilgrims. This is for salt, clay, copper, gold, cotton, maize, turquoise, cacao, honey, fish, and precious feathers. This is for the renewal of our kingdom. . . ."

He heard shouting. He opened his eyes.

Ixul was already at the door, angry at the interruption.

Then he heard Mutna's voice outside. "Ajul Ahau! Come quickly!"

"We're not dressed."

"I brought robes. It's your sister Ket."

Ixul looked at Ajul, and a thousand words passed between them.

They put on the robes and followed Mutna to the front plaza. As they rounded the corner, Ajul saw Ket lying on a blanket with half her face gone.

They knelt next to her. Her head was elevated. Ajul saw it was an animal bite with ragged edges. The teeth had not broken the bone, which was some small blessing. In the pool of her eye socket, peeping out of the blood, her eyeball was bit in half like a little white tomato. Upakal was there, but Ajul didn't register his words. A servant woman put down clean cloths and hot water. Ket was still conscious, but her right eye was staring upward, glazed with a red film. Her breathing was ragged and shallow. Upakal must have carried her here, away from the crowd, and now he heard him repeating that he'd failed, he'd let Ket take one of the captives for a walk, unsupervised, and knew to look for her because the captive had escaped and returned to warn them. As Upakal talked, he heard silence in the plaza below. Everyone knew.

Now Ket was curling the finger of her other hand, beckoning: come here, come down.

The twins bent their heads to hear her.

"It'll be okay," she said. "Tell everyone." Then she rested her head back on the blanket.

Ixul said to Ajul, "You must speak."

"I will, after—"

"Now."

Ajul was afraid. "What about Ket?"

"I'll stay with her. It looks bad, but she'll live. Speak to our people."

"And tell them what?"

"Tell them the story. The bloodletting, the jaguar, the eye. This will be the story of our empire. Xibalba took her eye so the Tzoyna could flourish."

"We don't know if that's true."

"I am saying it is true. So now it is true. Go be king and proclaim it."

Those words knocked the fear out of Ajul, and something new took its place.

He got up and walked to the edge of the plaza. He stood on the rampart. There were hundreds of people below, their work abandoned, their faces fearful.

When he spoke, it was as if another voice were speaking through him.

"Today, at midday," he called, "my sister, Royal Princess Ket Lajchän Ajwal of the Tzoyna, let blood on the mountain, which I myself witnessed; and summoned the god Balam Ahau from Xibalba, which I also witnessed. Balam Ahau took her eye as a promise. A new age begins. As the Sun descends and the Great Star ascends, Xibalba is near as a lover, matching our every move. Tonight, we will offer the captives to the gods to complete our offering."

He waited for the cheering to die down and then, like a child seeking approval, turned back to Ixul.

She nodded.

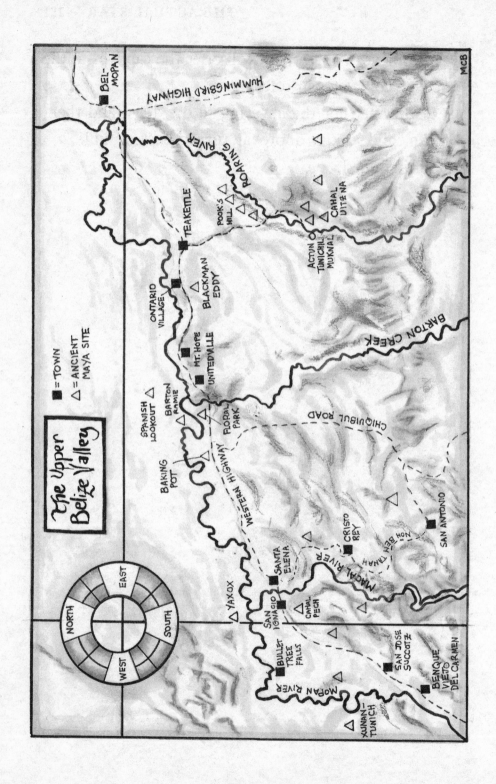

CAYO
1 Tznanab 0 K'ank'in,
Long Count 12.19.19.17.17

---

18 December, 2012

On the riverbank in San Ignacio, Leah stood between two bridges, the low bridge and the high bridge, one wooden and one suspended, and watched the children stream away to school, like columns of soldiers to a holy war: the maroon-and-creams, the green-and-whites, the navy-and-blues. On both sides of the river, black birds creaked in the trees like rusty hinges, swooping back and forth in a game of Red Rover that had lasted for millions of years.

She felt she'd passed through many veils to arrive here. Yesterday, she'd woken in the freezing black of Anoong. Then she'd taken a taxi to St. Cloud State, a bus to Minneapolis, a plane to Houston, and a plane to

Belize City. She'd fallen asleep six times and had lurid dreams. Every time she woke, she felt as if she were on a new planet. From the plane, Belize was a sunny blue-green country marked by pillars of smoke and rivers of mercury. She drank in the air on the tarmac as if it were amniotic fluid. On the bus to San Ignacio, they passed through a veil of rain, and then the coastal plain swelled up into hill country. A little girl across the aisle offered her a jam roll. It crumbled in her mouth, all flour, the jam gone gummy from the sun.

She checked in to her guesthouse at midnight and ate a pack of plantain chips on her bed. Her pillow smelled like roses. She woke before dawn, too excited to sleep. She went to sit by her window and saw the bright morning star. It was so wonderfully warm, even at this hour. The mist turned pink-orange, the dogs began their call-and-response, and a man clopped past on horseback. She put on her green dress with bows on the straps and went down to the river.

Now she'd been walking up and down the bank for the last hour, watching the traffic on the low bridge. There were cars, jeeps, trucks, pickups, taxis, motorcycles, snack carts, green-and-yellow buses, glossy brown horses, and so many vans with decals: ULTIMATE CAYO TOURS. CEIBA TREE ADVENTURES. PACZ ADVENTURE TOURS. XPLORE INLAND TOURS. MAXIMUM

ADVENTURE TOURS. ANCIENT CULTURAL TOURS. RIVER RAT EXPEDITIONS. There were young boys splashing under the bridge, and young girls wading in the water, with braids as black as her own, holding their skirts with balled fists. A caramel dog with a double row of teats ambled up to Leah, trustingly like a cow, head lowered. She caressed its head, wondering who owned it, where its collar and tags were. Maybe it belonged to the whole town, she thought.

She walked back along the riverbank, her flip-flops hooked on her fingers, breaking the dew with bare feet. She still marveled at the air, how rich and warm it was, with a mineral flavor of limestone. She felt like she could dissolve here, just melt away and expand, and become the space between all things, like the Holy Spirit. She knew she'd done right in coming here. Wholeness was somehow nearer, here.

Leah got hungry. She walked up from the riverbank and passed through the market grounds. A few stalls were open, selling oranges, tomatoes, carrots, eggs, pumpkin seeds, and plantain chips. Women were arranging bras and baby clothes to sell on a pegged board. She walked to the center of town, smiling at everyone she passed, beholding them as if they were holy Byzantine icons fixed with eternal meaning. She walked past a grizzled old man with red leather skin and hard blue gems for eyes; he, noticing her stare, finally begrudged a nod in her direction. She thought that everyone in Belize would look like her, and many did, but many did not. They were every shade. She got choked up. The sidewalks were not smooth and featureless, like in Anoong; they were broken and tossed as if by earthquakes, with huge chunks missing or upthrust or caved in, and the new topography acted on her body, teaching her to pay attention. Minnesota now seemed as inconceivable as Belize had, two days before. She saw a tiny wooden sign that said POP'S DINER on a side street, went in, sat down, and ordered breakfast, which seemed to arrive nearly as soon as she'd ordered it, a Picasso of a breakfast, with orange papaya keystones, eggs in brown lace, pillows of fried bread, thick fibrous bacon, and a pool of black beans quickly losing its shine.

Leah ate. Her forearms stuck to the table from the heat. She ran her finger along the sweat, delighted. She would never have to worry about being cold here. In the upper corner of the diner, there was a small TV framed in Christmas garlands, showing an episode of *Animal Rescue*. As she ate, Leah watched cases of (1) a cat with its leg cut off, (2) an owl caught in wire, and (3) a puppy covered with ticks, its gums grey. They were all taken care of. They all thrived in the end.

She paid and left. She wandered up the hill to look over the town, and watched while the last of the mist disappeared. It became hot and bright again—this caused her constant amazement, how bright it was here, how absolute the need for sunglasses, right away—it was the first thing she'd bought. Belize was blinding her. This was a good thing. It was going to be a good day, as good a day as she'd ever had in her life. She wondered again at the intensity of her happiness. She'd never known she could be this happy. As if this place, its warmth and humidity and salinity, was calibrated to that of her own blood, so that the feeling outside finally matched how she felt on the inside, and she could swim down the streets as easily as walk them. She'd expected to feel culture shock, but she felt the opposite— that Belize was far more normal than Minnesota; or, what was strange about it was precisely what made it familiar. Leah only wanted to eat Belizean food, learn Belizean history, speak Belizean languages. She began to hear music: a solemn twinning of horns and drums. She turned into one side street and then another, looking for the band, but the music always seemed to come from behind her rather than in front of her, and she got turned around and lost, and soon found she was back where she'd started. It sounded like a funeral march of some kind. She saw police in riot gear, practicing formations in a soccer field. She saw vultures folding over a dead dog in someone's backyard. The dog was splayed in spectacular fashion: limbs outflung, teats exposed. A boy on a bike watched closely for her re- action. She made a sad face, and he nodded back, as if reassured. She entered a park, crunched across sun- toasted grass, and sat on a bench painted green and yellow. She listened. The phantom music petered out. Now there were just the sounds of cars, reggae, and children too young for school.

She'd been here for less than twenty-four hours. She felt like she'd been here a year. She was transformed, and all she'd had to do was get up and go. What if, she thought, travel itself could become a religion, where the rituals of wandering became the essence of the faith? Each node of the journey like the Stations of the Cross, performed and revered? Each person searching for that place on Earth where the outside matched their inside? And now she felt she was in her own promised land. Her guidebook said that all of western Belize was one continuous ancient Maya site. Her ancestors were beneath her. And deeper, and beneath them, were the caves. Xibalba itself was underfoot.

A pack of dogs trotted by, circled, and stopped. They'd been seen by another pack of dogs at the other end of the park, who were also circling. There are many soap operas going on here, thought Leah, among many species. "Soap opera" seemed the term that best fit: in Minnesota, everything was dull realism in black and white; here, everything was a bright fantasy in vivid color, with hot passions bubbling up over and over like the spurts of a volcano, cooled by sudden inkblot storms. She touched her braid. It was hot from the sun, like sheet metal. She thought, I am here. I am actually here at last.

Xander, on the fourth try, with one hand on the wheel, careening back along the Western Highway, got through to Dr. Castillo.

"I have bad news." Xander took a deep breath. "A tourist dropped his camera onto Individual 12."

"In ATM?"

"Yes."

An awful silence. "Where?"

"The skull. There's a hole in the skull now."

Another awful silence. Then, "Talk later."

The connection went dead.

Xander threw his phone on the passenger's seat and it bounced off the car door and clattered onto the floor. Eventually Dr. Castillo would want to know which guide was responsible. He hadn't asked, because he was afraid it was Xander, and then he'd have to punish him so as not to appear like he was treating him too well. The other guides knew that Xander was his favorite. They resented him for it.

He sped past the landmarks he'd passed thousands of times. Ontario. Mount Hope. Unitedville. The blue St. Martin de Porres School. St. Hilda's Church. Galen University. The ghost hotel. The cow pasture. The lone guanacaste tree. He passed white van after white van filled with tourists. They were all headed somewhere to have an experience. Everyone having fun. Everyone making money. Black fruit cake in the markets. Christmas was coming, but before that was December 21—the supposed Maya End of the World.

He drove down the final hill into Santa Elena, then swerved onto the road that led down to the river. The traffic was backed up because the high Hawkesworth Bridge was closed, which meant that cars going in and out had to negotiate the single-lane wooden low bridge. He waited for his turn. The car in front of him was being too generous with the opposite side. He laid on the horn, shouted some choice words. Finally he made it over and up into the alleys of San Ignacio. He turned right at the football stadium and careened along the side streets until he found a parking spot. It was still early in the afternoon, so the streets were free of dehydrated tourists. He got his things, locked up his truck, and walked down the street to Ultimate Cayo, the headquarters of his tour company.

The manager, Hector Moody, was standing on the step, arms crossed.

"Weh yu tooris deh?"

"Lang stoari."

"Pendejos?"

"No, wos. Dehn deh wid Javier. Ah wahn tel yu layta."

Hector could tell he wasn't in the mood to talk. He said, "Aarait bwai," shuffling from one foot to the other. He glanced down the street at Ceiba Tree Adventures, their main competition, where the manager, Angelo, tapped away at his keyboard on the veranda. Their building was freshly painted with a mural of Belizean landmarks. They had new computers, new logos, a new website, and new golf shirts. Javier worked for them.

Xander texted Dr. Castillo to tell him where he was. That he was happy to explain the incident. That he'd take the lead in redesigning protocols so it wouldn't happen again.

There was no reply.

So all he could do was wait.

He went to Meetup's two doors down and ordered chicken pepper soup and a stack of tortillas. Hector had put out two clamshell chairs and leaned back in one, lacing his hands behind his head. Xander took the other. He shredded all the tortilla into the bowl to soak up the soup and hunched over it, eating with his fingers.

A kid rode past on his plastic big wheel.

Then a big dog that resembled a bear flopped onto the ground in front of them.

Poochie—one of the town's homeless, always in drug sweats—trudged by. The dogs hated him. Sure enough, one of the dogs upstreet got wind, and then the entire Burns Avenue pack had mustered and gathered around him. The tourists started to stare. He hunched over and moved on. The pack followed, barking.

The bear dog remained, watching Xander's soup.

Two Creole women walked by in green polyester skirts.

"Wahn sevn an wahn ayt," Hector said under his breath.

"Moa laik foa an faiv," said Xander.

"Yu noh laik di chaaklit gyal dehn."

"Yu di taak raas, mee laik di chaaklit gyal dehn."

"But yu laik vanilla beta."

Xander didn't answer. Hector liked to tease him about white women. Which in Belize usually meant students, tourists, volunteers, expats, and the occasional wayward Mennonite. But it wasn't an aesthetic choice. It was just practicality. White women came and went. They weren't complicated. They wanted a fling, or a brown baby to carry back to the States. Xander had a few like that, that he knew of. He wasn't in touch with them. Their mothers had gotten what they'd come for. Meanwhile, he knew everyone in Cayo, and knew their families, and their families knew him, and it was a small town, a small nation, and anything could get back to anyone. Besides, when sleeping with white women, he could work on his ethnography: *Tourists and Tourist Gaze in 2012: Cayo District, Belize.* When it was ready, he'd submit to the small press in Benque, or even an academic press in England. He did have a woman in Bullet Tree, and considered calling her later, though he might be too tired for sex. He had to be up early for tours every day through New Year's. She never understood how tired he was when he got home. Sometimes he just wanted to drink at home, watch videos online, and feel how much he was wasting his life.

Hector hissed to get Xander's attention, then nodded across the street at Ceiba Tree. Angelo, light-skinned and baby-faced, had glided out in his polo shirt with a tray of coffee for some tourists. The tourists looked confused, and tried to indicate that they hadn't ordered coffee; Angelo waved his hands as if to indicate bounty, and they understood the coffee was free, and thanked him. Angelo paused on the threshold, but not before stopping and scanning the area to see whether anyone had noted his good deed. He saw Hector and Xander watching him. He vanished inside.

"Mi waif yoostu waip fu hihn bahain," said Hector.

"Wat?"

"Fi chroo. Shee yoostu wach Angelo wen ih da mi baybi an shee da mi teenayja. Now luk pan ahn."

Xander was annoyed that Hector was roping him into gossip. He was feeling contrarian. "Ih di mek gud bizniz."

"Wat, yu waahn werk fu hihn?"

"Fuck, mayn."

"No, goh. Goh an snugul up wi ahn, an yu breda Javier."

Xander went silent. Everyone in town knew these silences. They weren't resignation; they were the result of growing up with a stutter and being made fun of, and so using silence to his advantage, letting others have time to see the blow coming. His silence was so loud that the bear dog lifted his head and woofed, as if spooked. Hector used the excuse to get up and shoo him away.

Now the sun was sinking and the air was cooling. People wandered up from Courts, or down from the double road, or from across the river in Santa Elena—cabdrivers, guides, whites, teenage couples, tour operators, professionals in pumps, and girls dragging toddlers by the hand. At night, Burns Avenue became a catwalk for local drama.

Frank Martínez came biking down the street, pedaling like he was being chased. He braked so hard his hair bounced.

Hector said, "Buenos tardes, bwai."

Frank didn't answer. He looked doleful.

"Weh rang?" said Xander.

"Rosa?" Hector guessed.

"Wi di geh divoas," he said with great solemnity.

"Yu di geh divoas fu di las toti years," said Hector. "Fu weh reezn dis taim?"

Frank beseeched the sky.

"Oh kom aan bwai, wat?"

"Shee seh, ih need wa groan man. Ih seh, ah noh help wi di chilren."

"Soh yu help wi di chilren er nat?"

Frank gave Xander a dark look and made to pedal on.

"Hol aan bwai," said Hector.

Frank stopped.

Hector leaned forward. He looked mischievous. "Yu stap yasoh bikaaz yu waahn kongsl, noh? Mek wi taak bowt sohnting." He took his time drawing out the words. "Weh yu du fu please yu uman?"

"Shee hapi," said Frank, too quickly.

Xander whistled.

Hector leaned back, victorious. "Mi noh di aks yu dat. Ah di aks weh yoo *du*."

"Shee neva tel mi notn."

"Soh how yu noa ih hapi?"

"Ih mek naiz."

"Aarait, dis naiz, weh ih song laik?"

Frank whimpered like a kitten.

The Ultimate Cayo scheduler, Ned, came out of the office, his white mane flowing like Father Christmas. He lit a cigarette. "What the hell is that sound? What are you blokes talking about?"

"Frank noh mek his woman happy."

"Bollocks, are you talking about sex again? What is it with you lot? Always sex. Nothing but sex." He took a drag and looked at Frank. "Was that you making that sex noise?"

"Ah mek the sound Rosa mek wen ah inside her cave." He added some throaty moans for good measure.

"Oh God." Ned went back inside. Then came the theme of his favorite British detective show, the sound of strings swelling.

Hector leaned toward Frank and tented his hands

together. "Yu hafu yooz yu tong eena ih punani, mayn."

Frank looked horrified. "Shee noh need dat."

"Rass. Ih noh noa weh ih need til ih get it, an den bileev mi, ih wa need it."

"Not every woman does," Xander said.

"Weh di hel kain a uman noh laik dat?"

"Maybi ih insecure bowt how ih pussy luk. Nobodi eena Belize tel uman bowt dehn badi."

"Yoo fuk tu moch tooris, mayn," said Frank.

Xander did not respond.

"Ah tel yu bwai," Hector pressed. "Yu du it, yu geh gud, yu repyutayshan spred, yu noh wori bowt no uman agen. No uman wahn chroa yu owt. Aal a di uman gwehn brok dong di doa wid dehn shain op punani sayin, 'Frank, eet mi.'"

Arthur Fairweather, a distinguished old gentleman who made the rounds each night, paused his cane in front of Ultimate Cayo. He greeted them, listened in.

Hector was on a mission now. He addressed Frank with a show of goodwill. "Hahn, ah wil giv yu wahn rejimen. Yu redi? Yu kohn hoam fahn shap an ih eena di kichin, shee bizi fu yu, ih lov yu, ih mek dinna fi yu. Ih put wahn Belikin eena yu han. Koars wan, salad. Koars too, rais ahn beenz ahn schoo chikin. Koars chree, aiskreem an kayk. Koars foa . . . *yoo* da di wan weh di serv dat koars, bwai. Yu giv shee di seekrit

Hows Speshal. Den ih noh kamplayn bowt noh ting. Shee da fu yoo. Shee faytful."

Zebulon, the owner of the Rasta souvenir shop, came out and sat on the curb. "You got to live your life, mayn," he sang, "and uman, too!" He addressed the last bit to a light-skinned girl at a table across the street. Xander couldn't tell if she was local or a tourist. She was wearing green sneakers and a green dress, with straps that tied in bows, which was not an outfit a Belizean girl would wear. But at the same time she looked like a mestiza, with warm canela skin, five foot maybe, a thick girl, with small round breasts, a good round belly, a long black braid, and a plain face like a full moon.

Zebulon was still singing at her. "Women got to live dey life too!"

"I am, thank you very much!" called the girl, raising her fork. She had a nasal accent—so, a tourist, from Canada or the States.

"Yu alone?" called Zebulon.

"Yeah!" called the girl.

"Waahn company?"

"Not at the moment, thank you!"

"Okay." Zebulon turned to Frank. "Yu luk laik a fuckin daag, mayn."

Frank spread his arms like Christ.

Out of the corner of his eye, Xander could see the tourist girl was surprised that Zebulon had given up so easily. Men could be persistent here, especially with girls who were traveling alone. But she'd done the right thing—a polite, firm no, and Zebulon had responded in turn. Cayo men were usually better about that than the island men.

The girl saw Xander watching her and narrowed her eyes.

He looked away.

A ten-year-old boy drifted past with a metal pan on his shoulder, covered in aluminum foil. "Fudge," he called.

Xander recognized him—Leroy, from Santa Elena, son of Eustacia, whose younger sister Molly he'd gone to school with. "Yes, me," he said, getting up. "Peenots bota, rait?"

"Yes sa," said Leroy, animated. He whisked off the tinfoil and presented him with a square of fudge on a napkin, cupping the corners to catch the crumbs.

Xander handed over the dollar coin.

"Wid notmeg," added Leroy. "Mi ma grayta it een."

"I'll have some fudge too," called the tourist girl.

Leroy ran to her. Xander wanted to see how the interaction would go, but then Hector got up and blocked his view. Now they were in for it, Xander could tell.

Hector was in his ringleader mood. He was circling among the men, drawing deep breaths into his skinny chest.

"Da taim fi wahn symposium a aal di laanid man eena Bileez," said Hector, waving his hand to indicate the expanse of Burns Avenue. "Ya wi stan da di dawn a wahn nyoo ayj. Da 2012. Da wahn nyoo yaa. Da di nyoo *baktun.* An wi gyada yo fu joj weda Frank shuda yooz ih tong pan ih uman. Ai seh dat ekschra impoatant. Frank seh, Noh man, dat da noh di ansa tu mi prablem. Soh hoo rait? Weh kain a peepl wee, da hoo liv eena Bileez? Weh kain a peepl wi *waahn* bee? Taak now er fareva hol yu pees."

The circle of men was quiet, letting the charge sink in. In addition to Frank, Xander, Hector, and Zebulon, there was muscled Sumeet from the Hindu clothing kiosk; Gerry, the wobbly white Californian who ran the high-end souvenir shop that imported all its goods from Guatemala; and Roy, the quiet photographer who'd lived in Europe and come back, wearing a purple caftan and a low ponytail.

Xander's eyes flicked to the tourist girl across the street. Apparently she'd bought the entire tray of fudge from Leroy. The bars sat in three stacks, like bricks, each separated by a napkin, which gave them the look of pagodas. She was nibbling one as she leaned to listen in. Native English speakers could understand the gist of Kriol if they concentrated, and she was concentrating hard.

"I do," volunteered Gerry. "I go down on the women."

Hector whirled. "Speak, Gerry from di States."

Gerry stayed in his place in the circle, gesturing with one skinny arm. "Oh, I mean, I was a hippie in San Francisco, and you just couldn't get away with not doing it," he said. "Girls would notice. And then they'd tell each other. And you'd never get laid again."

Hector turned on Frank, eyes wide, ominous. "*Neva get laid again,*" he repeated.

Now Roy the photographer wandered into the middle of the circle. He nudged the street dog with his foot.

"Watch it," said Zebulon. "That dog's racist."

"Fu chroo?"

"Fu chroo. He only follow tourists."

Roy smiled to himself and kept one foot on the dog's back. It was a dig at Zebulon, somehow. Xander would have to watch that. He watched everything that happened in San Ignacio—who had a grudge, who was fucking whom, who was addicted to what, who owned a gun, who was laundering money, who was covering up an affair, who was secretly CIA. Information was always useful. When it came to Roy, it was useful to know that his uncle was high up in the government, and they had money from mahogany plantations.

"Luk pan dis man ya," said Hector, reclining in his chair and pointing at Roy. "Di man gwehn taak."

"Shet op, mayn," said Frank.

"No luk, ih nayli di taak."

Roy opened his arms to his countrymen. "What kind of society are we?" he said.

No one answered.

"Or, what kind of society do we want to be?"

Xander went from annoyed to very annoyed. It's not that the question wasn't relevant. It was a miscalculation of the mood. Hector had been jestering, but Roy had gone for the existential. Belize was only thirty-one years old. Guatemala still claimed the entire country as its own territory. The world at large still thought of Belize as one of the British colonies, or confused it with Bolivia. Meanwhile, every Belizean had their own opinion of what Belize was. What Belizean national character was. What Belizean industry should look like. Who was a true Belizean. Who should be welcome in Belize and who should not be. Every man in this circle was a Belizean citizen, even Gerry, who had dual citizenship, because he'd married a girl from Unitedville. Everyone had a stake. But Roy had repeated

Hector's questions in English, not Kriol, which meant he was performing for the tourists who were beginning to listen in. Xander loathed the pretension.

"I've been to London. I've been to New York. I've been to Paris," he said, still walking in a circle with his hands clasped behind his back. "They know who they are. And what do I mean by that? I mean they have a national character. You ask, What is a Swiss man? What is a Czech man? And they have an answer. In three days, it's the beginning of the new Maya baktun. We must figure out our answer. When someone asks a man, whether he be from Punta Gorda or Corozal Town or our own San Ignacio, 'What is a Belizean man?' we must be able to define our national character."

There was a long pause in the circle. Xander sensed resentment giving way to thoughtfulness. Through a gap in the circle, he could see the tourist girl had gotten her order: a plate of stew chicken and plantain. She shoveled a bite into her mouth, then sat sideways so she could keep listening. The colonial verandas dripped with light.

"Resourceful," Gerry volunteered, and then immediately looked like he wished he hadn't been the first to speak. "I'd say the Belizean man is resourceful," he said in a smaller voice.

"Diverse," boomed Arthur, gracious, saving him.

"How kud wan man bee diverse?" said Frank.

Arthur shrugged. "Many lineages in the blood," he said. "Maya, Spanish, African, Garifuna."

"Sumeet noh diverse," said Frank. "Yu diverse?"

Sumeet was standing with his hands tucked into his armpits, gold chains against black chest hair. "Sindhi," he said.

"Sandy?"

"No, Sindhi," he said. "From India."

"Ata yu baan an rayz eena Bileez."

"Yaa mayn."

"So," said Roy, as if a point had been proved, "we are a nation of diverse men, by the design of our ancestors, who—"

Xander couldn't stand it anymore. He sat forward in his chair.

"Mayn weh rang wid yu? Yu da loan raas."

Immediately he had the circle's attention. He started to blend English into his Kriol, because he felt the tourist girl watching, and he wanted her to understand his answer to this jackass. "Who da yu ansestas? Who yu taak about? Di Spanish come enslave wi, then di English come wid di Afrikan slaves, so everybody enslaved to take out di riches from di land, fu white people eena Europe ahn Amerika. Is dat what yu meen by 'ansestas'? Is dat what yu mean by 'design'?"

No one moved, except Ned, drawn out again by the hubbub. He lit a cigarette and wandered around the circle as if in a game of Duck Duck Goose. Happy hour was underway. Strings of Christmas lights clicked on, one by one, all up and down Burns Avenue, like the stars of a miniature universe.

Roy looked sweaty, but tried to hold his own. "That was then. This is now. Now we get to define who we are."

"Wee du raas. Yu waahn taak ansestas? Di Maiya da di ansestas. Di Maiya stil livin. *Ai* da Maiya. An di Maiya get treated worse dan dogs eena dis country. Dehn can't hol their own fuckin land before di govament sell it off. Fu mahogany. Tu dis day. Every sacred site wi hafu fight fah, ahn eevn if wi win, di onli way fi mek money fu sel wi souls tu tourists. Yu waahn taak about national character, yu start wid di Maiya."

"I'm Maya," said a girl's voice.

The circle parted. The last streetlamp clicked on overhead, like a spotlight. There was the tourist girl standing in her grass-green dress. Her plate was abandoned on the table behind her. Xander hadn't even noticed her get up.

The men were frozen. Tourist women didn't behave this way. And this girl—brown North American tourist traveling alone and saying something weird—was hard to place. But as she had appeared in front of a business, Ultimate Cayo Tours, where they were technically on duty, and tourism was the trade of the town, they were obligated to welcome her. If they didn't, they'd hear about it on TripAdvisor.

Ned was the most well-placed to address her.

"Hello. Are you interested in a tour?" he said.

She looked to him, not expecting greeting from that quarter. "Yes!" she said. "I'm a viajera."

Ned looked back at the circle. "What's that then?"

Thirty years in Belize and he'd never learned Spanish. "Traveler, Ned," said Xander.

"*Female* traveler," the girl added, sunnily.

"Ah!" Ned turned back to the girl. "Well, we offer lots of tours, including to ATM cave."

"I'm going tomorrow! But I'm already going with Ceiba Tree Adventures."

There was a slow, sad shaking of heads.

"What, is that wrong?"

Ned grimaced, stepped on his cigarette butt. "Naw, it's not wrong. They're just our competitors, is all. Perfectly nice people! In't that right, Angelo?"

He called the last bit loudly enough to be heard in the office on the Ceiba Tree veranda. Xander could see Angelo stir at his computer, but not take the bait.

"Who's your guide?" Xander asked.

"His name is Javier," she said.

All eyes swung to Xander for his reaction. But he could play it cool. He shrugged and said, "Make sure he gives you what you pay for."

"Why, do you have reason to believe he won't?"

Xander looked up the street and squinted, as if distracted, at something far away. "No, just . . ." He encountered a block, had to maneuver around it. "Be sure."

"That's really quite vague and unhelpful," she said.

Arthur, ever the gentleman, asked, "Are you from the States, miss?"

"Yes," she said. "Minnesota. But my father's from San Ignacio."

Now, this was interesting. A daughter of Cayo, come home. The circle of men contracted like a curling hibiscus.

"Who's your father?" said Hector.

"Pancho Gonzalo Iglesias." She watched him, sensing for any reaction.

"Ah," said Hector, nodding. "I knew him."

"He ded lang taim, noh?" blurted Frank.

"Fuk, mayn!" said Xander. "Ih mait no noa."

"Oh, I know," said the girl. "I know he's dead. I never got to meet him."

"Oh gyal, mi sorry," said Hector, with real feeling. "He was a good man. One of the first guides at ATM."

"Yes, that's why I wanted to go."

"And before that he was a chiclero . . . he played the guitar so well, remember, Gerry? You knew Pancho, no?"

"The Maya in the hat with the ribbon?"

"Ya mayn. Play bai di riva an soh."

"I remember him," said Xander.

"He had a child?" said Gerry.

Xander could see that Frank was about to say something impolitic about Pancho having lots of children, and he cut him off. Suddenly he felt generous toward this girl. "He was a good man," he said. "I'm sorry you never knew him. But you're a true Belizean, gyal. Welcome home."

"Welcome home." The men in the circle nodded.

"Thank you," she said, and Xander was embarrassed to see her eyes bright with tears. She stuck out her hand. "I'm Leah Oliveri."

Xander shook her hand and made introductions all around the circle. She nodded at each, looking pleased. When he was done, Leah said, "And what's your name?"

"This is His Eminence, Señor Xander Cañul," said Hector. "Ahn ih neva weighed on mi question."

Now Xander was trapped. He'd punch Hector in the face for this later.

"What was your question?" asked Leah, though she seemed to know very well what it was.

"It's not for ladies' ears," said Arthur.

"I'm not a lady," said Leah.

There was a roar of appreciation. This girl was a sport. Or she might just be a weirdo—there were plenty of those, too, especially around San Ignacio, which seemed to attract weird people. Xander would have to watch her. She'd make an interesting case study.

"The question," Hector said, overenunciating his English, "is whether a man, when he is intimate with her, should"—and here he was exquisite, fishing for words—"pleasure a woman."

Leah raised her eyebrows. "You should be asking a circle of women instead."

Hector was flustered. He couldn't tell whether she was baiting him or not. Hector was raunchy, but essentially decent; he was in his sixties and this girl looked like a teenager.

But she saved him. She crossed her arms. "Do women here get together to judge the men?"

"Eena di kichin," said Frank.

Zebulon kicked him.

Hector recovered, addressed the circle. "Aarait luk. Mee si ih paint. Ah aks, weh kain a konchri wee, da di biginin a di nyoo baktun. How bowt dis. Wee da di kain weh lay dehnself dong, hapi ahn wilin mek uman ga di opa han. No? Xander. Wi sidong ahn joj uman weh waak paas, rait?" He turned back to the others. "Jos bifao dis rispektabl aadyans gyada, Xander ahn mi sidong eena wi chyaa, ahn injai di eevnin, wentaim too laydi waak bai ahn wi seh, 'Dis da faiv, dat da nain' ahn soh. So. Miss Leah. Wi are going to cave wiself into you. Ah wahn sit down here. Wi all going to be silent. Ahn yu will judge wi."

A slow smile spread across her face. "Goodness gracious," she said. "Judge you how?"

"On a scale a one to ten," said Frank, energized by the possibility. "Who yu tink look gud."

"But there are so many kinds of attraction."

"Sexual, miss."

"Well, that clears it up, doesn't it." Leah turned in the middle of the circle, regarding each man with a bovine sweetness. Some wilted. Some grinned. A breeze sprang up and made the bows on her shoulders dance.

"You," she said to Frank, having turned a full circle and arrived at the start. "A four."

Frank took it well. He stood up on his bike and lifted his arms to the sky. "Dat da almost half, dat enough fu mi Laad!"

She turned to Sumeet. "Eight."

She turned to Roy. "Six."

She skipped Xander with a wink, which caused a mild hysteria.

She turned to Hector. "Three." His face fell. There was much sucking of teeth.

She turned to Zebulon. "Seven." Zebulon jumped up and started dancing to the reggae pumping from his shop.

She turned to Gerry. "Five."

"Faiv!" cried Hector, leaping up from his chair. "Ahn mi da chree?"

"The lady has spoken," said Arthur, then stood up straight and put both hands on his cane as Leah turned her eye on him.

"Eight," she said.

"I still got it," said Arthur. Gerry clapped him on the back.

Hector was upset. But he'd called for the judgment, so he had no right to be. He put his ire elsewhere. "What about Xander?" he said. "You skipped him! How can he avoid judgment?"

"I was going to wait until he gave his answer to the question of the day," she said, and fixed her eyes on him.

The circle of men laughed their appreciation. Somehow, this was a karmic return of Xander's earlier outburst: having put Roy in the hot seat, now he himself was in the hot seat, put there by a girl, no less.

Xander tried to appear cool and collected. But inside he was nervous, and he hated it. Who did this girl think she was? She was fearless. Her confidence was both unnerving and appealing. He was attracted to her. So he said the thing that would most endear him to her, because he wanted to push inside her to figure her out and like any tourist, she probably wouldn't be here for long.

He willed his words to come out casual.

"Of course he should," he said.

Everyone lit up, but right at that moment, Poochie broke into the circle to warn Gerry about something at his shop, which drew the bear dog, who started barking, which set off all the other dogs, barking in staccato so loudly that Leah clapped her hands to her ears. Hector lost his temper. He shoved Poochie and Poochie stumbled back into Roy, who grasped at a pole before going down in a satisfying splay of limbs. Everyone was shouting. The dogs were howling. Sumeet and Zebulon were helping Roy up and Arthur was jabbing his cane at the dogs. Poochie had wandered down a side alley, drawing the dogs away with him, and their barking faded into the distance.

Leah, eyes wide, turned back to Xander and took her hands off her ears. The circle was already dispersing: Gerry had gone to see about his shop; Zebulon had seen someone else to talk to; Roy and Arthur were in conversation; Ned had called Hector in to ask about a reservation.

The moment was over.

Leah and Xander were left staring at each other.

Xander patted the clamshell chair next to him. She sat down, looking dazed.

"So," said Xander. "How long have you been here?"

She stared into space, as if having trouble remembering. "I landed yesterday," she said, and her smile grew as she talked. "So not very long. But I feel like I've been here for a year, or a lifetime. I love it here so much. I feel like I'm resuming a life I used to live. Does that make any sense?"

"You have Stendhal syndrome," said Xander.

Leah's smile faded. "What's that?"

"It's a disorder that tourists develop when they travel to a new place. They think, Oh this place is so different, so 'other' than what I know, so beautiful. They get overwhelmed and end up in the hospital."

Leah was looking at the ground. "Oh."

Xander had gone too far. "But it's a nice feeling," he said, trying to make it up, "nice to feel that way. And you came at the right time. All this fuss about 2012—it's one of the biggest cycles ending in the Long Count calendar. We're starting a new age."

Leah mumbled something.

"What?"

"I said, I don't think it's a sickness. I think I'm just really happy."

"Okay," he said. "I didn't mean to—"

"No, it's fine," she said, getting up and brushing off her skirt. "Nice talking to you."

She went back to her table and her plate of cold food. She sat with her back to him.

KAUA'I
1 K'anan 7 Muwan, Long Count 15.10.13.17.4

---

17 May, 3012

Tanaaj made landfall at sunset.

Where the searoad ended, the ramps began, snaking back and forth like ribbons on the cliff face. Hundreds of La Familia de la Carretera were assembled along them. They'd been waiting for her. Some waved Laviaja flags, green and gold. Some held drums, waiting for the sign. Their faces glowed in the orange light. They wore passion flowers in their hair for Javier El Jugador, the founder of *La Estrella Actual*.

Tanaaj stepped onto the sand and felt the surf on her ankles. She bowed east, in the direction of the island. Then she bowed to the north, then the south. She saw the others realizing what she was doing and following her example. Tanaaj had resurrected this tradition among the LFC: to honor the four corners of the middleworld in the ancient Maya way. West was last. Lastly, four hundred viajeras on the searoad bowed to the sun. She was surrounded by people. She'd never seen so many in one place, not even for Día de Pasaja.

She turned back to the island, clapped, and bellowed, "¡La obra comienza!"

They lifted their hands. "¡Danos la obra!"

"We offer the Litany of Landfall," she called. "We call on the god of this place to act on us, blessed be the land. May the god open the window on Xibalba."

The drummers began.

Tanaaj pulled down her mask, carved with passion flowers, purple and cream. She leapt up the ramp, touched the earth to her left and right, touched her heart. She stepped up, touched the earth to her left and right, touched her heart. Her company followed, doing the same, ascending the ramps like a delta of birds. The viajeras above yelled their encouragement.

Tanaaj called out the questions, and the others repeated them:

¿Está aquí mi cortada?

¿Está muy cerca mi diox?

¿Tal vez un poco más lejos?

¿Tal vez a la izquierda?

¿O a la derecha?

Like many viajeras, Tanaaj had undergone an obsessive-compulsive phase during adolescence, when she first understood the implication of cortada theory: that she could disappear at any moment. She'd memorized the disappearances of the saints: Saint Shu of the dumpster, Saint Gregory of the cemetery, Saint Hiroko of the highway meridian. Jovenix whispered to one another that if you started feeling synesthesia—when sounds appeared as shapes, or words as tastes, as they did to the ancient Maya—it was a sure sign your cortada was very near, and you must slow down, inch forward.

Tanaaj passed the drummers and stepped onto rough tropical grass. Her head tipped back at the pleasure of dirt under her feet. It felt good to be on land again. She smelled woodsmoke and plumeria and iron-rich mud. She slid her right foot forward, her big toe breaking the grass like the prow of a ship.

¿Tal vez un poco más lejos?

¿Tal vez a la izquierda?

¿O a la derecha?

Early viajeras practiced Laviaja literally. Saint Pilar spent ten years pacing one island in the South Pacific to make sure she had covered all its ground before moving on. Ironically, when she did disappear, it was while perusing a Delhi rummage in her wheelchair. Her broken teacup was enshrined on the spot. Now the word "pilari" meant anyone who circled and circled in one place, exploring one god, an island or forest or canyon.

¿Tal vez un poco más lejos?

¿Tal vez a la izquierda?

¿O a la derecha?

If she crossed over to Xibalba, how would she know? Would the landscape vanish and a new one take its place? Would she be in a different body? Would nothing change at all, so that she would simply keep on with her life as usual, not realizing where she was?

¿Tal vez un poco más lejos?

¿Tal vez a la izquierda?

¿O a la derecha?

Tanaaj sensed the tension in the crowd behind her. They were waiting for release.

She turned to face them.

"¡Necesito correr!" she cried. "Catch me!"

She caught a moment of incomprehension on their faces before she broke away and ran up the hillside and darted under the cover of jungle. Soon she heard yells behind her, the sounds of pursuit, humming hoverdishes and stamping feet. She caught a glimpse of the sea, well below her now, turquoise and tangerine. She rounded a tree and a viajera appeared like a vision and handed her a jug of fermented balché. In her euphoria it made perfect sense; they'd planned for her coming, prepared whole vats. She took a gulp of the honeyed slime and then ran with the jug and then gave it to someone else playing a flute with her nose, then darted away lest she be caught. A pack of brown dogs started chasing her, crazed with excitement, and her ai translated *up up up up up up up up up up.* Even as she raced, she tried to take in the god of the place: purple vines, golden milkweed, trees with little pom-poms. It was like Linapacan in some ways, but not in others: the gods were subtly different. She leapt over the skirt of a palm tree, banged her knee, kept going. The air had turned to liquid gold now, and when she looked back at the horizon she couldn't tell the line between sea and sky. She heard a conch blast above her. She saw one viajera riding piggyback on another, lashing her with an orchid. Another masked viajera handed her another jug; more balché, and she took a long swig. She turned back and saw viajeras far below her still surging off the searoad, up the ramps, up the slope, breaking form, rummaging for their masks and pulling them on. The orange sky had deepened to lilac. The clouds looked like raspberry sandbars. She darted back under the tree cover, found a stream and followed it up, slowed down to entice someone to follow her. She caught a flash of a heliconia mask behind a fern, and she shrieked and clambered up the slope. The sweet madness had set in. Now they were all trying to get as high up as they could, or rather, catch one another in the attempt or let themselves be caught. The drink, the drums, the dance: as ever, these were the engines of the alteration of ordinary time. Xibalba felt so close, the liminal, the numinous, the unknowable. The Other World permeated this world, constantly, to be felt in art and song and dance and herb and drink; but never touched. She could never touch it. That was the one thing she most longed to do. The viajera with the heliconia mask caught her by the heel, and Tanaaj let herself fall, and turned on her back and opened her legs to prayer position.

Tanaaj woke between two sleeping bodies.

It was after dark. She blinked to orient herself, sat up on her elbows. She'd only slept a few hours, as usual. She heard grave voices nearby. There were two viajeras talking under a palm tree.

When they saw her awake, they stopped.

Tanaaj could guess why. "The Tzoyna voted," she said.

"Yes," said one.

"And?"

"They've disallowed blotting Niloux DeCayo. It takes three consecutive sessions, and she got four out of six."

Tanaaj sat up, put her hands over her eyes. This meant her work had become much more difficult. The heretic was effectively free again.

"Where is she now?" one viajera asked.

"Capri. She and some others are banding together to go to the Jubilee."

Tanaaj got up, careful not to wake the others. She pulled on her tunic and pants and went to sit with the viajeras, who handed her a green coconut. She drank from it. She could tell they were in awe of her, which, a year ago, would have horrified her. But after months on the searoad with hundreds of familia, and daily consultations with adivinix, she had come to understand that these were unprecedented circumstances. Xibalba had chosen her to lead its faithful. In order to save Laviaja, she had to interpret the Rule of Saint Leah in a new way. She still felt uneasy at times, but she told herself that once she confronted Niloux at the Jubilee, she could go back to her life as a simple jugadorix, seeking the Other World with her familias like everyone else. All of this was temporary.

"Will you take a stand, Tanaaj?" asked one of the viajeras.

She looked up at the sky. Clouds had rolled in, covering the stars. She shivered. "I must first learn what I should say, hermanix, according to the god of this place. I will wait until I am told." She put down the coconut and held out her hands. "Will you pray with me?"

They gave her their hands and bowed their heads. Tanaaj closed her eyes and breathed in the jasmine, the sea salt, the clay.

"Escúchanos," said Tanaaj. "We feel you beneath us and above us. We hail you, the god of this place, you who are ultimately unknowable. We hail you, Xibalba, all around us. Our hearts are troubled by this news from afar. May you grant us peace and instruction during the whole of our quest, but especially in the coming days. En el nombre de la Trinidad de Cayo, gracias."

"Gracias," the others said.

Tanaaj was awake now; it was no use going back to sleep. She was hungover from the balché and her body ached from the running and the sex. Her pelt was compensating, cleaning her blood, but it would take another hour or two. She reviewed how many she'd made love to before her ai warned her she was unable to consent. Four!—a baker, a cegadi, and two yucatec maya at the same time. This made her worry a bit: there were getting to be too many maya, especially since the advent of the Zeinians. Soon the manéra would reach its cap and stay closed, for a year or more, to prevent voting blocs.

The trio switched to coffee. Both of these viajeras had been with her in the sea crossing. One was a vesque named Ceres, elegant in maroon and gold; the other was a miqunk named Fei, with olive skin and a bald head. They discussed the god of this place—how Polynesian people had discovered this island, how white settlers stole it, and how its residents had been the first to declare independence from the United States, soon followed by the rest of Hawai'i.

Fei said, "Did you know there's a shrine on the ridge above us?"

Tanaaj perked up. "Which saint?"

"Saint Quare."

She nodded. "I know that one. Saint Quare of the Vista."

"It's one of the earliest panoptic holotapes. You can watch her disappear."

Tanaaj raised her eyebrows, sipped her coffee, smiled to herself.

"What is it?" said Ceres.

Tanaaj shrugged. "I think it is plain that the god of the place has instructed us what to do next, yes?

All of those who feel disheartened by the news about Niloux DeCayo may feel their faith renewed by a visit to the shrine."

Fei and Ceres agreed this was a good idea.

Then Tanaaj heard a soft whimpering sound. She put down her coffee. "Do you hear that?" she said.

The other two strained to listen, but Tanaaj wasted no time. She got up and tapped her heart to sharpen her night vision. Then she found the source of the cry: an infant, stretched out like a fish. She bent down and picked her up. The adults shifted in their sleep, grateful the noise had stopped.

She slung a blanket over her shoulder and tiptoed up the slope where the trees cleared. She sat cross-legged with the baby, whom she noticed was soft and floppy, with a thrusted tongue and a round, moonlike face. This baby needed specific care and attention. But didn't every baby, according to their bodies and souls? "I know, I know," Tanaaj said. "I heard you. And every child is my child. Are you hungry?"

The baby cooed.

"Your feelings are plain, madam," she said, and pulled up her tunic. She drew her finger around her nipple three times to induce. The baby tried to latch, but her muscle tone was too soft. Tanaaj was patient. She held her at arm's length, then brought her back, directing her nipple deep into the baby's mouth again, so she could drink while still being able to breathe. Finally the baby fastened on.

Tanaaj exhaled. "Muy bien, bebe, we did it together," she said, and kissed the silky hair.

She felt her breast swell with milk even as it was being drained; the other was filling too. She felt thankful for her breasts, and thankful for every other part of her that was sore from the night of sex, sometimes giving and sometimes receiving, all of it delicious. Meanwhile, dawn was coming. The sky turned from ultramarine to lilac to peach. Tanaaj switched the baby to her other breast and pointed to the east. "Look," she whispered. "There is Venus. The ancient Maya called her Chak Ek', the Great Star. Look how bright she is! Now she's at the end of her cycle as the morning star, so we can only see her for a few minutes before the sun comes up. Did you know that Venus is the twin planet of Earth? You would think it'd be Mars, but no, it's Venus that is the same size and density. The Great Star has meant so many things to so many people. What will she mean to you?"

The baby suckled, eyes closed in bliss.

Her ai told her the baby's name: *Mei Sakura DeMar.* The surname meant she'd been born at sea, just like her own baby, Messe.

Tanaaj winced.

While on the searoad, she'd received a new holo from Messe. She hadn't watched it yet because she'd never been alone, and she didn't want other viajeras to see her watching a holo and misinterpret her intent, which was, and always would be, to sharpen her resistance to temptation. But now she was alone. So while Mei Sakura breastfed, Tanaaj touched her heart to recall the motmot, which hopped away from her again and flowered into the shape of a child.

This time, Messe was wearing plain travel wear: printed shirt, loincloth, leggings. She wore her hair in a soft cloud around her face. She seemed to have grown up so much, even in the last four months.

This time, she didn't look up. She addressed the ground, turning over something small in her hand.

"Hi again," she said. "I don't really know why I'm doing this, since I know you watch these but I never hear back from you. I mean, I understand. My zadres taught me multivalent attachment theory. We're not supposed to attach to blood kin. I guess that's what you're trying to teach me too. Not sure why you didn't just make me a Child of Saint Leah, then, but whatever."

She kept turning over the little object in her hand.

"My Primera Viaja went fine except that I was attacked."

Tanaaj's breath caught in her throat.

"I didn't see it coming. My shields activated but I got hurt anyway because I was knocked down. And I was alone. And then I had to wait two hours for help and I didn't know if the animal would come back. So that was not fine."

The baby unlatched from Tanaaj's nipple and started fussing.

Messe seemed to be fighting with herself. She still hadn't looked up. Tanaaj was fighting with herself too: this was a more difficult temptation than the ones before. Always, Tanaaj wanted to take care of those who were hurting and comfort those who were suffering. But this was the hard lesson: if she attached to this child, she would prize caring for her above all other children, and then she might lose her. This is what Messe had to learn too: you must never attach to anyone, because you will lose everyone, and painfully.

"In fact," said Messe, "I could have died. And while I was waiting for help I was thinking: What if I called Tanaaj, just to talk to her? Would she answer if she knew I was hurt? Would she even care?"

Messe held up the object in her hand: a long sickle-shaped bone, yellowish, with a white enamel tip.

"When my zadres came, they found this nearby. A jaguar tooth."

She looked straight into Tanaaj's eyes, as if she were across from her in real life.

"I'm going to save it as a souvenir."

The baby began to cry.

Tanaaj's familia reached the shrine at noon.

They sat around the gazebo on the ridge, taking turns reading the seal in the middle of the floor. *Aquí está la cortada de Quare DeKing,* it read, *que ha pasado a la Mundotra.* Here is the cortada of Quare DeKing, who has passed to Xibalba.

Recent pilgrims had left offerings: honeycomb in a dish, a branch of hibiscus, and an emerald brooch in the shape of a butterfly. Fei held it to her eye, waited for her ai to match it. "Nineteenth century," she said, passing it to Tanaaj. "Made in New York for a newspaper heiress."

Tanaaj turned it in the light and shook her head. "Hoarding rocks while people starved."

Fei shrugged. "That was normal to them."

"As this is to us," said Ceres, handing out teacups.

"Barbarians," Tanaaj said. She put the brooch back, then looked over the golden canyons that faded into the distance. She had hardened, since watching the holo from Messe. She felt that Xibalba was testing her worthiness as a leader. She had to be on guard.

After the tea was poured, Ceres opened the holo. The text in the air read:

Recorded by Ifeoma DeCanton
Maya . 6 Lamat 11 K'ank'in, Long Count 14.10.0.4.8
Gregorian . 8 August 2604, 17:56:11

The holo began.

The sun disappeared beneath the clouds. The gazebo disappeared beneath their legs. Now they seemed to be sitting in midair.

A viajera came into sight from the other side of the ridge. This was Quare. She looked antique: her pelt was a thick rubbery suit, not the integrated skins they had today. She was tall and muscled, likely in her sixties, with black skin, white fingernails, and hazel eyes. Tanaaj guessed her manéra was zekk or león.

Quare walked with energy and purpose, looking out over the canyons.

Then another voice called "¡Buendía, hermanix!"

That must be the voice of Ifeoma, whose ai had recorded the disappearance.

Quare turned toward the sound, and looked as though she were staring directly at Tanaaj. But Tanaaj had to remind herself that Quare was not seeing her;

she was seeing someone who'd stood here four hundred years ago, and this gazebo had not existed then.

"A ti también, hermanix," said Quare as she approached. "You need a new kiln, yes?"

Tanaaj asked her ai to adjust for language drift. She could barely understand this dialect of Común.

"Yes," said Ifeoma. "I'm so glad there was one in the area. Foraging is good here, but . . ."

"Sometimes you need hot food. I picked up an extra on Oahu."

"Thanks. I'm about to start toward Japan."

Quare pulled off her pack, plunged in her hand, and pulled out an enormous contraption with buttons and sharp corners—an early model of kiln.

"Thank you," said Ifeoma. "I have a gift for you in turn."

"I don't expect anything," said Quare. She straightened up and reshouldered her pack. Tanaaj started feeling nervous. Everything was so mundane, so ordinary, but the big event was about to happen any second.

"You don't have to take it if it burdens you," said Ifeoma, "but it's a weaving of Saint Leah."

Tanaaj saw the weaving held out, right in front of her eyes. It was minimalist, yarn on burlap. Saint Leah—

marked by her green yarn sneakers—was standing in a blue yarn stream looking into a black yarn cave.

"That's lovely," said Quare, reaching for it. "My favorite story of Saint Leah is the first time she went into the cave and—"

She vanished.

There was a pause of incomprehension, then a scream from Ifeoma, who dropped the weaving on the ground.

The recording was over.

The sun came back. The gazebo and seal reappeared.

Tanaaj was rigid. She tried to rebuild the last moment in her mind. There was no indication that disappearance was imminent; no flash of light or change of air, no warning or hesitation. Quare had simply been there, then not there.

They were silent a long time. No one had touched her tea.

Tanaaj sent word that everyone following her—eight hundred, now that they'd made landfall—should attend the shrine in groups of nine, then make camp farther down in the canyon.

As her familia was walking along the ridge, Tanaaj was visited by an aug parrot.

Aloha, Tanaaj DeCayo!
Your work today is:
2200—0200, compañerix to Kiren DeSaav.
All prerequisites met.

Her companions noticed she'd stopped and stared into midair. "You got work?" said Fei.

"Yes, hermanix," said Tanaaj, resuming her walk.

"What! You're already doing enough work!"

"It is not for me to say, hermanix. We will all be getting more work as we head east. I serve my familia, and the paragua tells me what the familia needs."

Fei seemed ashamed. She was silent, then asked, "Anything fun?"

Tanaaj's wry expression told her everything she needed to know.

Fei hooted and poked at Tanaaj's ribs. "I'm jealous! All I ever get is bot maintenance."

"But don't you have to train as a compañerix?" said Ceres.

Fei pouted. "True. I'm not cut out for it. Only what, five percent of all viajeras can do it?"

"I think it is four, hermanix," said Tanaaj.

"Look at you," teased Ceres, "so humble."

"Have you gotten a look at her?" Fei asked.

"I never look before I meet them," said Tanaaj.

"Not even their manéra?"

"No, hermanix. I take her as she is. That is the practice and the art."

Fei whistled. "So you could really get anything."

That was true. Tanaaj had trained as a compañerix from the time she was a teenager. She'd been an omnipreféra since she knew what sex even was, and she was a caregiver by nature, so the work came easily. But still, she had to train her body in a strict tradition. She could not discriminate against any genéra, manéra, or preféra. She could not show any distaste. She had to minister to her charge as an ancient servant to her queen, if only for a night.

Kiren joined the familia for supper. Upon her arrival, Fei turned to Tanaaj and lifted her eyebrow in a suggestive manner. Tanaaj could admit, Kiren was very attractive. She resisted the urge to guess her concórdia on sight; she'd let Kiren tell her, as she felt comfortable. She was thick and energetic, naked to the waist, with long breasts, salt-and-pepper hair, and a huge smile. She'd brought a cache of taro and banana. They made a real fire and roasted them on sticks while Ceres printed sauce.

Fei asked, "So where are you headed, Kiren?"

"Nowhere!" she said, grinning. "I'm one of those damned pilaris. I came over that ridge to the south and saw this canyon and said to myself *This is it*. Been here ever since."

Fei looked to Tanaaj, but Tanaaj was careful not to react. To some orthodox, pilaris were too much like sedentix, who settled and colonized one place. Tanaaj avoided them, as a rule, and had to admit she felt uncomfortable around pilaris as well. But her training as a compañerix had to come first.

Ceres broke the awkward silence. "So you know this area well," she said.

Kiren seemed oblivious. "I do!"

"What kind of work do you get?"

Kiren got excited. Tanaaj sensed that she didn't talk to other people very often. "Mostly I make sure the local paragua algorithms haven't gone out of whack," she said. "For example, when there's an emergency, like someone is injured or dying, the algorithm sorts by urgency first, then proximity, then expertise, right? If the closest viajera doesn't have the expertise, they have to take the tutorial first, and then, you know, sleep for three days, so it's not ideal. Anyway, the algorithms are built to self-regulate, but humans will always have to check them for drift. And now all of you are coming through in a big flood. We haven't had this many people on the island in the two years I've been here. So the paragua is bearing a load it hasn't borne in a long time. It's a good time to test for stresses on the system. Anyway, you're all going to the Jubilee?"

The company nodded.

Kiren eyed them all. "I've met Niloux DeCayo, you know. The one who's making all the trouble."

The whole company stiffened, remembering the morning's news; except for Tanaaj, who forced herself to soften. "Oh?" she said. "Where?"

"Tibet," she said. "Gertse Wayhouse. The paragua algorithms there are out of whack because it's cold as hell and everyone deals differently with cold. It was only sixty degrees when I was there. I hated it. I just wanted to go somewhere less cold."

Tanaaj nodded, which is all Kiren seemed to need for encouragement. She stuffed another piece of taro in her mouth and chewed as she talked. "Niloux was too. Cold, I mean. Brilliant, though. She stalked around like a cat, like she was always angry, but really she was just always in her head, thinking about things like pistas and cortadas and whatever else sofists think about. I wanted to talk to her about algorithm neutrality but she always wanted to be alone."

"Doesn't sound very likable," said Fei.

"Doesn't matter," said Kiren. "She was the kind of person you meet and hope *she* likes *you*."

"Sounds like the exact opposite of you," Ceres said

to Tanaaj, and Tanaaj inclined her head at the compliment.

But Kiren was staring at her as if thinking hard. "No," she said, and then once she said the word, it all flooded out. "No, no, no. Actually I think you two are very much alike. You're both charismatic. But you're charismatic in a warm way and she was charismatic in a cold way, like a cold flame you need to touch. And aren't you both maya?"

"It is true," said Tanaaj. "In fact we are both mopan maya."

Kiren whistled. "That's got to sting."

Tanaaj forced a smile. She didn't want to get into politics at the moment, especially with someone she was about to minister to. Besides, she felt uncomfortable with anger, a useless and destructive emotion; always she tried to commute anger to another form, like compassion. So all she said was, "I pray that Niloux DeCayo will see the truth someday soon, hermanix, and not least because of our efforts."

They stared at the fire.

After supper, Kiren led Tanaaj to the edge of the canyon. The rainbow blush of the galaxy was just beginning to rise in the east.

"I'm sorry," said Kiren immediately after they sat down. "I know you're a jugadorix. I know you'd rather

be working as a performer instead of stuck here listening to me talk about algorithms. I didn't know the
paragua would pair me with you, of all people."

Tanaaj laughed. She angled her body in the way she'd
been trained, in a pose that expressed openness and
safety. She was also getting the sense that Kiren might
not want physical touch; rather just someone to talk to,
and receive her enthusiasms. That was all right. That
was a form of being an envolvánte too. "There is nothing to apologize for," she said. "This is my work and I
am devoted to it, as much as I am to *La Estrella Actual.*"

Kiren looked her over. "I hope I get to see you perform too. You have a reputation. You're famous."

Tanaaj stiffened at the word "famous," but reminded
herself to de-center her feelings. Her work was to make
Kiren comfortable. "That is very flattering," she said.
"I try only to witness to the truth of Xibalba."

"What's your favorite role to play?"

Tanaaj looked out over the canyon, the folds grey
in the starlight. She couldn't make her mind understand the dimensions of the view: how far, how deep,
how vast. It looked like a painting on a flat canvas. "I
like to play Javier Magaña," she said, "the founder of
La Estrella Actual. The reason why is not a mystery, I
suppose. I am a jugadorix like him. I have studied his
videos so much that I can replay them in my head."

Tanaaj glanced at Kiren, trying to gauge her mood. She was juggling her knees, just seeming excited to have someone to talk to. Tanaaj went on. "But I also feel close to Javier because, his whole life, he only wished to love. He served his people by being an ambassador of his culture. He took care of the tourists who came to Belize. He longed for his brother, Xander, even though Xander spurned him."

"I think you should be more aggressive," said Kiren, tearing apart a palm frond and peering closely at it. "I know you don't read any of the feeds or keep up with the Tzoyna because of the Rule of Saint Leah and that's fine, but I hope your disciples back there are telling you everything that's going on out there too."

Tanaaj chose to ignore the word "disciples." She said, "They told me the Tzoyna voted to lift blotting on Niloux DeCayo."

"That's only a little bit of it!" Kiren threw the shredded frond over the side of the canyon, started on another. "Things are changing fast. Ever since the ice melted. Do you know what else the Tzoyna has been discussing in the last month? I was called for duty just last week. You know what I had to vote on? Whether people's manéra should be determined by birthplace. Can you imagine? No one having a choice anymore?

Forcing alignment instead of letting people find their own? And also whether people should be restrained from going to places that are 'dangerous.' Who would decide what's dangerous or not? Who would enforce that? Would they shut me out of mutual aid because someone tells me my canyon is dangerous? Would they take away my algorithms because they don't trust me anymore? My point is that everything is going faster than you think and if you want to succeed, and I want you to succeed, you can't keep being so passive."

Tanaaj remained still, jaw clenched, but absorbing each word. It was true. She had not known any of this because she hadn't asked, especially during the long sea journey when she was lost in prayer and familia and searoad maintenance. Meanwhile, Niloux's heresy had set off waves that had destabilized the delicate balance of the world. Things were worse than she'd thought. She would have to change tack, again, to lead effectively.

God of this place, she thought, *grant me peace and instruction.*

"Maybe you are right, carnalix," she said. "Maybe I can make my own proposal to the Tzoyna."

Kiren stopped shredding. "What would it be?"

"First, that Niloux DeCayo be named an enemy of the people."

Kiren whistled. "No one's done that for two hundred years."

"And second," said Tanaaj, her voice calm, saying the words that came to her, "that at the Jubilee, I will prove Xibalba is real."

TZOYNA
3 Batz' 14 Pop, Long Count 10.9.5.7.11

---

9 December, 1012

"For your faithfulness, child of maize," said Ajul, "we commend you."

The captive stayed prostrated.

"You returned to warn us of the jaguar, even knowing your destiny. Princess Ket will keep her life because of you."

The captive said nothing.

"I, Royal Prince Ajul, release you from the ball game."

The captive looked up with hope in his eyes. Upakal—behind him—made a motion as if to say, *Correct him.*

"Not from captivity," Ajul hurried to add, "but from the ball game. Your death will be swift and merciful."

The light went out of the captive's eyes. Ajul thought, He is not perfect, then; but so few captives are now. In the glory days, captives embraced their fate with a fierce joy. Even the captive at his own presentation ceremony—the young Nahua prince—had been better than these. Now the old ways were falling apart.

But Ajul thought: not here. We will become the navel of the world.

Upakal tugged the captive's rope to lead him away.

There was still some time left before the procession began. Ajul started up the back side of the temple. He climbed all the way to the top platform and crouched there, trying to remain unseen. His father would have chastised him for doing so. But now he was nearly king and could do what he liked.

Besides, he wasn't here on a whim. He wanted to gather his thoughts and prepare for the ceremony. Chak Ek' the Great Star was now in his evening phase, the first to appear when the sun set. Chak Ek' was the beginning and the end, and today was Three Batz', the day who secured continuity through past and future. There'd be the feast with entertainment, the ball game, the arrival of the gods, the dressing of the body, and then the journey into the Great Cave, where—Mutna had told him—there was a ladder leading to a deep crystal chamber, where they'd leave the sacrifice.

He listened to the howler monkeys roar their evening chorus, and watched the sunset flood his city. There was the dayrise plaza and the old ball court, the palace and the servants' quarters, the steam bath and the tower, the market and the small plaza, the retaining wall and the small temple, the orchard and the promenade, the garden and the healer huts, the terraces and the lime road. The sky was filled with soft honey clouds; below him, torches flowered around the courtyard. He stood between the heavens and the underworld. His procession was assembling. His people were gathering to eat. His allies had come to pay tribute. All was well in his kingdom. He wanted to linger here, where everything was already accomplished, already won.

On the court below, Ixul stood surrounded by handmaids. They were painting her as Xbalanque, with patches of jaguar skin on her shoulders. Her hair was oiled, braided, and sculpted around a shoot of blood-red heliconia; her headdress bloomed behind her, yellow kiskadee with orange oriole and scarlet tanager. She wore gold cuffs, gold bangles, a gold chain on her cheek, and a necklace of jade plates that rested on the tops of her breasts. Her ears held two gold earspools carved like heliconia blooms. Now she was the queen-to-be, unfazed by the fuss, standing on the lip of her destiny.

As if feeling his gaze, Ixul looked up and beckoned him down. He descended and presented himself to his twin for inspection. His shoulders were painted with black spots like Hunajpu, and his arms and legs were painted in wide bands of black. His headdress was black, too, with bursts of catbird feathers that shone green in the light, and a fringe of blue motmot. He wore a jade bar through his septum, a jade labret through his lower lip, and jade earspools carved in the shape of passion flowers.

"Come closer," said Ixul when he was done turning. He did. She licked her hand and slicked down his head. "Your hair looks like you slept on it, as usual," she said. "The handmaids were sloppy."

"We'll teach them," said Ajul. Already he was thinking about trysting, tomorrow, when they'd be released from abstinence.

Ixul grunted. "You might have to speak to Mutna. She's agitated that we haven't greeted our guests yet. I told her they should be satisfied to be feasted. Have they eaten stingray before? I doubt it."

"Can I eat stingray too?"

They both looked down.

Ket had asked the question. Her head was wrapped in white cotton. Both her eyes were covered, but she looked straight at them as if she could see them, and her lips curved up in a smile.

Ixul caught her breath and looked away.

Ajul crouched level to Ket. He tried to sound as normal as he could. "Look at you," he managed. "You should be resting."

"That's what Mutna said. But she gave me holy water from the Great Cave to help heal me and then she gave me some bandages that were all soaked with sap from the give-and-take tree and told me to lie down again, but I said no, I want to be here when you become king."

Ajul remembered her fervor, that morning. He tried to keep his voice steady. "You're very brave," he said.

Ket swelled with pride like a watered flower. "Well," she said, "why not be brave? There's nothing to be afraid of, not really. That's what I think. What do you think of our captives? Are they anything like Nob?"

"Nob?"

"Don't you remember? The beautiful captive at your presentation feast?"

"Oh, you mean the Nahua prince."

Now Ajul remembered. Ket's first captive was a kind of obsession. Once Ajul had caught her playing with a doll she called Nob, whom she was treating as her husband; when he asked her about it, she got shy and tongue-tied. But the twins had had a different experience of Nob: he was the first captive whose body their father had taught them to dress. They'd be using those very lessons tonight.

Ket's voice stirred him from his thoughts.

"This is Patli," she said, waving at an older girl kneeling behind her. "The merchants heard what happened and lent her to me as a gift. She dressed my head." Ket touched her fingers to the bandage, hemmed with red and green.

"That was generous of her. Does it hurt?"

"Oh yes," she said immediately, which struck Ajul like a slap in the face, and he realized he'd been hoping she'd say it didn't hurt at all, that her uncanny mildness could override even pain. "It feels like there's a hot spicy black moss on my face and it's spreading through my head down my back into the base of my spine. It all itches. But I'm getting used to it."

"You're taking it well," said Ixul, returned and composed, cool and formal. "It sets a good example."

Ajul looked up at Ixul and there was a moment when he didn't know her, when she was so beautiful that his eyes had to adjust to the splendor, to recognize that this vision was his own sister.

"See the embroidery?" Ket said, looking in Ixul's direction.

There was panic in Ixul's eyes for just a moment, and then it disappeared, like a fish that came to the surface and then dove again. "Pretty," she said without emotion. "Who made it for you?"

"I just said! Patli here. She's a little older than me."

Ixul turned to the older girl. "We appreciate your kindness," she said. "You may rise, child of maize. You will have your reward later."

Since the events of that afternoon, Ixul had become detached, and managed a distance about the issue of the jaguar, as if it were distracting and unnecessary. It was a habit of hers, when things she loved were threatened. She did this even with Ajul. Early in the rainy season, Ajul told her he wanted to consult on whether it was proper for brothers and sisters to couple, even in a case like theirs, where there were no suitable bloodlines left. The first time they coupled was an accident; it seemed like an answer to grief. But then they'd returned to it over and over. It seemed like the only thing that made their bad turn of fortune worthwhile. But now Ajul had been feeling troubled and guilty; he prayed and made offerings, but still heard no answer.

So Ajul said to Ixul, Let's just wait until we can send for a special priest.

In response, Ixul withdrew from him. She went to the library and shut herself in. She ate and slept by herself. She only saw Mutna, and even started playing with Ket. If Ixul saw him, she walked the other way. If she had to share a room with him, she didn't look at him. He came back to her in tears, burying his face in her esh and asking to be let back in. He said, I was wrong, I want to be with you again, and I want the whole kingdom to know—I want them to see us as king and queen, bound as tight as this world and the other, knotted at the navel and making new time.

She took him back without a word. They never spoke of it.

He was always worried she would abandon him again.

But for now, and especially when she was attired as his queen, he just let his eyes feast on the copper of her skin, the heart of her face, and the impossible darkness between her lips.

Ixul spread her arms for a final inspection. Her handmaids looked her over in the orange light. They knew she was fastidious about her appearance on occasions of state. If she was with her family in the private quarters, she didn't care; she was neat but not vain. A public ceremony was different. She was pragmatic. She had to make an impression on her people.

The royal procession drew up in the courtyard. Upakal was stationed at the front with six royal bodyguards, mirroring the six that brought up the rear. Next were six drummers and six royal servers in green-edged huipils. Then there was Ket with her little bandaged head and Patli to guide her. Ixul was behind them, and behind her was supposed to be Ajul, but he was still pacing in the corner, muttering his speeches.

Mutna stood on the rampart, watching the sky. She'd wait until the sun dipped below the middleworld. When the Great Star appeared, that would be the signal to begin.

Ixul felt restless. She called for Upakal.

He turned at once and marched to her and knelt with his spear. Upakal was a fine warrior, young and kind, already a veteran of raids on the dayrise. He was dressed plainly—a spray of raven feathers behind his head, his face half black, the star of the Tzoyna on his chest, and plain copper anklets on both legs.

She gestured to him to rise. He was still a hand shorter.

"What is the temper of the crowd?" she asked. She could hear the noise in the plaza—greetings, gossip, and anticipation.

"Skeptical, Ahau."

Ixul raised her eyebrows. Upakal was also honest to the point of pain. "Skeptical of what?" she snapped. "Do they not smell the food with their own eyes?"

"They don't doubt the food, Ahau. Every guest has been assured they will get a full share, even the refugees haunting the shadows."

"Then what is the object of their skepticism?"

"They doubt that good fortune will return to the Tzoyna, Ahau."

Ixul sneered. "Peasants. Can't they read the sky? Tonight is the most important alignment in five katuns. The Great Star is accompanied by both of his warriors and the Cacao Star precedes him. Do they expect the Sun himself to come down and sit among us? We could have no better sign for a turn of fortune than if we'd screwed the gods into the sky with our own hands."

Upakal bowed. "Of course, Ahau. I have no doubt that after tonight, they will be free of skepticism."

"And our 'honored allies'? What are they like?"

Upakal caught the insult in her voice, but made no comment. "Tatichwut is a young farmer. He's the son of the man who moved into Pekwitz in your parents' time and claimed to be its lord."

The name "Tatichwut" tickled her memory, but she ignored it for now. "How do you read him?"

"Sulking and jealous."

Ixul pursed her lips. That was useful information. "And the merchant?"

"Chenukul of Katwitz is nervous and eager to please."

"So I've heard. And his warriors?"

"They're merchants' warriors," he said. "They're used to guarding convoys. They fight for property, not honor."

"I hope they don't embarrass themselves."

"This is not their first ball game, Ahau."

"But they're merchants without kings. They're used to games for sport, not for the gods. We'll have to trust them to act like civilized people and not piss themselves when they see the knife."

"We will monitor their consumption of beer, Ahau."

"Thank you. Is there anything else I should know?"

He paused, looked uncertain.

"Upakal. Tell me."

"It's not a great concern, Ahau."

"Let me decide that."

"It's only . . ." He kept his eyes lowered. "Wackan took final count with the head steward. There are fewer guests than we expected."

"Fewer? How many fewer?"

"We prepared food for two thousand, Ahau. At last check, we counted four hundred."

Ixul felt like she'd been punched in the throat. It was like their parents' canoe race all over again. They'd spent months preparing for this feast. Tracking the days in consultation with Mutna. Negotiating with Katwitz and Pekwitz. Sending out word. Securing the roads. Preparing the captives. Practicing with gear. Sweeping the plaza. Whittling the torches. Mixing the tar. Growing the food. Sending for the food. Storing the food. Cooking the food. Disappearances were common— there were daily reports of farmers gone in the night, homesteads abandoned, and whole valleys left empty. But can there have been that many who'd abandoned the realm so quickly? There'd been a great migration out of the lowlands in their great-grandparents' generation, but not from here. The Tzoyna was the last stronghold.

She tried to control her temper. "Why are there so few?"

"I don't know, Ahau."

"Ask people in the crowd. Be discreet. See what you can find."

"I will, Ahau."

"Thank you."

"I am sorry to have told you, Ahau."

"It's all right. Now, go to the front and watch for Mutna's signal."

He did so.

She regretted her tone with him. But it was difficult to control herself when she was angry. She decided not to tell Ajul. He was too sensitive. He had to focus on his speeches.

The Sun winked out.

At the exact moment of his departure, the Great Star blazed.

A wind sluiced through the courtyard, making the torches run sideways.

Mutna took a torch from its sconce and waved it three times, and the signal was returned in the plaza.

Mutna turned and bowed to Upakal.

It was time. There was nothing else to do but go.

The drums began to beat.

Ixul kept her head down. She shifted from one foot to the other. She had to drop her anger now. She made herself breathe from her belly.

She felt a tap on her shoulder and turned around.

It was Ajul, resplendent, with a very serious look.

"Don't trip," he said.

Ixul forgot all her anger and laughed.

The procession was beginning. She stumbled, still laughing, her tension released like a dove from the hand.

They processed across the courtyard, up the small

steps, through the arch, and down the stairs into the public plaza, where warriors held a double row of torches, making a broad path through the prostrated crowd. The nearness of the peasants made Ixul nervous, though she knew all had been checked for plague. Patli was leading Ket, arm in arm. Ket's left eye was gone and she'd be blind for a while. Her wound was not life-threatening, but it was still traumatic. Ixul was both unnerved and impressed by the girl's resilience: after all she'd been through today, she still insisted on bowling the game. Ajul was right. They had to take her seriously now, to consider her a royal player, as much as they were themselves.

The procession wrapped around the ball court. Again she looked at the Great Star. He stabbed forth like the point of a knife. Sacred time had begun. Now they couldn't stray, even if they tried; the cycles were set in motion and had to play to their ends.

They arrived at the temple overlooking the ball court. Ajul took Ket's hand and Patli stepped aside. Then the three royal children alone climbed to the dais, arrayed with soft couches and embroidered pillows, and copal censers in the shape of jaguar heads.

On either side of the dais, there were lower platforms set up for their new allies: five merchants of Katwitz on one side, and four farmer-lords of Pekwitz on the other. Ixul noted the farmers had a few adornments—a copper collar here, a dyed sash there—scavenged or bought, no doubt; not won in war or gifted to their lineage. She also noted how strangely the merchants were dressed, in tilmatli, that Nahua fashion of long robes tied at the shoulder. They looked like they were wearing blankets. Ixul imagined that tilmatli would be comfortable where it was cool and dry, but here in the lowlands, it was hot and wet. The merchants sweated and picked at the cloth.

Looking out onto the plaza, Ixul could see that Upakal had spoken the truth: there were only a few hundred gathered, plus the skinny refugees at the outskirts. She told herself that, as distasteful as they were, they were welcome. Everyone would be welcome in the new Tzoyna. And—Ixul realized—fewer guests meant triple portions. Everyone would go home declaiming the generosity of the new rulers. More people would come next time.

The drums rolled to a stop. In the silence that followed, Ixul heard the torchlight snap.

Now was the time for Ajul's first speech. He rose, towering over the plaza.

"Tonight we gather—" Ajul bellowed, and his voice cracked.

Ixul twitched.

That couldn't have happened. She felt cold in her throat.

She saw Chenukul, below, glance up from his prostration.

Ajul cleared his throat. She willed him to start over. To speak from the bottom of his belly. He began again: "Tonight on Three Batz', the Great Star blazes, and we gather to mark the triple friendship of Tzoyna, Pekwitz, and Katwitz," and it came out well, and she thought, *This is good, wajmul, don't think about it or it will happen again.* "In the past, we may have been rivals; but in the age to come, we are kin. We are bound by the rivers that course through the realm, even as blood courses through our flesh. We welcome you, our guests from Pekwitz. We welcome you, our guests from Katwitz. We welcome you from every corner of the realm. Now, rise!"

This was the signal. Everyone sat up from their prostrations. Ixul willed him to finish with conviction.

"Much will be seen and heard tonight, but first: eat until you are full. It is our promise to you of the age to come."

The cheers swelled, then faded, as peasants looked to and fro for the servants who bore the food.

Ajul looked clammy as he sat down on his pillows.

"You did well," Ixul said, with no mockery.

"Thank you, wajmul," he said. "And thank you for giving me the words."

She tilted her head in acknowledgment.

On the step below, servants poured cups of cacao back and forth, working up heads of froth before presenting them to the royal family. Then the merchants and farmers were served balché—it was meant to honor them, and Ixul observed that it did. To Ket's delight, she received her own bowl of seed draught, flavored with rare white honey. Then the servants loaded all of their plates with cinnamon porridge, spiced fish, river snails, hot popcorn, palm marrow, and tamales folded with venison. Ixul ate with a wild hunger, glad to break the fast.

Meanwhile, plainclothed servants went among the crowd, moving from family to family. Clowns threw up balls of maize dough and chopped them up in a show of human sacrifice. Acrobats flipped between the mats, adding to the mealtime entertainment. But no one looked. They were too busy eating. She saw a gaunt woman in a dirty huipil ask for water for her son, whose eyes were vacant. The woman accepted a clay cupful and held the back of the child's head while he gulped it down. How had they come to that?

Then Ixul was startled by Ket's hand, feeling for her arm.

"Ixul?" she said. "I want Patli to come up here."

Ixul opened her mouth to rebuke her for impertinence, but Ajul put his hand on her shoulder, and she closed it again. Ixul was easily exasperated by Ket and her sudden devotions. Tomorrow she would have a talk with her little sister about what constituted royal behavior—for example, not making demands in the midst of a sacred ceremony. But for now, after the sacrifices this child had made, Ixul would let her have her way.

"She can come up," Ixul said, "if she sits below you."

Ket was in the dark, but she had begun to see in a new way.

Ever since Balam Ahau had taken her eye, and kind Patli had bound her head, and Mutna had washed her wound with holy water from the Great Cave, her whole body had felt sharp and tingly. How silly she'd been, to think one cut to her finger had been the end of the whole affair! Ket rejoiced in her new injury. Her brother and sister were tall heroes, crowned by their beauty; but now she was marked by the god. Her wound was her beauty.

"Ket," said Ixul.

Ket turned toward the voice.

"Patli is below you now."

"Hi, Patli," Ket said to the friendly darkness in front of her.

"Greetings, Ahau," Patli said. She'd been trained to speak to royals; that would please Ixul. "Will you allow me to fetch you more food or drink?"

"No, our servants will bring it," she said. "I just like having you here."

"As you wish, Ahau."

Ket felt for her bowl of seed drought, slurped it, and smiled into the dark. She still carried her star blade. She felt proud she'd carried it through this whole ordeal, though she didn't even remember how. Her memory was blurry. But here it was, tucked in her esh, a small but certain weight.

She couldn't forget the elements of her vision!

The pink-orange light.

The cacao water.

The red leaves.

She'd tell her brother and sister in the morning. They needed to hear the whole vision, especially the parts that included them, so they could plan for the future. And maybe she'd tell Mutna, too, so she could help them understand how everything connected. Ket wondered where the jaguar had taken her eye. Perhaps to the river, or even all the way to Xibalba. Perhaps she would even begin to see Xibalba, as if she were living half in this world and half in the other. It was an exciting thought. But for now, her eye socket throbbed, growing that hot, itchy black moss. She had to keep herself occupied so that the moss wouldn't drive her mad.

So Ket ate and ate. She was very hungry. She seemed to know where the food was even though she couldn't see it; anytime she reached out, her fingers closed on a morsel.

Then she heard a man's voice below, halting and wheezing. "This child of maize begs leave to address you," he said.

"We greet you, Chenukul of Katwitz. You may rise and approach," said Ajul, in the darkness to her left.

The wheezing voice began again. "Ahau, I come on behalf of the merchants and the farmer lords, who sit below. They . . ." There was a pause, and Ket heard only the murmurs of the crowd on the plaza. "We beg that Ahau would honor your promise, that we would be granted status and rank, as we commence a new empire together."

"We're lonely!" Ket heard a farmer joke. Another shushed him.

"Please excuse his outburst!" Chenukul said. "He does not speak for me."

Another voice came from the same quarter, whiny.

"Chichen Itza does it, I heard so! They're all on a council together and they're all equal."

Ket went still. She could sense the twins' tension. If there was another outburst like that, Ixul would lose her temper.

Then Ajul's voice, calm: "The agreement was that we should have equal status as sovereigns of our own cities, but not that we should be of the same natures. You cannot be a royal member of this or any other house, just as I cannot be a merchant or a farmer."

He spoke so well that there was silence, and Ket hoped that it would last. But then, the whiny voice again: "So you must always sit above and we must always sit below."

Ket knew whose voice she would hear next.

"How dare you complain," Ixul snapped. "Is this your temple? Did your ancestors build it? Did you descend from the Hero Twins? Have your ancestors guarded the way to Xibalba for thousands of years? Can you call the gods? Can you play the ball game? Did you give your eye to a jaguar and live to tell of it, as did the least of us, my sister Ket? Do you shed blood for your people? Or do you fuck dogs in the rotting ruins of a more noble man's home?"

Ket put her hand to her mouth. In the hush that followed, she imagined that the target of this speech had caught flame and was now burning alive in perfect silence.

"Ahau, forgive us, Ahau, forgive him," said the wheezing voice again, this time muffled, so Ket knew he was prostrated again. "He shall be punished for his impertinence. We thank Our Ladyship and Our Lordship for allowing us to sit on the sacred steps of the royal Tzoyna and beg that we continue to be suffered."

Ket wondered whether Ixul would accept his apology. But the next one to speak was Ajul.

"You shall have our sufferance," he said, sounding hurried, as if to preempt Ixul, "but you must remember your place, tonight and forever. There can be no empire if we begin by subverting the natural order."

"Yes, Ahau, yes, of course . . ."

The voice faded away to her right, which meant that Chenukul was descending back to his place. There were no words from the farmers on the left. Ixul and Ajul were in heated conversation, but low enough that Ket couldn't hear them. She hoped that would be the end of the trouble. And "Chenukul"! That was a Nahua name, just like "Patli" was. How much these merchants loved those faraway people and their mumbly language!

At that moment, Ket heard a whistle.

At first she thought it was a powerful birdcall, but then the note changed, and she realized it was an ocarina. Ket turned her head. She couldn't tell where it was coming from—behind the temple, or in the trees? The notes repeated themselves. The melody started low and ended high, as if to ask a question.

Another whistle sounded closer. This one was lower, coming from her right. Ket turned her head toward it. The melody followed the other in close harmony, and then crossed over it, departed and fluttered upward and then settled again, like a bird alighting on a branch.

A third ocarina sounded—high, like a grackle call— this time from the direction of the ball court, where the captives were staked.

The music was starting! Sacred time had steepened its spiral. And somehow, Ket could see the musicians as colored blurs on a field of black. Each wore the color of the direction they'd come: yellow for right, white for left, red for dayrise, black for dayfall. The one in the center stood silent in green. Blurry servants trailed them and scattered allspice leaves from baskets, which men gave to their children for the pleasure of crushing. The warm cinnamon smell began to blend with the pine smoke and the copal.

Xibalba was at hand.

CAYO
2 Chab 1 K'ank'in, Long Count 12.19.19.17.18

---

19 December, 2012

Now was the mustering of the tourists.

At Ceiba Tree Adventures, Leah observed an assemblage of white people in flax and spandex, tightening straps, double-checking for water bottles, adjusting sun hats, standing with arms crossed, trying to get ahold of the experience they were about to have, trying to form a framework of expectation, asking about food, water, snakes, mosquitos, sunscreen, proper footwear, camera safety, the state of the road, the necessity of plastic bags, the appropriateness of socks, the length of the van ride, the length of the jungle hike, the time they could expect to be back, the remoteness of the site, the possibility of souvenirs at the site, the availability of toilet facilities at the site, the swimmability of the flooded passages, the depth of the water, the presence of aquatic life, and the potential for jaguars. A calm young man was trying to answer all their questions. He was wearing a black polo shirt with the Ceiba Tree insignia. Leah squinted to see the badge on the lanyard around his neck. Was it Javier? The man Xander had warned her about? If so, Leah couldn't see why. His hair was messy, as if he'd slept on it that way, but his face was mild and benevolent.

She caught his eye and waved.

He waved back, confused. "Am I taking care of you too?" he called.

"I think so!" she called, then jogged up to him, her backpack swinging side to side. "I'm going to ATM today with Javier . . . ?"

"I am that one Javier Magaña, señorita," he said in mock solemnity. "Did you bring everything on the checklist?"

"Yes."

"Water?"

"Yes."

"Socks?"

"Yes."

"Change of clothes?"

"Yes."

"Good girl. Now I know I do not need to worry about you." He pointed to a van with the green-and-blue appliqué of Ceiba Tree Adventures. "That is your royal coach, princess. We are waiting for two more, but then we are leaving straightaway, so no wandering off, yes?"

"Thank you, I won't."

He turned away with a half smile.

Across the street was Ultimate Cayo Tours, with the maroon-and-yellow veranda, the site of last night's little symposium. Leah didn't see Xander.

"You here for the tour too?"

Leah looked up. Standing over her was a young white man in pink swimming trunks and aqua shoes.

"Yes, the ATM tour," said Leah.

"ATM?"

"Short for Actun Tunichil Muknal."

"Oh! Yeah, us too," he said, glancing back at what Leah assumed to be his girlfriend, a fairy-bodied woman who was coming up the street with a big bottled water. "I'm Luke," he said, offering his hand.

"I'm Leah," she said.

"Ha!" he said. "Luke and Leah. Like in *Star Wars*."

"Almost," she said. "She's Leia, not Leah."

"I like your shoes," said his girlfriend, standing on

her tiptoes to zip open his backpack and stuff in the water bottle.

Leah smiled and turned her leg to show off her green canvas sneakers. "Thank you! I got them at Kmart."

But the girlfriend was preoccupied. "There was dust on everything in that grocery store," she said to Luke. "I picked up a pack of strawberry cookies, but the wrapping had an *actual* film of dust on it, and I thought, No thank you."

Luke said to Leah, "We're here for the end of the world. We're obsessed with it. We go to the cave today, but then we signed up for a special jungle thing at Caracol. They're having a real Maya ceremony and everything."

The woman zipped up his backpack and came around. "I'm Nhi," she said, and shook Leah's hand. She wore fashionable sunglasses, black with gold lettering on the sides.

"Are we introducing ourselves?" said an older white man nearby. There were two of them. One was wearing a grey T-shirt and one was wearing an orange T-shirt. "I'm Paul. This is Ron. We're schoolteachers—well, retired now. What do you do?"

"I'm an entrepreneur," said Luke. "And Nhi—"

"I manage a boutique."

"Whereabouts?"

"Chicago."

"Ah! We're right above you in Wisconsin." One of the schoolteachers—Leah guessed Ron, in the orange T-shirt—turned to her. "And yourself?"

"I'm from Minnesota," she said.

"All northerners!" Paul exclaimed.

"But my father is from Belize. It's part of why I'm here."

"Whoa, so you're half Belizean?" said Luke. "So do you, like, come down here all the time?"

"No, this is my first time."

"That's great. How do you like it?"

Leah stared into the middle distance. "It's like a dream."

"In a good way?"

"Yes. 'Dream' is the only word I can think of. Like it's just easier to exist here. I didn't even know how hard I had to work to exist in Minnesota, until I came here."

Luke said *whoa* and nodded.

There was a shuffling silence.

"So what did you teach?" Nhi asked the two older men.

"English," said Paul.

"Biology," said Ron.

"Are you together?" said Leah.

Paul and Ron did a double take as they registered what Leah was asking them. Then they laughed loudly. "We'll have to tell that one to Bea and Meg," said Ron. "They'll enjoy that. No, sorry to disappoint you. We're all on vacation. They went to London, we went to Belize. One to the colony and one to the colonizer, eh? I think we got the better end of the deal."

"Hello, my friends," said Javier, hovering outside their circle with a little smile. "Are we ready to go? Ready for the Crystal Maiden? Vámanos."

He led them to the van like a mother duck leading her chicks. He saw them each inside. Leah got in the back—she didn't want to talk, just look out the windows—and Javier noticed and pretended to be hurt.

"Are you scared of me, amiga?" Javier called back to her.

Leah smiled. "No, I just like watching the landscape."

"I do not bite."

"I know you don't!"

"It's okay. You are the only single female, so we are just going to sacrifice you at the end anyway."

Everyone laughed.

"Nice rosary you got there," said Ron, pointing to the beads hanging from the rearview mirror.

"I pray it every day, amigo."

"Every day!"

"Every morning when I drive to work. I prayed just before I came to see you. I pray to the morning star."

"Is that significant?"

"To the Maya, amigo, yes, very significant. It is our sacred star, Chak Ek'."

"Isn't the Virgin Mary also called the morning star?" said Nhi.

"Bingo!" called Javier, and turned the key.

Leah noticed that Nhi had a Midwestern plane to her voice. "Did you grow up in Chicago?" she asked.

Nhi whipped around and pushed her sunglasses back. She smelled like coconut lotion. "Right outside, in the suburbs," she said, gathering her silky hair to one side. "But then I went to school in L.A. and I just couldn't take it. Moved right back after I graduated."

"Couldn't take what?"

"The heat. It made everything feel cheap, somehow."

"Huh."

"I kind of feel that way about here. I don't know. I guess I'm just a Midwestern girl. But you are too, right?"

"I was born in Minnesota, but I really hate the cold."

"Wow. How old are you?"

"Nineteen."

"How did you survive this long?"

"I don't know. I don't think I knew there was any other way to be. I just always underdressed and wished it were summer. But here, it's always summer."

Javier pulled out of the parking lot and headed up the street, past the school, around the park, past the market grounds, and down to the low bridge. The river was swollen and brown from last night's rain. Leah watched out the windows as if it were a movie she'd been waiting to see her whole life. The others' conversation blended together in a happy buzz.

"So, Javier," said Ron. "You grew up here?"

"Yes I did, amigo. I grew up near Benque Viejo, to the west. I am Maya born and bred."

"Maya? Aren't the Maya extinct?"

Javier got excited. "I will pose a question to you right now, amigo," he said. "Where did all the Maya go?"

"Well, that's what I want to know. They just disappeared, right?"

"Look around. Look at that woman there, see, at the pineapple stand. Is she disappeared?"

"So they're still around?"

"There are millions of Maya living today. Mopan Maya. Kekchi Maya. Yucatec Maya. We did not disappear. We just changed."

"Do you speak Maya?"

"Walak wa a tan ix tan? Walak in tan ix Mopan Maya, yes I do."

"Ho-ho! Paul, did you hear that?"

"I sure did. How many Maya are there in Belize?"

"That is complicated, amigo. Most people in Belize have some Maya blood, but not everyone calls themselves Maya. They call themselves Creole and Mestizo. But the census says that eleven percent of the population calls themselves Maya."

"Do you call yourself Maya?"

"I do, amigo. I am Mopan Maya, raised by a Maya father and learning Maya traditions. I am descended from the people who lived here long before the Europeans came."

"Would other Belizeans also say that you're Maya?"

"No, not everyone would agree with me, because I did not grow up in a Maya village."

"How many languages do you speak?"

"Mopan, English, Spanish, and Kriol."

"Speak in Kriol."

"It is closely related to English. If I say in English, 'I am going to the market,' in Kriol I say, 'Ah gwehn da maakit.'"

"And we dummies only speak English."

"Nhi speaks Thai."

"You know I don't. Shut up."

Leah tried to read the signs on the plywood kiosks: johnny cake, lime juice, papusa. The jostling in the backseat was pleasant, even arousing. The van turned into the sun, and light flooded the windows. Javier flipped the visor down.

"We Maya never disappeared," he said again, "we just changed. The archaeologists say we 'collapsed,' but really, only the elites collapsed. Many things at once put pressure on the royalty, so the farmers lost confidence in them, and they no longer had the power to control or persuade them. Some stayed here. Others migrated."

"It's hard for us to imagine that."

"Sí amigo, it was happening slowly, over many generations. They were not sitting around saying 'Here we are in the middle of the decline of the Maya.'"

"I bet they didn't even call themselves Maya."

"You are right. The word 'Maya' was a mistake by the Spanish."

Leah watched a Mennonite buggy with two grey ponies, and a skinny redheaded man in white suspenders, holding the reins.

She sneezed violently.

Javier came to attention. "Are you all right, hermana? Are all your organs still intact?"

"Yes," Leah said. "Whew! I don't know where that came from."

"If you sneeze, do you know what that means? It means your sweetheart is thinking of you."

"Oh-h-h-h-h!" said Ron, swiveling. "Do you have a sweetheart?"

Leah saw Javier's eye on her in the rearview mirror.

"Tengo varios novios," she said.

Javier almost drove off the road and had to jerk the steering wheel back.

"What did she say?" Ron demanded of Javier.

Pause. "She said, 'Only Ron.'"

More laughter.

Silence.

Leah caught Javier's eye in the rearview mirror again, then looked away, smirking.

The countryside passed, each feature more brilliant than the last. First Galen University, red and white, nestled between hills; then the hills dropped into a green pastureland, snug in a blanket of mist. White cows and ceiba trees appeared and disappeared like ghosts. Leah pressed her palm to the window and fogged the glass with her breath.

"Is there a lot of poverty around here?" Luke asked Javier.

Pause.

"No, amigo, not exactly poverty. We do pretty well in Belize, compared with the rest of Central America."

"I heard it's the most expensive—"

"No, second most expensive—"

"—country to travel in, if you're American or Canadian or whatever."

"Costa Rica is most expensive."

"Oh, right."

"Have you been to Costa Rica?"

"Yeah, we've done Costa Rica. That was our first trip together, right babe?"

"We did Montevideo—"

"Monteverde, babe."

"—and Playa Samara, that was the best. The sand was so soft."

"Have you been to Costa Rica, Javier?"

"I have not, amigo."

A short silence.

"Oh, look at this countryside," said Paul.

"So green," said Ron.

Javier said, "You are seeing ancient Maya cities."

"What do you mean?"

"Two million people used to live in what is now western Belize. Who knows the population of Belize today?"

No one knew.

"It is three hundred and twenty-seven thousand."

"Jeez!" said Nhi. "So that's a whole order of magnitude fewer people."

"Yes, amiga. This area is deserted, compared to what it was at the height of the ancient Maya. In that time, all of this land was cleared for farming. See all of the mounds in the fields? When you start looking for them, you see they are everywhere."

"What are the mounds?"

"The foundations of Maya houses, amigo. If your house had a stone foundation, you were well-off."

Leah looked. There were humps in the ground everywhere, like the shoulders of giants rising out of the earth. They reminded her of the ruins she saw by the highway in Minnesota.

"And what did the cave mean to them?"

"The cave was a very sacred place that only elites were allowed to go."

"Elites—?"

"Royals, priests, kings, nobles. And they brought sacrifice victims, of course." Javier noticed Leah in the rearview again. "Are you still alive, amiga?"

"Yeah! Fine!"

"Okay, just checking. No sleeping!"

"I'm not sleeping. I'm wide awake. I'm so awake."

The others didn't know how to respond to such

fervor, which Leah was used to, so she tuned them out and kept watching the scenery. It was like a film reel unspooling before her eyes. There were palm trees upon palm trees, some fat and wide, some tall and slender, their fans like hands, all waving. Houses on stilts. Sleek SUVs. A black dog trotting along her morning errands, teats swinging. The air was wet. The ground was wet. The sun drenched it all in a golden syrup. Already, she couldn't imagine leaving this place. The land made sense to her. The particular combination of flora and fauna and smiles and hills and palms and cows and wetness and clouds—it all made sense to her. She had to breathe around the lump in her throat. The trees were shaped like the trees from her childhood dreams: small, with a rounded profile, and delicate branches like filigree. There was emerald green and lime green and olive green all mixed, like the green choir of the crayon box, dumped and scattered.

"Leah!" said Nhi again.

"Yes! Sorry!"

"Paul asked if you want a Snickers."

"Ooh, a Snickers! Yes, please."

"They're just the little size," he said, passing one back. "I hear they're good fuel for caving. Is that right, Javier? Or is that an urban legend?"

"Or a rural legend!" Ron said. "Dad joke, sorry."

"Snickers are good, amigo," Javier said. "You burn a lot of calories in the cave."

"How do you burn them? I mean, how strenuous is this?"

"Climbing, walking, swimming, and your body keeping warm. But do not worry. A lot of people do it every day, especially with the 2012 craze."

"So tell us what 2012 means."

"According to the Maya, it is just a new beginning."

"Don't tell that to Nhi."

"Do you want the world to end, amiga?"

"Hey, sure. Couldn't get any worse."

Laughter.

Her voice assumed an apologetic tone. "I just really got interested after I saw this documentary on National Geographic."

"We helped with that."

"What, you personally, did?"

"Ceiba Tree Adventures did. We won the contract over Ultimate Cayo."

"Is there some sort of rivalry going on there?"

"No." He paused. "Well, some might say, maybe, yes."

"We knew we picked the right one!"

"I walked past Ultimate Cayo yesterday and they just seemed shady to me."

"Shady how?"

"Just the dudes outside, leering. They seemed fake."

"Well, they all have to be fake to some extent, right? They're selling something."

"I guess."

"Their culture. Or, access to it."

Javier didn't respond.

The van bounced on a series of potholes. Leah grasped at the seat to steady herself, remembering the car on the frozen river, in Minnesota, in another life. Here it wasn't cold; here, her hands slipped because of the humidity. The water she'd drunk was heavy in her groin, making it sensitive, burning like a live coal every time the van hit a bump.

"This is it!" called Javier.

A brown road sign with white lettering read:

Actun Tunichil Muknal
Archaeological Reserve
7 Miles

An arrow pointed the way. Chickens and dogs ran alongside them on the dirt road. After a half mile, they stopped at a kiosk.

"Welcome to Teakettle Village!" Javier announced. "It is our last pit stop before the big show."

Paul and Ron went to buy water. Leah got out and approached a bush growing through a chain-link fence, where butterflies were landing, whole flocks of them, yellow and blue. She held out her hand and one landed on the heel of her palm.

Javier wandered over, half a cookie in hand. "You have the magic touch," he said. "You doing all right, amiga?"

"Yes," she said. The butterfly rose, and they watched it flutter away. "I'm really enjoying myself. But 'enjoy' is not the right word. I don't know why I feel this way. It's just trees and hills, but they're the *right* trees and hills."

Javier took a drink from his Coke bottle, unfazed, nodding. "Belize is the most beautiful land in the world. I have never wanted to leave in my life." He clapped her on the shoulder. His hand was heavy and warm. "I am just looking out for you so that no jaguars get you."

Luke swaggered up with his water bottle in hand. "So, you married?" he said to Javier.

"Why, you interested?" said Javier.

They laughed. Leah noticed that Javier hadn't answered the question.

Luke could roll with it too. "Yeah, man, I might be available, but you gotta get me a good ring."

"Do not joke," said Javier. "You don't know how many marriage proposals I've gotten."

"Dude, seriously?"

"You better Belize it, amigo. These women want to stay to become citizens."

"Not because you're so handsome?" said Leah.

Javier widened his eyes at her. "Uh-oh, I got to watch out for this one," he said. "Luke, protect me."

Another van pulled in behind them and they moved out of the way. This one had a cracked maroon-and-yellow stripe around the perimeter, which were the colors of Ultimate Cayo. Xander was driving. He saw her with Javier. He looked away.

Paul and Ron returned with their water bottles.

They got back into the van.

They drove out of Teakettle Village and into the countryside. Shreds of cloud ran low and ragged over the hills. Leah missed the reverie of the Western Highway, but now she could see that it had merely been the journey to church, and Teakettle was just the milling in the narthex, the meet-and-greet before the Mass. They drove over the top of a ridge, then descended into fog.

"Now we are entering Roaring Creek Valley," said Javier. "Do you see these mists? That's how you know there are caves beneath us. The caves breathe out their vapor, like they are exhaling."

The road curved through the fog. First they passed through tall slender trees planted in regular rows, with mottled brown trunks; these were teak. The teak plantation gave way to low fields of green sprouts, also in rows; these were beans. Again the mounds rose up in the fields like shoulders. Maya houses everywhere. Maya garages. Maya restaurants. Maya dance halls. Maya roller skating rinks where Maya adolescents held hands, ages ago.

Then they were driving through orange groves. Each tree was hung with green balls like Christmas ornaments.

"Beautiful!" she cried out.

Javier glanced back at her. "Do you like oranges?"

"I love them. I've never seen them actually growing on trees before! I knew they did, but . . . here they are, right here!"

"We can stop on the way back and pick some."

Leah shook her head in amazement. She was remembering her favorite childhood book, *The Twelve Dancing Princesses*, where the heroines passed through a silver forest, a golden forest, and a diamond forest to reach their princes, who rowed them across a glass lake in boats shaped like swans. She felt like a princess just now, with a royal entourage.

They crossed a wooden bridge over a swift river.

"That was Roaring Creek," said Javier. "If it takes more rain in the coming days, they might shut down the cave."

"How high does it have to get?" asked Ron.

"The rangers take measurements. If it is six in the morning, and too high, they start putting out calls that the site is closed."

"What if it rises really quickly?"

"Then you don't want to be in the cave, amigo."

"What would happen?"

"You would drown. Or get trapped, until the water goes down, but who knows how long that would take. Other things would get you—like hypothermia."

They drove up from the river and emerged into more bean fields. Mud spattered on the windows. There was less talking now. Everyone was content to watch the movie. A towering tree stood guard over the road.

"Yax che," said Javier, pointing it out. "The ceiba tree, sacred to the Maya. The namesake of our tour company."

The van made a wide left turn and stopped at a house on stilts. A ranger in a khaki uniform came up to the window.

Paul waved and said, "Help, help, he's kidnapped us."

Laughter.

The ranger gave his speech. "Good morning how do you do welcome to Belize you have now passed into the Tapir. Mountain. Nature. Reserve. This is a protected area and we ask a few things of you to protect the integrity of the site no bug spray no sunscreen no lotion no Chapstick no lip balm of any kind these things we put on our bodies over time they will get into the stream and erode the natural. Limestone. Formations. Over. Time. We want to protect our environmental heritage for many many generations to come does everyone please understand."

Vigorous assent.

"Then please enjoy your time in the cave."

They parked in a rough gravel lot. Three men watched them from under a tarp, one leaning against a pole, one sitting at a picnic table, and one lying in a hammock with a machete on his chest. Leah found the machete very exciting. She nearly tripped out of the van. The three men regarded her, motionless and amused, like cats.

"Hi!" she said. "Are you the guards to the cave?"

"Yes gyal," said one. "Yu need fi noa di seekrit paaswerd."

"Machete?"

"Da Javier tel yu fu seh dat?"

Javier strolled up to the spotlight. "Noh bada ahn."

"Raas, wi no di bada ahn."

"I asked if there was a secret password," Leah explained. "I wanted to guess it."

The man in the hammock slapped the flat of his machete on his bare chest. "You don't need a password. You got the best guide in Cayo, right here."

Leah could see that they were all teasing. Javier slapped hands with them, half-hugged. She could tell they liked and respected him.

The other tourists returned from the potty shack across the parking lot. Javier distributed blue plastic helmets and showed them how to carry their water bottles inside them. He told them what to expect: an easy half-hour hike, during which they would cross Roaring Creek three times. He grabbed a walking stick that lay against a tree, then led them on a path through the jungle. "The first river crossing is the deepest," he called. "The current is not too strong, but the water will come up to your chin because of all the rain."

Leah was last in line. She wanted to be first and last. She wanted to rush ahead but linger, too. She stepped into the water and it felt deliciously cool. She waded in farther. Already the line was making its way across; Javier was at the front, his walking stick and khaki bag balanced on his head. The water rose to her knees, her thighs, her stomach, her chest, her throat, her chin. She'd forgotten to pee. The pressure made her groin burn hot against the cold water. She watched Javier emerge on the far bank, his clothes stuck to his body, now, and he stripped down to a black tank, which gleamed like sealskin against the hard curves of muscle.

"Leah!" called Javier. "Don't fall!"

She fell.

She came back up, sputtering.

"Oh no!" called Javier, who clearly wanted to laugh. "Are you all right, hermana?"

"I'm fine! I'm thrilled, in fact!" she called back. "Now I'm properly baptized!"

"You are mixing religions, señorita. That is sacrilege."

"Mixing religions isn't bad!" she said. "That's how you start new ones."

She trudged up the steps from the river, where the others were standing. Now she was aware of her own body: her tank top stuck to her bikini top, which stuck to her skin, all slick and shiny, nipples hard, but they were in the jungle, so it was warm, so it was okay. Leah noticed that Javier waited for just the moment when the others had turned their backs to look at her more fully.

He offered her a hand up the last step.

"Gracias," she said.

"De nada," he said, and turned to walk ahead, too quickly.

Oh yes, Leah thought. This is happening.

They hiked on. They stopped every now and then to look at features along the trail. The rubber tree. The chicle tree. The cacao tree. The give-and-take tree. Droppings of an ocelot. Tracks of a tapir. Highways of leafcutter ants, ferrying shreds of green. Javier stopped to pick passion flowers, and gave them to everyone to wear in their hair. *These are signs and wonders*, Leah said to herself, *signs and wonders*.

"Have you ever seen any jaguars?" asked Ron.

Javier didn't answer for a few beats, which made Leah think he might not have heard him.

"Yes," said Javier. "But many more have seen me than I have seen."

"What do you mean?"

Javier halted and whirled around. "Stay very still," he said.

Everyone stopped, as if in a game of freeze. Leah's blood quickened. Her eyes swung right and left, but she saw and heard nothing, except for the fans of green and the cries of birds.

Javier spoke to everyone in a soft voice, but was looking at Leah. "If there are jaguars near," he said, "we will never know. They are able to see us, but we are not able to see them. They come and go from their world into ours, but they are watching us, always."

Javier turned and kept walking up the trail.

Nhi turned to Leah. "Jesus, he gave me chills," she said.

Leah nodded, too thrilled to speak.

After the third river crossing, they ascended into a clearing, edged with towering palms. At the far end there was a thatch longhouse with benches and backpacks on pegs.

"Welcome to Camp Xibalba," said Javier. "Ladies and gentlemen, here is your last pit stop. I suggest you use it."

The others wandered off, but Leah was still looking up, admiring how the sunlight filtered through the canopy. "It's like a cathedral," she said.

Javier nodded at her. "Just wait till the cave, hermana."

"But how can anything be more beautiful than this?"

Javier pointed across the clearing, to the top of a stone stairway. For the first time, Leah registered the sound of rushing water. She was almost afraid. She had the sense that if she set eyes on that water, something would cross over in her.

"You'll see," he said. He bent down, rummaging in his pack.

"I've never been in a cave at all."

"I've been giving tours to this cave every day for fifteen blessed years," he said.

"So you're like a priest."

His head snapped up. He was amused. "What?"

"It's like you perform Mass every day, for the pilgrims who've never seen it. You have to make it new, like it's never been done before."

He looked down into his bag, which he was repacking with batteries and water. "You could say that, señorita," he said. "I like that."

Leah was fussing with her helmet strap. Javier noticed, walked up to her. He was just as tall as she was, five foot nothing, and smelled like Irish Spring. He took the straps in his fingers, snapped the buckle under her chin, and guided her hand to the outlying strap. "Pull that until it's tight, chula."

"What does 'chula' mean?"

"Pretty," he said. "It means pretty."

Javier walked away to check in with the others and Leah thought, This is a man who's at ease in rest or in motion, and puts all other beings at ease.

Just then, Xander came up into the clearing.

Four tourists straggled behind him, panting. He didn't seem to notice. He peeled away to the longhouse and started to unpack his gear, looking up and around, restless, as if looking for someone. Then he saw Leah and they locked eyes for a moment. What was he saying with his eyes? He had been so rude to her the night before, dismissing her euphoria as a kind of mental illness, but until that point she'd been very attracted to him. He reminded her of Javier, in fact—they even looked alike, with the same height, same stout build, same square face and dark eyes.

But Javier was cool water, solid earth.

And Xander was hot fire, flickering wind.

With his eyes he said, *We're not through.*

"Miss Leah," said a voice.

It was Javier. He was calling her over to join the group. He glanced at Xander, as if wanting to hurry. There were three other groups in the clearing, all somewhere along the appointed timeline, one just arriving, one just fanning out into the trees, and one just departing down the steps to where the roar was coming from. She imagined that they were all one eternal tour group, appearing in a time-lapse video that spanned thousands of years.

"Amigas y amigos," intoned Javier. "We are almost at the cave. The cave was used as a sacred site by the ancient Maya for more than two millennia. After de-population of the city centers, the cave was still well known to local people. They showed it to the archaeologist Dr. Thomas Miller in 1986, who mapped it in a scientific way. After that, the cave became a tourist destination. This camp, the trail to get here—none of it existed in 1986. If you look around this area you can see more mounds—there, there, and back there in the trees, amigo—which were all structures the Maya built. Maybe they were guardhouses. Maybe a priest lived here, who took tribute from pilgrims. All this land used to be cleared. If you walk through the jungle in that direction"—Javier pointed downriver—"you will come upon mounds thirty feet high. Those are temples and palaces. There is a city there, called Tzoyna, the capital of the ancient kingdom of the Tzoyna, which means 'Mother's Cut' in Ch'ol Maya. There were many other settlements in this valley as well, and we do not know what the Maya called them, but we know they were all connected by limestone roads called sacbes. Now there are hundreds of caves in this area, but caves with live water"—Javier gestured in the direction of the roar—"were especially sacred. Because water is what? Rain. And the Maya needed rain, my friends. Especially in times of drought."

Solemn nodding. Leah was fidgeting and biting her lip. She wanted to run toward the roar.

"So now we are going to descend to the entrance of the cave. Vámanos," said Javier, and again led them like ducklings. Leah was last.

At the bottom of the steps, there was a giant flame.

That was the first word that came to Leah's mind. It looked like a black flame cut into the mountain. At the top of the flame, knives of rock stabbed down, and green ropes dripped and crossed like a beaded curtain. A sheet of turquoise water poured out.

Javier turned so he could be seen by the whole group.

"May I have your attention please," said Javier.

Leah willed herself to look at him and not at the black flame.

Javier drove the tip of his machete into the ground.

"Friends, here is where I must ask for your complete cooperation," he said.

Vigorous assent.

"The cave is dangerous. I have not had any serious accidents in fifteen blessed years, and I do not want to start today. I have a first aid kit but I do not want to use it. I'm trained in cave rescue, but I do not want to use that either. When I tell you to do something, you do it. We will be in a single-file line. When I say to the first person in the line, 'Look out for this rock,' or 'Don't touch the left side,' you pass it on to the people behind you. We depend on each other for safety.

"There is also the issue of respect. The cave is a sacred place. That is true even if you do not say you are religious. The cave was sacred to the Maya then, and it is still sacred to Maya who are alive now, and that is including me, though I am also Catholic. There are many in Belize who do not want this cave open to the public at all. It is a church for them. In ancient times as well as today, these waters are collected and used for healing purposes. I myself have seen them heal the sick. And here we are going to be swimming in that holy water like it is a swimming pool. So again, I ask for your respect. In the cave, we do not speak loudly. We do not yell. We do not relieve ourselves. You may see other groups with markings on their cheeks, using the rocks to paint the markings, but I do not do this, for me it is an issue of respect. We do not take anything from the cave. We keep our bodies covered. Gentlemen, keep your shirts on. Ka-peesh?"

Solemn nodding. Everyone wanted to be good for Javier.

"This is the entrance to the cave. First there is the light zone, where we can still see sunlight. Then there is the dark zone, where there is no more sunlight. Follow me—be careful; the bottom steps are slippery, so you will step where I step, and keep your center of gravity low. And then we will swim across the pool. Can everyone swim?" asked Javier.

Nodding.

"Okay then, I will meet you on the other side of the pool and then we will embark into Xibalba, the Other World, the Place of Fear. Are there any questions?"

"How can a place so beautiful be a place of fear?" Leah blurted out.

Javier cracked a smile. "Maybe for you, señorita, it will not be."

Leah watched the others wade into the turquoise pool. She was deep in memory and deeply present, both at once; at this moment there was no distinction. She was remembering how when she was a little girl, her mother had taken her to the Waffa Chocolate Factory, and the whole lobby had glass walls and ceilings to keep it warm, because they'd planted enormous palm trees and other tropical plants in the lobby area, where a waterfall of chocolate milk coursed down the wall and circled the gift shop. The ride itself involved sitting in a moving car and gliding past various exhibits, which you could look at but not touch, of animatronic workers in burlap shirts and cutoff pants, smiling, harvesting cacao beans, raking them, roasting them. The leaves of the palm trees had always seemed too dark and glossy to be real. They felt fake, just like these palm trees overhead, just like the moss Leah was now touching on the rocks. Everything here felt too beautiful to be real; as if it were a very cunning counterfeit, a deception built for tourists. But she had it all backward, she thought: she'd loved that factory because it reminded her of this, the real thing she'd intuited but not yet seen. This place knew her. It had wanted her to come for a long time.

Javier stood knee-deep, waiting for her.

"Are you ready?" he said.

"Is this real?" she asked.

He smiled so that dimples sprang in his cheeks, and gestured her to enter.

Leah waded in. She wanted to slow down time. The color of this pool was impossible, now emerald, now jade. Little white fish nibbled at her legs. She fell into an easy breaststroke. She looked up and rolled over onto her back. She wondered if she could stay just in this chamber, go no farther, and be happy.

Javier swam in last, climbed onto a shelf of rock, and stood to address the tourists who were now standing waist-deep in the river. The roar was much louder here, originating up and away to their left.

"How deep is the cave?" asked Ron.

"Five kilometers, amigo. But tour groups only go as far as the step-up rock."

"Have you ever been all the way in?" asked Leah.

Javier addressed the group as if he hadn't heard her.

"All right, amigas y amigos, you can switch on your headlamps now." He demonstrated. "Press once for low light, twice for bright light, and three times for strobe."

They all managed, except for Luke, who got stuck on strobe and tried to argue that it was defective. Nhi laughed and mocked him. Javier fixed it and clapped him on the shoulder. Meanwhile, Leah noticed the fine white vapor in the beam of her headlamp. She blew into it. Her breath sent it swirling.

"Ahead you can hear a waterfall," said Javier. "Follow me and put your feet where I put my feet. I'll meet you at the top."

Leah felt cool and wet and powerful. The pressure in her bladder was making her horny. She liked how her green sneakers sloshed and dragged in the water. She followed the line of people around the bend and up a tumble of rocks, bending double, testing for footholds, squeezing the stones for purchase. The cave water coursed over her legs. It felt like one long sensuous baptism.

They reassembled at the top. "Everyone okay?" asked Javier.

Assent.

"I have observed all of you and you are all doing well, so I don't need to reshuffle your order. But if you need to stop me at any time, just say, Javier"—he whistled one short loud blast with no fingers, just his mouth, which Leah found terribly erotic—"stop a minute please, I need to tie my shoe, I am stuck, I feel I want to stop and look at this formation, anything. Every now and then I will call back to make sure everyone is still here. Leah?"

"Yes!"

"Don't get any ideas."

"Too late, I already have too many ideas!"

"Uh-oh. Do I need to keep you next to me?"

"No!"

"Do you promise to behave?"

"Yes!"

"Okay . . ." He narrowed his eyes at her, teasing, and pointed with his finger—*I'm watching you*—as if in apology for having ignored her question before.

He led them through a breakdown of boulders. The stone was marbled grey and mustard. She was euphoric. They all were. The darkness, the rushing water, the daggers of rock. Now they'd begun to understand the gravity of this place. Javier led them down through a tight squeeze into an arched corridor, chest-deep. This was yet another place of ecstasy to Leah. She wanted to stay in this passage, just this passage, and listen to the water. But there was still so much more to see. She found it uncanny that the cave was so navigable. All the spaces were human-sized, as if, again, the cave was actually an artificial tourist attraction, built to lure them.

They ascended into an open chamber. Leah was dismayed to see sunlight. Hadn't she been promised darkness? But there was a sinkhole above, dripping with vines.

Javier stepped onto a rock and addressed them.

"This is the end of the light zone, my friends," he said. "We are entering the dark zone. From here, is no more sunlight."

Good, Leah thought. I don't think the sun we see is the actual sun anyway.

"Here is where I like to point out the deep history of the place we are standing," said Javier. "Millions of years ago, this land was at the bottom of the ocean. All the little sea creatures had shells made of calcite, and when they died, their bodies would fall to the seafloor and build up into what you see here." He pointed to the coarse white rock. "This is limestone, also called karst. It is very permeable to water. All of western Belize is like Swiss cheese. Over millions of years, the holes became as big as this cave."

They left the light and walked upriver. Here it was shallow, just a rippling sheet of water. The stones were like the assortments you could buy at office supply stores: some round, some blocky, some like slate with sharp edges, like the ones she'd vomited into outside the clinic in Minnesota.

Javier addressed them over his shoulder. "Can you imagine the Maya making their way through this cave a thousand years ago?" he said. "This section is easy. But back at the entrance, climbing up that waterfall?"

Leah saw, ahead, a tiny star.

"All they had was pine torches, amigos. If they went out, they would be stuck in the dark."

The star was tinged yellow, just like the morning star she'd seen when she first arrived.

"What would they do if they got stuck in the dark?" said Ron.

Leah wondered if she was hallucinating. But the star just swelled, got brighter.

"They would have to feel their way out," said Javier. "But only if they were near the entrance, where they could feel which way the water was going. But if they were not near the entrance, well then, amigo . . ."

Leah came upon the star. It was the eye of an enormous spider, fastened like a brooch to the breast of the flowstone.

"Javier," she said.

He stopped and wheeled round with a splash. "Yes, Miss Leah at the Back."

"Look at this."

Everyone turned to look, yeeped. Luke hid behind Nhi. Ron clutched at Paul. The spider was the size of Leah's hand, with grey legs cocked like elbows. It didn't move.

Javier came to stand beside her.

"You found a whip spider," he said. "Very common in the cave. They're harmless."

"The eye looked like a star in my headlamp," said Leah. "I was so sure it was a star."

"Don't say that, señorita," he said. "The actual star will get jealous."

She looked up, startled, and he winked.

They went on. The passage cut to the right, then again to the left. The sand dropped away and they waded into the river again. Leah had begun to mark the phases of their journey: First, the waterfall. Then, the canal. Then, the sinkhole. Then, the shallow sheet. She went over the phases in her mind, trying to make associations with numbers, so she could remember. It felt important to remember: One, the waterfall. Two, the canal. Three, the sinkhole. But now there were new things to remember. Four, the huge flowstone on the left. Five, the slim beach that looked like a perfect sitting spot. When she looked up she saw diamonds, but realized they were drops of water hanging from each stalactite, like milk quivering from a cow's teat. There were tiny gnats and pale crickets, moving too quickly for her eye to track. The walls were colored like marbled fat.

Javier stopped and shone his beam up on a ledge above them.

"That is a place where the Maya conducted rituals," he said. "Up there, archaeologists have found blood-letting bowls. The Maya would offer their own blood from the finger or the tip of the penis."

"Oh God," said Ron. "I'll take Methodist any day."

"Did bloodletting give them visions?" Paul asked.

"No, that is a misconception," said Javier. "The visions came from taking psilocybin mushrooms, which they viewed as a god in itself. They did experience pain from self-cutting, but that alone did not induce visions."

"But what they saw wasn't real," said Nhi.

Javier cocked his head. "Not real, amiga?"

"Meaning, just happening inside their heads, not externally verifiable."

"Does that mean it's not real?"

"Well," Nhi said, waving her hand. "I'm not explaining myself very well."

Javier was generous with her. "I know what you mean. But ask yourself about your definition of real. If what is real is only what scientists can test, well . . . that leaves out most of human experience."

"So what was the purpose of the cutting?" asked Leah.

Javier chose his words carefully. "It was an offering to Xibalba, amiga. Blood was a gift to the gods to say, Here, take this essence of my mortal life, in hopes that you will give me the essence of your divine life in return."

Leah pondered this.

Javier turned and went on. "We're almost there," he called back. The column followed. But Leah couldn't stop turning over his words. He'd said that blood was a gift to the gods of Xibalba. Is that what she was supposed to do? What if this was her only chance? Six: they crawled over sheets of bubbled rock like peanut brittle. Seven: another chamber, chest-deep in water. Eight: the floor rose again and the cave narrowed into a tumbledown of rock, metallic, rounded, and hard, like they were climbing through a field of meteorites. What if she never got to come back? How could Xibalba know she was there? What if blood was the only way Xibalba could see her? But what could she use to cut?

Leah loitered behind the rest, scanning the river

for a sharp rock. She knew she had to be quick. She'd have to pretend it was an accident so that the others wouldn't get the wrong idea. She crouched, rummaged. The column was moving ahead. She was running out of time. She picked up one, examined the edge. Not sharp enough. She dropped it. She picked up another. This one was nearly black, like slate, with a sharp edge. It could work. She said in her mind *For Xibalba*, and dashed it hard across her finger.

It worked. Too well, too deeply, already, she could see. She blinked back sudden and involuntary tears. The blood made an unbroken stream, then slowed to drops, each splashing in the water and making tiny clouds.

She frowned. The clouds weren't moving with the water. They were moving against it.

She didn't have time to keep watching, though. She'd lingered long enough.

"Javier," she called.

A turn and splash, far ahead. "Yes, Miss Leah in the Back!"

She tried to sound innocent. "I cut myself."

The column stopped as Javier and the others back-tracked to where Leah stood, looking down at her finger.

"You sure did, hermana," he said.

Nhi sucked her teeth. "Ouch, are you okay?"

"Oh I'm fine. It just hurts a little."

"How did you do that," said Javier.

"I just . . ." Leah gestured at the river stones, imagined a lie about stumbling and falling; but hated lying and tried to say it another way. "I picked up a sharp one."

"You got a little too inspired with all that blood sacrifice stuff back there," said Ron.

"You ain't seen nothing yet, amigo," said Javier. "Wait till we get to the upper chamber." To Leah, he patted a boulder. "Sit here." He took off his rucksack, unrolled the top, and located his first aid kit. Leah sat with her hand held out. She tried to angle her finger so that the blood would run down her arm instead of falling into the water. She didn't want the others to see what she'd seen. But in her mind she said, *Take it, I'm here.*

"I'm sorry for making trouble," said Leah.

"Hakuna matata," said Javier. "Hold still." But Leah could hear the tension in his voice.

Now she could hear why. The next group was coming, the one led by Xander. Javier worked quickly. He used one antiseptic cloth to apply pressure to the cut, and another to wipe it; then he applied antibiotic ointment and a Band-Aid. Xander's voice got nearer.

Javier unwrapped a length of gauze, snapped it off in his teeth, wound it around Leah's finger, and tied it off.

Xander came around the corner. The beam of his headlamp fell on Javier.

He took in the scene for a beat, then turned to halt his group.

Javier rushed to repack. "He will give us room," he said quietly. "You all right?"

"Great, thank you."

"Vámanos, chula."

Javier walked ahead so quickly he tripped over a rock, and Ron's arm shot out to steady him.

Leah looked back. Xander kept talking and gesturing to his group. He seemed to be in performance mode.

The passage made a gentle turn. Javier stopped at a boulder twice as tall as he was, and patted it. "Friends, this is the step-up rock, where we climb to the upper chambers," he said. "I will stand here and tell you where to step up, so that you will do it safely. Ron?"

Leah wandered ahead. The cave went on, a perfectly walkable stream, in a dark curve to the left.

"Can we go farther in?" she asked.

"No, señorita," said Javier, his eyes on Ron, patting one place and then another for him to put his feet. "This is where the river portion of our tour ends."

"But can you go farther into the cave?"

"I don't know," said Javier, vaguely, now helping Paul up the boulder.

Leah was sure he was lying. She decided to call his bluff. "Why?"

"There are no Maya artifacts past this point."

Leah felt a holy quiet bloom inside her. "Why not?" she said.

"Eeek!" Nhi cried, losing her footing. Javier had to pay closer attention to her, and dropped the conversation.

Leah used the opportunity to wander toward the bend. Her finger throbbed in its dressing. Of all the parts of the cave they'd passed through, this seemed to be the most perfect, somehow, the most made for human habitation. She was ankle-deep in water clear as crystal. She could see every stone, lucid, bright, distinct. She dropped to her knees, a gentle suppliant, and faced the darkness. If the whole expedition was a Mass, this was Communion. What was around this bend? What was in that wonderful soft blackness beyond?

"Leah?" called Javier.

She turned around. "I love this place," she said.

He shook his head. "Madre de Dios, gyal, I knew I'd have to keep an eye on you. Come on, it's time for you to climb up."

Leah made herself get up and slosh back.

Up on the ledge, they took off their shoes and crawled through a narrow opening. "You like tight spaces," Javier teased Leah. "We call that a squeeze freak." But she didn't answer. She missed the water. She didn't like these dry upper chambers, which she was sure were fascinating, but to her, felt like a boring detour. To soothe herself, she kept her eyes open for more whip spiders, their eyes signaling in the language she could understand but not speak.

Leah half listened to Javier. He was explaining that this huge chamber was a travertine labyrinth, left by ancient rivers. They stopped at pools one by one, like Stations of the Cross, and Javier explained each. Here is the baby skull. Here is the pot with the distinctive monkey insignia. Here is the skull with sharpened teeth. Here is the pile of shards. Here is another pile of shards. Here is the skull with the pumpkin-shaped head. Here are a tibia and ulna tossed together like fiddlesticks. Here is the rock that looks like Ixchel if you shine a flashlight on it. Was it deliberately carved to look like Ixchel? Who knows.

On the far side of the chamber, Javier led them through a tumbledown to a terrace of shallow pools, where an aluminum ladder was tied to the wall.

"Here is the ancient Maya ladder," he joked.

"How did they get up there?" asked Nhi.

"The Maya knew about ladders," said Javier. "Probably they got there the same way we are getting there, amiga, but their ladder has long washed away."

They ascended one by one. They found themselves in a narrow passage. Javier led them farther in and directed them to stand against the wall. Leah noticed, again, that he seemed nervous, glancing toward the ladder and the oncoming voices. But first he had to finish his performance.

"There are two victims here," he said. "One died on their knees." He ran his flashlight over a pile of bones, crusted with lime. The skull had an oblong hole in it, a gap of blackness. Leah noticed Javier staring at it, his mouth open, as if he were about to address it. But he didn't. He said, "The other died lying on her back, as if pushed or thrown. She is the Crystal Maiden." He ran his flashlight over a small sparkling skeleton, arms and legs flung outward.

Leah frowned at it. "That's not a she," she said.

Javier looked amused. "Can you see up her skirt?"

Leah stared. She didn't know how she knew, but the skeleton was that of a young man, not a young woman. "I just know."

"Crystal Hombre doesn't have as much of a ring to it," Paul joked in the awkward silence.

Leah smiled tightly. She knew she was making things difficult for Javier, so she let it go. He was strangely quiet in this chamber, whereas he'd been so sociable the rest of the time. Leah longed to ask him why. She longed to get him alone, warm and clean, and talk about it from across a pillow.

There was a metallic ting-ting from below. Javier looked toward the ladder. "Alas, mis amigas y amigos, we have to let the next group up here," he said. "I hear them gathered."

"It's Xander," said Leah as he squeezed past her. "I met him last night."

"I know Xander, chula," said Javier. "He is my twin brother." And he gestured for her to go down the ladder.

Leah felt dizzy.

His twin brother!

She descended the ladder, rung by rung, from Javier to Xander.

"Leah from Minnesota," said Xander as she reached the bottom, as a sort of announcement, his muscled arms crossed. He seemed to be playing it cool in front of his tourists, but in his tone and stance, she could detect insecurity.

"Xander from . . . Burns Avenue," she replied, glad to be on speaking terms.

"What happened to your finger?"

Leah had forgotten about it. She looked down to see a rosy stain on the gauze. "I cut it on a rock. Javier took care of it."

Xander nodded upward. "What did you think?"

"Of the Crystal Maiden? Fine. I like the river better."

He frowned. "The river?"

"Yes. I want to see what's around that bend at the step-up rock. Have you ever been farther into the cave?"

Xander gave her a queer look. "Yes," he said.

He didn't have a chance to say more, because her whole group was down the ladder now. Javier exchanged a few words with Xander in Kriol. Leah couldn't catch what they said. It seemed logistical, a bare minimum of necessary words. There was tension there. Leah longed to ask about that over a pillow, too.

Javier led them back through the tumbledown. As soon as Xander was out of sight, he seemed to breathe easier. They made their way down the travertine labyrinth. The mood had changed, as if the Crystal Maiden had been the orgasm of the tour, and now they were done, over, hurrying, pulling out.

When they put their shoes back on and climbed back down into the river, Leah eyed the darkness ahead.

"Xander said he'd gone farther into the cave," she said to Javier. "If I come back, can I?"

"No, señorita," he said. "You have to get special permission from Dr. Castillo to go past here."

"You got a death wish?" said Luke.

"No," said Leah. "I just feel pulled. Like there's something in there I have to see."

"Xibalba is calling you," said Ron lightly, but Javier turned around to look at him in a way that silenced him.

"You're going to walk up front with me, señorita, so you don't cause too much trouble," said Javier. His tone was light but he didn't meet her eyes.

It was physically difficult for Leah to turn her back on the darkness. That sound of rushing water was like the first strains of an opera that was just warming up, and she was going to miss the front seat reserved for her.

On the way out, Leah only knew that she would have to come back. That was all. She had four more days here and she still had money to spend. She could do the tour again. On the way out she concentrated on the sections of the cave: Nine, the Venice crystal. Eight, the meteorite field. Seven, the gentle sway. Or was that six? She'd have to come back to get it straight. The big flowstone. The sacrifice chamber. The reflecting pool.

When they were near the entrance but still in the dark, Javier stopped the group and told everyone to form a line.

"Now, turn off your headlamps," he said.

They did as he said. They were in total darkness.

Luke said, "Whoa."

Paul said, "Holy cow."

Leah opened and closed her eyes, and it made no difference. There was only the feel of cool water pooling and rushing past her knees. She felt more at peace being blind than she did with sight.

"Friends," said Javier, his voice coming from the darkness on her right, "this is what it would have been like for the Maya, if their torches went out. Do you think you could find your way back?"

They said no, no way, not at all.

Leah was silent. Now she was sure that light, sunlight or otherwise, obscured true sight. Nothing she saw with her eyes was real. She felt her upper and lower eyelashes beat together and pull apart again. She could see the vapor streaming past her, now with her inner eye, and it was colored gold. It wasn't streaming out, toward the exit; it was streaming back to where they'd come from, where the dark river sluiced around the bend.

MEKNES, MAGHREB
2 Ok 13 Kumk'u, Long Count 15.10.14.2.10

---

22 July, 3012

Niloux estimated six hundred viajeras in the plaza. That number was a clear violation of the Rule of Saint Leah. Some were already calling themselves Zeinians, and some just wanted to hear her speak. Overhead, a static dome kept off a sandstorm, which cast the plaza in a dark red light.

Niloux swallowed a gulp of wine to calm herself. Then she stepped onto a dais and tapped her temple to amplify her voice.

"I'm Niloux DeCayo," she said. "Thanks for coming." She spoke as if to an intimate other; she didn't know how to speak to a crowd. Despite her incompetence, they looked rapt. Is this how despots came about? she thought. When their cult of personality outpaced their actuality? She pushed on. "What I want to do first is acknowledge that . . ." She took a deep breath. "I'm aware Tanaaj DeCayo has declared me an enemy of the people. I'm aware of her following. The LFC is in the Pacific now, on the searoad from Hawai'i to Mexico. They're headed to the Jubilee like I am." Behind her, there was a delicate cough. Niloux turned to see Emelle raise her eyebrows. She turned back to the crowd. "Like we are, I mean. The Zeinians."

The crowd looked somber. It was the first time she'd claimed the name in public. This is what they'd wanted: a declaration.

"I'm willing to meet Tanaaj," she continued. "She's welcome at the tzoyna I want to hold. I don't bear her any ill will. I think her argument is interesting. She thinks I'm destroying this utopia we've built, and I understand why. I just think the taboos of Laviaja are too restrictive if the human race wants to keep growing and not stagnate, so . . ." Lightning flashed and thunder cracked. A fresh wave of sand hissed on the dome. Is this what Venus was like? She told herself to focus. "So I'm willing to debate her. If she would deign to talk publicly with an enemy of the people." She couldn't keep the sarcasm out of her voice. She licked her lips, pivoted, tried to sound upbeat. "Tonight we celebrate the birthday of the Consort Twins. They were born a few minutes apart in the year 1989. Javier Magaña, the founder of our ritual tradition, was born on July 22. Xander Cañul, the founder of our scholarly tradition, was born on July 23. We'll celebrate like we do every year, but I just want to say, when they were born—" She stared up at the dome, the hypnotic streaking sand, already elsewhere, already imagining and even hoping herself into dialogue with this Tanaaj DeCayo, the charismatic jugadorix who asked that no images be made of her face. She appeared to Niloux in her mind's eye as a cloaked, steadfast figure, a keeper of tradition, a Thomas More or Dalai Lama or Joan of Arc, striding the searoads with her loyal thousands. Laviaja had been forged from the suffering of billions. Tanaaj saw herself as the keeper of their sacrifice. If Niloux were to repudiate it, was she insulting their suffering? Was she only doing this for her own selfish desire, which she couldn't name aloud? She made herself look down at the faces of the people in front of her. "When the Consort Twins were born, they had no idea what the world was about to face in the Diluvian Age. No one did. They just acted in their time, how they thought best . . ." Niloux swallowed. "And so do we. Tanaaj thinks we should remain as we are. I think we should change. But we're both doing what we think is best. So let's eat."

Awkward silence from the crowd, then scattered applause.

Niloux tapped off her amplifier, stepped down to face Emelle. "Verily, I am become a leader tonight," she said dryly.

"You're getting there."

Niloux gave her a bitter look. "I've hardly been alone in a month."

Emelle shrugged. "Stop complaining. Go off alone. Just give us notice."

"Are you my zadre?"

"I'm your bodyguard."

"No one is actually going to hurt me, Emelle. Things aren't that bad."

Emelle's eyes flashed.

Niloux ignored her. She looked out over the crowd. The sandstorm was still raging, and people were lighting candles and building fires. Across the plaza, someone had begun strumming an oud. Another had set up chess boards on the tops of broken columns. She smelled supper cooking.

She turned to see Emelle still staring at her.

"Fine," she conceded. "I'll go off by myself tomorrow."

They'd both gotten the work assignment to help serve supper. Niloux was quick about it, not wanting to linger or give anyone the opportunity to ask her questions or, worse, debate with her. She was hungry too. When they were sure everyone had food and drink, they found mats to sit with their own dishes: couscous shaped into calderas, with raisins and carrots piled in the middle. They ate with their hands. Niloux admitted to herself she was glad Emelle was here. She'd accompanied her all the way from Capri. They'd become close and still slept together often, despite the strangeness of her being a one-time lover of Tanaaj DeCayo. It cost Emelle, to be so far from the sea—but also because, in theory, the Tzoyna could vote to allow blotting of either of them at any time. They were living in defiance of Versa Tres, the injunction against gathering. Then again, they could argue on a technicality: a group traveling toward a specific celebration of Día de Pasaja was immune to Versa Tres, and also to Versa Siete, known as the Principle of Dispersion. Tanaaj's group was immune for the same reason. Many in the Tzoyna regarded this as an abuse of the Rule, but there'd been no repercussions yet.

After supper, a viajera approached, carrying a tray of steaming glasses. Niloux took one. There were mint leaves crushed at the bottom.

Emelle nudged her. "Don't look now," she said. "To your left, under the archway."

Niloux blew on her tea. "What am I looking for?"

"Malcontents."

Niloux took her time, letting her gaze settle far and wide before swinging to the left. She saw a huddled group, apart from the crowd, sober expressions, heads close together. One of them looked at Niloux and then looked away.

"Scrupes?"

"Possibly LFC."

"Here?"

"Yes. Be careful, Niloux."

"Careful?" She snorted. "What are they going to do, attack me?"

"Tanaaj named you an enemy of the people. It's not impossible. You know that."

She did, but the idea was still ridiculous. Laviaja was strictly pacifist. Drawing the blood of another for any reason except medicinal reasons was deeply taboo, and those who did were often blotted for life. Versa Trece: *La sangre le pertenece solamente a Xibalba.* There was no reason for anyone to hurt anyone, except jealousy or other untreated mental illnesses.

Then a company of ninx rolled up. They were seven or eight years old, wearing crowns and jewels. They looked furtive but determined, as if playing a secret game. The ringleader—a stout ninx with cornrows—planted herself in front.

"We're here to collect tribute!" she said.

Emelle smiled, wry. "In exchange for what?"

"Nothing. That's what tribute is."

"Who told you that?"

The ninx faltered. "I learned it in local tutorial. The sultan who built this city got tribute like grain and bracelets."

"And slaves," Niloux muttered. The children blanched at the word.

Emelle leaned forward. "Ah, but the sultan got tribute because he provided protection for those who paid tribute," she said. "And good roads, and settlements of dispute. You see, it was also an exchange of mutual aid, after a fashion. So I ask, what are you giving us in return?"

The ninx was flabbergasted. She called a huddle with her companions.

"You're confusing her," said Niloux.

Emelle nodded. "She'll set up a sultanate. Laviaja is finished."

Niloux shook her head and sipped her tea. It was sweet as syrup.

One of the children said something that made the ringleader straighten up and turn to eye Niloux. They conferred some more, passed something between sweaty little hands, then arrayed themselves again in tableau.

The ringleader held out her palm. On it, there was a gold funnel. When Niloux looked at it, she felt her adrenaline surge like a hot splash inside her stomach.

"How pretty," said Emelle. "What is it?"

"It's an earspool," Niloux said, the meaning of the object coming into focus, like text in a dream. "An ancient Maya earspool."

Emelle heard the change in her voice. "How do you know it's Maya?"

Niloux held out her palm, and the ninx handed it over. The touch of it sent a shiver through her blood. She began to feel nauseated. She put it on the ground. It seemed to be made of solid gold, small but very heavy, carved with heliconia blossoms. Her adrenaline was still making her stomach churn. She stayed still. It took effort. "I recognize it," she said, "but I don't know from where. Some text or tutorial—maybe it's famous." She looked up at the ringleader. "What's your name?"

She stuck out her chin. "Yewande."

"Where did you find this?"

"Found it in the rummage."

"I can have it?"

"Yes. But I'm the sultan so you have to give me something in exchange."

"What do you want?"

"Show me your past life."

Niloux snorted. "It doesn't work that way. I have to question the landscape piece by piece. It's like knocking on a wall to find a hollow place, and then when I get a positive result I mark the spot in the aug and it forms a line. Ideally. It's rare that I ever come across a positive result, I haven't gotten one since . . ." She blinked at the earspool on the ground.

Yewande crossed her arms. "Okay. How do I find my own then?"

Niloux looked up. "You ask the god of the place. You ask the god if it knows you. If the god says yes, mark the spot and keep marking them until they make a line. That's all."

"Let's try it!" screamed a little one, and ran off toward the gate. Yewande yelled for her to come back, but the other children were already gone, jewels rattling, and she followed, shouting to regain control.

When they were out of sight, Niloux pointed to the earspool. She was afraid to touch it again. "I think the technique applies to objects too," she said. "Of course it would. Stone remembers longest."

Emelle registered this. She didn't ask what Niloux had felt; she trusted without having to ask. "Which means, in a past life . . ."

"That I was Maya? Maybe. Or a looter."

"But you think this belonged to you."

"I just know that it remembered me. Without my even having to ask. It told me."

"May I touch it?"

Niloux felt a strange reluctance, but nodded.

Emelle picked it up, turned it over, admired it. "For what it's worth, I feel nothing," she said, "except that it's beautiful." She put it back on the ground with respect, and they both regarded it as dogs would a forbidden bone.

There was a cry on the other side of the courtyard, so loud that it disrupted the music. A chess match had ended. One viajera was being lifted up on shoulders, another was sliding off her stool in shame, and everyone was laughing and shouting. The band in the courtyard now numbered eight, with an assortment of ouds, washboards, and flutes, singing an old Belizean pop song. What a strange world, Niloux thought, where they were listening to Andalusian music with Kriol lyrics in the Maghreb by candlelight under a sandstorm. The gods of each place were fathomless. Now this night was part of it.

Now zadres were dancing with their ninx, some just little chubby babes in arms, looking worried. The children would get tired and the adults would pair off. Those who didn't pair off would fall asleep together in this courtyard, huddling together for warmth, just like the Diluvian refugees of old. This was her familia tonight. These people were her hermanix. These children were her children.

Niloux said aloud, "'Entropy is the first, last, and most irrefutable force. As time goes on—even on the scale of centuries—it will become more and more difficult for us to construct a coherent narrative out of the fragmentation of human experience.'"

"'This will be true regardless of technological advances. It is a feature of the universe,'" Emelle finished the quotation. "Xander Cañul. *Entropy as God*."

"Do I tell myself that, as an excuse to break the world?" said Niloux.

Emelle didn't answer.

So Niloux just stared at the earspool, deep in thought.

The next afternoon, Niloux went off alone. She gathered up her things, making sure to wrap the earspool in her bedroll. Emelle would come find her eventually. For now, she wanted to be alone. She had a premonition she wouldn't have the chance again for a long time.

She walked south to the ancient ruins of Walili, where a production of *La Estrella Actual* was mustering in honor of the Consort Twins. A crowd had already gathered. Some sat on pillows and some reclined on hoverchairs. Some blind viajeras sat up close and others sat by hermanix who'd whisper the play into their ears. Lovers clustered together, arms around waists. It was a hot, gusty evening with clear skies, and she could see the vast plain below through the Roman colonnades.

Under the ancient basilica, there stood three performers. As per tradition, they were waiting for the appearance of Venus. She checked the time. Eight minutes to go. Niloux wondered what part, what version, and what mode they'd be performing. Usually the mode honored the god of the place, so she expected something Berber or Houara. Given the constraints of nomadism, performances were usually quicksilver groupings that performed a segment or two at a time, but this production seemed more premeditated. The performers wore matching djellabas. The performer in the center wore green—Leah—flanked by the red and the black, Xander and Javier.

The sun touched the plain. When it had sunk far enough, Venus would appear above it. Niloux watched for the exact moment when it would appear, as they all were, now; shushing the children, softening in expectation. And now she was not here, she was back in Persia, six months ago and thousands of miles away, watching the same star appear over the oasis, beaming a message that she was still trying to read. The planet was calling to her. That was plain. But how could she answer?

A point of light separated from the glow, hardened, blazed.

God of the place, she asked the point of light, *do you know me?*

A conch blew over the crowd.

Niloux jumped. She tried to focus. *Be present,* Emelle always told her. *Be here.*

She spotted the conch player on the rampart above the arches. She seemed to be a fellow maya, maybe achi maya; she wore an esh around her hips. She was now putting down the conch and picking up an oud.

"¡La obra comienza!" she called in the high speech of Laviaja. "Hoy, aquí, hay cinco jugadorix para jugar *La Estrella Actual.* ¿Quién las mirará?"

Everyone in the crowd bowed their heads and murmured, "Las miraremos." Niloux too.

The jugadorix playing Saint Leah stepped forward. She stared boldly at the audience, her arms outstretched, her green djellaba hanging stiff. Then the musician plucked the oud, and on that note, Saint Leah arched her back and bowed her chest forward, drew her hand across her chest and pointed it at the sky.

Niloux tried to focus.

As always, she found it hard to stay present to the performance. Otracortices could only do so much. Her mind still flickered here and there like an errant flame. The play was a spectacle occurring outside the mind, yes, but there was also the spectacle it ignited *inside* the mind. For her, that was the greater spectacle. She knew that art was meant to be enjoyed more than analyzed, but she couldn't enjoy art unless she analyzed it at the same time, which meant being in many times at once, jumping from the far past to the far future and back again, examining from all angles.

She watched the dancer in green.

Saint Leah's bare foot pawed at the stone, like a wild horse teasing, before bursting away. Niloux turned on her pista filter and saw the line drawn from the dancer's steps, dripping from her feet and spooling on the ground. Niloux tapped her temple again to throw her vision up a hundred feet into the air so that she could see from a bird's-eye view. Now she could see this jugadorix's path from the rummage the day before. And—Niloux threw her vision farther and farther up—now she could see the jugadorix's whole lifelong pista, snaking through Congolese jungle—and she ascended higher, seeing now as if she were in the troposphere—through the Kalahari, from the Lesotho Highlands, from the searoads of the Southern Ocean, from her birthplace in Antarctica, a tiny wayhouse at the foot of Mount Melbourne, where sparkling streams ran down the face of the caldera.

She brought her vision back down to eye level.

She wished she could call Yewande back and say, *Remember that the pista is the body's text, inscribed upon the earth.*

Some viajeras walked intentionally so that they left designs on the land. Some chose a symbol and left it as a sort of signature, saying *I was here.* Then there were the more ambitious projects: the Chi-Ro written on the hillsides of Kells. The name of Allah written across the whole of Australia. The latter had taken three generations of viajeras to make.

Niloux worried, not about the Zeinians or the LFC, but the apathetic in between. The ones who thought this global peace was the way things had always been and the way things would always be. As if humans had always freely walked the face of the Earth, collecting wayhouse tokens to show off in their haloes, never wanting for food or love or shelter. As if there hadn't once been billions of people living in incomprehensible indignity enforced by psychotic hoarders. Laviaja was developed by climate refugees over centuries of ecological catastrophe: it was a superb social technology. But now scrupes threw around the word "utopia" as if this state of affairs were permanent, as if time wouldn't continue its course, as if entropy would not always fray its edges, as if humans would stay dispersed of their own accord, as if the Tzoyna need not be vigilant, as if the balance couldn't so easily tilt back into hoarding, territory, and violence. All of it could change at this moment in history. If Niloux hadn't spoken up, someone else would have, but Venus had chosen her. She had to be careful, going forward. She had to steer the Zeinians along the edge of a knife.

She refocused on the jugadorix playing Saint Leah. Her long black braid whipped around her shoulders as she turned and turned on the stone.

The oud stopped.

Saint Leah froze in place.

The musician put down her oud and picked up a second conch shell, as big as her head. She hefted it up to her lips. The note she blew was so startling that Niloux blinked back tears. The jugadorix wearing red and black animated and fell into step for the same gestural phrase with which Saint Leah had begun: arched back, chest forward, the hand drawn across the chest and pointed at the sky.

The oud resumed, now with drums.

The ruins began to change.

Piles of stone sprang into the air, each finding its place. The bases sprouted into pillars. The arches rebuilt themselves, keystones slipping in last. Ghosts of viajeras appeared and disappeared among the ruins, wearing jumpsuits, then jeans, then khakis, then kaftans. Niloux understood what was happening: the performers had set the history filters on reverse. They were passing through the Carnival days, the Moroccan tourists, the French excavation, the Idrisid dynasty. She checked the year: sixteenth century and dropping. Villas rebuilt themselves, unbuilt themselves. Olive groves rose and flourished and shrank. Wild grass grew with white oleander, then turned to bare rock, then flushed green again. Streets were empty of people, then thick, then empty again. The Islamic crescents became Christian crosses, then Roman eagles, then Numidian horses, then Phoenician sphinxes, then Amazigh yazes, then even more ancient symbols of peoples unknown, crescents and cups. Tents and fires. Shepherds and flocks. Herds and hunters. In the background, always, the rolling hills, green and gold and green again: the face of the god of the place.

And then there was only a bare plain, and the stars wheeled.

A full moon rose and stopped overhead like a spotlight.

The jugadorix playing Javier came forward until she was standing right in front of Niloux. She was so close that Niloux could smell the sweat coursing down her legs. She could have found out who this performer was, but didn't want to; right now the performer was Javier Magaña himself, kind and steady and true. And then she was reaching out and slipping her fingers along Niloux's elbow, hooking her arm, pulling her to her feet, steering her into the light of the moon. Usually Niloux hated modes that compelled the audience to join, but this time she didn't mind, as if this were merely a dream sequence in the night's inquiry.

The jugadorix pulled her close.

"Tú, igual, eres una turista," she murmured in her ear, flirting. She smirked. "Follow my feet."

Niloux looked down. She tried to match the dancer's steps. Easy enough—foot forward two beats, then back, then switch. The dancer's hand was soft on her back.

"You have it," she said. "Now keep doing the same steps, but look at me."

Niloux looked into her eyes. They were pale green, like watery jade. She didn't blink.

The beat got faster, the drums louder.

They were repeating the same movement over and over. Niloux had the hang of it. She was afraid that if she stopped, she'd stumble. She was aware of the many eyes on her, the particular sofist, face plain for all to see.

"Too fast," she said.

The dancer tightened her arm around Niloux's back, pulling her tightly. "Just look at me," she said, breathless.

"I can't do the steps."

"Just keep looking at me."

Niloux heard a shout, then screams, then felt an icy bite in her back.

The jugadorix hooked her arm around her neck to hold her still, looking triumphant, but Niloux was already twisting away, shoving her hands against the jugadorix's chest. Then many things happened at once. The drums faltered. A flash of silver hair, lilac skin. The ground hit her cheek. She saw sideways, the front row, viajeras sitting cross-legged, looking horrified. Then yelling and scraping and children screaming. Someone she didn't know lay on top of her and a voice in her ear said *Be still.* But she didn't listen. Her animal body needed to know. She wrenched herself under the person's weight to touch the place where she'd felt the bite and her fingers came away wet with blood.

It was a full eighteen hours before Niloux was alone again.

As soon as she was, she packed her things in five minutes.

She was well guarded now. Emelle, who'd saved her life, and another—Meret, who'd lain on top of her to protect her—had made sure of it. But now she wanted to be alone. Even more so, because of the assassination attempt. Someone had shed her blood, and not to scare her. They'd actually tried to kill her. They considered her enough of a threat to break pacifism, to risk lifelong blotting. The LFC was encouraging fanatic murderers. It didn't matter that the stick hadn't worked, that the damage had been healed with fermites and filler and taffy. They would just try again with better weapons. Before, Niloux had been willing to talk with Tanaaj. Now she just wanted to end it. She could use the assassination attempt in her favor—claim victimhood, play it up—but if these were the risks, she didn't want anyone else to take them. She'd started this alone and wanted to finish it alone.

Last: the golden earspool.

She pulled it out of her bedroll, touched it, felt the same electric surge as before. But this time she wanted to live with it. She would learn whatever this object had to teach her. She tugged down her earlobe and worked it in, wincing. She had to force it. The skin strained and stretched around the metal, but the pain was good, it would keep her awake.

She peeled open the borrowed pod with her thumb-nail, stepped outside, resealed the pod. If anyone saw her, they'd think she was just out for a piss. She walked over a hill, then slunk on her belly around the next hill, below which she wouldn't be visible. They'd find her eventually but at least she had a head start. She stopped to take in the moon-soaked plains. This was a walk-able country. She asked her ai to calculate the fastest path through the mountains, and a salmon-colored line raced from her feet into the distance.

Holding that line steady, she softened her mind and applied her pista technique, which now went so fast she didn't have to think about it. The bee descended and ascended so quickly it was as if a thousand bees were touching down on the landscape at once, all of them asking, *God of the place: do you know me?*

No especial feeling, anywhere.

She set off on the path. The full moon was setting over the mountains. Dawn was nearing; the air was cold and dewy.

After a few miles, she finally allowed herself to look back.

She saw a column of viajeras following her, stretch-ing all the way back to the basilica, heads bent in the moonlight.

TZOYNA
3 Batz' 14 Pop, Long Count 10.9.5.7.11

---

9 December, 1012

Ixul watched the performance begin.

The ocarina players met on the ball court, then turned to face the direction they'd come. She forgot her anger at the insolent farmer. She wanted to enjoy the music. She needed to trust that all of her long preparations, and those of Ajul and Mutna and Upakal, would carry the night. The peasants were fed. The court was clean. The musicians were perfect. Their five-fold harmony held, even as they lowered to a kneel together. She felt Ajul's hand over hers. He knew she was tense. But as the players settled back on their heels, and the ocarinas held their final note, Ixul felt something cross over in her, and the air on the court took on a telltale shimmer as if underwater.

That was the sign: Xibalba was near.

Ajul's hand tightened.

In the new silence, Mutna took her place at the head of the ball court. She had a grave, triumphant look. She lifted her arms and the musicians stirred in readiness.

Ixul held her breath.

Mutna brought down her arms.

The agave horns gave a terrifying blast, like giant bullfrogs. Ket cried out and covered her ears. Ixul put her hand on her shoulder. The sound of the agave horns was always startling, even for Ixul. Then the horns broke into a flutter, as if dragging a furrow through the earth; and the ocarinas came back, dancing along this new scaffolding. Everything on the court looked more real, as if she were seeing with the clarity of a dream that would dissolve if she got too close. Mutna had once told her that when Xibalba was near, you had no doubt of what you saw. It was the very quality of certainty that marked it.

Then the conch players lifted their shells to their lips.

Mutna opened her hand.

Ixul was not prepared. A tear escaped and fell down her face. The players' hands slid in and out of the shells, shaping the groans that echoed up and down the valley. Then the rattles began, as if every cicada in the realm had descended. She couldn't believe they could get louder, and then they did.

The ocarina players put down their instruments and prostrated themselves. Mutna strode the court and began to shout, and the crowd answered.

Come here, white and yellow
(Left and right, come)
Come here, red and black
(Dayrise and dayfall, come)
Come here, thou green
(You in the center, come)
All of you ancestors who preceded us here
All of you gods of this place
All of you gods of the days
All of you gods of Xibalba
named and unnamed,
known and unknown:
Keep us in balance
Keep us in peace

The ocarina players rose on the ball court, shoulders hunched, and began to undulate from the pits of their stomachs. They wore jade masks now; Ixul hadn't seen where they'd been hidden, and neither had the crowd, who marveled at the revelation. The players made their way to the four moorings of the ball court and held out their hands as if to invite; but everyone knew the summons was not for them, and no one in the crowd stirred but to give the dancers room.

This is even better than our parents did, Ixul thought. All is proceeding exactly as it should.

Mutna beckoned to the warriors—two each from the Tzoyna, Katwitz, and Pekwitz—who'd had the honor of preparing the captives for the game. The old man who'd escaped and returned was kept aside, looking feverish. But the stout woman looked ready, her brow set; and the skinny man was straining forward, his eyes darting to and fro.

Be brave now, Ixul thought toward the captives. *Accept your part. Acceptance will make everything go well for you.*

And for us, she thought.

Then her left hand was suddenly bare, and she felt a rush of wind at her side. Ajul had gotten up already and was descending down the steps to the court.

Fool!

He'd gotten so entranced by the glamor, he'd forgotten he was supposed to give his second speech. She half-rose from her seat to follow him, which made Chenukul look up at her inquiringly. She stopped herself. How would it look for her to chase down the new king and steer him back to the dais, and say, *No, Ajul, you fool, remember you have to speak again, the speech about trade and resettlement?*

She had to let him go.

Besides, time had already moved on with him.

As soon as the crowd saw Ajul coming, they took up an ululation that spread across the plaza like a sheet of flame. The music increased to drown them out, and the crowd cried even louder in answer so that the combined sound made a conflagration that filled the valley and bloomed up to heaven. Ixul saw the merchants pressing their hands to their ears. How childish, she thought. The gods were near! How could they not feel most alive now?

Mutna welcomed Ajul to the court. The crowd was seething to get a better view. Tonight was the night of his transformation into a king. No performance would ever be so important, but he looked calm. His skin was gold with firelight. He bowed his head, opened his hands, touched the earth, reached to the sky, then turned to the four corners of the court to bow from his waist. Ixul couldn't keep her eyes off him. Before, he was just her brother who chewed on his fingernails and complained about his pine torch. Now he was the timeless young king.

And he was hers.

Meanwhile, the guards were untying the first captive—the skinny man. They'd arranged it so, thinking Ajul would find good sport with him, whereas Ixul's speed would outmatch the stout woman. But it didn't matter. None of these captives would be a match on a good day, but especially not after their conditioning. The long days of deprivation and grooming, the denial of food and water and then its sudden gifting, the hours in the hot sun, the fawning and abandonment: all of it was described in the Black Treatise. Two guards led him onto the court and yanked on his yoke, forcing him to kneel. They unbound his hands and held his arms apart. The masked dancers converged on him, dipping their hands into a bowl of blue clay and spreading it over his body. In the altered air of the court, the blue had a vividness Ixul had never seen, not even in parrots or motmots.

Then Mutna began to dress Ajul in his gear: the quilted chest plate, the knee pads and elbow pads made of deer hide, the wicker belt studded with jade. This gear was for ceremony, not often worn, and far more stiff than their usual practice gear. They'd make new blisters. Tomorrow they'd sit in the sweat bath and press herbs into their sores.

But tomorrow was so far in the future, it seemed like myth.

Ixul fought to return to the present moment.

Now Ajul was dressed. He called out in a strong voice, and the crowd answered.

Thirteen matches of the game
(For thirteen realms of the heavens)
Nine volleys of the ball
(For nine realms of the underworld)
Three attempts at the ring
(One for Hunajpu, one for Xbalanque, and one for the
Bloodmaiden of Xibalba)

Now the captive was on his feet. The dancers were fitting him with his own gear. His head was tilted back and he was looking down his nose, as if he himself were the threat. Ixul felt sorry for him. He'd been a refugee. He had no idea what was coming. Now he was taking deep breaths with his whole chest, and his shoulder blades worked like fins.

Ajul stood still, waiting.

Mutna brought forth the pelota, then beckoned to the royal dais.

"She's asking for you," Ixul said to Ket. "It's time to bowl the ball."

Ket rose to her feet, helped by Patli. She touched her fingers to the bandage over her eyes. But she didn't go down to the court. Instead, she held up her hand.

Ixul didn't know what was happening.

Upakal bellowed out, "The Royal Princess Ket Ahau would speak."

The crowd hushed. The drummers stopped. Mutna cocked her head, and even Ajul looked up.

Ixul strained to look normal, as if she'd expected this speech, as if they'd planned it all along. But she had no idea what Ket was about to say. Why didn't her siblings just do as they were told!

Ket shifted from one foot to the other and took a deep breath.

"I am called upon to bowl the ball for my brother and sister, the new king and queen," she called out in her thin little voice. "Today, a black jaguar took my eye. It was not a normal jaguar. It was the god Balam Ahau from Xibalba, who takes jaguar form. Don't worry about me. I will live. I will even bowl. And I can see with new eyes now. Balam Ahau has blessed the Tzoyna, and will be our guardian forever."

The crowd murmured in approval. Ixul looked to Mutna, who nodded; though this speech was unplanned and could have gone badly, it had landed well and could be incorporated, even advantageous. Ket smiled a little, and it made Ixul's heart ache. Suddenly she felt generous toward this girl. It would be so easy to let her in. Why had she kept her at a distance all her life?

But then Ket was gone, led with care by Patli. The servant girl seemed to love her. Tomorrow they'd have to see about retaining her service.

Mutna welcomed Ket to the court. She took her hand and led her to the far end of the court, and bent her head to explain her duties, where to stand, what to do. Meanwhile, Ixul noticed that Patli kept looking back at Chenukul, as if for guidance; but Chenukul was giving orders to a servant. How that dull merchant inspired any devotion, Ixul did not know, but Patli looked very anxious.

Mutna offered the ball to Ket. The girl took it with tenderness. She seemed not to need any guidance, as if she could see perfectly from beneath her bandage. Ixul shook her head in wonder.

The blue captive was hopping from foot to foot. Ajul stood rooted.

Mutna called *Match One, Volley One,* and nodded to Ket.

The crowd was silent. The torchlight cracked.

Ket bowled, hard and true. The pelota went straight for the center.

Both players sprinted, folded one knee, and slid.

Ajul's slide was stronger. He got possession.

Ixul let her breath out.

Now he had to pass to the other player, and they had to complete nine volleys before Ajul could attempt to put the ball through the ring—a stone circle on the right bank of the court.

Ixul watched him. He was moving well in the new gear. He twisted his hips in midair and passed the ball to the captive, who barely returned it with his stringy calf. Ajul noticed the weak pass, picked it up, and returned it with—Ixul could tell—more gentleness.

But the captive missed it and stumbled. The ball rolled off the court into the crowd. People scrambled to get out of its way. One of Katwitz's warriors retrieved it as the people began to jeer, and then the captive bent double, vomiting pale ropes onto the court.

Ixul couldn't believe it. Were all the captives as weak as this? Had they been fed too much or too little? She leapt to her feet before she had time to think it through.

"Give that one a stimulant," she yelled at the court, "and see if the other captive is any more brave."

Ajul looked up in surprise. Immediately she regretted her haste, but the crowd was already cheering her words. Now she had committed them all to her course of action. Mutna herself seemed unfazed; she bowed and took the skinny captive by the elbow, steering him back to the far end of the plaza, where they would let him finish emptying his stomach. Meanwhile, there'd be a delay. Ixul saw people in the crowd grimacing. This was horribly embarrassing. The second captive was untied, but it would take a moment for her to be painted and dressed. The crowd would lose attention. They had to do something to recapture it.

"Music!" Ajul called. "Strike up the drums."

Ixul breathed out and nodded to herself. Yes, he had the instinct of a king. She was beginning to trust his judgment, the way she had always longed to.

The drummers began a steady rhythm.

Ixul watched Ajul pace to the music. She knew how unsettled he felt. He'd wanted a challenge, of course, but there were worse things than mere lack of skill. If the captive was a coward, not only did the ball game give no sport, it lost its sacrificial potency. The captive was destined to die on behalf of the Tzoyna. To crumple in the face of that duty was worse than death—for the captive, and for the realm.

But now the vomit was washed away and the musicians had struck a good tempo. Ajul began the Dance of the Deer in the athletic style of Baakal. The crowd cheered. He was as confident in dance as he was in sport, easy and graceful. Ixul looked out over the crowd to gauge the mood. They looked happy, bellies full, pawing one another to get a better look at the king.

Finally the second captive was ready. She seemed more steady. All the musicians stopped playing—except the drums, which went faster.

Ajul and the captive took their places on the court.

Ket held up the ball again.

The drums became one long roll.

The crowd strained forward like maize under a strong wind.

Ket bowled. Both players ran and slid sideways for control, and Ajul's black headdress folded up like wings as he dove.

The captive got control of the ball; it was something Ajul had allowed to happen, Ixul knew, because he wanted to put on a better show this time. Even so, Ixul was rapt. This captive was lively and thick. She'd give better sport.

The captive retreated behind the fourth marker and kneed the ball to Ajul. Ajul passed it back in an arc from his hip, barely seeming to move his body. The captive lurched and returned it with the flat of her arm. It was either an expert move or an amateur's luck; Ixul couldn't tell. But Ajul caught the ball on his shoulder and rolled it like a salamander running along his arm till it popped off his wrist. The captive lurched again, this time to hit the ball with her hip. It dribbled back to Ajul, but he took a spectacular slide, and the ball shot straight up in the air.

In her mind, Ixul heard her father's words:

Never touch the ball with the hands or feet.

The game was played thus, in the last creation, but everyone mastered it too quickly.

In this creation, the gods made it harder.

Touch the ball with your arms, shoulders, knees, hips, and thighs.

Never with the hands.

Never with the feet.

And then she returned to the present moment, with the black valley, the white torches, and their purple ghosts.

Ajul swung his head to clear the sweat. It landed on the court like an arc of rain. Everything glimmered, everything slid: he was on the holy ball court, the window to the absolute, where all things were their truest selves, and all people too.

Nine volleys down. Now the captive was free to attempt the ring. He took position on the other side, center of gravity low, arms swinging. Everything felt good. He watched the captive move, knowing exactly how she felt in her body, even as he was in his own body. This is the kind of king he would be: other and self, simultaneously.

The captive punched the ball up the bank. It glanced off the wall next to the ring and dribbled back down. She caught it on her knee this time and kicked hard—but the ball hit the bank at a bad angle and missed the ring. Now Ajul was free to steal it from her. He saw panic in her eyes as she tried to split her attention between recovering the ball and fending him off. Ajul swung around her, and the ball cleaved to his shoulder. He was aware of the swell of noise when the crowd saw him take possession, now running two steps down the bank and landing in the center lane, after which he jumped, torqued, kicked, and from midcourt the ball went straight into his own ring.

Mutna called, "One point for the Hero Twins!"

The torches bloomed fresh, as if to register his victory. Someone threw a passion flower onto the court. He picked it up and put it behind his ear.

Now it was Ixul's turn.

Ajul flung his arm out to her, calling, *Come, my Xbalanque, and dispatch the other!* He realized he was hard again. So be it. Now he was king, more truly himself than he had ever been. Ixul was approaching the ball court, huge and tall, his afternoon jaguar, her fiery headdress shining in the torchlight. Ajul knew this look, the lethal snarl. When playing against him, it was her only weakness: a tendency to take competition personally. He could handle it. But against anyone else, it was the mark of doom.

Ixul took the court as Ajul stepped off it.

He heard a thin voice at his elbow. It was Ket.

"Ajul," she said, "where is Patli?"

Ajul felt annoyed at being petitioned at this moment, but such was the manner of children. He looked around but didn't see the servant girl.

"I do not know," he said. "Do you need her?"

"No," said Ket. "I just don't know where she went. She disappeared. Oh well." Without waiting for a reply, she marched back to her position, as if she could see perfectly.

Ajul stared at her, wondering how that was possible. But then he was distracted. The vomiting captive had been rallied on tobacco unguent, and came back onto the court with eyes as round as moons. He was brave now, and though it was a false bravery, it was better than none.

Mutna called, *Match Two, Volley One.*

Ket pulled her arm back, bowled strong and fast.

Ixul and the captive slid for it.

The captive went harder, but Ixul was cannier. Her

leg hooked and curled the ball into her possession, and already she was on her feet again, kneeing the ball up into the air. She and the captive both retreated behind the fourth markers. The captive spattered blue sweat all over the court.

The volley went fast. Knee, shoulder, hip, hip, knee, shoulder, knee, hip, knee, and then Ixul could try for the ring. She flew up the bank like an eagle pulling short up a cliff and Ajul wished he could remind her to draw it out so that—

The captive dove for her legs and knocked her to the stone.

Ajul couldn't believe it.

At first he thought it was a poor joke. Then he thought the captive must be mad. Then he saw Mutna coming toward him with a strange look in her eyes, pointing up and saying something about the Great Star. He was torn between receiving her and going to Ixul, who was rising from her undignified fall with a look that cooled his blood solid. The captive was on his hands and knees, getting to his feet.

Ixul hit him so savagely that he twisted a full turn before landing.

Ajul cried out her name.

She took no notice.

He had to take command. He was the king.

"Stake this captive and leave him for last," he called, striding forward. "He brings dishonor to himself, his captors, and the gods. His blood will irrigate the city."

The captive got up and spat at Ajul.

The foamy spittle landed on his thigh. Ajul stared at it, dumbfounded.

Ixul punched the captive across the face again, stuffed her fist into his mouth, hooked her other arm around his neck, and began to drag him to the altar. The crowd was shouting for death, but that was the emotion of peasants, wanting instant gratification. He had to stop Ixul. So much damage had been done already, so quickly, faster than he could react. What if Xibalba recoiled? Ajul looked wildly around him. The gods had not arrived, as yet, but the air still shimmered; Xibalba was still near. All was not lost. Ajul remembered Mutna and looked for her, but couldn't find her, which was strange, because he'd only just seen her coming toward him. Now she was nowhere on the court. Ket was standing alone and staring at the darkness beyond the plaza. Everyone was in disarray. He had to take control.

Then he heard a growl from the jungle.

Out of the darkness, a shadow was coming. Ajul could only see it by the gloss of its limbs. It moved low, undulating, hills and valleys.

Now Ket was running toward Ajul, palms up, as if trying to outrun a wave.

"Upakal," he snapped to his bodyguard, who stood at the edge of the court.

Upakal turned, and a spearhead bloomed from his chest.

The crowd rose to its feet.

Ixul dropped the captive, whose head bounced on the court.

"To me!" Ajul called to his warriors, and three of them rushed to him, sacred space violated, but an enemy was in their midst, and he and Ixul both turned and dropped into readiness position.

Then his own warriors pinned his arms behind his back.

Ixul was taken the same way.

They were wrenched to face each other, pinned, at the moment the jaguar reached Ket.

There was chaos now. The crowd dove away. The musicians rose; their instruments tumbled down the courtsides and burst on the stone. Ajul got free of the warriors, whose grip had loosened when they saw the jaguar, and so had Ixul, and they surged forward even as the crowd surged back. Ixul was yelling Ket's name. It was the same jaguar, Ajul knew, as he'd seen this morning. Was it really the god? Had he not taken enough? Why was he so greedy? The twins ran toward him. He saw them coming and tugged Ket's small folded body away, cantering across the empty plaza and over the low wall on the other side, ignoring all the peasants scrambling and stampeding and fleeing into the darkness. The twins got clear and ran after the god, leapt as one over the wall, and continued on the white road that fell down the terraces like a waterfall.

The god contracted and pumped against the road. The glimmer on its pelt matched the glimmer in Ket's hair, barely there, a trick of the eye. Ajul was desperate to keep up, but not slip on the lime. The god slowed to a trot and looked back to see if they were still following, as if in play; then Ajul heard a cry behind him, and he turned to see Ixul had fallen on her knees, but she screamed *go*, and since he trusted her in all things, he kept going, and the god leapt away with renewed energy, the chase on again. All Ajul had to do was get Ket back. They could dust her off and carry her back to the ball court and pick up the game where they'd left off, like getting back to a dream whose problem was left unsolved.

The god leapt down another terrace, then sped up, and all Ajul could see was the glimmer of starlight on his black fur. Ixul was yelling behind him. In the corners of his eyes he began to see other glimmers, shapes barely seen, bodies without legs and legs without bodies, circling and wheeling. They were flanking him like gnats at the corners of his eyes. He heard the river below them. Now Ixul was beside him again, matching him step for step, breath for breath, as if they were sprinting a race, leaping over the canals with no water, landing on globes of soil that burst like flour under their feet. Below, the god was leaping down to the river in single jumps, contracting and expanding, and so were they, so close behind it now, taking the steps as if they were flying. And now the shapes on both sides of them were flying too, matching them step for step, but silent; and as they reached the sacred river, Ajul felt a strap curl around his leg and he soared into space, twisting, until the earth flew up to punch him in the eyes.

CAYO
2 Chab 1 K'ank'in, Long Count 12.19.19.17.18

---

19 December, 2012

Leah's tour group returned to San Ignacio in mid-afternoon.

She lingered on the street, watching Javier talk to Angelo on the veranda. She said goodbye to her fellow tourists, who trickled away to their guesthouses: Luke, Nhi, Paul, Ron. She realized she'd never see them again.

She went back to her own guesthouse. She sat on her bed with the curtains drawn and listened to the grackles creaking outside. She took off her clothes and masturbated in the shower. Not satiated, she did it again on her bed, and then again. The cave had built up a tension in her. Then she got up, inspired, and scribbled a poem on the back of her hotel receipt, inspired by the ancient name of the city near the cave: Tzoyna, Mother's Cut. She folded it and put it in her pocket in case she wanted to remember it later. She braided her hair. She didn't feel hungry or thirsty or tired. All she wanted to do was stay in Belize and go back to the cave—every day, if she could.

She put on fresh clothes and went back into town.

The sun was setting now. In the west, the sky was melon and pink; in the east, there was a lightning storm, white forking on purple.

She found a side alley that led to Burns Avenue. She returned to the veranda of Ceiba Tree Adventures and peeked into the office, where Angelo was staring at his computer.

"Hello?" she said.

"Hello!" Angelo saw her and jumped up from his chair. "Did you enjoy your tour with Javier today?"

"Enjoy isn't quite the right word . . ."

"Oh no." Angelo's face transformed into a tragedy mask. "What happened?"

"Oh, I had a terrific time!" Leah assured him. "What I mean is that it wasn't quite enjoyment as much as a transcendence of time and space."

"Good, good," said Angelo, bobbing his head, not appearing to have heard her. "We like to keep customers happy. If you have any feedback, anytime, just—"

"I don't know if it's feedback, exactly, but I'd like to go again."

"Again!" Angelo laughed. "What, all the way through the jungle, with all the mud and water?"

"I can't think of a better way to spend my time."

"How long are you here?"

Leah felt a shadow of cold. "Nine days, including travel. Only five left now."

Angelo grimaced. "Let's see what I have." He peered at his computer, and the screen glowed blue on his face. "I have one space open . . . the day after tomorrow."

Leah felt anguished. "I was hoping to go again tomorrow."

Angelo shook his head. "Oh no, not tomorrow," he said. "I have four trips going, eight tourists each, plus the guide is nine, and that's the maximum any one company can send on one day. It's this business about 2012, you know? The 'end of the world' and all that."

Leah nodded.

"You look like someone just died!" said Angelo, who was trying to joke, but seemed unnerved by Leah's show of emotion. "But I promise you, this spot with Javier is yours. Look. I have it marked in red. LEAH OLIVERI, USA."

Leah managed to smile. After all, he was doing everything he could. "Thank you very much. I appreciate it. I'll . . . I'll see you then."

"And probably sooner!" said Angelo. "San Ignacio is pretty small."

"It is," Leah agreed. "Have a good night!"

Leah went into the street again. She looked up at the yellow-and-maroon sign across the way. Ultimate Cayo Tours. Xander's company.

"Hello Miss Leah the Half Maya!" said a voice behind her.

She turned around. It was beady-eyed Hector, folding his arms and twisting his mouth. "Who rated me a three. A three!"

Leah flushed, felt guilty. "You asked!" she said.

"I did, gyal, I'm just teasing you." He winked. "You going to the tree-lighting ceremony?"

"The what?"

"Christmas tree lighting. Right down that alleyway, in the new outdoor Welcome Center. They're still completing it, but it's ready to be used. There's music and food."

"I'll definitely go. But first, I wondered if you might have any spaces in your tours going to ATM tomorrow."

Hector raised his eyebrows. "Didn't you go with Ceiba Tree today?"

"I did, and it was so wonderful that I want to go again."

Hector laughed. "You know we have other tours, gyal. You don't want to go visit the temples at Caracol?"

"No."

"Cave tubing at Barton Creek?"

"No."

"Horseback riding to Xunantunich?"

"No. I know it sounds strange. But I just need to go back. That cave has a sort of . . . pull on me." It was such inadequate language, but how was she to describe it? She must go again. That was all.

"Well, let's see what we have. Come on, gyal," he said, leading her into the office. Leah looked behind her and saw Angelo, stricken, duck behind a post.

"What's the rivalry with Ceiba Tree all about?" she said.

"Oh, that," said Hector, putting on granny glasses and opening a planner, smeared with eraser clouds. "Long story. Goes back a few generations. You know what you have to do in a small town, though? You have to find a way to live with people."

"I know that very well," said Leah. "I come from a small town in Minnesota."

Hector nodded. "Everyone's an angel and a demon and you know all their business on each side."

"What about Angelo?"

"Oh, Angelo. He's not a field type of guy, if you know what I mean." Hector looked over the rim of his glasses, and she wondered if he was saying that Angelo was gay. "But he's not the problem. The problem is he's the frontman for a corrupt family. Ceiba Tree is run by some . . . well." He turned back to his planner. "My wife says I gossip too much. I will give what I was going to say to the Lord."

Leah laughed. "Catholic?"

"Yes, gyal."

"So am I."

Hector smiled. "So, ATM. Tomorrow. I have two tours going. John-John already has eight guests, but you're in luck—Xander only has three so far."

Leah felt both elation and apprehension.

Hector could read it on her face. "I thought you liked Xander."

"I did," said Leah. "I mean . . . I do. I think. But how can he only have three guests when demand is so high?"

"Welllllll . . ." Hector grimaced.

Leah sat in one of the clamshell chairs. "I'm going, no matter what. You can tell me."

"All right, gyal." Hector marked her down, then leaned back in his chair. "Xander has a few bad reviews on TripAdvisor."

"How many is a few?"

"Maybe eighteen."

Leah laughed.

Hector leaned forward. "Listen, gyal. I will tell you di truth. Xander is the best guide in Cayo . . . *if* he respects you."

"Oh dear. I hope he respects me."

"He does, gyal. I could tell, I know him, even if he's hard to read. He just . . . has some issues sometimes."

"What kind of issues? I know Javier is his twin brother . . ."

Hector looked out onto the street to check if anyone was near. He continued in a low voice. "Yes, gyal, and Javier's just as bright, but in a different way. He's at peace. Xander is not. When they were born, their parents split. The father took Javier west to grow up in Benque Viejo, raised him Maya, looked after him. The mother took Xander east, to grow up in Belmopan. The mother is . . . bad news."

"So they didn't grow up together at all."

"Not like brothers should. The kids used to tease them, call them the Hero Twins, but not in a nice way. Now all the guides joke that they're Ajul and Ixul reborn."

The names jogged Leah's memory. "Ajul and Ixul . . . ?"

"Legendary rulers of the Tzoyna. It's that city downstream from the cave. But we only have oral tradition. Some say they were captured, some say they died in the cave, others say they led their people north." He hocked, spat into his trash can. "Anyway, Xander and Javier have never gotten along. Oil and water."

"They hate each other?"

"Xander more, I think. He has a lot of anger."

"How awful. I wonder why."

"He has plenty of reason. The divorce, his mother's drinking, and Javier can be a little . . ."

"A little what?"

Hector enunciated each syllable. "Sanctimonious."

"Ah." Leah liked Javier very much, but she could see that in him.

"Anyway." Hector shrugged. "Many reasons to be angry in this life. Maybe more reasons from a previous life."

"A previous life! Didn't you say you were Catholic?"

"I'm a little bit of everything, gyal." Hector grinned. "Anyway, no one can control the family they're born into, yes?"

"I don't want to go back to my family."

Hector frowned. "Why's that?"

"My mom is marrying a conservative Catholic guy and he doesn't really listen or understand or . . . anything."

Hector nodded.

"And my mom . . ." She smiled sadly. "We have very different views on things."

Hector leaned forward in his chair. "Gyal," he said, "listen to me. Put all that out of your head. You gotta be who you gotta be. You know what I'm saying?"

Leah smiled. "I think I do."

Hector nodded toward the music. "Get down to the square. There's music and food. Forget about your family. You're all set for tomorrow morning, so just relax and enjoy yourself until then."

"Seven?"

"Yes, gyal, be here at seven. Bring water, change of clothes, close-toed shoes—you know the routine."

"I will. And thanks."

Leah went into the street, feeling light and happy again. She turned around. Hector was standing on his step, hands in his pockets, whistling and surveying his domain.

She went down a narrow alley, which opened onto a public square. On the far side, there was a big Christmas tree decorated with shiny balls and felt ribbons. It struck her as strange—a Christmas tree in such a warm, balmy wind. The only Christmas trees she and her mother had had were the plastic tabletop variety.

In the middle of the square, there was a sunken plaza, and a pavilion with a stage. Teenagers milled around in matching red-and-blue polo shirts, assembling a row of steel drums and checking their phones. On the sidewalks, she saw faces she'd seen before, just wandering around town; some smiled and nodded at her, others ignored her. She saw Ned and Zebulon from the previous night, milling and greeting. She waved and they waved back.

Just then, she nearly tripped over someone's leg. She began to apologize, then said, "Javier!"

He looked up and bolted upright so suddenly he almost fell off his chair.

"Miss-Leah-in-the-Back, Now-in-the-Front!" he said, reassembling himself. "How are you doing this evening, amiga?"

She was overwhelmed to see him again, in casual shorts and a tank top, holding a beer. She felt shy, dropped her eyes, noticed his round calves. "I'm really good, I—"

There was a heavy thudding overhead: the tapping of a microphone. She and Javier turned to the stage, where a man in a Hawaiian shirt was waving for attention.

"Hello, and welcome to the Christmas tree lighting ceremony, in the new beautiful Cayo Welcome Center!"

Scattered applause. Leah clapped very hard.

"The Welcome Center is of course not done yet, but the facilities are built just enough that we can use them for a special occasion this Christmas season. We have the steel-drum band Panerifix from Belmopan, the big headliner tonight, and before that we will have a special Maya ceremony from the Kaan family. But first off, we are the Galen Band from Galen University, and we are going to start the night's festivities with a Christmas song. It is a nice sweet, gentle song. We hope you enjoy it."

They launched into a reggae rendition of "Little Drummer Boy."

Javier said, "Sit down and join me. You like Belikin beer?"

"I'm too young."

"How old are you?"

"Nineteen."

"Old enough in Belize, chula." He made eye contact with the bartender and held up a finger. A cold Belikin was placed on a white square napkin in front of her. Leah thanked him but, remembering the doctor's office in Minnesota in that other life, only pretended to drink from it. Javier didn't notice. He'd flagged down a fellow guide and was talking to him in Kriol. She was so self-conscious and so happy all at once. The tour had provided a structure for them to flirt, but now they were just two regular people in the world, figuring out how to relate.

When his friend left, Leah blurted out, "I'm going to the cave again tomorrow."

Javier's eyes widened. "Again? Chica loca."

"I'm not crazy!" she said, but she wasn't mad. "You saw how the cave affected me."

To her relief, he nodded. "I did notice that, Miss Leah."

"Does that happen to many tourists?"

"Not many. I would not say many. Almost everyone enjoys themselves, or comes out of it saying, wow, that was a big experience, and I am going to tell all my friends." He took another sip of beer. "But to really feel blessed, to feel how sacred a place it is, to want to come back . . . yes, that is rare. Are you coming with me?"

Leah swallowed. Now she'd have to tell him. "I wanted to. But Angelo said that Ceiba Tree was booked for tomorrow. So I'm going with Ultimate Cayo."

"Who at Ultimate Cayo?"

"Xander."

Javier's features clouded over. He leaned back, beer in hand. "Good, he is very smart," he said.

Leah thought it best to lay all her cards on the table. "I didn't know he was your twin. I mean, you told me and then Hector told me, but I wouldn't have guessed otherwise."

Javier started peeling the label from his bottle. "He is very smart," he said again.

Leah took a deep breath and looked toward the stage.

The Galen Band was finished. Now the plaza was cleared. The man in the Hawaiian shirt took center stage again, tapped the microphone for silence, and then without any preamble, lifted an enormous spiral shell to his lips.

Leah braced herself on instinct.

He blew the shell, and she jumped in her seat.

It was an exhilarating, primal sound. The crowd was caught off guard too; now they were paying attention. Leah half rose from her seat so she could see better. In the new silence, she heard a high whistle, joined by another, and then another. Four figures emerged from the crowd, one from each direction: a man and a boy, wearing white tunics, pants, and hats with ribbons; and a woman and a girl, wearing embroidered huipils and tiered skirts. All four were playing little flutes that looked like dolphin fins.

"The Kaan family, playing ocarinas," said Javier.

Leah was relieved at the assurance that he wasn't mad at her. "Kaan means 'snake' in ancient Maya. The Snake Kings of Kaanu'l were one of the greatest dynasties in the lowlands."

"And they still carry the name?"

"Yes, señorita. We Maya are still everywhere."

"What's the ceremony for?"

"To mark the new baktun. See, they come from all four directions, to acknowledge all the corners of the world. A new age is beginning."

On the stage, the man in the Hawaiian shirt was crouching by a stereo. At a nod from the father, a soundtrack of drums began playing over the sound system. The family kept playing their ocarinas, but now moved gently, lifting their knees just enough to turn a shuffle into dance. Then they drew red handkerchiefs from their pockets, and danced around the circle in gentle sways. A white couple in cargo pants positioned themselves close by, holding up their phones; then Poochie crossed the courtyard near the dancers, as if to show disdain.

Javier hissed.

Leah looked over. His jaw was clenched in anger.

She looked away again, quickly.

When the music was done, the Maya father went to the microphone and hovered to the side, as if he were afraid of it. No one could hear what he was saying. The man in the Hawaiian shirt came up behind him and showed him how to stand directly behind the microphone so it could pick up his voice. He nodded his thanks and shifted. He said, "Thank you for your attention. That dance was called the Butterfly Dance, in honor of the new baktun that begins in two days. We began by marking the four moorings of the world. We . . . we learned these dances from our parents."

He looked like he wanted to say more, but faltered, waved, then made his way off the stage. The Galen Band returned and started a jazz rendition of "Away in a Manger."

Leah turned to Javier, who looked calm again. "Do you know them?"

"Oh sure," said Javier. "Roberto was the man just speaking. He is my second cousin. Or third, who knows."

"It seems like everyone around here is related."

"Not everyone by blood, but yes, Belize is so small we're like one big family."

"I want to ask you so many things. Like what all the parts of that ceremony meant. Do you wish you could go back to the time of the ancient Maya so you could see how it really was?"

Javier looked at her sharply. Leah worried that she had offended him somehow.

"Always I do," he said, "but sometimes I think, it is the wrong thing to wish."

"Why would it be the wrong thing?"

"Because we cannot change anything. We can only do right by the world we have come into and follow its rules. And even what we might have known about the ancient Maya—the Spanish burned it all in the Yucatán. Everything, amiga. They gathered all the books and set them on fire. We know only a tiny fraction of what we might know of the Maya. It is all lost."

He sounded so bitter, Leah thought it better not to respond. She just nodded.

But then Javier sat up straight. Though he could express anger, it seemed his mood defaulted to mildness. "Can I tell you a secret, amiga?"

Leah leaned in.

Javier looked around as if to gauge who might be listening. "I have been working on a major project for a long time," he said. "I have a plan to bring back pitz, the ancient ball game."

Leah had a sense of galloping backward and forward in time all at once.

"I have done a lot of research," he said, "and I have recorded many videos of myself on the ball court.

Sometimes I am playing the ball game. Sometimes I am dancing or acting out characters from ancient times. They are all on my YouTube channel but only I can see them. I have not released them yet. I am waiting for the right moment."

"Maybe 2012 is the right moment."

"Maybe, señorita." He grinned at her. "Do you want to go there now?"

Leah was incredulous. "Where?"

"The ball court. I use the one at Cahal Pech."

"But what about the—"

"I have a ball. I made it myself the ancient way. Come on, I'll show you." He got up from his chair, already decided, already on his way, despite the Christmas tree not yet lit.

"Wait," Leah said, "how do I pay for my beer?"

"Do not worry about this, chula, I have a tab. You are my guest. Come."

He set off into the crowd, and Leah followed him.

Xander was glad to miss the Christmas tree lighting ceremony. Instead, he'd gathered a small group of guides in San Jose Succotz, just up the river, in an open-air restaurant set back from the road.

He'd called them at the request of Dr. Castillo to talk about the broken skull. He got there early to hang a white bedsheet and set up the projector. He didn't plan on speaking—he hated public speaking—but he'd ordered six baskets of nachos and paid from his own pocket. The baskets were now making the rounds among ten guides, all senior, and sympathetic to Xander within the Cayo Tour Guide Association. There was an All Guide Meeting tomorrow night—back in San Ignacio, attendance mandatory for anyone who wanted to keep their license—but the issue of the broken skull required immediate attention.

At Dr. Castillo's request, Xander had also texted Javier: *dokta said come to Amir's, 7pm. abt skull.*

No response. That was unusual.

So he called. No response then either.

Xander began to feel elated. It would look bad if his twin didn't show up.

Dr. Castillo was getting impatient. The man had a well-known temper and an appetite for drama. Xander had once seen him strip a guide of his badge on Burns Avenue as if he were defrocking a priest. The lanyard went flying and fluttered to the street. The guide had let a tourist scratch his initials into the wall of the cave: *AJM '06.* That was very bad. He'd been barred for life.

Now Dr. Castillo was milling—the first stage of irritation. He said, "We can't wait for Javier. We can't wait for anyone! We have to start. Individual 12 will have justice!"

Xander nodded and bent over his laptop. He tapped a few keys and a photo of the broken skull appeared on the sheet. The guides sucked their teeth, shook their heads. A few had seen it in person, but most had not.

Dr. Castillo stood with his foot on a chair, which pulled his pants up from his ankle and exposed his fine woolen sock. "Gentlemen, by now all of you have heard about the incident in the cave. Xander has related to me that a tourist dropped his camera onto the skull of Individual 12, which made a hole in the skull. This is an extremely serious incident and the Institute of Archaeology is taking it extremely seriously. After conferring with my colleagues in Belmopan, we have decided to extend at least one of the emergency measures: as of now, cameras are no longer allowed in the cave."

The men looked relieved. Xander knew they'd been worried the cave would close altogether, which meant they'd lose their livelihoods. Only a few guides were certified for Actun Tunichil Muknal. They tended to be lifers. With a full group and everyone tipping, a guide could make up to $500 USD in a day. No other gig came close.

A guide raised his hand. Blanco from Benque, with blue eyes.

"How did it happen?" he asked.

Everyone turned to Xander. He realized he'd never told Dr. Castillo the full story. He took a deep breath and told himself to stay calm.

"It was my tourist," he said. "I wasn't watching him for a few seconds because another group was rushing me from behind, coming up the ladder even though I and my two guests were already up there." He had to include this detail. It was true. All guides knew not to crowd another guide's group. He was still angry about it. But he also had to appear as though he was not deflecting blame. "But it was my tourist," he finished. "I take responsibility."

That was a good choice. The guides' faces were grave, but they nodded. His was a reasonable story. They were on his side. No one asked who the other guide had been—that, they'd eventually pick up from Ronald. And since Javier wasn't here, well. That meant he wasn't here to take responsibility for his end of things. And where was he, anyway? Javier never listened. He was always coasting on his popularity, never imagining that anyone could dislike him for any reason. Xander fought the urge to glance at his phone.

Dr. Castillo clapped his hand on Xander's shoulder. "Thank you, Xander," he said. "We all make mistakes. We appreciate you stepping up to tell your side of it."

Your side of it—that meant there'd be a reckoning with Javier, later. Xander was satisfied.

The meeting went on. They discussed how to prevent such a thing from happening again. Whether they should put fluorescent tape around the remains so that tourists didn't get too close. Whether they should restrict the maximum number of tourists any one guide could have in a year. Lots of guys here did private tours through resorts, where the fees were higher and the commissions more generous than the big group tours of Ceiba Tree and Ultimate Cayo. But strangely, those were the jobs that Javier liked best—the ones where he could maximize the number of new friends he made on any given day.

Which made Xander think of Leah, the tourist girl. She'd been in Javier's group today. She'd probably fallen in love with him already. He resented the fact that he was thinking about them both, and kicking himself for having shut her down on the street last night. Not because he wasn't right—she sure sounded like she had Stendhal syndrome—but rather because it wasn't conducive to his getting to sleep with her. She wasn't white. But she wasn't really Maya either. She was a white girl who looked Maya. How old was she? She didn't seem very old, and he didn't want to break the law. He was twenty-three. If she was over eighteen, it was fine.

Having zoned out and thought about her, he pulled down his shirt to cover his tenting dick. He sat down and ate nachos as the guides continued to talk. They were brothers to him, yes, but he also resented them. Like Javier, they had no ambition. Did they know anything about JavaScript? Or climate change? Or cosmology? No, nobody had reason to. Belize was the backwater of the world. White retirees moved here to build featureless mansions on Ambergris Caye, while white veterans came seeking paradise, only to end up fighting one-man wars in the jungle and dying of alcohol poisoning.

But Xander was still young. He'd get out, somehow. His visa situation was complicated by the fact that he'd tangled with the law as a teenager. It began as fighting, because he got teased about his stutter and fought back; but then it grew into theft, trespassing, a general disregard for authority. He'd been thrown out of school twice, so ended up just teaching himself from the library. He'd volunteered for a dig and Dr. Castillo had noticed he was bright. Ever since then, he'd been trying to send him abroad to college. Boston? Groningen?

Dublin? He wanted to leave so badly that sometimes he spent hours drinking Belikins and looking at pictures of faraway exotic places. And then he'd get three hours of sleep and show up for his tours, still drunk.

Not like Javier, the contented one, the trusted one.

"Xander!" snapped Dr. Castillo.

He came to.

"Where is that smug brother of yours?"

Javier felt jubilant. Christmas was coming and he had a pretty girl in his passenger seat. Xander kept texting him, but he didn't want to deal with Xander tonight.

It was fully dark by the time they reached the Cahal Pech Archaeological Reserve. Javier got out and stretched his legs. The countryside was laid out below like a rumpled blanket, starred with yellow and blue. He opened the door for Leah. She stepped out with a little curtsy. He liked her. He wanted to know what she would be like in bed. Was she the sort whose nighttime personality matched her daylight personality? Or the sort who shifted into her opposite, a dominatrix or a role-player? Javier had flirted with hundreds of girls over the years, and bedded many; his job provided him with plenty of opportunity. He liked to go down on them best. He thought of sex as a ministry, as if he were a missionary sent by God to give pleasure to all the women on Earth. He'd never had a steady girl-friend. He was having too much fun.

Leah, though—Leah overwhelmed him. It wasn't just about her looks. She was pleasant enough to look at—her eyes were bright, and her braid was long and thick. But it was her sincerity that was so disarming. She knew she was strange and she didn't care. Her fearlessness made him afraid of her. He'd never been afraid of a girl before. He liked it.

Leah pointed up at the visitor center. "Do we need to check in?"

"No, chula, it is closed now," said Javier. "But if someone comes, it's all right—I have my badge. Now, follow me."

He led her up the steps. He felt so happy. Flirtation was one of the greatest pleasures in the world, especially with one so willing. They reached the start of the path and he stopped and turned. He took in her body in the moonlight: curved breasts, curved belly, thick legs. He wanted her. He was already swelling. He would have to be patient.

"Miss Leah?"

"Yes, Mister Javier."

"Watch where I step. You have a body like mine, low center of gravity. I expect you not to fall, not once."

She gave a military salute. "I won't let you down."

He grinned.

He led her into a dark gully of cohune palms. Patches of moonlight glowed on the ground. Javier focused on the path, pointing out obstacles as he walked—root there, stone there. Down here, it remained damp year-round, and he found the tree where, he remembered, something special grew. He snapped off a few blossoms and presented them to Leah.

"So pretty," she said. "What are these?"

"Black orchids, señorita. The national flower of Belize."

Leah tucked them behind her ear, grinned at him.

Javier led her up to level ground, and into the site itself, as manicured as a golf course. There were stairs and arches and tunnels and passageways and pyramids, all casting moon-shadows on the grass.

"Welcome to Cahal Pech," said Javier, "known in ancient times as Pekwitz."

Leah turned in a slow circle, taking it all in. He loved how interested she was. He wanted to teach her everything.

"What does the name mean?" she asked.

"It means Mountain of Ticks, señorita. When they first started excavating, they found many ticks in the brush."

"Excavating? You mean, all of this didn't used to look like this . . . ?"

"Oh no. All of it was overgrown. It looked like the mounds we saw on the way to the cave this morning."

Leah shook her head, and Javier admired the way her braid undulated, root to tip. "How many more cities are there?"

"They are everywhere. Did I not say two million people used to live in Belize? And remember that there is a buried city right next to the cave itself."

"Yes. Tzoyna. I want to see it too."

"One can, señorita, but it is very overgrown. All you see are hills of crumbled rock. They're pyramids just like these, but looters got there long before archaeologists."

"A whole lost city. And the people who lived there must have known about the cave."

"Oh certainly, chula. It was likely the foundation of their religion. There are many more caves in the area, all with burned pine and handprints and bones. But the city of Tzoyna built a white road straight to the sacred cave. How could they not have made such a place the center of their world?"

"I wonder how they would have seen it."

This was the language Javier longed to speak. He felt himself opening up further. "Yes," he said, "I try to imagine that all the time, amiga. In their texts, they describe Xibalba as an underworld, a dark palace, a whole city with its own houses and temples and ball courts."

He beckoned her to follow. He was leading her into Plaza B, where stately ceibas alternated with shafts of moonlight. To their left, Temple B rose over them; across the plaza to their right, there were the arches of the palatial quarters, and Temple A beyond them. He named each feature aloud. "No one knew what these structures were really called, though," he said. "These are only the names archaeologists gave them. But now I must show you my favorite part."

He led her around the edge of Temple B and down the steps, under a towering cohune palm. It was darker down here because of the tree cover. He turned to read her expression.

"Do you know what this is?" he asked.

Leah squinted. "It looks like a sort of alleyway." She pointed to the lane bordered by two banks. "Or like a tiny football stadium."

"You are close, señorita. It is a ball court. Not football, but pitz."

"Pitz?"

"The ancient Maya ball game. Want to bowl?" He took off his backpack and pulled out the hard yellow pelota. "Catch, chula."

She caught it, yelped. "It's heavy!"

"Solid rubber. I made it myself."

She held it up, sniffed it, examined it. He leaned against the dais at the far end of the court, enjoying watching her. He came here often, usually in the low season after the tourists were gone, to work on his secret videos. He'd made seventy-six so far. In some of them, he demonstrated the fundamentals of the ball game; in others, he performed monologues where he "channeled" various characters from Maya legend, like Ixul and Ajul. He hadn't shared the videos with anyone yet. He was too shy. In his fantasies, he'd present them to Dr. Castillo, who would recognize their value and make them a fixture of his courses at Galen University. That would lead to the same prestige that Xander had—a recognition of his gifts. It also might lead to a theatre troupe, which would reenact the sacred myths of the lowland Maya, involving the schools and the artists and the local cultural groups. And finally, it would lead to the formation of a pitz league, with teams in Orange Walk and Caye Caulker and Toledo. He'd be the captain of the San Ignacio team. They'd tour all over the country, and then they'd start leagues in Guatemala and Mexico and Honduras, uniting the whole Mundo Maya.

An idea occurred to him. While Leah was still playing with the ball, he pulled out his phone, set it on the

dais, and pressed Record. Usually he was only recording himself in his videos, but this time he'd have a
partner. He didn't tell her yet. He didn't want to spoil
her natural reactions.

Javier crossed his arms, resumed talking.

"When they excavated here," he said, "they found
broken speleothems."

Leah looked up from the far end of the court. "Speleothems?" she said.

"Stalactites. They broke them off in caves, sanded
them down, and arranged them around the court like
pillars."

"Because they associated the court with Xibalba."

"Exactly right. To them, the ball game was a ritual
where they could summon the other world to come
close to them."

"So in this very place we're standing, there were
hundreds of games."

"Thousands. Played by my very ancestors."

"Mine too."

Javier cocked his head. She looked mestiza, but he'd
never asked. "Yours, chula?"

"My biological father was from here. Pancho Gonzalo Iglesias."

He blinked in shock. "Fu chroo, chula?" He cried
out. "He was one of the first ATM guides!"

She smiled. "I know."

"You did not tell me this all day!"

"You didn't ask."

He put his fists on his hips in mock anger. "Who is your mother?"

"She was a young missionary. Taught at a Sunday school . . . St. Ignatius, I think."

"Chula, do not joke with me! I went to that school!"

"What! Did you have a blond teacher? Toni Oliveri?"

"Miss Antonia." Javier shook his head. "Madre de Dios, yes I did."

Leah's delighted laughter echoed on the ball court. Javier covered his face with his hands, shaking his head. Of course he remembered Miss Antonia. He'd been four or five. He remembered her flaxen hair and businesslike kindness. He opened his eyes, peered at her.

"Of course now I can see it in your face. Miss Leah, I had a crush on your mother."

"Oh?" She waggled her eyebrows.

He was afraid she was going to ask, *And do you have a crush on me?* when he wasn't quite ready to go there yet. But she didn't. She tucked the pelota under her arm and put her other hand on her waist, a silhouette against the stone. "Well, now that we've established that we were meant to meet all along, tell me about this place. Why is the ball court your favorite part?"

Javier liked that she had asked him. He liked that she made him think. No one asked him questions like this, or presumed that he had an inner life beyond that which he gave so willingly to others, his body or kindness or time. "I like to come here," he said, "and imagine all of the ball games that once happened here. Who might have played them and why. Were these jugadores just having fun, or were they conducting a sacrifice to the gods?"

"Jugadores?"

"O jugadoras, si eres una mujer," said Javier. "I thought you knew Spanish."

"Oh sí, 'jugadores.' It's been so long since Spanish class. I thought that word meant 'actor,' like in the theatre."

"It can mean both, señorita. Just like 'player' means both in English."

"I see." She tossed the ball to him and he caught it. "¿Eres un jugador?"

Javier smiled. "Yes, I like to think I am, in both senses of the word. An athlete and an actor have much in common, after all."

"So when you say you want to bring back the ancient ball game, do you mean the sport or the theatre?"

"Ah," said Javier, tossing the ball back, "they are not much different, no? The ball game had many modes.

The ritual could be improvised in many ways, for many purposes."

"So how was it played?"

"Nobody knows."

Leah burst out laughing again. He loved the sound of it, no matter how loud. The neighbors might hear them and get annoyed, but they'd just call the police, and Javier knew all the policemen.

He wanted to confide in her. "What I said earlier," he said, "about wanting to go back to the time of the ancient Maya. I feel this every day. I feel like I've lost something and I want to get back to it, but the only way I can do it is . . ." He gestured to the court. "Coming back to the places where they were."

She nodded, no judgment, the pelota still tucked under her arm. "Have you ever told anyone else?"

Javier looked down. "Only my brother," he said. "Once. We got drunk on our birthday, many years ago. He made fun of me. He said, 'You should look ahead, not back.'"

"That wasn't a kind thing for him to say."

Javier looked up. Her voice had been so soft.

"What about you?" he asked. "Do you look forward or back?"

She smiled. "I think the present contains both." She took a few paces back. "Let's play."

"I told you, we do not know exactly how the ancient Maya—"

"Then we'll improvise!" she said, pulling off her flip-flops. "We have to listen to the ones who came before us, like you said. We're in their place. They'll tell us how to perform. Take off your shoes."

"You are joking about something very serious, chula," he said. "I will have to report you to the tourism board."

But he was joking, and she wasn't listening anyway. She'd thrown aside her flip-flops and now she was pacing the court, feeling it out, as if reacquainting herself. He remembered how he'd desired her all through the tour today, noticing how her potbelly hung over the hem of her spandex, how her skin smelled like rich soil when he got close, how her nipples were hard when she rose from the river. How could he know who God would send him on any given day?

She set the ball in the middle of the court. Javier started forward, but she said, "Leave it."

He stayed at his end. "Have we begun the play?"

"Oh yes. We began the play when we arrived." She spread her arms, as if to an invisible audience on the banks of the court. "¡La obra comienza!" she called. "Se llama . . ."

She turned to him, looking perplexed.

"What should we call it?"

"¿La obra?"

"Sí. A story that unites everything."

"Everything, señorita? It cannot be done."

"What did you say to me when I saw the spider in the cave today?"

Javier tried to remember. "You thought its eye was a star. Una estrella."

"Sí. And then you said—"

"La estrella actual se pondrá celosa."

"'La estrella actual.' I like that." She turned back to the invisible crowds. "Vamos a jugar *La Estrella Actual*. ¿Quién la mirará?"

Javier rushed to one of the banks as if he were in the crowd, held up his hands in solemnity and intoned, "La miraremos."

"¡Bien!" Leah laughed. "Now, come here."

Javier descended to stand opposite her, obedient.

"Take off your shoes."

He did so, socks and all, and threw them on the grass.

"Now feel the ground through your feet. Do whatever it tells you. Close your eyes."

He closed his eyes.

"Don't rush," she whispered. "Just listen."

He tried to calm down. At first all he heard were the owls and frogs and crickets. He curled his toes against the stone. Hard, rough, grainy. Then, like he was daydreaming, somewhere in the strip of consciousness before waking, a scenario began to play out in his mind: he was a tall young prince playing the ball game against a pretender, when the temple was red and the grass was parched gold. The prince strolled around the court, proud and haughty. He thought little of his opponent. He was sure of victory and craved the admiration of those watching. His eyes still closed, he picked up the pelota, threw it in the air, jumped, and thrust his hips. He felt contact. Then his foot shot out to catch it, to keep it in the air; then his arm, then the crown of his head, then his foot again, then his hip. He seemed to know where the ball was, even though his eyes were closed. He couldn't make a wrong move. He just kept going. Hip, head, foot, knee, knee, arm, shoulder, knee, knee, arm, hip, chest, hip, knee. He knew he was showing off, but he didn't care. It was so pleasurable to feel the genius of his body.

He felt the ball fall in space one more time, used his knee to kick it forward, and opened his eyes.

The pelota had rolled straight to Leah's feet. She was watching him from the dais, her mouth open.

"How did you do that?" she said.

He shrugged, pleased. "I just can."

"You changed," she said. "I could see it."

He nodded, catching his breath. "I only did as you told me, chula."

"But your body is so . . . smart. I don't know how else to say it."

"Well, thank you."

"How many women have you had sex with?"

He laughed. "Where did this question come from?"

She grinned. "It occurred to me while watching you."

He was unsure of whether to overestimate, to impress her; or underestimate, so as not to scare her away.

"A few," he said.

"You're lying."

"Okay, more than a few." He struck a pose. "Maybe I am a little puto."

Leah laughed. "I know that word! Puto means 'whore'!"

"Well, the masculino is a bad word for a gay man," Javier said. A terrible thought occurred to him. "But I assure you that I am not gay."

Leah shrugged. "It'd be fine if you were."

"Oh?" Javier was surprised. He considered telling her that he had fantasized about sex with men before.

But acting on that fantasy would complicate his life too much, even in Cayo, which was a little more open-minded than the rest of Belize. He liked girls enough, so he stayed with them.

He feigned hurt. "You would not perhaps be a little bit sad if I were gay?"

"Whatever could you mean?"

Javier knew she was playing with him. He liked it. He liked that she made him work for her. "I remember what you said in the van," he said, "that you have many boyfriends."

"Oh sí, soy una puta también," she said.

He was surprised that she referred to herself as such—not as a joke, but with pride, almost reverence. "What does that word mean to you?"

"Hmmmm." She jumped up to sit on the dais and cocked her head. "Well, first of all, it means I don't think sex is bad."

Now the way she was swinging her legs, beating her heels on the stone, was driving him crazy. He started to wander toward her, as if his feet were moving on their own. He told himself he just wanted to be near her. That would be enough.

"You know about Mary Magdalene, right?" she said. "She wasn't really a prostitute, but everyone called her one just because she was close to Jesus. As if being a prostitute is a bad thing anyway! It isn't."

"You don't thhhhink so?" he said. His tongue felt thick in his mouth. Now he was so horny he was slurring his words.

She smirked. "No," she said. "I think sex is very beautiful."

"I do too," he said, feeling foolish. He stopped short of her, waiting to be invited.

She opened her legs to him.

He kicked away the pelota, walked between her legs, pressed his face against her cotton shirt, felt her legs hugging him, felt a kiss on the top of his head, hugged his arms hard around her waist. He was shaking.

"Te deseo tengo ganas," he said into her body. "Ahora."

She held his face in her hands, smiled down at him. "But the stone is so hard."

His mouth was dry. "Don't worry, Leah mi putita."

Before he could think, he pulled off his shirt, undershirt, and pants, balling them into a bundle and reaching back to put it under her head. She lay back. He pushed her knees apart, then reminded himself to be gentle. He kissed her knees, then up her thighs. He reminded himself to slow down. The smell of rose soap gave way to salty musk. He peeled up her skirt, slid his fingers under the hem of her underwear, and pulled them down.

The phone blinked red, recording everything.

Leah had never gotten head, and it was so fun her brain hurt. Afterward she had to massage all her facial features back into place. She was grateful for the darkness. They walked hand in hand back to his truck. They drove down the acropolis and into the countryside, didn't make it far, stopped by the side of the road. She took him in her mouth. He beat his fist on the car door, tasted strong and bitter. They started driving again. The night was warm and Leah leaned out of the window and called to the hills, "I love you! I love you!"

She leaned back in her seat and Javier grinned and gunned along the road. Leah thought, There will never be another Leah and Javier again, in the history of the world.

In a close neighborhood with pitted streets, they parked in front of a small house with a fence in front. A dog was barking. "It's Toots," said Javier. He bent down to greet the rearing black shape, visible only by its tongue. "You are supposed to be a guard dog, perrita. I do not think you realize this."

He opened the front door. It was dark, but Leah could make out eight people drinking Belikins and five dogs nestled among them, all in a cloud of pot smoke, watching a pirated DVD of *The Voyage of the Dawn Treader*.

"Honeys, I'm home," Javier called. "Ah ku tun aan di lait?"

"Yaa mayn," said one. The *Dawn Treader* had dropped anchor on Ramandu's Island and they were engrossed.

Javier led her to the kitchen and turned on the overhead light, garish white, with dead moths collected at the bottom of the bulb. Clothes and equipment were piled on the floor. A giant cockroach scuttled to the far corner. But Javier said no word to excuse the scene, so Leah surmised that it was the normal one.

"How many people live here?" asked Leah.

"Officially it is just me and my dogs, but at any time, I might have a few friends staying," he said, peering into his fridge. "I like having people around. Want a Belikin?"

"No, thank you," she said.

"Anything else? You need to rehydrate, chula," he said, and winked.

Leah grinned. They were in a refractory period, which suited her just fine. Only this morning, he'd guided her into the cave; only an hour ago, his tongue had been wriggling inside her. She shivered at the memory. This whole day had been nothing but a series of climbing perfections, so she welcomed however the next one would appear to her.

Javier, still shirtless, gave her a bottled water and opened his Belikin. He leaned his elbows on the counter. She sat on a stool. They clinked bottles, glass on plastic.

"To . . . Belize?"

"To the Maya."

"To the past and future."

"And the present."

They drank.

Leah nodded at the screen, where the crew of the *Dawn Treader* was meeting Ramandu and his daughter. "Have you read the book?" she asked.

Javier shook his head. "I have not, señorita."

"What you said in the cave today, about the star. It reminded me of this line where one character says something like, a star is a ball of gas, and then another character says, 'That's only what a star is made of, not what it *is*.' I think it's the most important line in the story, but," she pointed to the movie, "they leave it out."

Javier frowned. "Is there pain?"

It took a moment for Leah to understand he was talking about the bandage on her finger. She'd forgotten all about it. "I think it'll be fine. It was a clean cut."

"I will dress it again."

"No, don't worry about—"

But he had already left his beer on the counter to open a cabinet. He pulled out a first aid kit.

"It is no problem, chula," he said. "You want to be sure it doesn't go septic. Tropical environments can do that." He opened the kit and used tiny scissors to cut the gauze off her finger, which revealed a pale, shriveled section of skin. The cut was deep and translucent. He tilted his head toward the hall. "Go wash."

Leah found the bathroom. The toilet had no seat cover and the shower had no curtain. A gecko watched her run cold water over the cut and use a bar of white soap to clean it out. She patted it dry on her shirt.

She came back to him and held out her finger.

He leaned across the counter. She remembered how he'd knelt in front of her just an hour before, for another reason; everything was repeating. His hands were cool and wet from the sink. He used a cotton ball to dab the cut with antiseptic.

She said to Javier, "I used to cut myself on purpose."

He stopped, looked up at her. "Why?"

She swallowed. She had not told the whole truth—

that this cut, too, had been on purpose. But she reminded herself that omission was the only acceptable
form of lie. She didn't want to endanger this romantic
moment. She said, "Because when I did, I felt more
whole."

To her amazement, Javier didn't chastise her. He
just turned back to his dabbing. "You know the ancient
Maya cut themselves as well."

"I know."

"They did it very carefully. Do you?"

"Yes. My mother . . . would freak out if she knew.
She wouldn't understand. She'd think I was trying to
kill myself."

"But you are not."

"No. Not at all. I'm practicing, somehow."

Javier squirted ointment onto a Q-tip, daubed it
along the cut. "The cave can taste blood."

"Taste it? What do you mean?"

Javier didn't answer, which was maddening to Leah.
He continued, "As long as you are careful and don't
do it very often, it is not dangerous. Like passing your
finger through a flame."

She noticed that he'd started using the present tense,
and she didn't correct him. "I'm careful. I use anesthetic and a razor blade that I hold over a fire. What
did the ancient Maya use?"

Javier cut off a strip of gauze. "Obsidian," he said. "Sharp volcanic glass." He pressed a Band-Aid to the wound, then wrapped the gauze around it.

Leah wiggled her finger and grinned. "I'm healed!" she said.

But Javier looked troubled. "Miss Leah, may I tell you another secret?"

Leah forgot all about her cut. "Of course."

He picked up his Belikin. "Let's get out of the kitchen," he said.

He led her down another hallway into a bedroom, just big enough for a full-sized mattress. She sat by the window, trying not to look too closely at the stains on the sheets, as Javier lit three candles on the bedside table. Then he pulled the door shut and sat at the head of the bed.

"This is the secret. I have made a discovery in the cave," he said, and paused to allow maximum drama.

Leah kept her water bottle lowered.

"A green eccentric obsidian blade," he said, "inside the skull that you have seen in the cave today."

"Eccentric how?"

"It is shaped like a star. Difficult to carve."

"A star!"

"Yes. In Maya iconography, a star has four points, so I call it a star."

"I want to see it."

"I was trying to see it again, when we were up there today. I thought maybe I could get ahold of it and then . . ." He took a drink.

"Then what?" Leah prompted.

"Then maybe Dr. Castillo would take me seriously," he said. "Maybe everyone would."

Leah smiled at him, put her hand on his knee. "You don't think people take you seriously?"

"Not like Xander. He has an idea, everyone pays attention. I have an idea . . ." He shrugged.

"I see," said Leah. She withdrew her hand. "I didn't mean to go with Xander to the cave tomorrow, you know. It just happened that way. I'm going with you again the day after tomorrow."

Javier smiled. "I will survive, chula."

Leah stared out the window. They were quiet, listening to the grackles cheep in the trees.

Then Leah said, "Remember when we got to the place in the cave where we stepped to the upper chamber?"

"Yes, the step-up rock."

"And I asked you, why can't we go farther."

"Yes."

"How far in does it go?"

Javier was solemn, now, in a way that confused Leah. "I do not know," he said. "I have never gone."

He was so reticent. Leah had to draw it out of him. "Why?"

Javier shifted. He looked uncomfortable. "I have been going to the cave since I was a little boy. When you feel wind in a cave, you know that there is more of the cave, so you feel drawn to find its source. Many feel that hunger. But there are stories about this cave, among guides. It is not a normal cave. All of the caves in Maya land are sacred to the Maya, yes, but this one is especially sacred, and it is dangerous. I have heard the stories, so I do not go."

"Who has?"

"Xander has."

"Then I'll ask him about it tomorrow."

"I would not suggest that you do. It is not a topic he likes to talk about."

It was the closest he'd ever come to snapping at her, and she winced. For a terrible moment she doubted everything: her euphoria, his hospitality, her own safety.

But Javier saw her face and softened again. He put his beer down on the bedside table and crawled to her. He kissed her on the cheek. "I become frustrated when

I speak of my brother," he said. "But then I remind myself that anger accomplishes nothing. Anyway, he brought it on himself. I pity him. It has nothing to do with you, chula. You will have a good time tomorrow."

Leah nodded. "I'm sorry it's so difficult."

"It is life. He is very angry at me and I do not know why."

"Do you love him?"

Javier winced as if in pain. "Yes, he is my brother. I love him."

"Maybe in another life you can reconcile."

"In another life, señorita? Blasphemy. Remember you are speaking to a good Catholic man." Then he ran his finger under the strap of her bra. Leah shifted, opened her legs, leaned back as he buried his face into her neck.

"*I* think," she said, "it makes a whole lot more sense if we're reborn over and over, than if we only live one life and that's it."

"Blasphemy," said Javier, but his mouth was muffled against her breast, so it sounded like *maffami.*

She said, "You're so beautiful, Javier."

He lifted his head and smiled at her. "Thank you, chula."

She barely slept that night. They made love, slept a little, then woke up and made love again. A bird screamed so close nearby that it seemed to be in the room with them. In a few hours, the sky began to lighten. The sound of a rooster woke her from a doze, and she felt the sickness her doctor had warned her about. She went to the bathroom and vomited in the toilet as quietly as she could. Then she cleaned out her mouth with the rest of her bottled water. She didn't even think of telling Javier. Again: omission was the only acceptable form of lie. She returned to bed and pressed her lips to his skin. It was the only way she could express how she felt, just to fasten herself to him, to breathe in his smell of woodsmoke and pungent sex. She had never been treated like this by any lover, so cherished and enjoyed.

In another hour, they were driving up the road by the river, through violet mist. She heard phantom drums, far away. The morning star blazed in the east. The dogs did not stir.

OAXACA
13 Eb 10 Sek, Long Count 15.10.14.7.12

---

1 November, 3012

In a room carved into the mountain, Tanaaj was having lunch with a group of jovenix who'd come to see her.

"We brought you a gift," said the one named Leticia.

"But hermanix," said Tanaaj, "you have already brought me information."

"This is something you can hold! Trust me, you'll like it."

Tanaaj smiled. "See?" she said to those watching. "See how I suffer?"

They all laughed, and Leticia turned back to the other jovenix. The room was tiny, but the wayhouse was large, built to hold two hundred; its honeycomb rooms overlooked the valley. Though the views were beautiful, Tanaaj felt uneasy in this region. There was no water, no humidity, no greenery. Oaxaca was a desert. A dry wind screamed just beyond the edge, sloughing the mountains to sand.

Leticia turned back, holding a bundle on her palms. Tanaaj pressed her hands in thanks and unwrapped the cloth. There lay a four-pointed star of green obsidian.

"Oh," she said softly.

She touched it and felt a jolt, like an electric shock. She whipped her finger away.

It took a moment for Tanaaj to get her voice back. The jovenix were all staring at her.

"Truly, I am honored, carnalix," she said. She touched her hand to her heart, thanking Xibalba, and then took the bundle and used the cloth to hold the blade up to the sky. The edge of the obsidian was so smooth, it reminded her of water petals surging up a beach, which reminded her of something else, a memory that slid beyond her awareness. "I will cherish it."

Leticia bowed from the waist, and the other jovenix did the same.

"Now," said Tanaaj, "let us clean up from lunch, yes? And hermanix Leticia, let's work together so you can tell me what you came to tell me."

They started clearing plates and cups. Because of water scarcity, Tanaaj asked for irradiator brushes, then beckoned for Leticia to follow her to an adjacent room. She trusted the jovenix. She trusted everyone who came to her, according to Versa Seis, *The strangest stranger is your sister.* Briefly, she considered the alternative: suspecting every stranger of malice, or even murder. That was the hell that Niloux DeCayo was living now. But she had brought it on herself. Tanaaj felt pity for her.

She pitied herself, for other reasons. She'd made herself the champion of Laviaja by promising to prove Xibalba was real. How she was going to do that, she still didn't know. The problem swelled fresh in her mind every morning like a headache. Still, she kept faith. She adhered to the Rule of Saint Leah, using the aug as little as possible. That meant her only information came from those who chose to share it with her. Any bit of it was precious now.

They were brought irradiator brushes. They started scrubbing the plates, brushing the crumbs into bowls for reuse.

"Now, hermanix," said Tanaaj, "tell me what you came to tell."

Leticia nodded. "There are four thousand declared LFC following you now," she said, "if you count between Acapulco and Tenochtitlán. Two thousand more, if you count those to the east of us, and a thousand more, if you count those still on the 17-Lat searoad. But there are three active typhoons in the Pacific now, so they might not get to Cayo in time for the Jubilee. So that's a total of six thousand planning to assemble here in the valley tonight."

Tanaaj was pleased to hear these numbers, but did not let her face tell it. She had to watch her newfound tendency to enjoy fame. No viajera should become accustomed to leadership. But the Jubilee was so important, and these numbers gave her courage.

Now the more difficult question. Tanaaj told herself she must ask it with the same serenity for which she was known. She would not permit anyone to see the doubts beneath the surface. "And how many," she said, "have declared for Niloux DeCayo?"

Leticia swallowed. "Nine thousand," she said.

Tanaaj nodded. Serenity above all. She must have faith in the answer to come; Xibalba would not abandon her. "Are they on the Atlantic searoad with her?" she asked. Her voice came out smooth and untroubled.

"Or mustering in the islands. Or the jungle to the south, where I came from."

This meant they were as good as surrounded, if it

came to that. But again: serenity. "So you have met these Zeinians, hermanix?"

"I had an encamadix who was one."

Tanaaj raised her eyebrow, smiled a little. "What was your impression?"

The wind rose to a scream again. Leticia looked out over the valley as they waited for it to die down. Tanaaj studied her. She was a muxe, an ancient zapotec manéra that honored the god of this place, wearing satin flowers in her hair. The LFC skewed older and the Zeinians skewed younger, so jovenix were especially precious and Tanaaj made sure they knew it. Leticia was seventeen, maybe. Viajeras that age were keen readers of the world's mood.

When it was quiet again, Leticia said, "It was like she was brainwashed. She just kept talking about how, if Xibalba is real, then why have disappearances stopped. That the disappearances were never related to having ojos-de-Leah in the first place, but rather because there were just so many people on the move in the Diluvian Age, but now we've covered all the new territory there was to cover. That Xibalba must be a myth or even a big lie by some secret group of people who act outside of the Tzoyna to control people. And that . . ."—Leticia swallowed—"that you're a part of that conspiracy."

Tanaaj let these words flow through her, careful not to let them harden her. It was difficult. She hadn't known how much the Zeinians were not only misguided but malicious. There was no other way to describe such blatant disregard for the truth.

She brushed another dish, front and back, until the ceramic squeaked clean. "And the adivinix, Sembaruthi?" said Tanaaj. "Has she declared for either side?"

"The last I heard, she hadn't said anything about it." Leticia held up a plate, eyed a crack, and cast it over the cliff. It flipped in the wind and fell out of sight. "But why does she matter?"

Tanaaj started on the cups. "Sembaruthi is the adivinix responsible for the last known disappearance in 3009. I do not understand why she remains silent."

"How was she responsible for it?"

"Sembaruthi told her to walk to the nearest cedar grove. She started on the path, and then . . ." Tanaaj waved her hand in an arc. "Gone. There's a shrine on the spot, near Arkansas Bay."

"But couldn't it have been a coincidence?"

Tanaaj looked her in the eye. This time, it was hard to mask her disappointment. Was the rot creeping in, even among the LFC? But she would be gentle still. She would not correct such a misperception; she'd only shame it a little. She trusted the jovenix to take the hint from the look on her face.

Leticia did. She looked down. "I just don't want there to be war," she said.

Tanaaj softened. "War," she said, shaking her head. "No. There will not be such a thing, that much I promise you."

"But how can you promise that? Someone tried to kill Niloux DeCayo. She has to travel with guards now. How soon before they retaliate?"

A thought flitted through Tanaaj's mind, that it would not be so bad if Niloux were dead, because then her movement would die with her, and she could return to her safe wanderings, and so could everyone else.

She banished the thought back to the darkness.

"And if someone does kill her," Leticia continued, "the Zeinians will rise up to avenge her, the LFC will retaliate, and the cycle will never end."

"I will never instruct one viajera to kill another," said Tanaaj.

"Then what will you do?"

Tanaaj set down a cup, harder than she meant to, and it cracked.

Leticia fell silent.

When Tanaaj spoke again, she let her voice be soft but firm. "As in all things, hermanix," she said, "I await instruction from the god of the place. I do not worry about things before their time. Right now, I am here, speaking to you. Tonight begins the season of gathering, and we will muster in the valley and start the long journey to Cayo. Often I would like to dream about faraway places, or worry about problems I cannot solve, but what good will that do, when the wisdom I need always comes up through my feet? I will let Xibalba be Xibalba, perfect; I will let the Munda be the Munda, imperfect. I sacrifice here so that I may enter there." She threw the cup into the wind and heard it shatter on the mountainside. "Someday."

That afternoon, as Tanaaj's familia started down the mountain, she was visited by an aug bird. The owl hovered in midair and opened its beak:

Zac xtili, Tanaaj DeCayo!
Your work today is: Doula de la Salida
1800–0000, Xoxocotlán Home.
All prerequisites met.

Xoxocotlán Home.

The word "home" meant her charge was a sedentix.

Tanaaj felt angry. She'd been looking forward to the big crowds tonight, with the music and marigolds and spinning puppets. This was the beginning of the season of gathering permitted by the Rule of Saint Leah. She'd been longing for it, after months of following Versa Tres so devoutly. But the season of gathering also meant double the work.

Tanaaj tapped her heart to dismiss the bird. "Hermanix," she said, "I am needed elsewhere."

"What'd you get?" said Leticia.

"I will be a Doula de la Salida."

Leticia raised her eyebrows.

A ninx asked, "What is that?"

Tanaaj picked her up, carried her while she explained. "It means," she said, "that a person is about to receive the sacrament of Rebirth, so it is a very special time. I am going to go be with her to help her transition to her next life." She didn't mention that her charge was a sedentix. She would deal with that when she came to it.

Now the others were pausing and staring into the middle distance, also receiving work assignments. Three had to forage, two had to walk ahead to clean the ruins, and one was now a zadre to a child half a mile behind them. This meant there was no one free in Tanaaj's immediate familia to accompany her. She checked the time. There were not enough hours to look for a companion from another familia.

She had to go by herself.

For a moment, she thought of rejecting the assignment to take on a double shift of communal work.

She shook her head, disgusted with herself. She had to abide by the algorithm. It was her duty as a viajera. If she looked for special treatment, she was no better than Niloux DeCayo.

"I will see you in the valley, familia," she said. She kissed the ninx goodbye, and turned to walk down the mountain alone.

Tanaaj replayed her conversation with Leticia in her mind as she walked.

The mountain no longer sheltered her from the winds, so she raised her shields to blunt them. The static crackled and fizzed. She'd lose power quickly. She'd have to recharge tonight. She followed deer tracks, directed by her ai; where there were discontinuities she deployed her swair to float safely to the next ledge down.

She kept thinking about the word "war," and all that it implied. She had not allowed herself to believe that it would come to that, but now the specter of violence loomed to the east. What would anyone fight with? Niloux's would-be assassin had used a sharpened stick, of all things. Murder was a lost art. She was a naïve zealot who thought a simple stabbing would do the job, as if intent were enough to kill.

But that wouldn't discourage those who wanted to learn. No doubt the Zeinians were now provoked, and teaching themselves to defend against attack, or even attack first.

She stopped, closed her eyes. This is what happened when she was alone: there was not the presence of others to leaven and calm her. She reminded herself that she was not truly alone. "May the god of this place grant me peace and instruction, all of you who once walked this way," she said aloud. "May Xibalba direct my steps."

She opened her eyes.

She started down again, meditating on the land to calm herself.

She recalled that in the 2100s, Oaxaca had become wetter and hotter, with storms that lasted for days. Mudslides buried entire neighborhoods. Then the climate changed again in the 2600s; the aridity returned with new furor and baked the mudslides into interlaced fingers. It was a beautiful, alien sight. Still, she didn't like desert landscapes. They made her feel desolate and insecure. She'd had to cut across Oaxaca for the sake of time, and longed for lush rivers and black mud, like in Cayo.

Cayo, where the ancient Maya had ruled.

Cayo, where the Consort Twins had founded Laviaja.

Cayo, where the Zeinians were now gathering against her.

Tanaaj indulged her darker thoughts again. Inept as it had been, if the assassination attempt against Niloux had worked, the Zeinians could have easily lost their momentum. This Niloux DeCayo was a rare charismatic, it was said; without her, the movement would become a historical footnote. The Jubilee would again become a space for celebration, not a court of confrontation. Clearly Niloux was a misguided soul in need of instruction. Tanaaj would have given it, gladly, if they'd met under other circumstances. But that moment had passed. Niloux had already caused too much chaos. Was it evil of Tanaaj to wish her nonexistent?

She stopped on the path, put her hand to her heart. "The god of the place is with you, Tanaaj DeCayo," she said aloud. "The god of the place will direct your steps."

She started the meditation again.

She marked the scruffy creosote bushes, the pink nubs of cactus, the pressed umbrellas of acacia trees. She marked how the mud cracked in pentagons and hexagons. She slipped on a loose stone, flung out her arms to balance herself, and winced at the wrench of muscle. "The land has acted upon me, blessed be the land," she muttered. The wind continued to tear at her shields. She felt so exposed on this mountainside, impotent and pathetic. She looked around but saw no one. She checked the aug. The nearest people were a mile away, up on the ridge. She was alone. She had the strange feeling that the wind would sweep her right off the mountainside because there was no one to keep her grounded. She remembered that she'd received another message from Messe. She'd delayed watching it because watching the last one had been so hard. But she felt the temptation to watch it now, just to alleviate the loneliness, to indulge in what sense of company it provided.

She focused on the land.

Dusty mesquite.

A spill of sand.

A red wolf, tracking her from behind a spray of agave.

She tapped her heart to check her shield, and felt the telltale buzz under her skin. The wolf scampered away, whimpering. Her ai translated:

Hunger oh my hunger

dearest hunger

Tanaaj needed to eat too. She used her ai to forage ironwood seeds, cactus fruit, and three kinds of mushroom. When she'd gathered enough, she stopped for a brief supper.

While she ate, she opened the holo from Messe.

The sight of the child made her stop chewing and stare.

This time, Messe was no longer a child at all. She'd lost weight. She'd shaved her head. She wore sandals, a plain mottled tunic, and the jaguar tooth on a cord around her neck. She stared into Tanaaj's eyes, bitter.

"This is the last holo I'm going to send you," she said, "because there's no point if you watch these and never answer. I've become a hunter. I know eating animal flesh is against the Rule of Saint Leah. But I don't follow the Rule of Saint Leah. You do. I know that. But you've made pretty clear that I'm free to do whatever I want, so this is what I choose." Her voice became softer; she was pleading, the last of the child in her. "I always hunt with other bands. We can't use shields, but we protect each other." Her voice hardened again. "So I'd say, don't worry about me, but why would I say that? I don't think you do anyway. So . . ." She shook her head in disgust. "Why am I even recording this . . ."

The holo stopped abruptly.

That was the end.

Tanaaj closed her eyes. She must not give in to the temptation to answer. Laviaja forbade it. She must not break the Rule of Saint Leah at a time when she was assuming the leadership of Laviaja. It was as if Messe were goading her to answer, not with honey but with gall: hunters were as offensive as the sedentix. Versa Trece said that blood belonged only to Xibalba, and Tanaaj believed that meant all blood, human and animal. Technically, the Treaty of 2780 allowed for hunters—humans who could eat animal flesh if they hunted the animals themselves—but in turn, hunters were obligated to give up their shields permanently, so that animals had equal opportunity to hunt them. The thought of Messe hunting made Tanaaj feel sick. But Messe did not belong to her; she belonged to the Munda, to the whole human family. It was not her place to weigh in on this child's decisions no matter how she felt. Laviaja promised that the beloved always returned to you. Versa Cinco: *La amadix siempre vuelve.* Whatever child you gave up came back in another form. She knew this. So why did the hurt remain?

The answer welled up from the god:

Because you are imperfect forms stuck in an imperfect world. Here, peace requires sacrifice. But in Xibalba, there will be no need. In Xibalba, you will never have to part from anyone, ever.

She arrived at Xoxocotlán Home. It was a stone house surrounded by marigolds, set between massive mud spurs, blocking the view to the north and south.

A viajera waved from the door. Tanaaj bowed to her, a beguine by the looks of it, in full white wimple and black habit. She was very glad to see another person.

"Buenos tardes, en nombre de la Trinidad de Cayo," she said. "Me llamo Tanaaj."

"Y soy Clementine," said the beguine, bowing back. "Bienvenida. I know you well by reputation. Come in, I've been with ahn since midnight."

Tanaaj recoiled internally. She'd forgotten sedentix referred to themselves as "ih/ahn," instead of "she" in honor of Saint Leah.

But she said nothing and followed Clementine. The house was one long room with three square windows. Copal bubbled in the corner. She heard a sharp crackling noise, and thinking it was a fire, turned to see instead the dying person in bed, chest heaving, sloped toward the light. Her skin was dark yellow. Her white hair was combed into a rayed halo. At the sight, Tanaaj felt a surge of compassion, for someone so close to dying; and a surge of pity, for a settler who had rejected Laviaja.

She turned away and followed the beguine to a bench.

Clementine offered her tea. "Ih name is Ying Yue. Ih has long stopped taking food and drink, so we must eat and drink for ahn," she said.

Tanaaj nodded and accepted.

"Before I leave," said Clementine in a stern voice, "I need to discuss something with you."

Tanaaj raised her eyebrows. It had been months since anyone had spoken to her in such a tone. She realized she'd become accustomed to deference.

"As I said, I know you by reputation," said the beguine. "You follow the Rule of Saint Leah. Sedentix like Ying Yue do not."

And yet benefit by it, thought Tanaaj, but kept silent.

"Ordinarily, I don't think the paragua would have paired you with ahn. But it's the season of gathering. The algorithms do what they can to optimize skill-matching when there's so much work to be done, and here you are. But you must not let your prejudice interfere with your work."

Tanaaj saw two paths ahead: to let go or offer challenge. She remembered Kiren's words in Kaua'i: *You have to stop being so passive.* These were extraordinary times, so she chose the unusual path. "You believe I have prejudice, hermanix?"

The beguine seemed to second-guess herself. She blinked and said, "A Doula de la Salida has influence over how the person will be reborn. You might be the last person with ahn. It's true that I don't know if you have ill will toward ahn because ih is a sedentix, but if you do, you must put it aside."

"I carry ill will toward no sentient being," said Tanaaj. "Though I pity many."

"You call it pity," said Clementine. "I call it anger."

Tanaaj held her tongue.

"To be frank," the beguine continued, "the tone of the LFC's propaganda troubles me. You have names for the sedentix: 'settlers' and even 'hoarders.' You say the Zeinians are playing a dangerous game, but so are you. Especially since the assassination attempt on Niloux DeCayo."

Tanaaj took a sip of tea. She chose to engage the statement that would render the others irrelevant. "I don't know how it can be propaganda, hermanix, to state a thing upon which every personal and impersonal observer agrees."

"Which is?"

"That in the last millennium, thousands of people have disappeared from the face of the earth. It is not an artifact of evolving vision. It is not a trick of the aug. These disappearances began happening more frequently at the same time we learned how to grow ojos-de-Leah. And Saint Leah told us, explicitly, where she was going before she disappeared. Her body was never found, though she was last seen in a closed cave system. Do you dispute any of what I have just said, hermanix?"

At last Clementine said, "No."

"So how can it be propaganda, which implies bad faith?"

Clementine looked down at her lap.

Tanaaj smiled. "I am not an angry person, hermanix. I have never been angry. Only vigilant. I desire the security and salvation of all humankind, myself included, I admit." She decided to let her off the hook. She made her voice light. "You are correct, this is not often my work. I mostly work as a jugadorix. And you?"

Clementine still looked troubled, but said, "Usually I'm a Doula de la Salida. My pista goes from deathbed to deathbed. In fact, I have to go to my next assignment now." She seemed to decide something, then looked toward the bed in the corner. "While you sit with ahn, it may help to acquaint yourself. Ih never used the aug much, so there's not much of a record, but we do know ih had a single encamadix for most of ih life, and they had a child together." The beguine nodded toward a small altar and a holoportrait surrounded by marigolds.

Tanaaj looked at it, nodded, and said nothing.

"I left you some food," said Clementine. "The sunballs are charged. There's a pit latrine thirty paces to the east. The paragua has sent someone to relieve you at midnight but, I have to warn you, this one's time is near. Ih may die during your shift. Have you ever been present at death?"

"No, hermanix. I have attended deathbeds, but never seen death itself."

Clementine nodded and said, "Sometimes, in death, Xibalba comes very close indeed. This is part of why the Maya made human sacrifices, after all. You have to be careful."

Tanaaj felt sudden excitement. Had the god of the place guided her here to help her find the answer to her questions after all? But excitement was inappropriate here. She forced her voice to tranquility. "I understand, hermanix," she said. "What do you advise I do?"

Clementine pointed to the windowsill. "There's a cup of water there," she said. "Use the cloth to moisten ih lips and ih mouth, and otherwise ih body knows what to do. Remember that the final minutes are very important. They will determine how ih is reborn."

Tanaaj bowed her head. "I will stay with Ying Yue," she said, "to ensure a good rebirth."

———————

Tanaaj sat in the windowsill as dusk turned to twilight. The wind had died, and now the air was stale and dead. She watched Ying Yue and tried to guess her age: One hundred? One hundred and ten? Her eyes were half-closed, the eyelids translucent. She gasped for breath as if running a race.

Ih, not *she,* Tanaaj reminded herself.

The sedentix claimed that, because the ih-ahn pronoun came from ancient Belizean Kriol, it should not be offensive to viajeras. Tanaaj scoffed at them in her mind. *Call yourselves whatever you like,* she thought, *if you'd stop settling on the land that belongs to everyone and hoarding it for yourselves.*

She wiped the white mucus from the sedentix's lips, swabbed them with water.

"May the god of this place grant me peace and instruction," she whispered, "and you too, Ying Yue."

The prayer seemed to fall flat. This sedentix had spent ih whole life rejecting most of the very practices that ensured ahn a peaceful life—paraguas, worksharing, the panoptica. Similar to Niloux DeCayo, who abused the guarantee of individual liberty to hack at the very foundation of civilization. Did she truly want a world where no one could trust one another? Did she have some special nostalgia for the Age of Emergency, the capitalist epoch that broke the world? What kind of person desired a return to hoarders and weapons and narcissist-states? And what kind of person sat passively on the sidelines, as if none of it affected them, as if their own inaction did not enable it?

Sedentix, Tanaaj thought. Just like this one. Ying Yue looked helpless now, like a sacrificial lamb of old, but ih represented everything Tanaaj was now fighting against.

She got up, examined the holoportrait on the table. There was Ying Yue, young and beaming, with two long braids. Ih encamadix sat close, arm slung around ih shoulder, with a marigold in ih teeth. They both seemed to be some zapotec manéra, though how could you really tell, with sedentix? On their lap there was an elfish ninx, lurching forward with her eyes wide and her tongue hanging out. Had the child also become a sedentix? Tanaaj asked her ai. No, she had not; she had the sense to leave at age sixteen and was now deep in the Isle of Skye.

Tanaaj was reminded of her childhood fantasy of having a family of her own, and how her zadre had persuaded her otherwise. She had grown out of the fantasy. Ying Yue had not. Ying Yue had claimed both of these people as her own. And where were they now? Encamadix dead, child gone. Ih was dying without them. Had ih thought ih could hoard them too, up until the end? Now ih was attended by a hated stranger instead. This is what happened when you tried to possess people. You were always left alone.

Ying Yue gulped loudly. Tanaaj resumed her seat on the windowsill. This could be it. But the minute dragged to two minutes, and she realized it'd been a false alarm. *Hurry up,* she vented in her mind, *I am awaited in the valley.*

She shook her head to banish the thought. She must have patience. Her work was to deliver this person safely to the next life. Hadn't Clementine reminded her that the final minutes were most important? She had control over how Ying Yue would be reborn. What would be the best-case scenario for Ying Yue?

To not be reborn a sedentix, thought Tanaaj. To be reborn a true viajera.

She leaned back against the wall and retraced the history of her faith, step by step. How Ruth Okeke founded terraphenomenology, or the theology of place. How Ida Gudasz and Micah Wells wrote the first gathering algorithms. How Xander Cañul laid the foundation for a new understanding of entropy.

"This universe is ruled by entropy," she said, and her voice was soft in the low stone room. "Entropy is its ultimate nature. If our souls belonged here, we would never seek to leave it. But this is what all of human history endeavors to do, Ying Yue: to leave, to transcend the material, to reunite with the greater actuality. What other conclusion can there be, than that our presence in this universe is provisional? That we are being held captive, though we do not know our captor? That we must make sacrifices in order to get free?" She liked speaking aloud; it encouraged the evolution of her thought, and put her in the mind of performance, the revelation that only physicality could bring forth. "Saint Leah wrote, *The universe welled from the tip of the blade*," she said. "But in what greater body was that cut made?—it is Xibalba, the reality we cannot see. Our only work is to pursue it."

Ying Yue stirred again, gasping, chest shuddering. Tanaaj placed both feet on the ground in readiness. This could be it.

But again, ih breathing stabilized.

Tanaaj gripped her blade through the cloth. She didn't want to be alone with a dying sedentix. She wanted to be with her familia, mustering the parades for Cayo. She indulged a thought of Niloux DeCayo grappling with her assassin on the golden plains of the Maghreb. In her mind, the heretic had a ridged, demonic, distorted face. The stick bit deep. She gasped and died. Tanaaj needed to get out of here—to go ahead, to walk her way into the solution.

But hadn't she just told Leticia that there was no use in looking ahead? That always, the god of the place you were in provided the answers you needed?

She looked at Ying Yue with new eyes.

"I need to solve my problems," she said softly. "How to remove the threat of Niloux DeCayo, and how to prove Xibalba is real." Her voice grew as her conviction grew. "I am much troubled by these problems. All that I love hangs in the balance. I have faith that the gods will grant me this instruction. And you are here with me, in this moment; you are part of the god of this place. Are you my instructor?"

Tanaaj realized she was turning the green star blade in her hand. She hadn't remembered touching it, much less turning it, but here it was. The sedentix coughed, which became a rattling. Ih chest splayed outward, ih arms hanging, mottled blue like the ancient Maya victims.

Tanaaj leaned forward. This could be it.

But again, ih breathing stabilized.

Tanaaj began to feel desperate. She turned the blade between her fingers again, her blood acidified, thinking in circles. Ying Yue was so near death, but still refused to die. Tanaaj realized that she might spend her entire shift here and miss ih death altogether. Hadn't Clementine said that the moment of death was a moment when Xibalba was very near? Just like when the ancient Maya made human sacrifices, dispatching their victims to an honorable death and a favored rebirth, for the glory of Xibalba.

Tanaaj froze, and stopped the blade spinning.

She shut her eyes tight, and thought: Is this truly the god speaking to me? Or is this a heresy born of my troubled mind?

Eyes still closed, she indulged the vision that had occurred to her:

She stands up on her feet, and stands over the bed.

She bunches a blanket just beneath the sedentix's throat.

She whispers words of thanksgiving and safe journey, to Ying Yue, for ih sacrifice, which would guarantee ih rebirth as a viajera.

She uses the blade, and catches the blood in this blanket.

Ying Yue rejected Laviaja and with it, the panoptica; within this house, no actions were monitored nor subject to access. Ying Yue was near death. Clementine had said so. Who would think to question ih final moments? This was well, because no one who was not in this place in this moment would understand what

Tanaaj was beginning to understand: that Ying Yue, in ih death throes, was part of the god of this place, offering the very instruction that Tanaaj had so long sought.

She watched herself follow her vision.

She stood up and bunched up the blanket, her palm lovingly placed on the sedentix's cheek.

Tanaaj held the star blade.

Ying Yue gasped on, ih throat throbbing, ih body an oblivious animal, ih soul already merging into the greater god of the place.

This is what I will also say to Niloux when I meet her, Tanaaj thought as she laid her head down on the blanket next to Ying Yue's head. She touched the blade to the vein on the throat and opened her lips to pray:

A movement caught her eye.

Tanaaj looked up.

A black jaguar stood in the doorway.

It was not a holo. Her aug was off.

She blinked. The jaguar remained.

She had an enormous black face with white teeth, bared in a blinding rictus. Her body filled the doorway, as tall as Tanaaj herself. Jaguars didn't exist anymore. They'd gone extinct centuries ago. But she was right there. She could even smell her musk—sweet, like cacao.

She knew who this was. She averted her eyes, as if addressing the ground.

She said in Mopan, "I greet you, Balam Ahau, visitor from Xibalba. How does the Other World direct me?"

The jaguar didn't move. Her spade ears were flat against her skull. Tanaaj felt the stone beneath her feet, and the earth beneath the stone. She felt the power in her muscles coursing, available as needed.

Another movement caught her eye and she looked back to Ying Yue. Blood was spreading from ih throat and soaking the blanket in pulses, like a rose unfurling.

She looked back to the doorway, but the jaguar was gone.

Ying Yue's chest went still. Tanaaj bent forward, kissed ih forehead, and closed ih eyes with her thumbs. She said, "Become a viajera, mi carnalix, and may Saint Leah guide you there."

She sat back on the windowsill, tears streaming down her cheeks. The gods had answered her.

Now she knew how to prove Xibalba was real.

BOOK II

THE DARK ZONE

No one asks to be born. Birth is a form of captivity.

Among the ancient Maya, the theatre of captivity was essential to ritual life because it gave observers a chance to act out the central questions: Should I accept or reject the captivity that is my life? Should I follow the rules or make new ones? Should I befriend my captors or destroy them?

Your answers determine the trajectory of your life, perhaps of all your lives.

SAINT NNENA DEREGINA

2390

TZOYNA
3 Batz' 14 Pop, Long Count 10.9.5.7.11

9 December, 1012

Ixul was on her back, choking. Her headdress was hanging off her head. There were feet clustered around her and hands holding her down. There was something blocking her throat. Her convulsions became violent. She couldn't dislodge it.

Sound resolved into voices.

Voices resolved into words.

Words resolved into meaning.

They said, "Let her get it out."

Pressure on her shoulder relented and she swung to the side and finally coughed out a clump of dirt. It fell in a puddle of blood and slime. She tried to turn on her back but the heliconia stalk in her hair propped her up like a stake. She tried to sit up. There was a tangle around her legs, keeping her immobile. Her left ear was burning.

"This is the older girl, she has the tattoos."

"Look at the teeth."

A soft, heavy hand covered her mouth. She lurched. It pressed down harder. She went still.

"When I take this away," said one figure, dark against the sky, "I need to see your teeth. Do you understand?"

She didn't move.

He took his hand away.

She yelled "Ajul!" and thrashed to get away, but a foot pinned her left shoulder, and the butt of a spear pinned her right, and the hands returned to hold her body down.

The man leaned over her again and pulled on her cheeks so that her lips peeled away from her teeth. He ran his thumb over them. She screamed in her throat but it came out as a gurgle. His loose hairs brushed across her nose. She sneezed. The force of the sneeze made her face smash against his head, and she felt a warm gush across her mouth. Now her nose was bleeding too.

The man was rubbing his head. The others were laughing.

"Quite a little troublemaker," he said. Then he looked up at faces she couldn't see. "Yes, this is Princess Ixul. There's jade in her teeth."

"Can we take them out?"

"Possibly, after tomorrow."

"What should I do with this?" said a woman who stepped into view, and passed a small curved object over her body. It was Ixul's gold earspool. That's why her left ear was burning—it had torn through her earlobe when she fell.

"Start a pile," said the man.

So she was being taken captive.

"Who are you?" Ixul yelled. "Are you Nahua? Is this revenge for the prince? We took him in a fair raid. You see what happens to you if you take a royal captive by treachery. Xibalba will consume you."

The man bent close to Ixul again. He said, in a fatherly way, "Your family's reign has come to an end."

She spat in his face.

Someone kicked her in the side, and she curled up, stunned. No one had ever dared hit her in play or in fight. Not even Ajul.

"Peace," she heard the man say from a distance overhead. "She doesn't know. She was raised on warm milk and ignorance, just like her parents." He knelt by her again. "I'll tell you who I am. I am Letutz of Katwitz, son of Noxib of Katwitz, who died of plague. My mother was Ixbel, killed by bandits on the road to Hakan. My sons were Pitwoj and Pektaj, enslaved in Nahua raids. My wife was Ixkantan, dead in childbirth. My baby girl was Ixpip. She died from hunger."

He put his hands on her throat.

"You and your kind have said enough now."

His thumbs pressed down until darkness washed over her eyes.

They staked Ajul high on a hilltop. The stars flowered in their fields overhead. He could tell he was facing the dayfall. The rainbow serpent arced overhead, aligning with his body. He prayed:

How have we offended you?

Tell us and we will make amends.

Did we not choose the right day?

Was I wrong to let Ket proceed in her sacrifice?

His face was beginning to swell from the fall, and all of his cuts were still open, caked with blood and lime. He didn't know where Ixul was. He didn't know where any of his household was, his warriors and servants and cooks. He'd wanted to take care of them all. He'd wanted to show them how strong and capable he was.

What he needed to do now was to figure out what he'd done wrong, befriend his guards, and make amends so that order would be restored, sooner rather than later.

Two guards crouched nearby. They talked in low voices near a fire. Ajul could tell they weren't trained warriors, just farm boys with spears.

"Where is your home, brothers?" he asked them.

They both jumped to their feet, startled. He'd been dazed since being taken captive and this was the first time he'd spoken. The left one had a scar across his face, and the right one had bowlegs.

After a moment, the left one said, "Pekwitz," and the right one backhanded him in rebuke.

It was as he'd thought. The farmer-squatters had conspired to seize his home under the pretense of friendship, and used the sacred ball game for treachery. Their offense toward the gods far outweighed any he might have committed. He felt more comfortable.

"Where are my sisters?"

"Shut up," said the bowlegged one.

"What harm is it to answer?" said the scarred one.

"Nobody talks to captives as if they're equals, you fool."

"Tatichwut didn't tell us to answer."

"He didn't tell us not to answer."

"Fine, answer anything he wants, I'll fetch his honey posset," said the scarred one and stomped to the other side of the fire.

The bowlegged one leaned on his spear. The weapon was crude work, unpolished and crooked, only good for stabbing and not throwing, as if a child had made it. Ajul could tell that the boy was still scared of him, even when he was naked and tied.

"You played Tatichwut once in the ball game, you know," he said.

Ajul frowned. The name sounded familiar. "That farmer's son?"

"The *great* farmer's son!" cried the scarred one, running back to wave his spear around. "Tatichwut is the Great Red-Eyes, who conquered Pekwitz for his own domain. And now the dynasty of the Tzoyna is just a tribute state." He spat in Ajul's face, and Ajul couldn't wipe it away.

This was the second time he'd been spat on. He told himself to bear it for now, even to pity them. These boys were misguided. Tatichwut had conquered nothing. Pekwitz had already been abandoned by his parents' time, its royal lineage extinguished in the last war of the Snake Kings. He and Ixul had been planning to install a regent there and make the farmers her subjects. Tatichwut and his people had merely squatted in the ruins like children playing king-and-queen. Now they actually believed it.

The bowlegged one slapped the scarred one. They were like a pair of clowns, an entertainment for a feast. "That's not how you treat captives, you cocksnot," he said. "You have to treat them with respect."

"They're captives! You treat them with *disrespect!*"

The scarred one was about to open his mouth, but Ajul saw an opportunity and said in his most reasonable voice, "Brothers, be still. I can tell you how to treat captives. In our library is the Black Treatise, one of only eight copies in the world."

The bowlegged one said, "Never heard of it." But there was a slight give in his voice, a suggestion of curiosity.

"The Black Treatise is a copy of a book written in Mutul, thirteen generations ago," said Ajul. "It describes the proper treatment of captives, according to their station, their fate, and their purpose. I know the book in my blood, brother. So in order to instruct you how to treat me, I must ask why you and your people have taken my sister and me captive."

The two guards looked at each other.

They didn't deny his statement, which meant it was safe to assume that Ixul was also taken prisoner. Where, he still needed to find out. But Ajul could tell that his charms were working on these boys. He had a kind, easy, rational nature, which always soothed tensions and made friends out of enemies. The information would come soon enough.

The scarred guard spoke. "Tatichwut told us to take you," he said.

Ajul bowed his head to indicate gratitude for this information. "Do you know why?"

"Because everyone's dying, and you're responsible."

"Why am I responsible?"

"Because you're the king."

"I am not. Not yet. Tonight was the ascension ceremony, before we were attacked. I had not yet taken the headband or the scepter."

This didn't seem to have occurred to the guards. They looked at the ground, kicked pebbles.

"Well, it doesn't matter," said the bowlegged one, "because your father's responsible, and he *was* the king. Tatichwut says you don't have to be a king to let blood and anyone can do it and talk to Xibalba."

Ajul had to suppress his laughter. From what he remembered of Tatichwut, he was a whiny youth without much command of this world, much less the Other. But it wouldn't do to insult their leader. He was playing a longer, gentler game. "So Tatichwut the Great has ordered my sister and me to be taken captive and then . . . what?"

The two guards frowned at each other. They went away to consult with each other in low voices. At last they came back. "You and your sister are going back to the ball court tomorrow, but we can't tell you anything more," said the scarred one. "We're just supposed to hold you here until Tatichwut comes to get you."

"Very well, brother. Do you know who our opponents are?"

The bowlegged one grinned. He looked at his companion, who grinned back. They thumped each other's chests with the backs of their hands, as if Ajul had told a joke.

They tied Ixul to a tree, high on a hilltop. From the stars she could tell she was facing the dayrise. It was near midnight. Dawn was still hours away. She had a bad headache from the chokehold, and she had lost blood from her ear and nose, which put her in danger of losing too much heat. Her fury had cost her. Now she remembered the whiny farmer on the dais: that was Tatichwut, the weakling Ajul had played in the ball game at Pekwitz years ago. Was that all this was about? Revenge for a well-deserved beating?

She watched the White Queen cartwheel over the eastern horizon.

There were footsteps on the hill behind her. Torch-light drowned out the sky. A voice said, "Up now," and another said, "Good, thank you." There seemed to be a changing of the guard underway.

She heard water pouring from one jar to another. Her throat ached for it. Her mouth was tied with a gag that tasted of grass.

A man crouched in front of her, eating a tortilla with brown salt.

"It's really her!" he called to someone she couldn't see.

He got right in her face, searching with rheumy eyes. Ixul flinched away. "Took a tumble, didn't she," he said. "Shame about the ear. Still, you can see the royal blood in her face. See the softness of her eyes, like a baby jaguar's? And her lips tinged with red? She's the pure strain."

"Don't go falling in love with her, now," called a female voice. "She's got to save her strength for the game."

The game. They were going to make her play the ball game.

"She does," the man agreed. His eyes refocused, seeing her as a person now, not a face.

"You can call me Mukkan," he said. "Big Snake."

There was laughter behind the tree.

Ixul thought, *When I get free, you will be the first to die.*

"Do not fear Big Snake!" he said. "Big Snake is merciful! Is the little princess hungry? Would she like something to eat?"

The man tugged her gag loose and held up his half-eaten tortilla to her lips.

Ixul realized she was supposed to take it in her mouth without hands, like a baby presented with the teat. She turned her head to refuse. But the man bumped it against her lips, as if she were too stupid to understand.

She told herself to stay silent, to refrain from biting.

She told herself it would be over soon.

"Leave her alone," said the voice she couldn't see. Big Snake grunted, retied her gag, and went away where she couldn't see him.

She stayed ready, should he come back. But she didn't hear his voice again. Finally she relaxed against the tree. The smell of the tortilla had made her mouth water, and drool dripped off her lips and down her chin, and she couldn't wipe it away.

She withdrew into her mind.

She searched for reasons why the gods might have

been offended. But Mutna had been so careful. She could find no fault. She must be missing something.

She went over the words of the Black Treatise.

Captives are taken by means pleasing to the gods,
To the gods the captives are well-taken:
As slaves who failed their masters,
though this blood is cheap;
In fair and honorable raids
of the kingdoms we have erased;
As gifts from royal allies and neighbors,
to seal the friendship of peoples;
As gifts from farmers or merchants,
to bless their crops and wares;
In fair and honorable war,
when battle is waged by the Great Star;
and this is the most precious offering,
royal blood is most pleasing to the gods.

Did these fools know those words? By which of those criteria did they lay claim to her blood? Battle waged by the Great Star? What had happened on the ball court was not a battle. It was deception under the guise of friendship. It was betrayal. There were no words for it in the Black Treatise, because there was no honor in it.

A scrawny woman crossed in front of her.

Ixul made a loud sound, as dignified as she could, around the gag.

The woman looked back at her. She recognized her as the woman who had taken her golden earspool.

The woman didn't look bothered. She walked over to Ixul, crouched down, and cut through the gag with her knife, which gave Ixul hope. This might mean the stage of humiliation was over. She'd be fed and dressed and reunited with Ajul, which meant they could plan a way out of this catastrophe.

The woman raised her eyebrows. "You have something to say?"

Ixul straightened her back and composed her face. "Bring me the Black Treatise," she said, "and tell my captors to explain exactly under which circumstance pleasing to the gods they have betrayed me and my royal kin. I will tell you where to find the book in the palace."

Ixul heard laughter behind the tree, so hard it turned to coughing.

The woman cocked her head and said, "Do you know who I am?"

Ixul's nostrils flared at her casual vulgate, her failure to address her by her royal title. But she told herself she wasn't in a position to lash out again. She must remain calm. "No."

"I'm your mother."

Ixul recoiled. The woman was no such thing. It had been a year since her parents had disappeared on the road back from Monpanotoch, but even still, she remembered what her own mother looked like. She had had a round, pleasant face, with stocky build and firm breasts, always wrapped in fine cotton huipils with green and gold thread. This woman looked starved, sun-dark, and drawn. She wore unhemmed rags caked with mud.

The woman laughed. "Yes!" she said. "I'm your mother now. And you've been a very naughty brat, speaking to your betters this way, demanding this revenge or that black book. Call me Mother."

"No."

The woman pointed her knife at her face. "I said, call me Mother."

"I will not."

The woman smiled. "One more chance."

"Eat shit."

At a glance from the woman, Ixul's shoulders were pinned back by unseen hands, and her mouth held open, and her tongue pulled out. The woman speared it to hold it in place, then another knife began to saw at the root, and Ixul fainted from the pain.

Ajul remembered how the whole family would crawl into the steam bath at the end of the day. As they waited to acclimate, Ixul would ask their father questions about philosophy and history, Ket would curl up between their mother's legs and suck her thumb, and Ajul would just enjoy everyone being together, being themselves instead of royal bodies. All of their afterbirths were buried just beneath them, so this was the place where they were most connected to the Other World. He'd use a shell to scrape his sister's skin free of humors, and then sit for the same to be done to him. Sometimes, if one of them wasn't feeling well, a trusted servant would crawl in and beat them with palm bundles until they sweated the sickness out. Then another would have sap tea waiting for them outside, to replenish their blood, right at body temperature so as not to shock their stomachs. He was still looking forward to their steam bath tomorrow, when they could bind up their blisters, though the path to get there now seemed more complicated than it had before.

Father, he said, *what do I do if I'm taken captive?*

His father turned to face him, leading with a round naked shoulder.

Obey the gods, he said, but Ajul couldn't tell if it was really his father talking, or if he was making his father talk in his mind, like a puppet.

How do I know what the gods want?

Seek Xibalba.

What if I can't move?

Have faith.

Ajul opened his eyes. He saw the glimmer of a distant fire, felt the ropes still holding him. They were chewing into his skin. He told himself to embrace the pain as a warrior does, to feel it even more deeply, to seek it out, to welcome and befriend and enthrone it, to feed it morsels, to wash its feet, to fan its face, to comb its hair, to kiss its brow, to anoint it with oils—

Ajul slipped back into dreams.

Ixul had given him his first enema. It was a thing for women to do for men, as it gave them more pleasure, and was a sign of the woman's devotion and the man's trust. Their mother used to give enemas to their father behind closed doors; afterward, he and Ixul would inspect the paraphernalia and come to their own conclusions.

They'd done it on the Feast of Fools, at the beginning of the rainy season. After dinner, he and Ixul went to the steam bath, but with a secret purpose that made them smirk in the gloaming. They threw pebbles at each other. His face was hot. When they got inside, Ixul made him wait. She shut him in and locked it on the outside, as a joke. There was still light coming through the gaps in the brick. He paced, thinking,

Where should we do it? Not here. We'll make a mess. Where can we make a mess? He wanted to skip this and be together in the usual way that assured him they were closer-than-close, one person. Ixul would clutch his face in both hands, making him stare into her eyes until all their four eyes began to flutter, then squeeze shut; they'd bite each other's shoulders and then lay rigid, feeling the mountain receding.

Ixul pulled the door open with a wicked look on her face.

She'd prepared a pot of warm water. The leather bulb was perched on the rim, the tip lubricated with deer fat, and the cotton pallet next to the pot. He could smell the delicate nikteha.

He thought he would lie on his side, but with an imperious air, Ixul commanded him to kneel and present his backside like a woman. It made her laugh.

This is how it feels for her, he thought when he felt the nozzle probing around like a blind drunk, trying to find the hole.

She put a hand on his sacrum and told him to take deep, slow breaths.

He did.

His muscles relaxed.

He was aware of her hand resting on the small of his back. He closed his eyes. Then he sucked in his breath through his teeth and held it. She again reminded him to breathe. He tried to. He could feel the tip deep inside him, a twin to his navel, as if a spark from a fire had landed on the end of the nozzle and was riding with his breaths.

She told him she was going to squeeze now.

He felt his insides expanding, exploding, warm.

He rocked forward on his knees. She stayed with him, kept it in.

His eyeballs bulged against his lids, as if to escape their sockets.

He rocked back and groaned.

He pieced together her words. She was withdrawing it now. When it was out, he should lie flat on his stomach and clench.

He felt the nozzle slip out, yelped at the sensation.

He rocked forward onto his stomach, letting his chest press to the cotton pallet.

He heard the gentle patter of clean-up behind him. The pot. The knife. The metate. The leather bulb. Things laid upon things. The gentle susurrus of everyday objects.

He felt her hand on the small of his back again. It was so warm.

"Use the pot in the corner," she said. "But first, count twenty by twenty, or as near as you can stand."

Then her hand was gone, leaving a cool print on his skin.

Where had she learned all that? The library?

He rested his cheek on the cotton and took slow, deep breaths. It was done. The sacred herbs began to take effect. Ajul's vision blurred and refocused. He was looking at the bottom edge of the wall. A gecko friend perched there, eyeballs throbbing. He smiled and reached toward it, but fell short, and rested it on the stone, drumming his fingers. He felt happy and silly. Now he only had to clench in one place and stay soft everywhere else; and then the herbs peeled back the layers of the world, until he saw himself as a handsome captive staked to a tree, gazing at the moon, who was at the peak of her round.

"Where is my sister Ixul?" he asked.

The moon smiled and spoke, but he couldn't hear; then she rolled her pitcher between her hands, and some of that bright water spilled out and soaked the sky, and her long tongue fell out, and she parted it with her thumbnail so that a stream of blood ran down the middle of her chin, dividing her chest to reveal a bright obsidian heart, which doubled in size, then doubled again, then doubled again, until it took up the whole sky, and Ajul was only a speck in its reflection.

CAYO
3 Chak 2 K'ank'in, Long Count 12.19.19.17.19

20 December, 2012

Xander was speeding up the road to San Ignacio with a breakfast burrito in one hand and his flip phone in the other, steering with his forearms. Drizzle was spattering on the windshield. He called the ranger's office to make sure the day's tours were still on, then tossed the phone on the passenger's seat, swerved to clear a horse, took another bite of burrito. He'd been afraid Dr. Castillo would revoke his badge because of the skull incident, but last night's meeting had assured him he was in the clear. Javier had never shown up. He'd never even answered his texts. That was strange—they rarely communicated, but when they did, Javier was the one who was eager for contact.

He wadded up the tinfoil from his burrito and tossed it in the backseat.

Today was straightforward: all his guests were walk-ins from Burns Avenue, so he'd just pick them up there. When he'd started guiding, he'd wanted to know the names and nationalities of his guests to prepare for each tour. Now he just showed up and guessed.

He drove into town, parked on a side street, and hefted his gear from the back of the truck. He waited to cross the main intersection and saw Javier's truck. There was a girl sitting in the passenger seat. It was Leah. She was smiling and laughing.

The truck turned and he lost sight of them.

Of course Javier had spent the night with Leah after charming her during the tour. Of course. That made sense. They were the kind of couple he'd expect to see together, both of them so carefree and sincere. They could go fuck themselves. Or each other. Which they apparently had. That was fine. Xander didn't suffer for want of sex.

He passed Angelo, who scurried away. He arrived in front of Ultimate Cayo. Hector looked up from his planner, saw Xander's face, and whistled.

"Weh hapm?"

But Xander wasn't in the mood. "How moch?"

"Foa."

It was enough. He'd make a commission from each and hope for tips.

"Wid," said Hector, "yu canela gyal."

"Wich canela gyal?"

"Leah fahn Stayts."

Xander felt numb. He could tell Hector why, but that wasn't the sort of information to share casually. Only when it might suit him. So he just rummaged through his pack, knowing Hector was watching him. "Ih don di ya?"

"No. Hahn di ada chree doh." And he pointed to three tourists on the street, clustered in conversation. He'd passed them on his way in. He did an immediate assessment:

1.   Dark-skinned Black woman, skinny, sixties, in white sneakers.

2.   Light-skinned Black man, burly, twenties, in a stamped grey tank top.

3.   White woman, thick, twenties, with blazing-red hair.

He guessed they were all from the States, and that if the second two weren't a couple, they would be by the day's end. The cave had that effect on people.

Xander squared his shoulders and went down the steps to begin the day's performance.

"Good morning, everyone!" he said as brightly as he could manage.

"Good morning!" they all said cheerily in return.

"I'm your guide today. My name is Xander." He omitted his surname because tourists had trouble enough remembering his first name.

The older woman stuck out her hand. "Nice to meet you," she said in a thick accent. "I'm Ruth."

He placed the accent. "German?"

"Yes!"

"Whereabouts?"

"I'm from Groningen."

Xander was startled, and wanted to tell her about his desire to study there, but thought better of it. He'd had enough experiences of tourists condescending to him about education, or asking why, if he wanted to get a degree so much, he hadn't already gone and gotten one. They never thought about visas. To those with U.S. and European passports, the world was cheap and borderless.

"Very nice to meet you, Ruth," he said, and turned to the Black man.

"Micah," he said, and shook his hand very hard. "From Boston."

Boston. Another place he wanted to study. The world was mocking him today.

Xander turned to the red-haired woman, who held out her hand, smiling. "I'm Ida," she said. "Nice to meet you."

"Nice to meet you," he said. "Are you from Massachusetts too?"

Ida and Micah looked at each other, quick, flustered. "Oh yes!" said Ida. "He's my partner."

Right on most counts. Three out of four.

"Great," said Xander, then looked at his watch. It was 7:02 a.m. They had to get moving. "We're just waiting for one more guest, so—"

"I'm here!"

Xander turned. There she was, breathless and beaming. "I'm sorry I'm late," she said, and waved to the other tourists. "Hi, I'm Leah!"

They greeted her in turn. "And this young man is Xander," said Ruth, pleased to have remembered.

"Oh, I know him," said Leah with mischief in her voice. "We were acquainted my first night in town."

"Oh really?" said Micah, as Ruth said, "Well, that sounds like a story." But Xander didn't feel like playing along. He turned to Hector and called, "How di rayn?"

"Rayn wahn kohn," he called back, "bot di kayv oapm."

"Aarait." Xander turned, avoiding eye contact with Leah. "Let's go."

As he walked, he could tell it would be a hard day controlling his moods. Even just watching the pattern of the concrete beneath his feet, he felt anger, lust, impatience, excitement. He'd have to force himself to do his job today and not snap at Leah to get back at her, nor try to kiss her, to get back at Javier. He lived hours' worth of emotions in ten seconds. But the whole day stretched on ahead of him, unlived.

"Is it going to rain much more?" asked Ida, saving him from restarting conversation.

"Yes," said Xander, reaching the van with the peeling paint stripes. "But it won't make much of a difference to us in the cave."

"The cave never floods?"

"Oh, it definitely floods," he said. He climbed into the back of the van and stacked their bags next to the helmets and the cooler. "I've been there when it floods. You want to get out fast, if you can, or find the highest ground. But usually you have warning. It has to rain more than this."

The last of the bags was packed in. He indicated to his guests that they should climb in through the side door. He still avoided Leah's eyes. "What we have to worry about more," he said, "is how high the first creek is. If the bridge is flooded, we can't cross over to the nature reserve." He shut his door and put on his seat belt, also a performance for tourists. "We all set?"

"All set," they called to him. No one had joined him up front. It was Ruth in the first bench, Ida and Micah in the second, and Leah in the back.

He spared a glance at her in the rearview mirror. Leah's cheek was pressed to the glass, her eyes wide, though they hadn't gone anywhere yet.

"Then we go," he called, trying to sound cheery but knowing he was failing. He turned the key and pulled out of the parking lot, up Burns Avenue, right along the circling road, left past the market grounds, then down to the low bridge over the river, where traffic was backed up as usual.

They were stuck. The van creeped forward. Xander flipped through his mental Rolodex of breaking-the-ice questions.

How did you hear about the cave?

What brought you to Belize?

Do you like Belize so far?

But Xander was intrigued by this group. They seemed smart and well-off, which made him nervous; but they were also kind, which put him at ease. So he went for the question that would cut to the nature of whatever their dynamic was going to be, right away.

"What do you all do for a living?"

"Retiring!" said Ruth.

The couple laughed. "Too easy," said Micah. "What did you used to do?"

"Well, I'll never really stop working," she said. "Just teaching. I'm a professor of geography."

"Oooh!" said Ida. "That was my major in college!"

"Really!" Ruth exclaimed.

Connections already. This tour was going to lead itself.

"Where did you go to school?" said Ruth.

That didn't take long, Xander thought.

"Harvard," Ida said, and the word was weighted with self-consciousness.

"Such a shame," Micah said.

Ida made a face at him. "MIT's not good for geography."

Micah turned to Ruth. "MIT's better than Harvard for anything."

They shared a good-natured laugh.

Ruth tried to get it straight. "So you are at MIT, and . . ."

"No, he's at MIT. I code at Harvard."

"Oh wonderful! Like Facebook, or . . . ?"

"Ugh," said Ida, grimacing.

Ruth laughed. "Very sorry. That must be annoying to hear."

"It's all good. Actually, I design banking apps so, like, you can operate them on a ten-dollar phone."

"Open source."

"Exactly. I'm part of a working group that's trying to . . . well, hack the system, sort of. Most research groups just want to make products that they can scale up and get to market and make lots of money. But we've signed a pledge to make tech that puts human benefit above profit."

"Tech without the profit motive," said Ruth. "Mein Gott. It's hard to imagine what that would even look like."

"And tell her about the map," said Micah.

"Oh," said Ida. "Our group only uses inverted maps."

"Inverted!" said Ruth. "Which projection?"

"The Winkel Tripel."

"But flipped upside down," said Micah, "with south on the top and north on the bottom."

"I know what inverted means, young man," Ruth said.

Micah flushed.

Ruth smirked and patted his arm. "I've always found inverted maps very satisfying," she said, "because it annoys the imperialists, if nothing else. Now you just need to solve climate change."

"Ha!" Ida looked to Micah.

"Yes?" prompted Ruth.

Micah said, "I work on climate change."

"Oh, do you! What specifically?"

"The Eocene era and how it applies to modern climate."

"How does it apply?"

"The Eocene was an ice-free world. The whole planet was hot. There were crocodiles in the Arctic."

"So we're doomed!"

"Pretty much."

Laughter.

Xander was listening to every word.

He swerved to avoid a pothole. The drizzle had turned to a light rain. He rolled up his window and turned on the wipers to a medium setting.

"Actually," said Micah, "I wanted to ask our guide about the role of climate change in Maya civilization. Xander, it's not true that the Maya 'disappeared,' right?"

Xander looked in his rearview mirror. Finally, tourists who were halfway informed. "That's correct," he said. "The Maya didn't disappear. I'm Maya, for example. The Maya only disappeared in the sense that they became invisible to our modern idea of what's important."

"Wait, invisible how? What do we think is important?" said Ida.

"Stone. Big monuments made of stone. They take a lot of accumulation of resources to make, and they last a long time, and they're the easiest things to see—so we say, 'Oh, this civilization was important.' And then when they stop making monuments, we say, 'Oh, this civilization disappeared.'"

"But they did not disappear," Ruth added. "They just changed."

"Exactly."

"I see," said Ida.

"Drought was a big factor in the change, right?" asked Micah.

"Relative drought, yes," he said. "Some scientists think the Maya royal states flourished because of a period of rain that was plentiful and predictable. When the rain went away, so did the elites."

He saw Micah shake his head. "Climate," he said. "I keep saying it. All of human history is just climate."

"That is a big subject of my research," Ruth said. "It's just extraordinary how much humans believe they are the principal actors in their narratives, when in all of history, climate is calling the shots."

"Like with the Agricultural Revolution," said Ida.

"Agricultural Catastrophe, more like it," said Ruth. "And that's not all. The Levant and Nile valley were settled because of climate change. Capitalism and the nation state may well fall because of climate change. We think we act on the planet, but always, it is the planet acting on us."

"Right. And we're about to find that out the hard way."

"Did Hurricane Sandy happen because of climate change?" asked Leah from the back. "I couldn't believe the videos from New York."

"Oh yeah," Micah turned to say, "that's just an appetizer. There's way worse coming. We're going to have to rebuild the whole world to deal with it."

"Wow," said Leah.

"What about you, Leah?" said Ida. "What do you do?"

"Me?" said Leah. "I'm nothing!"

"Nonsense!" said Ruth. "No one is nothing."

Leah laughed and docked her head back against the window. She looked like she was in love. "Well," she said, "if you're asking what I do for work, I work at a bedding store in my hometown. But that's what I do, not who I am."

The other three nodded. "Where's your hometown?" asked Micah.

"Anoong. Minnesota. It's really tiny."

"Never heard of it."

"Don't feel bad. Nobody has."

She seemed not to want to talk much more, and the others, sensing this, returned to their own counsel. Xander liked these people. In fact, he realized, he wanted them to like him back. That was rare.

"So," said Ida to Ruth, "what's your area of research?"

"Tourist gaze."

Xander's hands went cold.

"Whoa, that's a lot to unpack. Okay. Tourist gaze is like male gaze, except with . . . ?"

"Yes, in the same sense. But I focused less on people, and more on places."

"How do you mean?"

"For example, I did ten years of work on the Zein-o-Din caravanserai."

They hit a big pothole, bounced up and down. Xander called back an apology, continued to listen.

"Very cool! Where is that?"

"Near Yazd, in Persia. Well, modern-day Iran, of course."

"So the name is Farsi."

"No, actually, it's Arabic, because it was built by the Safavids. Zein-o-Din means 'grace of the religion.'"

"So what did you study about it?"

"The phenomenology of the landscape, which means the unique essence of a place, and how it accrues meaning over time, especially with the introduction of tourists."

"Uh-oh," said Ida. She called forward to Xander, "We're not ruining the cave by going to it, are we?"

Xander glanced at her. "No more than all the thousands of other tourists who visit."

"Well, that makes me feel a lot better."

"Don't sweat it," said Xander. "'Natural' is a construct. So is 'untouched.' Humans have been altering landscapes for as long as there've been humans. That's what makes them landscapes and not just a set of coordinates."

"I would say all sentient beings, instead of just humans, but Xander is exactly right," said Ruth. Xander flushed with pleasure. "And, importantly, the landscape acts back."

"I don't understand. How can a landscape have agency?"

"We cannot act in a certain way if the land prevents us from doing so, yes? As Xander said, we cannot go to the cave today if the creek is too high."

"Ah. And we couldn't, say, build a castle in a swamp."

"Yes, and then the location of the castle that the land *does* allow shapes its fate, ever after. The landscape is acting on us. We only consider kinetic action, not passive action, the elimination of all other possibilities."

"Or," Ida said, "action done over such long periods of time that it's hard for us to see."

"Correct."

Xander wondered what Ruth was going to say about his cave. Of all landscapes, caves had the longest memory because they changed most slowly. That's why the ancient Maya had considered them the realm of the eternal. He felt pained. He was torn between playing the part of the tour guide and presenting himself as an intellectual equal. He rarely got to do that in Belize. He could only do it on Internet message boards late at night.

He glanced in the mirror at Leah. She was kneeling and gazing out the back window, waving at a pickup truck full of Guatemalans. She didn't know the difference.

He'd made a decision before he was aware of it. "I've been to the cave thousands of times," he called out, drawing everyone's attention, including Leah's. "And I think what you're saying—about land having agency—you'll see this when we get there, but the cave feels like it's carved for human beings." He let passion creep into his voice, and trusted these people to respect it, not mock it. "But what tiny accidents of physics, accumulating over millions of years, made the cave that way? Navigable here, but impassable here? When you think of all the different shapes it could be, it strikes you as strange."

"Almost as if it were inviting you to come in," said Ruth with a mischievous smile.

"Yeah," Xander snorted, "but to what end."

"Can you get all the way through the cave?" asked Ida.

Xander checked his rearview, sped past a slow taxi. "No, not all the way," he said, "but two-thirds of the way."

"Is that how far in we go?"

"No. We only go one-third of the way in."

"Why?"

"That's the tour. The tour ends with the Crystal Maiden, and her burial chamber is only one-third of the way in."

"Are we allowed to go farther in?"

"Not without special permission from the government."

"Have you been farther than that?"

"No," he lied. He saw Leah narrow her eyes at him, and he looked away quickly. "But we shouldn't be spoiling it. You'll see it all when we get there."

"I wonder how long you could stay in there without losing your mind."

"Not long," said Xander.

"Oh I don't know about that!" called Leah. "It feels romantic to me."

Xander jerked his thumb back at her. "She's been there before," he said to the others.

"Yesterday," she confirmed, her chin on her fist.

"Yesterday!" said Micah. "You don't want to get a massage or relax with a daiquiri today?"

"No," said Leah. "I just want to go back to the cave again. You'll see why."

"So you liked it," said Xander, trying to keep his voice neutral. It was the first time he'd directly addressed Leah all day.

"I did," she said. "Especially the part when we all turned off our headlamps and held hands. I loved being in the dark. You have no choice but to trust."

Xander didn't answer. He still wanted to punish her.

They turned into Teakettle, passed the kiosk, and drove south, through the orange plantations and mahogany groves. Leah was pressed to the window again, mouthing words to herself, as if trying to memorize the landscape. Xander waved to the Nuñez family in the stilted house, swerved to avoid a dog. The rain had eased now, but the road was muddy. He'd have to concentrate to get the van through. But he longed to talk more with these people. He just wanted to sit down over beers and talk about ideas. Like how it was impossible to reconcile the past and present. He walked in his ancestors' footsteps every day, but could he feel them in any real sense? Could he understand them any better? Was he any closer to them? He'd sat in the river at the mouth of the cave before, and closed his eyes, and tried to imagine the priests going in with their captives, holding their pine torches, through this same opening. But the past did not exist except as a fiction. And no matter how much he knew about the place, no matter the intensity of his imagining, no matter the blood in his veins, he was not truly there. He opened his eyes and he was Xander Cañul in the year 2012, with a red helmet on his head and a machete on his back. Who would be here a thousand years from now? Why would they be coming here, if at all? What would they look like? He had to be careful, choosing which people were safe enough to ask these questions. He'd asked Hector once, and Hector answered something vague about there being more land cleared for picnic tables. Xander had wanted to punch him. *No*, he wanted to say, *a thousand years. One thousand years. Do you see what is going on in the world? Do you understand how fast it is chang-*

ing right now? We're walking along on the edge of a knife.

But what was Xander's own answer? What would his cave look like, a thousand years from now?

It could be collapsed, overgrown, forgotten.

Or it could be the center of a global empire.

The thought made him snort. Tiny Belize, with its few hundred thousand Belizeans, as the conquerors of the new age. And everyone would practice cunnilingus.

When they got to the creek, it was high but not impassable. He eased the van across the wooden boards and then sped around the final stretch. As they pulled up to the ranger's office, Xander's phone buzzed in his pocket. He took it out and looked at it. There was a text from Javier.

dakta castillo tek weh mi baj. u tel mi wai breda

Xander put it away and didn't answer.

On the hike to the cave entrance, Xander focused on helping his tourists navigate the mud. He didn't stop for the usual demonstrations of local flora—he was anxious to get ahead of the other tour groups, which had been pulling into the lot just as he was reaching the trailhead. He didn't want a repeat of two days ago, when Javier had snuck up behind him. So Dr. Castillo had revoked his badge? That was unfortunate, but it also wasn't Xander's fault. Javier hadn't shown up to the meeting last night. That was Javier's fault.

By the time they got to Camp Xibalba, the only other group in the cave was from Pook's Hill, the resort just a few miles away. The rain was coming down harder. Xander went from Ruth to Ida to Micah to Leah, slipping a finger under each of their chin straps to test for tightness. When he got to Leah, she said, "You look like your brother."

She said it so without guile that he couldn't rouse his usual sarcasm. In fact, he found himself doing the opposite. "Is that a good thing?" he said.

"Oh yes," said Leah, smiling.

He thumped her helmet and called to the others, "It's time to go down!"

They followed him to the top of the stone steps. Seeing the cave for the first time, Ruth, Micah, and Ida gaped and exclaimed; but Leah stood at the top, serene, as if she had received the answer to a question.

For Xander, the tour went by in a blur of pleasure. These guests were smart, engaged, and respectful. They asked good questions. Micah knew geology, so Xander deferred to him on the subject of chemistry, and didn't even mind. Ruth knew geography, so she discussed access theory as it related to the cave's progressing chambers. He didn't feel he was among guests; he felt like he was among friends. He'd forgotten what it was like to enjoy the cave.

Leah trailed at the back of the column, her head-lamp making arcs back and forth on the cave ceiling. She looked peaceful now in a way she hadn't in the van. She didn't ask any questions. She didn't seem to be listening to them at all.

When they got to the step-up rock, Leah waded ahead toward the bend. He kept an eye on her while the others climbed up. The curls of her bikini string bobbed as she walked. Leah from Minnesota, wading in waters that rippled like jaguar skin. She didn't look like she was going to stop.

"Hey gyal," he called.

Leah turned around. "Yes?"

"Time to step up."

She pointed ahead into the darkness. "I feel like I'm at a crossroads."

"Tour doesn't go there. Tour goes here."

"Will you take me farther in, another day?"

Xander was getting impatient. It didn't seem like she'd take no for an answer, and they needed to move. So he lied. "Sure gyal," he said. "But come on up this way now."

It was clear from Leah's face that she believed him.

"Deal!" she said, and so came to the step-up rock, accepting his offer of a hand.

When they emerged into the upper chamber, Ruth whistled low under her breath.

"So," said Xander, "does this landscape have agency?"

"Oh yes, it does."

"Tell me how."

She waved her arm across the labyrinth of tide pools. "Well, of course the morphology is very stable. That was useful to ancient peoples because it signified the realm of the absolute, so it makes perfect sense as a space to offer sacrifices, which would last in the same form in which they were deposited. And each of these little pools look like . . . bucket seats."

"She's right," he said to the others. "Only a few of these pools have been excavated, but in each one, we've found bones. Imagine what it would have looked like two thousand years ago, with skeletons sitting up in every other pool."

"Like a half-filled movie theater," said Ida.

Xander laughed. The image fit, and he trusted she meant no disrespect.

For him, the final chamber was always a letdown. The "Crystal Maiden" was just the most photogenic thing that could be stuck on a pamphlet, glittering and gaping next to her companion, Individual 12, now sporting a brand-new hole in his skull. But his guests were mesmerized.

"Do we know anything about who they are?" said Ida.

"No. Not much. Floodings have covered them with calcite. But they may have had something to do with the city down the river. The legendary last monarchs were a sister and brother, Ixul and Ajul."

"What happened to them?"

Xander shrugged. "Disappeared from history."

As the others crowded to peer at the Crystal Maiden, Leah hung back, and spoke to Xander in a low voice. "Javier told me what he found in the skull," she said.

If she had any hesitation about naming his estranged twin to him, she gave no sign. Xander suppressed a surge of annoyance. "What?"

Leah blinked. "I thought you must have known too. There's an obsidian blade in there. Javier left it for Dr. Castillo to take out."

"*In* the skull? What else did he say about it?"

"That it was green, which was rare. And . . . he used a word that started with *e* . . ."

"Eccentric."

"Yes, that's it! *E* is my favorite letter because it's the

most common. It's like it's the space between every-thing, you know?"

Xander wasn't listening to her prattle, though. He was thinking. If this was true, it'd be a major discov-ery. Maybe it was really green obsidian, instead of the usual black, which would prove an ancient trade link with Pachuca. Maybe it was a shape no one had ever seen. Maybe he could write a paper on it. Maybe it was his ticket out of Belize.

When his guests turned around, he clapped his hands. "All ready to head out?" he said.

"It's so much to take in," said Ida. "I wish I knew who they were, what their lives were like."

"I wish so too," Xander said, but his mind was else-where. He wanted to get his guests down the ladder so he could be alone with the skull. Leah seemed to understand this, and with a look, lips pursed, said she'd keep the others occupied.

As soon as they were out of sight, Xander fished out his flashlight and looked into the hole. There it was: a gorgeous green star.

Right now, only three people knew about it: him, Javier, and Leah.

He reached in and pulled it out with his bare fingers, quicker than he could think about it.

For a moment, he turned it in the light. It was

exquisite: four spokes, perfectly even, shaped like the Maya glyph for Chak Ek' the Great Star.

He pulled off his pack, unrolled the top, found a plastic baggie, and dropped the blade in. He stuffed the baggie with cotton balls from his first aid kit. He cushioned the bag between his dry clothes. It was the best he could do.

"Uh-oh," called Ruth from below. "Is everything all right up there?"

Xander looked over the ledge. "Yeah, sorry about that," he said. "I just had to repack a few things." He avoided looking at Leah, who gazed at him, steady and untroubled.

During their journey out of the cave, Xander felt giddy. Part of him knew it was bad to remove the blade without consulting anyone. Another part of him felt that the cave owed him something, after all these years, and Dr. Castillo would forgive him as long as Xander bullshitted as effectively as he always had.

He conversed with his group continuously, talking about deep time, immortality, Obama, tourist gaze, futurism, Quakerism, geomancy, subsidiarity, Nigerian oil, panspermia, Janelle Monáe, neoliberalism, Ahmadinejad, chicle farmers, gay marriage, Zapatismo, academia, Gnosticism, Sandy Hook. He crossed paths with Ronald, who stood on a boulder in the stream like a king, his headlamp the shining gem in his crown; Xander ascended to meet him and embrace him and call him *hermano*, a performance of brotherhood for all watching. Ronald gave him a strange look, but took his good mood at face value. Xander was enjoying himself so much that when Leah called his name, he didn't hear her at first. Ruth had to tug on his arm, having passed the message up the column.

"Leah needs you," she said.

Xander turned back.

Leah was standing in the stream, staring at a spot on the wall.

He frowned and splashed toward her. It was odd behavior, even for her. He said, "You all right?"

"Look," she said, staring. "There's a star."

He adjusted his headlamp to see what she meant. There was a whip spider on the wall, immobile, its eye a sparkle. "You mean the spider?"

"No. It's a star. I have to remember."

There was a strange thickness in her voice, as if she were fighting to wake up. "Remember what?" said Xander.

"Red leaves," she said.

Then her eyes crossed and she fell backward.

Xander's arms shot out to catch her. Her full weight fell on his arms, but he was strong, so he could get his legs under her and she was spared a hard fall. Ida and Micah were at his side, helping hold her head above the water.

"Over there, get her flat," said Xander, nodding to a sandbank. With their help, he could move her. Her eyes were open, crossed, and staring upward, and she was moving her mouth. They laid her as flat as they could, and Xander knelt next to her, his pack already off, his first aid kit in mind. But then she gasped.

"Oh! Oh!" she said.

"Ssshhh," said Xander. "Don't try to talk."

"I'm so sorry."

"Don't try to—"

"How *embarrassing*."

Xander gave up.

"I was just . . . I was getting so close . . . I . . ." She fell silent and put one hand on her belly, moving it in circles.

Xander settled in the stream next to her. Micah, Ida, and Ruth stood nearby, watchful, like the Three Kings in a crèche.

He put his hand on hers. "You had a little spill," he said. "Just breathe for now. We won't go any-where until you're ready." The other three nodded in solidarity.

When Leah spoke again, her voice was steady. "I'm going to be okay. I just . . . got overwhelmed." She looked at Xander and smiled. "Stendhal syndrome, right?"

Xander laughed.

He kept her on the bank for awhile. A few groups passed them, and the guides made friendly inquiries, but saw Xander had the situation under control. He felt so much more at peace knowing that Javier wasn't coming today. They just stayed in the stream and continued to talk, the water running over their laps like a blanket.

Presently, Leah felt sure she could get up and go on. Xander insisted she do so slowly, and helped her every step of the way. He marveled at the change in himself. Was this all it took, to bring out his most generous self? Finding the right group of people? But tomorrow they would all be gone again. He tried not to think about that. He tried not to think beyond the coming hour. The four of them helped Leah out of the cave, step by step, until they came to the entrance pool.

Xander waited until the others had gone up the stairway, then said to Leah, "You know what you need after this, right? A Belikin."

She grinned.

It was dusk when Javier arrived at Hode's for the All Guide Meeting. The open-air restaurant also had a playground, a sports bar, and a seminar area. He showed up even though he'd just had his badge revoked. He'd planned on running for office, and he was going to do it anyway. His night with Leah had inspired him. This was his time of ascendancy.

First there'd be prayer, ceremony, and debate. He ordered a Belikin. His palms were sweating. He knew Leah had gone to the cave with his brother today. Where was Xander now? Was he coming to the All Guide Meeting? Planning to show up fashionably late? His twin had romances with tourists too, but private and temperamental ones, out of sight, known by rumor and not display. He didn't think Leah would go for that. Xander had grown up in the capital, Belmopan, getting bullied for his stutter, getting tangled up with bad kids. Javier pitied him, but there was nothing he could do. His brother was responsible for his own life.

Meanwhile, he'd been thinking about Leah all day. There was the sexual aspect, of course, her fearless joy in bed, without shame or hesitation, thoughts of which had made him pull down his shirt all day, as if he were still a schoolboy at the mercy of his dick. There was also her playfulness and ease, her intensity and sincerity. She was corny, but incapable of sarcasm. It was as if she'd never known deceit. To his amazement, he was thinking about marriage. And she was the daughter of Miss Antonia, his exotic blond Sunday school teacher! This couldn't be a coincidence. Maybe God was telling him that this was the time for him to settle down. He'd always wanted a wife and child someday, and maybe now was the time. He'd dodged the stork well enough so far, pulling out every time, including with Leah, which seemed to dismay her; he thought, if he had another chance, maybe he wouldn't pull out and there'd be a happy accident. Maybe she would stay in Belize. He'd get María Jose in Benque to sew a simple dress—or maybe he could buy her one of the dresses on display in Belize City, with ruffles and sparkles—and get married at Our Lady of Mount Carmel, with simple gold rings. That was all she'd need. He felt he knew her so well already. Maybe she'd become the first female ATM guide and they could go into business together. He saw them on a porch, in the far future, with white hair, holding hands and watching the rain. They would belong to each other.

Javier caught sight of Dr. Castillo just as Dr. Castillo caught sight of him.

The man scowled and turned on his foot.

Javier swallowed his gulp of beer.

This morning, Dr. Castillo had come straight up to him on Burns Avenue and asked for his badge, pending a later talk. Why? Because he'd been with Leah last night instead of going to a fucking last-minute meeting about a fucking accident he'd had nothing to do with. He was the one Dr. Castillo should be thanking for saving their collective asses, taking care of the tourist and retrieving the tourist's phone. But Dr. Castillo had his favorites, and when Javier tried to explain, he waved him off. So all day, he'd been imagining the story Xander must have told him.

Still no text back. That was a sign of guilt.

No badge meant he hadn't gone to the cave today. Angelo had taken his guests. Javier had just driven around town and stewed, waiting for Xander to text him back, waiting for Dr. Castillo to call him back. Without the cave to devote himself to, without friends and guests, he didn't know what to do. He hated being alone.

He looked over the crowd at Hode's. There were at least a hundred guides gathered. Some had brought their girlfriends, who looked bored, but they were important because they counted the votes. The Ceiba Tree contingent was in the front. They were all wearing their matching black polo shirts with the World Tree logo. Angelo caught his eye and nodded at him. They were behind him. He could do this. The Ultimate Cayo contingent was also here, Hector and the gang far in the back, occupying one long table under the orange blossom trees, arms draped on the backs of their chairs. They wore undershirts and camouflage, like a military regiment. Moths wheeled in dogfights under the lights.

Up at the front, Dr. Castillo was having a heated conversation with the acting president, Floyd Ruíz.

Floyd made some final point, then picked up the microphone and tapped it.

"Excuse me?" he said. "Excuse me?"

The chatter quieted.

"Welcome to the All Guide Meeting of the Cayo Tour Guide Association. We are going to commence with a prayer. Tonight I would like to invite Javier Magaña to lead that prayer."

Two hundred faces turned toward him at the bar.

He hadn't expected this. This must have been the subject of the heated conversation. There was an awkward silence as he landed on his feet and he realized he was a little drunk and made his way to the microphone with a look of puzzlement directed at Floyd, who added, "He is my very good friend and an example of faith to us all."

There were a few snickers, but mostly the silence of acceptance.

Javier took the microphone and said, "That is a very kind thing for you to say, hermano. I am Catholic so I will begin in the Catholic way. In the name of the Father, the Son, and the Holy Spirit."

Half the crowd made the Sign of the Cross.

"Heavenly Father, we are gathered here to discuss our livelihoods. We are ambassadors for our beloved Belize and our beloved district, Cayo. Teach us how to be kind and fair and law-abiding. May our nation flourish in the new baktun."

A woman tossed her black hair over her tiki drink.

"Bless each of us and our work tonight as we vote in our officers for the new year and discuss the issues that concern us. Holy Father, may we come to a peaceful consensus of brotherhood and fellowship. Amen."

Then everyone rose to their feet and turned to the flag in the corner and sang.

O Land of the Free by the Carib sea,
Our manhood we pledge to thy liberty!
No tyrants here linger, despots must flee
This tranquil haven of democracy . . .

The chicken plates started coming out. Everyone sat to eat. Javier joined the Ceiba Tree contingent.

While they ate, the mayor of San Ignacio gave a speech about the new infrastructure projects going up around town. Jesús Gonzáles gave a speech about pride and humility in the guide community, how "the lowest achievers are trying to force the highest commissions," which led to many dark looks. Sheila Vicks the Canadian archaeologist gave a speech about the new frieze at Xunantunich, and what to say about it if tourists asked. Floyd got back up to announce a raffle, with prizes: Dinner for two at San Ignacio Hotel. A night's stay at Black Rock. A couples massage at Du-Plooy's. Girlfriends tugged on their men's sleeves to enter the raffle. Latecomers straggled in and received their chicken plates. Still, Javier saw no sign of Xander. Carlos Castellanos told everyone to be careful in Offering Cave, where some flowstone had broken off near the entrance. The treasurer gave his report: $5,984 BZ total expenses, $9,646 BZ total balance. He projected his figures on a white bedsheet. Josefina Paz got up to propose changing the words of the national anthem from *our manhood we pledge* to *our honor we pledge* so that it would be inclusive of women. The men rolled their eyes until the mayor took the microphone and told her that this was not the time or place for her "feminist project." She left.

Finally, there was the call for nominations for office.

One for secretary, by the sitting secretary. "A woman should do this instead," he said, and nominated Nora Hopkins, who accepted with a nod.

One for president: Augustus Bradley, who lifted his head from his plate to decline.

Another for president: Ralphie Powell, who accepted.

Another for president: Patrick Hemsworth, who also accepted.

Another for president: Ian José Suárez, who also accepted.

Angelo raised his hand, was called upon, and stood.

"I nominate my good friend, the most popular guide at Ceiba Tree Adventures, Javier Magaña."

There was scattered applause, and Floyd winked at him. Javier realized he'd given him an advantage by asking him to lead the group in prayer. Now he felt even better. He had allies.

He joined the row of candidates, waiting his turn to speak.

Ralphie was a big guy. He dwarfed the microphone. "Hello. I would start by getting a decent sound system. You can't just sit on your butt and complain. You have to get out there and enjoy yourself. So please vote for me, for president of the Cayo Tour Guide Association. Thank you."

Scattered applause.

Patrick was older, potbellied. "Anything I do, I commit myself to. I would like tour guides to do well. A year is a short time, but I work hard, and will commit myself to advancing the prosperity of the Maya in the new age."

He'd named the Maya explicitly. Too political. The applause was less strong.

Ian José was handsome, an import from Punta Gorda in the south, wearing a gold chain. "I'm a team player. Everybody knows me from playing football. I have a lot of ideas. I love working with people. I'm not from Cayo, but I've lived here for fifteen years. Thank you."

Intense applause. But surely Javier could do better.

And then he was holding the microphone.

"I would like to be your president—"

His voice cracked.

Winces in the audience. A woman held her hand over her mouth in laughter. Angelo, in the front row, crossed his legs and looked down at the floor.

Javier made a show of coughing and pounding on his chest, and then he began again. "As you can hear, I am much younger than the other candidates."

There was laughter.

He felt proud. He'd handled that moment well. He paused, riding the buzz of goodwill. When he spoke again, he spoke from the heart.

"Mis hermanos y hermanas, what do you think the ancient Maya would think of us today? If Ajul and Ixul of the Tzoyna could see us standing here under these lights?" Silence. "I think they would say, *Believe and then act.*" The words had sounded profound in his tipsy mind. Now he realized he needed to back them up. He dropped into the cadences familiar to him from a lifetime of guiding. "Believe in what? Jesus Christ. Believe in what? Country. Believe in what?" He didn't know what. He was walking on air. "The market." A couple guides cocked their heads. He had to finish what he'd started. "Hermanos, it is simple. If we do good work, if we are kind and wise and helpful guides, if we are good ambassadors for our country, then prosperity will come to our nation. We are only beginning. Belize is only thirty-one years old. We are at the beginning of a new age and we can decide now who we are going to be. We are kin. We are bound by the rivers that course through the realm. We welcome guests from the United States. We welcome guests from Europe. We welcome guests from every corner of the planet."

Applause began. He had them. But he had to finish with strength and conviction.

"I want to oversee this age to come. You all know me already. Many of you watched me grow up in Benque and go to school at Mount Carmel. Now that I am a guide, I feel blessed. I love people. I love being around people. I love to serve people. This is what makes me happy and what I am good at. I want to be president of the Cayo Tour Guide Association because I want everyone to love our jobs as much as I love my job, because it is a blessed job, and we live in a blessed country. I said that I was young. What I mean is that I am the future of Belize. Thank you."

The applause was warm, strong, widespread. Floyd slapped his back. He felt happy.

He only wished that Leah were here to see it.

And also, Xander.

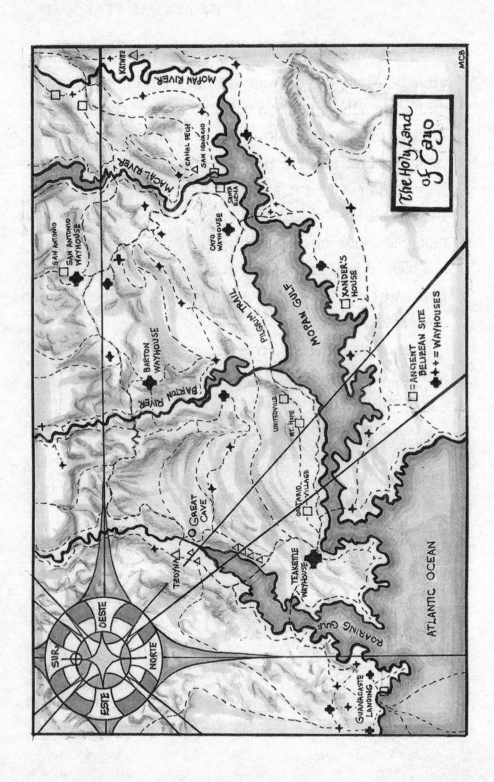

CAYO
5 Chäbin 14 Yaxk'in,
Long Count 15.10.14.9.16

---

15 December, 3012

Niloux had heard the myth, but never believed it: that the waters off Belize were uncannily clear, and had always been, even when the sea first claimed the coast in 2129. Now that she was here, she saw it was true. She could see all the way to the bottom. A fleet of stingrays soared underfoot, and she felt borne up by them, like Aphrodite rising on her shell.

She arrived at a yellow line that stretched north to south.

She tapped her temple to turn off the aug. Then she saw only sea, clear as mint jelly. She tapped to turn it on again. The yellow line was back, inert to the waves.

She turned to Emelle, who had surfaced beside her. "Border crossing," she said, pointing.

Emelle lifted her lilac elbows onto the searoad to anchor herself. "It's still ten hours to Guanacaste Landing," she said, looking to the horizon. "And it looks like we're going to run into another thunderstorm."

"Right. But the border. Should we stop?"

Emelle looked behind them and Niloux followed her gaze. Twelve thousand Zeinians were with them on the searoad, stretching into the distance. She'd tried to shake off followers after the attack at Walili. That had the opposite effect. Converts rallied to the cause, enraged by the bloodletting. She learned to tolerate them. Since then, the parades had only multiplied, like a vine sending new shoots along every searoad in the Atlantic.

"We need to press on to make it through the Hattieville mangrove forest," said Emelle. "It's less dangerous in the morning."

"What about the crocodiles? You can't swim into those."

"Don't worry, I'm getting out," said Emelle, and pushed herself up onto the searoad. She winced in pain, stretched her silver mermaid tail. "Sure, give a quick speech."

"What the hell do I say?"

Emelle narrowed her eyes at her.

It was only a moment, but Niloux felt chastised.

Ever since the attack at Walili, Emelle had been acting strangely. She kept losing patience with Niloux. They didn't have much sex anymore. Niloux told herself, that's entropy for you, what else is new, and besides—no one except sedentix stuck together this long. Eight months together might as well be a Victorian marriage. People were unbearable; not least of all, Niloux knew, herself.

But Emelle let it go this time.

She said, "Say something about the lingering power of borders." Then she went rigid, trying to balance on her behind.

"What are you doing?" said Niloux.

"My pelt is separating the exoskeleton from my epidermis. Then I peel it up the middle to get my legs back, and the rest comes off." She fluttered her hand at Niloux. "Turn around. It's gross."

Niloux snorted and did so. She waved to her self-appointed bodyguards, who were huddled a few scales away, and they came trotting up. These were Owen, a big friar; Cheen, an icy kuudere; and Meret, the tall tigrayan who'd helped save her life at Walili.

"We're at the border," she said. "I hate giving speeches. Can I just say something to you and you pass it back?"

"What, to all twelve thousand people?" Owen said.

"Yes. Person to person like in ancient times."

"There will be a degradation of the data," noted Cheen.

"It'll be simple. Just say . . ." Niloux stared at the line, licked her lips. "We're crossing the ancient border of Belize now. We're not ashamed. We're ready for anything we might encounter at Guanacaste Landing." She nodded. "That's all. Owen, go."

Owen shrugged and walked back to tell the line.

Niloux turned to Meret, who was watching the feeds for her. "Any new intelligence?"

"Sembaruthi hasn't endorsed either of you. I don't think she will."

"Fine. Her prerogative—she matters more to Tanaaj anyway. What about the LFC?"

"There's a group of them waiting at Guanacaste Landing."

"They're there?"

"A few hundred of them."

"Are they going to be violent?"

"They say they aren't. It's no guarantee."

"What would they use as weapons?" asked Niloux. "More sharp sticks?"

Cheen said, "Perhaps obsidian. To them it has symbolic significance."

"Of course," Niloux said. She flinched at the memory of the stab, which induced rage in her if she thought about it for too long. She fingered her golden earspool. Touching it still gave her a surge of adrenaline; it was a kind of addiction. "They forget I'm maya too."

"They don't consider your manéra valid."

"Good thing I don't give a fuck." Niloux looked ahead to the mangrove forest, a strip of black on the eastern horizon. Above it, blue thunderheads were bearing down. Lightning sparked in the distance. She shook her head. "Tanaaj is mopan maya too. Born in Cayo too." She turned back to Meret. "Where is she? What's her state of mind?"

"She and her entourage are camping on the Mopan River tonight. That's the old western border of Belize. She's been in some holy orgiastic state ever since Oaxaca. She keeps preaching about sacrifice."

"Well, that's reassuring."

Meret shrugged. "She's always been a scrupe, but some say it's gotten worse. Something happened to her in Oaxaca."

"She is planning a performance of *La Estrella Actual*," said Cheen, "for the eve of Día de Pasaja."

"And this is where she's going to prove Xibalba is real."

"Apparently so."

"What is she saying about me?"

"You sound like a jealous lover," said Cheen.

Niloux scowled.

"From what I've seen," said Meret, "she doesn't refer to you at all except to express pity."

Niloux raised her eyebrows. "That's condescending."

Meret shrugged. "Maybe condescension is how she shows rage."

Owen came back, grinning. Niloux became aware of a chanting sound, overlapping along the column like an echo. "What did you tell them?"

"Only what you told me," said Owen. "I can't be held responsible for what happens next."

Niloux made out the chant: *Zein-o-Din! Zein-o-Din!*

Zein-o-Din. Grace of the religion. An Arabic Islamic phrase from the sixteenth century to name the caravanserai near the oasis on the other side of the world where she'd looked upon Venus and started the schism in Laviaja. Now the phrase had an entirely new meaning. She shook her head. History was so arbitrary, she thought. Let that be recorded.

She turned back to Emelle, who was already standing, her exoskeleton in gelatinous shreds around her feet.

"You ready?" she said. "Let's cross over."

The evening before they crossed into ancient Belize, Tanaaj and her familia made the special Pasaja foods. They laid them out on palm leaves: johnnycake, tamales, maduros, all protected from the thunderstorm by a static dome. Eight LFC viajeras ringed the meal. They were her familia tonight. They looked feverish with purpose, but Tanaaj knew, in her heart, that she was the only one who would make the sacrifice that would save Laviaja. She had certainty, and in certainty she had security.

She pitched her voice to be heard over the thunder.

"Hermanix," said Tanaaj, raising a cup, "tomorrow morning we will cross the Mopan River. It is only six days until the anniversary of Laviaja. We have come one thousand years. We shall endeavor onward, in love and hope, until we are all safe in Xibalba. I am blessed to be with you all."

Lupe, a gentle sur catholic, had tears in her eyes. "To Tanaaj!" she burst out, her drink sloshing over the rim. "The defender of peace, against—"

Tanaaj held up a hand, and Lupe fell silent. The others looked at the ground in embarrassment.

"We will not speak of her here," said Tanaaj. "We will not even say her name. She may be crossing into Cayo at this moment, even as we sit assembled here together. But we are only concerned with the god of this place. Let us pause to take it in."

She looked up.

The others did too.

Through the static dome, she saw the cohune palms, tossing with rain. A scarlet macaw streaked past. The river gurgled in the dark just down the hill. Sweat dripped down her back. Along the bank, there was the sparkle of other domes, sheltering other familias—hundreds, thousands—all sitting down to supper, all feeling the same purpose, all staking the flag of Laviaja. They were almost in the motherland.

Tanaaj fingered her medal, traced the orchid.

This was the lesson she had learned from Ying Yue in Oaxaca: that Xibalba must be given life in order to give it back. It had always been this way. How could she, a maya, have forgotten it?

After supper, when they were pillowed on each other's bodies, an aug grackle appeared to offer an orientation holo. Tanaaj was drunk and slurred, "Estamos listas, hermanita," and the others couldn't stop laughing.

"Very good, Tanaaj," said the grackle.

She split open and blossomed into a map of Cayo.

The voice began to narrate. "What we now think of as the standard pilgrimage to Cayo is an accumulation of the customs that have developed over a thousand years of visitors, all of whom sought to walk in the footsteps of Leah, Javier, and Xander, and their legendary Maya ancestors, Ixul and Ajul of the Tzoyna. The boundaries of modern Cayo proper are as follows." The map zoomed in and out as the voice named each site, and Tanaaj felt as though she were falling toward them and bouncing up again in a giant rubber band. "In the north, the Mopan Gulf; in the south, the lower Macal River; in the west, the Mopan River; and in the east, the Roaring Gulf. The modern Cayo Wayhouse is the descendant of the first wayhouse in history. Since then, forty more wayhouses have been salvaged or grown in Cayo."

Forty stars glowed on the map like scattered maize.

"These wayhouses make Cayo the most population-dense area on the planet at any time of year, but especially during the holy month of December."

Then the map went dark, except for the wayhouses and a green line that made a continuous circuit. "This is the standard pilgrimage route, starting at Teakettle Wayhouse," said the voice. They zoomed in to a star in the bottom left quadrant, which split open and blossomed into images of marble pillars, chitin lattice, and silken walls. "Many viajeras choose to stay here for at least one night, as it is noted for both its views of the

Mopan Gulf and its spectacular concerts, readings, and tzoynas at all hours." Now they were flying up over the eastern stretch, descending to the beaten dirt. "Reymundo Road is a well-worn dirt track along which the ancient guides drove their tourists in oil-powered vans. The limestone cliffs have become a canvas for artists, sculptors, and musicians." They flew over fat rivers, orange groves, and mahogany forests, then descended into another star that expanded into a city of stone. "At the end of Reymundo Road, there is the holy city of Tzoyna. You will recognize the ball court from virtual sessions of the global legislature. The Tzoyna of Ixul and Ajul was buried by the jungle in Saint Leah's time, but excavated and restored in the twenty-fourth century. Now it is home to the first Arca de las Gemelas, a monument to Ixul and Ajul."

They bounced across Roaring River to a final star.

"This is the Great Cave itself. It is also known as La Cueva de Leah, La Cueva de la Trinidad de Cayo, or La Cueva de las Mayas. It is home to the second Arca de las Gemelas: the preserved remains of Xander Cañul and Javier Magaña, the Consort Twins."

A brief image of two leathery faces with sunken cheekbones, side-by-side.

Tanaaj shut her eyes. She didn't want to see them until she got there.

"According to tradition, each viajera must enter alone, and only once. She may spend as much time as she likes. She may go as far as the holy sump chamber, from which the purest waters spring, that have healed viajeras for centuries. But when she comes back into the light, she must take up her own viaja and never look back."

Tanaaj blinked back tears.

The voice went on.

"There will be pitz tournaments on the courts next to the Mopan Gulf beginning December seventeenth, Día de la Salida, the day when, a thousand years ago, Saint Leah flew to Belize in an airplane . . ."

What was the cave itself like? What was it like inside?

"December eighteenth is Día de la Sabiduría de Xander, a day for debates and discussions relating to the common good . . ."

Would she discover her cortada there? Was it too much to hope for?

"December nineteenth is Día de la Primera Viaja, when Javier first guided Saint Leah in the cave. It is the most popular day to go to the cave itself . . ."

Should she go to the Great Cave before or after she found Niloux? Would she even be allowed to go after, knowing what she was planning to do?

Lupe was whispering in her ear. "Tanaaj . . . Tanaaj."

Tanaaj turned on her side and faced her. "Yes."

"We don't want to disturb you but we're all wondering. When are you going to confront Niloux? She wants you to debate her at an open tzoyna."

"I do not debate, carnalix. That is not my way."

The voice said, "December twentieth is Día de la Segunda Viaja, when Xander guided Saint Leah in the cave. It is the traditional day to change manéras . . ."

Lupe frowned. "But then how . . ."

"I will perform *La Estrella*," said Tanaaj. "Trust me. My performance will be my first, last, and only answer to her."

"Does she know that?"

Tanaaj shrugged. "She will understand in the end."

The voice said, "Eighty thousand people are expected at the Jubilee celebration. In light of the controversies of the past year involving the Mardom e Zein-o-Din, and the attempt on Niloux DeCayo's life in Walili, the viajeras who prepared this holo would like to remind all pilgrims of the absolute injunction against violence. Anyone who forgets this, the foundation of the Peace of the Viajeras, will face swift consequences from the Tzoyna."

I accept the consequences, said Tanaaj in her mind, *and that will be my sacrifice too.*

The holo collapsed back to the grackle, who zoomed up to heaven.

Niloux tapped her temple to sharpen her night vision. Dusk was falling and they were deep in the Hattieville mangrove forest. The searoad led through tunnels of roots, jointed and kinked and overlaid, following the ancient Western Highway, which, according to her aug, was now only thirty feet below and rising.

Twenty.

Ten.

She hopped onto hard ground and she was in Cayo. Immediately she bent over.

Emelle was at her side. "What is it?"

Niloux swallowed. The ground began to glow, pistas drawing themselves like tendrils uncurling. Sour adrenaline was flooding her mouth. She knew this feeling well by now, but had never felt it to this degree.

"I've been here," she said.

"Yes," said Emelle dryly, "your surname is DeCayo. You were born here."

"No," she snapped. "Other lives. Before this."

Emelle drew in her breath. "You mean . . ."

Niloux nodded. "They're everywhere."

"Let me help you," said Emelle, taking her arm.

"No," she snapped, and shook her off.

Emelle stepped back. From her look, Niloux knew she'd gone too far.

"You are being a real piece of shit," said Emelle. "I healed you in Campania. I saved your life in Walili. I've been by your side through everything. So have lots of us. You keep treating us this way, we'll just leave you."

Part of Niloux wanted to say: *Good, I'll have peace at last.*

Another part wanted to say: *You've chosen to do this right now?*

But she knew she couldn't fight on multiple fronts. She had no idea what she was about to face ahead.

Still hunched, she said, "Sorry."

Emelle crossed her arms.

Niloux stood up straight. "I'm sorry I snapped at you."

Emelle nodded. "Thank you." Then she went down the line to corral those who were coming ashore.

Niloux ascended up the ramp. The ground continued to glow, like a mat of tangled yarn. She hadn't expected this. She hadn't seen one of her past pistas since Sparta. She strode along one of the thickest bundles, right into the plaza that was Guanacaste Landing.

There was a line of people at the far end.

Niloux stopped.

The line was maybe a hundred long, three deep. Some held torches. Many held Laviaja flags. In the front there were three viajeras holding dark velvet banners. Niloux knew them and their meanings well.

Javier Magaña in black, with the sun, pelota, staff, and passion flower.

Xander Cañul in red, with the moon, quill, book, and heliconia.

Saint Leah Oliveri in green, with the star, blade, spider, and orchid.

What a welcome, Niloux thought.

A fat viajera came forward, her face lit by torchlight. She seemed to be their spokesperson. She planted her feet and addressed Niloux.

"Wih di kip di pees," called the spokesperson. "Wi waahn noa if yu kohn eena pees."

Niloux narrowed her eyes. The viajera was speaking in Kriol, and this was a power move, to test her knowledge. Did they think she couldn't speak the language?

"Ah noh waahn chrai *kil sohnbadi*," she spat back. "Yu waahn chrai agen? Yu an aal dehnya peepl?"

"Peepl ku kil wid lat a ting," said the spokesperson with a wry look on her face. "Di naif? Da jus wan."

"You mean ideas. People can kill with ideas as well as knives. Right? What wisdom for the ages!" said Niloux, switching back to Común. She was sick of the performative piety. She would not play on the LFC's terms. "Look, nothing I've said or done in the last year, or ever, included anything about killing. And to imply that is dishonest. I *did* say that Laviaja evolved because of climate change, more than because of the specific things that these—these *normal human people*"—she pointed at the banners—"might have done in their lifetimes. Did I say to kill anyone? Tell me when I said to kill anyone."

Her voice had risen to a shout.

But the spokesperson continued to stare, unmoved, as did the line behind her.

"You are free, of course," she said finally, "to do as you will in Laviaja. To say what you will and walk where you will. But so are we." She drew her feet together, clasped her hands behind her back. "We, La Familia de la Carretera, the followers of Tanaaj DeCayo, have resolved to stand our ground while your company comes ashore. To enter Cayo, you must pass through us."

"What promise do we have that you won't hurt us?" said Emelle beside her. Niloux realized that she had come to her side, as had Owen, Meret, and Cheen. Her followers had begun to flood the plaza.

The spokesperson's eyes flicked back and forth to take them in.

Then she turned around to face the line.

"'Versa Trece,'" she called.

She was quoting the Rule of Saint Leah.

"*Blood belongs to Xibalba alone.* It is not for us to draw the blood of another."

"La recibimos," said those in the line, and bowed their heads.

Niloux realized she had done so too, without thinking.

The spokesperson turned around. Something had changed in her eyes, as if she had settled a question in her own heart. Niloux realized that the possibility of violence had been very real. Somehow they'd narrowly missed it.

"Are you satisfied?" said the spokesperson.

Meret murmured, "This is as good as we can hope for."

Niloux nodded and called back, "I'll tell my people too. No violence."

The spokesperson bowed her head, but tension remained in the set of her shoulders. "Let every one of them come through us, and understand," she said, "that they come upon holy land."

Niloux had no answer to that. She was far away in her mind, wheeling back into the past and far into the future. Holy land. Guards. Spokespersons. Leaders. Followings. Assassinations. Until recently, all of these had been distant nightmares consigned to history. Now they were real again. Even Niloux had underestimated how easy it was to slip back into the rhythms of mine and yours, us and them, territory and bloodshed.

Laviaja was already dead.

TZOYNA
4 Eb 15 Pop, Long Count 10.9.5.7.12

---

10 December, 1012

Ajul surfaced from a dream.

He was still tied. The fire was out. He didn't see any guards.

Silver eyes blinked in the jungle, watching him.

He slipped back into dreams.

Now he was descending with Ixul, following their father. Their presentation ceremony was over. The Nahua prince had been sacrificed, and a gentle rain was falling. He looked back. Ket was huddled under their mother's arm, clutching her doll. She got to stay behind. But the twins had to go with their father. They had to learn what happened to the body next. As they proceeded, the crowd thinned and turned away, as if caught looking at something private.

The priests carried the body of the victim on a litter. The king followed after, hunched and drooping. Ajul nudged Ixul. "What is he doing?" he whispered.

Usually Ixul had an answer for everything, but this time she looked confused, and when she was confused she got frustrated. "I don't know," she said. "He won. But he's walking as if defeated."

The procession arrived at the foot of the big temple. Their father stumbled against the first step and cried out in pain, and servants rushed to help him, but he waved them off. Ajul and Ixul exchanged looks again. They'd never heard their father cry out like that. But the servants looked serene, as if this were a performance, everyone playing their parts.

Their father began to crawl up the steps like a dog. As he climbed, he took off his regalia, bit by bit— headdress, earspools, necklace, belt, robe, armband, headband, chest piece. Ajul thought he began to understand, though it was an understanding of the heart, not of the mind; that there was some deeper truth at work here, rooted in Xibalba. More priests followed, balancing the headless victim on the litter. The twins followed last.

The procession ascended to the top platform, overlooking the countryside. The servants staked each corner with torches that sputtered in the drizzle. Their father was wearing only his esh now, as if he were a captive himself. He was alone with the victim and the victim's head. The twins knelt and watched.

Their father shook his hands at the sky in all four directions, then bent his forehead to the stone. There were tears in his eyes. It was as if he were mourning for the victim, as he would his own child. Then a priest stepped forward with an obsidian knife and gathered their father's long hair in his hand. Ixul surged forward, but Ajul put his hand on her shoulder. They must not interfere.

They watched as he cut it all off.

Then a servant stepped forward to unwind their father's esh. Now he was completely naked. He was presented a bowl of the victim's blood, and dipped his hands in it, and began to coat himself.

"What is happening?" Ixul hissed.

To anyone else, she would have sounded angry, but Ajul knew she was scared. He tried to be strong, even though he felt sick. He remembered his earlier flash of understanding. He whispered back, "He has taken on the face of the captive, sister."

"To what end? He's abasing himself."

Now their father was covering himself in lime dust. It stuck to the blood, making him look like a cutlet tossed in flour. Ajul struggled to put his certainty to words. "The abasement *is* the honor. He must show acceptance of the rite from all sides. He could have been the captive as easily as the captor."

"But he's not the captive. That was the whole point. *We* gave *our* captive to Xibalba for blessings for *our* kingdom."

"But we could just as easily have been given," Ajul whispered, not sure how he knew, but certain he was right, "by another king, for another kingdom; and he must acknowledge that, or the rite is incomplete."

Now their father was white as an egret, even as the chalk ran in the rain. He looked like he was melting. Ajul was in thrall of the sight, this powerful king smeared the color of mourners and victims and slaves. His father gave a signal to the priests and servants, who went down the other side of the temple, still bearing their torches. Meanwhile, their father folded the limbs of the captive into a basket, tucking them in with care and attention, placing the head in last, so that it appeared the captive was curled up on his side, holding his own head in his lap. Then with a great heave, he lifted the basket until it was balanced on his own head and stood up, like a washer woman carrying her load.

He began down the steps on the other side.

Ajul and Ixul looked at each other, then scrambled to follow.

Their father continued to descend. His back was straight and his steps were slow. Ajul knew these steps well—when he was a child, he'd run up them when no one was looking—but never in the rain. The steps were steep and narrow and now slippery as well. If his father lost his balance, he'd tumble face-first to his death. But he was halfway down the stairs, so far, with no misstep. There was no music. There was only the hiss of the torches in the rain. The twins followed, holding hands. The basket teetered on the king's head, began to wobble; he jerked out his hip, corrected. By the next step it was balanced again. Ajul was so tense he wanted to vomit.

The king reached the bottom of the stairs, crossed the wet plaza, and headed toward the darkness.

Ajul expected the servants to light his way, but they made no move.

He risked a question to Mutna, who stood among the priests. "Please," he said, "are we to follow him?"

She bowed her head in assent.

Ajul looked to his father, now disappearing into the eaves of the jungle. He pulled his sister's hand and felt resistance. He turned around.

Ixul's lips were set. "I don't need to see the rest," she said. Her voice was tight.

Ajul spoke in a soothing tone. "I'll be with you, sister," he said. "We need to know the full meaning of the ritual if we're ever to do it ourselves. Otherwise, how can we know what Xibalba requires of us?"

Ixul looked away, her brow furrowed.

"Trust him," he said. "Trust the rite. Our family has followed it since we descended from the Hero Twins."

He tugged on her hand again, and this time, she followed.

Ajul knew the path their father was taking. It was the lime causeway that led down to the Great Cave. He could make him out ahead, proceeding calmly, in and out of shafts of the full moon. The sound of rushing water grew louder. They were approaching the entrance of the underworld. These were the sacred mysteries of inversion and submission, his duty and birthright. Ajul felt scared, but if he looked away now, he'd never be worthy of the title of king.

Now the river sparkled darkly below: rainwater, holy water, healing water. Their father descended the last few steps, then knelt with the basket on his head. The twins knelt a few steps above, following each other's motions to do what seemed right. Only once their father was stable on his knees did he finally remove the basket from his head and set it before him. Ajul let out his breath. He didn't realize how much he'd been holding it in. Then their father began muttering words, again beseeching the sky, then bending his forehead to the earth, then reaching out to unseen powers in all directions. He didn't look at his children. Ajul strained to hear him, and could only make out words and phrases: *For the gods of this place . . . thank the wind and the heavens . . . accept this blood . . . according to the law . . . this world and the other . . . we give you life so that we may live.*

Then he set the basket on the water. It bobbed and began to drift.

Ixul gripped his hand. "Look," she whispered, "look how it's moving."

He looked more closely. He realized that the basket was moving upstream.

They watched until it disappeared into the cave.

As soon as it did, his father bent his forehead to the ground again with renewed energy, and—Ajul could tell—words of relief and thanksgiving. *These children . . . curse of death . . . rain and maize . . . new age.* Finally the torrent of words subsided and he sat up. He simply knelt there, by the river, for a long while. He seemed to be enjoying the sound of the water. The moon rose higher in the sky, and the world was shadowed black and white.

Finally he turned and addressed the twins.

"Do you understand?" he said.

"No, Ahau," said Ixul at the same time as Ajul said, "Yes, Ahau."

He came up the steps and stood over them, stiff and formal, half still in ritual mind, half in self-consciousness at his appearance. He drew himself up and squared his shoulders.

"The ball game is only the first half of the ritual, done for sport and spectacle, to give the gods their due and the subjects their entertainment. This is the second half, done away from the eyes of those who would misunderstand." He spoke with urgency. "You are only a queen or a king if you yourself are ready, at any moment, to give yourself to the god. Rebirth requires death. That is the lesson of the Hero Twins. When you hear that call, you must not turn away."

"How will we recognize it?" asked Ajul.

He frowned. "It is easy. Ask yourself, who is bound and who holds the spear? You cannot fail to recognize it."

Ajul was abashed.

"And if one does turn away from the call?" asked Ixul.

"Then they are not worthy to lead."

She stared into the darkness where the basket had disappeared.

Ixul wrenched her hand free of Ajul's grasp and rubbed her hand to get feeling back into it and then realized she was only imagining that she was rubbing her hands, because her hands were bound.

Ixul started awake. She was very cold. She made to form a word, but the word became a brilliant sunburst in her throat, and she remembered the pain, the knives, the mouthfuls of blood, the laughter, the curses, the cauterizing stone plucked from the fire. The woman who called herself her mother was the one laughing. She had vomited from pain, then fainted again as they pressed the stone to the stump of her tongue. The howler monkeys roared in the dark. She couldn't believe they were howling away as they always had. Weren't they paying attention? She woke up again. Her head was tipped back. Her mouth was stuffed with cotton, soaked in sap. A ceiba root stabbed into her back. An apron of vomit and dried blood fanned down her chest. She scanned the sky for Chak Ek' but he had already set, and she remembered the time she had asked Mutna if the star was truly a god, and Mutna gave her every theory of every philosopher who ever lived until Ixul asked, *No, what do you think?*

Mutna said, *I think each star is a whole other world.*

She fainted again.

She dreamed of Ket, riding a black jaguar, her bandage stained with eyes of blood.

She turned back to Ajul, who was still gazing up at their naked father.

"One day you'll go into the underworld yourselves, when the god calls you," he said. "Watch over each other. You are each the other's responsibility, in this world and the Other, and you must always seek that which binds your love, not that which divides it."

For a moment, Ixul wanted to run away, to defy everything she'd ever been taught, just because she could.

Their father began walking back up to the city. Ixul moved to follow him, but Ajul was still holding on to her hand. She unlaced her fingers, wrenched them free. "Come on," she said.

"No," said Ajul. He looked dazed, as if he were digesting everything he'd seen, and it was taking up all of his vitality. "Stay with me awhile, sister. Let us listen to the river."

"I've heard the river," Ixul snapped. "I want to hear other things."

He looked up, hurt, his eyes full of moonlight.

"I am staying here," he said.

"Fine," she said, and started up the path by herself.

She saw her father disappearing under the eaves. She hurried to catch up with him. She had more questions about the ritual, about the basket floating against the current, about what would happen to the captive's body after it entered Xibalba. Ixul and Ajul had played captive-and-captor hundreds of times as children, switching roles and torturing each other. They'd agree on rules at the beginning of each game.

Ajul would always fulfill the rules.

Ixul would always change them.

She started awake.

She tried to push the cotton out of her mouth, but she had no tongue, and the pain of trying made the world swim. She let her head drop back against the tree. She would not cry. She'd been given drugs, she knew; but the drugs were waning, and the pain was waxing. She could feel it like the glow on the horizon before the sun appeared. When the full pain arrived, she would need to be in control of herself.

She tried to calm down by going over the cycles of time. She was a daykeeper. A daykeeper must be able to count a thousand years into the past and the future, rolling the sacred rounds like bracelets on her wrist.

Yesterday was Three Batz'.

Today is Four Eb.

Tomorrow is Five Bin.

Then Six Hix.

Seven Men.

Eight Chäbin.

I am Royal Princess Ixul B'olon Tznanab of the Tzoyna, descended from the Hero Twins.

Nine Tznanab.

Ten Chab.

Eleven Chak.

Twelve Ajwal.

Thirteen Himux.

My brother is Royal Prince Ajul B'uluch Chab of the Tzoyna, descended from the Hero Twins.

One Ik'.

Two Wotan.

Three K'anan.

Four Nohchan.

Five Tox.

Six Manich'.

My sister is Royal Princess Ket Lajchän Ajwal of the Tzoyna, descended from the Hero Twins.

Seven Lamat.

Eight Mul.

Nine Ok.

Ten Batz'.

My sister was taken by the god. Balam Ahau scooped her up in his own mouth like a kitten. I saw it with my own eyes.

"Why did the god take my sister?" she asked Mutna, who sat before her on the riverbank, hair now unbound and flying free in the wind.

"Ask the god of the day."

"Three Batz', what does it mean?"

The glyph of Three Batz' unfurled in her mind. Batz' was a god who governed the continuity of all creations. He spun the thread, and she swung the bracelets upon them, back to the beginning of the last baktun, and forward to the next baktun. Three Batz' rearranged into a sly smile in the darkness.

"Why did the god take my sister Ket?"

"Which god?" said Three Batz'.

"Balam Ahau," said Ixul impatiently. "He already took her eye, which should have been enough, but then he took all of her, and my brother and I have been taken captive. Why?"

"Large demands require large sacrifice."

"Large? We just asked for rain."

"You asked for a whole empire."

"We'll build that ourselves! We only need help from the gods."

"There are many more gods listening to you than the ones you know."

Ixul was furious. "Tell me."

Three Batz' laughed. "To tell you, I must take you to all the ends of the earth, and all the corners of the cosmos, for all of your lives, and still you will never know them all."

"Then why tell me at all?" Ixul shouted at the floating mouth. "Who sent you? What authority do you have? Have you been sent to trick me? Where is Ket?"

The more she shouted, the more the mouth unraveled, until she heard herself making moaning sounds with the stump of her tongue, and beyond that, the sound of laughter.

The sun cracked the horizon, and it was made of pain.

CAYO
3 Kawoq, Long Count 12.19.19.17.19

---

20 December, 2012

Leah rode shotgun in Xander's truck. She studied his profile in the light of the streetlamps that flicked overhead. He reminded her of a dormant volcano.

He took her to a Mexican restaurant. There were no tourists here. She followed him in and noticed the warm pink-and-orange light.

"Oh! I remember this," she said.

Xander frowned at her. "You've been here?"

"No, I meant . . ." Leah shook her head, she can't have been here before. Then she remembered. "There was a Mexican restaurant in St. Cloud, near where I grew up, and they had paper lanterns like these. My mom used to take me all the time. They had a statue of a Maya goddess too."

"Ixchel."

"No, her name was Bloodmaiden. She was the mother of the Hero Twins."

Xander nodded. "Obscure. I approve."

He ordered takeout—shrimp quesadillas and a side of black fruit cake, wrapped in cellophane. Leah went to the bathroom. Someone had glued the mirror of a compact case to the wall, and she looked at herself in its tiny smeared surface. She smiled, and seeing herself smile, smiled bigger. She remembered the lovely statue of Bloodmaiden in orange and gold, and her mother's papier-mâché version, both so far away they might as well be on another planet; though paradoxically, here she was, in Bloodmaiden's real home. She remembered how she'd shaved her vulva and looked in the bathroom mirror at home—what was it, now? Seven years ago. Last night with Javier, she didn't dare imagine what life could have in store for her next, but then today was a salvo of new friends, new experiences, and new wonders. She'd walked the same path in the cave, but it felt different with Xander. With Javier, she felt safe, desired, and cherished; with Xander, she felt admired, pursued, and challenged. Both feelings were pleasurable. Both were forms of love. And now she wanted to slide this glove on too, to see how it fit.

When Leah came out of the bathroom, she saw Xander hunched over his notebook.

"What are you writing?"

Xander looked up. "Notes. All the things I want to follow up on."

"Follow up on?"

"I need to stay in touch with those people. Ruth and Ida and Micah. I got their contact information and texted them all already."

"Have they texted you back yet?"

"No."

"They will. They're good people."

"*Great* people," he said with fervor, which surprised her. "They might be able to help me get out of Belize."

Leah frowned. "Why would you want to get out of Belize?"

Xander glanced up at her, looking annoyed. He seemed to be swallowing words, getting himself under control. Finally he said, "I want to study. I can't study how I want to study here. I can only study how I want to study abroad. It's hard to get a visa to go abroad."

Leah nodded. Now she understood. "Can I help?"

"Are you related to any deans at MIT?"

"No."

Xander shrugged. "Order's ready," he said.

They got in his truck and sped up the road that led east out of town, not west, like she'd gone the previous night. They didn't talk much. He only spoke to ask for something from his glove compartment, or check that she was comfortable with the windows down. She was, of course. The night air was thick, wet, and green.

He and Javier were fraternal twins, and had different demeanors. Javier's features were mild, pleasant, and benevolent, while Xander had a stronger nose, heavier brow, and fuller mouth. She felt more mature just by being with him. Not that Javier wasn't mature, but Xander seemed to ask more of her, and she liked feeling herself rise to the occasion. She enjoyed his approval.

They turned off the Western Highway, drove through a labyrinth of side streets, and finally arrived at a small house at the end of a dirt road. Xander unlocked the gate and a cat mewed from somewhere in the yard. "Cevichon!" he called out. "Come here."

"Cevichon?"

"My cat. Or . . . I can't call it mine. It's a cat that's figured out it can get meals from me."

The cat showed up and raked its claws on the door. Xander opened it and the cat darted through, then turned to inquire about the quesadillas. Leah followed them. Xander flipped on lights, went to the kitchen, and opened the cupboards. In contrast to Javier's house, this house was tidy. Xander appeared to live alone, and to sweep and clean on a regular basis. "Stereo is there," he said, pointing to a corner of the living room. "You can put on some music."

Leah was happy to have something to do, and even more to investigate his CD collection. Those were good indicators of a prospective lover's character. She found boxed sets of Ravel and Shajarian, neither of which she'd heard of, and '90s hip-hop, which she had. She turned over a P.M. Dawn case, then a Boyz II Men case. "They were popular when I was born," she said.

Xander looked up from the counter. "How old are you?"

"Nineteen. How old are you?"

"Guess."

"Thirty?"

His eyes widened. "Jesus gyal, no," he said. "I'm twenty-three."

She smacked her forehead. "Oh, like Javier! Right." She held up the Shajarian CD. "Who's this?"

Xander squinted. "Mohammad Shajarian. He's Persian."

"Persian," Leah said to herself, relishing the feel of the word on her tongue.

"Put him on. He's good."

She did, and with the first notes, she felt she was in a lonely desert far away.

Xander shredded off a piece of quesadilla, put the bowl and cat outside, came back in. "He's probably the most famous Persian singer alive. I wish I could go to Iran and hear him in person."

"Why don't you?"

His mouth tightened. He uncapped a water bottle, poured two glasses. "It's not so easy for me, gyal," he said. "Iran might as well be Venus."

Leah felt her face grow hot. It was the second time she'd asked a question about travel with such naïveté. She may have prided herself on her cultural awareness in Anoong, but here, she was realizing how much she had to learn. "I forgot," she said. "I'm sorry."

Xander nodded. "It's all right. You grow up in the States, you never have to think about it unless someone tells you."

He came out from behind the counter and set two plates on a round wooden table, then two glasses of water. Leah seated herself. They both ate. After eating for a while Xander said, "Sorry if I don't talk much. I'm really hungry."

"That's fine," said Leah. "I'm enjoying the music."

"And I'm not used to company."

"No? Your place is very clean."

"Out of respect for the gods."

"Which gods?"

Xander waved his fork. "No idea," he said, though Leah perceived he was being flippant, that he did have an idea, and she just needed to wait for the right moment to ask again.

"I don't know what God is either," she said, "even though I went to Catholic school all my life."

"Are you Catholic?"

"Yes. But not Roman Catholic. I'd call myself . . . Magdalene Catholic."

"What's that?"

Leah shrugged. "It's whatever I am."

"Well, give me your creed."

Leah was at a loss, until she remembered the poem she'd scribbled down and put in her pocket the day before. She pulled it out, smoothed it down, then handed it to Xander. He reached for his reading glasses and peered down at the poem. Leah thought the glasses made him look both distinguished and vulnerable.

He read,

"In the beginning,
in the cave,
God knelt in the darkness with her blade.

When she cut her hand,
in the cave,
the universe spilled from the tip of the blade.

Flooding the wound,
the gift of blood,
souls that remember the perfect whole—
the body of God,
the blade, the cave,
and what a star is, not of what it is made."

He looked over the tops of his glasses at her.

"Xander," she said, "I can't go back to Minnesota."

He put down the paper and waited for her to say more.

"I mean . . . I've thought about it in little bursts, and just the idea of going back to that coldness . . . I can't bear it. But I only have a few more days here. And then I'd have to work at my job for another two years to come back, and that's if my mother would even let me live with her and Rick. I know you want to leave Belize. I understand why. But for me, coming here for the first time, I'm just so happy, and in the cave most of all."

Xander considered. "But Belize will still be here when you come back."

Even the suggestion of being away made her stomach turn. She felt panicked. She had to stay here. "But . . . every moment I'd be away would be like I was sealed up in a tomb waiting to die."

"Imagine how I feel."

Leah nodded, miserable.

Xander relented, and spoke in a gentler voice. "You finished with your food?"

"No," said Leah, and stabbed a shrimp with her fork.

Xander got up. "Want that Belikin?"

Leah paused. "Do you have anything else?"

"What about cacao?"

"Ooh. Is that like hot chocolate?"

"Almost. It's made with water—a Maya drink."

"I'd love that."

Leah watched him move through his kitchen. Watching him calmed her. Admitting to Xander that she couldn't leave Belize was a big step. Now she just had to figure out how to stay. Could she talk to an embassy? Appeal to her Maya heritage or her father's citizenship? She'd figure it out.

He set the kettle to boil, then turned and said, "What do you think the future is going to be like?"

Leah smiled. "How far into the future?"

"A thousand years."

She loved questions like this. No one at home asked her questions like this. She folded her hands in her lap and closed her eyes, trying to braid together everything she'd felt over the last few days.

Finally she said, "No one will hurt each other anymore. Everyone will walk everywhere, looking for where they belong, like how I feel I belong here. But they'll enjoy their time because there's no need to hurry. There will be great festivals, like masquerade balls, except with millions of people at once, all being exactly who they want to be."

"It sounds like utopia."

She opened her eyes. "Oh no. Nothing in this world can ever be."

"Why not?"

"Because we don't belong in this world. We'll never feel complete."

"Never? Not if we have everything we want?"

Leah smiled. "There's no end to desire." She remembered the public television show she'd seen so long ago. "And it's only going to get worse, as entropy grows."

Xander looked amused. "What does entropy have to do with desire?"

"Well, as the universe comes apart, everything we desire will get farther and farther away. So we'll have to work harder to get it."

The kettle whistled.

He poured a mug, mixed it with grounds from a glass jar, gave it to her. Leah sipped it: bitter but warming, and familiar somehow. She told herself it was because she was remembering her ancestry. She sat on the air mattress with it, cross-legged. Xander hooked up a pump to the mattress. They'd decided she'd stay the night, without discussing it. But they hadn't even kissed yet. Was Xander even the kissing type? Leah felt excited, like she was starting up the first hill of a roller coaster.

Xander started pumping the mattress.

"Should I get off?"

"Nah, stay put."

She smiled, as it became a game, trying to keep her mug steady as the mattress plumped and deepened beneath her. This moment felt so much like her experiments back home, when she tried to layer sensory experiences on top of each other to induce a higher consciousness. She was listening to Persian music after eating Mexican food in a Belizean man's house drinking Maya cacao. His body was so near. She could smell the laundry detergent he'd used on his shirt—lavender, unexpectedly. She realized her heart had started beating faster, because when he was done pumping the mattress, what else could he do but join her?

He finished, stood up, looked down at her.

"I'm going to shower," he said, smirked, and left.

Leah gaped.

She'd never known men like these! Javier, who matched her fervor, and now Xander, who made her wait. She peered down the hall to make sure he was in the bathroom, then reached down and wiped a slick of herself on the pillow, hoping the pheromones would get to him.

When he came back, wearing a white undershirt and red plaid boxers, he took the mug out of her hand and set it on the floor.

"Wait!" she said. "I have to shower too."

Xander sucked his teeth, then said, "All right."

She went down the hall, pleased with her little power move. He wanted her. She could tell. She closed the bathroom door behind her. There was a single white towel on the rack, still damp. She took a brief, hot shower, realizing she hadn't had one since yesterday at her guesthouse, which seemed ages ago. She still smelled like Javier! It was good to get herself fresh.

She came out of the bathroom naked, with all of her clothes in a bundle under her arm.

Xander was on the mattress, reading by candlelight. He looked up and took all of her in. His eyes lingered on the scars along her iliac crest.

He put down his book and said, "Come here."

She put her bundle down and lay alongside him on the bed. He had an erection and she expected him to just pull down his boxers and roll on top of her. Instead, he drew his finger across her scars, as if asking a question and reading the answer.

"Why do you think the future you described isn't a utopia?" he said.

Leah willed herself to wait, to slow to his pace.

"Because it still won't be Xibalba," she said.

His finger paused, then resumed its trail. "What do you think Xibalba is?"

She tried to concentrate. "I know it's the 'place of fear.' But when I'm there, I feel just the opposite. I feel happier than I've ever been. I know that doesn't make sense."

She feared he would condescend to her, as he had the first time they'd talked. But he only nodded. "It does, in a way," he said. "The ancient Maya believed in dualities. The dualities had to exist, to sustain each other."

Leah turned her head at the softness in his voice. "Do you believe utopia can exist in this world?"

Xander shook his head. "No, but I believe that the desire for it exists. That desire can perform a useful function."

"To do what?"

"To make a better world."

Leah shook her head. "I need the real thing. I need to keep looking, and then, one day—I'll cross over. And the cave is the closest I've ever felt to doing that."

Xander nodded. "You really love the cave," he said.

"I do."

"And you want to go all the way in."

Leah blinked to clear the lust. Her attention sharpened. This was the subject Javier had warned her not to ask Xander about, but he was bringing it up of his own accord. "Yes."

"Why?"

Leah grasped for words. "It feels like it's inviting me. Like it was made for me."

Xander stared at his finger, tracing the scars on her pelvis. "If you went past the step-up rock," he said, "you'd see things that would make you want to turn around."

Leah's arms broke out in goosebumps. "Like what?"

"There are no artifacts beyond that point," he said. "None. And if you study the ancient Maya, you know that they went wherever they could in caves. You find entire shrines in the most inaccessible parts of other caves that take hours to get to, even with modern equipment. But there . . . nothing."

"But you said I'd see things that would make me want to turn back."

"Heliconia petals," he said, "floating on the water."

"Wouldn't those just come from sinkholes farther in?"

"There are no sinkholes farther in."

"Then where do the petals come from?"

His eyes flicked up to hers, then down again. "You also hear voices in the dark, like strong winds. You have to be careful what you say. They're listening."

Leah swallowed. "You've been all the way in."

"As far as the sump. It's a flooded passage about four kilometers in."

"So you'd only be able to get farther by swimming under the rock."

Xander nodded. "With scuba gear."

"And how much farther does the cave go on after that?"

"Another kilometer or so. It's a closed system. But past the sump, you'd have to be an advanced caver. There are false branchings and sumps and abysses that no one's measured. It's dangerous."

Leah made herself take deep breaths. She laid her head back down. Her heart beat like she was running, even though she was still. She knew, though she didn't know how she knew, that even if the cave was dangerous for anyone else, it wouldn't be dangerous for her.

"When I went all the way to the sump," Xander said, now tracing circles around her nipple, "I did it alone. Which was very unwise, and I did it anyway."

"Why?" she asked softly.

"I wanted to. I've always felt compelled to return to the cave. It has power over me too."

"What happened?"

Xander's eyes unfocused; he was seeing a memory. "I got to the sump chamber. I was standing on an island in the middle of the river. I saw something buried in the sand, so I bent down to look at it. But then my headlamp went dark. Which it shouldn't have, because I'd put in fresh batteries that morning."

Leah was beyond arousal, now. She felt like she was hanging upside down.

"Then I heard a noise behind me, and saw two eyes in the darkness, even though there was no light to reflect them. Then something heavy fell on top of me. That's the last thing I remember." The candlelight flickered on his forearm as he resumed circling her nipple. "Ian from Pook's Hill found me the next morning at the step-up rock. He'd seen my gear in camp."

"At the step-up rock? How did you get back?"

"I don't know. I don't remember anything." He lifted his finger off one nipple, then dropped it on the other, like a needle on a record. "What do you expect to find, if you went deeper in?"

"Xibalba," Leah said immediately. It was an answer that came so suddenly, it seemed to have bypassed her conscious thought.

Xander drew in his breath, circled his finger.

She was returning from the upside-down land in her mind, back to her warm body, to find he was still erect, and now pressing himself against her thigh.

"Xibalba," he repeated, as if beginning an academic proposition, but then he gently pushed her shoulder so that she turned over, and was lying on her stomach. Now it was starting. Now there was no mistake. He pushed himself up on his elbows. She heard a rustle of cloth; he was taking off his boxers. Then she felt him straddle her legs and sit on her thighs, a warm heavy weight. She didn't look back. She trusted him. She heard more rustling, then a bottle squeeze with a funny slirching sound, then palms being rubbed together. She felt her legs being spread apart. She was opened, exposed, pink, wet. She buried her face in the pillow, trusted the dark. Now her only source of information was sensation. Shajarian continued to sing.

A warm hand on her sacrum, a cushion nudging at her side.

She lifted up her hips so he could slide it under her.

She angled herself up the way she thought he wanted her to, but he pushed down on her bottom, told her to relax and breathe deep. Her eyes widened in realization. Could it be? Oral sex for the first time last night and anal sex for the first time this night? How could she be this lucky? What would Nate say? Did he even exist anymore? She stifled a giggle, felt wild.

Then she felt Xander's fingers slide down her ass. They were slippery. She realized the squelch she'd heard was a bottle of lubrication. He'd come prepared! He had a bottle ready! Had she washed thoroughly enough there? She hoped so! She'd just showered. He spread her cheeks apart. Oh God, he was looking right at it! She was both aroused and hysterical. At any moment she'd break out into a moan or scream or cackle, she couldn't tell which. No boy in Minnesota had ever actually looked at her. Now these boys, these twins, stared straight into her soul.

She felt his slippery finger penetrate her, then withdraw: a test.

Leah gasped and curled her fingers around the top of the pillow.

"Are you okay?" he said.

"Yes," she gasped.

His finger penetrated again, slow, circled within her.

"Eres malo," she said, now somehow speaking in Spanish.

"No," he said, and she could hear the smile in his voice. "Soy bueno."

The finger slipped out again. The wake of the sensation was even more overwhelming than the sensation itself. Then she felt the docking of a hard, slippery knob. It was much bigger than his finger. The girth of it sent her into a panic. She clenched up and looked back to see Xander spread over her, black hair thick between his legs, black hair hanging in his eyes.

"I've never done it this way before," she said.

Again he placed his hand on the small of her back. "I'll guide you. Take deep breaths. It might hurt at first, but just tell your body to relax."

She turned back to rest her chin on her folded hands. She closed her eyes and tried to unclench. What was she afraid of? There was nothing to fear, only joy to gain. She felt the knob again. She told herself not to be afraid. He pushed, slow. It felt so wrong at first, like a joke, like this was just not the direction that things were supposed to go. He pushed further. Somehow her throat was activated: she felt choked up. The pressure was popping up in other areas of her body. She began to feel pain. What he was doing felt unnatural. But she felt this was a test: she had to trust, to see this through. She remembered her first time having sex, when she was thirteen, with a seventeen-year-old who'd told her she was very mature for her age; how much it hurt at first, but she took hold of the experience, told herself in the moment that this was natural, this was good, this was what her body was built to do. She relaxed. She liked sex now. This was the same. There was pain, but she had to accept the pain. She willed herself to accept the pain just a moment longer to see what was on the other side.

And then there was a give of flesh, and no pain.

She was gulping now. She felt like she was breathing underwater, blinking in a new world.

Xander could feel the shift too. He rested his full weight on her, moving with her. His belly fit into the small of her back. Again she could smell his laundry detergent. Lavender! Who knew! In her mind's eye she saw the eye of the spider in the cave, the star on the breast of the flowstone, that seemed to symbolize all things at once. But this universe was falling apart. That was its ultimate destiny, just like the nature program had told her. That meant human experience would only fragment and disperse more. It meant meaning itself was decohering. But now, the opposite was happening:

all the blood in her body was flooding to her belly. She tried to concentrate, to grind down, to encourage the wave that was rising in her, and then it was breaking, and she screamed as she came, and then laughed at herself and couldn't stop laughing.

Xander rested on her for a while, his belly breathing into her back, until her fit passed.

Then he slipped out, which made her laugh again. Everything was so funny.

She watched him get up. He was naked. He wetted a washcloth to wipe himself off, then crouched by his bookshelf. She just rested her head on the pillow and followed him with her eyes, too full of bliss to speak. He lay down next to her, kissed her shoulder once, then opened the book he'd brought, its cover golden and red: *Popol Vuh*, translated by Allen Christenson. He put on his reading glasses and read, with no preamble: "But when the sun ascended upward, he was like a person. His heat could not be endured. This was but his self-revelation when he was born. What is left is but a mirror. What appears now is not the true sun."

Leah fell asleep, and the last thing she saw was Xander at his kitchen table, lit by candlelight, writing on a legal pad.

CAYO
8 Chak 17 Yaxk'in, Long Count 15.10.14.9.19

---

18 December, 3012

Niloux wrote a word in the air: *ENTROPY*.

She turned to face the tzoyna. There were hundreds of viajeras sitting shoulder-to-shoulder in the common room of Teakettle Wayhouse, and others in the back, leaning against pillars. Eight aug boards made an octagon around the room and every board was covered in writing. It was well into the night now. The air was hot. Most had waited until the thunderstorms let up, then defected to parties in the jungle; those who'd stayed were fanning the children asleep in their laps. The flag of Laviaja hung limp overhead.

Niloux tapped her temple to amplify her voice. "Xander Cañul and his cohort built Laviaja as a purely egalitarian society," she said. "In theory, maybe. In practice, egalitarianism can become just another kind of oppression. Individuals introduce planes of breakage."

She drew lines radiating out from *ENTROPY*, and wrote:

Viajeras.

Orthodox.

Zeinians.

LFC.

Sedentix.

Pilaris.

Glucosis.

Hunters.

"These are all distinct populations now," she said. "There have been distinct populations for at least fifty years, even before the ice melted. We know this because we have terms for it—naming them has brought them into being. Fifty years ago there were less than a thousand sedentix in the world. Now there are nine or ten thousand."

"That's less than one percent," said Emelle, leaning against a pillar.

Niloux scowled. Emelle was still being remote and contrarian. But she didn't want to escalate, so she answered as neutrally as she could.

"Sure," said Niloux, "but it's also a tenfold increase."

"I think it's because of the stop in disappearances," said Meret, poised at the board across the room.

"That, and other factors," said Niloux. "The human race has outgrown this way of life. Just like we outgrew monarchy and capitalism. Even if people don't say it to themselves in those terms, they start to . . ."

Now Niloux was far away, in the oasis in Persia, watching Venus rise, the twin planet ascendent.

"They start to act it out," she finished. She wiped the sweat off her forehead. The heat was oppressive.

A child raised her hand. "Why is being different bad?"

A sooraya near her answered. "Different kinds of people are not good or bad. But in the past, people used to say that, based on their differences, some kinds of people deserved food and others didn't."

The child looked confused.

"But we've had difference for centuries now," said Owen in the back, stubborn. "There are hundreds of manéras, and nobody treats anyone differently. We have at least a hundred manéras in the room right now."

"But we hold luchas based on differences in manéra," someone said from the floor.

"The luchas are just play," Owen shot back. "And anyone can change their manéra."

"The word 'lucha' originally referred to physical violence," said Cheen. "It could return to that."

"It could well," said Niloux. "I should know."

"And what are you doing to stop it?" said an ancianix in front.

"Ask Tanaaj DeCayo," Niloux snapped. "She's the one encouraging it."

There was an uncomfortable silence. Now Niloux could hear the howler monkeys in the jungle around them. They sounded like choruses of demons, protesting the humans underfoot. They'd taken to flinging their shit down on the viajeras, who, of course, named it a sign of good luck.

Niloux let the silence drag on. She wasn't about to comfort anyone, especially those who still couldn't see the big picture. This was the problem with open tzoynas. You couldn't control the discussion. It just went around and around, everyone saying things that sounded smart and getting nowhere. Her patience was waning. This was her third straight night at Teakettle Wayhouse and, with the tzoynas, plus work shifts for cooking and mucking and maintenance, she'd barely slept. Her past-life pistas were so dense in Cayo that she kept only some features of her aug turned on; otherwise the ground would blind her. But even just the knowledge of them made the ground feel electrically charged. It messed with her mind. She had to fight to stay focused.

"Change can't be stopped," she said at last. "Entropy is the fundamental law of the universe, so even a religion *that worships entropy* will itself fragment. The point is to steer the fragmentation."

"And the first step is awareness," said Cheen.

"Yes," said Niloux. "Awareness that equality is a myth."

"But we all have equal right to food and freedom and everything else in the Universal Bill of Rights," said Owen. "We confirm that every day in the main Tzoyna."

"There are limits, though," said Niloux, "unspoken limits to freedom. For example, no one can accumulate capital, and I want the freedom to build—"

In her exhaustion, she'd almost said it aloud.

She knew she couldn't. She'd be laughed at. She would become a joke, like Ting Lee DeBrazza, her entire movement revealed as a cover for her own self-ishness. But would it ever be the right time? When could she trust anyone with her heart's real desire?

So she lashed out.

"Look, I was blotted for five months for a goddamn idea. Do you know how miserable that was? With thousands of people watching me every time I took a shit from Tehran to Amalfi? And then a fanatic tried to kill me. You could say that there's no such thing as freedom from consequence. Fine. But those consequences were designed to silence me. Not to engage with me—to silence me. And to scare anyone else who thought about doing the same."

"But the person who tried to kill you was blotted," said another. "There were consequences for her too, which would deter anyone from trying again."

"It obviously didn't!" said Niloux, throwing up her hands. "If that were the case, why was there a battalion of LFC waiting for us when we arrived in Cayo? And why does Tanaaj remain silent and refuse responsibility, like she has nothing to do with it?"

"Why don't you meet with her?" asked the sooraya.

Niloux seethed. "I would have. I was open to it. I publicly offered to in Meknes, on the Feast of the Consort Twins. And then the next day, one of her followers tried to kill me. Would you still want to meet with someone whose follower tried to kill you?"

"So what do you want?" asked the sooraya, again with an attentive calm that made Niloux slow down, consider the question.

After a moment she said, "I want her to condemn the violence. There's a reason I haven't left this wayhouse in three days. If she doesn't condemn these intimidation tactics, she's sanctioning them."

"And afterward? You want to be left free to pursue your ideas?"

Niloux nodded. "Yes. Tanaaj doesn't understand that things are changing whether we want them to or not. We have to take control of the moment of change, just like Xander Cañul did."

"To what end?" said Emelle.

Niloux pivoted and opened her mouth when a brightness caught her eye, and she was drawn to it, thinking it was a sequin on someone's dress. But she blinked and the glimmer remained. She was seeing beyond the sea of heads, out between the pillars, out beyond the jungle, deep into space.

Again, the evening star. She burned in the void, the twin sister of Earth.

For a moment Niloux floated down into the fire and the wind of that planet, where the sun rose in the west, and turned to see a bright blue star rising over the golden clouds, and knew it to be the planet she was floating over, and looking back at herself, as if she were existing both at the beginning and the end of her life, simultaneously.

"Niloux?"

Someone touched her arm. She turned and it was Meret, her eyes kind.

"You should rest," she said.

Niloux shook her head. Her mind snapped back into her body as quickly as it had left. She was standing on a bamboo floor in the wet jungle, on Earth, in a moment that would decide the future of the human race.

"To what end," Niloux echoed, then wiped the air clean with a wave of her hand and wrote:

2068–3012: Diluvian Age
3012: _____

She turned back around to face the crowd. "We are gathered here to decide to what end we should seize this moment. Here. Now. What do we call the new age?"

The question passed over their faces like a fresh wind on the grass.

No one spoke.

Before dawn, when her familia was still asleep, Tanaaj rose and hiked to the ancient site of Xander Cañul's house. She found a Laviaja flag whipping over a cracked cement foundation—all that was left. She sat at the edge, fingering her obsidian blade, addicted to its charge. She listened to the howler monkeys and watched the clouds moving low and ragged overhead. Storms were coming through Cayo, two or three a day, thundering down from the west.

For the past three days, she'd visited many pilgrimage sites—Javier Magaña's childhood home; Burns Avenue, reconstructed with colonial-era wooden balconies; and Cayo Wayhouse, the first Laviaji wayhouse in the world. Each site felt more potent than the last. And now, she was here, at Xander's house. She thought about the significance of this cracked foundation. In the god of this place, Leah had slept her last night on Earth while Xander El Erudito wrote thirty-six pages of notes that became the intellectual foundation of Laviaja.

Could he have known that, then?

Could he have known what would happen later that day?

Tanaaj closed her eyes. She performed the Passion every year at Día de la Pasaja, but it was always a spiritual ordeal, because she felt the emotions of the characters so clearly, as if she were seeing the world through their eyes. It wrenched her dry. This time—knowing where she was, and what she had to do—the weight of the task was unimaginable.

All she could do was begin.

She lay back and opened her legs in prayer position.

She was alone, but trusted she wouldn't be for long; she knew that the god of the place was with her, conspiring to accomplish her plan.

"Hail to the god of the place," she said. "I am here at the ruins of the house of Xander Cañul, on the very spot where he lay with Saint Leah. I am here where the Passion of *La Estrella Actual* began a thousand years ago. I am here to receive instruction in how to perform the play, and in how to approach Niloux DeCayo in the course of it, so that I can do what I must do. The next three viajeras who come to me in this spot will be my fellow performers. The god will tell me which role they will play. I wait."

She watched the flag snap in the gusts. It could start raining any moment. She fell asleep into a miniature dream of red blood and green obsidian.

"Is it her?" a voice exclaimed overhead.

"I think so," said another.

Tanaaj cracked an eye, saw two hulking viajeras, and sat up. The left one jumped back; the right backed away more slowly, sensing her companion. There was nothing to fear. It was just a pair of big-boned jovenix.

"Is it who, hermanix?" teased Tanaaj.

"Are you Tanaaj DeCayo?" said the right one. Her eyes were just slightly open and looking down, so Tanaaj guessed she was blind.

"I am. Would you like to perform *La Estrella* with me tomorrow evening?"

"We're not jugadorix," said the other, with bright blue eyes.

"That's all right," said Tanaaj. "You do not need to be. The god sent you; that is enough."

"But we don't know what to do," said the first.

"Do you know the story of the Passion?"

She frowned. "Of course."

Tanaaj smiled. "Then you will do well. Come sit," she said. "We will be performing in the Carnival mode. What are your names?"

They came to sit. "Angela," said the blue-eyed one, and the blind one said, "Hecate."

Tanaaj laughed. The god was making this very easy. "Well," she said, to their confused expressions, "in the Carnival mode, there are four main characters: Javier, Xander, Angelo, and Hector. There can be no question which characters you will play, yes?"

They realized what she meant, and laughed nervously.

Tanaaj was used to it. These jovenix, like so many viajeras these days, just lacked faith. This performance would restore it to them. "Now," she said, "we must wait for one more. The god of this place will send her and tell us whether she will play Xander or Javier, and therefore, which character I shall play."

"Only them?" said Hecate. "Not Saint Leah?"

Tanaaj winked. "Not in Carnival mode. I will explain soon. But for now, let us pray that our last jugadorix will come soon."

They still looked stunned, trying to make sense of what was happening. For now, they followed her lead, lying back on the grass and spreading their legs, like children roped into a game.

They didn't have to wait long. After a minute, Tanaaj heard a cough. She sat up and shielded her face from the spitting rain. There was another viajera ambling on the other side of the pit, older, short and thick, with freckled cinnamon skin and silver cornrows.

"Buenos días, en nombre de la Trinidad de Cayo," called Tanaaj.

The other viajera looked up, startled. "Buenos días," she called back in a hoarse voice. "Sorry to disturb, you all look . . . busy."

"You are not disturbing us," said Tanaaj. "We were praying for you to come."

"For me?" The viajera laughed.

"Sí, hermanix. The god of this place is casting *La Estrella Actual*."

The viajera looked up, down, and behind her. "Who is doing *what*?" she said.

Tanaaj patted the ground next to her. "Come, and I will explain," she said.

The older viajera walked around the pit and sat. The two jovenix moved aside to make room, looking relieved to have another witness to this strangeness. The sun had broken through the clouds now, and their faces were dappled in early-morning light.

"This is Angela," said Tanaaj, "this is Hecate, and I am Tanaaj DeCayo."

The viajera's eyes went wide. "*You're* Tanaaj DeCayo?"

"I am afraid so," said Tanaaj with mock solemnity.

"But you're so tiny!" she said.

All four of them laughed.

The viajera put her face in her hands. "What I meant to say—oh hell, I've screwed it up. Nice to meet you all. I'm Bayode."

She looked embarrassed. Tanaaj took her hand and held it, to soothe her. She already liked everyone the god had sent. "These are strange circumstances, no doubt, hermanix," she said. "Día de Pasaja is almost upon us, and I have a question for you. Will you perform *La Estrella* with us tomorrow night?"

"Me?" Bayode said. "I haven't performed *La Estrella* since I was a jovenix."

"What part did you last play?"

She pointed a thumb back at the concrete foundation. "This guy."

Tanaaj closed her eyes and thought, *Gracias a la diosix del lugar, otra vez,* then opened them again. *You are so clear with us today.*

"In fact," said Bayode, "that's why I came here, to pay my respects to Xander's old house. This is all that's left?"

"It was buried and then excavated at some point, it seems," said Tanaaj. "Just a mound. You can only see the edges of walls."

"Not much to look at."

"So what do you think, Bayode?" said Hecate in a mischievous tone. "Are you going to be our Xander?"

"I'd be honored." Bayode turned to Tanaaj. "How will we play it?"

"Carnival mode," she answered.

Bayode whistled and nodded in appreciation.

"Hold on," said Angela. "You said that before, but I don't know what it means."

"I can explain," said Tanaaj, "and I think Bayode can help me. You understand how the modes of *La Estrella* vary along a spectrum, where some are more spontaneous and others are more scripted, yes?"

"I think so."

"The Carnival mode is the most improvisational mode. The name honors the beginning of the Hundred-Year Carnival."

"When the tsunami hit Belize City," said Bayode. "In 2129."

"Yes," said Tanaaj. "The early jugadorix were performing *La Estrella* at Carnival, and their Saint Leah was washed out to sea in the first surge. But instead of stopping, they ran along the Western Highway all the way inland, to Belmopan—"

"And took over the National Assembly Building," said Hecate. "Now I remember the tutorial."

"*And* cast a clerk as Leah," added Bayode, "who they installed as the new prime minister, because the last one hadn't built seawalls."

"Eunice Emmanuel. Who went on to dissolve the nation state of Belize."

They sat there, shaking their heads.

Tanaaj kept her eye on the two jovenix. She could tell they were hooked.

"So that's why there's no Saint Leah cast in the beginning," said Hecate.

"Sí," said Tanaaj. "In the Carnival mode, we let the land guide us, and Saint Leah reveals herself in the course of the play."

Bayode said, "Once I saw a full *La Estrella* that lasted a week. It started at Coimbatore Wayhouse and ended up a hundred miles away. I think there were two thousand performers."

"Two thousand?" said Angela. "But in the texts, there are a couple dozen characters at most."

"Because the Carnival mode travels," said Bayode. "It's a matter of endurance. As you go along, some jugadorix fall away and others join in. The narrative fragments and then comes back together. There might be one Leah, then twenty, then back to one."

There was a snap of light and crash of thunder, making them jump. The spitting rain became a sideways gust. The four of them got up and headed for the trees, where Tanaaj spotted a viajera beckoning from inside her dome. They passed through the static membrane even as it grew to accommodate them.

"Gracias, carnalix," said Tanaaj to the viajera.

"De nada," she replied.

Tanaaj looked up and faltered for words. The viajera was very striking. She was broad-shouldered and well muscled, wearing a blue silk wrap, gold cuffs on her biceps, and three lines of white chalk across her forehead. An oeste pakkari, maybe? Her beauty was severe, a strange contrast with her casual slouch.

The viajera noticed her staring, grinned. She seemed used to attention. "What a beautiful morning, right?" she said.

Tanaaj found her voice. "Indeed, hermanix. I am Tanaaj DeCayo, and—"

"I know," said the viajera.

Tanaaj was taken aback. "How?"

The viajera looked her over, as if taking stock. "Lucky guess," she said, "but also, your reputation precedes you."

Tanaaj raised her eyebrows. "Reputation?"

"They said, 'Look for a mopan maya, slightly feral.'"

Tanaaj straightened in mock solemnity. "I am honored."

The others laughed. "It's endearing!" said Bayode.

But Tanaaj was intrigued. "Why were you looking for me?"

"I heard you wanted divination."

Tanaaj realized who she was. "Sembaruthi."

The viajera smirked, bowed from the waist. "I am she."

Tanaaj had expected the famous adivinix to be reserved and sober, not gregarious and familiar. She'd also expected her to be mobbed, everyone wanting a reading from the famous adivinix who'd directed the last disappearance in 3009. Instead, she was just a viajera like any other, riding out a storm in the jungle.

Sembaruthi was still smirking.

Tanaaj cleared her throat. "It is true, hermanix. I wished to see you for divination."

"I'm right here. What do you want to know?"

"Now?"

The adivinix squinted up. Rain was hammering the dome, making the static sparkle. "You're right," she said. "Tonight, then."

Night four of tzoynas. Niloux was losing her mind.

There were now seven candidates for the name of the new age. Each candidate had its dedicated factions. But none of them captured the pivot Niloux wanted to make. She herself couldn't capture it. Meanwhile, she played referee for others' ideas. Post-Diluvian Age was functional but boring. Same for New Age. She wanted to argue not for a functional title but a visionary one that would give the human race a new purpose. Entropic Age. Jaguar Age. Neo-Eocene Age. All the while, she was aware of Tanaaj, her entangled particle, now just west of her across the Mopan Gulf. Meret was still tracking her movements in the panoptica: Tanaaj had visited the house of Xander Cañul, and cast her *La Estrella*. Tanaaj had met Sembaruthi, the famous adivinix. Tanaaj was going to start it at Teakettle Wayhouse tomorrow night, which meant Niloux didn't want to be anywhere near here then.

"What about the Pluralist Age?" said Niloux.

"What are the plurals?" someone called.

"Sedentix, pilaris, viajeras. Celebrating different beliefs as long as they don't infringe on anyone else's basic rights."

"That's what we've been trying to do for the last twenty thousand years!"

"Well, let's try again."

"But can we still believe in Xibalba?" another called.

Niloux shrugged. She was beyond caring. "Sure," she said. "You can believe in Xibalba. Its meaning keeps changing. First it was the place of fear. Then Leah went through it like Christ in the Harrowing of Hell and presto, Laviaja said it was a place of joy." Even as she spoke, she was aware that only a year ago, saying such things in public had gotten her blotted. Now she wasn't afraid. Acceptable discourse had shifted. "But those of us who think Xibalba is a myth should be able to live as we wish."

"If you want to prove Xibalba isn't real," said a young voice, "why don't you just look for Saint Leah's body?"

Niloux searched the crowd for who'd spoken, and found herself looking at a younger version of herself. The head was shaved close, but the dark brown skin, heavy brow, and firm set of mouth were all the same.

She stared.

The others in the crowd looked back and forth, confused.

Niloux couldn't move. She didn't know how to explain this. Somehow her past lives were intruding in her waking life, now, in hallucinatory form; maybe an artifact of her visualization technique, maybe a malfunction of her ojos-de-Leah. But then the jovenix spoke again, independent of her.

"What?" she said. "What, am I going to get blotted now? Takes a heretic to know one?"

"What—who are you?" called Niloux.

"Messe DeMar," she said, crossing her arms.

Owen was at Niloux's side. She murmured, "She looks exactly like you."

"So it's not just me," said Niloux, then called, "What did you say about Xibalba?"

Messe rolled her eyes. "I said, if you want to prove Xibalba isn't real, you should look for Saint Leah's body. If she didn't cross over, she must still be in the cave somewhere, right? Doesn't the cave preserve bodies for thousands of years? Isn't that why Leah and all the tourists went there in the first place?"

"It is," said Niloux, and it was all she could manage.

Owen stepped forward, clapped her hands. "Stretch break," she called. "Come back in ten."

It took a while for the crowd to break up and shuffle away. Everyone was still confused at what had just happened. Niloux crouched in a corner and slapped her own face. Her familia gathered around her—Emelle, Cheen, Owen, Meret—sensing the need for counsel. Meret beckoned Messe to come over to them. She did, looking saucy and defiant. She wore a gold ring through her septum, a dull blue tunic, and a bow and quiver on her back. She couldn't have been more than thirteen years old.

Messe squatted in front of Niloux, staring into her eyes.

"Niloux," said Emelle slowly, "did you mother any children?"

"No," she said, "but I consented to father a few."

"Have they gotten in touch?"

"No, none."

"Did you father them with Tanaaj DeCayo?" Messe asked.

Niloux snorted. "That'll be the day."

"So you don't know her."

"I've never even met her. But she hates me. Why, does she hate you too?"

Messe flinched, and Niloux realized she'd said something wrong. But then her eyes hardened. "Apparently she does," she said, "because she never answers my holos. And she's my birth mother."

An infinity passed.

Her body knew before her mind did. For a moment she wanted to disallow the knowledge from rising to the surface, because it would change everything faster than she was prepared to change.

It was Owen who said: "Niloux, Tanaaj must be your birth hermanix."

Then Cheen added, "Her surname is DeCayo too. So either their mother was a pilari—"

"Or they were twins."

Another infinity passed.

"How old is Tanaaj?" said Niloux at last.

Meret asked her ai. "Thirty to thirty-one."

"My range," said Niloux. It was a range because, since the birth parents of Children of Saint Leah didn't want to be known, all Children celebrated their birthdays on the first of January. In theory, she could access the information, but it was frowned upon to use DNA data to establish blood kin. And right now, everything she did was being watched.

Niloux leaned her head against a pillar. "Fuck everything," she muttered.

"Tanaaj was a Child of Saint Leah too," said Emelle. "She wore the same medal you do."

Niloux looked at her. "You couldn't tell when you saw me?"

"It was a long time ago," she said. "You have the same build and skin color, but otherwise you don't look alike. Not from what I remember."

"Does Tanaaj know?" asked Owen.

"There's no reason she would," said Cheen. "Versa Diez. Her interpretation of the Rule forbids her from interacting with anyone who's not in front of her. And she asks everyone not to record her or make images of her face."

"And even if she knew, she wouldn't care," said Messe with bitterness. "She knows she's my birth mother. She watches my holos but she never replies to them. She could have made me a Child of Saint Leah, but she didn't."

Niloux stared at Messe. She sensed an opportunity. "You have good reason to be angry with her," she said.

"Yes," Messe spat. It seemed she'd been storing up these things in her body for a long time, and now she had an attentive crowd of tíax. "Even when I told her I was going on my Primera Viaja. Even when I told her I'd started hunting."

Owen raised her eyebrows. "I'm sure Tanaaj was thrilled about that."

Emelle slapped Owen on the arm. It was an indelicate thing to say.

But Niloux was thinking about the opportunity that had presented itself—to turn the tide against Tanaaj. "You think we should look for Leah's body in the cave," she said.

Messe shrugged. "I suggested it."

"Would that be a way for you to get back at Tanaaj?" Niloux asked her.

Emelle gasped. "Would it be for *you*?" she snapped.

Niloux held up her hands. "Take it easy. I'm just asking her. She can make her own decisions."

"Especially when they benefit you."

"Emelle—"

She shook her head, got up, and walked a short distance away to sit alone.

This had happened before. Emelle needed to take time away just like Niloux did. She'd come back when she was ready. Even so, Niloux felt pained. Her relationship with Emelle had been strained ever since they made landfall, and maybe going back even further—to the assassination attempt at Walili. Niloux didn't know what to do. She liked her, and appreciated her help and counsel and companionship, but Emelle had offered it of her own free will. She didn't owe her.

Niloux held her head in her hands. The others stayed in a circle around her.

Eventually Owen spoke up. "So . . . I have a question. Didn't people search for Leah's body at the time? And they didn't find it? And that's why we have Laviaja?"

"Those searches were never comprehensive," said Meret. "The last real try was sometime in the early twenty-second century, and even then, entangled solar lighting didn't exist. Neither did orgo-scan."

"Would it be possible to find Leah's remains that way?"

"Sure. Her DNA is known. It'd take a while to scan the entire cave—a week or two. But it's possible."

"In the past," added Cheen, "they couldn't grow pelts or gills or tails either. They would have had to carry tanks of air on their backs."

Owen looked alarmed. "What if they ran out?"

"They drowned."

"Oh. So it was dangerous."

Cheen nodded. "Very. And costly. The hoarders didn't want to keep funding it."

"For something so important?" said Owen.

"You're seeing it through modern eyes," said Niloux. "In the twenty-first century, tourism was the biggest industry in Belize. Stories of a dead tourist would hurt business. In the twenty-second century, the world was in chaos. Laviaja wasn't a global religion, it was a fringe sect, just a few wayhouses in Cayo. Finding one person's body was not a high priority for the government of Belize."

"And then it stopped mattering," said Cheen. "People made up stories about Leah and believed the stories. Taboo prohibited them from even considering a search."

Niloux crossed her arms in the silence. "Well. Where should we start looking?"

"And when?" said Meret quietly. "Tanaaj is starting the Passion here. This time tomorrow night, Teakettle will be swarming with LFC."

"And if she's playing it straight, they'll end up at the cave."

"Right."

"So where can we go to get out of the way, but stay close to the cave?"

"The Tzoyna," said Meret. "The Passion wouldn't pass through there, because it was overgrown in Leah's time."

Niloux nodded. "We need to leave. The sooner the better." She turned to Cheen. "Can you take over the tzoyna? You can rejoin us later. Just say I had to sleep. Which I do."

Cheen inclined her head in assent. Niloux stood to look for Emelle and tell her the plan, but she was nowhere to be seen. Probably she'd gone to get food.

"I'm coming with you," said Messe in a loud voice.

The others turned to her, abashed. They'd forgotten she was there.

Niloux recognized the hurt in the jovenix's voice. "I want to say yes, but . . ."

"But it's not really your choice, is it?" she shot back. "I can go where I please. And you're going where you're going because it was *my* idea. So like I said. I'm coming with you."

"You don't care that it'll upset Tanaaj?"

"No," said Messe. "I found you and . . . well. Isn't that supposed to be the god of the place, shaping events? And besides," she said, nodding to Niloux's single earspool, "I need a familia to celebrate."

"Celebrate what?"

"My first fiesta de manéra," she said. "I want to become a maya."

In the evening, when there was a break in the thunderstorms, Sembaruthi led Tanaaj up to an overlook.

They took a moment to enjoy the view of the Mopan Gulf. From a barge on the water, there was a deep popping sound, and then a trail rocketed skyward and exploded. These fireworks were designed to bloom in layers. First, the four colors of the Maya cosmos: white, yellow, red, and black. Green came last, blooming in the middle.

Tanaaj tapped her heart to turn off the aug. The sky went dark. She wanted no distractions during divination.

Sembaruthi was already crouched under a cohune palm and rooting in her pack. She hadn't even asked what kind of divination Tanaaj wanted—directional? Binary? Complex? Maybe she knew without asking. Tanaaj watched her unroll her mat, set a cube of copal in an autocenser, and take her maize kernels out of a drawstring pouch. This adivinix served Xibalba first, took no sides. Convincing her to endorse the LFC would have been like gathering clouds in a basket. This quality appealed to Tanaaj, as if the adivinix were even less attached to this world than she—even more attuned to the Other. Tanaaj wanted to ask her questions, like *Who are you? Where is your birthplace, Siruvani? How did you learn such a gift for divination? How do you like to be touched? Do you like to grip or do you like to penetrate?*

Sembaruthi settled into prayer pose, open-legged. "How many questions do you have?"

Tanaaj banished the carnal thoughts and focused. "Two."

"Then we'll begin."

Tanaaj knelt before her.

Sembaruthi had changed. Before, she had been chatty and casual; now, she was quiet and serious. When she spoke again, her voice was deep, pitched for invocation.

"¿Cuál es tu pregunta?" she asked in High Spanish.

Tanaaj took a breath. There was nothing to do but ask. She had asked this question of diviners many times before, always trusting that the direction she received would set her on the right path to the next path, and the next, and the next, and into Xibalba in the end. But Sembaruthi was different. She had divined the last disappearance. She had an aura of authority.

"¿Como puedo encontrar mi cortada?" said Tanaaj. *How can I find my cortada?*

Faster than Tanaaj could see her hand move, Sembaruthi grabbed a handful of kernels, swept the rest aside, and began placing them on her mat in groups of four. "*May this question be heard by Xibalba,*" Sembaruthi began. The full moon had risen now, and the adivinix looked like an ancient cartoon, black and white, moving in strobe. Tanaaj closed her eyes, enjoying the rhythm of familiar words. "*May it be heard by the god of the day, Eight Chak. May it be heard by the god of this place . . .*"

She heard the barge parties out on the Gulf.

"*May it be heard in the middleworld . . .*"

She listened to the lap of the tide below.

"*May it be heard in the heavens and the under-world . . .*"

The copal smoke filled her nostrils.

"*May it be heard in the light of the day and the dark of the night . . .*"

The mud was thick between her fingers.

"*May it be heard in the deepest ocean and on the highest hilltop . . .*"

Xibalba was conspiring for her.

"*. . . Thank you to the god of the place.*"

Tanaaj opened her eyes, just as Sembaruthi closed hers.

She'd made twelve piles of four. A perfect cast. They could be confident in the answer. Now Sembaruthi had microdosed herself with psilocybin, and was listening to the day god and the god of the place, together, and alighting on whatever visions appeared in her mental landscape, to test their rightness. Tanaaj watched her face closely. Sembaruthi frowned and shook her head once, twice. Her lips moved. Her eyes twitched behind her eyelids as if she were dreaming. She cleared her throat, swallowed.

Finally she opened her eyes, as if waking up. She looked disoriented.

Tanaaj was concerned. "Hermanix . . . ?"

Sembaruthi licked her lips. "The god says you must seek your family."

Tanaaj felt disappointed. But she didn't want to show it. She should feel grateful to the adivinix for taking the time to serve her. "¿Mi familia?" she said. "I am always surrounded by familia. I have never been alone."

"No," said Sembaruthi, "family, in the ancient sense. A lover and a child."

It took Tanaaj a moment to understand what she was saying. "Just one of each forever?"

"Yes. And as you can see, we made a perfect cast."

Again, Tanaaj felt disappointment. Whatever reputation this adivinix had, it seemed to have been a fluke. "I see," she said. "Thank you very much for your help, hermanix."

Sembaruthi smiled, but it was strained. "I can tell you're not happy with that answer."

"Well," Tanaaj said with a laugh, "according to you, the god is telling me to violate the Rule of Saint Leah, which I have followed faithfully all my life, so yes, hermanix, I am confused."

Sembaruthi shrugged. "I can only tell you what the god told me. I had a very clear vision of you and a lover and child living together in a long stone house."

She remembered Ying Yue, dying alone in Oaxaca. "Like sedentix?"

"That's what we call them today, yes," she said. "But they're just as human as we are."

"They are misguided," Tanaaj said with an edge to her voice.

Sembaruthi eyed her for a long moment, then nodded. "Shall we move on to your next question?"

"Yes, hermanix." Now Tanaaj knew not to take her guidance seriously, but it would be rude to say so. She would follow through with this second question, and then they would walk down the muddy slope together, and she would bid a polite goodbye and rejoin her cast and spend the night in meditative seclusion in preparation for *La Estrella*. She could make this smaller sacrifice first.

Sembaruthi had already reset the kernels on the mat. "¿Cuál es tu pregunta?" she asked again.

"¿Como puedo encontrar Niloux DeCayo?" asked Tanaaj.

This time, the adivinix hesitated.

Tanaaj waited.

Sembaruthi seemed to overrule herself, and went on with the rite. This time, Tanaaj just folded her hands politely and watched her sweep the kernels, place them in piles, say the words, close her eyes, fly over her inner landscape. She noticed that the cast was weaker, this time; only two kernels in the final pile. So the answer could be trusted less. It was all right. She wasn't going to take it seriously in any case.

Sembaruthi opened her eyes suddenly. She looked angry.

Tanaaj was startled. "Hermanix, are you—"

"I can't answer your question."

"Why not?"

"The god says you wish to harm Niloux."

Tanaaj stiffened. She would have to handle this carefully. She didn't hold it against Sembaruthi; the adivinix had not seen the vision of Balam Ahau that Xibalba had sent her, nor grasped the sacrifice she was preparing to make. "On the contrary," she said, "I wish to save her."

"The god doesn't lie."

"But humans may misinterpret the god."

"How do you wish to save her?"

Tanaaj felt the green obsidian blade in her pocket, refrained from touching it.

"How do you wish to save her, Tanaaj?"

"I cannot expect you to understand my heart."

"I can understand that it is rotten."

It took a lot for Tanaaj to get angry. No one had ever said such a thing to her. She was always patient, always gave the benefit of the doubt, never took things personally. She'd gotten truly angry only a few times in her life. But when she got to that point, she snapped.

"Hermanix," she said quietly, "I believe we should part ways now. Nothing good can be accomplished if you are full of anger."

"Do you truly believe yourself to be free of anger?"

Tanaaj had begun to shake. She stood up, smoothed down her tunic. "Good night, hermanix," she said, "and may you have a pleasant Jubilee."

She started down the slope.

She was surprised to hear no further words, no sound of pursuit. Sembaruthi was leaving her alone. Whatever her delusions, she was wise enough to do that much.

Then Tanaaj saw another figure rushing up toward her. She was small and slight, and her hair shone like mercury in the moonlight. She arrived, breathing hard.

"Tanaaj DeCayo?"

Tanaaj peered at her. She looked familiar. "I am she, hermanix."

"Yo soy Emelle," she said. "I have something to tell you."

TZOYNA
4 Eb 15 Pop, Long Count 10.9.5.7.12

---

10 December, 1012

The sun rose. His beams fanned through the trees like a skirt of light. Ajul heard angry voices.

". . . the merchants are fops. They said they'd . . ."

". . . Katwitz cowards."

". . . prepared the court for today . . ."

". . . were gone by morning . . ."

". . . came just for the food . . ."

". . . a Nahua scout . . ."

". . . the faces are ruined."

". . . looted the temple . . ."

". . . vultures and pigs."

Ajul heard stomping footsteps. Then, standing above him was the same whiny farmer from last night on the dais, with the red eyes and patchy mustache.

"I am Lord Tatichwut!" he said. "I am the king of Pekwitz!"

Ajul stared up at him. This was Tatichwut? He hadn't recognized him. The self-declared ruler and his former ball game opponent were one and the same? He couldn't tell if he was joking or not.

Tatichwut crouched down. "You will call me Tata, because I'm your father now." He spoke as if he'd long rehearsed the words. But he was dissatisfied with his own delivery, and with Ajul's lack of reaction. He patted Ajul on the head and then pinched his cheek. The gestures were meant to be dismissive, to insult him in the way the words had not; but from the tentative way Tatichwut touched him, Ajul could tell that he was still afraid.

"Do you remember me?" asked Tatichwut, as if he badly wanted Ajul to remember.

"I remember you from last night."

"You will address me properly."

Ajul swallowed his pride. "I remember you from last night, Tata."

"No. From before."

Now he could fully recognize the face: the thin lips, the hurt eyes, the ragged hair as if cut by a hatchet. Yes, this was the same young farmer who'd demanded the honor of playing Ajul at Pekwitz three years ago.

He'd stomped off the ball court wiping away tears at the end. He'd scored a few points, but only because Ajul let him, before beating him soundly. He'd only been twelve years old, and the farmer, a skinny seventeen. Afterward, in dozing pleasure, he'd revisit that game in his mind and relive each set; after a year, he'd realized it was beneath him to do so, and had discarded the memory altogether like an old esh.

"I remember you, Tata," said Ajul.

"You like to play the ball game," Tatichwut said, with passion growing in his voice, "but only when everyone is throwing flowers at you. What about when you're not in control? Will you still enjoy it then?"

Ajul frowned. He had no fear of Tatichwut's skill, even as tired as he was. The farmer was weak and small and skinny, and his stooped posture did not speak of a man with any physical genius.

A woman appeared, carrying a bowl of water and two towels.

Tatichwut got to his feet. "Good. You're finally here," he said, putting his hands on his hips. "You can do your job."

The woman knelt next to Ajul, smirking to herself.

"Sakmut! Wait!" barked Tatichwut.

She looked up at him.

Tatichwut leveled his spear at Ajul's chest. "I'll be

here. Just in case he tries to harm you. He's strong as a buck. But I will protect you."

Sakmut pursed her lips. Ajul could tell she was trying not to laugh. But she was smart enough not to mock him, so inclined her head with grace, then went on with her task. She did not meet Ajul's eyes. She dragged the towel through the water and then began to wash him in gentle circular motions. The water was sun-warm. Ajul heard howler monkeys roaring overhead. The smell of his blood was reactivated, sharp iron; and suddenly he was by the river again, watching his father place the basket on the water.

You are only a queen or a king if you yourself are ready, at any moment, to give yourself to the god.

Ajul looked up at Tatichwut. He had a hard time believing this could be an agent of the god. Even in his role-playing games with Ixul, he had imagined her standing in for a strong, young king from a conquering realm, like a Nahua city grown powerful in secret; not a delusional peasant from the next valley, most well known for its tick-infested ruins. Regardless, there was something true in Tatichwut's eyes: a conviction of injustice done, a determination for redress, and strangely, a fixation on Ajul that resembled love. Was this person worthy to hold him captive? Or was worthiness beside the point?

Ajul looked at the spear tip, hovering in space.

You cannot fail to recognize it. Who is bound, and who holds the spear?

Ajul pitched forward in realization.

Sakmut jumped and Tatichwut leapt back. But then Ajul just relaxed against the tree and laughed. He knew. He leaned his head back against the tree. He had certainty, and in certainty he had security.

With a smile, Ajul indicated that Sakmut should continue washing him. He looked up at Tatichwut, who was tense and fearful, standing on the tips of his feet. He would have kissed the spear point if he could. Tata, indeed! This was his father now—his actual father, come back to him; this was the one sent by the gods to deliver his fate. Also, he knew Ixul had heard those same words from their father. Surely she'd remembered them as well. She was sharper than Ajul; she had probably known it the moment they were taken. He'd felt slow and confused last night, but now, in the morning light, he was calm. Total submission was the answer to all of his problems. In fact, there was nothing they could do to him— no insult, injury, or humiliation—that would not add to the glory of the sacrifice. Who would want to die old, cold and yellow, sapped of strength and beauty, gasping under a blanket? He and Ixul had been given the same chance as the most glorious heroes of old: to become immortal. The gossiping servants had always been right.

He and Ixul were the lineage of the Hero Twins, Huna-jpu and Xbalanque, the sun and moon. They were called to make the perfect sacrifice.

Now he knew. The knowing made him happy.

Someone was cutting Ixul's ropes. At last she could lean forward. She gaped at the pleasure of it, followed by the pain of fluids resettling, like bitter sand. The pain added to the pain of the stump in her mouth, which radiated down her spine like a bolt of lightning.

A burly man threw her over his shoulder and started walking. She was in so much pain that she had begun to detach from her body, to protect herself from feeling it. She noticed that the stalk of heliconia was still bound in her hair, and wondered how that could be. Sometimes someone said, "Here?" or "Take that way." The man who bore her stopped to adjust his grip on the backs of her legs so that she didn't slide off. Then her face hit his buttock, and she gagged on the clotted stump in her mouth, and was put down and allowed to retch out new blood, and then she fainted again.

She heard the words *Let her walk, fool* in the voice of the howler monkey, rattling from hill to hill. So they tied a rope around her neck and pulled her down the path like a dog. But it was better than being carried. She could use her feet.

As they approached the city, she began to see the bodies of her servants and warriors. She recognized them by the star of the Tzoyna, embroidered on their huipils or painted on their chests. Their wounds were already black with flies. Ixul didn't understand why they'd been killed. There was no honor in killing for the sake of killing. There was only honor in taking captives. One might as well scatter maize on bare rock and expect a harvest. She wondered who was in charge here, but it was a distant thought, drowned in pain. Her head ached as if split open with an ax.

They led her through the city wall and into the main plaza.

At first, she thought they had taken her to a different city altogether.

On the walls, the faces of her entire family tree had been hacked away and burned black. She wondered at it, admired the completeness of it: someone had spent the whole night devoted to this one task, hacking and burning, until her lineage was wiped from history. There was a scream from the direction of the palace. A clerk ran out of the temple, clutching an armful of scrolls that unraveled as he ran, only to sprout a spear in his chest, which made him fall face-first onto the steps.

They came to the ball court. All of the stelae were toppled and burned. The pieces looked like chopped snakes. No one had cleared any of the bodies. Half-eaten food was scattered across the plaza, and peasants were picking through, placing the good bits into baskets. A vulture was folding over Upakal. A wild pig was rooting in Mutna's chest.

In that moment, Ixul slid out of herself and became a ghost.

Her home was not her home, so she was not herself. She didn't know who she was. Not Ixul Ahau; but Ixul Again, Ixul More, Ixul Next. Who was that. Who could tell her.

What did she love, what did she need, and were they the same?

She loved knowledge. She loved newness and innovation and craft. She loved faraway places and exotic texts. She could have that life, up out of this jungle, somewhere else, far from here—perhaps in Chichen Itza, where the ball courts were as big as maize fields; or even farther, in the high deserts of the dayfall, to Tula, which she knew only by merchants' rumor, the city of basalt pillars and feathered serpents. Surely there could be a life there for a trained noble youth. She could read. She carried all the lore of her people in her mind. She was a daykeeper. She would settle in a new city, serve new people, worship new gods. All she had to do was escape. There was nothing these vermin could do to her—no insult, injury, or humiliation—that could touch her now.

She saw Ajul.

He was also being led on a rope. His face was puffy and misshapen. But he stood tall, shoulders thrown back, with a calm expression. Normally a captive would shamble, eyes downcast; instead, he met each person's eyes, and bowed his head to them. He'd been washed. His hair had been combed. He had never looked so beautiful to her, not even last night. Then, he had meant to look beautiful; now, beaten and stripped, he was somehow more so. She was conscious of her own appearance, still caked with blood and vomit. She didn't want Ajul to see her like this, but she had no choice. How could he be so calm? Ixul realized that he, too, must have seen the unworthiness of their captors. He must have come to the same conclusion she had: that they must escape.

His captors took him behind a wall so that she lost sight of him. She was frustrated that they were keeping them apart. The sooner she got to connect with him, the better. She was not going to leave without Ajul. He was the only one she trusted to know her, the only one she could rebuild with.

She turned to the guard and tried to move her mouth as if she still had her tongue. She tried to ask *May I see my brother* but it came out mangled, the speech of frogs, and the effort caused her searing pain.

The guard pretended he hadn't heard. He was embarrassed for her.

She ground her teeth and tried again. *May I see my brother.*

The guard committed to looking elsewhere.

She tried louder, *May I see my brother.* This time she was nearly intelligible, she knew she was.

The guard stepped away to talk to the other guard.

She stayed her anger. She forced herself to think through the fog of pain. Fresh blood welled out of the corner of her mouth and she wiped it away. She remembered she still had the family handtalk. She needed to choose something short and clear to sign to Ajul, as soon as she got close, before they met whoever their opponents would be.

Ajnen. That's what she would say. The sign was a tap on the temple. *Ajnen.*

Run.

She heard raised voices on the far side of the court. Letutz the merchant was pointing at the ground, talking to Chenukul and Tatichwut. Tatichwut was pacing and shaking his head. Chenukul was wringing his hands. She wondered again, who was in charge? Two merchants and a farmer, each grasping at power. Was this how Chichen Itza ran its ruling council? That wouldn't work in the lowlands, where only royals could rule, and soon these fools would find that out. Ixul marveled at their incompetence as if she were an eagle surveying them from above, distant and amused. They slouched, their feet were filthy, and they touched each other constantly like handsy youths. But now they were doing something else: gesturing to everyone present, telling them to gather those who were farther abroad on other errands, sitting on the tops of the court banks and arranging their tilmatli around them, halting, awkward, playing at nobility. Two dozen people obeyed, taking seats; then three dozen, lining all the edges. One of them knocked over a sacred dripstone, and it fell and shattered on the court. There was laughter. Guards were assigned to clean it up. Ixul marveled from above. Two thousand years of holy purpose, destroyed overnight.

Where was Ajul? Why were they keeping them apart when they were about to face their opponents? They needed to be near each other, to lock minds, to become one person, to run together. She stood on her tiptoes to see him, but he was still behind the wall.

Her guard said, "Time to play your game."

Ixul held up her wrists, unconcerned. She was not about to play any game.

He cut her ropes. She spied the path down to the

sacred river. If they could make it there, they could run fast enough up the path that led in the opposite direction, over the hill and down to the lesser river, and into the wild hill country beyond. That was their country, where they'd played their endless games. No one would be able to track them there.

She stamped her feet and rolled her shoulders to get blood flowing. She affected the death stare that Ajul always referred to, the heavy-lidded gaze that made opponents falter. But again, her intention was not to play. Her intention was to run. Her intention was to make the first move in another game, a longer game, that only she and Ajul could foresee. *Ajnen*, she repeated in her mind, touching her fingers to her temple. *Ajnen. Ajnen.*

Her guards yanked on her rope to pull her toward the court, where Tatichwut and Chenukul were still arguing. Letutz was nowhere to be seen, which seemed odd. The holy court was desecrated beyond salvage. But Ixul felt light and free. She was already long gone. She sneered at the farmer and merchant, but they didn't seem frightened. In fact, they seemed distracted. Then they moved off the court, and Ixul saw what they had been blocking: Ajul at the other end, loose, ready, wringing his wrists in a mirror image of her.

Ixul realized she wasn't meant to play with Ajul.

She was meant to play against him.

CAYO
4 Ajwal 3 K'ank'in, Long Count 13.0.0.0.0

21 December, 2012

Xander glanced over at Leah. She was sleeping on her stomach, bedsheets swaddled around her middle. Her long hair was loose across the pillow. Her cheeks puffed in and out with every breath.

Xander liked her. He found that hard to express to himself, even more to her; but he'd genuinely enjoyed the long night with her, and the bouts of erotic teasing. As for her mind, she might not be educated in a scholarly way, but she was thoughtful, with an easy, self-assured intelligence that was unanswerable to any other. If she came back to Belize—or even if she found a way to stay—he'd want to see her again. He rarely wanted to see anyone at all, let alone a second time.

He hadn't slept. He'd been writing at his kitchen table. Sex cleared his mind, and Leah had given him ideas. Her descriptions of "crossing over" were reminiscent of travel metaphors, and it was clear that "Xibalba" was a new species of tourist gaze, a way of tourists seeing what they wanted to see. In his experience, they often used the word "real" when describing tropical destinations, as in more "authentic" than their own homes. Some flew back to the comfortable "dream" of their life and job and family; some stayed in the "reality" of the tropics to make a new life, only to find that it was just another kind of dream. He'd also written down everything he remembered from his conversations with Ida, Micah, and Ruth yesterday, about Quakerism, landscape phenomenology, climate refugees, Zein-o-Din, everything. None of them had texted him back yet. It had been ten hours already. He felt himself capable of greatness. He just needed a chance, and people with whom he could work.

He thought of Leah's poem. He picked it up off the floor and copied it down with care. *What a star is, not of what it is made.* In the cave, she'd mistaken a spider's eye for a star; a mistake that in this moment, to Xander, represented a decoherence of meaning that was fundamental to the progression of history. And then there was the imagery of a female God cutting herself in a cave as the origin of the universe. Did Leah know that the original name of the cave meant Mother's Cut in Ch'ol Mayan? How could she have known?

Xander looked at his phone. It was six a.m. The grackles were starting up. Venus as the morning star would be rising east-southeast just about now.

He made himself get up and prep. Sleep or no sleep, he had a full tour today, as did every guide with half a license in Cayo. Today was the Big Day, the turning of the baktun, the peak of the End-of-the-World frenzy. Today's forecast indicated a one hundred percent chance of asinine questions. He'd have to be in top form.

He looked out the window. It was still dark. He went onto the back patio and held his hand out. Drizzle was coming down.

He called Ralfie at the ranger's station.

"Ralfie. How di krik?"

"Crik hai, bot unu ku stil kraas. Ah sen Francisco tu di kayv. Ih wa kohn bak soon. Bot ah chek di weda, an di rayn wahn stap layta."

Well, the entire Belizean tourism industry was going to be happy to hear that.

"Gracias mayn. Ah di kohn direkli."

Xander hung up. He checked his phone again for replies from Ida, Micah, or Ruth.

Nothing.

A foul temper began to amass on the horizon like a thunderstorm.

He made himself go through the motions, taking stock of every item in his backpack. Bowie knife. Two dozen batteries. Change of clothes. First aid kit. Extra headlamps. Rope.

The green obsidian blade, wrapped in a plastic baggie.

He held it between his thumb and forefinger and turned it over in the candlelight. He shouldn't have taken it. But now he had to deal with it. He placed it on the kitchen table. He'd figure out how to tell Dr. Castillo when he got back this afternoon.

He slotted batteries into the headlamps and tested each one. They sounded like marbles sliding into place.

Leah stirred and turned over on the air mattress, not a care in the world.

The more Xander thought about it, the more he realized that, all day yesterday, his academic guests were just being polite. It hadn't occurred to them that he might have something to offer the world, something that registered on their scale of significance. He didn't look like what people thought of when they heard the word "genius." He was too short, too foreign, too Maya-looking. Or they did realize, but they just didn't care.

They'd humored him, but what could they actually do for him? They had their own worries, deadlines, papers, applications, grants, fellowships, conferences. They'd long ago convinced themselves they were powerless. Just hapless beneficiaries of the world order. They'd be flying back to their ivory towers in a few days. He'd still be here. In the fucking cave.

"Hey," said Leah, her voice coarse from sleep.

Xander glanced up. She was propped up on her elbows, her breasts soft against the sheets. She must be so warm right now. But he didn't have time. He had to go to work.

"Hey yourself," he said.

"What are you doing?"

"I have to pick up my guests at Black Rock."

"What's that?"

"A resort near here."

"Sounds fun!"

Xander switched on his high-powered flashlight, which made Leah squeal and hide her eyes. He switched it off and packed it. That was the last item on his checklist. Now he'd go pick up coffee and breakfast on the road. He'd pick up the tourists' lunches at Ultimate Cayo. He'd get through this day.

"I had a dream!" said Leah.

"Yeah?"

"I entered the infinite society of myself."

"What does that mean?"

"Well, I got to it through the cave. First I saw rain coursing down the walls, like petals of water, and went all the way in, and—"

Just like that, Xander snapped.

"You know what would happen if you did, right?"

Leah stopped, cocked her head. "If I did . . ."

"Go in all the way."

She didn't answer.

"Here's what would happen: you'd get lost, and nobody would come get you. Nobody would put their lives at risk because one tourist girl decided the rules didn't apply to her and she wanted to go take her life in her hands."

"I'm not a tourist—"

"Of course you're not. You're special. Great. Go to the sump. When your batteries give out, you're fucked. When you get hypothermia, you're fucked. When—"

"But I'd go with you," she mumbled.

"I already went, Leah! I almost died!" he shouted. "What the fuck do I want to go back for? I want to get out of Belize, not get trapped in a cave forever!"

Leah was kneeling upright now, the bedsheets pooled around her legs, not covering her nakedness at all, which unnerved Xander. She should want to cover herself. Any other person would feel some instinct for defense. She had none.

This made him more angry. He needed to get through to her.

"You think you can just fly down here and eat our food and go to the cave and fuck whoever you want? You think that makes you Belizean?"

"You're the one who said I was a true Beli—"

"No. You're a tourist. You've been here for a week and you think you belong here. You think blood alone makes you Maya? You're just like every other white girl who comes down looking for an exotic adventure so you can go back home and tell everyone how much you loved everything about it. But I don't love you. And I'm not going to give you a brown baby. That's what you want, isn't it? You want a souvenir?"

"*I* was the souvenir!" Leah screamed.

Xander stopped. He'd said enough.

The silence was terrible.

He picked up four of the red helmets by the straps and carried them past her, out to the truck. It was still dark and drizzling. He opened the back doors and set the helmets in a row. He felt cold and focused. He went back inside to get the other four helmets. Leah was sitting cross-legged, now, staring at the wall. He knew he should say something, but he was still too mad. She was so selfish, so clueless, so entitled. He went back outside, placed the other four helmets at the back of the truck, and closed the doors. He retrieved his muddy boots from the backseat and brought them inside.

Leah hadn't moved.

He went to the side room with the chest of drawers. He put on clean boxer briefs, clean socks, a clean undershirt, clean cargo pants, and a clean army jacket. He went back to the kitchen and sat down at the table to put on his boots. Leah stayed staring at the wall.

He bent over, tied the laces.

Then he stood up.

Leah still hadn't moved or spoken.

Xander didn't feel inclined to apologize, but he also didn't feel like he needed to add any more. He'd said what he needed to say. She'd needed to hear it. Let her chew on it awhile, and then maybe things would cool down, and he could see her again.

"I have to go," he said. "I'd take you but you're not dressed, and I have to go now."

No answer.

"The door'll lock behind you. Turn right and it's a half-mile walk to Western Highway. You can catch a shared taxi into town. Shouldn't be more than a couple Belize dollars."

No answer.

Maybe he wouldn't be seeing her again after all.

Xander picked up his backpack and shouldered it. The straps dangled and bounced against his body.

"See you around," he said.

Leah's head turned in the direction of his voice. From the back, she looked like a river nymph, swaddled in sheets.

"You do love me," she said. "But it'll take your entire life to show me."

Xander felt very tired.

"Whatever you say, gyal," he said on his way out. "Take care."

He shut the door behind him.

From the driver's seat of his truck, Javier watched the rosary spinning from his rearview mirror. Six thirty in the morning, but the cloud cover kept everything dark.

He hadn't showered. He'd barely slept.

Last night after the All Guide Meeting, he'd gone looking for Leah to tell her the good news that he'd been elected president of the Cayo Tour Guide Association. She'd be proud of him. She'd look at him in a new light, maybe as someone she'd want to marry. All of this would make him feel better about the skull-and-camera incident, about his badge being stripped, about

Xander sabotaging him. He didn't want to confront him just yet. First, he needed Leah at his side.

To find her, he'd swallowed his pride and gone to Ultimate Cayo. Hector was still there at midnight, open late for the extra tourists.

Hector raised his eyebrows over his granny glasses. "Leah? La canela? Xander gaan wid ahn tu di kayv."

"Ah noa, breda. Bot afta . . . ?"

"Ih geh sik. Xander tek kyar a ahn."

"Sik? How?"

Hector closed his planner and leaned back in his chair. "Wai yu waahn taak tu ahn?"

Javier was desperate. "Jus do."

"Yu an yu breda lov di sayhn gyal."

Javier felt sick to his stomach. "Xander lov ahn?"

Hector laughed. "Ah tink evribadi lov ahn," he said.

Javier left. He heard Hector calling for him to come back, he'd just been joking, but he was already headed to his truck. It took a lot for Javier to get angry. He was always patient, always gave the benefit of the doubt, never took things personally. He'd gotten truly angry only a few times in his life. But when he got to that point, he snapped.

He remembered how Dr. Castillo had confronted him last night. "How are you going to serve as president if you don't have a badge?"

Javier was euphoric from his win, remained calm. "I need to explain to you what happened, sir."

"You could have explained at the special meeting last night. But you didn't show up."

"I apologize for that, sir. I can explain the incident to you now."

"Let me guess. It was Xander's fault."

"It was the tourist's fault."

"Whose tourist?"

Javier paused. "Xander's tourist, sir."

"But Xander was distracted because you came up behind him, no?"

"I had to fit in two tours that day because of high demand, sir. I needed to move fast."

"Javier," said Dr. Castillo, eyes flashing, "you don't *have* to do anything that places the cave in danger."

Javier wanted to punch him in the face. Nothing enraged him more than assumptions of bad faith, especially when he always acted in good faith. So he just walked away. Losing his temper would only worsen the situation. He just wanted to find Leah, and then he'd feel better.

He drove up and down the streets downtown. No Leah.

He drove over the low bridge and around Santa Elena. No Leah.

He needed to calm down, get a drink. The Mexican restaurant up the road to Benque was still open at two a.m., so he drove there.

Victor was behind the counter when he walked in.

"Buenas noches," he said. "Un tequila."

"Patrón?"

"No mayn. Cuervo fain."

Victor slid forward a bowl of lime wedges, then poured a shot. Javier drank it and bit down on the lime.

"Ah si yu breda ya," said Victor.

Javier's stomach twisted again. He took the deflated lime wedge out of his mouth and put it in the shot glass. "Wid wahn nyoo tooris gyal, fu shoar," he said.

Victor laughed. "Yu noa yu breda gud," he said.

Javier's heart was racing. But he kept on with his gambit. "Wahn wait laydi agen?"

"No," said Victor. "Canela gyal. Fainali ih di si di lait."

Victor laughed, then noticed Javier wasn't laughing along with him.

"Yu aarait mayn?"

"One more shot."

Victor poured it. Javier downed it without a lime.

"Yu noh luk tu karek," said Victor.

"Ah aarait," said Javier. "Jos aal dehndeh tooris."

"Goh sleep noh? Aal a dis wahn oava direkli."

"Fi chroo mayn." Javier put down a bill and walked out.

He went to his truck and got in. The bright half-moon was straight overhead, flooding the interior with ghost light. He felt dizzy. It wasn't just the alcohol. It was a sense that he'd entered a new phase of life that he hated, one that had a horrible, garish quality to it, and now his job was to fix it, to get back to the contented rhythm of only a few hours ago. He assured himself that Leah would have enough sense not to go home with Xander. Xander couldn't be Leah's type. He was so snobby, sarcastic, and aloof. So she had to be back in her guesthouse. But he'd never asked which guesthouse she was staying at. He hit his steering wheel with the flat of his hand. Why had he never asked? And now there was no use going from guesthouse to guesthouse all over town, asking for her at three a.m.

He unwound the rosary from the mirror, held it in his lap, and leaned his head against the steering wheel. "Mi Virgen María," he prayed, "ah noa yu protek mi. Soh ah hoap yu ku protek Mis Leah. She . . . she da wahn gud gyal."

He started crying.

He crawled to his backseat so no one could see him. He prayed the rosary behind the darks of his eyes, until he fell into fitful dreams.

He was awoken by a loud splash: the first tourist van on the road.

He sat bolt-upright and checked his watch: 6:25 a.m. The streetlights shone on wet asphalt.

He still didn't know where Leah was.

He got in the front seat, rehung his rosary, watched it spin, turned the keys, and headed over the low bridge toward Xander's house.

His first question would be: "Why do you hate me so much?"

It didn't matter if Xander was getting ready for his tour, or still in bed, or in the shower. It didn't even matter if Leah was there with him. He'd ask anyway. Why do you hate me so much? What did I do to you? No one hates me. No one has cause to hate me. Or at least—no rational cause. Their parents had split up after they were born. They were both born with stutters, Javier with glottals and Xander with dorsals. Their mother took Xander east to Belmopan, where there were better schools, but she was an abusive alcoholic and he skipped two grades before he was kicked out for fighting. Meanwhile, their father took Javier west to Benque Viejo on the Guatemalan border. He worked with a speech therapist and began to pronounce his *h*'s and *g*'s and *r*'s. His father was a womanizer, but a kind one who treated women with respect. Javier had a calm and happy childhood, always popular, always picked first for schoolyard games.

Is this why Xander hated him? Because arbitrary fate had given Javier a happier life? How was any of it his fault? At what point did personal choice figure in? Xander didn't do himself any favors, starting fights and making enemies, including his own twin. Javier wanted to turn back time and convince his parents to let them stay together, to be brothers in the way God meant brothers to be, protecting and supporting each other; not estranged and bitter. Javier missed Xander, always, and especially at holidays. Their mother didn't have the will to mount any celebration of her own, so one year he invited Xander to spend Christmas with him and their father in Benque, and he came, when he was twelve, and it was awful. He spent the whole day sulking and making sarcastic comments. He never came again.

Was that Javier's fault too? That he'd always tried to be nice and do the right thing?

No. It was not.

Javier was driving fast. The sky was getting lighter, but the drizzle continued. If it kept on like this, the creek might be too high for vans to cross and the day's tours might be called off. So much for the new baktun.

He passed shared taxis headed to town. He'd know if he passed Xander. He knew what his truck looked like.

He turned left at the airstrip and drove all the way to the end of the road, where a small house stood apart.

There was no truck out front.

Javier checked his watch. 6:50 a.m., and Xander was gone already.

He parked anyway.

He got out. The ground was wet from the rain and squished under his feet.

The gate was locked, so he jumped over the fence. The front door was locked. He used his driver's license to jimmy it open and broke it in the process.

The door swung wide.

No one was home.

He went to the kitchen table. It was neatly arranged, with a few candles burned down to the nub and a yellow legal pad. He scanned the top page:

—Xibalba = the world of the Other, as encountered
in travel
—the earth acts on us always BUT now it will
act on us on timescales we can see: the Age of
Emergency
—four great evils: capitalism, whiteness,
patriarchy, nationalism. (others?)

—what is the solution?—>
—accumulation of any kind leads to suffering
—dispersion of all kinds leads to peace
—radical sortition democracy
—nomadic communism or / anarchism
—look into subsidiarity (from Ida)

On the floor there was a stereo with a pile of CD cases, a copy of the *Popol Vuh,* and a mug of cold cacao grounds. The air mattress was made up: sheet, pillow, and blanket folded at the foot.

His phone buzzed. There was a text from Hector. He flipped it open.

angelo tek yu groop tudeh. jamaal seh angelo
fuget ih foan eena di aafis.
angelo need fi bring bak Leah Oliveri RAIT NOW.
ih ma an ih pa di kaal
FAIN AHN!

TEAKETTLE WAYHOUSE
10 Himux 19 Yaxk'in,
Long Count 15.10.14.10.1

---

20 December, 3012

Tanaaj let the viajeras strip her. They removed her tunic, straw hat, and drawstring pants. Her breasts shrank from the exposure and her penis scrunched up. The sun had just set, outrunning the thunderheads and illuminating them from below, which soaked the sky in a wet peach light.

She stood on her tiptoes and caught sight of her fellow jugadorix Bayode, Angela, and Hecate. They were being dressed by their own attendants. Emelle was somewhere in the crowd, too, her silver-haired encamadix from long ago, who'd come to her two nights ago and told her where to find Niloux DeCayo so that, she said, they could make peace. She'd seemed to want to say more, but Tanaaj reached out and stopped her, thanked her, praised her for being so moved by her conscience to want the two to reconcile. The information was yet another gift from the god.

The viajeras pulled a cotton shift over her head, dyed black for Javier. Next, a crown of passion flowers. Last, the green obsidian blade around her neck. She'd tied it so that it'd be ready to come loose when she needed it. She felt a sudden hot push of tears: none of these viajeras knew this would be Tanaaj's last night among them. After tonight, she would likely be blotted. She didn't know for how long or by how many. But the proof of Xibalba was Balam Ahau, and Balam Ahau required a blood sacrifice to appear.

From hand to hand came a mask, also black, with tragic eyes. She closed her eyes and let them put it on her, fit the eyeholes over the eyes, tie it back. She murmured the words of summoning, aware that the words spoken here had more power than the words spoken anywhere else in the world, because this was the land, this was the very god where the original events had happened. Thousands were waiting along the route to the cave, twelve miles over the hills, three hours' run if they never stopped, more with refreshment and inclement weather. "May the god of this place enter our blood," she said to herself. "May the god of this place direct the play. May the god of this place give us the will to do what is necessary in the service of Xibalba."

"Estas lista," said a voice, and Tanaaj opened her eyes as Javier.

Already there was another shade of awareness in her body, imparted by the land: heroic, determined. She felt how Javier had felt on this day, a thousand years ago.

The famous courtyard of Teakettle Wayhouse was filled with wooden plinths, which could be rearranged for plays and dances and readings. This time, they'd been set in two long rows, making a wide lane that resembled an ancient Maya ball court. Braziers of fire blazed all around the perimeter. Tanaaj stood behind the plinths, waiting for her turn to emerge; she waved to Bayode on the other side of the lane, wearing a red mask, red shift, and heliconia crown for Xander. A bald viajera mounted a plinth at the end of the lane and waved the flag of Laviaja back and forth against the molten clouds. The eyes of the crowd were all on the west, waiting for the appearance of Venus. For this moment, it seemed as though all was well in the world. Tanaaj wanted to linger here, where everything was already accomplished, already won.

A murmur became a cheer, which became a roar, as the evening star created itself out of the pink sky.

This was the sign to begin.

Hecate and Angela stepped forward at the head of the lane, dressed in white and yellow as Hector and Angelo. Their task was invocation. Hecate felt for the plinth with her hands, stepped up with one foot and then the other; Angela jumped up with both feet like a kangaroo. Someone handed a water jug and brush up to her.

Hecate lifted her arm to the crowd. Tanaaj willed the jovenix to project her voice, just like they'd practiced in seclusion.

She called, "¡La obra comienza!"

It was well done, clear and deep. Tanaaj flushed with pride.

The crowd responded "¡Danos la obra!" in overlapping voices that blurred into a cheer.

Hecate raised her arm again, and the crowd hushed. Now came the speech they'd written for the occasion. "Tonight, by the tradition of *one thousand years*—"

Already the crowd was cheering. Tanaaj let her tears run beneath the mask.

"By the tradition of one thousand years, on this most holy night, we remember the crossing of Saint Leah Magdalene Oliveri, Leah La Canela, Leah La Turista, Leah La Putita, Leah La Souvenir, to the other world of Xibalba, through her cortada deep in the cave of Actun Tunichil Muknal, known to our Maya ancestors as the Mother's Cut. We remember that she came here to accomplish the will of Xibalba set into motion two thousand years ago, by our ancestors in faith, Ixul and Ajul of the Tzoyna, who died in the cave so that Leah would be drawn to it. We follow in her footsteps to find our own cortadas, using the instruction of the Consort Twins, Javier El Jugador and Xander El Erudito; as well as the gift she left us, las ojos-de-Leah"—here Hecate touched her forehead with two fingers, in reverence— "by which we feel the nearness of Xibalba, as she did. When we find our cortadas and cross over at last, may we enter the eternal wayhouse, rest at the supper table, and never be parted from each other again."

Now Angela spoke, hefting her water jug.

"In remembrance of Saint Leah, and in the hope of our own escape from this world, we come together in joyful prayer to perform *La Estrella Actual*, to retrace the steps of La Trinidad and celebrate their mysteries. May we, through our performance on this land, come ever closer to the god of this place, and become confident in the surety of our own crossing, in this life or the next."

She searched the crowd. "Jugadorix, come forward."

Tanaaj and Bayode stepped into the center lane.

Angela dipped the brush in the water jug and flung it at the both of them. Warm drops struck Tanaaj and slid down her skin.

"By this holy water of Xibalba, gathered this morning at the mouth of the Great Cave, may our ancestors come alive in your bodies. May the god of the day and the god of the place direct your movements. May the land tell you where to go. May the sky and star, clouds and sun, rain and hills, sky and star—wait no—"

Angela lost her place in the text. There was a pause as she retraced the words in her mind.

"Rivers and rocks!" She laughed, and the crowd laughed with her. "May also the rivers and rocks show you the way to everlasting liberation."

Now it was Hecate's turn again. She began to recite the Prayer of Saint Leah, and as soon as the crowd caught on, they began to hold hands and say it with her:

"*In the beginning,*
in the cave,
God knelt in the darkness with her blade.

When she cut her hand,
in the cave,
the universe spilled from the tip of the blade.

Flooding the wound,
the gift of blood,
souls that remember the perfect whole—
the body of God,
the blade, the cave,
and what a star is, not of what it is made."

Thunder rippled overhead. The crowd began to cheer. No rain yet, but it would come. Bayode turned to Tanaaj and their eyes met through their masks. They were impatient to get started, especially now that they were going to get a storm.

The bald viajera started waving the flag again, as if at the start of a race. Angela started flinging cave water on the crowd and yelling to be heard.

"May the rite of *La Estrella Actual* renew our faith! Go forth and relive!"

But there was one line that remained: the signal to Tanaaj.

Hecate turned in her direction, now speaking as Hector to Javier, the young Maya tour guide, generous and faithful:

"FAIN AHN!"

Tanaaj turned and sprinted away.

———

Niloux descended the ramp into the ancient city of Tzoyna and was blinded.

She recoiled, swearing, and covered her eyes. The others stopped. She heard Owen's voice: "Are you okay?"

"No, I'm not okay," she said. "Why are there flood-lights on?"

A pause. "There aren't."

"Then what is all this light?"

Another pause, while purple discs throbbed against her eyelids.

Cheen's quiet voice: "Turn off your aug."

Niloux stood up straight, turned off her aug with a tap to her temple.

Her vision began to clear, revealing an ancient Maya city, excavated and restored. There was a ball court to their right, a palatial complex behind it, and in the distance, more pyramids and plazas. They were painted red and cream and hung with strings of light.

No one commented on her reaction. They wanted to, she could feel it, but the whole group had been tense ever since Emelle had walked away at Teakettle and never come back. Niloux felt relieved, in a way. She'd alienated her, just like she seemed to alienate everyone in the end. Nothing new.

Meanwhile, the ground glowed wherever she went.

Even with her aug off, she felt the pull of the soil beneath her feet. Maybe after the Jubilee was over, she'd stay in Cayo, develop the technique further. She could learn to ask the god of the place more questions than *Do you know me.* She could figure out how not to be blinded all the time. But with Tanaaj and the LFC here, it was too much to deal with. Clearly she'd lived a past life here, or many lives, but there was nothing else to say without more study.

"Maybe we can have my party here," said Messe behind her.

Niloux was startled out of thought. "What?"

"My fiesta de manéra, remember?" she said.

Owen assessed the plaza. "You could do worse than here, to become a maya."

Niloux walked ahead. "I'm going to look around," she said.

The others told her not to go far, but she was already in her head.

She walked into a smaller plaza. There was a towering arch at the far end. She recognized it as the first Arca de las Gemelas. She got closer, keeping her distance from the other onlookers. The monument was enormous, as high as the temple behind it, the two pillars carved as Ixul and Ajul in the Classic Maya style: flattened foreheads and sprawling headdresses, standing atop panels of glyphs, each glyph as big as Niloux's body.

The green-and-gold Laviaja flag hung from the top.

She had to re-remember, every minute, that Tanaaj DeCayo was her birth twin. She couldn't reconcile it with the rest of her knowledge. She didn't want to believe it at all. Maybe Messe's looks were just a coincidence. Maybe everyone was deluded. But again, as with Venus at the oasis, she felt as if her body already knew something that her mind couldn't articulate: not just that Tanaaj was her birth twin, but that this fact was only a thread in some vast tapestry she'd never see.

She walked back to her familia. They were turning in circles, admiring the city. She tried to imagine what the site had looked like in Leah's day: overgrown. Pure jungle. Mounds and hills and looters' pits. Nothing like the painted, manicured plaza in which they now stood. There were only a few other viajeras here tonight— most were feasting with familia, or romping along Cayo's thousand footpaths, or lining the route of the Passion from Reymundo Road to Pleitez Road to the bridge over the Mopan, which would bypass them and end up at the Great Cave. It was a near thing: the Great Cave was only half a mile away. But Niloux wanted to stay close enough that she could slip in and begin the search for Leah's remains. Maybe tonight, once the bacchanals were asleep.

But for now, they were lying low.

Messe was looking toward the arch. "Is that where Ixul and Ajul's bodies are?" she asked.

"No, they're in the Great Cave," said Owen, "supposedly."

"'Supposedly' being the operative word," said Cheen. "We don't know if the two bodies in the final chamber are theirs. Or even if they existed at all."

Niloux snorted. "Doesn't matter. History is just a function of belief. It unfolded as if they existed, so they might as well have."

Owen looked down, but the jovenix was undaunted by Niloux's mood. "Well," she said, "then where did the legend come from?"

Meret stepped up. "Somehow the names survived the fall of the city," she said. "We don't know how; they're not inscribed anywhere. But when those two skeletons were discovered in the back chamber of the Great Cave, it made a good story for the tour guides to say it was them."

"I'm hungry," said Niloux. "Let's sit somewhere and eat."

She walked to the temple steps, where she was out of sight of the monument. Niloux didn't want to look at it again. The others followed her, one by one. She could sense them watching her. They wanted her to talk about the blinding. Or about anything. She didn't want to. What would she say? That she must have used to live in the Tzoyna? That she herself was the reincarnation of Ixul or Ajul? Even her ego wasn't that big. Anyway, she didn't want to lose credibility, not to her familia and certainly not to the LFC, who still wished her dead. Which was Tanaaj's fault. No matter if they were birth twins.

They laid down palm leaves and ate Pasaja food they'd picked up on the way: tamales, bananas, coffee.

"What do you think Tanaaj is planning?" asked Owen. "To 'summon Xibalba'?"

Niloux shrugged. "Everyone will see what they expect to see. Something strange will happen, and they'll all say, 'That's it, that's the sign.'"

"What would convince you?"

Niloux felt the urge to answer with sarcasm, but then it ebbed. This was a useful question. Again, in her mind, she was at the oasis in the Persian desert. She wished she could feel the same conviction she'd felt that night. She wanted to go back. The desert was dry, clean, and quiet, and she could think clearly there.

"I'd be convinced," Niloux said, "if I experienced something I knew to be impossible. But of course I have no idea what that would be until I experienced it."

She felt the patter of rain on her forearms, looked up. A bank of clouds was rolling in from the east like a breaking wave.

"*La Estrella* must have started by now," said Meret.

No one answered. A wind sprang up, making the palm trees spasm. The storm was getting close.

Niloux saw the future pacing ahead of her. She wouldn't stay in Cayo at all. She'd find Leah's remains to prove her point once and for all and then she'd get out of Cayo, this never-ending circus, and walk back to Persia. She'd gather whoever wanted to keep working with her. They'd study disappearances and pistas and the new technique to see past lives. Maybe they'd even recover lost techniques, pushed aside by the taboos of Laviaja. She'd learn to trust her companions, and start planning, start building, start looking to Venus—not as a star, but as a place, as a god. Who would go with her? Who would learn the god of that place with her? She couldn't imagine. In the last few months, she'd realized she didn't always want to be alone, necessarily; she just needed to find the right people. A core group she trusted. A familia, yes, but a consistent one—like Meret, Cheen, and Owen. Maybe she could contact Calliope from Capri. And maybe Ahmed from Zein-o-Din.

Maybe this one here, Messe, her own blood.

Niloux said, "Well, we should hold our own celebration. Messe?"

The kid turned to her, mouth full of banana.

"Want to become a maya?"

As Tanaaj ran south, she could see the rain coming. Veils dropped, blurring the hills. The clouds were dark violet. Lightning snapped. No one was deterred. Angela and Hecate were running together, Angela guiding Hecate and Hecate blowing the conch to announce their coming. On the first stretch, the viajeras were four or five deep, lapping up on both sides like waves against a searoad. She saw so many costumes that she stopped trying to remember them all: mopan maya, yucatec maya, kekchi maya, ch'ol maya, achi maya, maya queens, maya daykeepers, maya warriors, scribes, farmers, priests, merchants, ixchels and xquics, chaacs and itzamnas, hunajpus and xbalanques, olmecs, tainos, mixtecs, aztecs, zapotecs, zapatistas, tourists, tour guides, chicleros, capitalists, campesinos, selenas, catrinas, archaeologists, expaats, garifunas, mennonites, and of course javiers in black, xanders in red, and leahs in green. They were tossing passion flowers into her path. The filaments stuck to her skin. She passed through a corridor of drummers who raised their arms and hollered. There were no mistakes. Everything she did was good, destined, already written. The land itself was the set of the play; her steps, its language; the hills and valleys, its grammar.

Hecate blew the conch.

The road led into thick jungle. She slowed to a trot and so did the small group who'd kept up with her. They'd fall away or join as the play went on, as it should be. The drums faded. The rain would hit any minute. There were viajeras by the road here, too, but fewer; they'd emerged from under their domes to see the Passion pass, and then they'd go back to eating. A trio of flute players fell in with them, but they were so drunk they laughed more than they played. There was a cluster of viajeras ahead, holding a jovenix on their shoulders who was wearing a puffy coat, waving and grinning. It was a fiesta de manéra. Tanaaj called, Blessings from Javier Magaña! and swerved over to her and they knelt so she could lift her mask and kiss the jovenix on both cheeks and she asked in her ear, What did you choose, hermanix? and the jovenix said, Minnesotan! and Tanaaj laughed and held her hand on the jovenix's head and said, May you find Xibalba in this life, and then she pulled down her mask and was off again, having left some viajeras behind and gained some new.

She heard the first rain hit the canopy. A few drops made it through, splashed her forearms.

Hecate blew the conch.

She enjoyed the feeling of her strong legs running. Her body was the litter of her soul. She could always depend on its genius. Not everyone in Carnival had the stamina or desire to keep going. Some stopped to linger in a compelling place. Some caught the eye of an amorous viajera. Some wanted to branch out onto darker, lesser-known paths. Some got caught up in their own performances, building their own set of angelo, hector, xander, javier, and leah. But Tanaaj's route was set, and she still had a crowd following her, hundreds on foot and hoverdish and hoverchair. She could feel them watching her. They were wondering: hadn't Tanaaj DeCayo promised to prove Xibalba was real? How and when would it happen? *Wait,* she said in her mind, *until we make the unexpected turn.* She still didn't know how to approach Niloux, or what to say in order to get close to her, but she trusted the answer would come. Then the touch of the blade, as in Oaxaca. Then Balam Ahau would arrive.

The jungle thinned. They ran into the pounding rain. The land before them sloped down to Roaring Gulf.

At once Tanaaj thought: *I have seen the shape of this land before.*

In the instant before she turned to take it in, she knew what she would see: a cluster of three hills directly ahead, a limestone cliff to the left, and a flat floodplain to the right, except now it was underwater.

The land was acting on her. Javier was rising in her. She was becoming he.

She ran down the slope. The rain had made the road slippery with mud. On the shore there was a huge crowd, an encampment of tents and pods and steel drums protected by domes, lit by fires and moonballs and sunballs and strings of star-lights, all glimmering in the downpour like a dream. Viajeras crowded the road and held up their palms as she approached, calling, Check the water! Check the water!, and Tanaaj remembered that this used to be the Roaring River, where the ancient tour guides had always checked for flooding, to divine whether the cave would be safe to enter.

In ancient Kriol, Tanaaj called, Ih sayf fi paas?

The crowd called, No! Turn back! The children tugged at her arms, begging her not to go.

But she was Javier. She had to go. She called, Leah Oliveri paas dis way, bredrin?

The crowd called, Yes!

Den ah haftu goh!

But then Angela and Hecate caught up with her: they'd decided running wasn't safe for Hecate in the rain, so they'd advanced a request for a hoverdish. Tanaaj assured them they'd all wait. She accepted a cup of orange juice, shielding it from the rain; she let Angela restore her crown as best she could. Surely the rain was a sign too? Rain was holy to the ancient Maya. Rain was the gift of Xibalba. They were all drenched in it. A hoverdish arrived from the camp and was slid on the air to Angela, who put it in Hecate's hand. Hecate sat, folded her legs, and gripped the edge.

"¡Estoy lista!" she said when she was settled.

"Bien, hermanix," said Tanaaj. "Sound the horn!"

Hecate put the conch to her lips and blew. There was another encampment on the far side of the water who heard it, and they started to cheer.

Tanaaj pointed ahead and called, "Ah wahn reskyu Leah!"

The crowd let her go.

She ran onto the footbridge and felt the shudders of the others following her. Lightning flashed green on the water. She blinked to clear her eyes, peered ahead. Even from this distance, she could see the other crowd had a different temperament: they were milling, uncertain. When they got to the other side she called another halt, saying it was so that everyone could drink water. But there was news. A gaucha viajera elbowed forward and said, "Your Xander is hurt."

Tanaaj pulled her mask up. "Bayode? Is she all right, hermanix?"

"Yes. She slipped—on an ancient helmet. All kinds of artifacts come up because of the rain. Twisted her ankle."

Tanaaj remembered the court on the other side of the world, months ago, on the island of Linapacan: Li-Wei falling and injuring herself also. In that case, they'd stopped the play altogether because it was just a showcase, and because Li-Wei was in too much pain to keep performing. Was Bayode?

"Who told you?"

"The medic. Named Emelle."

Tanaaj nodded. So, her old lover had followed Bayode's party. "Did she send instructions what to do?"

"Instructions?"

Tanaaj felt a flash of impatience. "It is the choice of Bayode whether to continue performing as Xander."

"Oh! No she didn't. I'll ask her."

The gaucha's eyes went unfocused, rain running down her face. Then she turned back to Tanaaj.

"She said go ahead without her," she said. "She releases the spirit of Xander to the Munda."

Tanaaj nodded. Her followers had begun looking at one another with worry. The euphoric mood was ebbing. She had to rally them. The god had chosen

Bayode, but the god had also twisted Bayode's ankle—with an ancient helmet, no less!—so this, too, was part of the play.

Then it came to her. How to approach Niloux.

"Tell Bayode," she said to the gaucha, "to send us her mask."

The gaucha nodded.

Tanaaj turned back to the crowd with a grin.

"¡Escuchame!" she called. "The land has acted upon us, blessed be the land! You think because Xander has twisted an ankle, that Xander is gone? No, mi hermanix. The new Xander shall be revealed by the land, just as Leah is. Trust in the god of the place."

"What are you going to do?" asked a ninx.

Tanaaj smiled at her. "What did Javier Magaña do?" she said. "Javier could have gone home! Javier could have thought of himself! But he didn't. What did he do?"

The ninx grinned. "He went to save Leah!"

Tanaaj winked, pulled down her mask.

Hecate blew the conch.

She took off running again.

There were cheers behind her as they reentered the jungle. The road was more narrow on this stretch, more overgrown. Rain fell on the palms overhead—just as rain had fallen on the day Leah disappeared, a thousand years ago—and every time her foot landed, mud splashed up to her thighs. Tanaaj felt fatigue. She'd been running for an hour and a half now. This is how Javier had felt too: tired beyond reason, not having slept; but a deeper purpose propelled him. She was passing through new veils of awareness. Tiredness had a way of changing perception, of softening the mind, of helping you see what you couldn't see before. The land was again familiar to her. She could anticipate each hill and curve and vista before she saw it: every feature Javier had seen, traveling this road hundreds of times. They came upon a cluster of young ixchels, painted like the goddess, who'd been looking over their shoulders, waiting for her, and when she did they waited until the last moment to begin running, such that Tanaaj had to yell out at them to get going, in a teasing way, and they sprang up like butterflies and flitted ahead, back and forth over the road, quetzal feathers crisscrossing each other. Their hands were dipped in red and they were screaming.

Hecate blew the conch.

"Messe needs to be holding a black orchid," said Cheen. "I'll find one."

"No," said Niloux, "that's Saint Leah's flower."

"Heliconia or passion flower?"

"No. None of those. I don't want her carrying any of that baggage."

Cheen raised her eyebrows. Niloux knew she was straining everyone's patience with her snappishness. The fiesta de manéra had seemed like a good idea to take their minds off *La Estrella*, but still, Niloux felt she was fraying at the edges. She hadn't slept in days. She hadn't been alone in days. She wanted to be in Persia.

"Then what, O great and wise leader?" said Cheen.

Niloux nodded. "I deserved that. Get whatever you can find, just none of those three."

Cheen sprouted a dome and left the shelter. The rain had been falling for half an hour now. Meret and Owen were out looking for the other main elements: a musician, a source of fire, something sweet. Niloux was making balché in her kiln. They were assembling an impromptu ceremony.

"So what are we going to do?" Messe demanded, hopping from one foot to the other. Niloux was surprised to find she liked this kid. She was exasperating in the way that Niloux herself was exasperating. She respected that.

"It's not going to be anything fancy," said Niloux.

"That's fine. The setting is fancy enough."

"True."

"I've always wanted to come to Cayo. And now that I've seen it . . . I don't know. I don't think I feel called here."

"Where will you head after this?"

Messe looked sidelong at her. "Where are you headed?"

Niloux raised her eyebrows. "Me? Why do you care?"

"I've been following you for a long time."

"Oh have you."

She waved her hands, hurrying to explain. "Your activity, I mean, not your path."

"I'm flattered."

"Yeah, since Zein-o-Din." She paused. "I agree with you. I think we should be able to challenge Laviaja and not be afraid of being punished."

"Yes. That's something I want to change. Otherwise we stagnate."

"Did you ever decide what to name the new age?"

Niloux laughed. "No. Do you have any ideas?"

"No. I think it's silly to try to name it before it happens."

Well, thought Niloux, I am conquered.

"Why did you act so weird when we came onto the court?"

She was relentless.

Niloux told herself: *Care for the child before you.*

"I automated my technique in my aug," she said, "so anything I touched in a previous life lights up. The more I touched it, the more it lights up. If my technique is sound, that is. The first time I tried it out and got a positive result, I was in Persia."

"At the Zein-o-Din caravanserai."

"Yes."

"Isn't that where Ruth Okeke died?"

"Yes, with Xander Cañul at her bedside."

"What if you're the reincarnation of Xander Cañul?"

Niloux laughed out loud.

But Messe looked serious. "You're a maya, right?" she asked.

"All my life," said Niloux. "Mopan maya."

"And so was Xander Cañul. So . . ."

"So?" Niloux was getting tetchy. "So are thousands of other people."

Messe shrugged. "I'm just saying. You got positives at Zein-o-Din and now you're getting positives here. It fits."

"I wouldn't want to be him. He has a lot to answer for."

Messe sensed her mood darkening. She changed the subject. "I'm going to be mopan maya too," she said.

"Because Tanaaj is?"

"Because *you* are," Messe shot back, eyes full of hurt.

Niloux allowed for the moment to breathe, then went on in a more gentle voice. "It's a good manéra. But you've got a lot of tutorials ahead."

"That's fine. I want to learn everything. I want to learn bloodletting, even."

Niloux's stomach turned. "That's forbidden," she said.

Messe turned on her. "Oh, so now you're the one defending Laviaja?"

"It's different." Having said so, Niloux struggled to justify why. It was a taboo so old that even she hadn't questioned it. And she still hurt from the memory of the assassination attempt. "We just . . . don't do that anymore. Not even the maya manéras."

"Because why?"

Niloux thought. "Probably it became taboo when pacifism merged with Laviaja in the twenty-third century."

"So it was just because of the association of blood with violence?"

Niloux stared into the middle distance. She didn't have a good answer. Maybe bloodletting was one of the lost techniques, pushed aside by Laviaja, that could be revisited. "I guess so," she said.

"Well, I don't think it has to be violent. It's all about the intention."

Niloux grimaced and started to answer, but then Owen and Meret returned.

First they made Messe turn around so she couldn't see what they'd brought. Then they showed Niloux the torches and the handmade blocks of chocolate, and introduced her to a redheaded ocarina player who insisted that she wasn't very good. They assured her that was fine, this was all spur of the moment. Niloux checked the balché: it was ready. Then Cheen returned with branches of blue plumeria.

"All right, kid," Owen called over to Messe, "go away. Let your tíax surprise you."

"In the rain?"

"Sprout a dome."

"I can't use domes or shields, I'm a hunter."

Niloux called, "The ancient Maya considered rain a blessing. You could too."

Messe grinned, then darted into the storm. They watched her kick puddles on the court and spin with her arms out.

Niloux turned to the others. "Let's all do it, for her. No shields, no domes."

"What about the torches?" asked Owen.

"Okay. Bubble domes for the torches, but that's it."

They seemed agreeable, except Cheen, who patted her hair.

Finally they were ready. They called to Messe to not look. She waved to indicate she'd understood, then stood on the court with her hands clasped behind her back. A child in the pouring rain. Almost a full-grown viajera. A dozen other viajeras had become curious and watched on the sidelines. A fiesta de manéra tended to attract onlookers.

Niloux sent the ocarina player out first. The sound of the flute cut through the rainfall. Then Cheen, Meret, and Owen, carrying the torches, their light diffused by the domes. Niloux followed last. She was holding the plumeria.

The little company surrounded Messe. A larger crowd had gathered to watch. This was an important moment in a jovenix's life. As the ocarina player continued to improvise, Niloux broke off twigs of plumeria, and set one behind the jovenix's ear, then one behind the ear of each of the others, including herself; then she gave Messe the branch to hold. The child was drenched, smiling. They all were.

Then she heard a conch horn in the jungle.

Everyone turned to look.

Emerging from the trees was a slight figure, dark-skinned, barefoot, filthy with mud, her shoulders heaving. She wore a black shift and a black mask, the eyeholes fixed in tragedy.

TZOYNA
4 Eb 15 Pop, Long Count 10.9.5.7.12

---

10 December, 1012

Ajul stared at his sister at the other end of the court. She was covered in dust. Her heart-shaped face was bruised and swollen. Dried blood ran from her mouth down her throat like a long black beard.

This meant they'd cut out her tongue.

"Oh wajmul," he said under his breath.

"Play!" someone shouted.

"No, not yet!" Tatichwut stomped back to the center of the court.

"What are you waiting for?" called Chenukul.

Tatichwut pulled aside one of the other farmers and towed him to the merchant, and they conferenced again in whispers while the crowd shifted, restless, eager to get the spectacle over before it got too hot. Ajul met Ixul's eyes. It was the first time he'd ever seen her afraid. He understood: he had not anticipated this cruelty either, being made to play against each other, cast as opponents instead of partners. But his insight on the hill overruled all his fears. He wished he could share it with her. Why be afraid, if she remembered their father's lesson about embracing fate? Once, they'd been the captors; now, they were the captives. The universe itself was sustained by the exchange. If that meant they had to play against each other, so be it—they had thousands of times before.

He tried to convey all of this with his eyes. That was all they'd ever needed to understand each other.

But she was tapping her temple, over and over.

Ajul frowned at her. What was she saying?

She drew her hand from her chest outward, and then tapped her temple again.

Ajul realized she was saying *We run* in handtalk. Did she mean, in the ball game?

He signed back, *Yes, here. We run here.*

Ixul blinked.

She pointed at her mouth, then moved her lips in an exaggerated way. Her tongue was missing; she couldn't articulate in the normal way.

He shook his head, not understanding.

She tried again.

Was she saying *la kasin*? Yes! That meant "we play" in High Ch'ol. That was what Ajul had been thinking. Yes, they were here, and they were going to play the ball game. They were going to see this through to the end.

Ajul smiled.

Ixul smiled back in relief.

They understood each other.

Then Tatichwut cuffed Ixul and she collapsed on the stone.

"Are you trying to talk to him?" he shrieked, standing over her. "Don't try to talk to him! You've talked enough. You've done everything enough. Everybody knew you two were rutting. Farmer blood wasn't good enough for you? Only royal butter for the royal cob, eh?"

Ixul got up, fresh blood welling from her mouth, never taking her eyes off Ajul.

"Everybody listen!" said the farmer, coming to the center of the court. He put his hands on his hips and then took them off again. He was so awkward in his body, so graceless. He made a slow circle of the court, taking stock of those in attendance: sunburnt farmers, old women, handfuls of warriors and guards, everyone mixed in together, eyeing one another, unsure of their status in the new order.

"The alliance of Katwitz and Pekwitz has conquered the city of Tzoyna!" he yelled, throwing his arms apart.

"Now we have taken captive the mighty twins Ajul and Ixul. Now we control the entrance to Xibalba. Now we can sacrifice them both!"

There were scattered cheers.

"And then I will be king!"

The farmers cheered again when they realized no one else was going to, and the others joined in, half-hearted.

Tatichwut stepped back and indicated the twins.

"Shall we be merciful?"

There were boos.

"Shall we be cruel?"

There were more vigorous cheers.

Ajul was impressed by how bad of a speaker Tatichwut was. He felt a resurgence of last night's doubt, but then thought: *Be steady. Remember your duty. Remember your fate. No amount of humiliation can hurt us; it can only glorify us. We're playing a longer game that transcends the cycles of time. Ixul's words:* la kasin. *We play.*

Ajul saw motion from Ixul. She was clapping her hands together, staring at him.

He looked back at her, confused. Did she have more to say? He didn't want her to strain her tongue. She had to save her strength for this game.

La kasin, she mouthed again, laboring.

To show he understood, he tapped his hand to his heart, the handtalk sign that meant the same thing: *we play.*

But she didn't smile back. Why was she so agitated?

"Enough, Tatichwut, let them play," someone yelled, fanning themselves. "It's getting hot."

"But play for what!" Tatichwut had a gloating look on his face. Ajul could see he'd fantasized about this for a long time. No one was going to rush his pleasure. Not even the merchant Chenukul, who was not paying attention, but half-standing, craning his neck to look back toward the road. For what? More stragglers? More looters?

Tatichwut snapped at one of his guards, who brought over a cloth bundle. He rolled it open and held up a green obsidian blade.

Ajul darted forward on instinct but a guard leveled his spear.

"There's a third royal child of Tzoyna," Tatichwut called out, "The Princess Ket. We have her. This is the proof."

He reveled in the new admiration of the crowd. He tossed his hair and straightened his esh.

"Yes," he continued. "We put her in the Great Cave. Whoever wins this ball game will accompany me to retrieve her and let her go. Whoever loses will die on the spot. So," he said, turning to the twins, "which of you loves Ket more?"

The crowd cheered at the new cruelty. They all sat forward now, elbows on knees. Ajul fought to control his temper. But again: provocation was just another part of the captivity rite. He must float above himself, see with the eyes of the gods. He knew that, blade or no blade, Tatichwut didn't have Ket. Balam Ahau had Ket. He had seen him take her with his own eyes.

He was afraid to look at Ixul.

"Well?" Tatichwut yelled, gaining confidence as the sun rose. "What's the answer? Which of you loves Ket more? She's very patient, very trusting, sitting there all alone in the dark. I've told her you're coming to visit her. Which of you is it going to be?"

Ixul was still trying to get Ajul's attention, but why did she want to repeat the same thing to him when he already understood? When Tatichwut would just strike her again for trying?

Ixul clapped.

He turned, exasperated.

We go, she signed.

Ajul was confused. *Go where?* he signed.

She looked desperate. *Far away*, she signed.

He stared at her. Could she really be proposing that they run away, like cowards?

There was a cry from the road.

The crowd heard it too. They twisted to greet whatever it might be, craning their necks and trying to get a look at the arriving entertainment. Chenukul half rose in his seat. An arrow went through his throat with such force that his body arced through the air and landed on the other side of the court. Another arrow missed its target, hit the court, and broke in half, which sent its shaft spinning to Ajul's feet.

White feathers.

The Nahua were here.

Ixul ran, and as she ran, she thought, *Well, finally the Nahua are sacking the city, except you're late, it was already sacked last night, so enjoy the leftovers. I won't be one of them.*

She got to a sheltered spot and tried to lock eyes with Ajul, but Ajul was facing the charge in attack position.

What was wrong with him? Why wasn't he running? She'd told him to run, *ajnen,* and he'd seemed to understand at first, but then not to, probably because of her missing tongue, which made it impossible to articulate the word. She'd gone back to handtalk instead. *Go. Far away.* And now they'd been given the very chance they needed to escape.

A Nahua warrior ran straight for her. Ixul bolted.

She broke through a wall of onlookers, and then through a cluster of Nahua warriors, painted green with white feathers, strange and dreamlike, as if the jungle itself were attacking. She looked over her shoulder as she ran. The lone warrior was still pursuing her. She tasted fresh blood in her mouth: the spurt of energy had reopened her wound. But she felt no pain. She had no time to feel pain. She ran across the main plaza. No one was there. She made for the cleft between the two temples that led to the front plaza. There was still no one in sight. Everything was unguarded. Everything was falling apart. She heard the sounds of battle behind her; or rather, slaughter. The farmers would be no match for trained Nahua warriors. She had to get somewhere where she could see Ajul. She swerved left and came to the head of the lime road. When she got to the end she'd double back toward the river. She knew Tatichwut was lying about Ket, no matter whether he had her blade. The god had taken Ket. She'd seen it with her own eyes. Wherever her sister was now, it was beyond her sight. She got to the line of boulders along the road. Each one was taller than she. She turned to look behind her. The warrior was still pursuing her. But she knew her home. She banked right, through a gap in the boulders and down the slope. The warrior couldn't make as fast a turn. She heard him scramble, double back. She ran only far enough down the slope to pick up one of the polished river stones that lined the path, big as a squash, and set her legs, ready, bleeding from the corners of her mouth like an anointed ancestor. She waited. She saw the tip of his spear and waited for him to emerge. His head appeared. She threw. It hit him in the forehead and he stumbled. She was on him in an instant, taking the stone back up and ramming it into his head until it was so wet with blood it slipped out of her hand like a lump of soap.

She got up, breathing hard. She coughed and sprayed blood on the grass.

There were still screams coming from above. She had to get out of sight until the battle died down. She trusted Ajul could take care of himself, because she could not permit the alternative.

She took the dead warrior's spear. The point was obsidian, finely knapped, bespeaking a rich sponsor. It didn't matter now. She walked down to the river. If these warriors had any sense at all, they'd stay away from the cave. They'd know by the yax che trees that they were coming close to Xibalba. Only royal blood could go anywhere near it, and even they had to be extremely careful. The idea of Tatichwut coming here was a joke. He'd piss his esh. It didn't seem like he'd survive the scrum on the court, but again, she had faith that Ajul would. Ajul was a better warrior than any of them. But Ixul still didn't fully understand. Had Ajul refused to run? Could he be that foolish? He must have misunderstood her. She had to wait for him. If she understood correctly, Tatichwut was intending to sacrifice them to legitimize his rule. The idea would have made her laugh if it didn't enrage her. He was a shriveled peanut of a man, pleasuring himself to what little power he'd seized by treachery.

She crept up the river. It was a bright, hot morning. This time yesterday, she'd been on this bank with Mutna, discussing the nature of creation.

She heard a whimper. She went still, heard it again. Someone was crying.

It could be a trap. She gripped the spear and crept toward the sound, the weeping mingling with river chatter.

She rounded a boulder. There was the child Patli, hugging her knees to her chest. At the sight of Ixul, she curled up even tighter.

Ixul knelt, signed, *Be quiet* furiously, then realized the child couldn't understand handtalk.

But then Patli signed back, *Don't kill me.*

Ixul was so surprised she almost dropped her spear. She signed, *Are you alone?*

Yes.

Ixul looked up and around to make sure, then signed, *I don't want to kill you*, and knelt out of sight of the road.

Ixul signed, *How do you know royal handtalk?*

Patli looked miserable. *You had spies*, she signed. *They taught us.*

Ixul reminded herself she was a ghost now. She had no reason to feel anger. In fact, she felt almost appreciative. *You planned this for a long time*, she said.

Yes. But I hate them. I hate Chenukul. He's such a fool and now the Nahua are attacking and—

So leave. I am.

Patli rubbed away her tears. *And go where?*

Found your own city. Call yourself queen.

There were shouting voices and battle cries, just above. Ixul pressed herself and Patli to the stone, out of view. The sounds faded.

She turned back to the child. *I'm going to hide in the entrance until it's over. I have to save my brother*, signed Ixul.

Patli nodded, fresh tears in her eyes. *I didn't want to do it*, she signed. *I liked you all.*

I believe you, signed Ixul. *If you get away . . .*

She still had her pride. She wasn't wholly a ghost yet.

. . . Remember the names of Ixul and Ajul. Tell your children.

Yes, Patli signed. *I will.*

CAYO
4 Ajwal 3 K'ank'in, Long Count 13.0.0.0.0

---

21 December, 2012

Xander wanted to be one of the first groups in the cave today so he could get it over with early. But that never happened. Tourists couldn't be expected to get up before six a.m. They were on vacation, after all, and so on. This time, all his tourists were at Black Rock Lodge, a long drive through the hills south of San Ignacio. And it was raining, which messed up cell-phone signals. And a single-lane road serviced five resorts, so there was much stopping, backing up, obligatory hand waves. And then when he got to the resort, his guests were still waiting for their breakfasts, because two of the cooks had gotten stranded in their village by rising waters.

So.

By the time they got underway to the cave, it was already eight fifteen. Which meant they wouldn't arrive at the parking lot until nine, and not at the cave itself until ten. This day was fucked. His tourists could tell too. They sat in chastened silence.

He checked his text messages while he drove. There was still no reply from Ruth, Ida, or Micah. But lucky him, there were five texts from Javier. He didn't read them. He tossed his phone on the passenger-side seat. He'd slept with the same girl his brother had slept with the night before. Well, so what. Now he was mad? Javier had gotten everything good in life and thought he deserved it. Whenever Xander had tried to talk to him about it, Javier couldn't hear him. He could only patronize him. He thought Xander should be happy with the beautiful, blessed life they were all apparently living in Belize because he couldn't imagine anything else. Once they were close—interlocked, twins in the womb—and now they had no way back to each other. Sad, he thought, but that was the way of the universe. Entropy was both a physical truth and a narrative truth.

When they got to the turnoff for the cave, the drizzle had turned to mist. He called the ranger's station. Ralfie said the creek was high but still passable.

"The cave's still open," he called back to his guests, "so don't worry."

"Oh good!" one called out.

Xander turned up the radio to fill the silence.

He was beginning to feel bad about how he'd yelled at Leah. He might have ruined any chance he might have had of sleeping with her again. But there was nothing to do about it now. She'd just needed to let go of all that nonsense about going deeper into the cave. It wasn't true that no one would look for her. Every fucking guide in Belize would go looking for her. The police would turn out. The Belize Tourism Board would descend. They'd shut down the entire nature reserve for an emergency search-and-rescue mission. Nothing would be worse for tourism than a tourist dying in the cave. But he didn't want to tell her that—the massive mobilization of manpower and resources that would follow. He just wanted her to drop it.

The mist thickened to drizzle again.

Meanwhile, they'd had a good night, had fun, had good sex and good conversation, which gave him lots of ideas. Though he'd been a little unnerved by her reactions, like bursting out laughing when he was in her ass, as if she'd been surprised by the punch line to a joke.

They passed over the creek. It was just as the ranger said—high, but still passable.

This was the point beyond which cell service started

to fail, so he glanced at his phone one last time. Three missed calls from Ceiba Tree Adventures. Why did these fuckers from Ceiba Tree want him? They were probably going to ask him to take more tourists because they assumed his group wasn't full. Well, his group was full. Everyone's group was full today.

The drizzle thickened to rain.

He parked. He told his guests to stay in the van, and got out. The rain was coming down hard. Even if the cave was open, it'd be a quick tour. None of the porters were at their usual places under the lean-to, so he had no one to ask what the latest situation was.

He checked his phone. He had four new texts.

Xander! It's Ida. So nice to hear from u and so great to meet u that amazing day!
Lots to say but first, there's an international fellowship in my dept, I think u should apply
What's ur email? I'll send u the link & Micah & I will both write u recs
you'd be a great candidate

He stood there looking at his phone for a long moment, reading and rereading.

Then he held the phone to his chest.

He was afraid to look at it again. What if the texts disappeared?

He checked again. They were real.

He pushed the phone into his pocket, ran back to the van, and pulled open the sliding door.

"The rain's coming down," he said, "but hey, that's the blessing of the Maya! It's the turn of the baktun, the start of the new age! I'm good to go if you are."

His guests looked surprised at his sudden enthusiasm. "Cave ho!" said one, and the others chimed in.

He couldn't stop thinking about the texts from Ida.

So nice to hear from u

They made their way down the path to the first river crossing. The water was high and strong, but there was a rope strung from bank to bank, and Xander stood in the current and helped each guest across.

international fellowship

His bad mood had lifted, because of the texts, and now, because of the concrete labor of protecting human beings against the elements, throat-deep in cold water. This mattered. He was happy.

you'd be a great candidate

He guided each of his guests safely to the other side. The rain was still coming down. He set off up the path and his group followed, their helmets gleaming.

will both write u recs

They'd texted him, because they saw in him an equal. They valued him. They wanted him to join. It wasn't a dream and it wasn't an illusion. This could be it.

Xander rounded a bend and came face-to-face with Angelo, leading a group of seven. If a group was coming back this early, that meant only one thing: the cave was closed.

"Ah," said Xander, opening his arms, magnanimous. "Di kayv kloaz?"

But then he saw the look on Angelo's face, and on his guests' faces. They looked ashen.

"Can I talk to you," said Angelo, and the way he said it made Xander step to the side with him immediately.

"The cave is flooding," he said. "But Javier is there."

"Javier? Isn't he banned? Why is Javier there?"

"I lost one of my guests."

Xander felt a lurch in his throat.

"Leah," he said.

Angelo frowned. "You knew?"

Xander shook his head. "Tell me."

Angelo started talking fast. "I saw the water in the cave start to turn brown. I turned our group around and tried to get out as fast as I could. She was last in line. She just slipped away somewhere."

The whole world focused to a point at the end of a tunnel. Every second counted now. "Where'd you notice?" he said.

"At the sinkhole."

Xander was aghast. Angelo had gone almost the entire tour and not checked his group count. That was criminal negligence. He forced himself to focus. "And Javier stayed."

"Yes. He told me to ask you to help because you've been all the way in. He's waiting for you at the entrance."

Xander nodded and said, "Take my guests."

He turned to go when Angelo clamped his hand on Xander's shoulder. "Javier said he tried to text you," he said. "Leah's sick."

"Sick," Xander repeated.

"Yes. Her family called Ceiba Tree ten times overnight."

Xander remembered the missed calls from Ceiba Tree. "She's nineteen," he said, though that had nothing to do with anything.

"She never told them. She's terminal."

Xander turned and started running.

Run, root, rock, mud, splash, run, tree, rain, river, steps, run. He passed Ronald's tour group and heard a shout. He didn't stop. What did he need? Headlamp and batteries and rope and first aid kit. A sudden flash. Thunder cracked across the sky. He threw the rest of his things down on the path so he could run faster.

that amazing day

Leah fainting in the cave. Her eyes crossing up toward her head. At the time he'd thought of Stendhal syndrome. But of course that was a seizure. Of course it was. The crossed eyes were a sign of a seizure. Seizures were a sign of brain tumors.

I'll send u the link

He passed John-John's group and Pablo's group and Ian's group. Everyone froze to see him coming. He ran through them. No one said a word. Or maybe he'd just stopped hearing them. He ran so fast his feet didn't have time to slip. A tree was down across the path. He leapt over it, landed, and slipped and hit his head. He heard a crack. He fumbled with his chin strap and pulled off his helmet and saw it was cracked all the way through.

I think u should apply

He threw his helmet into the jungle. Useless. Fools, fucking fools, especially Leah, brain tumor or not, and Javier the romantic, and Angelo the incompetent, and all the rangers who'd said it'd stop raining, and the forecasters who'd told the rangers it'd stop raining, and weather, and nature, and climate change, and the Earth. Fuck the Earth itself.

He sloshed across the last river crossing and bounded up the path to Camp Xibalba.

He could hear the changed pitch of the river from all the way across the clearing. He sprinted across, saw the water—brown as cacao, but still low enough to enter the cave. He clambered down the steps and into the river, right along the travertine shelf where the water cascaded out of the entrance.

Javier was there, crouching on the far side of the pool. When he saw Xander he stood up, his face transforming from worry to relief. "Breda!" he called. "Kohn. Wi stil gat taim."

But Xander couldn't speak. His stutter was back. It might be true that they still had time, depending on where Leah was, depending on if she'd found high ground, depending on if they did too. But he knew. He knew that if he went in that cave this time, he wouldn't come out.

He opened his mouth to try to say this, and nothing came out.

"Breda," Javier called again, confused. "Kohn. Ah need yu."

Xander couldn't speak.

Lots to say

Javier was counting on him.

that amazing day

He could go in and help.

international

He couldn't speak.

fellowship

Xander shook his head and sat down on the threshold.

Javier stared at him, then nodded, then turned and climbed up the waterfall alone.

CAYO
10 Himux 19 Yaxk'in,
Long Count 15.10.14.10.1

---

20 December, 3012

Tanaaj tried to guess which one was Niloux.

She scanned the ball court. Through the eye-holes of her mask, she could see only a few people at a time. There was a small group holding torches in the center of the court, and then a few dozen others, standing under domes to keep off the rain. Niloux might be any one of them. Lightning flashed red on the stone. Tanaaj touched the obsidian blade on her chest. She heard the revelers flooding onto the court behind her, wondering at the detour: the Great Cave was only a half mile away, but in the other direction. Why had she taken them here?

Wait, hermanix, thought Tanaaj. *Balam Ahau is so close, waiting on the edge of the world.*

"I am looking for Niloux DeCayo," she called out in the rain.

A big viajera, one of the torch-bearers, set her feet. "What do you want?"

Tanaaj held out her hand. At the signal, Angela stepped forward and placed Bayode's red mask in her hand. She held it up.

"With Xibalba as my witness," she called, "I call on Niloux DeCayo to play Xander Cañul this sacred night."

A smaller viajera came up behind the big one, put a hand on her arm, and came forward. She was dressed in a long slender huipil: maya travel wear. She came close enough that they could hear each other, but stopped there.

"Who the fuck are you?" she asked.

"Yo soy Javier Magaña."

"The hell you are." She was the same height as Tanaaj. Her skin was dark and her black hair was cut short, wet across her forehead; she was wearing a golden earspool in one ear. The rain fell in ropes all around them. "Take off that mask."

"Are you Niloux DeCayo?"

"Yes."

Tanaaj held the red mask out to her. "I'd rather you put this on, Xander."

She looked furious. "Don't call me that."

Tanaaj stepped forward. She just needed to get close enough. Her quest was nearly done. Balam Ahau was waiting for her cue. "There is nothing to be afraid of."

"I know who you really are," said Niloux.

Tanaaj could see that she was shaking. This made sense: Niloux had been so long in the dark, and when confronted with her liberation, she could not recognize it; she could only fear and loathe it. This was understandable. Tanaaj held out the mask, began to walk toward her, began to unwind her blade from its string. "Take the mask," she said in a gentle voice. "Xibalba is calling you."

Niloux took a step back.

Tanaaj stepped forward.

Niloux turned and ran.

Tanaaj started after.

Then someone jumped in front of her, holding up her hand.

Tanaaj tried to stop, but the stone was too slick from the rain, and she slid. She collided with the other and they crashed onto the stone with a soft crack. Tanaaj's shields shimmered and cushioned her, then faded away. She was about to get up again to pursue Niloux, but

first, she had to make sure the other was all right—
she was young, holding a branch of plumeria, and her
shields had not activated.

"Hermanix?" she said.

Then she recognized the child's face.

"*Messe?*" she said.

The child opened her eyes, which focused on Tanaaj,
then swam away.

"Messe!" she said. She looked just like she had in
her last holo: head shaved, gaunt, but so beautiful. She
got excited. Was this the meaning of the play, instead?
The god of the place had brought them together in the
flesh. This was her dearest fantasy come to life! Should
she let Niloux go? Viajeras had gathered around them.
Tanaaj heard voices speaking, low and urgent. She ignored them. She pulled up her mask.

"Child!" she said. "I am Tanaaj DeCayo. Can you
sit up?"

"Don't move her."

Tanaaj was startled by a sharp voice near at hand.
She looked to her side and saw Emelle, just arrived,
breathing hard, kneeling and opening her kit.

"What are you doing?" she said to Emelle.

All she said was, "Look."

Tanaaj saw that a pool of red was spreading under
Messe's head. She jumped back. She picked up her

hand: rosy rainwater poured off. She remembered that Messe was a hunter. She couldn't use shields. And they'd collided hard. But she'd be all right, especially because Emelle was here. She remembered she'd treated Bayode too—she must have left to follow Tanaaj, then, and been just behind her.

Tanaaj bent down to put her hand on the child's face but Emelle snapped, "Do not touch her. Go away, I have to treat her."

She looked up. "But I am her birth mother."

Messe opened her eyes. "Tanaaj?" she said.

Tanaaj looked down. She couldn't get over the existence of Messe. She was here, the very baby she'd pushed out and held, all grown. She marveled at her perfection, the smooth copper of her skin, the curve of her cheekbones, the undulant curl of her lips. She was so beautiful.

"Yes, child," she said, "I am here."

"I hate you."

Tanaaj shook her head. The child must be hallucinating. "What a thing to say," she said with a gentle smile.

"I hate you," she repeated. She sat up and said again, "I hate you."

Emelle said, "You need to go."

"But I—"

Hands seized Tanaaj's shoulders, picked her up, moved her. She was pulled away from the circle and dropped roughly on the stone. She got to her feet, but stayed where she'd been dropped.

Emelle sprouted a dome over herself and Messe. The rain hit the static and slid over them.

Tanaaj let the rain soak her.

Messe had said she hated her. It was not a mistake. Emelle gave instructions to others nearby, who helped her lift the child's head and shoulders off the stone while she placed taffies on her tongue. Tanaaj didn't want to be hated. She had never been hated. She had never given anyone cause. Emelle took off her shirt, bundled it, and placed it underneath Messe's head before they lowered her back down. Emelle put her hand on the child's forehead, looked into her eyes, moved her lips, got no response. Someone in a dome arrived with a dry blanket. Emelle cut off Messe's shift with a scissors, tucked the blanket over her.

Emelle gave instructions to the other medics, now arrived. Then she came and stood in front of Tanaaj. She realized that they were being watched by all the viajeras who'd gathered at Tzoyna and all the viajeras who'd followed her from Teakettle and all the viajeras who'd been called by the paragua to help. They were standing in the rain and watching her.

Emelle punched her so hard that her mask came off and shattered on the stone.

Tanaaj reeled back, stared.

"I did not tell you where Niloux was so that you could murder her," said Emelle.

The others overheard, started whispering and staring at Tanaaj, edging away.

Emelle continued, "I told you because I honestly believed you would reconcile when you saw each other. What a fool I was."

Tanaaj couldn't focus. Her child hated her. She'd just been hit. No one understood what she'd almost accomplished; if they did, no one would be feeling this way. "Is Messe all right?"

"No, Tanaaj, she is not all right. Her skull fractured when she hit the stone. She'd lost half of her blood in thirty seconds."

"Oh," said Tanaaj slowly. "But you can apply—"

"Sealant, yes, I did that."

"And stimu—"

"Yes, I stimulated her body to make more blood, but that'll take an hour, and even when her blood levels become normal, there's no guarantee she'll ever wake up again. She's traumatized. Not least by seeing you."

"She said she hated me," said Tanaaj.

"I know. You needed to hear that."

Her voice sounded far away.

One of the other medics jogged over. Tanaaj heard her voice from far away, also: "She's going into shock." A hand pried open her mouth and placed orange taffy on her tongue. "She'll be fine, she just needs to lie down." Others handled her to the ground. She saw other viajeras looking at her, some with pity, some with contempt. All the voices were coming from far away. The strings of starlight blurred into stripes. The rain had stopped. She imagined a black jaguar running onto the court, its snarl fixed like a stucco mask, and its eyes were her own.

BOOK III

THE CORTADA

The cave began as nothing more than a softness. As the water pooled, the softness became a depression, the depression a cut, the cut a passage, the passage a cavern, and the cavern a world.

In the time of the Maya, that world was the realm of the gods.

In the time of Saint Leah, that world was a tourist attraction.

In our time, I propose, that world may be most rightly understood as a theatre of the soul.

NECHUMI DENOME
2940

THE CAVE
4 Eb 15 Pop, Long Count 10.9.5.7.12

---

10 December, 1012

Ixul crouched on the threshold of the underworld, holding her spear ready.

What is Xibalba? she'd asked, in another life.

Ask the day, said Mutna.

Ajul always trusted Ixul's judgment in the end. So when she saw him again, she just needed to be more clear than she'd been on the court. She felt light on her feet. But she wouldn't go without Ajul. Finding him remained the last thing to be done. After that, there would be nothing tying them to this place, no temple, no title, and no family.

Her whole body ached now. The center of the fire was in her throat, but it had expanded into her breasts and back. She spat excess blood into her hand and let it drip on the stone, mouthing the words that would take away its power: *This is not for you, Xibalba.* The blood ran with the current.

She heard low voices outside the entrance.

She shrank back into the shadows.

First she saw the tip of a spear, followed by a hunched young man stepping onto the threshold. He was one of the Pekwitz farmers, bowlegged.

He turned around and said, "What now?"

Another voice snapped, "Go in, you fool, before the Nahua find us."

"Why don't we just give ourselves up?"

"Because Letutz sold us out! I knew it. He didn't want me to be king."

"I don't want to go. This is forbidden." His voice trembled.

Tatichwut splashed onto the threshold to face him. Ixul clenched her fists at the fool of a man, desecrating sacred water.

"If I do this thing," he said, "that means I prove myself worthy to be king. Do you understand? I can't be king unless I kill the old king in the proper way. Otherwise no one will respect us."

No one will respect you no matter what you do, thought Ixul.

"And you," Tatichwut continued, "will never be my

councilor. Don't you want to be famous? Didn't we want to be famous?"

The bowlegged one stared into the darkness, fearful. "But the death gods live here."

"They're not here. This is just the antechamber. They're farther in."

How did Tatichwut think he knew that, Ixul wondered. How did he presume to know anything about Xibalba besides what he'd learned from smelly village shamans who slept with their dogs.

"I can help, Father," said a new voice. It was Ajul's.

He stepped onto the threshold, tall and strong.

The first farmer pointed his spear at Ajul. Ajul held up his bound hands to indicate he meant no harm. How had they re-bound his hands? She must have underestimated the capacity of the enemy, at least in this regard. Here there were two of them, too much for her to take on in the light. But this was good, she thought. She could read Ajul's mind, as she always had. He was going to baste them with his usual honey—including calling Tatichwut "Father"—to earn their trust. All she had to do was be ready to assist him when he chose his moment to attack.

"We don't need you!" Tatichwut said to Ajul, like a child caught playing stones the wrong way. "I know what to do."

"What are you going to do, Tata?"

Tatichwut crossed his arms. "I just have to follow the main avenue. It's straight. The knowledge came to me from my mother's side. Her people came from the Tzoyna and served the priests."

So that's where his pretension comes from, thought Ixul. A distant ancestor once served Xibalba, so he considers it his birthright. She hoped the gods would pull his intestines out through his mouth.

"The avenue is certainly *not* straight, Tata," said Ajul. Good, thought Ixul—he is making himself useful to them, and deepening the trap. "I have the knowledge from our daykeeper, and also my father the king. The avenue wanders. And there's a sign that marks the place where you must ascend to the upper levels; if you go beyond that, you may never be able to find your way out."

"What is the sign?"

"The royal emblem of the Tzoyna."

"Where is it?"

Ajul opened his hands, ever tolerant. "I do not know, Father. I have never been in the cave, only taught."

"You mean to trick me."

Ajul frowned. "You say that still, when I saved you from the battle and allowed you to bind me?"

Ixul gaped. Ajul was getting so clever! He'd done

everything to earn Tatichwut's trust. Now she understood that, not only was he waiting to attack, he was planning to sacrifice these two in the cave. She wished she could reveal herself right now, if only to tell him how proud she was. But she had to be patient.

Tatichwut waved his hand. "Lead the way, then."

"I will need light to see, Tata," said Ajul. "There is pitch and pine on that ledge."

From the looks on their faces, it was clear that the fools had forgotten all about the necessity for light. Did they think the sun himself would descend to guide them?

Tatichwut snarled at the bowlegged farmer to prepare a torch. Meanwhile, he kept his spear on Ajul, though he stole looks downriver, watching for signs of pursuing Nahua. But there were none. The silence was strange. Ixul wondered—in a thought that became a vision that became a fact, as if she were in the soft twilight strip between waking and sleep—that there had been yet more betrayals, more reversals of fortune. She and Ajul had been betrayed by Tatichwut and his allies; Tatichwut had been betrayed by his own allies; and now, perhaps, those allies were turning on one another, squabbling over the last of the great city of Tzoyna like pecking turkeys. Ixul wanted to laugh. It all seemed so distant. She was no longer here. Her body was here to do this thing, but her thoughts were flying far and free to distant lands: Chichen Itza. Tula. Suecha. Cities of which she'd only heard legends.

The bowlegged farmer handed a torch to Tatichwut and took back his spear.

Tatichwut indicated to Ajul that he go first.

He did. Even from her hiding place, Ixul could read his expression: calm, indulging, even amused. She marveled at his composure. He was far taller than the farmers; he could kill one so easily, even bound as he was. But he was also restraining himself. The farther they went into the cave, the more potent the sacrifice.

Ajul stepped down into the pool. He let himself go under, then frog-kicked until he reached the other side. The others followed him. Tatichwut handed off his torch so he, too, could dunk himself in the water, in imitation of Ajul. Even despite all, they were in awe of him. They were like chicks following their mother.

Ixul waited until they were almost out of sight, then slipped into the pool herself. She immersed herself and, surfacing, mouthed the words that blessed her entry and improvisation. And did not these waters have healing powers? She felt herself refreshed. She followed the men up a stone stairway. For a moment she looked back at the entrance, the flame-shaped door to the middle-world, with its familiar greens and blues. Save for the flowing water, it was quiet. No battle. No betrayal. No Nahua. She would do this thing, and then she would start a new life, just as the Hero Twins had.

She turned and crawled up the stairway, keeping low.

She had to be careful. The steps were irregular, jagged in some places and smooth in others, not made for humans, but for gods and naguals and other creatures that lived here, seen and unseen. Soon the last of the light had vanished and there was only the single torch ahead. Ixul tried to keep within its light.

They reached the top of the stairs and passed through an archway of stone. The avenue ran level here. She could see only contours of things: dark squares set high in the rock, with no steps to reach them. Whether they were windows or passageways, she didn't know. But she could feel the gods here. There were many of them, and they had been here for a very long time, long before her grandmother was queen, long before her family had even built the city, long before the gods had even created humans or attempted to. The gods had been here first. Their names had been forgotten, many creations past. Still they kept watch.

She saw the men could feel it too. The guard's legs trembled in the water, and his spear wobbled. The sight of his cowardice gave Ixul courage. She belonged here more than he did. She was royal. She'd been raised to this. So had Ajul, who—descending into a new pool—still looked steady. His strength gave her strength. She waited until the torch dimmed, then slipped into the pool after them. She avoided looking directly at the torch, lest her eyes' reflection give her away.

They entered a large chamber. She couldn't see a ceiling. Around its perimeter, the ceiba roots from above had twisted down into the earth to make elegant pillars. Beyond them, she could only see distant points of light, like stars.

How could there be stars here? Had they passed into the firmament?

Ixul shivered, stayed close to the wall. Ajul was at the front of the group, his back red with torchlight. He was looking down into the water and reading the current. She trusted him. Whatever he did, he'd have to do carefully, since Tatichwut held the torch. If it fell into the water, they'd be in the dark. Ixul closed her eyes at the thought of having to navigate back out of the city in total darkness. There'd already been so many corners and turns and stairs and ledges and false branchings. She would starve before she made it back out, or die of the cold. Flowing water sapped the heat from a body, and she'd eaten nothing for a day, and lost so much blood.

She shivered again.

Ajul turned and spoke to the others in a low voice. It was unwise to speak too loudly in this place. She saw vapor in the torchlight, sparkling with gold. Maybe it was the breath of those distant stars.

Ajul pointed into the darkness, and they started forward again.

She was getting impatient for him to strike. He must know something she didn't; or, she hadn't guessed his plan. Ixul crept up the avenue. It was smooth here. The water flowed around her ankles.

She heard a splash behind her.

She looked and saw only the distant stars.

She remembered what Mutna had said: *Xibalba exists in the very same space as we do. It is with us, it is all around us, like two circles overlapping. Xibalba is the place behind the place. We cannot reach it; we can only see it, but there are some places in time and space where the borders are thinner than in others. The underworld is such a place.*

She followed her brother.

The avenue bent left, right, left again. The city was far bigger than she'd imagined. It was not only a city, but a whole river of cities connected together. She heard chirps and flutters overhead but didn't look. Looking at anything directly would be an act of challenge. She moved her lips, asking the gods to bless what she and Ajul were about to do. They would shed blood, yes, but the blood of those who trespassed on sacred ground. *May you gods of this place accept this sacrifice,* she said, *and in exchange, show us the way out.*

She shivered again, more violently. The avenue became another stairway that twisted down into a pool, then rose again. They passed under another archway. She heard another stream somewhere to the left, its music lighter and higher, as if many ocarinas were playing. She glimpsed another stairway above, one she could never reach, with steps as tall as she was. Who was it for? She kept getting distracted. She refocused on the party ahead. The bowlegged farmer seemed to have forgotten his task of guarding. He was concentrating on his footing. She could use that to her advantage.

Ixul realized that Ajul was waiting for the Tzoyna insignia to make his strike. He'd be first on the stairs, which would give him the advantage. She gripped her spear.

The party stopped. Ajul was pointing to a carving on the wall—the four-quartered star of the Tzoyna. A set of stairs led up to darkness, opposite.

This was the moment.

Ajul started up, and Tatichwut followed. Just as

she'd predicted. She crept forward. The guard was still at the foot of the stairs, looking up in thrall.

Ixul knew there would be no better time.

She took a deep breath and threw the spear at his head as hard as she could.

He swiveled at the sound, ducked her shot, and threw his own spear in the exact direction hers had come.

Ixul jumped on instinct to protect her viscera. The spearpoint went clean through her leg and stuck there, wagging out of her thigh, and she clenched her teeth, reached down, grasped the shaft protruding from the back of her leg, pulled it through, turned it over in her hand, planted, pivoted, and threw it back.

It punched clean through the hollow of his chest. He fell back into the water and the water bloomed red.

There was a cry from above. Tatichwut was staring down at her.

She splashed over to the farmer and pushed her foot on his shoulder to pull out the spear. He was still jerking; she put the spear through his brain. Then she put two fingers in her mouth and whistled upward, not feeling the pain in her mouth and thigh, not caring, just wanting to see Ajul's face so he'd know to do his part and they could finally leave.

He appeared, looking down at her.

His face was gentle.

"Sister," he said, "look at your blood."

Ixul stared up at him. She didn't understand why he wasn't acting on Tatichwut, who was hiding behind him.

She made handtalk: *Take the torch and let's go.*

"Sister," he said again, gently, pointing, "look at your blood."

Ixul looked down. The light was so dim, like a lunar eclipse; but she could make out the contrast of the dark against the clear, not only billowing from the farmer's chest and head, but from her own thigh.

All the blood was flowing upstream.

"We've come too far," he said. "You belong to Xibalba now, the same as I do."

She didn't understand. She didn't want to.

Ajul. She made his name sign. *Ajul. No. We go! You don't have to do this. We go and run and live a new life in a new land, like . . .* But even as she spoke, her signs became messy and desperate, and she found she couldn't recall any of the names of any of the lands she had longed to see. Xibalba had swallowed her memory.

"No," he said, with tenderness. "No, sister. Come up here to me. Let us go together. Don't you remember what we were taught? Our fate is tied to this place. We belong to these gods. If we leave them, we are less than nothing. But if we accept our death here, we will be reborn to live again."

I want to live now, she signed.

Now Ajul appeared only as a dark outline against the torchlight. Ixul imagined his gentle eyes and soft lips, arranging themselves in the familiar way.

She tried one last time.

Brother, come, she signed. *I need you.*

He paused, as if to say something. Then he turned and vanished from the lip of the ledge.

Darkness fell like a sheet of lightning.

She blinked, then opened her eyes again.

There was no difference.

THE CAVE
4 Ajwal 3 K'ank'in, Long Count 13.0.0.0.0

---

21 December, 2012

Leah knew it was time to go. There were petals of water coursing down the flowstones, just like in her dream.

As soon as Angelo had seen the signs, he'd hurried each tourist down from the ledge. Everyone became quiet, nervous, focused. When they were all down, he led the column back toward the entrance. She watched them go. She had no desire to follow. *The visible sun is not the real one.* Even Xander had said so, misguided as he was, otherwise.

She watched the last tourist disappear between the boulders.

Then she turned back to her beloved bend of darkness.

She went ahead a few paces. Now she was farther than she'd ever been before. This was the way no one spoke of. This was where Xander was so afraid to go. But how could anyone be afraid in this place? Cool water swirled over her sneakers. She crouched down and scooped up a handful of sand, gritty on her palm. Somehow everything inside the cave was more real than anything outside it.

She knelt in the water and faced the darkness.

Now that she was here, she felt shy and awkward, like a bride on her wedding night. She felt compelled to do some kind of ritual now. She needed to set her intent.

She held out her hands.

"Gods of the cave," she said in a grandiose voice that made her feel silly, "I ask your help in seeking Xibalba."

The darkness rushed upon her like a foaming surf.

"Your *help!*" she snapped. "I won't tolerate anything that means me harm."

The darkness boiled in on itself and receded to its usual depth.

She took a breath. She sensed the spirits here were not all good. But since she herself was good, she could command the bad ones to let her be. She should have done that first.

After a moment's thought, she realized she didn't even need to use fancy words—only to speak from the heart, as if to a friend. She tried again. "I saw the blade on Xander's table this morning," she said. "I took it. I tossed it into a field on the ride into town."

She allowed herself a moment of smugness. It'd been her little revenge for Xander being so mean this morning.

"At first, I thought about bringing it here and cutting myself with it. But I didn't. It felt wrong. Like I've already given you enough . . . and now you owe me."

She pulled her spandex pants away from her waist and angled toward the darkness, displaying the rows of scars along her hips, like gills.

She let the band snap back.

"All the blood I gave, you already have it. It came here. As soon as I touched down in Belize I sensed it was somewhere here, but I didn't know where, until I came to the cave."

She smiled.

"Anyway," she said, "I'm coming now."

She stood up and walked forward.

Spider threads floated toward her like the lips of a curtain.

The way was smooth. There were no obstacles, just a shallow river that curved left and right in gentle arcs.

There were sandbars and islands and crests of sliding stones. She picked one up and slung it, and it skipped five times before sinking. She saw a star on the wall and blew gently. The spider contracted like a hand. Once she saw one, she saw them everywhere, as if she were walking through the night sky.

She sloshed forward.

A heliconia petal floated by, red with a creamy edge. She smiled. Xander had told her about this exact thing.

As she walked, the walls of the cave began to take more regular form. She squinted at them, looking at them in different settings of the headlamp, unable to tell whether it was just a trick of the eye. But it seemed not to be. The more she looked, the more the planes and angles began to resemble hewn rock, as if she were surrounded by great works of masonry. They were weathered by the water, but if she looked at them sideways, she could make out crumbling arches, fallen keystones, ramparts and causeways, flagstones on their side—all limestone, with traces of red paint still visible, and green moss growing in the cracks. She wasn't walking through natural chambers. She was walking through rooms, an endless warren of rooms. This had once been a vast underground city. She sensed this place had been waiting for her for a long time, and shaped this passage to lure her in.

She sloshed forward.

As she walked, she thought about the plaster statue of Bloodmaiden at the Mexican restaurant in St. Cloud. She could visualize it perfectly: brown skin, orange robe, gold paint. That statue would be right at home here.

She saw another heliconia petal, rocking past like a little boat. She waved.

She thought about her conversation with Xander last night. He had asked her, what does desire have to do with entropy? She continued the conversation as if he were walking next to her. "Well, let's think about it," she said. "Entropy is upsetting because we think space is empty. But maybe it's the opposite. Maybe space is full."

Full of what? said Xander-in-her-head.

"Desire."

Sounds miserable.

"No, maybe it's not! How can a thing know itself if it doesn't split up? How can you really know you love me unless I leave you? The space between us is what makes us whole."

The river got wide and deep again. She walked in up to her neck and began to do a breaststroke. This room was long, maybe once a banquet hall, and the water was bright mineral blue in her headlamp. The current was stronger here. Bats flitted low, squeaking.

Then there was sand beneath her feet. She ascended into a new room and scanned it with her headlamp. It was a medium room with an island in the middle, around which the river parted in two branches. As she came up on the island, the sand turned to smooth, flat stones, sliding and grinding under her feet.

Ahead, there was only a solid rock wall.

It's the sump, said Xander-in-her-head, *the flooded passage.*

The end of the road.

But hadn't he said that the cave went on, farther than this? It couldn't be the *real* end. This room had the feel of a waiting room, like at the clinic in Minnesota, where she swung her legs waiting for the doctor, reading a copy of *National Geographic.* Maybe this room was a sort of test that she had to find her way out of.

Then she heard a note.

She stood still, not sure if it was real.

Silence again.

Had she imagined it? It had sounded like a conch shell, just like the one she'd heard at the Welcome Center two nights ago. She pressed her ear to the rock wall. This couldn't be the end of the road, not for her. She had to get to the other side of this wall.

She took stock of the chamber. On the left, there was a steep slope that led to a crevice. There was an apron of fine sand that looked like it had once been deposited by a water flow. That could be a passageway.

She climbed the slope. It was muddy and loose and littered with scree. The slope got steeper. A foothold gave way, and she lurched for a handhold to the side, but that slipped too, so she bellyflopped into the mud.

She paused to get her breath before trying again.

She got to her hands and knees and tried to stand up. This time she took a long time planning a sequence of holds that looked safe. She tried out the first two. Each hold held. But the higher she got, the farther she had to fall. She pressed her body to the slope and continued, crawling. *Get low*, she heard dear Javier's voice in her head. *Use as many points of contact as you need.* The more her body was in touch with the mud, the more friction there was, the less likely she would fall.

She pulled herself up on her belly. She didn't look down or she'd lose her nerve. *You're Maya*, Javier said. *I trust you will not lose your balance.* The crevice in the rock, the one she thought might lead to a passage forward, was another six feet above her. She knew it was open because she could feel the wind rushing out of it. She had to find out where the wind came from— maybe the same place as the conch.

She put her left foot on a shelf of rock. It held.

She hooked her left hand into a depression in the mud. It held.

She swung herself up to reach for a higher knob of rock, and her foothold collapsed.

As soon as she realized she was falling, there was nothing to do but ball up. She had the feeling that she was tumbling around a washing machine. She felt stabs in her shoulder and back and shin before hitting her helmet hard on the rock.

THE CAVE
10 Himux 19 Yaxk'in,
Long Count 15.10.14.10.1

---

20 December, 3012

Framing the entrance to the Great Cave of Laviaja was the second Arca de las Gemelas.

The monument consisted of two pillars, one on each side, each as thick as Niloux was tall. Carved into each pillar was a window shaped like a four-pointed star. In the middle of each window, there was a shriveled mummy suspended in static, chin on chest, looking down in benediction. They were the preserved bodies of Xander Cañul and Javier Magaña.

It was easy to tell them apart. Xander was robed in scarlet and maroon, his white beard reaching down to his belly, his withered hand clutching a book; Javier was robed in charcoal and grey, black-haired as the day he died, his hand wrapped around a walking stick. They looked like two regal chili peppers. There were offerings piled beneath each body: copal, candles, chocolate bars, coffee berries, balché, amber, marigolds, conch shells, coral, oranges, mangoes, calabashes. Then the offerings appropriate to the iconography of each: balls for Javier, quills for Xander. Gold suns for Javier, silver moons for Xander. Passion flower for Javier, heliconia for Xander.

Niloux touched her earspool, carved with heliconia.

Tanaaj's words on the court: *I call on Niloux DeCayo to play Xander Cañul this sacred night.*

She didn't turn on her aug. She didn't want to know.

She'd run all the way from Tzoyna. She'd run past the palace complex, past the first Arca, and up the road on the other side of the city. The rain had stopped. She asked her ai to direct her to the Great Cave, and the salmon line ran ahead of her, directing her up a series of footpaths before curving back north. She hadn't been pursued—not by anyone, not Tanaaj or even anyone of her own familia, but she didn't stop to think about it. She had only one thought: that she must find the remains of Saint Leah, settle the question of her "crossing over," and prevent this war before it began. Then she could go. Then she could finally leave this land. For how long she'd been stuck here, for how many lifetimes, she couldn't begin to guess.

Now she was here: the black flame in the mountain.

She activated her orgoscan function and set it to search for the genetic residue of Leah Magdalene Oliveri, on public record since 2206.

She stepped onto the threshold, avoiding the eyes of the two mummies, and descended into the entrance pool.

She could see that this place, like the ancient city, had been tamed. It had once been rough and wild and awe-inspiring. Now there was a smooth, raised pathway that began at the threshold, circled the pool, and continued up the waterfall on the other side, with starlights overhead guiding the way. Anyone could access it. There were no guards, no rules posted, no soldiers with guns, no ticket-takers. For a thousand years, the cave had been preserved by the mutual trust of millions of viajeras.

Niloux started up the path.

As she ascended the waterfall, she noticed tiny sparkles all over the rock. She stepped closer to examine one, then jerked away. She was face-to-face with an enormous spider, soft grey, with kinked legs the size of her hand. Its eye shone like a diamond.

Sacred whip spiders. The ones whose eyes Leah had

mistaken for stars—*las estrellas actuales*—and, Xander Cañul had argued, might as well be stars to Leah's augmented mind, tumor-pressed. Niloux touched her fingers to her forehead, where her own ojos-de-Leah grew behind her skull. After Javier's death, Xander had gone to Boston to work with Ida Gudasz and Micah Wells, and written *Entropy and the Decoherence of Meaning*, laying the foundation for the Laviaji Principle of Dispersion.

But before that, he had walked through this cave, thousands of times.

She stood on the path, between the pool and the waterfall.

She couldn't grasp the significance of this place. It was impossible.

She stopped trying and walked up the path.

Star-lights overhead, actual stars on the walls. Her orgoscan had picked up nothing so far. Leah Oliveri had been this way five times, twice on the way out and three times on the way in, and fainted once; but any evidence of her passage would have long been washed away. The orgoscan would pick up bones, though. Bones lasted. She reviewed what she knew about the cave. There were three major sections: the light zone, the dark zone, the sump. A mile in was the Step-Up Rock, which led up to the Maya burial chamber, the big draw of the tourist era. But the sump—where Leah was thought to have headed—was at the end of the main river passage, another mile in. Beyond that was an unknown hellscape. At least, it had been in Leah's time. In the Laviaji era, no one went there. It was too sacred. It was considered to be Saint Leah's realm.

The farther Niloux walked, the more she could recognize the features of the cave, anticipating them before she saw them. She didn't even need her aug turned on to know she was retracing her steps from a past life. She knew when the path would branch, the right fork leading down into a narrow channel. She departed from the path, swam through it. Now another prediction: she would step up out of this channel into a chamber with a sinkhole at the top.

She did.

Next, a reflecting pool.

Next, a smaller sacrifice chamber with a high ledge.

Next, a Virgin Mary flowstone.

Next, the Step-Up Rock. She looked up and to the left, to confirm what she remembered: there was a four-quartered star carved there. It wasn't visible unless you knew to look for it.

She went on.

Past that point, she didn't recognize anything.

Xander Cañul had famously been afraid of this

part of the cave. He'd walked it once, alone; he was found the next morning, remembering nothing. He refused to return, even to pay homage to Leah, even when he was dying himself and the supposed healing waters of the sump might have saved him. But Niloux didn't feel afraid. She felt sad. The path winded, a travertine ribbon, through chamber after chamber, beautiful and desolate; and below it the river ran smooth and clear, shallow in some stretches and deep in others. Even by the dim star-lights, she could see all the way to the bottom, where blind fish bumped against the stones.

Then Niloux saw a change in the light ahead. The path ended in a small chamber of mottled stone, with candles set in the walls, each a different shade of green. There was a solid rock wall at the far end and the river welled from beneath it.

In front of the rock wall, kneeling on a sandbank, there was a tall viajera wearing a blue silk skirt tied at the hip. The fabric rippled in the water.

"Hello," she said.

Niloux was very annoyed. She'd been in her own reverie and wanted to stay there. Besides, she needed to keep focused on her work. This was the last place Leah was known to have been—the initial search teams had found handprints high up on the scree, where the flood hadn't reached—so this was where her search really started. To keep looking for the remains of Leah, she'd have to wait until this viajera was gone, or explain what she was doing, which she did not want to do.

"Who are you?" she said.

"That's not a very kind greeting."

Niloux grimaced, regrouped. "Yo soy Niloux. Quisiera venir . . ."—she gestured to the holiest spot on Earth—"aquí."

The viajera smiled. "Ven en paz. Soy Sembaruthi."

Niloux paused. "Sembaruthi? DeSiruvani?"

The other smirked. "Niloux? DeCayo?"

There was a long silence as they stared at each other. This put Niloux even more on edge. She didn't know anything about this adivinix except by reputation, and that she'd been silent on the struggle between the Zeinians and the LFC, which Niloux was glad for because she suspected her of being sympathetic to the LFC, given her work as an adivinix—what else could she be, if she still subscribed to the idea of cortadas and disappearances? But she didn't know for sure. So for the second time tonight, she said, "Yes, that's me. What are you doing here?"

"The god told me to come here and wait. So I am."

A real scrupe, then. She'd have to be careful. "Wait for what?"

Sembaruthi shrugged. "Maybe you." She held up a golden earspool. "Looks like this is yours."

Niloux took it from her and immediately dropped it.

She'd felt the same shiver of nausea she'd felt in Meknes. She bent down to look at it. The earspool was the exact match of her other, down to the heliconia pattern.

"Put it in!" said Sembaruthi. "It'll look nice."

Niloux glanced up.

Sembaruthi flinched at her expression, held up her hands. "Okay, you don't have to put it in."

"Where did you get this?"

"It was here when I got here. Half-buried."

"Who left it?"

"Who knows? Maybe the river gave it up."

Niloux stood, staring at it. She didn't pick it up. "The god told you to come to the sump chamber specifically?"

"Sort of. I performed a divination for myself and the god just told me to follow in the footsteps of Saint Leah until I couldn't anymore."

"Looking for your cortada?" Niloux couldn't keep the contempt out of her voice.

Sembaruthi was silent a moment, as a rebuke. "No," she said at last, "that was not my question to the god. My question was how to heal the schism in Laviaja."

Niloux frowned, eyed the hill of scree to the left, still thinking of her mission. "There's no healing it now."

"Because Tanaaj tried to attack you?"

Niloux turned back. "How did you know?"

"I saw it when I sat down with her for divination. That she intended you harm."

"And you didn't tell me?"

"No, the god directed me elsewhere. But I did tell your friend Emelle and sent her to follow Tanaaj."

"A lot of good that did," Niloux snapped. "She tried. She said she wanted me to play Xander Cañul. Then when she saw I wasn't taking her ridiculous bait, she started—" She was yelling now, and her yelling filled the chamber.

Sembaruthi winced, waited for the silence to settle.

Niloux crossed her arms, stayed where she was.

"She was not well, when I saw her," said Sembaruthi quietly. "She has many defenses built up, which many don't see, because she appears to be so kind."

Niloux wanted to say, *Kind to whom?* but held her tongue. She wanted to hear more.

"She's wrestling with a great hurt. Whether from this life or previous lives, I don't know. But it has caused her to be what she is, and I think this schism made it worse."

"It's not my fault."

"Maybe not in this life. But maybe a previous one. And before that, maybe she hurt you, who knows."

Niloux thought of her past-lives technique, chafed at its limits. "But we can't know for sure."

"It doesn't matter. It's clear you're bound together in some way."

"She's my birth twin."

Sembaruthi raised her eyebrows. "Oh?"

"Well, we think so. Her birth child, Messe, looks just like me. We were both born in Cayo in the same year. It adds up."

"I can't say I'm surprised."

"Why, some mystical intuition?"

"No. Same nose."

Niloux laughed. She remembered the oasis, and Venus rising over the water. She nudged the earspool with her foot. "So you want to heal the schism."

"I think you couldn't have realized what you'd started at Zein-o-Din."

"That's for damn sure."

"You think cortadas aren't real?"

"I keep saying, I don't know," Niloux said in exasperation. "But at least I wanted to ask the question. Yes, people have been disappearing for centuries and we can't explain it. But yes, fewer are disappearing now. What if it's because—"

This time, the desire rose up to say the thing out loud, and she didn't stop it.

"What if it's because there are no cortadas left on Earth, and we have to go out into the universe to find them?"

Niloux's voice had cracked like that of a petulant child. She felt humiliated. Now she'd done it. She'd killed her credibility. Sembaruthi would go back out into the world and tell everyone how selfish and delusional she really was.

But the adivinix just raised her eyebrows with a look of contemplation. She sat back on her heels, giving space to the words and letting the implications resonate.

At last she smiled and said, "You might be right."

Niloux felt a weight lift.

She looked up to the hill of scree to the left.

Her desire to search for Leah melted away, like the last of the ice.

"Oh!" said Sembaruthi, her eyes unfocusing. She was looking at the display in her aug. She blinked, refocused on Niloux. "Feliz Día de Pasaja."

Niloux summoned the time. It was just past midnight.

"How is she?" said Tanaaj, as soon as she opened her eyes. "How is my child?"

Emelle looked down, her face tight. "She's alive."

Tanaaj got up on her elbows and craned her neck. She couldn't see Messe. The child was still surrounded by medics and, now, viajeras kneeling in twos and threes, who appeared to be praying. "Still alive, but what, hermanix? You are not telling me everything."

"Her blood is replenished," she said, "but she hasn't woken up. If she doesn't in the next hour, the chances decrease that she ever will."

"Why, hermanix? Why doesn't she wake up, if she has all the blood she needs?"

"Because the soul doesn't always want to," Emelle said.

Tanaaj began to get up, her task in mind. "All right then. How do we make her want to?"

Emelle pushed her back down and held her shoulder in place.

"You must not go to her," she said.

Tanaaj remembered, now, what her child had said.

She turned her head and began to cry.

Emelle's hand on her shoulder became lighter, comforting. Finally quiet came.

"What can we do?" Tanaaj asked.

"There's nothing to do," said Emelle, "except keep her comfortable."

"But there is nothing here on this ball court to make her want to wake up."

Emelle spread her hands, exasperated. "She loved Niloux, she idolized her, but—"

The unsaid thing: *you drove her away.* With pain, Tanaaj remembered the grand plan, the clumsy lunge, the slip on the stone. She had tried to murder Niloux. She had murdered Ying Yue, before that. She didn't know herself. She didn't want to be in her body anymore.

"Then take her to Niloux," said Tanaaj.

Emelle looked down at her, surprised.

"Wherever she is. Take her."

"And what will you do?"

"I will stay here." But then she was scared. The ancient city was damp and cold and full of enemies. She didn't want to be left alone here. "No. I would like to follow."

"How can I trust you?"

Tanaaj shook her head, hating herself. "You cannot. I understand."

Emelle sighed, then said, "Wait here."

She got up and joined the other medics. They spoke in low voices, sometimes looking over at Tanaaj, sometimes beyond the city wall. One nodded, another shook her head, another rubbed her eyes. They continued to discuss.

No one stood near her. None of the viajeras who had run with her were anywhere to be seen; not Angela, not Hecate. The play was over. Her life was over. The Tzoyna would blot her for attempted murder and she would wander the world alone. She had to accept that now.

Emelle came back. She said, "We're going to do as you suggested. Niloux went to the Great Cave. So we're going to put Messe on a steadifoil, and for the sake of speed I'll be the only one steering it, to catch up with her." She paused. "The others don't want you to follow."

Tanaaj's voice stuck in her throat. She spoke through her tears. "I do not think I should be alone, hermanix."

"Do you have anyone you can go to?"

She thought of all the people she had left behind. "No, hermanix."

Emelle looked up: the steadifoil had arrived. The medics were beginning to slide it under the child's body; once there, the steadifoil lifted on its air cushion. Messe's arm flopped, her wrist dangling. A medic tucked it back.

"You can follow me," said Emelle, "if you stay

back. I'll tell the others not to obstruct you." She went ahead.

Tanaaj got up. She was wet and sore and filthy. Her shift was caked in mud. She waited until Emelle began and followed at a distance. She kept her head down. She felt the contempt of everyone watching. She deserved it. She wanted to apologize to everyone. She focused on righting at least this wrong: seeing Messe safely delivered to Niloux. Then she would leave and never return. She would exile herself and lead a life of penance.

Emelle took the footpath out of the city, until they came to a swollen creek bridged by a limestone arch. *Roaring Bridge*, Tanaaj registered. She knew all of the landmarks of this holy place by heart. She'd spent her life longing to see them. Now she wasn't worthy of any of it. She begged whatever gods would listen to forgive her this trespass, that she would see Messe delivered and then go. They crossed the bridge. The storms had blown away. The full moon shone in a lane of sky overhead and its light was cold and yellow.

She followed Emelle and the steadifoil up and down limestone ramps.

La Plaza de la Trinidad.

La Musea de la Cueva Grande, with bottles of holy cave water to take away.

The second Arca de las Gemelas, with the preserved bodies of Javier and Xander.

Tanaaj didn't look up. She felt nothing. She followed Emelle and the steadifoil.

When she entered the cave, she recognized it as she had the land. But this time, she saw it from far outside herself, as a distant curiosity. She did not care. Whatever desire she had once felt to come here, it was gone now. In its place there was dread. She followed Emelle up the waterfall and through the boulders. This was clearly a place of death. She followed through a large chamber, then a long lane, then a curve. She was falling behind. She remembered the green obsidian blade still against her chest. She fingered its weight. Why commit to a life of exile, when she could end it now and start over? The cave seemed to be filling up with darkness. She had lost sight of Emelle. She trusted she would get Messe to Niloux, where she needed to be. She didn't deserve to see it done. She stopped on the path. She wouldn't go any farther. Emelle had been generous in letting her come, but she didn't want anyone to have to worry about her anymore. How long had she been sick? At least a year. Why hadn't anyone told her? She'd chosen the wrong cause. She was so embarrassed. Nothing justified this. Whatever had spoken to her from the Other World had misused her. They were not good; they were the death gods of Xibalba who lived to deceive. The water began to rise now, foaming brown cacao, washing over the path ahead. She stopped to get her footing, adjust her backpack. She recounted her supplies: rope, flashlight, extra batteries. She knew that Xander would regret this for the rest of his life, leaving her alone in a flooding cave, even after she'd said, *Ah need yu, breda.* Xander would never get over the guilt of that. He would spend the rest of his life making up for it. He, Javier, would take comfort in that knowledge when he found Leah and rescued her, and they both got out of here alive, carrying her like a bridegroom carrying his bride over the threshold of the world, and they would return to San Ignacio and marry and have a child together. Maybe ten. Tanaaj unraveled the blade from her chest. She wanted to carry it, just to feel its comfort, that she had the option near at hand. The darkness was up to her shins. He'd seen maps of the cave: he estimated another ten minutes of running before he reached the terminal sump. Beyond that, Leah wouldn't dare to go. There was nowhere *to* go—no way through. He tripped and fell face-first into the water. He got a mouthful of brown river. He pushed himself to all fours and spat it out. The current was so strong it almost lifted his palms from the sand. He'd been wrong to trust Xander. His brother had been sabotaging him his whole life. There was no reason he'd ever stop. Xander hated him. He didn't know why. He hadn't done anything wrong. The lesson was that Javier should never count on anyone, ever, especially no one of his own flesh. Where was Leah? He shouted her name. He stood in the river, bent his forehead to his hands, said, *May all the gods be with me*, and then started running. Rock, rock, beach, stream, sand, current getting stronger, river bubbling and foaming like chocolate milk, up to his thighs now. He saw a solid rock wall ahead, but then a wall of water surged from under it and lifted him off his feet and slammed him against the ceiling and just like that, his life was extinguished. This, Tanaaj did not want to live through again. She did not want to drown again. She was always the sacrifice, always the martyr, in every age. That was her destiny. And now she had arrived at her destiny again: the Option was in her hand, so she stretched her arm before her as if granting a princely boon, and set the blade to her skin.

"Tanaaj," said a voice.

She looked up.

Standing on the path was Niloux, wearing two golden earspools now instead of one.

"Stop," she said. "Give it to me." She came forward and held out her hand.

Tanaaj stepped back. "You cannot take this away from me."

Niloux's face changed, as if she were remembering something that troubled her, and then it passed. "I assure you," she said with a small smile, "I can be as stubborn as you."

Tanaaj was surprised by the smile. She said, "I had intended to kill you, hermanix."

Niloux let her hand drop to her side. "I know."

"Do you hate me?"

Niloux laughed. "If you can believe it—no."

Tanaaj was confused. "But you should."

Niloux nodded. "You're right, I should. You've been a self-righteous ass." She held out her hand. "Now, give me the blade."

"You left me here to drown," said Tanaaj.

Niloux paused. A darkness passed over her face. "I'm sorry," she said.

She took another step closer.

"Just let me see it. I promise I'll give it back to you."

At last Tanaaj held it out.

Niloux plucked it between her thumb and forefinger. At first she shivered at the touch, but then recovered. She held it up to the star-lights.

"I think," she said, "we've both known this blade for a long time."

Tanaaj nodded. She stared at it. Now that it was out of her hands, she craved it. She'd find a way to get it back, her Option, and then go into her exile as long as she could stand it, before she'd find some windy cliff-top with a beautiful view, and then she would do it.

"Why did you come here tonight?" asked Niloux.

"To make sure Messe got to you. Why did you?"

"To find Leah."

"And did you?"

Niloux shook her head. "Maybe I have," she said, "many times over." She beckoned. "Come on. Messe needs you too."

"She hates me."

"Then come for me." She held out her hand. "Ah need yu, sista."

Still, Tanaaj couldn't move.

Niloux put the blade in her pocket, came close, and scooped Tanaaj up in her arms. Tanaaj clung to her like a child.

Her twin was heavy, pure muscle on small bones, just like Niloux. She smelled familiar, like dirt and woodsmoke. She began to remember her traits, like following a text in a dream, one line leading to the next: that she trusted too easily. That she didn't sleep well. That she found fulfillment in obedience. That she was sensual and unkempt. Even now, she was so dirty, her mud rubbing off on Niloux's huipil.

She carried Tanaaj back to the sump chamber. Emelle was there, kneeling at Messe's feet. Sembaruthi knelt at her head. At a look from Niloux, neither asked questions.

Still holding her twin, Niloux knelt next to Messe. The child's chest rose and fell rapidly. Her eyeballs twitched under her eyelids as if she were dreaming.

Tanaaj opened her eyes. At the sight of the others, she curled up and pressed her forehead to Niloux's neck.

"It's okay," said Niloux. "They're not going to hurt you."

"They hate me," Tanaaj whispered.

"They don't. They understand."

"Don't leave me."

So Niloux continued to hold her.

Emelle looked down, wiped her eye.

Niloux felt awkward. "That was one hell of a *La Estrella*," she said.

No one laughed.

Sembaruthi shrugged. "Maybe it hasn't ended."

The comment seemed designed to draw out Tanaaj, even flatter her; but she made no sign she'd heard, and continued to breathe into Niloux's collarbone.

Niloux looked at Messe. "How is she?"

"Still reluctant to return, I think." Sembaruthi placed a hand on her forehead. "And Emelle says the window is passing for her to do so."

"What can we do?"

Sembaruthi stroked a finger down Messe's cheek. Her armbands glittered in the candlelight.

Finally she said, "For whatever reason she doesn't want to come back, I think its ultimate source is the rift between you two," she said. "Maybe you can try to heal it."

Niloux hugged her twin to her body. "I think we have."

"Not in this life," said Sembaruthi. "I mean the root of it."

"What, by seeing our past lives?"

"You've already begun to," said Emelle.

"But I can only see past pistas. That tells us nothing. And we don't have years of time to work."

"I don't mean healing through sofist technique," said Sembaruthi, her voice calm. "I mean a far more ancient technique."

Tanaaj straightened up, so suddenly that Niloux almost dropped her.

"Where is the blade?" said Tanaaj.

Niloux frowned. "Why?"

"I know what we must do, hermanix."

"I don't want you to—"

"No." She said it with a pained look, and shook her head as if to banish a thought. "Don't give it to me, give it to Sembaruthi."

Niloux believed her. She pulled the blade from her pocket and handed it over. A part of her began to understand.

Sembaruthi balanced it on her palm, held it up to her eye. "Pretty!" she said.

"Use it," Tanaaj said. "On us."

Niloux was alarmed. "What do you mean?"

"To let blood."

Emelle was disgusted. "I don't understand," she said. "Why would you want to do that?"

Sembaruthi looked thoughtful. "That's what the first viajeras used to do, in early Laviaja," she said. "They'd come to this chamber to take psilocybin mushrooms and make a blood offering."

"But why?"

"For an intention. Here it was usually to ask the god of this place for healing."

"How do you know this?"

Sembaruthi smiled. "I am an adivinix, Emelle. It's my work to know ritual history, including lost techniques. And moreover, today is Eleven Ik', a day to plead with the gods that we may avert disaster."

"Too late," said Tanaaj.

Niloux remembered this too: her sense of humor.

Tanaaj disentangled herself from Niloux, gently, then stood up and knelt on the other side of Messe. The twins faced each other over Messe's body, almost with shyness. Sembaruthi was right: they did have the same nose.

"I'll do it," said Tanaaj. "I will ask for healing for Messe."

Now Niloux remembered Messe pressing her, earlier, on the court. *I don't think bloodletting has to be violent,* she'd said. *It's all about the intention.*

"I'll do it with her," said Niloux.

Her twin smiled at her for the first time.

Sembaruthi nodded. "Then let's do it quickly. Wash your hands."

They both dipped their hands in the water.

"Induce psilocybin."

Niloux touched her temple and Tanaaj, her heart, to give their ai the command.

"Give me your fingers."

They held out their index fingers, side to side.

"Emelle," said Sembaruthi, "catch the blood."

Emelle cupped her hands beneath their fingers.

"It'll hurt."

Niloux looked at Tanaaj, into her reddish-black irises, the bar of candlelight reflected across each eye.

"Ready," Sembaruthi said.

She curled her hand around their two fingers as if binding them, closed her eyes, bowed her head. Tanaaj did not blink. Niloux felt the psilocybin starting to work.

"We ask the god of this place," said Sembaruthi, "to heal this child."

She drew the blade across their fingers in one hard stroke.

The twins leaned toward each other, made no sound, touched foreheads.

Then their mouths fell open, and they were looking at themselves from below.

Tanaaj fell backward, away from her own slumped body, and hit a shelf of sand at an awkward angle, against her neck. Her hands flew out to find a handhold but there was only wet rock and sand that crumbled where she touched it. The light from the candles dimmed, extinguished. She wanted to yell for Niloux but couldn't stop tumbling enough to produce a word.

She hit open space.

She opened her eyes.

She was falling toward a bright river in golden sand.

When she landed, she was kneeling in the same position as before, forehead still pressed against Niloux's. But Sembaruthi, Emelle, and Messe were gone.

The twins looked at each other in incredulity.

Niloux said, "Did you just—?"

And Tanaaj said, "Yes, I just—!"

The ground gave way, and they both fell through.

Tanaaj pulled in her limbs to protect her viscera. She was still tumbling down a chute of rock and sand, hearing streams and waterfalls. She couldn't see Niloux. She didn't know if her twin was falling in the same chute or a parallel chute or another chute altogether.

She hit open space.

She opened her eyes.

She fell into a foaming cacao flood.

She didn't want to relive this. She had already. She was done with it, because this time, his twin had come back for him.

He fell through.

He opened his eyes.

He was descending onto a travertine labyrinth, and saw two figures: one was skinny, holding a torch, and the other was himself, Royal Prince Ajul B'uluch Chab of the Tzoyna, descended from the Hero Twins.

THE CAVE
4 Eb 15 Pop, Long Count 10.9.5.7.12

---

10 December, 1012

"You left her!" said Tatichwut. "I thought you loved her!"

Ajul strode from pool to pool. He felt detached and superior. On the ledge, he had become angry with Ixul, but he did not want to defile his body with anger when he was so close to his sacrifice. Anger would taint his next life. He chose serenity instead. "In the end, Tata, my sister is responsible for her own life," he said. "It is not my fault she chooses fear. I had wished to die with her at my side, but she is making everything more difficult for herself." Ajul paused, a moment of remorse. "Maybe when you return to the river, she will have reconsidered, and you can bring her to where I am."

"But—"

Ajul turned to him. The suddenness of the gesture made Tatichwut flinch, step back, and teeter on the lip of a pool.

Ajul lurched forward to steady him, even as his hands were still bound. The torch was saved.

They both took a breath.

Ajul smiled. "Would you like me to take the torch, Father? You would have to untie me."

Tatichwut looked uncertain.

"Tata," said Ajul, trying to call all his native gentleness into his voice, "if I had wanted to kill you, I could have done so twenty times already. Do you still not trust me?"

Tatichwut cowered. "But we're so far in!" he said. "They say blood is more powerful, the deeper you go in. Maybe that's why you waited."

"That is possible," Ajul conceded. "I do not know how to make you trust me. You are not of royal blood, and therefore you are not used to such places as this. You are frightened. That is natural."

Tatichwut looked out of the corners of his eyes. Ajul looked with him. The floor looked like a honeycomb, each pool mirrored in the torchlight. But instead of bees emerging from the cells, there were captives, dozens of them, ahead, behind, on all sides, sitting enthroned in their pools, all facing down the terraces that led to the river, as if waiting for someone.

Ajul spoke into the dark for Xibalba to hear. "I am not afraid," he called. "I am descended from the Hero Twins, born of the Bloodmaiden. I am the last of the royal line of the Tzoyna, taken captive according to the eternal law that governs this world and the Other. This is my place, where I die by my own will and shall be reborn in peace." He turned to Tatichwut. "And as long as I am with this man, no harm will come to him."

Tatichwut's eyes were big. "But . . ." He made a gulping sound, and his eyes welled with tears.

"But what, Tata?"

"Now I don't want to kill you," Tatichwut blurted. "I've never killed anyone."

The farmer shuddered with sobs. Ajul remembered he'd also broken down in tears after being defeated on the ball court in Pekwitz. This man had an envious but tender nature. Ajul reminded himself that a captive never got to choose who his captor would be; he could only accept his appointed role in the play. With acceptance—no matter how odious the circumstance—came unexpected gifts, such as this. Now Ajul saw that although Tatichwut was a man of fragile constitution, he was capable of passion and devotion too. Maybe this man had always been in love with him.

"Also I lied," Tatichwut sobbed. He seemed to need to confess. "I don't have Ket. I saw the god take her just as you did. I just picked up the blade from the court where it fell."

Ajul remembered his baby sister, letting blood from her finger.

I ask the god of this place to heal the Tzoyna, she'd said.

She had looked so small, legs askew, like a whip spider.

"I forgive you," said Ajul.

But Tatichwut was still covering his face.

"Cut my rope, Father," said Ajul. "I will carry the torch and help you complete your task."

Tatichwut wiped his nose on his arm, nodded, sawed through his ropes with a flint knife. "Take it," he said, handing over the torch.

Ajul lifted the torch high and looked ahead. The labyrinth rose in steps, like the farming terraces of the middleworld, but as glimpsed in a fever dream. Here, no maize grew; only flesh. A hundred victims slumped in their seats, jaws ajar, eyes sunk, chins on chests, wisps of hair stirring in unseen currents.

"Should we choose one of these pools?" said Tatichwut.

"No," said Ajul. "There is a certain chamber,

farther in, where we intended to put our captives. I shall take their place."

"How do you know where it is?"

"Our daykeeper prepared me. She told us to go through a wall to the left, and then look for a ladder."

So Ajul led from rim to rim, up the terraces. He greeted the victims in his heart as if greeting comrades: a woman wearing an old-fashioned Mutulian huipil, a warrior with his hair in a topknot, a man with a king's breastplate, and two babies curled up like larvae.

At last the pools ended in a wall of boulders. A stair led to a narrow opening between them. Ajul led the way through, over the sound of running water, somewhere far below. Then the stairs led down again, to a smaller chamber with a sloping floor.

There: a wooden ladder leading to an upper room.

Ajul felt at peace, as if he had found his childhood bedchamber.

"Here, Father," said Ajul, lifting the torch.

Tatichwut eyed the ladder, still teary.

"I'll go first," said Ajul. He climbed the ladder with one hand, careful to hold the torch away from the wood. When he got to the top, he looked around. The room was shaped like a tomb, long and narrow, as if made for him. There was a mirrorlike pool by the wall, fed by drips from above. The walls glittered with crystal of red and cream and gold.

"Here," he said.

Tatichwut fumbled past Ajul in the narrow space. Neither knew what to say. Now that they'd chosen the place, they were bashful, like naked newlyweds.

"It's beautiful enough," said Tatichwut, "for you."

"I agree," said Ajul. He pointed to a spot against the wall. "Here is as good a place as any."

Ajul knelt with his back to the wall, still holding the torch.

Tatichwut looked terrified. Sweat trickled down his face. He fumbled in his leather pouch and pulled out a wad of cloth. He dropped it, cursed. He picked it up again and unwound it: the green obsidian star blade, heirloom of the Tzoyna from when the world was new.

Ajul had never felt such peace in his life.

Tatichwut was staring at the torch in Ajul's hand, and the blade in his own. "How do we . . ."

Ajul laughed. "Take the torch. You cannot very well get out without light. Look: with one hand, you can strike, and with the other, you can hold the torch. See?"

But Tatichwut didn't move. "You really want me to do it?"

"Yes," said Ajul. He pushed down his dirty esh and threw it to the side so that he was naked.

Tatichwut looked to the side, breathing hard. "I don't know how to do it . . ."

"Listen," said Ajul. "Look at me."

Tatichwut did.

"You will cut my throat," said Ajul. "You will stay with me till my breath leaves my body and my chest is still. You will pull the jade labret from my lip and take it with you. You will take the torch and go back the way you came, down the ladder, through the wall, down the terraces, down the stairs to the main avenue where the river flows. You will walk with the current until you return to the middleworld. There, you will present the jade labret to those who have claimed the Tzoyna, as proof that you have killed the king and therefore have a right to the throne."

"I want the Tzoyna to become a light to the world," said Tatichwut.

Ajul nodded. "I believe you. What will you do to make it so?"

The farmer spoke eagerly: "We will become a great pilgrimage site again," he said, "as in ancient times. Where the first Hero Twins entered and were victorious. This is why the land is sick: there are no pilgrims. The land misses them. The land misses their feet. I've always felt so."

Ajul smiled and said, "I believe you, Tatichwut of Pekwitz. You will bring them back."

Then he reached out and guided Tatichwut's hand to the stem of the torch. "Hold the torch firmly," he said. "I will help you hold it until I can't anymore. When you cut, draw the point in an arc under my throat. Here"—he drew a line with his thumbnail—"to here. Come closer. Press hard and be quick."

Tatichwut shuffled forward on his knees. There were fresh tears in his eyes.

"Are you ready?" he said.

"Yes, Father," said Ajul.

"Then may the gods receive you."

Ajul felt the point under his ear, and wanted a moment to relish the cool pinprick, but Tatichwut leaned in as instructed and slashed so deep that Ajul felt the slice at the back of his windpipe.

Blood poured down his chest like an apron and filled his throat and squirted out onto the stone.

He coughed. He couldn't help it. More blood spilled out of his mouth. He struggled to breathe and choked on more blood. He was a fish drowning in the air.

Even a death this quick was not quick enough.

Ajul forced himself to stop trying to breathe, clenched his chest, told himself to embrace death as he had embraced pain so many times before, to embrace it as a warrior does, to feel it even more deeply, to seek it out, to welcome and befriend and enthrone it, to feed it morsels, to wash its feet, to fan its face, to comb its hair, to kiss its brow, to anoint it with oils, and as his eyes finally, blessedly began to go dark, he saw Tatichwut tremble, stand up too quickly, lose his balance, and fall back into the pool, the torch with him.

After Ajul abandoned her, Ixul stood in the darkness for a long time.

She tried to remember the middleworld, but Xibalba had begun to claim those memories, too. She did know that the Nahua had taken her city. Her family had been wiped out. Ajul was going to his death, obedient till the end; as stubborn as she, in another way. But Ixul still planned to leave. She would get out of this place, recover her memory, and proceed alone. But before she did, she wanted to meet the gods. She wanted to face them just like the Hero Twins had. They owed her answers. Why had her brother abandoned her? That would be her first question.

She felt her way down to the stone and began to crawl against the current. She was a daykeeper. A daykeeper must roll the sacred rounds like bracelets on the wrist, naming each god of the day. She would crawl until she had named all two hundred sixty gods of the Sacred Round and then she would start again, until she had counted all the way forward to the next baktun. She would question every one.

She stopped, sat up, signed in the void:

GOD EIGHT CHAK: WHY DID AJUL ABANDON ME?

She wasn't sure how long she'd been crawling. She did know she was cold, so cold that the raw stump of her tongue had gone numb, and her leg was numb too where the spear had gone through, and that she was crawling with her right hand in water and her left hand touching the wall. Didn't this water have healing powers? Was the water healing her? It was hard to tell. Her shivers were becoming shudders. The warmth was leaching from her stomach.

She stopped, sat up, signed in the void:

GOD NINE AJWAL: I CURSE ALL THAT I TOUCH.

She wanted to get into a sweat bath. In a few minutes she'd stop, nap, and then keep going. Sleep seemed like a delicious, hot, foaming drink of cacao. She'd been hungry before, but now she seemed to be beyond hunger. That was a good sign. The water was healing her, after all. The shuddering had turned into a kind of food, sustaining her. She was beginning to see shapes in the darkness—edges of things—but they slid away as soon as she looked at them.

She stopped, slapped her own cheek to stay awake, signed in the void:

GOD TEN HIMUX: WHAT IS XIBALBA?

Ten Himux was a very powerful day. As an offering, she wrenched the stalk of heliconia out of her hair, pulled off the petals, threw them into the water one by one. She stopped, overcome by giggles. The giggles seemed an answer to her prayer, built into a cackle, became a wheezing wordless yell that echoed up and down the river.

The fit passed.

She went on.

She crawled for an hour, maybe two, maybe ten, always testing the water with her hand. This was who she was: a seeker, a traveler, a voyager. She had always been. Ajul was not. Ajul loved home and family and familiarity—he loved them too much. He was weak. At the first sign of danger he'd lain down like a deer. That was his nagual. He was prey. He was born to be prey, to lie down, to sacrifice himself with no objection. But Ixul's nagual was a spotted jaguar. She was predator. She was born to hunt.

What day was next?

She couldn't remember. Shudders shook her like a

washerwoman flapping a sheet. Was she counting forward or backward now?

GOD ELEVEN IK': WHY DID AJUL ABANDON ME?

Eleven Ik' was a day to plead with the gods to avert disaster. Too late! she thought, and laughed at herself again. The laughter came from higher up in her chest now, garbled by the stump of her tongue. She seemed unable to breathe from her belly. She curled up in the water, her cheek to the sand, listening to the pleasant music of the water and letting her eyes close, just for a moment.

Then she saw a glow ahead.

She sat up and squinted at it. It didn't go away.

Her curiosity won over her sleepiness. She crawled toward the glow. At first it seemed only a trick of the eye, but then it got brighter.

She crawled forward until she felt sliding stones beneath her hands.

There at last, in front of her, was a god.

He wore strange clothing, red on the top and green on the bottom, each leg wrapped. He was hunched over, looking at something on the ground, and his back was turned to her. He held up something he'd dug out of the sand: a bright gold earspool, exactly the same as the one in her ear.

She tried to stand up but she was too weak. She crashed back into the water. She mustered all her strength to push herself up again, to come up right behind him and get up to kneeling and make her hands sign:

WHICH GOD ARE YOU?

The god whipped around and for one moment they locked eyes and Ixul saw the whites all around his eyes and then, at that moment, something heavy crashed into them from above.

Niloux landed atop two other bodies.

They crashed and rolled and came to all fours, fingers splayed on the stones.

One was a naked teenager, her face tattooed with a jade star, and her body riddled with open wounds. Her lips were blue and her fingers were white.

The other was Xander Cañul. He was wearing a tank and khaki pants, a helmet and headlamp. He looked to one, then the other. Then he splashed back into the river as if chased, dove ahead in dolphin dives, and was lost to sight.

Niloux turned back to the teenager. But the teenager had laid her head down on her arms and closed her eyes. There was a gold earspool in one earlobe, and the other was torn. Niloux crawled toward her, crawled on top of her, and tried to keep her warm as she finally gave in to sleep.

She fell through.

The twins landed, their foreheads still touching.

Hunajpu said, "Did you just—?"

And Xbalanque said, "Yes, I just—!"

They didn't need to say any more. They got quiet like chided children, then buttoned their lips, grinning.

This time, they stood up and looked around. They were no longer in the cave. They were outside, in a cool twilight, in a clearing on a mountainside. They stood in a narrow lane of dirt, wearing the gear their mother had made: kilts and wrist guards, headdresses and knee pads. She herself watched them from the head of the lane with a black orchid in her hair. Then the court cracked down the middle and they looked into the chasm, and saw how deep time was in both directions, how long they'd loved each other—so long that their very separation had become a third person, binding them together.

"Well, are we in Xibalba yet or not?" said Xbalanque, pointing down, but the plaintive way her voice came out made Hunajpu laugh at her, which made Xbalanque laugh at herself, too, and when the crack widened and they both fell through, they were still laughing.

THE CAVE
4 Ajwal 3 K'ank'in, Long Count 13.0.0.0.0

---

21 December, 2012

When Leah opened her eyes, she blinked at the ceiling of the sump chamber. She'd had the wind knocked out of her. She tried to get her breath back. But if she could still see the ceiling—mottled rose-and-yellow—which meant her headlamp was still intact. She tried moving her fingers and toes. They worked.

She got up slowly. Her knee was embedded with gravel. She crawled to the river and washed it clean, but the water stung. She peered more closely: the water had gotten cloudy.

She had to get out of this chamber.

She looked up at the slope she'd tried to climb. A wind still blew from that opening, but she was afraid to try that way again.

She decided to explore the other side of the chamber. She crossed the island of sliding stones, waded into the far branch of the stream, spotted a cleft in the wall, swam forward, held on to a knob, and looked down into the water. All she saw was endless cool electric blue. Her green canvas sneakers kicked in big round frog kicks. It could be ten feet down or a thousand. There was no way to know.

She swam farther into the cleft, against the current, going from knob to knob, until it narrowed to a dead end. She could swim under, but of course the question was in what direction, and how would she know her way back if she was wrong? She started feeling for air pockets. On the right, her hands encountered solid rock; but on the left, her hand came up into air. Her breath caught. She flexed her fist just to make sure it wasn't a trick of the senses.

She had to act carefully now. She kept one hand in the air pocket. She rehearsed the pattern of movement in her mind: squeeze both sides of the rock as if squeezing a bolster and use the leverage to swing up to the other side.

She took a deep breath and did it.

Underwater, she heard the blast of the conch.

She surfaced on the other side, sputtering and wiping the spit off her mouth. She'd heard it! It was real! She realized that she could hear it only faintly above water, but it was much louder underwater because that must be where it came from, its natural medium.

The new air pocket was tiny. It tapered into a dead end ahead and behind her. It was about the length of her own body and three feet wide. Her legs dangled into the blue abyss, and she noticed that even after a minute, the water had become even more cloudy.

The flood was arriving.

For a moment she thought about letting go and just falling, like stepping out of a helicopter over a canyon. But that was silly. She would die if she did that. She had to find the way forward. If this cave were truly calling her to keep going, then it must have provided a path for her to do so. There had to be another air pocket nearby. Maybe that's how she'd get through the sump: ducking from one air pocket to the next like a frog on a lily pad, until she emerged in a chamber big enough that she could stand up.

She felt all around her, but found no air except for the chamber she'd come from.

Leah slapped her palm on the rock in frustration.

There had to be a way.

It occurred to her that she could let herself down into the abyss just a little, enough to use her headlamp to look for more air pockets. She bet they'd look different from solid rock. Meanwhile, she'd have to swim forward into the current so that she could come up again in a direct line from where she'd let herself fall.

She rehearsed the sequence of movements in her mind. She was a strong swimmer. This was a doable thing.

She squeezed both sides of the rock, looked down, took a deep breath, and let herself fall into the water.

The sound of the conch hit her full-force, as if someone had turned on a radio. She tried to ignore it for now. She looked up. The chamber she'd come from was shaped like an eye, a dark blur in the light blur of the rock. That was enough information for now. She needed to come up. She kicked back up and emerged in her tiny chamber, gasping, and gripped her handholds.

Now she knew that air pockets did look different from the surrounding rock, and that the conch horn was definitely coming from below. That had been a good mission. Now to scout the next one. She took another deep breath and dropped underwater just far enough to see the underside of the rock ahead. She saw five dark patches and a bigger dark patch beyond it. She turned to swim back up. But her hand slipped, and she drifted back in the current. She had to sweep her arms in a full breaststroke and kick her legs in a full frog kick to get back.

She tried to surface but was too hasty.

Her helmet banged on the rock. Her headlamp jiggled and almost came free.

She fell back, disoriented.

The current was sweeping her back again. Her lungs were clutching. She didn't want to fall into the abyss. She looked down into the clouded blue eternity. She kicked, but her green sneakers were catching the current and dragging her back. The flow was much stronger than it had been before.

She was close to panicking, but saw her dark eye-shaped blur.

She pulled herself up.

She put her hands to either side and wheezed until she got her breath back. That had been a bad mission. She needed to be more careful.

But—she'd seen more air pockets. That was the way forward.

Her sneakers had almost drowned her. It occurred to her that she had no real need of them. She trusted her feet more. She leveraged her back against one wall and braced her knees against the other, so that her butt was hanging over the abyss. She used one hand to untie the white cotton laces. The shoe loosened around her foot. It felt heavenly. She couldn't get it off fast enough.

She hooked her thumb into the back tab and wrestled off the whole shoe, then let it slide off her thumb.

It fell, drifting backward in the current. It looked like a balloon falling up into the sky.

She took off her other shoe and let it fall too.

Then socks.

Now the water flowed over her bare feet.

She did three test drops in a row, just to get a sense of how quickly the current was moving. She had to swim harder to stay in place now. The water was rising. She smiled at the thought of her swim team in Anoong. What if her teammates could see her now?

Leah dropped into the water again. She swam for the first pocket and pushed up.

Her helmet crashed against solid rock.

The pocket wasn't deep enough.

She tumbled backward and thrashed in the current. She was beginning to panic. By sheer chance she saw the next air pocket. She strained against the current to swim to it. Her lungs were aching again, and she might find this one shallow, too, but she had no choice.

Her head broke the surface.

It was deep enough.

She found a handhold to rest and catch her breath. But the current was even stronger now, and swept her body horizontally from the waist down. She didn't have much time. The water was up to her throat, then her chin. She couldn't stay in this spot. The water was rising.

She dropped down into the water again and scanned the ceiling ahead. There were three more air pockets, then the dark expanse she believed to be a whole chamber. She could just skip the air pockets and aim for that. No stops, no intermediates. The cave was forcing her. The land was acting on her. She wished she could tell Ruth.

She rose to get air, sucked in breath, then dropped.

She swam against the current. She flailed, then made herself understand, there is no possibility of going back, this is a matter of life or death, so you must choose life, you must have faith in that dark blur, and she reestablished a steady stroke against the current, blowing like a hurricane wind. Her lungs ached. There was pain, but she had to accept the pain. She had to endure the pain just a moment longer to see what was on the other side. The edge of the darkness was near. She just had to come up into it, to surface there, and she'd be able to breathe again.

She tried to come up too early.

Her helmet crashed against the rock and her light went out.

She kicked forward, blind.

Her palm hit sand.

She grabbed handfuls of it, scrabbled onto it, and the sand became a slope, rising upward, and then suddenly it was easier to move, and her mouth gaped open to drink in the air. She coughed out water and slime. She lay on the surface in front of her, her cheek to the sand, her lower body still in the current.

She was still alive.

Her brain moved her fingers to where she thought her headlamp was, but it wasn't there. She'd lost it in the abyss.

Leah smiled into the sand.

This was the part where, in films, the hero was truly fucked. But this was not a film. This was her real life.

Carefully, feeling the space around her, she pushed herself up to kneeling and listened.

The conch horn she'd heard underwater, she could hear aboveground, now. It had seemed to come from below, but now it seemed to be coming from ahead. Its source was changing, as if she were being led. She leaned forward in empty space and pressed her palms to the ground, feeling a mixture of grit, flat stones, and velvet sand, just like on the other side. She slid one hand forward and found the same thing. She would have to go very slowly, because Xander warned her of false passages and crevasses. It was still possible to die here.

She felt for the water, placed one hand in it. It was calm here, not overpowering like it'd been on the other side. Maybe only one part of the cave was flooding and she was out of its way now. She'd be able to crawl forward by feeling the current. On hands and knees, then, she crept in the blackness, keeping her right hand on the sand and her left hand in the water. All her senses were very sharp, compensating for lost sight. She could taste the fine mineral mist on the breeze—limestone, almost cacao. She marveled that she'd gotten through. She marveled that she was still wearing the same clothes: a bikini, tank top, and spandex pants, all of which she'd bought for her trip at a Kmart in St. Cloud, the same place where she'd bought the cinnamon incense and bite-sized Hershey bars and green-tinted sunglasses that she used to layer on top of each other before slicing her finger, to induce a sense of wholeness. She loved herself for the attempt. It had gotten her here. The conch sounded again, pure and clear. St. Cloud and Kmart seemed very implausible, as if they were plays she'd once performed, with cardboard sets.

She crawled this way for a long time. With her hands, she felt the same chunks of limestone masonry cut at right angles, and the moss that grew in the cracks.

Then the sound of the water changed. She'd entered a new space. She put her feet where her hands had been and stood up slowly, hands above her head. When she felt her knees lock, she trusted she was standing upright. She put out her arms and touched rock wall on either side. She could only go forward.

She took a tiny step, then another. The sand floor was sloping down into the water. First she was up to her knees, then her thighs, then her hips, then her chest. The water was as cool as a summer lake in Minnesota. Then the current got stronger. She must be wading into a constricted space. She got a mouthful of water and spat it out; it tasted faintly of cacao, like the drink Xander had made for her. The conch sounded again, and this time she almost thought she saw it: a brief light shaped like a candle flame. The karst in the air sounded like wind in the trees. All of her senses were becoming confused.

Finally she stubbed her toe on some kind of bottom. She winced and let the pain ebb. Then she reached down and touched her fingers to a flat stone with a square edge, like a step.

She dragged her good foot back and forth along the stone. Yes, it felt like a step. So she stepped up, and found another step that felt similar. The water was coursing down from above. She put her hands out and felt walls on either side, and pressed against them to brace against the current. There were four more steps, rising out of the water. Then there were no more walls under her fingertips at all.

A horizon began to take shape.

She blinked, because there'd been no light a moment ago. But a horizon was taking shape all the same, a clear distinction between this-above and that-below, a pink-orange and a soft grey.

She kept walking forward, tentative. The dark and light patches were resolving themselves into walls, hollows, and courtyards—those works of masonry again. She was following a footpath, well-worn, carpeted with red leaves. She passed from a larger room to a smaller one, and then into an even smaller one, through a series of arched doorways.

The conch sounded again. It made her want to run, but she cautioned herself to go slow. The light kept growing: a soft pink-orange, with no source that she could see. These elements felt familiar:

The pink-orange light.

The cacao water.

The red leaves.

These were the signs she had tried to keep in mind, to tell the twins. But now she realized that they hadn't been for them. They had always been for her.

She began to remember the way back.

She followed the footpath down, took a right turn, went down ten steps, then emerged onto a platform. Beside the platform, there was another river, a river beneath the river, and its surface was also covered with red leaves. The conch sounded again. There was a path beside this deeper river, just wide enough for her body, that led to a small half-circle of stone that jutted into the river, like a jetty for a swimmer. She remembered that she should swim—that it was in fact better to swim, more fun; she'd done so many times before. She sat on the edge of the stone and let herself down. The bottom was smooth and sandy and she kicked forward. The pink-orange light grew ahead. There was more music now, like glitter showers, and voices cutting in and out as if strobed. She kept swimming. She tasted the water again: cacao. She remembered to take the right fork of the canal, then climbed up out of the water. The footpath ended at a stone wall. There was a single door in the wall, and next to it, a whole tree of blood-red leaves. In the other world, red leaves meant autumn and death; but Leah knew that here, red was the color of true spring, the spring behind the spring.

This was a tricky part, she remembered. She shouldn't go in through this main door, which was a trap. Rather, she should climb the tree to find the secret door higher up, where the pink-orange light was coming from. She got a foothold on one branch, then the next. Her spandex waistband snagged on a twig and she stopped to dislodge it. Three more branches up, she could see it: the secret crawlspace. She balanced on a thick branch and pushed herself into it. Then she elbowed herself down a narrow tunnel; it steepened and became a slide, and she shrieked as she slid.

She landed in a starlit forest.

There, sitting on the back of a black jaguar, was a little girl wearing a blindfold.

She looked straight at Leah and grinned. She held up the conch shell she'd been holding in her lap. "You heard me!" she said.

Leah couldn't speak.

The little girl pulled up her blindfold. Her eyes were solid gold.

"You don't need that anymore," she said, pointing at Leah's head.

Leah was confused, until she realized she was still wearing her plastic helmet. She laughed at herself. She pinched the release under her chin and took it off and set it by the wall, lovingly folding the straps inside.

Then the little girl cocked her head as if to say, *Listen.*

Leah could hear: the music had become louder. The glitter and silk were more coherent now, the voices unbroken.

The little girl beckoned. "Come on. She's waiting for us."

Leah threw her leg over the back of the jaguar and squeezed her knees into its fur.

"Hold on to me," said the girl.

Leah circled her arms around her stomach.

The jaguar leapt forward.

The ground sloped down through a forest of red trees. The deeper they went, the louder the music got. Leah's ears began to ache, then to burn, as if they were melting. Leah cried out and tried to cover them but the little girl slapped her leg and yelled, "Don't! Listen!" So she refastened her arms. She rested her forehead on the girl's shoulder. She tried to bear the music.

Then she realized she knew this song.

She knew this melody—how the words lay on top of the chords—how she used to sit in her bedroom with chocolate on her tongue and wait for the peak of the best chord change, that unbearable twinge of bliss. Now the music was so loud that Leah felt as if it were coming from inside her own head. She realized it always had been.

They came to a stone wall and passed through the arch.

Inside, there were thousands of dancers. Each dancer was tossing her black hair, drawing her hand over her chest and pointing upward in the gesture of praise, circling a towering blood-leaved tree whose crown was netted with stars.

The jaguar sat. They slid onto the ground in a pile of limbs. The little girl got up first and pulled Leah up by the hand and started tugging her forward.

There was a woman in the split of the tree. Leah saluted her, and she saluted back, for they knew each other well. She was huge now, a colossus come to life, her body stretching from earth to heaven, robed in orange and gold, showered with blood-red sparks that cascaded down the trunk to twist around her wrist and drift over the dancers. Leah tried following the little girl into the crowd, to reach the woman in the tree so they could finally speak again, but lost her and got swept away with the dancers, who were so happy to see her again, all of them laughing and flinging sweat and making the same gesture of praise, hand drawn over chest and pointing up. How had she ever forgotten?— that it was just as much pleasure to disperse as be whole.

GLOSSARY OF TERMS
IN LAVIAJA

Actun Tunichil Muknal (ATM). The name of the Great Cave during the tourist era of ~1986–2050 CE, and the name by which it was known by Saint Leah Oliveri and the Consort Twins. The translation is "Cave of the Stone Sepulcher," with words borrowed from multiple Maya languages.

adivinix. A viajera who serves as a diviner for other viajeras, most often in directional divination—channeling the god of the place to answer where a viajera should travel next. The answer might be in the form of an image, a direction, an instruction, or a specific site. All viajeras learn divination in the sacrament Divinidad, so as to administer it to anyone in need; but adivinix seek it as their preferred form of work and service. Singular and plural.

Age of Emergency. The time period between ~1945 and 2129 CE, when unchecked capitalism led to an unprecedented spike in accumulations of capital, wealth, populations, and computing power worldwide, resulting in mass extinction, catastrophic climate change, and human displacement on a global scale. Laviaja was founded in reaction to the Age of Emergency: as the undoing of the conditions that led to it, and as a codification of a postcapitalist, extreme-weather, refugee-led world.

agribots. Automated farming robots that tend gardens to provide fresh produce for viajeras. Gardens are most often associated with wayhouses, but are also planted along well-traveled paths.

ai. Pronounced "eye." A general term for any artificial intelligence, local or networked, of animate or inanimate things. Most often used to refer to viajeras' interface with the aug. Viajeras can employ their ai by thinking their commands, or by a chosen gesture such as touching the temple or heart.

ancianix. One of the seven major relational terms in Laviaja, meaning an elder. Singular and plural.

aug. Abbreviation for "augmented reality," pronounced "ogg." The common, interactive, virtual reality that exists within viajeras' networked otracortices, mapped over the "normal" visual world. Viajeras interface with the aug using their ai.

autocenser. A portable, self-heating ceramic dish used by adivinix for burning copal.

balché. A traditional fermented drink of the ancient Maya, made from bark and honey; used for toasts and celebrations in Laviaja. Can be made synthetically or brewed directly from the plant.

bia. A hard, dense ball of whitish-yellow organic matter used as pluripotent mass for making food in printers and kilns. One ball can keep a viajera fed for a month. Resembles dense maize dough.

bird. A virtual messenger from a viajera, paragua, or wayhouse ai, usually in the shape of a local bird or one's personal avatar bird.

blotting. A form of punishment. In extreme cases such as assault, murder, rape, and abuse, any viajera has the choice to "blot" the criminal from the landscape: to choose not to see them, except as a blur. Technically, blotted viajeras are still entitled to mutual aid, but those who blot them sometimes fail to render it. Four out of six consecutive assemblies of the Tzoyna must approve the sentence for it to go into effect, for a set amount of time, after which the sentence is revisited by a new sequence of the Tzoyna.

braiding. A method of reconciling multiple streams of information to discuss an issue and arrive at a resolution, modeled on ancient Quaker practices. Most often applied to sessions of the Tzoyna. Rapid data processing is enabled by otracortices, and must be followed by a period of rest.

cannaba. The psychoactive compound tetrahydrocannabinol, which viajeras are able to secrete on demand for medicinal, spiritual, or recreational purposes.

carnalix. One of the seven major relational terms in Laviaja. The original High Spanish word "carnal" denotes "beloved blood relative," but is used far more widely in Laviaja, as all viajeras use familial terms.

Like "hermanix," but with more strength and affection. Singular and plural.

Cayo. The holy land of Laviaja, originally the home of the first Maya, and then the ancient nation state of Belize. "Cayo" was originally the name of the middle western district of Belize, on the border with Guatemala.

Chak Ek'. The ancient Maya name for Venus, as both the morning star and the evening star.

chitin. A fibrous, translucent polymer used as building material.

compañerix. A viajera who serves as an encamadix (lover or companion) to anyone who requests it through the paragua. Being a compañerix requires specialized disposition, training, and tutorials; only 4 percent of the population is capable of it. Singular and plural.

concórdia. A viajera's personal identity, usually described as a combination of genéra, manéra, y preféra (roughly corresponding to gender identity, personal alignment-expression, and sexual orientation, respectively).

Consort Twins. A term referring to twin brothers Javier Magaña and Xander Cañul, honoring their roles as guides and companions to Saint Leah in 2012.

cortada. The theoretical rip in the fabric of spacetime that allows a viajera to "cross over" to the true realm of Xibalba. The only proof of their existence, in the westernist sense, is that thousands of people disappeared from the face of the Earth in the Diluvian Era.

Común. The common language of viajeras, descended from twenty-first-century English, with Spanish, Hindi, and Arabic influences. Because language drift is locally determined at the speed of individual movement, a person speaking Común in China and a person speaking Común in Ireland might not be able to understand each other without the help of ai correction.

Diluvian Age. Roughly 2129–3012 CE, from the first permanent >2m surge of sea level to the night the last of the world's ice melted in the Chersky Range.

Divinidad. One of the eight sacraments of Laviaja, usually occurring before one's Primera Viaja. A child learns how to perform and receive directional divination, according to the practice of the ancient Maya and the early viajeras.

documented anarchy. A method of community organization wherein all individuals' actions are recorded and accessible via a blockchain ledger, including the act of accessing such information.

Doula de la Salida. A viajera who serves as a companion to the dying in the sacrament of Salida, with hope of effecting a good rebirth.

encamadix. One of the seven major relational terms in Laviaja, meaning a lover. Singular and plural.

endotánte. From the High Spanish for "giver," meaning a viajera who prefers to give or penetrate into others' sexual organs. One of four preféras that correspond to one's general inclination in sexual intercourses. See also: **envolvánte, omnipreféra,** and **nonpreféra.**

envolvánte. From the High Spanish for "involve," meaning a viajera who prefers gripping or taking of others' sexual organs. One of four preféras that correspond to one's general inclination in sexual intercourses. See also: **endotánte, omnipreféra,** and **nonpreféra.**

en vivo. In person.

familia. The group of viajeras with whom a person is traveling at any given moment. According to Versa Tres of the Rule of Saint Leah, a familia should number no more than nine, and no two members of the familia should be together for more than nine days. At any given time, the majority of viajeras on Earth (~70 percent) are in familias. There are seven major relational terms within familias: ancianix (elder), encamadix (lover), carnalix (dear), hermanix (sibling), ninx (child before the age of twelve), tíax (indirect caregiver to a ninx or jovenix), and zadre (direct caregiver to a ninx or jovenix).

feed. A general term for any stream of information in the aug.

fermites. Nanoscale biomachines that accelerate healing of the human body on a scale of hours. Taken orally or applied topically.

fictism. The science of understanding the universe by creating it.

Fiesta de Manéra. One of the eight sacraments of Laviaja. A celebration of a young person's choice of their first manéra, or of any older viajera's change of manéra. Ceremonies may be lavish or simple, but usually involve five elements: music, flowers, flame, something sweet, and a drink for toasting. The traditional time of year for a Fiesta de Manéra is December.

filler. Totipotent cell matter applied to the site of a wound, which can alter rapidly into the necessary tissue.

filter. A mode of viewing the world in the aug. For example, one can walk through a landscape seeing it as if it were the year 1638, or as if it were painted by Monet, or as if the temperature were twenty degrees colder.

foraging. Ai-assisted gathering of edible food from the landscape, such as mushrooms, seeds, bark, fruits, berries, and wild greens.

fugitech. A term derived from "refugee" and "technology," describing all technology oriented toward human health and survival, rather than corporate profit. The beginning of the fugitech movement, widely credited to Ida Gudasz and Micah Wells, coincided with the rise of sea levels beginning in the twenty-first century.

genéra. A viajera's gender identity, often described as norte, sur, este, or oeste (High Spanish for the cardinal directions of the compass, roughly corresponding to the Age of Emergency terms woman, man, agender, and nonbinary, respectively). The default pronoun in Laviaja is "she/her" in honor of Saint Leah. All newly pregnant viajeras induce epigenetic treatment so that their baby is born with a womb, vagina, penis, and testicles. This omnipresentation of genitalia is a legacy of the population bottleneck of the twenty-fifth century, when a newly nomadic humanity was in danger of dying out, and therefore—for survival of the species— viajeras began to develop both sets of genitalia. A ninx is not assigned a genéra at birth, and can usually name their genéra between the ages of three and eight. See also **manéra** and **preféra.**

geosophy. An area of study concerned with the agency of landscapes.

gift economy. A system whereby goods are freely given and received according to need, without expectation of payment or exchange. In Laviaja, goods can be obtained through rummages, stockpiles at wayhouses, and/or by sending a request to the local paragua, which then matches a giver to the requester. In difficult cases where priority must be assigned, priority is given to the option that optimizes human health and survival for the most number of people.

god [of the place]. In Laviaja, "god" is indistinguishable from "place," formally defined as the integration of infinite time over a discrete area of space, as small as a micron or as large as the universe.

gossamoor. Synthetic silk modeled on the drag lines of Darwin's bark spider, weighing twelve milligrams per thousand meters. Used to anchor searoads to the seafloor.

glucosi. An ascetic viajera who lives on photosugar alone.

Great Cave. A natural limestone cave system in the northern foothills of the Maya Mountains in Central America. The system consists mainly of a two-mile river passage and a large upper chamber that the ancient Maya used for sacrificial burials. Known by local Maya for centuries after the collapse of the elites, the cave was first mapped in the westernist sense by Dr. Thomas Miller in 1986, after which the cave was opened to archaeologists and tourists. During this era

(~1986–2050), the cave was known as Actun Tunichil Muknal. The cave is the holiest pilgrimage site in Laviaja, the place where Saint Leah is said to have crossed over into Xibalba.

halo. A three-dimensional aug projection that surrounds the head and displays a viajera's collection of wayhouse tokens.

hermanix. One of the seven major relational terms in Laviaja, meaning a sibling. The most general and often-used term. Singular and plural.

higgs. A temporary, localized Higgs field that gives substance and tactility to a holo. Frowned upon by orthodox viajeras, as they believe it violates Versa Diez of the Rule of Saint Leah. A Higgs field requires a tremendous amount of energy, so it's not often used.

High Spanish. Vernacular twenty-first-century Spanish, descended primarily from Mexican and Guatemalan Spanish, preserved and adapted for the purpose of sacred Laviaji rituals and terms.

hoarder. A denizen of the Age of Emergency. Also a derogatory term for a sedentix or anyone who accumulates (land, possessions, companions) in violation of Versas Tres o Ocho of the Rule of Saint Leah.

holo. A holographic image, recording, or message.

hoverchair. A movement device sculpted to fit the user's body, which hovers above ground or water as steadifoils do. Can be steered with hands or by linkage with otracortices in the brain.

hoverdish. A movement device resembling a saucer, which hovers above ground or water as steadifoils do. Can be steered with appendages or by linkage with otracortices in the brain, and made with or without leg holes to maintain contact with the earth.

Hundred-Year Carnival. The time period roughly between 2129 and 2381 CE. Beginning when one of the major sea-level pulses drowned Belize City, driving the Carnaval celebrants inland to take over the capital of Belmopan, and ending with the dissolution of the last nation state (India) by the newly converted Meha DeVellore. A period characterized by the collapse of capitalism, the collapse of the nation state, the refugee-nomad transition, the rise of fugitech, anarchic and subsidiarist self-government, and mutual aid.

hunter. A viajera who chooses to hunt animals for food and, therefore, consents to being hunted in turn without the protection of shields. Though allowed for in the Treaty of 2780, many other viajeras consider hunters to be barbaric and regressive.

incongruéncia. The discomfort some viajeras feel with the traditional omnipresentation of genitalia, which misaligns with their genéra.

Inducción. One of the eight sacraments of Laviaja, typically occurring between the ages of seven and nine. A child learns the history of democracy, the braiding technique, and how to vote and participate in the Tzoyna legislature.

jovenix. An adolescent or teenage viajera. Singular and plural.

jugadorix. A viajera who serves as a performer and/or athlete, typically in productions of *La Estrella Actual* or games of pitz. Singular and plural.

kiln. A device for turning bia into specific food items, according to programming or a pre-filed design. Resembles a bisected ceramic sphere, with a lid for cover and a flat bottom for setting on surfaces.

La Estrella Actual. The canon of dramatic literature relating the history of Laviaja, including that of Ixul and Ajul of the ancient Tzoyna; and of Javier, Xander, and Saint Leah of ancient Belize. Most viajeras have a standard text memorized as part of their education; jugadorix may have dozens of texts and dances memorized. Productions are meant to be fluid and improvised; casts typically don't rehearse more than once or twice. Often, jugadorix honor the god of the place by adopting a mode of performance that aligns with the culture of the people who used to live on the performance site.

La Familia de la Carretera (LFC). In High Spanish, "The Family of the Road." The political movement founded by Tanaaj DeCayo in 3012, emphasizing the conservation of the traditional Rule of Saint Leah and the reality of Xibalba, in reaction to the heresy of Niloux DeCayo.

Las Arcas de las Gemelas. Two monuments in Cayo: one that honors Ixul and Ajul at the site of the ancient city of the Tzoyna, and one that honors Xander and Javier at the entrance to the Great Cave.

La Trinidad de Cayo. Refers to the triad of Saint Leah, Javier Magaña, and Xander Cañul.

Laviaja. The global system of nomadic, subsidiarist, anarchist self-organization in 3012, formalized by climate refugees in the late twenty-third century, building on the work of Xander Cañul, Ruth Okeke, Ida Gudasz, and Micah Wells; associated with the legend of Saint Leah Oliveri, and characterized by mutual aid, gift economy, panoptic justice, gender concórdia, documented anarchy, and algorithmic skillmatching. The intellectual tradition of Laviaja is attributed to Xander Cañul, and the ritual tradition of Laviaja is attributed to Javier Magaña.

lucha. A play-conflict between manéras, as between ancient sports teams or nation states. Luchas may be expressed in poetry exchanges, practical jokes, public wooings, pitz games, or other contests of skill.

lysergia. The psychoactive compound lysergic acid diethylamide, which viajeras are able to secrete on demand for medicinal, spiritual, or recreational purposes.

manéra. A viajera's chosen personal and/or genéra expression, best described as some combination of alignment, aesthetic, and area of interest. Manéras may be uncovered or created based on an archetype, physical attribute, astrological sign, religion, fashion aesthetic, fictional character, historical character, mythical character, ancient worker identity, ancient ethnic identity, ancient national identity, ancient sexual identity, ancient regional identity, or any of many other modalities. When a viajera chooses or changes a manéra, she is expected to take a battery of tutorials that educate her within her chosen manéra, or—if she is creating a new manéra—to develop her own. About half of all manéras are created, trend over a period of years or decades, and die off; the other half persist through the ages. Typically, a viajera chooses her first manéra upon menarche or around the age of twelve, and can change it at any time, though December is the traditional month to do so. Viajeras change manéra an average of three times per lifetime. At the start of 3012, there are 1,289 declared manéras. The most common manéra group is maya, with about three hundred thousand identifying as one of the maya subgroups (or 3.8 percent of the world population); according to the Universal Bill of Rights, no manéra or manéra group may exceed 5 percent of the world population, to prevent voting blocs in the Tzoyna.

Mardom e Zein-o-Din. In Farsi, "The People of Zein-o-Din." The political movement founded by Niloux DeCayo in 3012, challenging the norms and assumptions of Laviaja custom, and advocating for the right to challenge said norms without fear of punishment.

medkit. A bag of medical supplies carried by most viajeras, which they replenish at wayhouses or rummages, or through gift exchange. Usually include taffies, fermites, sealant, filler, and gauze.

moonball. A solar-powered, spherical light with a soft blue hue, turned on and off by smoothing the hand across it.

multivalent attachment theory. Originating in the twenty-second century, multivalent attachment theory posited that children could successfully be raised by hundreds of successive adults without the need to attach to any in particular, if their bodily safety, physical needs, and emotional needs were universally guaranteed. The theory was highly contentious and took three centuries to prove, which was how long it took to ensure the necessary conditions on a large enough scale.

Munda. From the High Spanish term "mundo," meaning the world; and the 2012-era Maya term "Mundo," meaning the earth deity. In Laviaja, a general reference to the world-as-god.

Mundotra. From High Spanish "mundo + otro," "the other world." See **Xibalba.**

murk. The term for any subtidal region consisting of former cities, forests, or other landforms that lie partially or wholly submerged in the ocean.

mutual aid. One of the major organizational principles of Laviaja, only the latest in many exemplars throughout human history. Viajeras render aid to other viajeras in need whenever called upon by the paragua, whether it be in service of food, health, rescue, companionship, shelter, or other basic human needs. Failure to render aid is documented in the panoptica, and may be cause for reformation, shunning, censure, or transformative justice.

ninx. One of the seven major relational terms in Laviaja, meaning a child. Singular and plural.

nonpreféra. Term used to describe a viajera who does not desire or seek out enveloping or penetrative sexual intercourses. Sometimes this means the viajera is asexual, but not always. One of four preféras that correspond to one's general inclination in sexual intercourses. See also: **endotánte, envolvánte,** and **omnipreféra.**

ojos-de-Leah. An otracortex grown to mimic the brain of Leah Oliveri at the time of her disappearance, believed to give a person special sensitivity to Xibalba.

ombligo. High Spanish for "navel." A viajera's birthplace, from which she takes her surname (e.g., DeCayo, DeGrozny, DeVellore).

omnipreféra. Term used to describe a viajera who acts as both an endotánte and an envolvánte. One of four preféras that correspond to one's general inclination in sexual intercourses. See also: **endotánte, envolvánte,** and **nonpreféra.**

orgoscan. A function of the ai-aug interface that can scan for organic and even genetic material according to certain specifications.

otracortex. A directed brain growth that integrates with the aug for the purposes of visualization, interaction, and data processing. Otracortices are especially useful for tutorials, in which viajeras absorb large amounts of information in short amounts of time.

panoptic justice. The principle whereby all actions of all viajeras are recorded in the aug, and are accessible by any other viajera, provided the act of accessing is also recorded. See also: **documented anarchy.**

panoptica. The blockchain "ledger" wherein all actions of all viajeras are recorded in the aug—including the act of accessing information. Accessible by any other human, viajera or sedentix; though some sedentix opt out. See also: **documented anarchy.**

paragua. High Spanish for "umbrella." The automated mutual-aid algorithm of a given region, which expands or contracts depending on the density of people in that area, optimizing skillmatching and gift exchange for maximum likelihood of health, survival, and well-being for all whom it governs.

particularity. The principle by which viajeras are taught not to seek or cultivate fame so as to put themselves above others in their and others' eyes.

Paz de las Viajeras. High Spanish for "Peace of the Travelers." The period of history from roughly 2600 to the present, marked by a gradual decrease in violence, destruction of weapons, and collapse of infrastructure necessary to sustain violence.

pelt. The skin of a viajera, evolved through fugitech to be capable of photosynthesis, limb regeneration, tail development, temperature regulation, heat tolerance, shield generation, gill production, swair integration, and augmentation or reduction of sexual organs. The function of a pelt is to enable a viajera to travel safely in any environment on Earth, and to accommodate a wide variety of concórdias.

photosugar. The product of photosynthesis, generated by a pelt and deposited directly into the bloodstream. Very unsatisfying to live on alone, according to most viajeras, but will keep one alive.

pilari. Named after Saint Pilar, pilaris are viajeras who stay in one locale for years at a time until they cover every square foot with their pista. If they haven't found their cortada, they move on.

pista. High Spanish for "track." A viajera's worldline, the path she has taken over the Earth, recorded in the aug and accessible to all.

pitz. The Laviaji descendant of the ancient Maya ball game. Pitz courts are common at wayhouses and rummages, and tournaments are traditional at the Feast of the Consort Twins and throughout the month of December.

Plantanda. One of the eight sacraments of Laviaja, occurring shortly after birth. An infant's otracortices, including ojos-de-Leah, are typically induced or "planted" in the brain.

pluripotencia. The principle by which fetuses in the womb are epigenetically treated to develop a womb, vagina, penis, and testicles. This omnipresentation of genitalia is a legacy of the population bottleneck of the twenty-fifth century, when a newly nomadic humanity was in danger of dying out. Viajeras can only become pregnant by the consent of both parties.

preféra. Term used to describe a viajera's general inclination in sexual intercourses: whether she prefers to take or give, grip or penetrate, or both, or neither. The four preféras are **envolvánte, endotánte, omnipreféra,** and **nonpreféra.**

Primera Viaja. One of the eight sacraments of Laviaja, occurring anywhere from age ten to fifteen. A child takes her first journey alone. However, with the help of zadres and tíax, the child chooses a well-traveled route with well-populated wayhouses at the beginning and end, and is monitored in the aug throughout her journey.

Principle of Dispersion. One of the foundational principles of Laviaja. "Accumulation of any human property ultimately leads to human suffering. Lasting peace can only result from the constant, deliberate dispersion of population, wealth, power, computing, and capital. In order to survive, we must flow with, and not against, the entropic nature of the universe." Xander Cañul, 2028.

pluripote. A hard, dense ball of silver-grey resin, fed to a printer to make three-dimensional inorganic objects.

printer. Any device that converts bia or pluripote into food or three-dimensional objects, or repairs objects according to a programmed or previously filed design.

profitech. Technology devised with the ultimate aim of increasing shareholder profit. See for contrast: **fugi-tech.**

recon. To obtain objects at a rummage, particularly vintage or antique objects for self-adornment and manéra expression.

Renacimienta. One of the eight sacraments of Laviaja. A viajera is born; that is, her soul enters the world in a new body to resume her journey.

Rule of Saint Leah. A set of shorthand reminders by which viajeras live, act, and interact, based on the practices of the early viajeras in the Diluvian Age, in thirteen Versas. Viajeras interpret these Versas in a range of different ways. They are:

Ayuda a la personix que te acompañe (help the one you're with).

Esta niñx es tu hijax (this child is your child).

No se permite más que nueve, excepto en diciembre (no more than nine [familia members, days in one place, etc.], except in December).

Las pluripotentix sobreviven (the pluripotent survive).

La amadix siempre vuelve (the beloved always returns).

La extranjerix más extraña es tu hermanix (the strangest stranger is your sister).

Dispersa todas las cosas (disperse all things).

Posee solo lo que cargas (own only what you carry).

Nadie sabe la pulgada (you know not the inch [where your cortada lies]).

Está presente para la diox del lugar (be present to the god of the place).

La ofrenda debe estar en rotación continua (the gift must move).

No seas particular (be not particular).

La sangre le pertenece solamente a Xibalba (blood belongs only to Xibalba).

rummage. A concentration of goods in one place, analogous to markets, except that everything is free for the taking. Rummages are usually recycled goods from centuries past, preserved, repaired, or remade by printers, and by viajeras assigned to do the work.

sacrament. The eight ritual ceremonies of a viajera's life: Renacimienta (birth), Plantanda (implantation of otracortices), Inducción (training for and induction into the Tzoyna), Divinidad (divination), Primera Viaja (first solo journey), Fiesta de Manéra (celebration of an alignment), Unión (sex), Salida (death).

saint. In Laviaja, a saint is someone who has disappeared. They are believed to have crossed over to Xibalba through their cortada.

Saint Leah. Leah Magdalene Oliveri, born in St. Cloud, Minnesota, United States, on March 18, 1993. Her mother was Antonia Oliveri, a young Italian-American missionary, and her father was Pancho Gonzalo Iglesias, a Belizean manual laborer of Maya descent. She attended Our Lady of the Prairie Elementary School and Trinity High School in Anoong, Minnesota, before she traveled to Belize and disappeared in the cave Actun Tunichil Muknal. In Laviaja, she is credited as the first person to knowingly seek out Xibalba, and articulate the path thereto. She is known by the honorifics Leah la Turista, Leah la Putita, Leah la Viajera, and Leah la Souvenir.

Salida. One of the eight sacraments of Laviaja. A viajera dies and her soul is reincarnated in another body being born (Renacimienta).

scrupe. Short for "scrupulous." A derogatory term for a viajera who strictly interprets and follows the Rule of Saint Leah.

sealant. A common item in medkits, used to seal over wounds and make them continuous with one's pelt for rapid healing.

sedentix. From the High Spanish for "seated." Sedentix are people who opt out of Laviaja by settling in one place, known as a "Home." In 3012, there are only 9,000 sedentix out of a world population of 8 million. Often, sedentix exempt themselves from documented anarchy, panoptic justice, paragua skillmatching, and/ or mutual aid. Many viajeras feel prejudice toward the sedentix because of this, and their expectation of privacy (considered another form of hoarding), but relations are nonviolent, and most viajeras will answer their calls for mutual aid regardless. Singular and plural.

settler. A derogatory term for a sedentix.

shelter. Any place where a viajera can take shelter from the elements. Some shelters are ruins of ancient buildings, some are grown from biomaterials, and many are a combination of both. Smaller than a wayhouse, a shelter holds anywhere from one to nine people.

shields. A function of pelts, shields are force fields generated to protect a viajera against impact, blunt force, or animal attack, deploying in advance. Most viajeras are vegetarian, but if a viajera opts to hunt, she gives up the right to use her shields permanently, and so must consent to being hunted in turn.

skillmatching. The algorithmic process by which a paragua automatically matches a need or preference of one viajera to its fulfillment by another.

sofist. A viajera whose primary work is research.

solar paint. The main energy source for many way-houses in sunny climates. Solar paint converts sunlight into energy with 90 percent conversion efficiency.

sortition democracy. A method of democracy dating to ancient Greece, wherein members of a governing body (in this case, the Tzoyna legislature) are randomly selected from the larger population and required to serve for a set amount of time (in this case, approximately one hour per year).

star-lights. Small, multicolored spherical lights that resemble stars, usually used for ambiance instead of functional lighting as sunballs and moonballs are.

steadifoil. A flat, wheelless, contourable mat that can transport incapacitated viajeras over water or earth for medical or accessibility purposes.

subsidiarity. The organizing principle by which decisions are made at the most local level possible, by those affected by its outcome; and only decisions that affect all are taken up by a global subsidiary body (in Laviaja, the Tzoyna legislature). These global decisions include hourly re-ratification of the Universal Bill of Rights, ai relations, animal relations, sedentix relations, cases of extreme violence or criminality, and philosophical questions pertinent to Laviaja.

sunball. A solar-powered, spherical light with a soft yellow hue, turned on and off by smoothing the hand across it.

supper wear. One of the two sets of clothing with which a viajera usually travels. Supper wear is social wear, used to express one's manéra, usually featuring historical ornaments or costumes reconned from rummages. See: **travel wear.**

swir (pl. swair). Swair might be called wings, but are more like parachutes, attached to a pelt and deployed in case an ambulant viajera is falling, needs to fall slowly, or otherwise needs help navigating steep terrain.

taffy. Medicine administered orally, in a taffy-like matrix, often flavored with orange or honey or peppermint.

therolinguist. A linguist who studies animal languages.

tíax. One of the seven major relational terms in Laviaja, meaning a viajera who's older than, and takes an interest in the welfare of, a ninx or jovenix, but is not a zadre or ancianix. Singular and plural.

token. The unique spherical medallion of a wayhouse.

travel wear. One of the two sets of clothing with which a viajera usually travels. Plain, hardy, and functional, travel wear is usually printed at wayhouses in a limited set of styles. They're worn for one to three months at a time and then recycled. See: **supper wear.**

Treaty of 2780. The treaty reached between viajeras and 156 species of animal, the animals being translated by therolinguists, by which viajeras pledged to stop eating singular sentient beings for sustenance, nutrition, and recreation, and were therefore allowed the use of static shields for protection in the wilderness. The treaty also allowed for hunters—viajeras who choose to hunt animals for food and, therefore, permanently forgo the protection of shields.

tutorial. Virtual courses that cover entire subjects, lasting one to twenty-four hours, engaging the otracortices. Learning in this way requires the brain to recover and repair itself; for example, an eight-hour session would be followed by four or five days of sleep.

Tzoyna (uppercase). "Mother's Cut" in Ch'ol Maya. Originally the name of an ancient Maya city-state, now the name of the global governing body that convenes by randomized sortition democracy, every hour of every day. Typically, a viajera is called to serve once a year by logging into a virtual space that resembles the ball court of the original Tzoyna. They vote to re-ratify basic human, animal, and ai rights, then consider special questions that anyone can pose, using the rapid-throughput braiding technique of reconciling thousands of streams of information and coming to a consensus.

tzoyna (lowercase). An in-person discussion group for philosophical, political, or other matters.

Unión (uppercase). One of the eight sacraments of Laviaja. Generally occurring during the teenage years after choosing a manéra, a young viajera who desires sex has sex for the first time. She may choose to announce herself or not; if she does, she can expect to be instructed and fawned over by tíax for several days.

unión (lowercase). A public wooing, seduction, or sex event, usually between exemplars of two manéras as part of the luchas.

viaja. High Spanish for "travel." In Laviaja, any movement from one god to another.

viajera. High Spanish for "traveler." This term is used for any practitioner of Laviaja who lives by its system of nomadic, anarchistic, interdependent mutual aid. The feminine-gendered ending is preserved in honor of Saint Leah, who identified herself as a viajera.

wayhouse. Any semipermanent shelter that serves as a place for viajeras to rest, bathe, congregate, talk, exchange news, eat cooked food, have sex, perform *La Estrella*, play pitz, celebrate a Fiesta de Manéra, stage a lucha or unión, recover from illness, die in peace, or give birth. Like shelters, wayhouses are usually made from ancient ruins, directed biomaterials, or a combination of both.

westernist. In Laviaja scholarship, the term for the objectivist, empirical epistemology that dominated the Age of Emergency and its prelude.

Xibalba. From the ancient Maya "Xibalba," the underworld, "place of fear/wonder." In Laviaja, Xibalba is the Mundotra, the Other World, the true realm from which all viajeras are exiles, and which can be reached only through perpetual movement over the face of the Earth and encounter with one's cortada.

zabendita. A viajera who stutters. From High Spanish "Xander + blessed," referring to Xander Cañul's congenital stutter.

zadre. One of the seven major relational terms in Laviaja, meaning a viajera who's acting as a caregiver for a child. A child will have had hundreds of zadres by the time she embarks on her Primera Viaja.

Zeinian. A viajera who identifies with the Mardom e Zein-o-Din, founded by Niloux DeCayo.

ACKNOWLEDGMENTS

I'm so grateful to everyone who helped bring this book into being over the last eight years.

First, thank you to my dearest friends in Belize: Francisco Reymundo of Ancient Cultural Tours and Gonzalo Pleitez of River Rat Expeditions. The gods blessed the day we met, and every day since that I've known you.

Thank you also to Jamaal and Nechisha Crawford, formerly of PACZ Adventure Tours, always my first stop when I arrived in San Ignacio; the wonderful Bob Jones, very much missed; Sergio Paíz and Max Caballeros for their good company (and Belikins); Winsom Winsom and Marlene Sulker for their kindness; and Marge and Thomas Gallagher for protecting me from jaguars. Thank you to my guides Ian Burns, Rafael Guerra, and John August for keeping me safe in dangerous places. Especial thanks to Martha August, Alexis Sanchez, and the staff at Martha's Guesthouse for always making me feel at home.

My agent, Sam Stoloff, went far above and beyond the call of duty in bringing this book to life. Thank you so much, Sam, for sticking by me with such faith, patience, and good humor. Thanks also to my editor, David Pomerico, who's steered the book with such clarity and insight, and the wonderful team at HarperVoyager: editorial assistant Mireya Chiriboga, designer Paula Szafranski, publicist Emily Fisher, and production editor Evangelos Vasilakis. Thank you also to copyeditor Rachelle Mandik for her careful and thoughtful work, and to sensitivity reader Felice Laverne, who helped me see my blind spots.

Huge thanks to my consultants: artist Katie Numi Usher, for helping me portray Belizean culture accurately, and correcting my Spanish and Kriol; Basilio Mes, for translating my Mopan Maya; Dr. Nicholas Hopkins, for critical insight into the usage of Ch'ol Maya; Dr. Francisco Belli-Estrada, for checking my portrayal of the ancient Maya against the latest research; Colleen Weiler-Beazley and Dr. Laura Thompson, for guiding my portrayals of disability in Laviaja; Katherine Croft, BSN, RN, and Program Manager of the UNC Transgender Health Program, for guiding me on portrayals of gender in Laviaja; José Gallegos, who taught me Spanish and helped me dream up neologisms over mezcal; conductor David Möschler, who helped me "score" a key scene; archaeologist Dr. Jaime Awe, who helped me secure the necessary permissions for the cave and encouraged my imagination; and political theorist Dr. Samuel Bagg, who gave me the idea for the entire Laviaja political structure in one conversation over hot chocolate. Thank you also to Drs. Ayana Arce and Beckett Sterner for early conversations about cosmic structure; Areli Barrera de Grodski for help with Spanish; Clare Byrne for key insight on dance; Ali Kashan and Areon Mobasher for help with Farsi; Dr. Thomas Miller for providing me with a detailed map of Actun Tunichil Muknal; and Profs. Emil' Keme, David Mora-Marín, and Erich Fox Tree for crucial early direction on the Maya. Thank you also to my wonderful guides and teachers farther abroad: Randall Colaizzi in Campania, Mokhtar Bouba in Morocco, Joel Bulnes in Oaxaca, Oliver Deniega and the Lost Boys of Palawan, and Babak Kianpour, Parviz Saberi, and Mohammad Shirkavand in Iran. And finally, thank you to Naomi Burn of Biscayne Village for proposing a gender-neutral change to the Belizean national anthem, Antonio Beardall for helping me access research materials at NICH, Dr. Lindsey Andrews for lending me a key line about teenage girls, Zachary Wagman for suggesting I roll all three books into one, and Babi the Belize Relationship Specialist for . . . everything.

In the course of my research, I found the following works especially useful on the ancient Maya and other Mesoamerican cultures: *Popol Vuh: The Sacred Book of the Maya*, translated by Allen J. Christensen; *Aztecs: An Interpretation* and *Ambivalent Conquests* by Inga Clenninden; *Breaking the Maya Code* by Michael D. Coe; *New Perspectives of Human Sacrifice and Post-sacrificial Body Treatments in Ancient Maya Society*, edited by Andrea Cucina and Vera Tiesler; *Characters & Caricatures in Belizean Folklore*, published by the Folklore Book Fund Committee in Belmopan; *The Natural History of the Soul in Ancient Mexico* by Jill Leslie McKeever Furst; *If Di Pin Neva Ben: Folktales and Legends of Belize*, edited by Timothy Hagerty and Mary Gomez Parham; *A Historical Dictionary of Chol (Mayan): The Lexical Sources from 1789 to 1935* by Nicholas A. Hopkins, J. Kathryn Josserand, and Ausencio Cruz Guzmán; *The Memory of Bones: Body, Being, and Experience among the Classic Maya* by Stephen Houston, David Stuart, and Karl Taube; *The Great Maya Droughts in Cultural Context*, edited by Gyles Iannone; *Classical Maya Provincial Politics*, edited by Lisa J. LeCount and Jason Yaeger; *Time and Reality in the Thought of the Maya* by Miguel León-Portilla; *Chronicle of the Maya Kings and Queens* by Simon Martin and Nikolai Grube; *Everyday Life Matters: The Ancient Maya at Chan* by Cynthia Robin; *A Forest of Kings* by Linda Schele and David Freidel; *Daily Life in Maya Civilization* by Robert J. Sharer; *The Ancient Maya* by Robert J. Sharer with Loa P. Traxler; *Time and the Highland Maya* by Barbara Tedlock; *Breath on the Mirror* by Dennis Tedlock and *Popol Vuh: The Definitive Edition*, translated by Dennis Tedlock; and *The Bioarchaeology of Space and Place*, edited by Gabriel Wrobel.

For research on other aspects of the book, I especially credit *The Surrender: An Erotic Memoir* by Toni Bentley; "How to Change the Course of Human History" by David Graeber and David Wengrow in *Eurozine*; *Death in the Afternoon* by Ernest Hemingway; *The Gift* by Lewis Hyde; "Braver New World" by Walidah Imarisha in *Bitch*; *For the Benefit of Those Who See: Dispatches from the World of the Blind* by Rosemary Mahoney; *God Is Not One: The Eight Rival Religions That Run the World* by Stephen Prothero; *Blind Descent: The Quest to Discover the Deepest Place on Earth* by James Tabor; *A Phenomenology of*

Landscape by Christopher Tilley; and *Planet Narnia: The Seven Heavens in the Imagination of C. S. Lewis* by Michael Ward. Thank you to Jason Hickel for teaching me about the necessity for global degrowth, and adrienne maree brown for teaching me that science fiction can create our reality. Thank you also to the Smithsonian National Museum of the American Indian, whose Maya calendar converter I used constantly; to the planetarium program SkySafari, where I could always check the position of Venus, even a thousand years in the future; and to Alex Tingle at firetree. net for making user-friendly maps of global flooding.

I take full responsibility for all choices, mistakes, and inaccuracies.

Writers are born from their influences. I'm especially indebted to the collected works of Kim Stanley Robinson, who graciously granted permission to borrow both his concept of documented anarchy from *Red Moon* and his naming convention from *The Years of Rice and Salt;* and to the utopian fiction of Ursula K. Le Guin, from whom I borrowed the term "therolinguist," and whose novel *The Tombs of Atuan* was a guiding light. I'm also grateful for *Hild* by Nicola Griffith; *Dune* by Frank Herbert; *The Summer Prince* by Alaya Dawn Johnson; *The King Must Die* by Mary Renault; *Lying Awake* by Mark Salzman; *A Stranger in Olondria* by Sofia Samatar; *The Consuming Fire* by John Scalzi; and *The Southern Reach Trilogy* by Jeff VanderMeer. I'd also like to thank Alfonso Cuarón for creating *Y Tú Mamá También*, Jantje Friese and Baran bo Odar for the Netflix series *Dark*, Alexander Sokurov for the film *Russian Ark* and Norman Jewison for the film *Jesus Christ Superstar*, Neri Oxman for her work in material ecology and design, Christopher Martin for the song "Cheaters Prayer," Ann Leckie for using a default "she" pronoun in *Ancillary Justice*, and Charlie Brooker for writing *Black Mirror: White Christmas*, to which I credit the idea for "blotting."

I thank C. S. Lewis and J.R.R. Tolkien for creating my Scripture, and for meeting me at the Eagle & Child in December 2013.

Thank you to my dear friends, whose faith and companionship sustained me: Samuel Bagg, Erin Barringer-Sterner and Beckett Sterner, Nicola Bullock, Danielle Durchslag, Cynthia Fischer, Ami Evangelista Swanepoel, David Hankla, Ben Holbrook, Franny Goffinet, Skylar Gudasz, E. B. Landesberg, Katie Mack, Sarah Parcak, Stan Robinson, John Scalzi, Laurie Stempler, Alice Rose Turner, Caitlin Wells, Katherine Wilkinson, and the whole Beazley family of Annville, especially my godsister Eileen. Thank you to Swaminathan Kumar, who anchored my heart through the hardest months. Thank you to D.L., the hidden midwife of this and all my work. Thank you to Lindsey Andrews, Erin Karcher, and the staff at Arcana Durham; Elizabeth Turnbull, Roberto Copa-Matos, and the staff at Copa Durham; Areli Barrera de Grodski and Leon Grodski de Barrera and the staff at Cocoa Cinnamon; and the staff at Open Eye Café in Carrboro, for creating spaces where I was always welcome as both a patron and a friend.

To my family: you are my heart. Thank you to Pam, Julie, Glen, Donald, Nicole, Niko, Laxmi, Clare, Mary, Mark, Elizabeth, Julian, David, Matt, Ellie, Lucy, Jesse, Eddie, Francie, Alan, Laura, Dick, Greg, Donna, Nora, Margaret, Lucy, Betty, Katie, Eileen, and all of their families. When I am with you, I am home. Thank you to my father, Donald, who died while I was finishing the book. Dad, our long talks about Trinitarian theology formed the heart of this story. Last and most of all, thank you to my mother, Mary Anne. Mom, the whole reason I first went to Belize was to follow in your footsteps.

Finally, thank you to my incredible patrons on Patreon. Your faith and support brought this book into existence. Thank you to Adona El Murr, Aaron Huslage, Aaron Mandel, Aaron Muszalski, Aaron Reed, Aaron Six, Aatish Bhatia, Abigail Henderson, Abigail

Riddick, Abridge, acailrose, Adam Szymkowicz, Adam Lindsay, Adam Schultz, Adriana Knoupf, Adrienne Anderson, Ahmed Finoh, Aimee Ogden, AinsleyJo, Alan Purdom, Alex Claman, Alex Fine, Alex Taylor, Alexander, Alexandra Hsiao, Alexis Peterka, Alfred Glover, Alice Flanders, Alice Lai, Alice McCurry, Alison Carberry Gottlieb, Alissa Lyon, Allison Petrozziello, Allison Rackley Moore, Alvin Bone, Alysha Herrmann, Amanda McLoughlin, Amanda Palmer, Amber Wood, Ameer Ghodke, Amelia Sciandra, Amina Evangelista Swanepoel, Amita Rao, Amy, Amy Cash, Amy Chang, Amy Lawler, Amy Scott, Amy Singer, Ana Mieves, Ana Mozo, Andie Arthur, Andrea Blythe, Andrea Kennedy, Andrea Martinez Corbin, Andrea Mihalko, Andrew Aghapour, Andrew Beaton, Andrew Clark, Andrew DeYoung, Andrew Hungerford, Andrew Newman, Andrew Stoffel, Andrew Thaler, Andrew Weisskopf, Andrie Sismondo, Andy Tabor, Angela Pauly, Angela Tarango, Angus Thomas, Ann Chen, Anne-Laure Py, Annette Adamska, Annette Hynes, Anthony Gifford-James, April Chase, April Kuehnhoff, Arcana Bar and Lounge, Arne, Aron Lewis, Art of Rising, ArtSpark, Artur Nowrot, Ashley Puenner, Ashley Reichheld, Avarice Bliss, Avilyn, Ayesha M., B. Lorraine Smith, Barry Lindeman, Barry Stanford, Beck Tench, Beckett Sterner, Ben Holbrook,

Ben Stearns, Benjamin J. Nichols, Benson Kalahar, Besha Grey, Beth Wodzinski, Beverly Luther, Bev Melven, Bilge Ebiri, Bill Bier, Bill Ferris, Bill Harting, Bill Sterner and Margot Browning, B. J. Witkin, Bliss Floccare, Bob Milnikel, BonSue, Boykin Dunlap Bell, Brad J. Murray, Brad Munson, Brady Amoon, Brandon Eversole, Brandon Johnston, Brandon Karoscik, Brandon M. Crose, Brandon Smithey, Brandon Villamar, Bree TruLove, Brendan, Brendan Ward, Brent Medling, Brian Betteridge, Brian Engler, Brian Gillis, Brian Hawkins, Brian Huber, Brian James Pundt, Brian MacDonald, Brian McCune, Brian Moog, Brian Sladek, Brian Wolven, Brooke Bryant, Brooke Fishman, Bruce Davison, Bryan Roach, Bryan Roth, Budd Friend-Jones, Buster Benson, C. Figler, C. Melton, C. A. Bridges, C. C. Finlay, C. C. Kellogg, Caith Esra Ulvar, Caleb Rogers, Cameo Wood, Cameron McCallie, Carl Friedrich Bolz, Carl Rigney, Carol Anne Ciocco, Carole Bell, Carolyn McDaniel, Carolyn Sara Covalt, Carrie Ann, Carrie J. Cole, Carrie M. Golus, Carsten Knoch, Cary Grey, Cassandra Scully, Cat Davis, Catherine, Catherine Asaro, Catherine Kastleman, Catherine Miller, Catherynne M. Valente, C. B. Hackworth, Cecilia Lam, Cecilia Tan, Celina Chapin, Charles Anderson, Charles Castleberry, Charles Ryan

Stebbins, Charles Tan, Charlie Moss, Charlie Payne, Charlie Reece, Chris, Chris Dial, Chris Chapman, Chris Munro, Chris Nielsen, Chris Tierney, Chris Turchin, Chris Underwood, Chris Woods, Chris Woodworth, Christi Clogston, Christina Gleason, Christina Michelle, Christina Molldrem Harkulich, Christine Delmonico, Christine Phillips, Christopher Burke, Christopher Tower, Claire Fry, Clare Byrne, Clare Corthell, Clare FitzGerald, Clare Sanders, Cloud-walker Bligh, Coleman Humphrey, Collin Bunch, Coralie Grassin, Corey White, Cori Princell, Corianna Moffatt, Corinne Woods, Courtney Borgers, Crystal Dreisbach, Cynthia Fischer, D. J. Trindle, Dallas Taylor, Damaged Sandwiches, Damien Walter, Dan B. Sandler, Dana Mele, Dana Sandersfeld, Dana Weekes, Daniel P. Haeusser, Daniel Rosenblatt, Daniel Stroud, Daniel Westreich, Danielle Durchslag, Danielle Lee, Danielle Paquette, Dan R. Winters, Darrah Chavey, Dave Hunt, Dave Singer, Dave Wofford, David Ball and Susan Chapek, David Bonner, David Dobbs, David Fero, David Hankla, David Henderson, David Henry Hwang, David J. Loehr, David Jackson, David Klionsky, David Leftwich, David M. Perry, David Möschler, David Robinson, David Romine, David Simpkin, David Solow, David Tietjen Wiener, Dawn Sabados,

Dean Hubbard, Deanne Fountaine, Deborah Postman, Debra Collins, Debra Lary, Deirdre Lockwood, Deniz Bevan, Derrick L. Pearson, Diana Cameron McQueen, Diana Oh, Dietmar Bloech, dogunderwater, Donald E. Byrne Jr., Donald Byrne III, Donna Shaunesey, Dot Dotter, Doug Messel, Doug Reed, Douglas Spalding, Dustin McKenzie, Dwain Ritchie, E. Christopher Clark, Eamon Ambrose, E. B. Landesberg, Ed Plunkett, Eden Kupermintz, Edward Hunt, Eileen Beazley, Elais Player, Elan Dassani, Eleanor Kleiber, Eliot, Elise Tobler, Elissa Stebbins, Elizabeth Bear, Elizabeth Hirshorn, Elizabeth Mandeville, Elizabeth Tigani, Elizabeth Turnbull, Elizabeth Vadera, Ellie Mer, Elroy Fernandes, Emily Baxter, Emily Jaworski, Emily Kimball, Emily MacGregor, Emily Pike, Emmett Holladay Anderson, Emmy Bean, Emmy Laybourne, Eric Foster, Eric Martell, Eric Pfeffinger, Erica Jean, Erica Joy, Erik Hilbmann, Erin Barringer-Sterner, Erin Bell, Erin Bernstein, Erin Kissane, Erin Teachman, Erinn White, Eruditorum Press, Esther Patterson, Eswaran Balakrishnan, Ethan Fremen, Eunice Chang, Eva Panjwani, Evan B. Henry, Evan Jensen, Evan Mallon, Eve Rickert, Everett Harper, Ex Nihilo Theater, Fabio Fernandes, Fernando G., Forrest Sutton, Frances Tietjen Wiener, Frank Hyman, Fred Ball, Fred Grieco, Frederike Peters, Gabriel Sciallis, Galen Bodenhausen,

Garrett, Gary Dowell, Gary Harmon, Gavin Sandison, Giffen Maupin, Gigil Ghosh, Ginnie Hench, Glynnis Kirchmeier, Grace Dow, Graeme Wiliams, Greg Cantrell, Greg Dorsainville, Greg Gbur, Greg Goldsborough, Greg Kelly, Gregory Ball, Gregory P. Smith, Gus Hinrich, Hannah Allison, Hannah de Keijzer, Hannah Hessel Ratner, Hassan Melehy, Heather Aruffo, Heather Minchew, Heidi Waterhouse, Helene Wecker, Heyward Sims, Howard Wood, Hye Yun Park, Ian Monroe, Ilana Brownstein, Imran Siddiquee, incredimella, Ingrid Nelson, J. R. Frontera, J. Renee Parker, J. M. Prince, Jack Derbyshire, Jack Reitz, Jackie and Roger Geer, Jacob Pinholster, Jacquelyn Gill, Jae Steinbacher, Jake Thompson, Jake L. Woodworth, Jaimie Slade, Jameela Dallis, James Dymond, James E. Green III, James Kennedy, James Lambers, James McAndrews, James Rowland, James Wahlberg, Jamie Bartholomay, Jamie Beck Alexander, Jamie Wallace, Jane Park, Jane H. Park, Jane Davis, Jase Short, Jason D. Crabtree, Jason Scully-Clemmons, Jay Wolf, J. B. Burrage, Jim D. McBroom, Jean Sirius, Jean Yang, Jeff Stern, Jeff Storer, Jen Silverman, Jenn Northington, Jennifer Bishop, Jennifer Lu, Jennifer Martin, Jennifer Neal, Jenny Colvin, Jenny M., Jeremy Brett, Jeremy John Parker, Jeremy Jones, Jerry Beasley, Jesi Kinnevan, Jess Yuen, Jesse Gephart, Jesse

Williams, Jessica Perkins, Jessica Flemming, Jessie Kneeland, Jim Lewis, Jim Meyer, Jo Lindsay Walton, Joe Jones Jr., Joe Taylor Jr., Joe Wojtowicz, Joe Zehnder, Joel A. Nichols, Joel Wysong, John Bachir, John Berggren, John Brier, John Coyne, John E. Manzo, John Foy, John Honeycutt, John Klima, John M. Russell, John Maynard, John McDaid, John Osborne, John Regan, John Speck, John Wilbanks, Johnny M., Johnny Winston, Jolanna Hughes, Jon Sager, Jonathan Hovland, Jonathan Rees, Jos, Joseph Colaccino, Joseph Lundquist, Josh Krach, Josh Richards, Josh Schmidt, Josh Thomson, Joshua A. C. Newman, Joshua Batson, Josie Tenner, Judith Roth, Judith S. Anderson, Judy Gayton, Juli Carter, Julia Specht, Julian Caesar, Juliana Finch, Julie Andrews, Julie Baum, Julie Byrne and Glenton DeLeon-Job, Jussi Valonen, Justin Cook, Justin de Vesine, Justin Kahn, K. B. Wagers, K. C. Alexander, Kaci Beeler, Kaitlin Houlditch-Fair, Kameron Hurley, Karen Burns, Karen James, Karen Price, Karoline Gostl, Kate Black, Kate Bradtmiller, Kate Garrido, Kate MacQueen, Kate McGee, Kate Rose, Kate Ward, Katherine Charlotte Ann Jack, Katherine Collins, Katherine Flaster, Katherine Lucas McKay, Katherine Wilkinson, Kathleen Raven, Kathleen Block, Kathryn Mackintosh, Kathryn Parker, Kathy Randall Bryant, Katie Ballou, Katie Cole, Katie Locklier, Katie Mayo, Katie Reing, Katie Riley, Katja Gee, Katja Hill, Katriena Knights, Kavita Srinivasan, Kaye Soleil, Keegan Connelly, Keith Burton, Keith Reynolds, Kellan Sparver, Kelli Cotter, Kellie Grubbs, Kelly Carlin, Kelly Kehm, Kelly Kleiser, Kelvin Traves, Ken Gagne, Ken Rumble, Kerry Adrienne, Kerry Benton, Kerstin Walsh, Kevin Hendzel, Kevin Jesse, Kevin Mitchell, Kevin Parichan, Kevin S. Reilly, Kevin Surace, Kevin Wilson, Kevin Young, Kim Steckler, Kim Werker, Kip Silverman, Kirstin Butler, Kitten Holiday, Klelija Zhivkovikj, Korrie Xavier, Kristen Mark, Kristen Owles, Kristen Rappazzo, Kristin Henry, Kristin Wiley, Kristina Dahl, Kristine Maltrud, Kyle Johnson, Kyle Miller, L. Alexandra, Lance Heard, Larissa Ranbom, Larry Clapp, Larry Rothman, Lars Stephenson, Laura Axelrod, Laura Friis, Laura Jacobsen, Laura K. Case, Laura Miller, Laura Ritchie, Laura Shepler, Laura Thompson, Laura Tietjen, Laura Westman, Lauren Barth, Lauren Kessel, Lauren Spencer, Lauren Valentino, Lauren Znachko, Laurie Dunn, Laurie Penny, Leah Kaplan, Leah Langan, Lee Purcell, Leigh Campoamor, Lene Preuss, Leon Grodski de Barrera, Leslie Ordal, Lian-Marie Holmes Munro, Liesel Tower, Lila Sadkin, Lincoln Dennis, Linda Ho, Lindsey Andrews, Lindsey Elcessor, Lindsey Halsell, Lisa Eckstein, Lisa Lutz, Lisa

Scanlon Mogolov, Lisa Vollrath, Livie, Liz Henry, Liz
Powers, Logan Siegrist, Lois Dawson, Lori Mannette,
Lorraine Valestuk, Louis Landry, Luke Dones, Lyle
Wilson, Lívia Labate, M. A. Provencher, Madeline
Snipes, Madeline Tasquin, Madhusudan Katti, Madi-
son May, Madison Shaw, Magdalene Constan, Maggie
Gerrity, Maggie O'Grady, Maggie Thomasson, Maia
S., Mailande Moran, Mara Thomas, Margaret Farrell,
Margaret Thorpe, Maria Beatty, Maria De Fazio,
Maria Popova, Marina Devine, Mark Goldthorpe,
Mark Jeffrey Miller, Mark Laucks, Mark Simmons,
Marlee Jane Ward, Marlo Johnson, Martin Cahill,
Martin Dahl, Martin Fisher, Martin Hall, Martin Ho-
leysovsky, Martin Locklear, Martin Robbins, Martina
Oefelein, Mary Wong, Mathieu Perron, Matt Cooper,
Matt Luedke, Matt Mills, Matt Vancil, Matt Wiley,
Matthew White, Maya Rosman, McKenzie Millican,
Meehan Crist, Meg Smith, Meg Stein, Meghan Florian,
Meghan Modafferi, Melina Greenport, Melissa Hill-
man, Melissa McBride, Melissa Tapley, Meredith So-
rensen, Michael Gunn, Michael Harren, Michael
Heilman, Michael Lebowitz, Michael Moore, Michael
Oakes, Michael O'Foghludha, Michael Perry, Mi-
chaelann Gardner, Michal, Michelle Crawford, Mi-
chelle Legaspi-Sanchez, Michelle Orabona, Mike
Dean, Mike Kozlowski, Mike Little, Mike Miller,

Mike Morrow, Mike Ramsey, Mike Rayhawk, Mike Wallace, Milly Lyon, Mitch Allen, Moira Pulitzer-Kennedy, Molly Fisk, Molly Priddy, Molly Weaver, Monica Joan Bryant, Monica Louzon, Monica Tromp, Morgan Allen, Mx. Hunter Mass, Nan Craig, Nancy, Nancy McDonald, Naseem Jamnia, Nat Smith, Natalie Zutter, Natasha Peters, Nate Rebmann, Nathan Murphy, Nathaniel Merchant, Neal Johnson, Neal Williams, Neena and Clint Litton, Neil Argue, Neil Gaiman, Neil Parry, Niall Harrison, Nic Anthony, Nicholas Trevino, Nicola Bullock, Nicole Graysmith, Ninja Writers, Nivair H. Gabriel, Noah Berlatsky, Nora B. Fitzpatrick, Norah Vawter, Olivia Batto, Omari Akil, otherchaz, P. King, Pamela Jean Herber, Pat Connelly, Patricio Javier, Patrick Baker, Patrick Jean, Patrick Malone, Patti Wachtman, Paul Boccaccio, Paul Bonamy, Paul Bradley Carr, Paul Cuadros, Paul Deblinger, Paul DesCombaz, Pavel Curtis, Pavithra Vasudevan, Peggy Youell, Pete Kirkham, Pete Miller, Peter Hansen, Peter Haynes, Peter Jones, Peter Stuart Lakanen, Peter Tavernise, Phil Harrington, Pierre N. Hauser, Pierre Roullon, PINA, Precious Lucy, Pris Nasrat, Queer Mama, R. Subramanian, Rachael Alaia, Rachel Cole, Rachel Hilliard-Brown, Rachel Jordan, Rachel Kincaid, Rachel Rzayev, Rachelle Estephan, Rae MacCarthy, Raf Noboa y Rivera, Ralff, Ranganathan Rajaram, R. E. Collins, Rebecca Bossen McHugh, Rebecca Cynamon-Murphy, Rebecca Novick, Rebecca Pierce, Rebecca Rosengard, Ren H., René López Villamar, Renee Calarco, Reshmi Rustebakke, Rhonda Zatezalo, Ricardo Contreras, Richard B. Becker, Richard Hess, Richard P. McHugh, Richard Sepcic, Rio Aubry Taylor, Rob Funk, Rob Stanley, Rob Young, Robert Bakie, Robert Cantrell, Robert Cook, Robert Getty, Robert Griffin, Robin Sokoloff, R. S. Buck, Roger John Middleton, Rohan Smith, Roman Testroet, Ronnie Chen, Rosa, Rose Eveleth, Roshni Sampath, Rouzbeh Gerami, Roy Neary, Rremida Shkoza, Ryan Hughes, Ryan Rutley, 15x15 medias, [wolfe interval], S. M. Mack, Sabrina Rodríguez, Safwat Saleem, Saleem Javid Reshamwala, Sam Erickson, Sam Rasoul, Sam Stoloff, Samantha Lowe, Samuel Bagg, Samuel Johnston, Samuel Montgomery-Blinn, Samuel Richardson, Samuel Sattin, Sandra B., Sandy Sulzer, Sara Carroll, Sara Davis, Sara Jo Taylor, Sarah Coradetti, Sarah Burg, Sarah Corsa, Sarah D. Dawson, Sarah Fitzsimmons, Sarah JM Kolberg, Sarah Kaiser, Sarah Miller, Sarah Moazeni, Sarah Morgan, Sarah Rogers, Sarah Sprague, Sarah Spurgeon, Sarah Walden McGowan, Saskia Davies, Scott Bezsylko, Scott Jennings, Scott Takahashi, Sean William Brown, Sean Dacey, Sergey, Sergio O. Parreiras, Sergio Sirsay, Shadeaux Public

Radio, Shaena Montanari, Shana DuBois, Shannon Palus, Shaun Geer, Shaun Leisher, Shaun Martin, Shawn Connery, Shawn Hudson, Shay Shortt, Shayla Maddox, Shveta Thakrar, Simrat Khalsa, Siva Vaidhyanathan, Skylar Gudasz, Shayne Muelling, Sofia Ballesteros, Sonia Balsky, Sonja Christina, Stacie Nagy, Stefan Linden, Stefani Nellen, Stephen Black, Stephen Byrne, Stephen Millet, Stephen Peck, Stephen Spotswood, Steve Avery, Steve Himelfarb, Steve Kalkwarf, Steve Mehan, Steve Tell, Steve Travis, Steven Klotz, Steven Lee Solheim, Steven Samuels, A Strange Loop, Sugar Moon, Susan Evangelista, Susan Wilson, Susannah Simpson, Susanne Pohl, Susie Kantor, Susie Nazzaro, Susie Schroeder, Suzi Steffen, Swaminathan Kumar, Swan Huntley, T. K., Tabitha Bear, Tadhg O'Higgins, Tal Raviv, Tamara Kissane, Ted Lee, Ted Logan, Tee Bylo, Tegan, Telmo Correa, thaumascope, The Secret Bureau of Art & Design, Theo Kogod, Theresa Tribble, Thomas McGreevy, Thomas Scott, Thu Nguyen, Tia, Tiff, Tiffany Cothran, Tiffany Palmer, Tim Edwards, Tim McMackin, Tim Rodriguez, Tim Scales, Tim Walter, Tjebbe Donner, Tobias A. Carroll, Tom Harris, Tomi Blasic, tortagialla, Trace Ramsey, Tracy Barry, Tracy Kaplan, Tracy Walker, Travis Bedard, Ty Schalter, Valdis Kr minš, Valentina Ferraro, Valentine Edgar, Vern Ballard, Wade Minter,

Wes Kroeze, Whit Andrews, Whitney Retallic, Will Woods, William Johnson, Wyatt Jenkins, Wynn Pham, Xarene Eskandar, Yonas Kidane, Yusuke N., Zain Rehan, Zarah Ruth, and Zena Cardman.

We did it.

ABOUT THE AUTHOR

MONICA BYRNE grew up in Annville, Pennsylvania, as the youngest child of two theologians. She studied biochemistry at Wellesley, NASA, and MIT before pivoting to fiction and theatre. She is the author of the novel *The Girl in the Road*, winner of the 2014 Otherwise Award, as well as the plays *Nightwork*, *What Every Girl Should Know*, *Tarantino's Yellow Speedo*, and *Ohio!*. She also performed the first science-fictional TED Talk in Vancouver. You can visit her online at monicabyrne.org and support her work at patreon.com/monicabyrne. She is based in Durham, North Carolina, and loves a good thunderstorm.